Sweet Strings

ALY BECK

1

"HELLO, boys, my name is River West, and I'm your new band manager. Congratulations," I say, cocking my head.

My heart pounds against my ribs. Pain encases my chest, tightening like rubber bands and constricting my air. Every ounce of oxygen stalls in my lungs until I blow out a calming breath, forcing myself to stay in the present—with them—the boys who broke my heart five years ago.

Who knew staring into the eyes of the four exes who screwed you over five years ago after they ran away would be so fucking nerve-wracking. I should despise them. Hate their fucking existence. I should want to see their careers spiral down a dark hole and hit rock bottom as I laugh maniacally at their demise.

Instead, with as much confidence as I can muster, I utter the fourteen words that will forever change our lives and throw us down a wicked path of devastating revelations and wreckage we may not come back from.

Varying degrees of emotions cross their pale faces, sending victorious goosebumps down my spine. Their utter fear empowers me to sweep my gaze around the room.

Callum blinks rapidly like a flickering mirage stands confidently in front of him. And he has yet to believe I'm actually here in person.

My eyes move with ease to Rad, who stares at me with those big, brown puppy dog eyes I used to get lost in for hours and hours on end. Quickly, though, he turns away to study the conference table, avoiding any more eye contact.

Kieran's face twitches in disbelief, and his jaw pops open. A reddish tint takes over his flesh, starting on his neck, and slowly seeps color onto his cheeks. Sooner rather than later, I see an outburst in our future.

And Asher. My breath catches in my chest, stopping me cold. Never in my life did I think I'd see the day Asher Montgomery would freeze in place with horror lining his face.

An array of feelings slams through me. Fear. Sadness. Utter betrayal. Wide, unblinking eyes look up at me in horror, and disbelief pulls their muscles rigid in their chairs. One by one, the realization of what's happening slams into their chests, and they're nothing but frozen men with gazes glued to me—the star of the damn show.

Something deep inside me bubbles with excitement, yet the fear and utter devastation they left behind reside there, too. Reminding me of what happened when I ran to their doorstep with pregnancy tests in my back pocket, begging to see them. I vividly remember Gloria, Kieran's sadistic mother, answering the door and throwing me a life-changing grenade of knowledge. Kieran, Rad, Callum, and Asher were gone— vanished into thin air without a goodbye or explanation. The most devastating part of it all was the way they left without a word, leaving our child and me in the dust with nothing more than a restraining order forbidding me from speaking with them.

And they knew. They acknowledged the existence of Lyric by having Gloria toss me a check, advising me to 'get rid of it' and stating they didn't want her. They denied my daughter having fathers. Sure, she knows them by name and calls them daddy by choice, but she'll never have the chance to know them in person unless they step up to the plate. But that's only if I let them. They can hurt me all they want, but I'll be fucked if I let them hurt her, too.

Somewhere in my mind, a little voice begs for revenge against the men who callously threw us away like yesterday's stale bread. Like we had meant nothing to them—like I wasn't someone important to them. Like I hadn't had an instrumental impact on their ability to even enter the Battle of the Bands competition— let alone win it.

Oh, how the tables have turned in my favor. No longer am I the scared girl with a baby in her belly and vengeance on her mind. I'm a woman, a mother, and I'll fucking get what I'm owed. Professionally, of course. I can't simply destroy these men without consequence. This job, my daughter, and this entire record company are my life force that kept me going when I thought my world had fallen apart. I wouldn't have made it this far without the loving support of my brothers, Seger and Zepp, and their family. They've taken me in and given me everything I've ever dreamed of and accepted me as one of their own.

These men are at the root of it all, and karma is quite the bitch when she wants to take back what is owed. Whispered Words will 100 percent get everything that's coming to them—all in due time, of course. Whether by me or by the universe—Karma is on her way to lay claim.

"How about we get started?" I hum, letting the shocked silence embrace me in a warm hug and revel in their awkward expressions.

"What-what are you doing here?" Asher utters through his shocked expression, gripping his chair so hard, I swear he'd choke it if it were breathing. "Why are you here?" he mumbles again, shaking his head.

I'm the ghost of your fucked up past coming back to haunt you— is what I desperately want to say, but I bite my tongue. I'm a goddamn professional. I won't let Whispered Words screw up my career. Besides, Zepp and Seger are watching my every move from behind the damn glass.

"So nice of you to ask, Mr. Montgomery," I say as politely as I can and add, "I'm working." Shrugging, I set the thick folder my brothers gave me on the conference table and spread their paperwork out for further examination.

Clearing my throat, I drag myself out of my thoughts and focus on the plans before me.

On the outside, I'm completely unaffected by their presence with the right kind of professional smile and squared shoulders. But on the inside, that's a completely different story. I can act as tough as the next person. But a tornado unleashes my emotions, sending mixed signals throughout my trembling body.

"Working?" Kieran asks in a deep voice. "There's no way," he says in a cold tone, tinged with disbelief. "You can't work here! What the fuck?" he growls, narrowing his eyes at me with suspicion.

"There is a way," I retort with no emotion, thumbing through a few more pages, finally finding the numbers I should have been able to study yesterday. You know if my stupid brothers hadn't sprung this on me ten minutes ago. Right, that reminds me. Murder is definitely still on the table. I wonder how my sister-in-law, Kaycee, will take the news when her twin husbands disappear off the face of the planet.

"Relax," Rad says in a bored tone, forcing himself to stare at the phone clutched in his white-knuckled grip.

"You fucking relax, dickhead," Kieran snaps. "This can't be possible."

"Believe it or not, but I'm standing right here," I say, still staring at the messy, down-turned numbers lining the page with a crease forming in my brow.

Fuck. This is worse than I thought.

When my brothers, Zepp and Seger, hired me, I never imagined it would lead to this. I completed my college education, garnered a degree in music business, and set out to make waves within the company with my ideas. The Fixer. I'm the person West Records turns to when a band is on their last leg and needs intervention before they're expelled from their contracts and kicked out on their asses. We give them a chance at redemption to show us they can still perform and bring in money again. Or else, they're out.

Over the past three years, since I took on this position, I've seen countless bands. Some work hard and regain their contracts, going out to make a new name for themselves. Others, well, they snort coke out of groupies' assholes and ruin their careers. *Looking at you, Break.* Idiots.

This time, though, it's them—Whispered Words. The four men I tried my hardest to forget, which is hard when one of their mini-mes calls me mom. My heart jumps, pounding against my ribs in a rhythmic drumbeat. Lyric. My daughter. His child. My eyes glide across Kieran's twisted-up face, reddened by boiling anger that's simmering beneath the surface of his skin. His mismatched eyes, so similar to the little girl who holds my entire heart now, burn into me with hate so visceral a shiver runs down my spine.

Letting out a low whistle, I shake my head with disappointment. How could a band at the top of their game for years suddenly fall so fast and hard?

"Your numbers," I say, scrunching my nose.

"What numbers?" Asher asks cautiously, losing his breath when my gaze slams into his watery, hazel eyes filled to the brim with worry and concern.

"I'm so glad you asked," I reply in a professional tone, sliding the paper in front of his face. His brows furrow when his eyes gaze over the page. "It's your performance numbers. The amount you're bringing in through ticket sales, online sales, and everything in between. It's the numbers we evaluate every year to see if our investment is still paying off. And by the looks of it, Whispered Words is on their last leg," I say, pacing back and forth at the head of the table. What they can't see are my hands clasped firmly behind my back, trying to keep the shaking away from their eyes.

"Last-last leg?" Callum breathes, finally speaking up after staying silent for so long. The room falls away when his eyes finally connect with mine. A dark bruise rests beneath his eye, blackening his skin. Quickly, his eyes dart to the table once again, sinking his teeth into his bottom lip and losing himself in the pattern of the table.

My heart hammers in my chest, nearly knocking me back into the past. Callum. Sweet, lovable, caring Callum has marks on his flesh. But from what? Who could have caused him so much damage? And what the hell has changed? It's only been a few years. The last thing I could ever do was picture Callum putting his fists into the air and fighting with someone.

How much has each of them changed?

"I think you're lying," Kieran says, jumping to his feet and readying himself for a fight. "This is a fucking joke. There's no way some Central girl could be working here. Let alone be our new band manager. This is bullshit!" Kieran explodes, slamming a hand down onto the wooden table. Everyone flinches away from his outburst, watching his contorted face twist with hate.

Ouch. Is that really what he thinks about me? A painful pang spears through my heart. My eyes barely recognize the boy who held my hands under the stars and told me I'd be okay. Who is this man standing before me? Has this ruined him? And why the fuck does Kieran hate me so much?

"Well, you should know that you're here because West Records has placed your contract on probation." I raise a brow when Rad's face crumples, and his dark eyes glare down at the table, refusing to meet mine.

Tension laces every inch of his muscles, locking him in place, which gives me a chance to give him a once-over. Ashton Radcliffe may look the same as he did back in Central City with his dark and curly mullet and his lanky physique, but there are crucial differences shining through, hardening his closed-off exterior.

"This isn't a joke. Believe me; I wouldn't be here if it was some big ruse. You're stuck with me. Like it or not." I shrug again, taking a huge breath to relieve myself of the hurt brewing beneath the surface.

Anger vibrates through the entire room, setting my teeth on edge. Never in my life have I been met with such hostility, but I guess there's a first time for everything. But what the hell do they have to be so hostile for? They left me. They left her. Not the other way around. I'm the one who should hate their guts. I mean, don't get me wrong, I fucking do. But my professional duty binds me to their cause.

"What the hell is that supposed to mean? Probation? We haven't done anything wrong. This is bullshit," Kieran growls, slamming his fist into the table again. His hulking body heaves with every breath he takes, and those mismatched eyes glare at me head-on, ready to take me down.

"Well, that's why we're having this meeting, Mr. Knight," I say, tilting my head. "We're here to discuss your future."

Kieran's fiery eyes slam into my gaze, hardening the longer he stares, filling to the brim with hate and unsaid wrath ready to unleash on me. My breath leaves me, and my head spins until I collect myself and my heart off the floor.

His stare is a stark reminder of the little girl just a floor above us, patiently waiting for her Aunt Kaycee to collect her for a sleepover. It's the reminder that he left her. They left her knowingly, refusing to listen to me. They gave up their responsibility with the flick of their wrist and signatures across restraining orders.

Fuck them.

"We have no future here with you. I'll speak to my agent about this. There's no way in fucking hell I'm working with you," Kieran barks, twisting on his heels and stomping away.

Oh, cue the dramatics from the biggest dickhead around. Of course, he'd stomp and throw a fit at the sight of me. Idiot. *Deep breaths, River. You have to reel them back in.* Kieran always did have a flare for the dramatics, but this is pushing it too far. He's running away like the big fucking coward he is instead of facing me. Sounds way too familiar for my liking. I'd rather him go back to the boy who strummed his guitar on the hill behind our apartment complex, singing songs he envisioned during school. Instead of that man, the one I fell in love with twice, I'm left with the angry shell walking away from me.

"Fucking Kieran," Asher growls, climbing to his feet with determination. "You can't fucking walk away. Not because it's her." His eyes follow Kieran's slow, angry retreat, almost afraid to take his eyes off him.

My eyes narrow at the emphasis on the word her. Again. If they say it one more time like I'm not standing in front of them, I'll lose my shit. Seriously, though. Who, me? Little ole River West? The girl you dumped so fast after witnessing Van Drake, my stupid ex, forcefully kiss me without permission in my kitchen as I nursed my grief alone. Alone! They left me at my own mother's funeral without so much as a "sorry for your loss, Riv." Anger simmers beneath the surface of my skin, bubbling and aching for me to act on it at the harsh reminder of their betrayal. My mind begs me to lash out and put them in their place, but I bury that piece of me. I'm not here to talk about the past. I'm here to discuss the future of their band. Nothing more. Nothing less.

As Kieran drifts farther away from the group of men staring at him with wide eyes, I slip back into my professional persona. With one last deep breath, I become River West—The Fixer. Not River West—The Brokenhearted.

"I can do whatever I want. I can't be in the same room as her," Kieran growls, picking up his pace toward the French doors on the opposite side of the room.

My edges harden at the word her again and how it's implied. Maybe I should remind them of who they're fucking with. I discreetly rub the handle of my old knife nestled in the pocket of my dress pants. Images of Kieran behind the counter at the old record store I worked at come to mind. I smirk. This time Kieran wouldn't get a boner when I sit the edge of my knife near his dick, which I'll promptly cut off if he keeps up this defiant rock star bullshit attitude. He's on thin ice, growing thinner. Soon, he'll drown at my hands.

Asher looks at me and back at Kieran with wide eyes, expectantly waiting for him to come back to his seat like a good boy. But if there's anything I know about Kieran, he's not a very good boy.

Every step Kieran takes is a step closer to him forfeiting their contract. I could let him go and walk out into the hall and wipe my hands clean of them and never look back. I could laugh as they realized they'd fucked themselves over by not staying in the same room as me. No more concerts. No more fangirls willing to suck their mediocre dicks on their tour bus. And no more West Records. Bye, bye Whispered Words. You can return to Central City and explain to your mommy why you're back penniless and contract-less.

Inwardly, I groan, staring at the ceiling and counting backward. I'm better than that. I'm more professional than that petty behavior. Plus, my brothers would never let that fly. For some fucked up reason, despite knowing exactly what they did to me, they like their music.

The moment Kieran's hand touches the handle, I sigh. My responsibilities nag at me to do the right thing, just this once, and I comply.

"Mr. Knight, you should know the moment you step out of this meeting, you void not only your contract with West Records but all their contracts as well," I say in a smooth voice, crossing my arms over my chest and surveying the room.

Someone grumbles. Another gasps. And Asher, the once smug bastard, fucking begs—much to my delight. There once was a prideful man named Asher, who never got on his knees to beg another human being for anything. And yet, here he is, about to drop down and save face. I shouldn't have a giggle bursting up my throat or joy humming through my body at the stark difference.

But I do.

"Kieran, you have to give this a chance. It's a second opportunity for us to continue with our dream," Asher pleads with desperation, falling back into his chair with a desperate huff, never taking his pleading eyes off Kieran's retreating form.

"Bro, you can't walk out." Rad finally slides his gaze to me, quickly darting away with a twist of his lips and a shake of his head. His brows furrow, almost in confusion or maybe pain, but he shakes it off, running a hand through his curly mullet. I can't believe he's kept it after all these years.

"I can do whatever the fuck I please," Kieran sneers, twisting away from the door. "You can't be our band manager. You don't fucking belong here. You belong in the gutter like the rest of Central City. Is this a fucking joke?" Kieran barks out, throwing his arms all around like a child.

"Oh, ouch. Awesome," I mutter with so much sarcasm I swear one of them chokes on my tone. So much for biting my tongue. *Must. Remain. Professional, River.* Ugh. As much as I want to bash my fist into his dick and make him drop to his knees, begging for mercy, I don't.

"You can't be," he hisses again like a hysterical child, readying himself to drop to the floor and throw a full-blown fit.

You'd think our daughter Lyric was in front of me, throwing herself around and screaming at the top of her lungs because I refused to let her eat unicorn ice cream for dinner—cue the eye roll. Somehow, my four-year-old manages to regain control of her emotions better than this full-grown man. Pathetic.

Cracking my neck, I straighten my posture and ready myself to face the bull. There's no doubt in my mind that he'll fight this every part of the way. And I say, bring it on, Kieran Knight.

"I am your new manager. That's something you'll have to get over right here and right now. I am in charge of you, officially, this time. You fuck with me. I fuck with your career. Do we have an understanding?" I ask with an even tone, trying not to let my boiling anger get the best of me. "This is a professional environment. We will not disrespect each other. The past stays in the past. This is the present. I will not be disrespected again. Got it?" I ask, narrowing my eyes on each of them as they nod in unison, still giving me the stink eye. Reaching into the paperwork, I pull out a thick copy of their contract with West Records and throw it down the table. "If you want to read for yourself, it's on page fifty-seven, subsection B. It'll lay out everything you need to know when dealing with me and the professional services I offer at West Records."

Kieran grunts, shoving the paperwork at Callum, who sits rigidly in his seat, clinging to the armrests of his chair.

"You read it," Kieran barks out his order, pointing at the stack of papers.

Callum doesn't flinch when he reaches for the contract and flips through the pages, using his photographic memory, no doubt. "Fine," he mutters, stopping on my part of the contract, and he nods. "It's-it's all right here," he says, heaving his breath while pointing at it.

A pang pierces through my chest. The old Callum was doing so well and coming into himself. Now, it seems like he's reverted back to the stuttering, shy man I helped come out of his shell.

Those beautiful, gray eyes spare me one glance, and my heart thunders. Despair rests deep in his gaze when he flicks his eyes up and down my body. A familiar redness tints his cheeks until his gaze hardens again. Every ounce of life spirals out of his eyes, leaving me with his blank stare. My lips pop open when I zone in and really examine the faint remnants of black surrounding his slightly swollen eye, and then he turns away.

"How?" Asher mutters in a shaky voice, rubbing circles over his ghostly white temple, bringing me back to the conversation.

"I still don't fucking believe it," Kieran growls, throwing himself back into his chair. His fists clench when he leans forward, placing his elbows on the table.

Ignoring their questioning glares, I pull out another copy of their contract, flip it open to the page marked by Zepp, and scan the words.

"Well, believe it. As a matter of fact, don't forget it. I've been doing this for three years now, and this is how it will go. There are moving vans on their way to all your residences right now." I raise a brow when Kieran glowers at me with an unrelenting stare, but I shake him off. Nothing he can do will deter me from doing my job. "You're to pack whatever you want to take with you on a six-month vacation."

"Six months?" Rad gasps with wide eyes, finally looking up at me again. My heart pounds as memories of him and I on his dirt bike come back to mind but quickly dissipate. I don't have time to rehash memories that bring me nothing but pain. The quicker they get this done, the quicker we can move on with our lives.

"You'll never have to worry with me, Pretty Girl. I'll fight off the monsters and keep your brain in your head," he murmurs, shoving the helmet over my head with force and buckling it under my chin.

I shake myself out of that stupid, childish memory. I did have to worry about him. He loved me with his entire soul and pursued me the hardest. Only to drop me for whatever reason. Was it the Van kiss? Or did they decide they'd gotten their use out of me with Battle of the Bands? I did my job. They just didn't hold up their end of the bargain.

"You can't be serious," Kieran shouts. "I can't leave my place! That's mine. There's no way—"

"It says it in the contract," Callum cuts in with a quiet but authoritative voice.

"Why the fuck didn't we read that better?" Kieran grumbles, pinching the bridge of his nose. "Why didn't you?" He glowers at Callum, who reads through the contract again, shaking his head.

Clearly, their friendship is falling to pieces. Judging by their cutting glances at each other and snarky attitudes, they can't wait to leave each other's presence. The Kieran I knew before was never *this* cruel to anyone. Sure, he had an attitude problem. But this? This seems like more.

"Yes. You owe West Records six months of total dedication.

You've had time to sow your wild rock star oats, and now you need to prove that our investment was worth it. Six months at the Band House. Six months of practice, therapy, and rebuilding yourselves up. Six months of being mine." An ominous grin spreads across my face, making each of their expressions drop. "And if you fail, you can say goodbye to your contracts and hello to unemployment. No other record company will dare to sign you after you leave us. They'll all know you failed my program because I'll make sure of it. The choice is yours. Music or nothing. At any time during this process, you're free to leave. But your contract will be void. Oh, and I'm the ultimate judge. So, piss me off again, and you're done." I hold Kieran's stare when his gaze hardens again. But for the first time since stepping foot in this room, he bites his tongue.

Good boy.

One point River. Zero for the boys.

"What the fuck did we sign up for?" Rad asks, swallowing hard, apprehension crossing his face.

"Bullshit, that's what," Kieran so helpfully adds with a huff.

"Glad we have that settled. Moving vans are at all your places now. I suggest grabbing everything you'll need for the next six months. Your new home will be furnished, and a recording studio will be in the basement. I expect all your instruments to be there. We'll start practice at 8:45 a.m. Monday morning."

"Eight AM?" Kieran shrieks again with wide eyes. "What the fuck?"

"I'm well aware of your extracurricular activities, Mr. Knight, which include not waking up until two in the afternoon, but this is rock star boot camp. Welcome to your new hell," I say, gathering my papers into the folder and nodding at each of them. "You're dismissed. A limo will pick you up at your respective homes, and they will escort you to the Band House. There we will have another meeting of expectations, rules, and another six-month contract for you to sign."

Each of them nods, looking more confused as I step away

from the table, clinging to the file folders resting against my chest. It's the only thing grounding me. I hold my breath the entire way through the back doors, only releasing my breath when they close behind me and block me from the boys I once loved.

My brothers rest on the loveseat near the wall, cautiously eyeing me as I rigidly stand there. Everything inside me wants to crumple into a ball and not exist for a day just from seeing them. I'm all for putting on a brave face, but right now, tears burn the back of my eyes. Once upon a time, they meant the world to me. Apparently, I meant nothing. An ache forms in my chest as I collect myself, swallowing the hurt and betrayal.

"You did good," Seger sings his praises, rising from his seat. Having observed the entire encounter through the two-way mirror, he probably watched me like a hawk.

Immediately, he engulfs me in his arms, holding my shuddering body. "So fucking good, River. You're going to knock them into shape; I can see it now. We know your history with them, but you've got this."

I give myself a moment to break down. And then, I back away, lifting my chin at their praises.

"Very impressive," Zepp says, nodding his head as he approaches me. Placing a hand on my shoulder, he gently squeezes, taking me out of my momentary freak out that I'll save for later. "We believe in you, River. We would never have made you do this if we didn't think you could handle it."

"This feels like a shitty test," I grumble through a quivering lip, recalling the ugly name the band used. Central Trash. It fucking hurts to be reminded of where I came from. But then again, it proves how far I've come from the girl stumbling through life.

"You're a fucking rock," Seger adds, sidling up to me on the other side. "No one in this fucking place can do better than you. We know you'll be able to help them turn their fucking life around." He raises a sharp brow, emphasizing his belief in me.

A belief I don't feel.

I came into that room with revenge bleeding through my veins, begging for vengeance against the men who fucking ruined me. And now, I have to face them daily, organizing their lives and hoping they don't wreck me all over again.

We all flinch away from the two-way mirror, watching in horror as Kieran practically destroys the conference room with his anger.

Instead of running in there to stop him, Seger chuckles. "Ah, that one will be the fucking worst to tame."

"You've got this," Zepp mumbles with reassurance. "We'll give you a raise after this."

"Much deserved," I quip, shaking my head when Kieran storms away.

"Miss West!" Kat, my assistant, comes rushing in with a grim expression on her lips.

"Kat, call me River. Miss sounds way too damn formal," I grumble, noting the pale expression she's wearing.

"River," she murmurs softly, leaning in. "It happened again." My heart fucking drops into my ass, and I numbly nod.

"Um, thanks for that... I'll deal with it." Something seriously has to give. First them, now this shit. How much more can I suffer through in one day? Ugh.

"Okay. I need to..." She motions out the door, and I dismiss her with a wave of my hand.

"Is she doing okay?" Zepp asks, watching her retreating form.

"As good as she'll get," I say with a shrug. "Still needs some improvements, but she'll get there."

"There you fuckers are!" Chase chides, walking into the tiny room with his arm around their wife, Kaycee. Her brows dip as she looks me over, examining my ruffled expression. But before she can speak, Chase interrupts with his usual cheerful disposition, dipped with concern. "What did you do to Little West?" Chase asks with a frown, eyeing my face and heaving chest.

"Not now," Seger gripes, running a hand down his face. "We'll explain later."

Waving a hand, I shake off the doom sitting on my shoulders and plaster on my best fake smile. "Nothing. I'm fine. Just a hard job ahead." Hard is the understatement of the fucking century. "I'll run and get Lyric from the daycare and meet you in the lobby?" Kaycee nods, brows furrowing like she wants to ask what's wrong, but decides against it.

"Okay," she says with a tight smile. As I walk past her, she grabs my elbow and stops me. "Something is off. We'll talk about this later, right? Maybe a girl's night?" She examines my face when I nod, promising to fill her in later over a glass of wine. Scratch that; make it four glasses.

With that, still clutching their files to my chest, I make my way through the large skyscraper and head to the daycare to get Lyric the hell out of this building without being noticed.

2

Asher

My HEART DROPS into my ass when the ghost of my fucked up past strolls into the room with her head held high and stops right before us. *What the hell is she doing here? In our domain?*

Determination lines her sharp face, not giving any indication our presence affects her. No heavy breaths. No tears. There's nothing hiding behind the face of the girl I purposely screwed over and forced my best friends to leave behind.

Shit.

Pain spreads across my chest as the repressed memories I locked away long ago flood back into my mind, released from the confined space I shoved them into. Everything about River I've blocked and purposefully forgot about her. Our time together. The moments I spent between her luscious legs and shared with my bandmates. She went so far to help us get here, and then, I shit all over her existence. Imploding everything she'd built by one single lie I had orchestrated.

How has she been? Why is she here? How bad did I fucking break her with my betrayal because I was so damn desperate to get away?

Familiar pangs of guilt churn in my gut, and burning bile rises in my throat. I've avoided everything River West for the past five years. I never sought her out.

Out of sight. Out of mind.

Besides, there was no trace of her anywhere, with all her social media accounts shut down after we left. For me, it was a godsend. I didn't have to look at my mistake head-on and acknowledge the fact I fucked up. My refusal to think about her had me locking my memories away behind several heavy doors in my mind. My survival on this planet relies on her nonexistence. And today, I'm coming face to face with the karma I deserve by seeing her again.

Goddamn. What did I fucking do? Sometimes I don't understand myself. But if there's one thing for certain, it's that I'm not worthy to be in her presence. Kick my ass and lock me away, it's the least I fucking deserve for the vile actions I perpetrated against her.

Eyeing her up and down and taking in her appearance is its own form of torture. My heart pounds double time. My fingers fucking tremble around the arms of the chair. Staring at her is like looking too hard at the sun, and I'm bound to be burned. Not that I don't fucking deserve it. I deserve every ounce of ire this woman has, even if she doesn't know what I did. No one does except Gloria. Not a soul. Not even the men around me. I intended to purge my sins and confess them when we were famous, and she was long gone, but the words never left my tongue. I couldn't—wouldn't. We were good for so long, and then, we weren't.

River's long, brown hair remains the same as it always had, hanging past her shoulders. Only now, it seems smoother and more professional, framing the edges of her filled-out face. No longer does she look like the poor girl from Central City, barely eating and running herself ragged. She's filled out and looks healthier than I've ever seen her. More defined curves fill out the professional black pantsuit, highlighting just how much she's grown up.

Something beneath the surface of her calls to me again, much like it used to. River is a siren standing in a room full of sailors, begging them to come to her. Her aura hasn't changed one bit. I shift in my seat, determined to, once again, not heed her call.

"Hello, boys. My name is River West, and I'm your new band manager. Congratulations," she says, cocking her head.

I swallow the lump in my throat when all the oxygen leaves and suffocates me. Her voice drifts through the room with authority. Together, Callum, Kieran, Rad, and I sit like statues waiting for her to speak again. Every agonizing minute she stands there in silence, watching us with an eagle eye, is torture.

Her inspecting moss-green eyes take in the changes each of us has experienced in the past few years of a harsh rock star lifestyle. We're rougher. Maybe edgier from our time in the spotlight, entertaining millions, but yet, slightly more damaged than before. I always thought if I removed myself from the beast roaming the halls of my home, I'd heal the demons darkening my soul inside me. Boy, how wrong I was.

A new demon followed me around, relentlessly taunting me. Guilt. Over the years, I've tried to lock everything away in a small box and forget my transgressions. Who could forget, though? I never realized what I had, until it was gone. It was too late. Now, everywhere I look, my stomach turns, and bile rises at the simplest of reminders.

The longer she stares, waiting for us to acknowledge her, I swear fucking sweat breaks out across my flesh. Instinctively, I reach for the package of antacids in my pocket and toss one in my mouth, discreetly chewing the chalky substance to settle the nausea swarming in my gut.

The more I look at her, the more I see the ghosts of what I left behind.

Flashes of our intertwined past roar through my mind, leading to the worst decision I've ever made. Her name sits in the back of my mind, chanting like a prayer, patiently waiting for me to acknowledge the peak of our downfall. The person who cleverly built us up and helped us to succeed by granting us the golden ticket, only for us to turn our backs on her and leave her in the dust like she never meant a damn thing to us all. And that's the core of it all. I was young, stupid, and demented enough to think I could erase her from our lives without repercussions. But if there's anything I know about karma, she always comes back to bite you in the ass and take back what you put out into the world.

"How about we get started?" River hums with more confidence, not bothering to look up at us again.

"What-what are you doing here?" I swear I utter it without permission. "Why are you here?" I mumble again, trying to shake the specter from my vision.

"So nice of you to ask, Mr. Montgomery," she says in a polite yet professional tone.

The mere mention of my name sends shivers down my spine and goosebumps down my legs. Fuck. No, she can't affect me like this again. I can't let River work her way under my skin as she did before. I resisted so well back then, but with my guilt currently eating me alive, I don't think I can ignore the call she gives out.

"I'm working." Shrugging, she spreads massive amounts of paperwork out on the table. Her eyes look through the pages, humming under her breath until she comes to one that shocks her into silence.

Kieran says something snarky. Rad retorts. The entire room moves on without my conscious mind present. The only thing I can focus on is the past, instead of the present or future—where my mind should stay firmly planted. She mentions numbers, and I respond, staring at the dismal view of our existence at West Records. We're fucked. Kieran keeps babbling on, but I tune out his shitty attitude. The only reason he acts this way is because I'm a fucking tool and made him think she betrayed us.

Since then, I've lost touch with him. Hell—even myself. We aren't the same people we were rocking out in Callum's basement with stars in our eyes. We've changed. And we've ripped apart at the seams. I locked myself into music, focusing on the words and melodies. I tore myself away from the guys, promising myself I'd come clean. But I never did. In turn, they've collected their own vices, leading them away from the once tight-knit, brotherly bond we had.

My fingers white-knuckle around the armrests, hoping to choke the mirage standing before me from my vision. I blink hard, wishing her away. Many times before, my guilt chased me down with a vengeance. From the woman standing in the crowd of our performance to another walking down the sidewalk—she haunted every waking moment of my life, reminding me of the bullshit I pulled.

River tilts her head, looking us over with such confidence my heart aches in my chest. I swear someone utters a question of what she's doing here, and why the fuck is she standing in West Records, but I don't hear it. I hear nothing but the past calling back to me, forcing me to recall the bullshit I put her and my brothers through.

It's the one thing that keeps me staring at the ceiling night after night, until my eyes are bloodshot and burning. It's the rumbling in my stomach when I can't keep the acid from burning me from within. It's the itchy skin, pulling taut over my bones, and the patches of eczema reddening my damn flesh. An itch I can't fucking scratch because my guilt manifests in unpredictable ways.

It's consuming me whole. Before I know it, I'll be nothing but hollow bones wandering this earth.

Fuck. My gut churns, praying the constant loop of my nightmare rolling around in my brain will leave me for good. Sometimes I wonder if this is how Callum feels, reliving everything in vivid detail with his photographic memory. Sinking further into the darkness of my wicked mind, the memories of the only girl I've thought about since the moment I put my stupid-as-hell plan into motion comes back to haunt me, seizing the breath in my lungs.

"She's been cheating on us," I growl, tossing down my phone as the video on my screen plays at full volume, filling the room with her illicit hook-up with Donavan Drake, the thorn in our side—but my

secret ally.

The lie rests like sour milk on my tongue, begging me to break free and tell the truth. I suck in a breath. *Am I doing the right thing for us? Am I doing the right thing for River? Would she be better off without us? Probably. We'll do nothing but drag her down into our brand of fucked up bullshit if we stay. But this? Is this too much? Taking it too fucking far?*

Quickly, I avert my eyes at the image of River climbing on Van's lap and his low voice murmuring dirty words. Or it would be dirty words. *God, he fucking sucks at everything he does. I fucking hate his face. My only hope is we never have to see his stupid ass again. From here on out, River is only his and...* My eyes squeeze shut as Callum cries out in anguish. My heart fucking breaks as they grasp what I've laid down in front of them.

"No-no!" Callum sobs out, jumping to his shaky feet, nearly falling over. Fat tears well in his eyes, and he shakes his head, gripping the ends of his hair tightly in his fist. "That-that can't be true! That can't be her," he says, swallowing the lump in his throat. "That..." he trails off, covering his mouth with his fist, trying to hold back the rampant emotions surging inside of him.

"I've tried to tell you. Something was off," I say, running a hand down my face like I'm exasperated with the entire situation. "That's why we needed to stay away." I swallow the lie over and over. If I do, maybe they'll plant themselves inside my brain and sprout like it's the truth. Then, I might believe the words coming from my mouth.

"No," Callum says with conviction, shaking his head. "That can't be true. She'd never do that to me...or us," he whispers, letting the tears fall down his pale cheeks. Callum shoves past me, bumping my shoulder angrily with his, pacing near the front door of the home we've all made our own. I squeeze my eyes shut and grab my phone, mentally fighting with myself on the rights and wrongs of this entire scene.

I have to do this. We have to go to the Battle of the Bands without her. If she comes, they'll never get over her and move on with their dreams. If she can't go, then we'll never have the opportunity to leave this town. We'll live in this hellhole for the rest of our lives, wondering what our future would have been like if we had gone to California. And I can't let that happen to them. This is all for their own fucking good. In five years, they'll thank me for the sacrifice I made for them.

With my mental pep talk fizzling out into reason, I turn my back on my friends, as I've already done. I type out a single message to my stupid fucking ally and hit send. There's no going back now. Even as an elephant sits on my chest and compresses my breaths. Sweat forms on my brow when I return to the anger-filled conversation happening around me.

ME

Go.

He doesn't utter a word back, but I know he's seen it and is all too eager to get to the girl he's obsessively had his eyes on like a fucking stalker. Heavy iron sits in the pits of my stomach as I continue to tune out the mess I've created. My brows furrow as it all smacks me in the face at once. Van is a fucking stalker. We've had to fight him off her in more ways than one. And yet, I've fed the lamb to the mighty lion. Just like that. Gloria's words about talking to him come back to mind. How the hell did she know what kind of videos he had? Burning bile singes up my esophagus, begging to expel through my tightly held lips.

What the fuck have I done? I'm doing what's right. Shut the fuck up, mind! I'm putting this whole thing into motion. Fuck the consequences. Fuck everything else! We need this. This is our time to shine, and we can't let some Central City girl hold us back any longer.

"Where are you going?" Rad rasps, interrupting the guilty thoughts rushing through my mind and dragging me back to the conversation at hand. Holding back his emotions as he stands, Rad blankly stares, giving nothing away.

"To see for myself," Callum growls, clenching his fists. "You

can't just believe some video. He could...could be fucking her over. Again." With those parting words, Callum shoves out the front door with a bang. The rumble of his car fills the air, followed by screeching tires, and then he's gone.

It's not him fucking her over—it's me. I'm the one doing this to us. But it's for the damn best. It's for the damn best! My chest heaves.

If I don't get them away from her, then we'll never leave. I'll be stuck with Nigel and his fists for the rest of my life. Our dreams won't mean anything if I'm six feet deep at the hands of my father. And I can't let that fucking happen. This is for the best. For all of us. We'll be happier in a few years. And I'll be fucking free.

"I can't believe it," Kieran says with a stunned expression, running a hand down his face. "This is fucking unbelievable." His face pinches when he looks up at me for confirmation, and I nod. "But fucking why? I don't understand why she'd go back to him so easily. There's no way, man. She wouldn't go back to him like that. There has to be something going on that we don't know. Maybe he's blackmailing her," he grunts again, pulling at his hair. "I should go with Callum. I should..." He shakes his head, pacing the small living room with a pinched face.

"Fuck," I grunt in false anger. "How'd we let it get this fucking far? Huh? This was supposed to be simple! We weren't supposed to actually fall for her. How could you assholes let this happen? See what she did! I've been telling you for weeks that River has been up to something when she lets Van come into the record store. There's more to their relationship than she lets on," I growl, trying to weave more lies into the equation. Truth is, I've been doing this for the past few days, trying to implant false information into their brains. So, when it came time for this whole thing to go off, it'd be easier to make them believe.

"This was all your fucking idea!" Kieran shouts unexpectedly, with harsh emotions warring on his face. He's torn between not wanting to believe what I've laid out and firmly believing what I've shown him. And the latter is obviously winning when, within three *steps, he's in my face and fisting my T-shirt. Kieran teeters on the edge of being a loose cannon and is minutes away from slamming his fist into my face. It wouldn't be the first time, and it won't be the last. When they find out what I've done, they'll kill me. "You made us... I'm going to fucking murder Van for this."*

"I didn't make you do shit," I grunt, pressing my nose against his. "You all fucking agreed to this plan. Remember what we did it for? We wanted her for West Records and look at what we have now."

"But we didn't need her," Rad whispers, running his hand through his mullet. "We just..."

He fell in love; that's what he did. Head over heels with his ass in the air, his heart in his hand, and blood on his sleeves. They fucking love her, and I'm...fucking destroying them. I'm dismantling their love for her brick by brick; they never saw it coming. Day by day, since we've separated from her, I've been planting things in their heads. Hint by hint, I've been forcing them to conclude that this is what she did to us—betrayed us in the worst possible way. And this video? This is the nail in the coffin for our relationship.

No matter how badly I want to pull back and prevent this from happening, I can't stop myself. It's a necessary evil in my plan for our future. One day, when this comes out, I hope they can all forgive me for what I've taken away from the five of us. I'll get on my knees and fucking beg for their forgiveness. But for now, I must keep pushing through before it's too late. We have one week to get to California for the competition, and I need their heads in the game. Not on her. Not on their hopeless love. Us—the band—Whispered Words.

"And see where it got us?" I snark, knowing the quicker we move on, the faster we can get out of here and never have to think about this godforsaken town again. Goodbye Gloria, Goodbye fucking Nigel. And Goodbye River—may your life be what you always wanted it to be.

My chest squeezes when Kieran's expression falls, hurt lining every inch of him. "I just don't fucking understand, man," he growls, squeezing his eyes shut. "I need to fucking see for myself. I need to fucking talk to her and square this away. This can't be the fucking end." His fingers squeeze into fists, glaring at the front door.

Rad plops down onto the couch again, gripping the roots of his hair, muttering words I can't understand. "She wouldn't go back to Van," he says, scrunching his crumpled face and shaking his head with disbelief. "She wanted nothing to do with him. He's a stalker. Why the hell would she sleep with him behind our backs?" he asks, trying to rationalize the situation. "I'm with Cal. We need to talk to her and figure this out. There's something so fishy about this. We need..."

"It's all true," Callum says through heavy breaths, shuffling in through the front door. Deep, soul-crushing despair paints his long expression with tears staining his reddened cheeks, and his gray eyes darken in anguish.

"What's true?" Rad asks, lifting his head to meet Callum's eyes.

"Van was there," Callum mumbles through quivering lips. "He fucking kissed her. Before I left, I saw it. I...I saw it. They were there together. He brought her dinner, and then they fucking kissed. I couldn't-couldn't stay after he leaned in. How could she?" he gasps out, clutching his chest as mine tightens, feeling his misery from where I stand. Reaching into the depths of his pocket, he pulls out his phone, displaying one picture of Van shoving his tongue down River's throat.

Kieran leans forward with a scowl, taking the phone from Callum's hand. Without a word, he throws it back into Callum's hands and storms out of the house without a glance back, going to do whatever it is he's doing.

My dinner threatens to come up my throat and out my mouth for everyone to see. From where Callum stood, she looked so willing and compliant to Van's advances. That's all it takes for them to never question the accusation again. It is the nail in the coffin and all the motivation they need to pack their bags and turn their *middle fingers up to the city we are leaving behind. There's no going back now. I've set everything in motion to get us to the Battle of the Bands without a distraction. Without the woman who helped get us there.*

So, why do I feel like the human equivalent of a pile of shit in the front yard on a rainy day? This is my shining moment. The point I'd hoped to get to when I discovered that they'd stay behind and live normal lives for her. Only it's not.

By the time we made it to California and won, I knew I had made the biggest mistake of my life, leaving her behind. A wide crevice developed behind my ribs. Nothing in this world could fill it besides her. The love I gave her, without knowing it, shattered the moment we left town, leaving my insides a mess. I prided myself on not developing feelings and keeping my distance, but I was not only a liar to my best friends, but to myself. After our departure, something fundamental changed within the guys and in me. Almost as if they developed the same black mass inside them that ate away at everything it could get its hands on. We were never the same as we were in the small town of Central City, where we became famous.

Monumentally, I fucked up the best thing in our lives with one single lie that blew everything away. That tiny white lie was only the beginning of our story. Staring at River now has more thoughts and plans formulating in the back of my mind. I epically fucked up their lives by tearing them apart in the worst way possible. Maybe now that River is in front of us, I can fix this all. Maybe, just maybe, I can weave our lives together again and confess my bloody sins.

Even if they hate me—they'll still have her.

3

Asher

"You're dismissed. A limo will pick you up at your respective homes, and they will escort you to the Band House. There we will have another meeting of expectations, rules, and another six-month contract for you to sign," River declares, turning her back on us with her head held high.

My heart sputters, threatening to pop out of my chest. Until she slips from sight out the back door, leaving the four of us to wallow in the anger brewing like a dangerous storm around us.

"Well, this has been entertaining. Said no one ever," Rad snarks, lazily climbing to his feet. With ease, he grabs his motorcycle helmet from below the table and cradles it under his arm. "Apparently, I have a house to pack up. See you nut jerkers later." Pulling his phone from his pocket, he stares at it as he walks out of the room without a backward glance.

Since we settled in East Point, he's had this unaffected air about him. Almost as if River was just a blip on his radar and nothing more than some floozy, he messed around with on the Ferris wheel. Not the love of his life.

The thing about Rad is, he's put a mask on since the moment we left Central City. And now, he never lowers it and lets us see the pain he's hiding away from us.

The walls press around me. Over and over, I've lived with the damage I inflicted on four other human beings due to my selfishness. I, alone, crushed the love from Rad's veins the moment I pointed my fingers at her with my cheating allegations. More guilt builds in my chest, crushing me where I sit rigidly in my chair, basking in the silence of the other two who stay in their seats.

"Does this not bother him?" Kieran asks with a deep scowl, watching as he disappears through the door leisurely. "We left for a fucking reason. We..." Kieran grunts, jumping to his feet and throwing the chair across the room until it bounces off the wall with a thud. We don't even blink at his outburst. Kieran's been nothing but fumes, waiting for the match to strike. And here it is...

"We left because she...she...fuck!" he shouts, pounding a fist into the edge of the table. Releasing a pained grunt, he stands tall, gathering his emotions. Emptiness fills his blueish eyes, and he shakes his head. "I'm out," he says, clearing his throat and taking off out the door at a quick pace.

This is going to go swimmingly. The four of us, stuck in a house together. Throw in the girl they think cheated on them in the worst betrayal ever. What was past me thinking?

Pinching the bridge of my nose, I huff and climb to my feet. "You coming?" I ask Callum, who sits ramrod straight in his chair, most likely reliving the worst night of his life on repeat.

I swear I've never seen a man go from one extreme to another. From full of love and life, to an empty, speechless shell of a man. River's ghost may have haunted me from the moment we leapt on stage at The KC Club and swept the competition, but the remnants of what I did stood right before me, slowly falling apart at the seams.

All of this is my fucked-up masterpiece of manipulation. I took good men and molded them into angry beings. I robbed them. I fucking robbed her of our promise. God. If I could create a time machine, I'd go and change the past. We may have our freedom and money, but at what cost? I take a deep, painful breath, begging the oxygen to fill my glass-coated lungs and squeeze my eyes shut.

Callum solemnly nods, slowly rising to his feet with the contract we signed years before clutched tightly in his hands. Slowly, he makes his way out of the room with his head hanging low, leaving me here in the silence of the conference room to suffer in the hell of my own doing.

Tears burn the back of my eyes as I stare at the tile ceiling with self-deprecating thoughts swirling a million miles a minute. I take a few moments to gather myself and push the looming guilt to the bottomless pit of my soul.

As I walk out the door, shoving my hands into my jeans and balling them, massive amounts of guilt swim in my gut, churning until bile hits the back of my throat. My only sensible solution after all these years is to set the truth free. I squeeze my eyes shut, assaulted by another memory lurking in the shadows and ready to strike.

"Are we ready for this?" I ask, flexing my fingers around the steering wheel of my Tahoe, eagerly awaiting the moment we leave Central City behind.

"Fuck this town," Kieran grunts, shoving his middle finger into the air. "Fuck her," he mutters with venom lacing his tone. Nothing but hurt sits on his twisted-up face. Proving to me that pushing River away was the best option for us. Eventually, I'll have my brother back. Eventually, I'll have my best friends back.

"Yeah, let's roll," Rad grumbles with less enthusiasm, staring out the window with a blank expression, losing all the spark he once held. Hell, he's barely blinked since the night they discovered what River's been up to. Or, what they think she's up to.

Peering at Callum through the rearview mirror, I note the nod he gives me. Not bothering to say a word. Since he's come back from watching Van kiss River, he's spoken less than usual. Nearly turning mute in our presence. If I can get them out of this River funk and into our bright future, we could turn ourselves around.

I swallow thickly and pull out of the driveway, driving us toward our new destination—East Point Bluff, California. Where dreams come true. My mind endlessly wrestles with me on the rights and wrongs of this entire situation.

"Let's start a new chapter in our life," I say with confidence I don't exactly feel.

The more distance we put between River and us, the more my heart aches in my chest, cracking from the wool I pulled over my friends' eyes. Even though it's for the best. It's necessary. It needed to be done. Right? I had to do it. She would have just slowed us down. They would have turned away from our mission—the Battle of the Bands.

"Fuck," I gasp out, clutching my chest as the pain engulfs me once again from the inside out, hollowing me further and opening the dark pit of despair inside me.

The world tilts when I collapse against the wall, holding my face in my hands. No matter how hard I tried to tell myself it was the right thing to do, I knew in my heart I had thoroughly fucked up and made a sticky fucking mess of the whole thing. I took each of their trust and crushed it in my hand. And for what? This? We're fucking miserable together. Sure, we're still making music, but apparently, we're on our last leg. It's only been five years. And our career is already in the damn toilet. Worst of all, we haven't been brothers since we stepped foot in California, because we left our glue back in Central City.

And it's all my fault.

They weren't the only ones who fell for River's whims and free spirit—I did too. I held off for so long, the fear of getting close holding me back. Once I got my hooks in her, it was hard to release her from my grasp. It tore me apart to run to Van Drake. It still tears me apart that I climbed into that vehicle and planned the ultimate betrayal against her with a damn predator. But I did what I did because I thought it was what was best for the band. For what I thought was for our own good. Selfishly, I erased her from existence and ran away like a pussy.

"Fuck," I mumble, digging my palms into my eyelids, pushing away the pain of my past.

Silent, pent-up tears stream down my face at the reality of it all. In a few hours, the four of us will be locked in a house together for six months. I've held this secret for way too long, and it's time I come clean. And maybe we can get back to the people we were before I ruined everything. It's like fate came and slapped me on the head. And...

"You're crying," says a little voice from in front of me, getting a front-row seat to my breakdown.

Sucking in a breath, my whole-body jolts, and I'm knocked out of my spiral. My gaze snaps forward, locking on a little girl standing before me. Her tiny dark brows furrow, and a frown pulls at her lips. Discreetly, I wipe away the tears streaming down my cheek and shake my head. Looking up and down the long, empty hallways, a lone thought filters through my mind. Where the hell are her parents?

I swallow hard when she gasps, looking me up and down. A tiny smile lights up her little face, and she taps my shoulder, gently squeezing in a comforting manner. "It'll be okay, Daddy." She pats me again and leans her tiny head on my shoulder with a dramatic sigh. "No tears," she coos, gently squeezing again, sighing contentedly on my shoulder.

I lick my lips, sitting rigidly beneath her grasp. "Uh, kid," I say, clearing my throat and feeling an odd heat billowing up my neck. She has to be wrong. There's no way I could be anyone's daddy. I haven't touched a woman since... River. That night at the castle house on the lake was the last night I ever sunk my dick into someone.

"I'm not..." I swallow my tongue when she raises her head, looking directly into my eyes. She smiles again, taking in my face as I take in hers. My breath leaves, and confusion swirls in my mind at the familiarity. It's like looking at a small River with darker hair and... "Your eyes," I mumble, unable to look away from the blue, mismatched eyes much like...like... Kieran's.

They're so damn rare to have; I've only ever seen one person with them.

Long, dark hair hangs over her shoulders, nearly down to the middle of her back, her mismatched eyes take me in, and her cherub face fills with light and love. Gently, she clings to a small white rabbit held against her chest.

"Bunny makes me feel better when I'm sad. Here," she says, thrusting the tiny stuffed animal into my hand. "Now you'll be okay," she says with truth behind her words.

I scrunch my brows, staring down at the poor ripped rabbit, filled with light food stains and a ripped ear.

"Aunt Ode gave her to me," she says, fiddling with the little ribbon secured around the intact ear. "She came out to see me. Do you know her, Daddy?"

I'm completely frozen, staring at this child. I shake my head, lifting a hand to touch her cheek almost out of instinct when a piece of her hair falls in front of her face. It's odd to look into the eyes of a stranger and find comfort in the loving gaze she sends me. Like she knows me somehow. Like I should know her.

"What's your name?" I ask cautiously, removing the piece of hair from her face. Her expression crumples from the beautiful smile she once held, and her brows furrow.

"You don't know my name?" she whispers in a heartbroken tone, pulling at my heartstrings.

"I'm sorry, kiddo," I whisper, shaking my head. "Where are your parents? Are they around here somewhere?"

She sucks in a breath, heavily fidgeting with her bunny until she snatches it out of my hand. "It's okay," she whispers. "Mommy said..."

"Lyric!" I drop my hand the moment a frantic voice echoes from down the hall. I swallow hard as River comes hauling ass in our direction with determination taking over her expression. And then she stops right beside us, silently shaking her head. Every ounce of color drains from her face when she sees my tear-stained face standing so close to...

"You," I whisper, furrowing my brows, watching intently as she collapses to her knees and pulls the little girl away, shaking her head frantically.

"Lyric, I've told you before. You can't go wandering off on your own, okay? Even here." River's voice evens out into a soothing one, something my mother used to coo at me when she tucked me in at night and told me she loved me.

"I love you so much, my Asher," my mother's soothing voice echoes in my mind. Her hazel eyes stare down at me filled with so much love, I beg her to lie beside me. "Just for tonight," she murmurs, kissing my hair as her warm arms envelop me in a hug. "Stay my little Asher Bear forever," she whispers one last time before my eyes flutter shut, and my chest feels whole.

"Mommy," she whines, pointing a finger in my direction and making my body lock up. Lyric's lip puffs out in a pout with puppy dog eyes that could give Rad a run for his money. "He doesn't know my name," she says with more sadness, breaking my fucking heart. "It's Lyric," she says through a pout, eyes threatening to spill tiny teardrops.

"I know," River soothes, side-eyeing me with apprehension, but shakes me off. "Aunt Kaycee is waiting for you," she says in her mom voice again, successfully steering the conversation away from her child and me.

Her fucking child. Jesus. My heart gallops so damn fast in my chest that I swear it's going to finally take the leap and kill me. River has a kid. When the hell did that happen? Fuck. I run a hand through my hair, gripping the roots. She has a kid who has mismatched eyes and...

Every ounce of oxygen expels from my lungs. The entire world tilts on its axis and stops turning. Little pieces click together without her having to say a word. I snap my gaze to River, who swallows hard in my presence and silently shakes her head. Long gone is the woman who confidently walked into the conference room with her head held high. In her place is a woman scared shitless that I'm here in front of her daughter.

"And Maggie!" Lyric squeals with excitement, tightening her tiny fists, seeming to forget my mistake.

"And Maggie," River confirms, shaking off my presence and taking the little girl's hand in hers. With one last look in my direction, River drags the girl away from me with worry lining her face.

"Bye, Daddy," Lyric says, waving with her bunny in her hand and a bright smile on her face, reminding me so much of the woman holding onto her for dear life.

"Bye, Lyric," I rasp, waving back as a multitude of emotions roar through my body.

"Mommy! Daddy said my name!" she squeals, breaking away from her mother's grip and charges me with a grin. Her tiny body slams into mine, still seated on the ground. Her tiny arms wrap around my neck, and she nuzzles her face into my neck. "I knew you'd remember me, Daddy," she whispers into my flesh. "Please, don't forget me again." My heart fucking cracks inside my chest and splinters into pieces. I don't know what River has told her. Hell, I don't know how the fuck this happened, but I'll get to the bottom of it.

"Lyric, babe. We have to get you downstairs. Maggie is waiting," River's voice cracks when she says those words, slowly peeling Lyric off me.

"Bye, Daddy! See you tomorrow!" she says in a cheerful tone, waving to me one last time until they disappear around the corner and out of view.

"See you tomorrow," I whisper a promise I can't keep to no one but the empty hall.

I sit there for another five minutes, staring at the same spot they disappeared through. Rampant thoughts roll through my mind at hyper-speed, sending my heart into a damn frenzy. She called me Daddy. Daddy. Me? Fuck. I bring a hand up to my mouth, contemplating throwing up the acid still burning holes through my esophagus. This is my fault. Every ounce of this situation is on my shoulders. More tension mounts inside me, wreaking havoc. A pounding headache hammers through my skull, pressing me down onto the floor. The weight of the fucking world rests on me because I did this.

I'm to fucking blame. The guys have no clue River had a baby. Fuck. I didn't know! And here she is, this beautiful little creature calling me daddy and begging me to never forget her. Goddamn. Kieran is going to break my face open when he finds out.

And I'll deserve it.

I rub my eyes and lean my head against the wall. Fuck. I have so much to do, but I can't seem to get myself to move from this spot. Just as I'm about to rise from my spot, a figure comes marching down the hall with gritted teeth and balled-up fists.

"Why're you still here?" River asks with suspicion when she walks by, only stopping right beside me. "Shouldn't you be packing? I'm sure you have a lot of stuff to do." She raises a pointed brow, taking out a key from her pocket. Like a silent invitation, she opens the door I'm beside and walks in. It isn't until I climb to my feet do I read the plaque outside the door.

'River West–Manager–Fixer'

God damn. She really went and made something of herself, like she had always hoped. All her hard work and determination have paid off. How many days and nights did she work herself to the bone to achieve her dreams?

My heartbeat roars in my throat when I step into her office and stop short in the middle. River's brow furrows as she leans over her desk, running her finger over a piece of paper. She swallows hard, turning to another page.

"You had a baby?" I question through a rasp, startling her from her stupor.

"Great deduction skills, Asher. You're a regular detective," she bites back. "You're as smart as I remember. How long did it take you to remember her?" She scoffs, tossing whatever she was looking at back into a large envelope with her name on it. But I note the tremble in her fingers and the shiver that runs down her spine. Quickly, she picks up her phone and types out a message with pursed lips, not letting me see her emotions. Paleness erases all the color from her face, and she mutters a name under her breath, shaking her head. "Fucking, Kat."

"Remember?" I ask, furrowing my brows. "What the hell are you talking about?" I ask, rolling my shoulders back.

She rolls her eyes and sets her phone back in a large purse. "Don't you have more important things to do? Like pack and get your ass in the limo?" Cocking her head to the side, her green eyes narrow at me as she waits for my answer.

"Yeah, I have important fucking things to do. But you had a baby, and you're evading the question, Little Brat. Is it his?" I ask, crossing my arms over my chest and matching her aggression. Her nickname feels foreign on my tongue, but yet, oh, so right. I don't know what it is about River West, but she brings this side out of me. This demanding prick that begs to put her on a string and force her to my will.

"It's none of your business now. And my name is River, River West to you," she says with a simple head shake and collects her purse. "Now, get out of my office. I have a meeting," she demands, pointing toward the open door and shooing me away.

"No," I say, grabbing her arm and halting her retreat. "Is that little girl my brother's?" I whisper, looking deep into her wide, moss-green eyes. "Tell me."

"Why the fuck do you care now?" she grunts with emotions bubbling through her words, tinged with hurt and so much rage, it punches me in the gut. With defiance, she pulls her arm out of my grip and rights herself. "Five years of knowledge that, yeah, I kept our fucking kid. But why now? Why care now, Asher?" she growls, taking a step back, but keeps her eyes on me. "Explain it to me because I'd love to hear the words come out of your mouth."

My throat constricts at her tiny admission, and I press forward, pushing through the confusion. "You seem to be under the impression that I know what you're talking about. I didn't know you had a kid, let alone Kieran's baby. If we'd known..." I stop myself, running a hand through my hair and gripping the ends.

God fucking damnit! Guilt tears me in two, bringing fresh tears burning in my eyes. My stomach churns more, and I barely suppress the dry heave constricting my throat.

What? Would we have turned around? Giving up our dreams? Shit. Does Kieran know? Fuck. My heart sinks. Did he throw them away because of me? Did I... I heave a breath, tamping down the panic swelling like a surging storm in my chest. I did. I fucking destroyed a family. We could have had something wonderful, and I fucked it all up by being an asshole with my one little lie.

Not only did I fuck over River and my bandmates, but I fucked over his kid—our kid. Jesus, she called me daddy.

Time stands still around me as this pinnacle moment smacks me over the head, forcing me to see every mistake I've made flash before my eyes. We have a daughter. With River. Our time is running on fumes. I need to sew these wounds shut and fix our issues. For Lyric. For us. For River. I've been complicit in this for far too long and sitting back without opening my mouth. It's time to set everything in motion and bring our family back together. It's time I make this up to everyone.

She blinks a few times, staring at me, and shakes her head. "Out," she barks with much less fire in her voice, and her shoulders slump.

With reluctance, I follow her out, staying close as she locks the door and watching her every move.

"River?" I ask when she turns to walk away without glancing in my direction.

"What?" she asks in a sharp voice, stopping in the middle of the hall.

"Why did she call me daddy?" I ask, furrowing my brows. She's clearly not my blood, but I'd love her just the same, even if she wasn't.

My heart pounds when her shoulders rise and fall with her

heavy breaths. Without turning to look at me, she utters words I never thought I'd hear.

"Despite you assfaces deciding to ditch me for no reason or letting me explain. Even after the restraining orders and the fucking check I tore up, I wanted Lyric to know where she came from. She knows exactly who each of you is." She shakes her head and turns on her heels, glaring at me when my mouth hangs open in shock at the tears rolling down her cheeks. So much hurt sits behind those beautiful eyes. My damn mouth goes dry.

"My mother never gave me the chance to know my dad. But don't mistake her calling you daddy as a chance for you all to swoop in and play fathers of the year. I won't let Lyric get hurt like you hurt me. Because you all discarded us like trash, and I won't let you do that again. Not to her. She deserves better. *I* deserve better than some fuck boy rock stars who break their promises." River's eyes screw shut as she heaves a breath, collecting herself before she speaks again. When her mouth opens, every ounce of hurt and emotions wipes from her tone as she says her next words, "Now, go get your shit and go to the band house. Or your contract will be voided immediately." Wiping the tears from her face and with one last huff, River marches away, leaving me in a confused-filled fog that threatens to send me on my ass.

The world spins as I move down the hall, attempting to find the exit and get the hell out of this place. River's words live rent-free in my mind when I finally stumble to my car. Resting my head against the headrest, my thoughts continue to swirl. But there's one thing she said that stands out and makes me question everything from before.

What fucking restraining orders? What fucking check? What the fuck is she talking about?

4

Kieran

ME

Anything? Can we get out of it?

CONSTANCE

Short answer? No.

I GRIT MY TEETH, my fingers tightening around my cell phone. Anger storms through my body, tensing every inch of me. But that's nothing new.

ME

No?

CONSTANCE

It's in the contract, K. Nothing you can do about it unless you walk.

ME

Any other offers?

I drum my fingers on my thigh, nervously bouncing my leg. All we need is another offer, and we can flip West Records the finger and walk. We don't need them. We don't need her.

CONSTANCE
I'll keep my eyes open. But right now? No.
Good luck. Stay nice.

"Fuck," I mumble, pinching the bridge of my nose, eager to lash out at the gym and relieve myself of all this anger festering inside me. It's the only thing that chases any sort of feelings away. I can't afford to feel around her.

"Didn't go well?" Rad asks, staring down at his phone with longing in his dark eyes.

The edge of his finger runs over the picture he doesn't think I know about. The one he stares at day in and day out like a hurt puppy dog, waiting for his master to come back and claim him. It's never escaped me that he's still madly in love with her, even after what she did.

Rad sighs heavily, biting into his bottom lip as we pull up to Callum's condo. The limo comes to a complete stop, idling on the curb as we wait a solid three minutes for him to appear. Callum's bulky form comes into view with his hands tucked in his pockets. A large, black hoodie swallows his body whole, and the hood covers his eyes. The moment he flips it down, I know the evidence will be on his face in the form of blackened bruises and swollen flesh.

Callum doesn't utter a word as he shuffles into the limo and finds a seat next to Rad, not bothering to meet our curious gazes. Leaning back, he rests his head and closes his eyes, tuning us completely out with his earbuds snug in his ears. Like so many years before, Callum only speaks when spoken to, but worse. He only opens his mouth if it pertains to the band, and that's it.

Lead fills my stomach at the onslaught of memories banging around inside my head. Five years ago, something fundamental fucked us all up. We've thrived in our own ways. Some more than others, finding hobbies to take our wandering minds off the woman who crushed us with one single action. We don't speak her name. Or mention our past in passing. Together, we've avoided the topic altogether and moved forward. Well, mostly. Sometimes the ghost of my past comes back to haunt me, pulling me into unwanted memories.

Marching through the parking lot of River's apartment building, I tightly ball my hands into fists. Rage consumes every molecule in my body when I see the familiar red Mustang parked right in front of River's apartment. I stand, frozen next to it, when the front door of River's apartment slams open, and out walks Van with a victorious grin spreading across his face. His shirt hangs over his arm, and he whistles gleefully under his breath.

"You fucking her?" I accuse, stepping out of the shadows with a scowl and folding my arms over my chest.

Seeing the picture Callum had taken didn't satisfy my curiosity one bit. I had to see for myself. River and I have way too much history for me to just walk away without investigating what the fuck is going on. But now, the scale is sliding in an unfavorable direction, leading me to believe that everything is true.

"For a few months," Van says with a cocky grin, pulling his shirt over his head.

My fists clench at my side, and before I know what the fuck I'm doing, I grab Van by his arm and throw him against the side of his car. "You've been fucking her for months?" I hiss, getting right in his face.

"Yeah, bro. Aren't you happy I told you? God, she was going to let you all think you were hers when she's fucking half the town," he sneers, pushing his forehead against mine. Without a thought, I throw my fist into his temple, crumpling him to the ground, and taking my frustrations out on his curled-up body.

As the memory ebbs away, I come back to the reality of it all. I never made it inside to talk to River after witnessing Van walking from her apartment. For the next few days, I snuck away from the guys and watched him come and go from the parking lot, convincing me that the truth was right in front of my eyes the entire time. She cheated and felt nothing for us.

"We're stuck," I say, sucking in a ragged breath. "My agent

says it's in the contract that we have to put up with this for the full six months, unless we get another deal from somewhere else."

"Somewhere else?" Rad asks, raising his brows. He heaves a sigh, shoving his phone into his pocket. "Like that'll happen."

"Like where?" Callum mutters, peeking an eye open.

"EJ Records across town has always been interested," I say confidently as the car takes off across town toward Asher's massive house on the damn beach.

I squeeze my eyes shut when visions of River walking into the conference room fill my mind and refuse to let go. For five years, I've wiped her existence from everything. I pretend she never existed. I pretend she never shattered my heart into a million pieces. But she always seems to show her face in my nightmares. Now, she's here in the flesh, ready to haunt me more.

And it pisses me off more than anything. How can she walk around like nothing happened between us? What we had was more special than anything. And she gave it away for a good fuck in the back of a Mustang.

A picture of Van and River in her kitchen. Kissing. His fucking lips are on hers. Her lips on his.

I see red. My mind goes haywire. Accusations sit on the tip of my tongue. Anger rises in my chest and crushes my ribs, ripping my heart from inside me. Opening a deep, dark pit of nothing in my chest. Numbness prickles at my mind and tingles down my limbs.

And then I feel...nothing.

A part of me wished what Asher had said wasn't fucking true, and that it was all some sick joke on us. It was a video; it could have been staged. Some last blaze of glory for Van to try and win her back without us in the picture. I was prepared to march to her apartment and spank the truth from her ass. Then Callum came and set me straight with his picture.

There it was in bright colors. The truth I've been dreading with a sickening knot in my stomach since Asher opened his mouth.

How had I fallen so hard again? With her? Only to have to

force myself to put one foot in front of the other and leave her behind, forgetting she ever existed.

I used to think my heart only beat for her, but now it beats for no one. Not even me. I'm a broken man without my River Blue. Or not mine. Was she ever? Was it all fun and games? Did I not make myself clear who owned every inch of her?

Apparently not. Because Donovan Drake swooped in and stole her back like he had planned. Maybe we were just a way to pass the time, and we were never exclusive. Whatever it was, I'm done, but not before I find out for myself. Without a word or a glance back, I throw open the front door and storm away, hellbent on finding the truth for myself.

I blow out a breath, shaking the stupid memories out of my mind just in time to retrieve a pale-looking Asher. Something plagues him when he settles in his seat beside me, fiddling with a key between his fingers. Nervously, he darts his eyes around the car and swallows hard, before looking out the window again. It's always the same with him. Since we moved here, he's been sketchy as hell. Always locking himself in his room, unless it has to do with the band. Then he'll come out and play with us. He's always so quiet and so damn reserved. It drives me fucking nuts to see him act so differently from the guy I used to know.

He hasn't been the same since River.

"What is wrong with you?" I mutter, wrinkling my nose.

I've never seen my perfectly put-together stepbrother—or I guess not anymore—lose his shit like this. Sweat beads on his forehead, and he heaves another breath.

"Nothing," he murmurs so quietly, gazing out the window as we take off down the road with all of us settling in.

"Anyone know where this mysterious band house is?" Rad asks in a lazy tone, keeping his eyes trained out the window at the blurring colors passing by.

Rad may seem like the same old goofy dude, but he's not. He's thrown himself into music, girls, booze, and parties. All to forget her. She who shall not be named. The one who ruined us all with her selfish ways. And that idiot? Yeah, he still pines for her every night.

Sometimes I think River West was our one true love. Something we'll never find again.

"I'll find it," Callum says, pulling out our contract from some mysterious place in his hoodie. Flipping through a few pages with trembling fingers, he points to a spot on the page. "Number Four, Lyric Lane, is the official address listed in the paper."

Rad snorts. "Lyric Lane? Sounds made up."

Asher's breath beside me shudders in his chest, and he shakes his head, drawing my attention to him again. He's acting fucking weird. I've never seen someone who is all business all the time, so fucking rattled by this situation. I run a hand down my face and shake my head.

"Don't let her get to you," I offer, sitting back and getting comfortable. "We'll get out of this. I'll never let River rule my life ever again."

Asher swallows hard, snapping his hazel eyes at me. Licking his lips, he looks at the other two and leans into my personal bubble.

"You know River had a kid?" he asks in a soft voice, trying not to draw attention to the other two.

I snort. "Of course. Gloria called me," I spit, rolling my eyes. "I've known for the past five years." My heart beats heavily against my ribs at the thought of her having a kid. *His* kid. After all that time together, she still went back to him before we even left and opened her legs.

"You knew?" Asher asks with furrowed brows, and his face twists in disbelief. "You knew about her? And you've never..."

I scoff. "Why the fuck would I care?" I wave a hand. "River can do whatever she wants. She's not my concern. Not anymore." A pain stabs my chest, tightening like rubber bands constricting my breath. Even after all these years.

I loved her once. Hell, more than once. She was my best friend. I really fucking loved her, to the point I would have jumped off a cliff for her without a second thought. Until that night when I watched with my own eyes as she jumped into that psycho's lap and fucked his brains out, and then Callum's proof was all I needed. We used her at first, hoping to get by on her name to get here. Then, somehow under our noses, she used us right back, faking Van's stalker interest in her. Using us to defend her honor and all that shit. It's the only explanation I've come up with after all this time.

"River has a kid?" Rad asks, the conversation piquing his interest. Leaning forward, he rests his elbows on his knees, staring between the two of us. "Since when?" His face twists, and more betrayal spears through his dark eyes.

"Five years," I say with a shrug, focusing outside the window.

Rad gives a brief whimper, letting me know he's still affected by her presence, too. I wasn't the only one hopelessly in love with her. We all were. And she fucking decimated our hearts. Even after all these years and the betrayal of a lifetime, we're hopeless.

The conversation ceases, and only our breathing can be heard through the large cabin as we sit in the first conversation we've really had in a long ass time. It's hard to remember when it happened, but at some point, we fell apart. Right about the time Asher started retreating into himself and avoiding us at all costs was about the time Callum did the same. He barely speaks these days. Hell, he barely looks at us. And Rad...the poor, poor guy hasn't lost himself in enough pussy to get over her yet. It'll happen eventually, but I'm sure with her being our new boss, it won't help one bit. One day, I'll help him get over her and bring the rest of them back on board. Our band hasn't felt like a family for years, but they're the only ones I have. If I don't have this band, then I don't have shit.

Iron gates come into view with a large metal 'W' lining the entirety of the ornate metal. A guard shack, complete with a guard, who pokes his head out from the little window with an inspecting eye. His words to our driver are murmured through the separating glass, and his voice barely registers.

"A guard?" Rad raises his brows, eyeing the thin man nestled inside his office, complete with a small TV visible to us. A large badge displaying the name of 'D&D Security' clings to the upper arm of the dark blue uniform.

"What the hell does she need a guard for?" I snark as the gate opens wide, allowing us entry to the long, winding driveway. "Spoiled ass princess," I mutter, sulking as I eye the guard who is already sitting back in his chair with a drink in hand, lazily scrolling through his phone—some guard he is.

As we make our way down the drive, a bright blue street sign confirms what I already guessed. We're on Lyric Lane, heading to the house that will be our home for the next six months of hell.

Anticipation buzzes across my skin as we keep going, not seeing a home in sight. Grassy lands surround us, and to our right, a long beach with white-tipped waves greets my eyes. Jesus. West Records really went all out for this. We're secluded. Maybe fifteen minutes from West Records offices.

I can still hear Gloria's smug voice over the phone as she relayed the information on River's little secret. Like I cared at that point. Still don't. River can live the life she deserves far the fuck away from me. All I want is to fix the band. Not that we need it. We sold out shows last year. We packed the stadiums. Maybe we've had some mishaps and exposure to our mistakes, but we've always pushed through.

The limo comes to a stop in the short driveway of a simple two-story white mansion. There's nothing particularly special about it. But what catches my eye when we pile out is the matching house across the street with an SUV in the driveway. The license plate reads RWest.

"Whoa, dude," Rad says, turning in circles, admiring the luxurious view around us. "This is... Wow," he settles on, looking around both properties in awe.

I sigh when my phone buzzes. Pulling it out of my pocket, I frown when her name flashes across the screen. Everything in me tenses, and I shake my head. Of course, she'd ask this today.

GLORIA

I need some more money.

"Hello, boys," comes a sultry voice from the garage as the door lifts, revealing River in a tight red dress with matching come-fuck-me heels. A scowl forms at the idea of her outfit change, going from completely professional to this. This... God. Even if I hate her, she's fucking beautiful. "Welcome to your new home. If you'll follow me, we have some rules to discuss."

I swallow hard when her moss-green eyes connect with mine, and she tilts her head. Immediately, I look away, hiding the sadness resting in my soul every time I look in her direction, and snarl instead. If I can't show the fucking hurt bleeding my heart dry, then I'll turn to the rage I've felt since the moment I realized it was all true and punish the woman who crumbled my heart into a million pieces.

My heart can't take another round with River West again.

5

River

"*You seem to be under the impression that I know what you're talking about. I didn't know you had a kid, let alone Kieran's baby. If we'd known...*"

What the fuck does he mean he didn't know?

Tears cascade down my cheeks at an unstoppable rate when I finally park in my driveway. Bone-crushing emotions surge through my body as his words repeat in my mind. Deep anguish grabs hold, sinking its claws deep into me, letting everything I've held in over the last five years out. Even if I wanted to stop the waterworks, I couldn't. Not now. Placing my forehead against the steering wheel of my SUV, I allow myself a moment to grieve the fathers Lyric could have had.

Thankfully, Lyric is with her cousin tonight, because I don't think I could hold it together with her here asking me questions like she did before. So, for now, I cry for all the things they missed out on and the family they could have had. I cry so I won't cry when I pick Lyric up and bring her home. That's the thing about moms, we put on a brave face even when we're drowning in misery.

The late-night feedings, diaper changes, and the quality time getting to know the men who could have raised her alongside me. Only, they didn't. They walked out without a goodbye, leaving me to do it all by myself because it inconvenienced their chance at a better life. But what about mine? Where would I have been if Seger and Zepp hadn't tracked me down and handed me more money than I knew what to do with?

Confusion swims in my foggy brain, making a groan escape my lips. Asher's words reverberate in my mind, ping-ponging over and over again.

He acted like he didn't have a clue Lyric existed, and he should have known. Shouldn't he? Shouldn't they all? I shake my head, second-guessing everything that happened. Gloria called them right in front of me. I heard her from the vacant living room of Callum's old house. So, why did he act like he'd seen a ghost? Why was it such a damn shock that she was with me?

The way he gazed at Lyric with tears in his eyes and held her in his arms when she hugged him broke me in half. I will forever tattoo the scene in my thoughts. Through my efforts, Lyric holds strong feelings for each of these men after years of seeing their pictures and asking me about them.

What was I supposed to tell her? That they refused to acknowledge her? That she was a mess up, and they didn't want her? Fuck no. I did what any good mom would do; I let her know them through photographs and music, letting her sing their songs at the top of her lungs. No matter how hard it hurt at the time. I told her stories of our times together and the adventures we had as a unit. Then came the ending of our union. It's something I've kept hidden from her small ears. There's no way I can break her heart like they broke mine. So, for her sake, I keep them on a shrine for her to worship.

"But where?" Lyric's little lip pouts as she holds up a picture of Kieran, Asher, Callum, and Rad from some red-carpet event this past weekend on her tablet. Her big eyes zone in on their fancy suits and smiles on their faces.

"Ly," I murmur, curling a piece of her dark hair behind her ears. "Sometimes parents aren't ready to be parents. And your daddies weren't ready to be that just yet." It's all I can manage to

say to my broken-hearted daughter, who will never understand the magnitude of the betrayal that sits heavy on my heart.

"Do they not like me? I'll be better! I won't hit cousin Rome anymore. I promise. Just call all my daddies and tell them. I be good," she says in a hurried tone, tinted with emotions.

Her big, mismatched eyes well up with tears and spill over onto her reddening cheeks, ripping my heart from my damn chest and splintering it into a million pieces. Sometimes I think I'm doing the wrong thing by telling her where she came from. I'm leaving her with these high expectations of four daddies who can't be with her yet. Lord knows our relationship was unconventional. But I'm thankful everyday Lyric has Kaycee, Seger, Zeppelin, Chase, and Carter to round out her yearning for her fathers.

I have to remind myself every day when the guilt slams into me that I wasn't the one who walked away. They were. She'll know their lives and faces like the back of her hand if I can help it. And one day, when she's old enough to understand, I'll explain it all to her the best I can.

"I'm sorry, Ly," I gasp out, pulling her into my arms. Rocking her back and forth, I kiss the top of her head, holding my tears at bay. "They'll come back when they're ready, I promise." And maybe I shouldn't have promised her something so massive and life changing. I assumed one day, they'd come knocking and admit their mistakes, wanting to be present in her life. After five years, I'd given up hope for Lyric to ever know them.

"Maybe he didn't know," Odette, my best friend from Central City, says through the speakers of my SUV. Breaking me from my morbid thoughts. Because why cry by yourself when you can call your best friend and cry with her?

"But she-who-shall-not-be-named called them. Right in front of me, Ode," I sigh, rubbing a hand down my face. "I watched her do it. I heard the conversation. They knew. Or, one of them knew and didn't tell the others. Fuck. My head hurts. I'm so confused. Why is this happening right now?"

Ode snorts through the phone. "Did she? Seriously, Riv. That crazy bitch had it out for you the whole time you were with them. You have no idea what happened, girl. She could have pulled a fast one or something. The only way you'll find out is if you ask them. And I know, I know, that's the last conversation you want to have. I think you all need to hash this all out, once and for all, before you murder them, or Ly apparently tackles them and loves them to death."

I snort, pinching the bridge of my nose. "Yeah, yeah. I know you're right. I'll talk to them at some point."

Whenever that is. How the hell do I sit down and say, *"Heya, assfaces, we need to discuss our child. And oh, why the hell did you leave so quickly?"* It's one of those scenarios I've envisioned many times in the shower. You know, the anxiety-filled fake conversations that happen only inside of your head as you shampoo your hair and mock fight with people. Yeah, that type of situation, and it always goes one way—them laughing at me and me punching their nuts.

"And Jesus, I can't believe your brothers pulled that shit. Want me to kick their asses? I'm not above hopping on a plane and laying the smack down," Ode quips, lightening the mood instantly.

"Please," I grumble, wiping the tears from my face. "I need someone to help me dig their graves."

"Oh, we're hiding bodies now, babe? I'm on my way," she snickers. "I'm always here for you, Riv. But..."

"But?" I question, leaning back in my seat with a huff.

"But I think you're entitled to some answers. They owe you a hell of a lot of words," she encourages. "You know I've never felt right after they left. Something stunk really fucking bad. And the way Gloria did you dirty with those restraining orders. I don't know; it didn't settle right with me." I envision her shaking her head in disbelief and running her fingers through her wild curls.

Longing hits me square in the chest. Years ago, I could walk to Ode's apartment to visit with her, Leon, and their mom, Korrine. Now, she's halfway across the country running my former bar,

Dead End, with Leon and raising a family with her boyfriend Ricky.

"I miss you," I confess with a groan.

"Miss you, too. We need to vacation, or hell, you could come home. Mama is..." She sucks in a breath, stopping her emotions.

"Worse?" I whisper, feeling my heart sink.

"The chemo is kicking her ass. You know Mama, though, she's fighting tooth and nail," she says in a soft voice. "She misses you, too, Riv. Say you'll come home soon?"

"Yeah. I think I will soon." No matter what, my chosen family has always come first. Korrine helped to raise me. Ode was my sister. And Leon was my annoying brother. They've always shown up for me. So, I do the same for them. They were my damn rock when Ly was brewing. They helped me with everything I could have needed. And the moment I came into the money my father left me, I took care of them right back.

Now I'm stuck helping the guys get their dream back on track. The same dream that left me and my growing belly behind in another state. What does our future hold? Will we butt heads the entire time they're under my orders or will they get over themselves and forge ahead?

Ode is right, though; they owe me some answers, and I'm going to get them one way or another. I deserve that after so long. First, I have to get through this first meeting with them at the house and not stomp their balls with my heels.

"Now tits up, bitch. Go show those boys who is really in charge. Show them no mercy!" she says through a chuckle, making me smile.

"Fuck, Ode. I have to face them again," I groan, leaning my head back into the chair.

"How long?" she asks.

"Maybe an hour until they get here with all their shit."

"Good! Now, push your tits out and put on your best outfit and heels. Demand the damn room. Show them what they walked out on, babe."

I blow out a breath, staring at my tear-stained cheeks, and nod. "You think it'll be cruel if I give them a 10:00 p.m. curfew every night?" I ask, wiping under my eyes and removing the wetness from my flesh.

She snorts. "Hell no. Leash them to that damn house. Show them how a big girl gets petty revenge."

"Petty revenge?" I ask with a laugh. "I don't know about that..." I trail off.

"Think about it. Talk to them, get a little closure, and revenge, and move on. It's time to stop letting Whispered Words rule your life. Now, go get them bitch. You got this. And text me after."

"Bye, love you!" I chirp, hang up the phone, and head into my house.

Maybe it is time for a little petty revenge, right? It can't hurt. So, with that in mind, I open my laptop and start typing the new contract they'll have to abide by for the next six months.

6

1:49   4:10

Tits up, girl, you got this. Totally fucking got this. Whispered Words won't know what hit them soon.

I puff out my cheeks and release the air through my parted lips, hoping Ode's words of wisdom are just that—words of wisdom. I need all the damn encouragement I can get to not storm away from these assfaces and continue my life. Screw them. Screw our future talk. But, ugh. I can't. This is my livelihood, and I won't have them ruining the steps I've taken to get my life back. Plus, Lyric would be disappointed.

So, after refreshing my makeup following my woe-is-me pity party, I decided that taking a sliver of revenge was in order, thanks to Ode's wise words. I may be unable to buzz their body hair while they sleep and laugh as they look in the mirror with no eyebrows, but I thought of a creative way to get back at the assfaces taking residency across the street from me. So, after finagling my curves into a smoking hot red dress, I apply a little makeup, including deep-red lipstick. What? I want them to know what the hell they walked away from and what they'll never have again.

After sending Ode a picture, she assured me it would do the trick and have them drooling within two seconds. I quickly put on a pair of slightly unprofessional six-inch heels and made my way to the band house to greet my new neighbors with a smile.

The moment I walked in and showed them to the dining room table was fucking priceless. Their faces tightened, and lust swam in their eyes. For a fleeting moment, at least. Until they all averted their gazes, sat in their seats, and awaited my direction. But who says I can't saunter through the damn house, swaying my hips and making them regret every minute of walking out on me without a goodbye.

So, here I stand nervously in the kitchen, tapping my damn toes, anxiously waiting for them to finish the read-through of their final contract. The one they must sign before they settle into this place, and I take total control of their lives. My mind screams *run, bitch, go back home,* but my body remains rooted where it needs to be. Who knew being in their presence for only a few hours would have my skin fucking crawling with the need to run and hide like a coward. Did I ever want to face them again? Nope. Not a chance. But here I am, facing the bulls head-on.

My eyes drift toward the dining room, where all four of them sit quietly, discussing the paperwork I handed them an hour ago with civility. Well, kind of. The occasional huff, scowl, or grunt comes from their direction, letting me know how delighted they are to be here, too. Thankfully, I haven't been verbally attacked in the last hour. I'd call that an improvement. So far, so good. I guess.

Only the tiniest spark of tension hangs in the air like a persistent rain cloud between the five of us. It's so small I barely notice the divide. All bets are off when I step into the room, and by the down-turned look on their faces, they're getting a glimpse of my fun stipulations. But what can I say? I typed these rules up an hour before they showed their faces. So, I had plenty of time to set the boundaries they must adhere to without question because I'm the damn boss this time.

I glance at my phone, hoping for a text back about the

package I received this morning, but get nothing in return. I shrug it off. Sometimes my other best friend Olivia is prompt with her responses. Sometimes, she's chasing her three-year-old son around the house while wrangling her five husbands. Other times she's hard at work as an agent at Veritas. She's a ridiculously busy woman. So, it's a toss-up on what she's doing.

I take a deep breath and reign in the antsy feeling crawling over my flesh. Leaving my phone on the counter, I head into the open-concept dining room. Bright afternoon sunlight streams in through the floor-to-ceiling windows from the spacious living room and bounces off the dark wood floors adorned with the most comfortable couches and recliners money could buy. Three years ago, I invested my own money into this home across from mine, hoping to make something of my new position—my damn dream job. My brothers agreed without protest, letting me take the lead on my newest project. And since then, I've blossomed into this, restoring one band at a time to its former glory.

Kieran snorts in anger, flipping through the pages of rules. "Seriously? We're not babies," he complains with a shake of his head. "We're grown damn men. If I want to stay out all night, then I fucking will. I don't need to be here twenty-four seven."

Heat spears up my neck and onto my cheeks, as my rage builds. I'm getting sick and tired of his mouth running, and I've only been in his presence for a few hours. Whatever is going on between us, we're going to have to solve them, just like Ode suggested. Before I do something stupid like explode or stab them.

Maybe this is all a sick and twisted test from my brothers, so they can watch me squirm and laugh at me as I stumble my way through this. Sounds like them. Those assholes. Usually, this is easy. The bands respect me the moment we meet, eager to build themselves up again and follow my lead. Instead of respect from Whispered Words, I'm getting verbally abused by four whiny babies stuck in the past. *You are, too, idiot.* I huff at my inner voice and shoo it away. I'm not as stuck as they are. I've moved on with my life and made something of myself. I have a kid, a house, and a damn beach all to myself. It's everything I've ever dreamed of. So why do I feel like a piece of me is still missing?

Taking a deep breath, I soothe my rage monster. "Absolutely," I say with a shrug, slowly pacing the space around the table. "Go ahead. You're free to do whatever you want to do. Go gallivant in front of the cameras again with your arm around a different chick every day. See what West Records does. See what *I* do," I say, crossing my arms over my chest, begging him to test me and my thin patience.

"You sound jealous, River Blue," he goads, spitting the name like poison. Slowly, he climbs to his feet, ready for a fight. "Is that it? Did it tear you apart to see me on TV?"

No, but it killed your daughter, you buffoon.

I'm tempted to shout in his face. But for the sake of my profession, I sink my teeth into my tongue and quickly stop my burning retort. If he wanted to be in her life, then he'd make it happen. So far, he hasn't stepped up to the plate like a man. He hasn't even asked about her or seemed to care that she exists, which is going to make our conversation in the future all the more difficult. He's either in or he's out, and that's the end of story. Whoever else wants to step up; I won't stop them. Lyric wants a daddy—more specifically, these four idiots. I'm not about to deny her a relationship with them if she wants it, even if it kills me a little on the inside.

I raise my brow. My heart pounds against my ribs when I lock my challenging gaze with his. *Bring it on, Kieran.* I can go as many rounds as you want, but I will always come out on top.

"Jealous?" I ask, seething on the inside, but soothing out the rasp of emotion in my voice. "Not by a mile. It's the rules, Mr. Knight. Every band that's lived under this roof has had these rules." My index finger pokes into the wood of the table, stabbing it with every word. I swallow the lie, expertly perfecting my indifferent mask as if this doesn't affect me.

"Leave her alone," Asher pipes up, shaking his head at Kieran, and signs his contract without question. "Just sign the damn papers."

Sure, every band has rules, but never ones like this. Am I a fucking professional? Yes. Am I keeping Whispered Words on a shorter leash? Also, yes. So, sue me if I want to enact a little petty revenge for leaving Lyric behind. I can't cut off all their hair and then glue it to their balls as a form of retribution without blinking. So, I do the next best thing and professionally tie them to this house after 10:00 p.m. It's genius if you ask me.

"Bro, sit down. Sign the papers," Rad grumbles, grasping Kieran's forearm and setting him back in his seat with a reluctant huff. Picking up his pen like a good boy, Kieran flips to the last page and signs his name in messy cursive, pouting the entire time.

I bite the inside of my cheek when he grumpily throws the pen down and crosses his arms, glaring out the windows, refusing to look in my direction.

Callum's head stays down, studying the rules one at a time, memorizing them at a glance with his photographic memory. It's always stunned me to know he can replay anything at will in full detail. In the past, the memories from his parents and sister's death held him by the throat and didn't let him go. I wonder how moving out here has helped him cope and grieve properly, or is he still stuck in the same damn relentless loop? Does he think about the kiss Van forced on me when he stood in my kitchen and watched it happen?

"A 10:00 p.m. curfew? No parties? No alcohol? And no guests?" he murmurs, running his finger over the words with furrowed brows. "Band practice every Monday through Friday at 8:45 a.m. Weekly shows at undisclosed locations. IE; The KC Club South, The KC Club Shores, and River's Run, on Saturday evenings. A once-a-week group therapy session." Swallowing hard, his gray eyes meet mine with confusion.

"Whoa. Therapy?" Rad asks, holding my stare, and I shrug.

"Pretty Girl, I don't need therapy. I'm as right as rain," he says with a lop-sided grin, brushing off his shoulders like this is nothing more than a little stop before he returns to his fame.

My breath hitches at the nickname, and my lungs squeeze in my chest. Seeing the same old, carefree Rad from five years ago sitting before me liquifies my insides. A multitude of memories hit me square in the chest, reminding me of our adventures together. From the man who insisted I was his girlfriend when I wasn't to the man whose eyes drop to the table, filling with sadness. Rad refuses to look at me again like I broke his damn heart, and maybe in his mind, I did. But that's on him. If only they had come to me and let me explain what happened, we wouldn't be in this damn mess.

"Right. No matter how right you feel, it's required of all bands that stay in this house." I give a sharp nod. "This isn't a negotiation," I say with authority, reminding them I'm the one in charge here. Not them. The sooner they realize they're stuck, the sooner we can move on to fixing their career and getting them the hell out of my house.

"I can't fucking believe it," Kieran murmurs once again, letting his attitude out to play. Still glaring out the window, he rubs a hand down his face.

"Well, believe it. That's why you're here. This is a unique opportunity for each of you. So, don't blow it. No matter our past, you have a better future. And whether you or I like it or not, this is happening," I say in a calm tone, clasping my hands in front of my body. "Does anyone else have a problem with that?" I ask, staring around the table at each of them shaking their heads. All except shithead Kieran, who glares at me with a scrunched-up face filled with more rage than before.

"Unless we get a better offer," Kieran mutters more to himself than anyone.

I really shouldn't punch him, should I? You think one knock to his stubborn as hell head would do the trick? I'd love to find out.

"Sure, go ahead and try."

I know my fucking worth and what I bring to the bands. So do other record labels out there. Try and see where you get, you insufferable dickhead.

Collecting the contracts from each of them as they sign, I place them into a folder to file later.

"Your belongings should be here at any moment. Please unload your possessions into one of the rooms you select upstairs. There is storage in the attached garage for vehicles and such. I will allow you all to get settled in for the rest of the weekend and explore your new house. There's a home gym in the basement with anything you may need. There's also a recording studio down there for when inspiration strikes." My eyes scan the boys, as they sit attentively, listening to my speech.

"Remember, we will start band practices on Monday with no exceptions. Same time, same place, in the practice room. Every amenity possible is here that you could need. Per the rules, you're permitted to leave the property to get groceries or some fresh air. But please remember, you represent West Records and always have. Your public image is also important." My eyes zero in on Kieran when he scoffs, muttering under his breath again like a petulant child.

"Also, under no circumstances are you allowed to visit the house across the street without warning. That's my home. So, no unannounced visits. The moment you step foot inside, your contract is terminated unless you are given permission to do so. If you need me, my direct phone number is on the fridge. I am your contact for anything you may need now. I am your boss. This house—this opportunity is your last chance with West Records. If you fail, there is no more. Are we clear?" I scan the guys again when they each nod their heads in reluctant agreement, not wanting to accept the fact that I'm now in charge of their every move.

"Good. I'll return with copies of your signed contracts on Monday. I'll also put a copy of your new schedule on the fridge for practices, therapy sessions, and your performances." I give them all a tight smile, deciding this is as best as any time to walk out the front door and let them unload their things. The next six months will test them and me beyond belief.

The moment I step into my house, I release my frantic breath. Fuck. That was worse than I thought, but I survived the ordeal unscathed. Besides a few snarky comments here and there, they all seem to be settling with the fact I am momentarily back in their lives as their damn boss.

My phone buzzes in my pocket, alerting me that my other best friend, Olivia, has texted. It's useful that my friend has connections to higher powers and is a badass agent with Veritas—the government agency resembling the FBI, only more secretive and illusive.

OLIVIA

> Sorry, Riv. Busy day on the home front. Just saw your message. Is it the same content as before? Anything new?

ME

> It's okay. And yeah...same shit... Same flowers... Somehow it ended up on my desk.

OLIVIA

> Really? Your desk? Did Kat leave it there?

That reminds me. My assistant and I need to have a very serious discussion again about the packages I receive from the obsessed psychopath who loves to watch my every step. Hell, she even scheduled the installation of my home security system and cameras when I felt threatened enough. She should know this is serious and not something to mess around with. Yet, she leaves the reminders of his obsession on my desk.

ME

> Yeah. Going to talk to her. Want me to pass it on to Carter?

OLIVIA

Yeah. I'll get it from him tomorrow. So sorry, Riv. We'll get them, I promise.

ME

It's escalating, Liv... I'm starting to freak out... What if this gets worse? Effects Ly?

OLIVIA

Don't. Not now. Let Veritas handle it, ok? We got this. We got you guys. We'll always protect you.

ME

Ok. Thanks, Liv.

I blow out a breath and close my eyes. The moment I saw that package on my desk with my name scribbled in perfect cursive and a million stamps placed on the corners, my heart sank. For a brief moment, I hoped they had forgotten me and moved on to something else productive. But they didn't. They never do.

The package is a silent reminder that they're still there after three years of anonymous harassment, watching my every move from afar with a camera in their hand. I've been down this road before. We've looked for suspects left and right. Hell, they even looked into Van as a safety measure, given his previous stalking ways.

"You're positive it's not him?" I mumble, tracing the picture my stalker sent me. It's nothing but my grinning face, roasting in the sun. Lyric had a dance recital that day, near the lake on an outside stage. It could have been anyone.

Olivia runs a hand down the left side of her face, drawing my attention to the faint scars lining her flesh. I can't imagine going through what she did when she was a teenager. She rarely talks about the trauma of the fire or losing her three best friends.

"Yes. We've looked into Donavan Drake several times. He's been overseas with the production company he works for, for several

months now. There's no way he could follow you around and be halfway across the world."

My only saving graces are Liv and Veritas having my back, or I'd be up shits creek without a paddle. A hopeless feeling envelops me, not knowing what to do about this stupid stalker. When will it end? It's been three miserable years of watching my back, and now I have to worry about Ly, too. I'm tired of looking over my shoulder and making sure whoever they are isn't there lurking in the shadows.

I rub circles over my temple, trying to settle my rampant heartbeat. It pounds in my ear, taking over everything around me. It isn't until a distinct rumble coming down the drive, vibrating my entire house, brings me back to reality. As four moving vans park on the curb and open their back doors. Peeking out my window, I raise a brow when Rad wheels out his old dirt bike and places it in the garage.

I'd recognize that bike from a mile away. It's his winning bike, the one he raced around Raccoon Run, and the same one he finger-banged me on before spreading me over his winning eight-hundred bucks. *Fuck.* I close my eyes, trying to erase those happy memories from my brain permanently. Seeing them again awakens something odd inside of me. Something I never thought I'd have to face again. Maybe they're my nightmares, or maybe they're here to set things right.

Back then, when we first met, we were thrown together in a whirlwind and fell hard for each other. We were simplistic kids with enormous dreams, just trying to find ourselves. Then it all went to shit, which is something I won't let go of easily. They used me, intentionally, and admitted it. They invited me along on a trip they never intended to take me on and then left like I meant nothing after witnessing something they didn't fully understand. Forgiveness is not in my vocabulary at this moment in time; maybe, if they make it up to me somehow, but I highly doubt that.

I've moved on with my life with Lyric by my side. I don't need them anymore.

7

Rad

"SEE YOU, assmunchers, later. I'm going for a ride," I grumble, running a hand through my hair, trying to distract myself from her—River. The woman I fell head over heels in love with. Only to have my heart ripped violently out of my chest and spit on. "Fuck," I mumble, squeezing my eyes shut as the pain of her betrayal sears through me again. Stopping before the garage door that connects to the house, I recover my breath and sigh. I have got to get a handle on my fucking self. I'm being ridiculous. I can't fall apart because she's back in the picture. Not now. I've fought too damn hard to get back to the easy-going, carefree guy everyone loves to see. No matter the dark cloud floating over my head whenever I'm alone.

Once upon a time, she was my pretty girl. The most beautiful woman in the world. And I called her mine. All mine. And well, theirs, too, I guess. I thought she felt a semblance of what I felt for her. Love. Adoration. Major attraction. God damn, the sex was off-the-charts hot, too. Even thinking about spreading her ass out on a pile of money makes little Rad perk up. Even now, after all this time, she's still on a shrine in the back of my head with candles and a curtain concealing her memory. If only I could contain it from ever spilling out into my waking thoughts. Then I might be okay.

I guess I was mistaken about us, though. She managed to jump into Van's arms again, like the moments we had meant nothing to her. She threw out the Ferris wheel ride, the way she built our band, and the fucking dining room table incident like they didn't play on repeat in her mind, too. Because fuck, even through my hate, I fuck my hand to the memories of River's cries at the top of the Ferris wheel. *Fuck.* Not only am I sad, but now I'm saluting in my damn pants.

Hell, maybe I pushed my pretty girl too much and way too fast. I did kind of stalk her and put a flag in her ass, claiming her as my girlfriend. She had no choice. So, that's on me, I guess. She didn't want me the way I desperately wanted her. She didn't want any of us.

I huff a breath when the familiar burn behind my eyes threatens to spill tears again. I'm so damn tired of crying myself to sleep. It's been fucking years. Why can't my heart move on?

"You're going for a ride?" Callum asks in a soft voice, placing a hand on my shoulder. I grunt, shrugging his hand off, and nod, clutching my keys.

"Yeah, man. I gotta clear my mind," I mumble, wiping away the tears leaking out.

Stupid tears; I don't need you right now. Never again. I'm tired of crying over her; she's not worth it. She broke my heart once; I won't let her trample it again. Lesson fucking learned. Not even those sexy as fuck six-inch heels that accentuated her long, lean legs under that come-fuck-me-dress she wore over here for our meeting can win me over. God. She's amazing. I love her. But I fucking hate her. And what's wrong with me? My heart tears into two different pieces, going in two separate directions.

When I turn to look up at Callum, my brows furrow, there's a hint of something brewing in the back of his determined gray eyes, and suspicion hits me hard in the chest. That fucker is up to something.

"You're not thinking about going tonight, are you?" When he

darts his eyes away toward the ground, I get my answer. "Bro, we can't leave, remember? Not even for that."

His jaw clenches tight, and he nods. "Thanks for the reminder, Dad," he grumbles, working his jaw back and forth, biting back all the rage consuming him.

I swear, my brother Callum hasn't been the same man since he witnessed River kissing Van. It's like the sweet piece that made him, him—was left behind in Central City and with her. She stole that from him. He had just started opening up and becoming the person he wanted to be, and now, he has effectively shut down completely.

"Sorry, Man. I didn't make the rules. Take it up with her," I say, throwing an arm out toward River's house, which sits just across the street from us.

Thankfully, she hasn't shown her face today, giving us the weekend to move in and settle into our gigantic new home. I'd rather not face my past head-on. Until Monday morning, of course, when she'll meet us for our very first band practice under her new rules. Shit. I feel like I'm back under my strict parents' control. The ones who forbade me from getting tattoos and staying out past ten. Now here I am, twenty-seven, and on full lockdown enforced by my ex. Life is fucking weird.

"Look, I know it's Saturday, and I know that's what you do, but I can't lose this contract." If I don't have music, I don't know what I have.

Emptiness? More time to focus on my heartbreak? I'll self-destruct in no time. Even if we haven't been the same since we got signed, I never want to lose my grip on what makes me whole. Music. The tunes. The way I smash my sticks into the drums. It helps me to remember I'm alive, and if that's gone, what will I do?

Kieran snorts, walking past with a piece of pepperoni pizza hanging from his mouth. "Sneak out. No one will know," he says nonchalantly like he doesn't even fucking care we're in this predicament because of him.

He's why Whispered Words is failing, and it hasn't gone

unnoticed by Callum either. Sometimes I wonder what life would have been like if we had never met River. We wouldn't be here, that's for sure. But we'd still be brothers and damn happy about it, too, unlike now, where we can barely be in the same house without bickering or wanting to throw punches. Or, in Callum's case, beating the shit out of Kieran every chance he gets. Been there. Done that. Cleaned up enough of their blood to last a damn lifetime.

"Why? So, you can move on without us?" Callum asks in a low, deadly voice, cracking his knuckles.

Kieran grunts, tearing into his pizza again. "Going to kick my ass again? Hmm?" He raises a haughty brow, practically begging Callum to punch him in the face. I'm rooting for that. Maybe it'll knock him back a peg or two and pull his ego out of his ass. Stupid fucker.

"No fighting. You're an asshole. Go eat your damn pizza and leave them alone," Asher gripes, walking past with a plate of pizza. He shakes his head when Kieran narrows his eyes at him, grinding his teeth. "Just shut the fuck up. We're here to stay. Get over it," Asher says, softening his voice. "This is our last opportunity. If we don't take this seriously, then we can kiss our music career goodbye."

"Not if I can help it. I've got my agent on the lookout for better contacts. Away from that lying, cheating, manipulative..."

"Don't be so insulting," Callum grumbles, cutting Kieran's words off.

"Right, because you still love her?" Kieran asks, stepping into Callum's face. "How can you love someone who went behind your back and kissed and fucked and cuddled another man? Why?" Kieran growls every word, pressing his nose into Callum's as they face off.

"I don't," Callum growls back, pressing further into Kieran.

"Right," Kieran scoffs like he isn't still pining for his childhood best friend.

"Fuck off," I say, laying a hand on Kieran's chest and pushing

him away from Callum's rage-filled body. "Go eat. Leave him be,"
I growl, narrowing my eyes at Kieran, who smiles through the
whole damn altercation like he has since we left Central City.
River did a number on his ass, and I can't wait until someone
fucks him up and straightens out his attitude problem. Fuck. My
fingers curl. A man can dream, right? But could I forgive River for
what she did? I don't fucking know.

Once Kieran saunters away and shuts himself in his upstairs
bedroom with the slam of his door, I can finally breathe. Turning
to Callum, I put a hand on his shoulder and level him with my
best serious stare. "Don't get caught, okay?" I mumble, squeezing
his shoulder, and he nods. I know he needs this more than
anything, especially after the two days we've had under River's
rule. But fuck me if he gets caught sneaking out. "Be discreet or
some shit. There's a guard, remember?"

"I never do," he mutters, pushing my hand off his shoulder,
and heads into the basement, where the gym punching bag calls
his name as he prepares for what the night has in store for him.

Tension rises through my body, locking my muscles in a tight
grip. Now more than ever, I need to hop on my old bike and ride
until I can't feel this black hole swirling inside me and swallowing
my insides. I swear, she decimated me—all of us. They may not
admit it, but I know it's true. Callum resorted to violence to take
his ache away. Kieran's attitude needs a good fucking punch, and
if he didn't have such a talented voice, I'd sock him one. And
Asher? He's completely flipped from the man I knew in Central
City. Sure, he's still domineering and anal, but for someone who
didn't even like River as he claimed, he's been a wreck ever since,
mostly keeping to himself. The same vibe we had on stage has not
carried over since we left Central City. It's like all drive, passion,
and love stayed behind. Now, we're a shell of who we once were.

I walk out into the garage and run my fingers over the worn
paint of my beloved bike; I couldn't leave it behind. We only made
it back to Central City once after winning the Battle of the Bands,
and this is what I brought back with me before the real work

began. I knew I'd always need it, no matter how much money I made and how many new bikes I could afford. This one holds a special place in my heart for various reasons. Not only did it help me win multiple times on the racetrack, but it's where she sat with me and helped me christen it for good luck. God. I'm so hopelessly fucking in love with her still.

Fuck! How? Why does my heart continue to squeeze like it's been put in a vise, draining it dry?

Even after the heartbreak and all the shit she did to us, I can't help myself but to think of her and feel flutters. Stupid heart. Stupid fucking dick. Why can't I work her out of my system? She cheated on you with that scumbag! And then, when I'm almost to the point of getting over her, she shows up in a short, come-fuck-me dress, begging me to tear it up to her hips and fucking punish her for breaking my goddamn heart. I squeeze my eyes shut and take a deep breath.

The video of her and Van screwing lingers in my memories in the background. As always. Yes, I absolutely will always love River West. But fuck. My heart cracks into tiny pieces again. Usually, I take that emotion-filled feeling inside me and utilize it the best way I know how—beating the shit out of my drums. I can never seem to shake her, though. She's a ghost living rent-free in my mind whenever I close my eyes. And it's very fucking irritating not being able to let go and long for someone who was a passing phase in my life and fucked us over so hard.

Rifling through a tall box situated near my bike, I throw on my helmet for safety and ignore the burner phone vibrating in my pocket. At least I made one good decision since I got famous, never giving out my real phone number to groupies.

Since there's nothing other than the sandy beach on her side of the road and a mile-long driveway down to the gate, I'll have to stay on the pavement or take a joyride through our grass lawn. I smirk, imagining her yelling at me for being so damn loud and tearing up her grass. I'd love to get her all fired up and witness it once again.

Once I'm seated on my bike, the entire world disappears. It's nothing but me, the wind in my mullet—or my helmet since I'm a responsible guy—and the long road ahead of me. I rev my engine and book it down the light-up drive, going full speed until the gate comes into view, forcing me to stop suddenly. With heavy breaths, I can't help but to let my head fall back and laugh to myself. Shit. This is what I needed to let loose.

Adrenaline pours through my veins, breaking a grin across my face. Happiness and relief I haven't felt in days lifts me to the clouds like a damn drug keeping me in its grip. Thank fuck. I revel in the heady feeling when I race up the drive again, jostling over rogue rocks and tiny bumps in the road. I whoop, returning to the road's end nestled between each house, and my heart soars with excitement and pure fucking joy.

"Rad!" I whip my head toward the figure standing at the edge of her grass, clutching a large sweater around herself. Hell, even dressed down in her starlight pajama bottoms, a messy bun, no makeup, and a scowl—she's still hot as fuck. It's too bad she went and broke my damn heart.

"Can't hear you, Pretty Girl!" I yell, cranking up my engine again as I sit and watch her with amusement. A smirk pulls the edges of my lips when she narrows her eyes, sparkling in the bright moonlight. Yes, Pretty Girl. Give me all your anger, baby.

"It's nine-thirty at night, Ashton!" she barks, stomping toward me with determination.

"I still have thirty minutes, Mommy!" I shout again, revving it until she's standing right beside me and clasping my wrist.

"Yeah. You still have thirty minutes until you're grounded," she quips, shaking her head. Running her fingers over her bun, she finally meets my eyes when I throw my helmet off and give her my best grin.

"Then give me thirty more minutes to blow off some steam. Unless you want to help with that, Pretty Girl?" She sucks in a breath, and her eyes dilate before she shakes herself out of it.

Huh, she's still horny for the Rad Ride. I'll store that in the back of my mind for later, whenever I need it. Like tonight, when Mr. Fist meets Mr. Dick, and they come together with Mrs. Strawberry lube. It's a fantastic union, and she'll be the center of my fantasy.

"Not happening, assface," she says, glaring at me when I shrug.

"Had to try. If I can't have booze or girls over at your other mansion, you're all that's left." I cock my head, letting my hurtful words dig deep into her heart like her actions did mine. Would I invite other girls over? Fuck no I wouldn't.

Instantly, I know I've landed my mark when her face hardens, and she steps back. "Listen, my kid is asleep on the couch. Can you at least wait until tomorrow? She isn't feeling the best," she says softly, avoiding my eyes.

My brows furrow. Right, the kid she had after we left. Who more than likely belongs to Van's dumbass. Why couldn't she have been mine? Why couldn't my swimmers have won the damn race and given me my mullet baby? I clench my jaw and slam my helmet back on my head.

"No can do, Pretty Girl. Now, if you'll excuse me," I grunt, revving the engine and taking off.

Or I would have if a little dark figure didn't run right in front of me, screaming at the top of her lungs and stopping in front of my accelerating bike. I grunt, overcorrecting myself, and narrowly miss her by a fucking millimeter. My heart pounds when my bike wobbles, jostling my entire body until it tips over. I go fucking down onto the road. Hard as fuck. All the breath leaves my lungs as I'm dragged an inch, but it's enough to inflict some damage. My back scrapes against the pavement as my bike dies and flies somewhere in the middle of the road.

My breaths come in short pants as I stare at the twinkling stars mocking my luck. My entire body heats as pain envelops me, and I groan, thankful for the helmet protecting my damn head from scrambled brains.

8

Rad

"DADDY!" a little frantic voice yells above me, drawing my eyes to her. "He's dead!" she dramatically cries, laying her head on my chest. "No, wait! His heart is still here," she says softly, wrapping her little arms around me and squeezing with all her might. "You'll be okay, Daddy, I promise."

"Daddy?" I groan, trying to regain my breath as her words register in my mind.

Daddy? Who the hell is she calling daddy? I'm no one's daddy. I mean, Pretty Girl could call me that as I spank her ass. But, no. Fuck. She wouldn't.

"Lyric," River says softly, but I hear the concern laced there when she pulls her child off my chest. Grunting, I reach up and tear off my helmet, throwing it to the side. Fuck. My head pounds. "Hey, Rad. You, okay?" she asks, gently running a finger down my cheek. Slowly her fingertips run down my chest, poking through a new hole produced by the fall in my shirt. I hiss, trying to slap her hand away, but my body doesn't cooperate with me. "You took a hell of a spill."

"Yeah," I groan, sitting up and taking stock of my injuries. "I'm good." The world spins in an array of colors when I go to stand, stumbling into River as she catches me and wraps her arm around me. Her fingers dig into my side as we take a few unsteady steps, wobbling on my jelly legs. She grunts, continuing to hold me up. "Fuck," I hiss, trying to regain myself and pull away from her. She smells too damn good and fits too perfectly to my side. I can't fall down this River rabbit hole again because I know where it leads—to heartbreak.

See? My fucking head is all over the damn place.

"Yeah, I don't think so," she murmurs with a resigned sigh. "Come on, let me check you over before you go to sleep. Can't have the talent dying before you even get started."

"I'm fine, Pretty Girl," I murmur, leaning into the warmth of her side.

A pounding headache roars through my brain as she drags me through the front door of her house and settles me into a chair situated in her spacious living room. I squeeze my eyes shut, pinching the bridge of my nose, pleading for the room to stop spinning before I puke. Fuck. My stomach churns, and a knot forms in my stomach when the sweet scent of River's body wash hits my nose.

"You got some hellacious scratches, Rad," River murmurs, poking at my aching back. I flinch away from her touch, and she sighs. "Want me to clean the wounds?" I nod without thinking, giving her permission.

"I got bandages!" says the little voice again from in front of me. "Mommy, I'll help," she says in a serious voice filled with determination. "Daddy needs them all over."

"Ly, you and I need to have another discussion about running in front of cars and wandering off. You can help, but we'll discuss this more later," River sighs, tugging at the back of my shirt and lifting it to expose my back. "Do you want me to help?" she asks me cautiously in a soft voice.

"Uh, yeah. Thanks," I murmur, secretly loving the way her fingers feel as they ghost over my aching flesh as she pulls my shirt over my head and places it over the arm of the chair.

I hope she sees the pain I etched into my back via lyrics and musical sheets. I hope she sees the agony I've lived in for the past five years inked into my flesh in the form of skulls, knives, and anguish.

"Barbie or fishes?" the little voice asks until I peel my aching eyes open and focus on the little beauty standing before me.

The world ceases to fucking turn, skidding to a halt as my eyes widen. My body weaves back and forth. I suck in much-needed oxygen, trying to clear my vision. Rubbing my eyes, I finally focus on the little River standing before me with her dark hair bordering between brown and jet black. She gives me a toothy grin, holding up two boxes of Band-Aids with colors swirling through them, obviously made for children. I blink a few times, staring into her eyes that look an awful lot like someone else's who lives across the street.

"River," I say in a low voice, leaning forward. My lips pop open in surprise. "Either I have a concussion, Pretty Girl. Or I'm staring into the eyes of..." I whip my head to her as she stands beside the chair, shaking her head with tight lips. I go to stand, but River pushes my shoulder down and frowns.

"I'll get the alcohol," she murmurs, stepping out of the room, muttering something about a fifth of vodka and needing something to drink.

I turn my attention back to the little girl standing in front of me and really take her in, feeling my chest cave in.

"You want fish, Daddy?" she asks, holding the box up. "You have a boo-boo right here," she says, roughly poking her finger onto the spot on my forehead. "There's blood," she says with a frown, holding her little finger right in front of my eyes. "See?" she asks until I wrap my fingers around her wrist and inspect the small dot of blood soaking into her fingerprint.

"Fishes are fine," I mumble, blinking rapidly at her as she pulls out a small Band-Aid, poking her tongue out until she's huffing, trying to peel it open. "Here," I say, taking the tiny piece from her and peeling back the paper. Her unmistakable mismatched eyes search my face, looking for more injuries. "What's your name?" I whisper in awe of the little girl roughly sticking a Band-Aid on my forehead.

She frowns, pouting out her bottom lip. "You don't know my name, either?"

"I'm sorry, Little Pretty Girl," I whisper, shaking my aching head. "I hurt my head. I can't remember right now. I totally know." I try to give her my best smile, but she sighs, staring down at the ground. Her entire demeanor falls, and her shoulders sag in defeat.

"Mommy said my daddies weren't ready to be daddies. But you don't even know my name," she murmurs, sniffling a little. "You don't remember me. You don't love me."

Jesus Christ. Talk about someone reaching in and tearing your heart out. Only she's itty bitty and holds my beating heart in her hand with just those simple words. My face falls as I try to recall if she's said her name, but my goddamn brain rattles in my head. God. I haven't taken a spill like that in years.

Reaching forward, I put my hands on her shoulders, forcing her eyes to meet mine. I swallow hard, staring into the eyes of my former best friend, and my stomach falls out of my ass.

"Your eyes," I murmur in amazement. "You have such beautiful eyes." The same brown spot located on the same side as Kieran's twinkles back at me.

"It's Lyric," River says, coming back into the room with cotton balls and a bottle of alcohol. "And I didn't know it could be hereditary. Apparently, genetics are a hell of a thing."

My fingers tremble on her tiny shoulders, slightly shaking her. That's all the damn confirmation I need to send my heart into a flutter. Question after question runs through my mind. Like how? Why didn't she tell us? Fuck. What the hell happened after we left?

River had a kid—that I knew of as of yesterday, at least. But she had our kid—Kieran's kid—and no one knew. Fuck. Fucking Kieran. That dog dick. His words from yesterday echo in my rattling mind, and I groan. I'm too injured to think this damn hard about anything. He knew. And he doesn't give a shit about her.

I curl my fingers into fists and grind my teeth. Not only from the pain of the alcohol on my back but from Kieran's betrayal, too. Even if River fucked us over, he has a living, breathing human with his DNA walking around, and he discarded her existence. For what? Fame? Fortune? The band?

"Lyric," I confirm, turning back to the little girl, slowly wiping away the fat tears dripping down her cheeks. "Hi, Lyric. I'm Rad."

Her little eyes narrow at me. "I know. You're my daddy. Mommy said," she says in a small voice, waving a hand at River, who stiffens beside me.

"Why don't you give Daddy a little slack, Ly? He hit his head, remember? Always remember to wear a helmet. How about you cover his boo-boos in those bandages and make him feel better." A sly smirk tugs at the corner of her lips as the scent of rubbing alcohol fills the air. "Might hurt a bit," she murmurs before placing the cold as fuck alcohol on my stinging wound, which I don't think she minds doing one bit. In fact, I hear a sadistic laugh from under her breath every time she cleans a wound.

I hiss through my clenched teeth, making Lyric smile as she pulls out a wad of bandages, and I know by the determined look in her eyes she's about to punish me for not knowing her name by placing those brightly colored bandages filled with images of ocean life to my skin.

"So, Lyric," I start, grunting when she climbs onto my lap and starts placing Band-Aids on certain spots on my jaw, cheek, and chest. "How old are you?"

"I'm four. Mrs. Harper is my teacher; she's not very nice. Apple says she's only mean 'cuz she had to poop." I snort at her story, cracking a smile as she continues rambling and placing three more Band-Aids on my face.

"Lyric," River chastises, shaking her head with a laugh.

"Go on, Little Pretty Girl. Tell me all about Mrs. Harper and how mean she is," I indulge her, fighting through the pain of River dotting my wounds with more alcohol.

"I'm in preschool," Lyric says, poking her tongue out again when she sticks a Band-Aid right over my pierced nipple. Her nose crinkles. "Are you a robot?" she asks, touching it through the bandage with a scrunched-up face.

I chuckle. "Nah, Little Pretty Girl. It's a piercing. Like this one," I say, pointing to the septum piercing I've had for years. "And a few more." Like hell am I telling a four-year-old there's metal in places she's not allowed to see below the belt. Only her mother would get that honor. If that ever happened again, that is.

Her little eyes light up, tearing the shadows away from my heart. If this is what happiness is, then I never want to leave. No matter what River did, this tiny human calls me daddy, and that's all that matters to me.

"Mommy, I want my booby pierced, too. Just like Daddy," Lyric says, causing River to choke on her own spit. I bite the inside of my cheek, trying to cover the smile begging to emerge. This kid is something else.

"Jesus, Ly. No booby piercings for you. Where did you even hear that word?" She shakes her head, and a red tint spreads across her cheeks. "You have got to stop watching TV," she murmurs to herself.

Lyric shrugs, looking over my face and chest with satisfaction. "All done!" she beams, wrapping her arms around me. Gently, she squeezes herself against me and pulls back, cupping my cheeks. "All better, Daddy," she murmurs with furrowed brows. "Will you come see me again?" She blinks a few times.

"As long as your mom says it's okay," I whisper, pushing a few strands of her hair out of her face, and she lights up. "I'm right across the street now."

"And my other daddies?" she whispers.

"All there," I breathe without thinking about my words.

"Okay, Ly. I'm sorry. But it's your bedtime. It's ten-fifteen, and you, my love, need your beauty rest." River offers her a hand, and she quickly takes it.

"I'll see you tomorrow, Daddy," she says with the biggest, heart-melting grin as they disappear behind the wall separating the living room from the rest of the house.

"See you," I whisper, clamping my eyes shut, letting everything I've learned in the past forty-five minutes really sink in. I have so many questions for River and so few answers to go on.

My head still pounds when I stand from the chair, checking out the pictures lining the bookshelf near the fireplace across the room. Young River with baby Lyric in her arms, nestled in a hospital bed. Wet tears line River's cheeks, but her smile lights up the damn picture.

"It was right after she was born," River says, standing stiffly beside me. "I was two weeks overdue, and she refused to come. Longest day of my life," she says, blowing out a breath. "Nine pounds, three ounces, and twenty-one inches long."

"She's amazing, Pretty Girl," I rasp, trying to keep the brewing questions at bay when she sighs.

"She's something else. She's special," she says, side-eyeing me with glossy eyes. "Just don't make promises you don't intend to keep. She's four. She won't understand when you walk away."

"Whoa. Wait. Walk away? That's awfully presumptuous of you," I say, curling my hands into fists at her accusations.

She shrugs, wiping her face, and turns to leave the room. But I'm hot on her trail, shoving her gently against the wall. Her jaw tightens when I cage her in, trapping her body against mine. Fuck. The warmth of her breath feathers across my cheeks, and her heaving chest bumps into mine. Do not pop a chubby. And do not—Shit, I looked at her tits in her tiny sleep shirt. I shouldn't have done that. I shake my head and tame the wild little Rad and reel myself in before I end up poking her in the stomach. Yeah, she'd chop little Rad off before she ever let that happen again. I happen to like my damn disco stick intact, thank you very much.

"Why didn't you tell us?" I ask, scrunching up my nose,

refusing to acknowledge the burn tingling the tip. "Pretty Girl, we would have come back no matter what. I just..."

Every muscle in River's body freezes. Squeezing her eyes shut, she blows out several controlled breaths until two small tears fall from her eyes, cascading down her reddened cheeks. Her fingers curl into fists, and her entire face scrunches angrily.

"You don't still have a knife buried in your pajama pants, do you?" I quip, watching her hands like a hawk, so she doesn't hold my balls hostage with her little knife. The River from before would most definitely kick my ass and stab me sideways with no regret.

She lets out a cruel laugh and shakes her head. "If I had my knife, you'd know," she says, taking another ragged breath.

Well, thank fuck for that. I don't need any more holes than I have in my body.

"It was two weeks after my mom died," she confesses with stirring emotions, choking me up as much as her. With tear-filled eyes, she glares directly at me with a hardening stare. "Two fucking weeks, Rad. Two weeks of silence. Two weeks of being thrown away like I was trash. If you had known, you'd have come back? Yeah right. You know what I did? I ran to Cal's to tell you all that I had found out. I just wanted to talk to you and resolve whatever happened. But you were gone, and Gloria called you. And you fucking rejected my child. You said it was probably Van's. And then..."

"Back up," I say, holding up a finger and jumping headfirst into the past when we left Central City. Every word River spits in my face, my heart breaks a little bit more. "You said Gloria called us? When? She never called us or told us anything. As far as I know..." My brows furrow, thinking back to the time we left and the time we got here and won our music contract. She didn't bother to call Kieran until after, and it was only to let him know about his stepdad. And that was a doozy of a call. Besides, he would have mentioned it to us, right? Fuck.

"She did it right in front of me. She said..." River closes her eyes, reliving the moment over again as if it's dragging her under and drowning her. Pure emotions reach out from her soul when she opens her eyes, and the tears fall, squeezing my damn heart. No matter what happened between us, this moment broke her for eternity. "You guys didn't want Lyric. And then she handed me four restraining orders, Ashton. So, what am I supposed to believe? Huh?"

I cringe at the sound of my first name, reeling back. Ashton. She only calls me Ashton when she's upset with me or fucking me. But this time around, she's pissed as hell. I'd rather get back to Rad.

Wait a minute... My lips pop open. "Restraining orders?" I question, furrowing my brows. My damn churning stomach drops. "What the hell is happening?" I groan, rubbing my fingers over my forehead as my headache continues to rattle around in my brain, putting pressure behind my damn eyes. Maybe I have a concussion after all. Is this shit even happening right now? Or am I hallucinating? Shit. I know I'm not. She's breathing heavily against me, crying out in frustration I don't understand. But I want to. Something about what she says doesn't sit right with me. There are things not adding up. I'll get to the bottom of it.

Just as I'm about to grill my Pretty Girl like a damn delicious steak and hash this out, the loud rumbling of a familiar motorcycle echoes from outside, rattling the windows. My heart drops.

"Fucking Cal," I hiss, hanging my head at his totally discreet retreat. If he wanted to get out of here unnoticed, then he failed...miserably. So, fucking miserably I'm now missing the opportunity to have an important discussion.

"What the hell was that?" River asks, stiffening where she stands. Her eyes whip to mine and harden when I give her my best innocent smile, which isn't very innocent looking. "Rad," she barks with authority, pushing me back without a fight, and heads toward the window, peering through the blinds. "Is that Cal? Where is he going?" she asks as his lone headlight lights up her house and takes off down the mile-long road, where he'll use his code to leave the premises. If he was trying to be sneaky about leaving, he fucking failed spectacularly. "Ashton," she holds out my name like a damn song, and I lose all control of myself.

Blowing out a breath, I sigh. "He's gone to fight."

Her eyes widen, blinking several times. "I'm sorry. You said fight?" she asks skeptically. "Like..." She holds up her fists in a mock fight until I nod. "Why?"

"Why do you think?" I asked as softly as I can. "You broke us. When he saw..." I shake my head. "It's not my place to tell his story."

She snorts a humorless laugh. "Right. When I kissed Van and he saw? Maybe he should have been there ten minutes earlier when that fuck nugget pushed his way into my house. Didn't you idiots ever think, I don't know, to try and communicate with me about it? That asshole forced himself on me in my kitchen. Forced. Himself." She punctuates every word with venom, punching the organ in my chest and pounding wildly.

I swallow hard, memories of her history prickling my mind. That stupid, wild party and the unpleasant night River and I shared. The moment I picked her broken body off the hard ground and put her in my car after her assault, and carried her into the hospital, always stayed with me. She was so small, so fucking broken then.

"What?" I ask, scrunching my brows. "He forced you? He..." He fucking took what he wanted, and she didn't have a say in it.

"We'll talk about this later," she says, pulling out her phone and calling someone.

"Later?" I ask, stiffening. I want to continue this conversation, but fuck, if she thinks... "No. Fuck Cal. I want to talk about this right now, Pretty Girl," I plead, cradling her jaw in my palm, trying to learn more about that night and about the entire situation.

"Yeah, later. You're taking me to wherever Callum has run off to if you want to keep your contract." She raises her brow and steps away from me, while bringing her phone to her ear and sighing. "I never thought I'd ever say this, but I need your help. Can you come over? Mhmm," she mumbles and hangs up. "Let me put some clothes on, and then we'll leave."

Fuck. Fuck. Fuck. Not only did I find out a whole stack of shit I had no clue about, but now I was about to take River into a fighting den full of angry assholes looking for a fight or pussy. Shit. I may not know all the information about what happened that night, and I'm getting the sneaking suspicion that someone is lying. And that someone is not her. But who?

A soft knock lands on the front door as River races down the hall, shoving her foot into a pair of worn sneakers. My eyes light up at the tight band shirt clinging to her chest and hugging her curvy sides. Tight jeans cling to her legs and fuck. If I could shape-shift into fabric, I'd be the denim between her thick thighs. Shit. Discreetly, I fix my dick who has a mind of his own. Asshole. That's three times now he's tried to show himself. But I guess when he smells the sweet pussy of his girl, he gets a little too excited.

"Hey, thanks for coming over," she says in a soft voice, ushering someone in.

"Ash," I say, stiffening when he meets my eyes.

"Your bike's in the middle of the road," he says, disregarding my greeting and avoiding my eyes. Bastard! He knew! He fucking knew! That's why he said that shit to Kieran. Mother fucker.

"Yeah, I almost ran my kid over and had to bail," I murmur, rubbing my chin. "You know, don't you?"

"I know," he says slowly, confirming.

"Only since yesterday. It's amazing. So many people know. Now, you," River demands, pointing a finger in my direction. "Take me to Cal. And you babysit, please. She's sleeping soundly down the hall. She shouldn't wake up. Just please don't snoop," she says, folding her hands together, and he nods.

"Anything for her," he says in a low voice full of emotion. Swallowing hard, he continues to avoid my gaze.

"Perfect. Thanks. Now, Let's roll." She waves a hand, begging me to follow her out the front door, and I do once I grab my torn-up shirt.

"We'll talk about it later," Asher murmurs as I pass, staring straight into my eyes.

"Somethings not right, man," I say softly, watching the shadows outside swallow River until she jumps into her SUV.

"Yeah," he says, looking away. "You're right. It's not."

9

Callum

HER SMILE HANGS in my memories like a memorial of something I once had—my Little Star. The girl who brought out the best in me, helped to build me up, and then let me crash and burn in the worst possible way. I rub my chest over the masterpiece plastered on my skin in her honor.

Her lies eat away at my every waking thought, drowning me in the pain of her betrayal, even after so many years. No amount of distance eases the pain of watching your life fall apart at the seams.

Low music hums in my ears through my earbuds, low enough to be aware of my surroundings. Music eases some of the pain tearing through my chest. I focus on the words wrapping around my brain and unclench my fists, preparing myself.

My second reprieve stands opposite me behind the cage of the octagon, staring daggers in my direction. With a menacing smile and a scar running the length of his left cheek, he should send shivers of apprehension down my spine. But I wave it off, focusing on the screaming and heavy drums in my ears easing my soul. If he wants to fuck me up, then I'll serve myself up on a platter for the taking. Knock me around. Bash my fucking skull in. It's what I crave when I step into the cage—anything to momentarily numb the memories trying their hardest to resurface. I eye him again as a small man whispers to him, standing on a stool to reach my opponent's impressive six-foot-seven height.

"He's going to annihilate you, man." I peer over at the fight coordinator, Ruthless, as he likes to be called, nervously biting his bottom lip with a frown. Worry sits behind his dark gaze, and he shakes his head, running a hand through his dark locks and grunts.

He's an intimidating man himself, running this entire operation with his brothers. Standing at six-five, with his body covered in tattoos and a part of an underground gang, he should frighten me, too. Hell, there are a lot of things that should scare me. Not him, though. He's as harmless as an annoying gnat fluttering around. However, he's rarely on edge like now, bouncing on his toes and forming fists. He shakes his head.

"Seriously, Cal. You need to rethink this entire thing. He's going to bash your damn skull in," Ruthless grunts with irritation, glaring at me. What does he care? I'll make him money tonight by taking a few punches. "Not to mention he fights fucking dirty. I better not have to scrape your brains off the damn mats after he razor blades you."

"That's what I'm hoping for," I mutter, pulling my arm across my chest and stretching out. Ruthless continues his spiel on how I'm about to die and that he's not responsible for burying my body or carrying me out of here when The Beast tears me a new asshole and takes my heart.

"You have a damn death wish every time you come in here," he huffs, pushing away from me with a frown deepening the wrinkles on his forehead. "Just be careful. And watch the damn Beast's moves," he hisses out a warning with finality, nodding toward the tall asshole across from me, jabbing his hands out an excessive amount of times.

The crowd wanders into the old bleachers on either side of the gym we're currently taking residence in. An old panther's logo, peeling from the walls, stares back at me with its mouth wide open, and the words East Point Prep splattered above it. I've never asked Ruthless how he came upon this empty campus. Years before, it was a prestigious prep school, then turned into a public school. Somewhere along the way, it was abandoned for good and left to rot.

I've never inquired on how he uses this without getting caught, despite the parking lot full of cars. Somehow, we're never interrupted by law enforcement, and I'm forever grateful for the reprieve from real life. This is my haven. It's where I go when my head fills with too many memories that my brain refuses to erase and knocks them into a black box.

The rising voices of the crowd crescendo through the vaulted space, infiltrating my ears over my soft music, which is another nuisance. I close my eyes and take several deep breaths, calming myself down and drowning out their cheers and taunts by tuning into the heavy melody playing through my earbuds.

My mind drifts to a faraway time, when I was nestled in the arms of the girl, I thought I loved—my Little Star. Even now, butterflies flutter in my stomach, heightening my nerves. That woman opened me up on so many levels, bringing out the confidence I shut away.

Fuck. I take several deep breaths, focusing on the smile she'd give me out of the corner of my eye, giving me tingling skin and tied tongues every time. Or the way we laid so many nights under the artificial stars placed above her bed. The memory of sneaking in through her unlocked sliding glass door, slipping beneath her sheets, and holding her tight, always rests just within reach in my mind. There's something so precious about River West and what we shared for all those months until the rug was pulled from beneath my feet.

Ultimately, in the end, she ruined it by turning her back on us and sneaking around. So, we did the same when we left without a goodbye. Some days, I wish I had that closure to grasp instead of wondering how she took it or how she was. No matter how badly she tore my heart in two, she's always with me.

My breath shudders when another unwanted memory

resurfaces in the forefront of my mind. I stand rigidly as it flashes like a movie flickering to life, unable to stop it as it advances on me like a waking nightmare. Only this time, I don't try to tune it out. Instead, I keep it close and let the rage, pain, and heartbreak overtake me as fuel for the deadly fight I'm about to endure.

Van growls, locking his eyes on me when I emerge from the shadows of the hallway of River's apartment. My brows furrow when he pushes her up against the kitchen counter, slamming his lips into hers. Taking a step back, I shake my head, swallowing the bile rising in my throat. Out of instinct, I take my phone out and snap a picture of her infidelity. I may remember every detail of this moment, but my brothers need proof to move on. If they didn't believe it before, they will now, just like me. There was no way I believed anything that came out of Asher's mouth. He was never ready for her, always standing on the sidelines like an observer.

"She's been cheating on us." Ash's voice echoes in my mind as I witness the deepening of the kiss and the unmistakable sound of her pleasure. "Cheating." Again, it plays, forever haunting me as I retreat from the situation with haste and don't look back.

The world sits on my shoulders when I throw open the sliding glass door, and I halt my exit, listening to the muted conversation down the hall. It's barely a whisper in the wind, and I'm unable to make out what they're saying.

Every inch of me splits into two at the heartbreak soaring from her betrayal. Fat tears track down my cheeks, but I quickly wipe them away. She doesn't deserve my tears. Or my heart. Or anything that has to do with us. She took our love and crushed it in her palm, easily throwing us to the side for Van fucking Drake.

"Callum." My name is a plea on her lips as she reaches for me, begging me to stay and saying more words I can't understand over the roaring emotions turning inside me.

"Goodbye, River," I mutter, giving her one last tear-filled look as I retreat and memorize her horror-stricken face.

She mutters more words, calling me back into her apartment. But the loud pounding of my heart drowns out her voice until I've made it to my car and hop in. For several minutes I stare through the front windshield and collect myself, turning every ounce of feelings I have off.

For the first time in years, I felt alive in the arms of the woman I grew to love. She brought me out of my shell and helped me face the world. I gave her my first, and I gave her my last. No longer will I allow women in my bed to manipulate or use me. My only future is the one in the limelight, playing my bass and living out my dreams, trying my damnedest to forget River West ever happened.

A drum pounds in my chest again as I revel in the anger her memory stirs and savor it for later. Never will I forget the kiss she shared with Van in her kitchen as I watched from the shadows. His shirt was off. His filthy hands were all over her. She didn't protest when he leaned in and kissed her lips. That's all it took for me to turn my back on her and walk out the door. Yet, here she is again in the flesh as our new band manager, living directly across the street from us, sent straight from the devil himself to torture our already fractured band. She'd never know it, but she's the reason we're four separate people who happen to play music together instead of one brain creating masterpieces.

She's also the reason I'm here tonight, eager to have my memories erased. One kick and punch at a time if that's what it takes.

Blood pumps through my veins as my steady heart speeds up, thumping against my ribs, while adrenaline pours through me. Steadying my movements, I watch my opponent's every move, memorizing his strike and speed. In the back of my mind, I catalog them, storing them for later when we square off. So I can use it against him. No one here knows my superpower. They'd never suspect I use the very thing I'm aching to be relieved of to become the champion.

I blow out a ragged breath, bringing my shirt over my head, and lay it on the stool beside me. Finally, I take out my earbuds, letting the full effect of the audience overtake me. I continue stretching out, getting everything limber for the chaotic fight I'm about to jump into.

As the minutes tick by and Ruthless calls our names at the center of the beat-up octagon, all my thoughts leave, finally giving me the blank thoughts I've longed for since yesterday when I came face to face with my most bothersome nightmare.

I shake out my limbs and stretch my neck from side to side, forgetting everything. Inside the cage, there's no past, present, or fucking future. It's only my opponent and me. My fists against his. His kicks against mine.

The crowd grows louder as bets are placed around us when the bell rings, and we descend on one another. The Beast smirks in my direction, lazily making his way toward the center of the ring, where I wait for him to advance, and we tap fists as a sign of respect.

Rolling my shoulders back, I take the first hit to my right temple, and then the predicted uppercut knocks me back a few steps, knocking the air from my lungs. Swerving right, I barely miss his next throw and regain my stance with a sadistic grin.

A small cut opens on my forehead, trickling warm blood down my cheek, dripping to the mats below. I grin more in his direction when he advances with a frustrated growl again, with a cockiness dictating his every move. He's so damn confident he's about to take me down, but I have more tricks up my sleeve.

Stepping to my left, I throw up my arms and block his next hit, thudding against my flesh. A chuckle bubbles up from my throat when I leap back, putting my fists to my side.

"That's all you got?" I ask with a light tone, smiling more when his nostrils flare. Like a bull running at full speed, he advances toward me in a fury of fists and kicks my thighs as his answer.

Around and around, we go trading punches and kicks. With a grunt, my foot lands in the middle of his abdomen, knocking him back a few staggering steps. Exhaustion sweeps through his fallen expression as he stumbles into the cage, bouncing off it with a huff. With one final growl, he advances on me, pummeling me with a fury of fists against my skull and jaw. Black dots spot my vision until adrenaline blasts through my veins one last time, and I knock him back with one single blow to the head.

Victory rings through the crowd, howling my name so loudly the walls shake and clap with enthusiasm. I grin, raising my tired arms in the air, as The Beast lies flat on his back with his arms curling in the air, looking lifeless with his eyes closed. Bruises line his body and face, swelling from the intensity of my hits, and peace washes over me.

"Rock Star! Rock Star!" they chant over and over as Ruthless grips my bloodied hand in the air, waving it around in victory.

"You fucking did it," he mutters with an impressed grin.

I snort. "And you doubted me?" I raise a brow, gazing through the crowd, memorizing all the usual fans heading toward the betting desk to cash in on their winnings. All thanks to me.

My mind melts into static with no visions of my memories coming to the surface. This is the moment I live for. The minute I stand in victory with my arm raised and my emotions buried so damn deep, even my photographic memory can't touch them and torture me.

Standing on my throne above the rowdy crowd, I gaze around, taking everyone's faces. My eyes grow wide, and my entire body stiffens when a pair of familiar green eyes stare back at me with her arms crossed and her brow raised.

"Fuck," I mutter as Ruthless lets my arm go and pats me on the back in congratulations.

"Your cut is at the booth or..."

"Donate it to the usual charity," I say, unable to break my gaze.

Satisfaction roars through me when her eyes wander down my bare chest and widen at the art adorning my flesh. All the air leaves my lungs when she stiffens, eyes locking on the intricate tattoos carved into the skin over my heart. Her jaw falls, and her brows furrow with confusion. It's a special piece I knew she wouldn't miss once her eyes locked on it. If only I had wanted her to see it yet.

"You got it," Ruthless says, stepping to the side of the ring and demanding one of the workers clear the blood off the ground and get ready for the next fight.

My heart pounds when Rad tenses beside her, discreetly shaking his head at me. Guilt swims across his features, and he swipes a hand down his face, shrugging over the situation like he had no choice but to come here with her.

I know the moment I walk over there; my ass will be facing the music. My fate—our fate—lies in her hands. But it was all worth it. The sneaking out. The fight. Even if it means our music career is completely over. It was a good fucking ride. Maybe I'm ready for it to be over because you never really know what you have until it's yanked from your grasp.

I long for the brothers I had before. The ones who looked after me and never turned their backs on me. I long for the basement concerts. Something that was just for us. Sure, I love the stage and more than appreciate my fans. I wish I had more time to live for myself and enjoy the music again. An ache forms in my chest, longing to turn back the clock to a simpler time.

My mind turns off momentarily, letting me forget the persistent memories knocking around in my head. For one fleeting moment, I had peace. And now, I'm about to shatter it with the reality of what I've done.

I take one last long sweep of the crowd, finally breaking River's standoff. The usual suspects dot the crowd, talking with their buddies and drinking beers with smiles. In the corner of the room, I take stock of a large man near the bleachers, huddling with three other men. Something in the back of my mind tells me to pay attention to this moment because, in these parts, they're strangers.

"They newcomers?" I ask Ruthless, nodding to the men in question, and he nods.

"Friends of The Beast," he says with a shrug. "Been here a few times before." I rub my chin at the new information and purse my lips. "That one is Adrian something or other," he says pointing to a larger man, scowling at his friends. "Then there's Kaleb, Derek, and Greg."

I narrow my eyes when the large man, Adrian, leans down, having a heated discussion with a shorter man dressed in black, hiding his face from view under a ball cap. Shaking my head, I shrug off the odd feeling building in my chest in a warning. Whatever they're discussing sends Adrian on his way with a scowl. By the way, his head soars above the crowd; he's a few inches taller than the Beast I destroyed. Speaking of...

I peer back at the giant still laid out in the octagon, mumbling to the shorter man who was with him until they hoist him up and cart him off the mats.

Collecting my shirt and earbuds from the stool where I left them, I take a few steps toward River and Rad, standing in the back of the crowd, just as the big man knocks into both of them, flinging River to the ground. My damn heart jumps out of my chest, and my jaw clenches. She shrieks angrily, her entire body disappearing from view.

My lip raises in disgust when he looms over them, poking a finger into Rad's chest. With every poke the big man gives, Rad's face tightens, and his nostrils flare as he goes toe to toe with him and doesn't back down. Fuck. I have to get over there and help him, despite our differences these days. He's still my oldest friend, no matter the weird tension we've felt lately between the band. We've never been the same since we left Central City. Or since River West.

I curl my fists, laying my shirt over my bare shoulder, and beeline it toward Rad, whose reddened face gives away his rising rage. He's two seconds away from snapping on the man, just like I am.

"Watch yourself," I grunt, getting into Adrian's face and bumping his shoulder as he continues leering down at River, sprawled out on the sticky floor.

"You watch yourself. You think just because you won against him, you could win against me?" he growls, grinding his teeth together.

He inches his face toward mine, snarling as he takes me in. I roll my eyes at his attempt to rile me up and shove a hand into his chest, knocking him back a step.

"Shut up and leave," I say, folding my arms across my bare, sweaty chest. "Or you'll have the same fate."

Blinking a few times in my direction, he chuckles at me. A smirk lifts at the edge of his lips when he peers down at River again, letting his eyes roam the entirety of her body. A deep growl works its way up my throat at his apparent interest, and I step up again, forcing him to look at me. Not her. No one looks at her like that.

He smirks at me and waves a hand like I'm not worth the effort. "Sure, I will," he chuckles without another word and leaves the building without fanfare.

"Fuck's sake," River grumbles, slapping Rad's awaiting hand away, climbing to her feet.

Rad frowns, bringing his hand to his chest. "Rude," he grumbles, shaking it out.

River's nose wrinkles as she brushes the dirt from her jeans and rights herself. "What an asshole," she huffs angrily, watching where he disappeared. Turning her gaze to mine, she raises an expectant brow. "So, fighting. Huh?"

I blow out a breath, running a hand down my face. How the hell do I explain this to her and keep our contract intact? I might not want this anymore, but Kieran's sanity depends on this damn gig. If he doesn't have music in his life, I don't know what he'll do. And the other two haven't said they're ready for a change. Not that we talk anymore, but still.

"Um, yeah-yeah," I stammer softly, getting lost in the expanse of her green eyes that soften at my voice. "Better than drugs," I mutter as dread fills my system.

That was a different time when my open wounds still bled

from the lies, and I took things into my own hands to forget the misdeeds of the woman I loved. The poison was too accessible, and we had too much money at our fingertips. Only, it didn't work. It never took the pain locked in my damn bones away. It didn't even numb the ache in my chest and left me craving more. After days of detox, I sought other forms of relief. Then came fighting. One knock to the skull, and all the pain hidden inside my body disappeared into thin air, and sweet oblivion took hold, letting me forget my misery.

Blowing out a breath, she shakes her head almost in disappointment at me. "Okay, well. Obviously, we need to have a little chat. So, let's roll," she says, waving a hand and taking off toward the door without another word or looking back.

"Sorry, man," Rad murmurs, standing close to me as we follow her through the exit and step out into the warm air. "But you weren't exactly discreet with your escape. Next time, roll your bike to the damn gate or something." He side-eyes me with disappointment.

I shrug, poking at a children's bandage plastered to the side of his face. "Why are you wearing so many?" I grunt, pulling my shirt over my head and situating it against my sticky skin.

He rubs the back of his neck, looking at River, who walks ahead of us and then back to me with apprehension.

"I, uh, fell off my bike, and her kid patched me up," he says softly, keeping his voice low.

I snort. "With fifty bandages? Damn. You hurt?"

"So, you don't know either, do you?" he whispers with discretion, stopping our retreat by curling his fingers into the front of my shirt and bringing us chest to chest. His dark eyes widen with desperation.

"Know what?" I ask, trying to pull away from him, but he clings on.

"You should see her, dude." His whisper comes out with strain, holding back tears and swallowing the emotions. Shaking his head, he swallows hard. "She's the spitting image of him." His lips roll together, and he shakes his head. "Do you ever feel that something isn't right about how we left and what happened? Like something feels so fucking off right now. Have you ever felt that way? Like everything was set up just a little too easily?"

"What are you talking about? Who is she? And who's the spitting image of who?" I ask through my confusion. My heart falls into my ass as the past rushes forward at his words. He had the video. I had the picture. It was as clear as day as to what happened. She cheated. We left. End of fucking story.

"Lyric," he mumbles, wincing when River calls our names from the parking lot and puts her hands on her hips. "River's daughter. Kieran's daughter. *Our* daughter." The way he says our gives me pause.

My entire body locks up. "What?" My breath leaves my lungs as my mind reels. "Kieran's? Ours?" What the hell is he saying?

"Yeah," he whispers, letting me go and heading down the path toward the darkened parking lot.

"What the hell are you talking about?" I hiss, stomping after him and grabbing his shoulder, stopping him again. My brows furrow. "What do you mean Kieran's kid and her kid? Our kid? She...." I stop dead, reliving that night over and fucking over, like so many times before. It never leaves, especially since she walked back into my life a day ago. Maybe I missed something. Perhaps my damn emotions ruled my decisions that night. But fuck. I trust Asher with my entire life. So, would he lie to us?

"She called me daddy, dude. She..." He shakes his head again, wiping a hand down his face looking more heartbroken than I've ever seen him. "River and I talked. But I think you need to talk to her, too. Especially about what you saw, bro. I think..." He shakes his head wearily. "I don't know what to fucking think anymore." With that, he walks away with his head hung low.

What the hell was going on? I shake my head, trotting after him at a quick pace, meeting them at River's SUV.

"Fuck," she grumbles under her breath, patting her pockets. "Did I bring my phone?" she asks Rad, who shrugs in response.

She blows out a frustrated breath. "Monday morning, we'll talk about this, okay?" she says, cocking her head to the side when I nod.

"Yeah, okay," I mutter, shoving my hands into my pocket.

"So, you're not kicking us out yet, Pretty Girl?" Rad asks with an easy grin, rubbing his hands together.

"Your contract is safe for another day. Believe me. You're not the only idiots to try and press my buttons. But next time, let's have a discussion before we sneak out. I know you guys had lives before I became your warden. At least you didn't snort coke out of some groupie's ass," she mutters the last part with a wrinkle of her nose.

"What?" Rad chokes, bending at the waist.

"Out-out of the ass?" I ask, clearing my throat and trying not to laugh.

She snorts. "Oh, long story. Can I trust you'll be a good boy and go back to the band house? I don't need to follow you around and document your activities for the label?"

"Scouts honor, Pretty Girl. He'll head straight home," he says, giving me the stink eye.

"Yes-yes. Straight home, boss," I say with a smirk lifting the edge of my lips.

"Fine," she says with a heavy sigh. "Let's go."

I stand back as River starts the car, and Rad pops into the passenger's seat with an animated smile. There's something there with him as he leans closer to her and whispers something. She shakes her head with a small smile before taking off down the highway.

I meander toward my bike and pop my helmet on, starting my Harley. The loud, echoing boom from my exhaust bounces off the abandoned administration buildings of the old prep school. Ruthless once told me why this place shut down so many years ago and why so many people from East Point Bluff refuse to step foot here or pretend this place doesn't exist. It chills my blood to know such a powerful and murderous cult walked the same streets I do now.

Taking off down the highway, everything hits me at once. Rad's words. The fight. My memories. Most importantly, Kieran's daughter. His comments from the limo fester under my skin, and my teeth grind.

If he fucking knew about River's daughter, why hasn't he said anything? Why hasn't he stepped up and taken responsibility for her? Fuck. My brain screams at me as I travel along the highway and finally make my way to the gates separating our new home from the outside world.

10

Asher

"DADDY," a small voice rings out through the darkness of my mind, rousing me back to the land of the living.

I groan, wiping the damn drool from my lips, getting my bearings. Where the hell am I? I swipe my palms along the textured surface of the chair I'm resting in, bringing back the memories of River's frantic call from earlier, asking me to babysit so she could chase Cal. Wherever the hell he goes at night when he thinks no one else is listening. And I fell asleep.

My brows raise, and I peel my eyes open, staring into the eyes of my tear-stained daughter. Daughter. Shit. I don't think I'll ever get used to that. I adjust myself in the recliner I'm sitting in and sit forward.

"Daddy," she whines again, pulling on my shirt with a little grunt, waking me up completely.

"Lyric," I rasp, quickly clearing my throat when she snuggles her bunny close to her chest and sniffles. "Are you okay?"

"Mommy is gone. Other Daddy is gone. You're here," she says tiredly, rubbing at her eyes with a frown. "Why?" she asks in a small voice, eyeing me up and down.

"I said I'd see you tomorrow, right?" I ask with a soft smile. "Here I am."

"Okay," she says without question, climbing into my lap with the most trusting grin. With a heavy, sleep-filled sigh, she snuggles into my chest. I wrap my arms tightly around her, securing her to me.

"Why're you awake?" Running my fingers through her long dark locks, I pull them from her cherub face and marvel at her familiar features. Up close and personal like this really brings out her mix of features. Kieran's nose and eyes. River's bone structure. Tiny freckles.

"A dream," she sniffles, wiping her nose across my shirt, leaving a snot trail behind.

In normal circumstances, I'd be repulsed by the snot shining on my dark shirt. But this isn't a normal circumstance. This is a little soul who calls me Daddy. And I robbed her of the experience of having us in her life because of my desperation to leave town. I owe her so much more than snot on my shirt and cuddles after a bad dream.

Guilt presses down on my chest, stealing my oxygen until I take a huge, relieving breath.

"What kind of dream?" I ask, running my fingers soothingly through her hair, hoping to ease the little trembles rumbling through her body.

"Mean monsters outside my window," she mumbles with a sniffle. Her bright, mismatched eyes search my face as it softens for her. "Tap. Tap. Tap," she mumbles, moving her little finger along with the words.

"I won't let the monsters get you, Little One. Ever. None of your daddies will allow that," I murmur soothingly, as her eyes flutter, and her long lashes brush against her cheeks.

Her body wiggles a few more times as her whimpers die down, and she relaxes in my arms. It dawns on me that she trusts me, feeling safe in my presence. After a few minutes, her soft baby snores fill the room as she clings to my shirt. "I'll never let anything bad happen to you ever again," I mutter, studying her face again, getting lost in the soft glow of her skin.

How can I already love such a small human after only a few

days of knowing she exists? It shouldn't be possible. But fuck, since the moment she uttered daddy, I was a goner. Lost to the way she held me close and asked me never to forget her again. My emotions have been haywire and spiraling since that moment. Lyric may not biologically be mine, but I'm here for this. I want this. Need this. Need her. She's a piece of me I never expected to find, and now that I have, I can't give it up.

Since River walked into that conference room, I've been biting my tongue. On the one hand, the guys deserve to know the truth about our departure. They've earned the right to know why I did what I did—what I had to do for us to get us here. Back then, it all made sense. All the pressure that was on my shoulders forced my hand. But that was me then, and this is me now, looking back and realizing I was an absolute idiot. Since coming into the spotlight, I've been forced to grow up.

On the other hand, I'm being a selfish fucking prick. If I confess my deceitful sins to the boys on why we had to leave and why I told so many goddamn lies to get us here, then I'll lose everything. The band. Lyric. Hell, even River. My life would implode, and I'd be left to pick up the pieces by myself. There's no way they'll stand beside me after I tell them.

Fuck. The indecision wars in my mind, giving me a damn pounding headache.

I stiffen when the front door bursts open in a flurry of movement. Shielding the little girl in my arms from any harm, my eyes widen as Callum races through with wide eyes and a heaving chest, followed by Rad sheepishly entering the front door with a frown.

"Bro," Rad says, tapping Callum's chest and nodding toward Lyric, situated snuggly in my lap. Callum's face softens at the sight of her dark hair and tiny snores.

"Shut up," I growl, nodding toward Lyric sound asleep on my lap. "She's asleep."

"You assfaces are not supposed to be in my damn house. You keep pushing my damn buttons," River snaps in a sharp tone, marching into the house and shutting the door. "Has anyone seen my damn phone?" Quickly she checks her pockets and looks around the room with a frown and shakes her head, worry lines creasing her forehead. Her nose wrinkles taking in the bundle in my arms and sighs. "What happened?" she asks, eyeing the position I've found myself in.

"Monsters outside her window," I mumble, clutching her to my chest, rising with a groan. I didn't hold her for that long, but my muscles protest from the stiff position and my refusal to move an inch while she was in my arms.

River blows out a breath, running a hand down her face. "Yeah, that's been happening a lot lately."

"Is it not normal, Pretty Girl?" Rad asks, stepping forward with a grin and staring down at Lyric's sleeping face.

"Oh shit," Callum mutters in the background, stumbling over his feet to get closer.

"Told you," Rad mutters smugly.

"Want me to take her back to bed?" I ask River, who reluctantly nods and leads me down the long hallway of her one-story home toward the bedroom at the far end.

Footfalls softly sound behind us as all four of us step into the purple princess room. Fairy lights decorate the edges of the ceiling, hanging down the walls like rainfall, illuminating the medium-sized bedroom. Clothes, toys, and even snack wrappers line the floor, causing River to frown.

Gently, I place her in the middle of the bed, covering her with the plush comforter designed with princesses and crowns. Perfect for our little girl. Running a finger down her cheek, I bask in the tiny sleepy smile she gives me.

"Night, Daddies. You come tomorrow?" she asks in a little voice, melting my fucking heart all over again. Jesus. All she has to do is call my name, and I'm already wrapped around her tiny little finger. I'll do anything for her, and I don't think I'm the only one.

"Yes, Little One," I murmur.

"Yes, Little Pretty Girl," Rad says at that exact same time with enthusiasm and a grin.

"Yes-yes," Callum stammers in awe, stepping forward and meeting her barely open eyes. She grins at him and yawns.

"Other Daddy," she murmurs, looking up at him and examining his face. "You came, too," she says in tired awe, staring up at Callum with stars in her eyes.

"I did," he manages to whisper, staring directly into her eyes. I see the moment everything truly clicks for him, and he shudders. I'm sure Rad opened his big mouth and told Callum everything.

"Okay. Night, Ly. Sorry, Mommy had to run an errand. Now all your daddies are going to leave. But you'll no doubt see them again," she says with a pointed stare in our direction, silently ushering us out of her house where we're not supposed to be in the first place.

Rad snorts at her sarcastic remark but doesn't utter a word when she shoots daggers in his direction. As quietly as we can, we shuffle through the bedroom door, shutting it behind us. On silent feet, we follow River out to the living room, standing awkwardly in a spaced-out circle, with her putting more distance between us. Looking around the room, she awkwardly shifts from foot to foot and heaves a sigh.

"Um, thanks for the last-minute, late-night babysitting," River mumbles with a cringe. If I could see the inner workings of her mind right now, I'd be able to hear the warring thoughts displaying on her transparent face. "I appreciate it," she says again with a tight smile, standing rigidly in the awkward silence surrounding the four of us.

"It's no problem. I wasn't doing anything, anyway," I say with a shrug.

To be honest, I liked getting to spend a little time with Lyric. Even if it was for a short time. There are still so many questions sitting on the tip of my tongue that I need the answers to. And there's only one woman who can offer those up—Gloria. I'm sure she'll be eager to see my face at her front door this week when I make time to visit her in her penthouse apartment. Courtesy of Kieran's bank account, but that's a whole other story.

River's body turns rigid when Callum looms over her with furrowed brows, staring with confusion. Her eyes avert to the wall behind my head, avoiding his questioning stare at all costs.

"I'm confused," Callum mutters, rubbing a finger along his forehead. "You-you had a baby? She's—" He halts his words and shakes his head. "When?"

River pinches the bridge of her nose in agitation. "Let me guess; you weren't informed, either?" she asks in a low, emotion-filled voice, still refusing to look in Callum's direction.

"None of us were, Pretty Girl. Well..." Kieran. That's what he wants to say.

Maybe that asshole knew and decided he didn't want to tell us because of our new gig. He didn't want to jeopardize our future like I didn't want to either. But she's a child, and she needs us to be in her life. How could he make that decision without telling us, too? It affects us all. *Hypocrite,* my subconscious shouts at me as a familiar burning pain tightens my chest and trickles up my throat. Reaching into my pocket, I grab my antacids and pop two into my mouth. The relief isn't instant when I chew them up, but at least it'll tamp down the pain for a few more hours.

"No. I wasn't aware you had a baby. Let alone... She called me other daddy," he whispers, heaving a frantic breath. "You told her that..."

"I wasn't going to hide where she came from," River cries out in frustration, taking another step back from us and shaking her head. "She knows all about the four of you. For five years, I've been under the impression that you all denied her and didn't want her. You all walked away from me. You didn't say goodbye. You ignored my fucking texts! And then Gloria said you wanted nothing to do with her. I don't fucking know what the hell to think right now." Confusion swims through River's eyes, and her brows dip, creasing her forehead. Moisture pools in her eyes, most likely from frustration and rage. It's on the tip of my tongue to tell them that they'd been tricked into leaving, but I hold my tongue like a coward.

"Gloria?" Callum asks us softly, furrowing his brows again. "What did she do?" Fuck. What didn't she do? She had her hands in our doomed relationship before we even left.

River's jaw works back and forth, and her fingers curl into fists, whitening her knuckles from the pressure. "Listen, it's late. Could you all go? I really don't want to talk about this right now. I shouldn't have to defend myself any more than I have. It's you all who owe me an explanation. I'll see you all on Monday, okay?" River stands firmly where she is, watching wearily as we all nod in agreement.

"Sure thing, Pretty Girl," Rad says softly. "But this isn't over. You know that, right? We'll talk more." He raises a brow when her eyes narrow into slits, and I know a snarky reply sits on the edge of her tongue, ready to tell us all off if I don't get everyone out of here.

"Let's go," I say, grabbing his shoulder and pulling him out of the house as Callum follows slowly behind us with his hands in his pockets.

The moment we're outside, the warm summer air smacks us in the face. I take a breath, listening to the hypnotic sound of the ocean waves crashing against the shore behind River's house. Oh, how I ache to run down the beach, exerting myself into forgetting my sins.

"Fuck," Rad grumbles, picking up his discarded dirt bike from the middle of the road, looking it over under the streetlights shining down on us as brightly as the sun.

"Looks fucked," Callum says, stopping beside me as Rad looks it over.

"No shit, Einstein," Rad grumbles with a frown. "Old reliable has finally met his match," Rad pouts, running his finger over the deep scratches in the metal. "And all it took was one little girl to bring her down. I could have squished her." He touches the side of his face covered in brightly covered bandages and sighs.

"What the hell is going on?" Callum finally asks, shaking his head with frustration. "What was she saying about Gloria?"

"Don't forget the restraining orders on top of that," I grumble, rubbing my chin, still perplexed by that statement.

"That's what she told me, too! She fucking said Gloria handed her four restraining orders," Rad growls, wiping the beads of sweat from his forehead as he lifts his bike off the ground.

"With our signatures on it," I point out.

Callum's gray eyes bug out of his head. "Restraining orders?" he asks, looking to Rad for confirmation. "What the hell? We didn't do that."

"I told you. Something fucking stinks like a dirty coochie fish on the beach." Rad scrunches up his face, grunting when he tries to roll his dirt bike forward.

"But she-she kissed Van," Callum's voice dips low with accusation and hurt, shaking his head in denial. "I saw it with my own two eyes. Right after you showed us the-the video."

My stomach churns at the thought of the video, starring River and Van from when they were together. It was my only tool at the time to convince them we needed to leave without her. I was so convinced she'd drag us down. Now, look at her. She runs the damn show. If only I'd given her the chance.

"Did she? Or did he force her to?" Rad shouts out in frustration, wheeling around and letting his bike drop again. "Because, according to her, he forced himself on her, and you just stood by and took a fucking picture," he growls with flaring nostrils. "And then you walked away, leaving her there with him. Fuck! We all walked the fuck away because of you!" Rad barks, slamming his foot into the dented rims of his turned-over bike. Over and over again, he slams down on the metal, ruining it further. Only stopping when he's sweaty and breathing heavily from the exertion. "Why didn't we talk to her first?" he growls, advancing on Callum with malicious intent, curling his fingers into fists. This is one fight Rad would not win. Callum stiffens, tensing his body and waiting for impact.

"Whoa," I say, jumping between them and putting a hand on Rad's chest. His heart accelerates against my palm when he heaves a breath. "Fighting gets us nowhere," I say, pushing him back a step.

"Well, I want some fucking answers!" Rad shouts through the anguish, pushing me away and nearly knocking me off my feet. "I just want to know why I left the love of my fucking life. What the hell is real?" His chest heaves beneath my palm until he steps back, shaking his head.

"We'll figure it out." My voice trembles as I speak, knowing the truth of the situation already. Although, there seem to be certain factors I never planned that were put into play.

"Where'd you get the videos from?" Callum asks, spearing me with his knowing gaze. I swallow hard and blow out a breath.

"Van sent them to me," I say, rubbing the back of my neck, actively avoiding their stares.

"Out of the blue?" Callum asks again, scrunching his eyebrows.

"Yeah. Out of the blue." I shrug, crossing my arms so they can't see the tremble of my fingers.

"No idea what prompted it?" Callum asks again with more suspicion.

"No, man. I just assumed he wanted to rub it in my face that he was banging her behind our backs. You know how he was back then. He was fucking obsessed with her and following her around everywhere," I huff, throwing my arms around. "I thought I was doing the right thing!" I shout, pulling at the ends of my hair. "I thought..."

I thought I really was doing what was best for us. She was a distraction. Someone they were willing to stay behind for.

Rad frowns, staring at me. "I get it, man. I guess. But looking back now, I don't think we did the right thing." He swallows hard, staring off at the dark house a few feet away from us, housing the girl we intentionally left behind. "We should have talked to her and heard what she had to say. Like now. But..."

"She probably won't talk to us about it anymore," Callum mumbles, rubbing his chin.

"I don't think we did, either," I sigh, biting into my bottom lip as the guilt tears another piece of my soul into the void of no return. I rub my hand across my aching chest, praying the acid doesn't bubble up my throat as punishment.

One day soon, I'll tell them. I just want more time with Lyric before I'm thrown to the side for my atrocious actions. But I don't blame them. They'll never forgive me. River will never forgive me. If I have to sit on the sidelines and watch them happy together, that's a sacrifice I'm willing to make. I just need a few more happy memories to cling onto when I'm tossed to the side and forgotten about.

Callum stops, cocking his head to the side. "Did you hear that?" he asks with furrowed brows, looking into the dark shadows surrounding River's house.

"Hear what?" Rad grunts, picking up his discarded dirt bike.

Callum's face twists, and he shakes his head. "I thought I heard a click or tap or something."

"All I hear is the ocean waves," I offer, looking toward her house with a twist in my gut.

"The monsters coming for you, Cally boy?" Rad taunts, heaving his messed-up bike forward on its damaged wheels.

"Fuck off," Cal grunts, shoving at Rad's shoulders.

"What are we going to do about Kieran?" The three of us halt outside the open garage, listening to the silent house. All the windows appear black, hopefully meaning his grumpy ass went to bed.

"You think he knows? Like for real knows?" Callum asks, licking his lips. A deadly expression captures his face, brewing a fire behind his eyes.

Rad's teeth grind when he throws his bike into the garage without care and growls. "I'll fucking murder him," he grunts, kicking the bike one more time. "If he knew..."

"Doesn't seem like him, though." I shake my head. "If Gloria could concoct restraining orders, then who's to say she told him the truth?" I raise a brow when Rad and Cal exchange a look, and they sigh.

"What do we do then?" Rad asks, shoving his hands in his pockets.

"We don't say anything yet. The ball is in River's court."

"Fine," Rad agrees. "But if all this turns out to be bullshit, I'm reclaiming what's mine," he says, pointing a finger toward her dark house. "And that's a fucking promise." With that, Rad walks away, sauntering into the house without another word.

"What do you think?" I ask Callum, who narrows his eyes at me suspiciously.

"I don't know yet, but I'll find out." With those foreboding words, he turns his back on me, leaving me to stew in my own fucked up mess I made, now with more complications.

11

Asher

THE TALL BUILDINGS of East Point surround me, shining in the bright morning sunlight. I squint my eyes, taking a deep breath as I psych myself up for my rendezvous with the devil herself. Who knows if I'll make it out alive to tell the damn tale.

All around me, people bustle by, entering the high-end stores lining the area with bright smiles on their faces and exiting with an armful of bags, giggling about their purchases. Speaking of... two stores down, two brunettes dressed to the nines in expensive clothes and jewelry stop abruptly on the sidewalk with shock splayed on their faces.

"Oh, my God," one woman squeals ten yards away. Her big eyes widen, and her jaw drops, staring at me with awe like I'm a fucking rare God standing before them. "That's Asher Montgomery from Whispered Words!" she hisses with excitement to her friend beside her while jumping in place.

"Oh, my God! It is!" her friend shouts, promptly covering her mouth in embarrassment as high-pitched giggles escape from behind her hand. A pinkish tint takes over her cheeks as she stares in my direction with wide eyes.

"I heard they were living closer now." The first girl says in what she thinks is a whisper, but her voice carries loudly to my ears. Quickly, I hold in the cringe, making me want to melt away from the situation.

Inwardly, I groan, loathing this evil side of fame. For one split second years ago, I adored the attention and fucking ate it up with a spoon. I fucking encouraged it with a sick grin, craving the attention of the crowds coming to see us. It took me a long time to realize that no one wanted to know the real me. They didn't want to sit down and have an easy conversation. They wanted my fucking dick. Not conversation. Maybe a baby to claim what's mine. The fans want the man I portray on stage with the cocky smirk and sexy swagger. They want Asher Montgomery, the guitar player of Whispered Words. And that's a straight punch to the gut because the Asher on stage and the Asher walking the streets are two very different people.

This is all part of the gig. I know it is. But it's fucking annoying that I can't walk out of the house without someone approaching me for pictures and autographs. Some people—no matter their gender—offer themselves up to me on a silver platter. Years ago, I was tempted by their sexy curves and golden smiles. Tempted, being the key word. I've kept my dick firmly in my pants since the night I fucked River on that dining room table and came happily in her eager cunt. Believe me, that moment repeatedly sits on a high pedestal in the back of my head. Especially when the loneliness I've imposed on myself crushes my soul one squeeze at a time. My heart has only beat for one annoying Little Brat, even after all these years. It'll never change. No matter how much she loathes us. My heart is hers and has been for the past few years. My guilt has sat with me for too long to settle down, let alone bone another chick.

Politely, I wave as the fans drag their phones out and snap several pictures of me standing before my self-inflicted doom. I try to plaster on a fake smile and greet them with the kindness I don't currently feel.

"Can we take some selfies?" one girl asks, dragging her friend by the hand and stopping before me. She grins when I nod, and we take several selfies together, huddling in a tight hug. Our smiles light up the photos, despite the annoyance I feel.

"Make sure you tag me on FlashGram," I say as she squeals again, nodding in agreement, and they walk away without another word.

I blow out a breath, swiping a hand down my face, trying to forget the dread building like a damn storm coming. Lead sits heavy in the pit of my churning stomach when I take a step forward, continuing to tell myself this is a good idea. Yeah, a really good fucking idea to come here. I hang my head, peering around again and avoiding the issue at hand. A war is about to begin in the confines of this apartment building.

There's absolutely nothing cheerful about the situation I'm walking into. My stomach turns as I walk through the belly of the beast, waving hello to the front desk clerk, and then enter the large elevator. When I hit the top floor button, my fingers tremble from the uncontainable anger rising through my body.

As the elevator whirrs to life, my mind drifts to River's statements about the restraining orders and abortion check she tore to pieces. Oh, how I wish I were a fly on the wall when River told Gloria to fuck off.

The more I think about the shit Gloria pulled, the more my rage consumes me. Sure, I played an equal part in River's demise, but I never barred her from speaking to us permanently. I never told her to get rid of our kid. I just...did something almost equally as wrong. I grip my hair at the mounting frustration and heave a breath.

"Get a hold of yourself," I mutter, squeezing my eyes shut. "Fuck," I grunt, lightly tapping my forehead against the mirrored wall.

As the doors slowly slide open, I step out into the luxurious hallway illuminated by the sun leaking through the tall windows. Opulence decorates every inch of the space. From the beautiful chandelier to the gorgeous paintings lining the walls to the expensive luxury apartment I'm about to walk into—number forty-seven—on the top floor of the largest, most expensive apartment complex in East Point. Only the best for dear old Gloria—she can't seem to hold down a job or take care of her child. Since my father met his fate and got carted off to prison, Kieran's mother has been our problem. Five years of hell in her presence, why not another minute?

I raise a hesitant fist to the inconspicuous white door, halting mid-knock. Do I really want to look into the eyes of the woman who ruined my life without a second thought? No. I'd rather avoid Gloria as I've successfully done for years. Our only interactions are at Christmas when we return to see Camilla and dote on her as she deserves. But Fuck. This is something unavoidable. It's the only way I'll get to the bottom of everything, and then I can start repairing it one piece at a time.

Annoyance rises inside me as I pound my fist into the door with much more force than necessary, gleefully watching the hinges shake. On the other side, tiny footfalls flitter through the air, and the door swings open, revealing Gloria still in her red silk pajamas and glazed-over eyes.

"Asher, what brings you here?" Gloria's face scrunches as her eyes rake up and down my body with a disapproving frown. "I wasn't expecting you today." Gloria tilts her head, and a look of concern crosses her twisted-up face.

"We need to talk," I demand, pushing into her apartment and whirling around. I cross my arms over my chest, glaring in her direction as she softly closes the door.

"Talk? Sure, why don't you just come on in," Gloria snaps, furiously storming toward the large kitchen. "Could I interest you in a drink, Asher?"

I run a hand down my face in exasperation and nod. "Sure, a drink would be nice." And make it fucking stiff—is what I want to say, but I hold my tongue as she flitters into the kitchen, humming angrily about uninvited guests.

"So, what brings you to my neighborhood? I barely see you boys, and we live in the same damn town," she says with disdain, entering the elegant living room with two coffee cups. I raise a brow, noting the steam wafting from one cup as she gently hands it to me, and the familiar smell of coffee hits my senses, perking me up. Sitting beside me, she cocks her head to the side. "How's the band going? Any new tours ahead of you?" She sniffs her cup with satisfaction and takes a gulp, only slightly grimacing when she pulls back.

Of course, she wants to know about any new tours to line her own damn pockets. She's been bleeding Kieran dry since he's struck it rich, and she loves her walking, talking, piggy bank.

"So, have you heard from my father?" I know the answer as soon as it leaves my lips. Gloria scoffs, taking a sip of her drink, gearing up to defend herself for her actions. But fuck that, I let my tongue take the lead—consequences be damned. "That's right, you don't really talk to him after you sent his ass to federal prison, do you?" Not that I fucking care his ass is in prison. I'm glad he's behind bars where he can't hurt another soul on the outside. He's where he belongs, and now, we can protect ourselves and Cami from his wrath.

She blinks several times, and I know I've hit the mark on the head. "Well, I had to do what I had to do," she retorts quickly without missing a beat. "What was I supposed to do when the FBI showed up on my doorstep with evidence? Turn them away? Go to prison with him? I think not." She sniffs haughty, sticking her nose in the air. "I turned him in like he deserved. It was a win-win for all of us."

"It might have been a good place for you," I mutter under my breath, earning a death glare. Perhaps she's not too drunk yet and still has her wits about her. I need to hold my damn tongue until I can get more information out of her.

"You'll do well to remember who helped bring you to where you are now. If it wasn't for my contribution and the car I allowed you to take, you'd be no one," she says, tossing her hair over her shoulder and lifting her chin. "If it wasn't for me, then you'd be in prison yourself, and I'd still be stuck in that loathsome little city. This is where we belong, Asher. You'll do good to remember what we deserve." What we deserve? Is the alcohol making her dumber as we speak? What the hell kind of high horse shit is she on? "So, who cares if your father is spending the rest of his life in prison for embezzling everything? I sure don't."

"Of course, you fucking don't." I grind out. "Nothing has changed for you. We still pay your way." Because of our little sister Cami and that's it.

"If you're going to continue to insult me, then I'm going to insist you leave. Is this really what you wanted to talk about?" she growls as multiple veins pop in her forehead and her face flushes.

"No, that's not what I wanted to talk to you about," I say, running a hand through my hair. "Since we're bringing up the past, let's have a little discussion."

"Oh?" she questions with a frown, probably seeing her future being ripped away.

"Yeah, Whispered Words is officially on probation. Apparently, our sales have been down, and now they're trying to fix us, or we're fired." I blink a few times as her expression falls, and deep worry takes over her sadistic eyes, which widen in horror at our new reality.

"What do you mean your sales are down?" she snarls in my direction, acting like it's all my fault we aren't performing well.

She wouldn't be wrong, though. We've sucked it up this past year, unable to mesh any fucking more. It was only a matter of time before someone pulled the plug. At least this way, we're getting a second chance. Her body sits rigidly next to me, fury blazing through her veins.

"Just what I said," I say through gritted teeth, glaring in her direction. "Our sales are down, and now we have a new band manager. Can you guess who that is?" My fists clench in my lap when she sneers at me.

"No, I don't know who it could be. Why would I know?" she asks with innocence, moving her body away from mine. She takes a small sip of what I can only guess is alcohol in her coffee cup, and I sigh.

"Because you spend enough of Kieran's money, I figure you'd know all our business," I snark, gnashing my teeth together.

Get your shit together and stop letting her stupid face get to you. Fuck. I take a deep, relieving breath to blow the frustration away. There's nothing that gets my blood boiling more than Gloria Montgomery.

I know why Kieran and I decided to move Gloria closer. I only wish we didn't have to. Her broke ass should have stayed in Central City. Back on the poor side, where she came from. Maybe a little humbling could do her some good.

But we did it for our teenage sister, Camilla. She means the absolute world to us, and we wanted to protect her from Gloria's manipulative ways. Luckily, she got away from my father's abuse before it was too late. But Gloria is a whole other story. So, with strong suggestion, our little sister now attends the new East Point Prep a few miles away on the edge of town, safely tucked away in her dorm room. Far the fuck away from the toxicity, sucking the life away from this apartment. When we aren't on tour, we make sure to take Cami out for lunch and catch up on how middle school is going.

"If you just came here to insult me, you can leave," she says, sticking her nose in the air. Her finger points toward the door, and by the look in her eyes, she's shutting down fast.

"River West is our new manager." There. I said it. Let the fucking pin drop.

Gloria's face falls, and her hand comes up to her heart. Slumping back onto the couch, she vigorously shakes her head in disbelief. "But-but, we got rid of her. There's no way that slutty little Central girl is your new manager. She must have slept her way to the top, like every other girl from that side of town. There's absolutely no way. You have got to be joking," she scoffs, leaning down to take a massive gulp from her coffee cup.

Funny. That's precisely what Gloria did to snag my father as her prize. She slept around and climbed her way to the top, one man at a time, until she locked down the wealthiest man she could with a baby, and he couldn't deny it. And yet, here she is comparing River, who worked two fucking jobs and went to college all by herself with no help. Oh, the irony of it all.

"Yeah, and she's had some pretty interesting things to say about you and what happened after we left," I say, raising my eyebrows when her face pales, and she purses her lips, looking far from innocent. In fact, as the statement settles, the shock evaporates, and she smirks with victory. No doubt reliving the moment she permanently booted River from our existence.

Imagine what could have happened if River had been able to call us and explain her pregnancy. No matter how angry they were at her, they would have wanted to know Lyric. Something I'll forever feel guilty about. Fuck. The burning in my chest rises again, sending the nasty taste of acid up my throat and onto my tongue. I rub a hand over my burning heart, wishing the pain would stop before an ulcer forms.

"And by the way, River isn't just some Central girl. River is worth way more than you'll ever be. And I can't believe I let you talk me into doing what I did," I retort without thinking, letting my brewing emotions take the damn lead. Thankfully, I keep the essential part of the equation to myself. For now, at least. She doesn't deserve to know she has a grandchild who will never know who she is.

"Oh please, don't tell me I didn't do the right thing. That Central slut was going to ruin your lives. And you boys were just going to stand back and let it happen. Not on my watch! I had to do something to get her out of the way completely. Even after she told me that little lie about her being pregnant, all she was ever after was your money. She was so damn desperate, too," she says with a roll of her eyes, dramatically huffing.

I study every freckle on Gloria's offended face. True evil lies behind her eyes. She may not look like somebody that could take you down, but in her own unique way, she can. Every emotion hits me at once, amplifying the guilt closing my throat. Gloria unabashedly used me. She took my feelings, my anger, my desperation and put them in the palm of her hand, effortlessly using them against me with her sly, perfectly placed words.

I pull at the collar of my designer shirt and swallow hard. I swear my heart pounds in my ears, drowning out everything else. Gloria expertly manipulated me into doing what she wanted. With her twisted words and helping hand, she got exactly what she desired—getting rid of River. For good. The money she offered me and the promise to keep my father out of it had me where she wanted me, on my knees and begging for more.

Slowly, I get to my feet and chug the rest of the warm coffee she brought me, grimacing at the bitter taste on my tongue. As I contemplate my next moves, I look around, taking in the grand elegance of the home we've provided her with.

Gloria has everything from professional paintings hanging on the wall to the tiny one-of-a-kind designer statue sitting in the corner. And now, her end is near. I will never let another human being manipulate me the way she did.

My gut churns and bile rises at the entire situation. "So, after you manipulated me into this with the promise of money and my father out of the picture, while the boys and I were away and we won, you swooped in and ensured that River would never be able to talk to us again. Did you really think we would never find out about the restraining orders? Or the check you gave her?" My voice rises with every word, making her cringe back.

"Why do you care what some Central girl has to say? So what if I gave her four restraining orders? Judge Drake had no qualms about helping me secure your future and Van's," she says with a wave of her hand like it means absolutely nothing that she ruined not only River's life but Lyric's. "Besides, look at you now. You guys are the biggest rock stars around. What is she going to do?"

"River is in charge of our contract, Gloria. If we fuck up, then River sends us on our way. Our contract will be void. No more money. No more rock star status." I shake my head, running a hand through my hair in frustration. Tightly, I grip the longer ends, basking in the release of my festering temper. Talking to Gloria is like talking to a four-year-old who doesn't understand the word no. Hell, Lyric understands better than this grown woman, and I've only had brief conversations with her.

I slam my cup down with more force than necessary, praying a crack forms. Glaring down, I take in every inch of Gloria's pathetic form. What a conniving, money-hungry woman she's become. If only she'd known what an exceptional little girl Lyric would become.

"And you're wrong, by the way. River wasn't lying about the baby. Congratulations, Grandma," I say just as I maneuver through the front door, slamming it in her shocked face before she can utter a single word.

Racing down the hallway toward the elevator, I press the bottom floor button and slump against the mirrors as every inch of my flesh tingles and trembles with the exhaustion sweeping through me. So, it's all true. Everything River has been adamant about. Gloria served River with actual restraining orders, signed by a real sneaky judge, hellbent on getting everyone away from River and isolating her. I may have driven the guys out, but Gloria put the nail in the coffin. No wonder I never found River online whenever I snooped. She'd either erased herself off social media or blocked us long ago.

As I make my way out of the building, I clutch my chest and let the entirety of the situation crash down on me. I made the most monumental mistake of my life. Not only did it affect me, but it affects five other people. Old Asher was selfish, stuck up, and a manipulative asshole, and I let Gloria rule over me, bending my will for a few thousand dollars. She dangled my little sister's safety in front of my eyes like a carrot on a string, playing with my need to protect her. I knew it was the only way to drag them to safety, away from my controlling and abusive father. So, I did what I did to protect the people around me. When the only thing that my heart truly wanted was the girl I left behind on purpose.

Leaning against the sleek high-rise, I take several deep breaths and process the conversation I just had. Nothing prepares you for walking into the lion's den, and that's what I just did. As I search the distance and all the stores surrounding me, filled to the brim with shoppers and happy mothers and daughters and sons, a familiar person catches my eye across the street, coming out of the phone store with a perplexed look adorning her cute face. In a split-second decision, I make my way across the street and loom over her small frame as she stares down at a new phone in her hand. Before I open my mouth, I take the time to examine the woman River has become. And boy, do I like what I see.

12

Asher

"NEW PHONE?" I ask in a low voice, hovering over River as she stands on the sidewalk, oblivious to her surroundings.

Her brown hair sways with the light breeze brushing down her back. I swallow thickly when her scent envelops me, knocking me back a step and straight into forbidden memories that tickle at the back of my mind—reminding me of the times we shared. Now it feels like a lifetime ago. Seeing River and being around her takes me back to the simpler times when all I had were dreams and aspirations and my girl at my side. Even if we fought like cats and dogs, I'd take that feeling of playing at Dead End and watching her over the fame and fortune I betrayed her for.

"Jesus!" River yelps, jerking her body back from mine with a slight screech. Several shoppers walking past stare intently in our direction with curious eyes, startled by the noises coming from her.

Her expression morphs into a deadly scowl aimed in my direction as the fright wears off. From one scathing look, my balls shrivel, and I swear a fire starts breaking out across my flesh, causing me to pull at the collar of my shirt.

She huffs, putting a hand over her heart, and mutters words I can't quite understand. "You can't just sneak up on people like that, Asher," she barks, heaving a breath. "It's rude."

"Sorry," I say, putting my hands up placatingly. My teeth sink into the side of my cheek, concealing the small smile trying to pull at my lips. "I didn't mean to scare you. I was just in town and saw you over here. Thought I'd come over and say hi." She blinks at me a few times as my words register, deepening the wrinkle on her forehead.

Jesus Christ. What the hell has gotten into me? I'm suddenly transported back to when I was a teenage boy, nervously talking to the first girl I ever laid eyes on. Nerves bristle under my skin. My palms friggin sweat so much, I'm wiping them down my jeans.

River rolls her eyes and sidesteps me, moving along the sidewalk slowly. "Why exactly are you following me?" she asks, shoving her new phone into her pocket.

Good fucking question. Why am I following her down the sidewalk when my car rests a block away from here? Why not just turn on my heel and walk in the opposite direction? The short of it is, I can't. There's a pull between River and me, begging me to tag along as she actively avoids looking at me. Perhaps my crushing guilt pushes me to fix things, or maybe, I genuinely miss her—my Little Brat.

"It's a nice day for a walk." I shrug, shoving my hands into my pockets, and fiddle with the lone key poking into my finger.

The sun's heat blasts down on us as we walk side by side toward the middle of the square that makes up the center of downtown East Point Bluff. Several restaurants feature outside dining, where guests drink their coffees and enjoy a spread of breakfast items while chatting with their loved ones.

"I guess," she says, unconvinced, peering around at the other people walking past on the semi-crowded sidewalk.

All trepidation leaves her face, falling to the wayside when we step into the square and stop directly in front of an unfamiliar shop bustling with noisy customers.

The glorious scent of rich coffee wafts through the air, perking up my senses. The absolute shit Gloria offered me stains my taste buds with its awful flavor, making me eager to wash it away. Not to mention, it did nothing to perk me up.

"Want some?" I ask, gesturing behind us as she looks around at the other shops around the square, still avoiding my gaze.

The remnants of the heated conversation between Rad, Callum, and River hang heavily in the air. Every muscle in River's body seems to tighten with my suggestion, and her mossy green eyes find mine. Apprehension rests behind her gaze as she silently questions whether she should take me up on my offer. "Maybe a muffin, too?" My stomach rumbles at the thought of stuffing my face with sugar. I couldn't touch food this morning without my stomach tightening into knots, but now that the conversation is over—all bets are off.

Her eyebrows furrow as she looks between the shop and me again. "This is really fucking suspicious, Evil Ash," she says, pursing her lips while looking me over for ill intent. I'm unsure what is going through her mind, but it seems to be racing. My breath hitches in the back of my throat at the sound of my old nickname leaving her lush lips. Once again, bringing back the raging memories of our long, complicated past. "As long as you're buying," she says with a slight shrug, throwing open the front door.

I snort when she rushes into the shop without ensuring I am following, seeming so confident that I will be by her side and buy her the things she demands. Something so simple and small settles inside of me being this close to her again. River West has this aura about her that drags you in like a moth to the flame, and I can't seem to help myself. No matter how badly this turns out, the moment River finds out my role in the entire situation, she won't want anything to do with me. I will take my time and truly show River how sorry I am even before I confess my sins.

The smell of delicious coffee permeates the air as I slowly stroll behind her. Radiant energy cascades from her as she smiles at the people around her, pulling them into her happy little bubble. River waves to a few people around the shop, only stopping once to say hello to an elderly gentleman who greets her like she is family. She smirks back at me the moment we head toward the counter, making butterflies burst in my damn belly. The moment the barista's beady eyes set on her; I swear his entire face lights up like fireworks exploding.

"River!" he happily shouts, smiling as we make our approach together. An eerie feeling settles in my gut when his eyes roam her body, greedily taking her in. A deep red blush takes over his neck and cheeks when she smiles at him again in greeting. Something odd bubbles inside me, and on instinct, my fists curl at my side, ready to bash his way too happy face into a pulp. There's just something about him that doesn't settle right with me. "Same thing today?"

"Hey, Nathan. Same coffee. Same breakfast muffin. But this guy is paying for everything. And also, whatever he wants," she says with a sly smirk, patting me on the chest. The moment she indicates she's with me, the barista cuts his gaze to me, giving me a withering look.

"Sure," Nathan says tightly, dropping an octave and oozing with disapproval. "What can I get you?" His teeth grit, popping a muscle in his jaw. I would never notice the slight hostility dripping from him if I wasn't such an observant person. But there it is in his unwavering stare.

It's pathetic at best, but I offer him my friendly smile. "Thanks for asking," I say, looking at his name tag and leveling him with a condescending smile. "Nathan. I'd love your best Peppermint White Chocolate Mocha and a chocolate muffin." Discreetly, I scratch my nose to hide the grin tugging at my lips when he scowls. Begrudgingly, he puts in the order, pressing his lips into a tight line.

In some sick and twisted fate, an intense possessive feeling washes over me when he side-eyes River with a romantic interest. To her credit, she stands utterly oblivious to his affections, without an ounce of interest. Instead, her eyes lock on her new phone as she types something out quickly.

"Your name?" he asks as I give it to him, and he writes it down. "Okay, that'll be thirty-four, ninety-nine," he says, reclaiming his smile when I pull out my wallet and hand him a fifty.

"Keep the change."

I want to tell him that she is way out of his league and that he should set his sights on somebody more his speed. River West would chew him up and spit him out in two seconds flat. Believe me, I know. As I waltz to River's side, I make a show of it, leaning in a little closer than necessary. My shoulders brush hers, and surprisingly she leans into my side without conscious thought.

Nathan's hands curl into fists on the counter until he sharply turns away, mumbling under his breath. If I were a betting man, I'd say he's 100 percent going to spit in my drink as revenge.

"So, you never found your old one?" I ask, peeking over her shoulder as she signs into her cloud, sets up her new device, and gets back all her old pictures, messages, and everything in between.

"You're very nosy this morning," she grumbles, shoving her phone into her pocket again and hiding it from view.

"Just observant," I mumble, staring deep into her gorgeous eyes that further pull me into her. I don't know how I ever thought I'd get away from River and feel complete. The black hole that once swallowed my selfish heart slowly closes the more I'm in her presence.

She rolls her eyes. "I don't know where it went. I think I lost it at that fighting ring." Blowing out an angry breath, she crosses her arms in aggravation. "How long has he been doing that?" She quirks a brow as her eyes silently beg for answers.

"Right," I say, stroking my chin.

Callum's fights. The one he runs to whenever things get too tough, instead of opening up and confiding in the people who have always been his family. Well, until he was scarred for life, witnessing Van shove his tongue down the love of his life's throat. Fuck. No wonder we are falling apart at the damn seams. We can't even confide in each other anymore. All we do is argue, and it fucking shows in our performances. There's so much tension between us I have a hard time understanding where it came from. But the moment that thought enters my mind, I stare at why we fell apart. Years ago, I thought River would be the cause of our demise. I swore up and down that she would be the reason Whispered Words would never make it. And it doesn't hurt to admit I was so fucking wrong.

"Um, a few years," I say, clearing my throat. I can't pinpoint when Callum started sneaking away and returning with bruises and broken ribs. All I knew was that he came back lighter and full of life. If only for a few days, that is. Somehow, he managed to get on stage with a smile and makeup covering his wounds.

"River!" shouts Nathan, standing behind the counter with her drink proudly lifted into the air. "And Asser," he says with a tiny smirk pulling at his lips, slamming my plastic cup onto the counter, causing it to spill.

Huffing, I grab our two drinks and muffins from Nathan, who again gives me a nasty look when I bat River's hand away as she tries to take her drink. Without handing them over, I secure a booth, hellbent on getting her to sit with me. I know the second I give her a chance, she'll scurry away with her free meal, and I can't let that happen. Making amends starts now, and I'll throw everything in my arsenal to earn her forgiveness.

"But why?" she asks, snatching up her large blueberry muffin and coffee from my side of the table. Studying the blueberries adorning her muffin, she nibbles her bottom lip with contemplation. "Doesn't seem like his style," she adds, biting into her muffin with a happy groan.

"No, it doesn't, but it seems to ground him. I guess," I say with uncertainty.

The reality is Callum erected thick walls the moment we left Central City. The entire three-day drive from Illinois to California was painfully silent on his end. So much so that you wouldn't even know he was there. He barely uttered his food orders, let alone let us in to witness how deeply he was hurting. Hell, he still is. Callum has never divulged why he fights on Saturday nights, letting guys bash their fists into his skull, but I have a sneaking suspicion it all loops back to River. All our failures and our successes have always been because of that girl. And here we are again, in an endless circle of leaving and finding each other.

Her eyes meet mine as she sips her coffee. "Grounds him? He snuck out, endangering your contract, and you have no idea why he did it?" She raises a knowing brow. "What the hell happened to Whispered Words, Asher?"

You. That's what happened to us. Everything about you is embedded in our souls. Apparently, we're unable to function properly without you in our lives. But I don't say that. Instead, I smother my words by taking a hot sip of my coffee, risking the damn spit that might be in there.

A deep sigh rocks through me, letting my eyes roam out the windows, taking in the bright sun beaming down on the people outside and continuing their shopping. "A lot of shit happened to us. Fame and fortune." I shake my head, losing myself in the memories of our past.

"Where the hell is Callum?" I bark, pacing the backstage area with my hands gripping my hair. All the control I've carefully crafted over the past few months slips between my fingers like fucking sand and blows in the damn wind.

Kieran sits back, watching me with a calculating eye. "Where the hell do you think he is?"

"I don't fucking know, but we go on in less than an hour. He wasn't here for sound check and isn't here now. Rad, where is he?" I growl, stomping up to Rad, who twirls his drumsticks between his fingers and shrugs.

"Bro, I'm not his keeper. He'll be here," Rad says with indifference, frowning as he taps out a beat on his knee.

"Find him!" I bark again, pulling at the collar of Rad's shirt, bringing him to his feet.

"*Get the fuck off me, Asher,*" *Rad hisses, pressing his nose into mine as violence storms through his eyes.* "*Do you want to know where the fuck he is? He's trying to drown away her memory. Something I wish I could fucking do, too. One day I'll forget, but you know he won't. Ever. What he saw... What we all saw from that fucking video will live in his genius head forever. Give him some slack. And get the fuck off me.*"

"*He's here,*" *Kieran says lazily, pointing to the door blankly. The light disappeared from his eyes when we left Central City, changing his entire demeanor for the worst.*

Silently, Kieran has been falling apart behind closed doors, growing angrier and angrier by the damn day since we left Central City a few months ago and started this gig. For now, we're playing at smaller venues and trying to expand our fanbase. We're in the studio during the day, recording our first album with approved songs from our old playlist and new ones we've been forced to write. Every piece of this career is worth it, but slowly it's breaking us apart. Sometimes I wonder what would have happened if River had been with us all along.

Fuck. The familiar guilt swims through my veins, crushing through my chest again. Someday soon, this feeling will leave, and I'll be able to forget about River West and what I did to make her go away. I had to do what I had to do to manage to get us here. No matter the sacrifices I cut off. First, I must keep the damn band together before we implode. I can practically taste success on my tongue because we're just getting started.

"*Callum.*" *All the breath leaves my lungs at the sight of him slumping against the door frame of our green room. Heavy bags plump out the flesh beneath his eyes.* "*You look like you've been run over by a fucking truck,*" *I say with horror, marching forward and getting in his face.* "*Where the hell have you been? And... Have you showered?*" *I sniff the air, catching the hint of body odor and heavy amounts of alcohol.*

"*Fuck off,*" *he grunts, pushing past me and plopping on the couch next to Kieran.* "*I'm doing just fine.*" *A whimsical smile falls over his lips when he leans his head back and shuts his eyes. "So, damn good."*

Kieran raises a brow, examining Callum's face. "Yeah, he's high as a damn kite right now." Shaking his head, he leans back and pinches the bridge of his nose.

"High?!" I shout, throwing my arms out. "What the fuck, dude!"

"Chillax, Ash. You're giving me a damn headache with all your anal bullshit. Dude, take a shower and wash the stink from your ass. We're on in like thirty minutes," Rad says, shoving Callum off the couch as he stumbles toward an adjoining bathroom, catching himself on the door. Turning to look at us through hazy eyes, he nods in agreement and promptly slams the door in our faces. The moment a wall separates us from view, the sounds of his retches and gags, followed by vomit hitting the toilet, fill the air. I cringe with my stomach turning and try to tune out the disgusting sounds from the bathroom. There's no way in hell that we can continue like this and stay together. Something has to give...

"What the fuck?" I hiss, continuing my frantic pacing in front of the guys.

"He's just trying to forget," Kieran pipes up again with an indifferent shrug, staring down at his phone. "Leave him alone. Get the stick out of your prude ass."

I blink a few times, listening to the shower turn on and sigh in relief. Soon we'll be out on stage, and nothing will take away from that, not even Callum's newfound drug addiction, which he'll hopefully leave behind very soon.

I shake myself out of the memory drowning me. It took Callum twenty minutes to shower, which gave us enough time to find him some clean clothes. Our show went without a hitch, despite Callum's head not being in a suitable space. As soon as the show ended, he disappeared into the night again, only coming back the following day with a black eye and renewed life flashing in his eyes. That night, he promised us he'd leave the drugs behind. And he did. He was somehow giving it up without a fight. Only his new drug was the fight nights he found through the grapevine and aligned himself with some mafia family taking residence at an old, abandoned prep school.

"And you?" River asks, narrowing her eyes, taking the last piece of her muffin. "You're nothing like the Evil Ash I knew back in Central City. You seem..." She taps her chin several times, trying to find the word she's looking for. "More settled. Not as uptight as you used to be. Did you finally pull that stick out of your asshole? What changed in your world? Did you finally drop the demon?" Her eyes memorize my passive face, finally meeting my stare, and she smirks. Quickly, she turns away and licks her lips. A red tint explodes across her cheeks as she sits up straight.

I smirk at her outburst, noting how uncomfortable her posture seems, and sip my coffee. "Times change," I say with a shrug. "People change." I hum, take a bite of my muffin, and sip my coffee.

The moment I left my hometown, everything lifted from my shoulders. My father was no longer on my back to join his company. In fact, he was no longer in my life. After finding our way to East Point Bluff, I severed ties entirely with the man. The only time I ever heard about him was the news when the bars slammed on his face, and he was sentenced to prison for his crimes, leading to a whole new crock of bullshit. The only feeling that followed me from home was the constant guilt, crushing my soul for manipulating the girl sitting in front of me. Nothing prepares you for that when you decide to betray someone.

"But do they, really?" she questions, sitting back and folding her arms.

Licking my lips, I distract myself by pulling apart my muffin and shoving it in my mouth. "Sometimes," I say, staring out the window. For good or bad, people change every day, and I happen to be one of them.

"Why did you leave?" she exclaims, adjusting herself in her chair with a grimace.

I raise a brow at her, staring off at the apartment complex in the distance. Why did we leave? Because I felt like we had to.

"You see that apartment building over there?" I ask, pointing out the window toward Gloria's home.

River huffs. "You know what? Forget it. I've explained a lot of shit to you assfaces over the last few days, explaining myself over Lyric. But you assholes can't even answer one question I have." Slamming down her cup, she moves to get up, but I catch her by the wrist. When my flesh touches hers, a fire ignites beneath my skin, and electricity darts up my arms. Taking a deep breath, I ground myself.

"Gloria lives in that apartment complex." Her expression falls, and a paleness washes across her face. "That's why I was downtown before I saw you. I had questions for her myself."

She swallows hard, settling back in the chair. "What did that conniving bitch have to say for herself?" River asks, a flame burning bright in her eyes, ready to burn the world at her feet. That's the River I remember. The girl who took no one's shit, especially mine.

"Well, you have the conniving part right. I went to have a friendly discussion with her. After what you said to me in the hallway, I had a lot of questions I needed answers to." River blinks rapidly, grinding her teeth so hard a vein protrudes from her neck. With a wave of her hand, she silently encourages me to keep going. I sigh, running a hand across the back of my neck. "We didn't sign restraining orders, River," I say in a low tone, reaching across the table and chancing my fingers when I brush against hers. She doesn't pull away from my soft touch, but I can tell she wants to back away and put as much distance between us as possible.

"You didn't?" she asks, pursing her lips and keeping her emotions locked tight behind the fire in her eyes.

"She admitted to getting Van's dad to sign the papers without our signatures," I say, gripping her hand in mine. "Believe me. We didn't leave on those terms. We..."

"Then why the fuck did you?" Pulling her hand from mine, she shakes her head and abruptly stands from her chair. "One day, you guys were my fucking world, and then the next, you left me a grieving mess and deserted me like I meant nothing. Did I not deserve a text or a phone call that you were leaving without me? You promised me that we would go together. I played my part, Asher. Why didn't you? Huh?" Every word she speaks slowly gets louder and louder until the eyes of the other customers fall on our little spat.

River's chest heaves as her fists curl at her sides. She's kept this in for so long that I can tell it's worn her down, and she cannot gain the answers she needs. And it's all my fucking fault. I need to piece us all back together. It's my responsibility now. Whatever happens to us in the future, I will make this better. Even if I have to sit on the sidelines and watch my best friends be happy, this is what I deserve.

"I'll tell you everything if you sit," I murmur, pointing to the chair, and silently I beg her to follow my direction.

With a huff, she sits on the edge of her seat, preparing to dart off if I don't give her the answers she wants. I swear my heart skips a beat, and my tongue sticks to the top of my mouth. I could tell her nothing but the truth. I know that. I could get on my knees, beg for forgiveness, and explain my role in everything. But in the back of my head, I know the consequences if I lay the reality out for her. Lyric's sweet face pops into my mind, calling me daddy with a grin lighting up her tiny face. My conscience yells at me to confess and reveal my bad decisions, but my mouth works faster than my guilty conscience, covering my damn tracks.

"A few weeks before we left, you asked for space after what happened to your mom. It was hell being away from you when you were hurting so bad. Kieran was clawing at the walls to get back to you and take you in his damn arms. But—uh—someone sent my phone a video of you and—um—" I blow out a breath, working myself up to say what I need to say. My fingers fiddle on the table, twiddling my damn thumbs.

"Spit it out, Asher. I'm getting pretty pissed off," she snaps, running her tongue across her teeth.

"Someone sent me a video of you and Van screwing around in the back seat of his Mustang." River stops moving. Hell, I swear she stops breathing at my confession and narrows her eyes. "It came with a text that you'd been screwing him behind our backs just after we'd gone exclusive with you. And..."

"So, let me get this right," she says with a thunderous expression clouding her face. "You all got a video of me and Van doing the nasty. The same Van who had stalked me for months and never really stopped until I left. The same fuckin Donavan Drake who broke my heart as a teen because his mommy and daddy fucking hated my guts. And your first thought was, yeah, that's what River would do when she wasn't with us?"

I swallow hard, feeling the hints of her anger squeezing around me. It's so palpable in the air everyone within a five-foot radius moves away from the hurricane building inside her.

I lick my lips, lying through my fucking teeth. "Callum saw you," I say, trying to clear my throat. "He..."

"Ah, yeah. That's the proof you need then, huh?" she asks with her face twisting in anger. The vein in her forehead expands, and a redness encases her entire face. "He waltzes in uninvited, just like fucking Van did. Then Van forcefully shoved his tongue down my throat, and you know what? Fuck. You. All. We were adults. Do you know what adults do? They have conversations. They communicate with each other instead of leaving without a goodbye." Promptly, River stands, slamming her chair back, and looms over the table with ragged breaths. "Let me make this very clear: Van and I were done, and so are we. Have a good fucking day, Asher. I'll see you at band practice tomorrow. Prepare yourselves," she growls an ominous warning, stomping away and rushing through the door without a backward glance.

"Fuck," I mutter, staring out the window until she gets into her vehicle. That's not how I wanted this conversation to go at all.

Fuckity. Fuck. Actually, I don't know what I expected from her. I knew she'd be upset to find out why we left.

Movement whirls around me, dragging me back into the restaurant. Several pairs of eyes glare daggers in my direction, including the scowling older man who shakes his head in disgust. Feeling the awkwardness crashing down on me, I throw my barely-drank coffee and half-eaten muffin into the trash and walk out the door with my head hung low. I have a lot of shit to talk to the guys about if they'll fucking listen. I need to make this better without revealing the absolute truth. There will be a time and a place for me to tell them what happened, but I need to tell them what I discussed with Gloria. Fuck. I rub a hand across my tightening chest, crumbling under the vise, viciously squeezing it.

As I walk out the door, I reach into my pocket and pop two more antacids to tamp down the rising heartburn, eating away at my insides.

13

River.

"I HAD coffee with Asher this morning."

Accidentally, might I add. The little bastard followed me from point A to point B, trailing after me like a lost puppy dog. I couldn't shake him off. So, I made him buy me breakfast. I was starving, and he was offering. So, I took the opportunity to drag information out of him.

Something tells me Evil Ash had more to say but wasn't willing to give it all up.

Olivia chokes on her glass of wine. "What?" she croaks, wiping her mouth.

"I had coffee—"

"No, I got that part. I'm just...surprised, is all. Asher Montgomery? Really??" She gives me that—you're not falling for his shit again, are you?—look.

Kaycee watches me with an intense stare and nods after soaking in the information. "Was he informative?" she asks, cocking her head to the side.

"Very," I croak, forcing myself to gulp down the rest of my white wine.

"Do tell," Olivia says, grinning wide.

I sigh, explaining how I stormed out of the shop after learning about the video someone sent him, causing them to leave. Not to mention the whole, they had no idea about the restraining orders thing.

A shiver of disgust rolls through me, imagining why Van decided to do that and then sharing it with everyone. Was he really that obsessed with me? He was the one who broke it off with me because of his parents. Yet, he kept trophies on his phone like a creep.

"Also, apparently, Kieran's bitch mom lives right here in town," I groan, refilling my glass. If I had known that, I would have been more cautious walking around.

Thank God for my bestie's sober husbands. Or I'd be sleeping on this uncomfortable couch and have a headache in the morning before facing the guys.

Tomorrow is the day. The day I face these assfaces with confidence and determination. It's up to them now whether they succeed or crash and burn.

Kaycee wrinkles her nose. "I can drain her bank account if you want. Or hack into her FlashGram." Kaycee shrugs when I snort. "We can set her house on fire. I have connections." She wiggles her brows playfully until I'm bending at the waist with laughter.

"I'll pretend I didn't hear that," Olivia murmurs into her glass, slightly cringing at the mention of fire but plays it off by laughing at Kaycee's dedication.

I'll mention that to her later. Fire makes her uneasy. I don't blame her though. After what happened when she was a teenager, she's overcome a lot. But to be locked in a house while bleeding out and then having to fight her way through a blaze? Yeah. It was brutal for her. So, even at the slightest hint of fire, she cowers away. Yet, she's a badass Veritas agent, fighting the good fight and taking bad guys down without fear.

Trauma is a hell of a thing.

"I'm just saying I can help," Kaycee says, taking another sip.

"I'll remember that," I groan, rubbing at my forehead. "Is this reality?" I murmur, looking at my best friends. "How am I going to survive this?"

138ALY BECK

"Because you're a strong, independent woman who don't need no man!" Olivia shouts, shoving her glass into the air.

"She's right. You're you. Strong, sassy, and you don't take any shit. I could have used you as my bestie in high school," Kaycee says, blowing out a breath.

"Pfft. You did fine on your own," Seger says, sauntering into the room with a grin. "When you hacked into that bitch Hadley's FlashGram, that was a fucking riot."

Kaycee's grin lights up her face when she stares at him with dopey eyes. "I guess," she says with a shrug.

"So, fucking modest, Angel," Seger coos, kissing the tip of her nose.

"Yuck! Gross!" I playfully say, throwing a couch pillow at Seger's head.

"Umph," he grunts, tossing it back with a frown. "Rude." I grin in return as he grabs a magazine off the table and whacks me in the head.

"Asshole!" I laugh, clutching my head.

"I love ya, Sis. But I think we would have murdered each other back in the day." He grins, kissing Kaycee one last time before disappearing out the door, humming under his breath. Probably heading upstairs to continue watching Lyric, and the rest of his children–Maggie, Axel, Dash, and Roman.

"Back to this topic," Olivia chides, tapping on the table. "What the fuck is happening with you right now? Them?"

"Absolutely nothing. I'm their boss. That's it." I feel Olivia's eyes on me as I guzzle more wine and ignore her snort.

"Sure. That's it."

"They fucked me over, Liv. Like...so fucking bad. I can't fall into that trap again."

As I empty my glass, I finally feel the effects of the wine swimming through my veins. Instead of stopping like I should, I pour another glass, clinging to it like a lifeline.

"You don't feel anything for them?" Kaycee asks.

"Hate. Disgust. Wanna punch them in the dicks. Does that answer your question?" I ask with my brow rising high.

Liar! I may hate their guts and hope they rot in the desert. But dear God, they're fine as hell. Hot. Fucking smoking. I'll never understand why I'm being punished so much with their chiseled rock star looks.

Couldn't they be, I dunno—less attractive? Mouth-watering, assfaces.

They're like my damn wine, getting finer with age. I may despise their asses, but I have fucking eyes. I see the way their clothes fit snugly against their bodies, emphasizing their goodies. And I do mean goodies. Asher's ass alone is biteable...pinchable. I could bounce a quarter off it.

Jesus, what's wrong with me?

It's the damn wine, that's it. Nothing more.

Colors swirl before my eyes, blending in a rainbow. Fuck. When did the room start spinning? I squeeze my eyes shut, groaning at the sensation.

"Shit. I think the wine's kicked in," I snort, covering my mouth. "Fuck."

"Why? Because you're thinking about them naked now?" Olivia quips, drunkenly poking me with her index finger. "They were hot back in the day, weren't they?"

"No, not naked!" I hiss, swatting her away. "Okay, fine! They're hot as hell."

"No takesy backsies!" Olivia sings, taking another swig of wine with a grin.

"But they're not forgiven," I mumble, taking another sip. "Not one bit. I loathe them. They're dirty little brats." I pout.

"Absolutely not," Kaycee agrees with glossy eyes. "This is really good, by the way. I think we need more. They were so mean to you. How can you look them in the eyes? Do you look at their dicks? Dickmatized, am I right?" We cackle together.

"Dickmatized!" Olivia shouts, folding in half with a cackle. "Seriously, though? It's because she's braver than anyone I know,"

Olivia says with a grin, recuperating from her laughter by wiping her eyes and taking a breath. "Who else could face their exes like a professional?"

Professional, my ass. I want to drown them. And get dicked down. And... I should never drink wine again when I'm conflicted.

"Speaking of... Have you found any more information about my little stalker yet?"

Good! Change the subject. No more thinking about their cocks and... I wrinkle my nose, glaring at the wine.

"Sorry, babes. We looked into it and kept the pictures as evidence. But per his usual, he didn't leave any fingerprints behind. He's like a damn ghost."

"No one can be that good," Kaycee says.

"And you're like 100 percent sure it's not Donavon Drake?" My heart pounds the second I utter that stupid name. That scumbag doesn't deserve an ounce of my time or space in my brain.

"Still in Europe working with his company. He only has a few ties to East Point. A cousin and aunt live in town, but that's it. He hasn't been here for over ten years. He's out."

Fuck. It'd be easy if it were him. I'd at least have a clue as to why he was stalking me. With a stranger, though? I'm drowning in anxiety.

"And you've checked into Nathan down at the coffee shop? He's gotten extra clingy these days." I shiver at the thought of his eyes following me around the damn cafe every morning when I show up. If their coffee wasn't the best in town, I'd go somewhere else. But nothing beats the smooth taste of theirs.

"Nope. As far as we can tell, he's not it. Doesn't own any sort of digital camera and we checked through his photos on all devices. We've looked through his apartment and his background. We even followed him for a few weeks to make sure. There's nothing tying him to you or the stalking. He may be a little creepy, but he's innocent."

"Who the fuck could it be?" I grumble, massaging my temple.

"I don't know, Riv. But we'll get him. The good news is he hasn't escalated into something more yet."

"Yeah, just pictures of me and Lyric. He isn't hiding in my house or anything," I groan, throwing myself back into the couch.

"And it's still nothing digital?" An odd sparkle forms in Kaycee's eyes at the prospect of hacking.

She's the best in the nation. On par with her husband, Carter. If she weren't a stay-at-home mom with her other husband, Chase, she'd have joined Veritas, too. Olivia has been gunning for her to be on her team since they met in high school when Olivia saved Kaycee and the guys from some weird cult. Something they rarely talk about.

"No," Olivia snorts. "You'd have to be on my team to join the hunt." She smirks when Kaycee huffs.

"Can't leave the boys at home just yet. Maybe Carter will let me sneak a peek," she blurts, quickly taking a sip of her wine.

"He does, doesn't he?" Olivia laughs, shaking her head. "I should have known he'd never come up with half the stuff he does."

Kaycee snorts. "I am the brains of the operation."

I cackle when a grin explodes across her face. I don't know how I ever lived my life without these girls. Since I came here and this whole thing started, they've been Team River. We've had so many of these nights where the kids play, and we drink while the guys cook and babysit us.

After an hour more of laughing, Chase offers to drive me home as Seger follows with my car and Lyric in tow.

Tomorrow is the first day of the rest of my whole damn life. And even though I'm all wined up, my bravery is dwindling.

14

River.

It all started this morning as I pulled out of the driveway with Lyric in the back seat, chatting away as we began our adventure to school. It was at that moment, as I exited the gate and waved to the guard, that Asher emerged on the side of the road. Sweat dripped from every inch of his body as he huffed and puffed, bending at the waist to catch his breath. The moment our eyes connected; a flush worked its way up my neck.

Memories of our night on the dining room table emerge from the darkness, taking hold. The ghost of his dirty mouth wrapping around my clit has my damn pussy throbbing. Having these sorts of thoughts about any of them is just bad for my health. Back then, I went into our relationship with sex on my mind. They were a good time, and then, it all got real for me. Way too real.

Then they vanished like the dickless pricks they are. If history has taught me anything, it's that no matter what these boys say, I should stay the fuck away and keep my pussy, heart, and ass to myself. I groan, thinking back to when I was forced to halt our drive so my beautiful daughter could lure her daddy into the car with one simple smile.

"Mommy, stop!" Lyric screeches from the backseat, sending my heart into a damn frenzy.

Slamming on the brakes, I whip my head in her direction as she rolls down her window with a happy squeak. Fuck. I forgot about the damn window locks again. I grit my teeth when she grins in Asher's direction, who falls for her trap. Peering into the car with a smirk, he leans his bulging forearms through the open window.

"Daddy! I'm going to school!" Lyric says with a toothy smile, peering up at Asher as he pokes his head in and places a quick kiss on her forehead. Lyric's tiny hand immediately reaches for him, squeezing his arm with excitement. "Can you come with me? Please?" she asks with the biggest, roundest, and most pleading eyes I've ever seen. Puppy dog eyes, be damned. Lyric wins every damn time. It's so hard to tell her no, but I've had some practice. Asher? Not so much.

"Ly, Daddy probably doesn't have time," I say softly. Immediately, her face falls, and her grin disappears, replaced by a pout.

"Please, Mommy? I want all my daddies to see my school," she says in a little, pleading voice on the verge of begging.

Asher chuckles, turning his gaze to my narrowed eyes. "Well, Little One. That's up to your momma."

"Please, Mommy! Please! I want Daddy to see my school and meet my friends!" she insists again, folding her hands together until I'm huffing and unlocking the door.

"Sure," I say, smiling at her while dying a little on the inside.

The door slams with a thud, and Asher's half-naked body rests against my leather seat. His manly musk fills the air.

"Daddy, I can't wait for you to meet my friends! There's Maggie and Kaitlyn and Dorothy and Connor."

"Connor?" Asher's head whips toward her, and she freezes, pursing her lips.

"Yeah, my boyfriend, Connor. He says..." Asher cuts her off, putting a hand in the air.

"My daughter has a boyfriend?" he asks in a low voice, raising his eyebrows at me.

I huff, pushing the accelerator. "It seems to be that way," I say with a shrug.

"He's nice, Daddy. He got me a flower!" she says happily, blabbering on more about school and her friends.

As soon as Lyric jumps out of the car in the pickup line, Asher's gaze turns to me in all his half-naked glory.

"Expect me tomorrow," he says with a smirk. "I can even buy you some of your favorite coffee from your favorite barista."

"Don't hold your breath," I grumble, pulling out of the line with one last wave to Lyric as she holds her teacher's hand.

I glare in the direction of the house across the street as if it's the cause of all my problems. Because, well—it is. They are, I should say. They're sick, evil bastards who marched their way back into my life and give me so many damn emotions. I'm trying my hardest to be patient as they meet Lyric and bond with her. Lyric deserves to know who helped create her, even if they are jackasses.

Heaving a sigh, I grab the copies of the contract I promised them and make my way across the street, dragging my feet. Today's the day the boys find out what exactly I have in store for them. Our time together won't be fucking daisies. Happy Monday, boys. Your nightmare is about to walk through the door.

As I smooth out my form-fitting black lace tank top and pull my hip-hugging jeans up, I brace myself for the real test. For the last few days, we've danced around each other. They've tested the boundaries of the contract like I knew they would. Now the real work begins. Much like a sergeant, I'm about to tear them down to bare bones and build them back into the rock stars they were before. It'll be hard and somewhat complicated, but I believe they can do it. If they put their heads down, get to work, and obey my commands, we won't have a problem.

Like that's going to fucking happen.

With one last look around the scenery, I let the ocean waves take me over and calm everything inside of me. Without knocking, I use my key and enter the silent band house. Nothing stirs around me as I walk on light feet through the abandoned living room filled with the sunlight beaming in from the tall windows. My eyes narrow when I walk down the stairs into the basement. There by his lonesome, Callum sits on the couch with his bass in hand, listening closely as he tunes it.

His gray eyes widen, taking all of me in as a familiar blush pinkens his cheeks.

"I take it everyone else is still sleeping," I question, raising a brow.

Callum clears his throat giving me a stiff nod. "Yeah-yeah." He swallows the lump in his throat, quickly averting his gaze toward the ground. "I haven't heard a peep from them this morning," he says softly, reminding me of the boy I knew before.

"And you didn't wake them?" I ask, raising a brow.

"They-they're adults," he murmurs again, still refusing to look at me.

Pulling my phone out of my back pocket, I check the time, noting that it's 8:45 a.m. on the damn dot. Late bastards wasting my time. It seems that they're still trying to push my buttons and their boundaries. I guess it's time to show them who the boss really is.

"Don't worry. I'll take care of them." A small smile pulls at the edge of my lips when Callum's gaze snaps to mine, and he stiffens with momentary fear.

"What are you going to do, Little Star?" he breathes, turning slightly.

Every so often, when their little nicknames break through, my heart cracks a little more than before. Like the duct tape and pins keeping me together are fraying at the edges. It knocks me back in step, transporting me to the past when I was on top of the world in their arms. I may not have been in the best financial state, and I may not have had the best home life, but I had them. I had those nicknames. I was alive and full of energy, ready to conquer the world. Now I don't. I let the name slide this time because the way Callum looks at me now makes fire erupt under my flesh.

Clearing my throat, I straighten my posture and turn on my heel with determination. Looking over my shoulder, I gaze at him, sitting there fiddling with his bass guitar. The most mischievous grin spreads across my lips as my brain cooks up genius ideas for waking two sleeping idiots.

"They're late. I'll do what any good boss does," I say without context and make my way up the stairs. Half of me expects Callum to follow me. And the other half of me is thankful that he didn't because he'd try to talk me out of it.

Standing by the stairwell, I peer up where the bedrooms are, listening closely for any sounds of movement. When no one makes a move, I start the first action of my plan at the kitchen sink and fill a bucket with ice-cold water. As it fills to the brim, I grab a handful of ice cubes and toss them on top. For good measure, of course. With the bucket in hand, I make my way up the stairs just as Ash emerges from the steamy bathroom with a white towel wrapped around his toned waist.

Jesus fucking Christ in a handbasket. Don't look at the damn V near his waist. Fuck. I pretend I'm looking anywhere but his toned body as I stand before him. If he sees me checking him out, he doesn't utter a word.

His jaw drops when he sees me carrying a heavy bucket, and he shakes his head. "River," he says, drawing out my name with suspicion. "What are you doing?"

I shrug. "Last Friday, I told you guys my expectations. At 8:45 a.m. on Monday, you were all to report to the basement for your first band practice under my rule. And now three of you are late," I say, holding up my phone and showing him the time that says 8:50 a.m. "Is that water? And ice?"

"Seems pretty self-explanatory to me," I say with nonchalance, sidestepping him as he watches me closely.

A distinct chuckle greets my ears when I look back at him and his reddened face. "Let me get dressed, and I'll be down there in a second," he says, holding a fist over his mouth to cover the laughs. "I don't want to be up here for this. Especially Kieran. He's going to hate you."

"That won't change anything," I mutter, hobbling with

the bucket another step. "You're safe then. This will make them think twice about sleeping when they should get to work like Callum." I give him a pointed stare as he wanders toward his bedroom, watching my every move, and goes inside. As the door shuts, I stand, debating which door to choose. Rad or Kieran? Who deserves this more? Without a second thought, I veer to the right, opening the first closed door.

As I step through the door, I nearly screech.

"Jesus Christ," I say, covering my eyes and blocking the view of Rad's naked ass in the middle of the bed, sprawled out like a starfish.

He doesn't stir at the sound of my voice or when I walk in further with the sloshing bucket of water and set it down. As he softly snores, I take the time to examine the man that once held my heart.

A deep, burning blush creeps up my neck, covering my cheeks when I walk around the bed and fold my arms over my chest, examining the naked man before me. New tattoos adorn his entire body, from head to toe, leaving little naked flesh. Even his bubble butt has ink covering it. Shit.

"Rad," I whisper, shoving my foot into his butt cheek and rattling him around.

And nothing. He doesn't respond when I do it again, shaking him even harder. Instead, a loud snore escapes him, along with several mumbles telling me to fuck off.

I roll my eyes toward the ceiling in agitation. Okay, I tried to be nice. If he won't respond to his name, then I'll give him something to respond to.

"Okay, you asked for it," I say, heaving the bucket of water into my arms and dangling it above his naked body. With a grunt, I pour the frigid liquid right onto his bare ass, earning a startled yelp as his entire body soaks up the liquid.

"What the fuck!" he screeches, twisting and sitting in the middle of the sopping-wet bed.

With wide eyes, he looks around the room and finally settles his narrowed gaze on me.

"Pretty Girl, what the hell are you doing?" he asks through several heaving breaths. His long fingers search the sheets, scowling when they come back wet and dripping. "Did you pour water on me?" he asks incredulously.

I smother the snicker trying to escape from my lips when he stares up at me in utter disbelief. Regaining my control, I nod. "Yeah, I just poured a bucket of water and ice on you."

"Not just on me, Pretty Girl. You poured it on my ass," he says as his voice escalates around the room. "My precious bum! God, that shit was cold. I think little Rad went into hiding! Pretty Girl, that was not cool," he squawks every word, growing louder and louder by the second.

"It's Monday morning, Rad." I raise a knowing brow when he shrugs and tosses his arms in the air with subdued anger.

"Yeah, happy Monday, Pretty Girl," he says, narrowing his eyes at me with a mischievous glance bolting through his dark eyes.

Keeping my eyes locked on him and refusing to look down at his utterly nude body. I smother another laugh.

"Yes, happy Monday indeed. It's now 8:55 a.m., Rad," I say, holding up my phone so he can examine the time. "What is supposed to happen at 8:45 a.m.?" I purse my lips when he shrugs in response and suddenly stills.

Before I can even think, move, or protect myself, Rad wraps his arms around my waist at lightning speed and throws me in the middle of the bed. I screech when he throws his body over mine, and the wet blankets over us with a grin, soaking us both to the bone with cold as fuck water.

"Is it bed wrestling time?" he says, pushing his body onto mine and holding me down as I wiggle, trying to get away.

"Rad, get off of me," I grunt, struggling beneath him as he laughs.

"No can do, Pretty Girl," Rad says with a gigantic grin, mocking me as I struggle.

I try with all my might to remove my hands from between our bodies, only stopping my struggle when the stark realization hits me square in the chest. Oh god. Something hard and heavy rests against my thigh, jumping every time I move. Swallow me up, world, and take me away! An unwanted blush heats my face when I lock eyes with Rad, who wiggles his brows.

"I swear to God, if that's your dick on my leg, I'm going to slaughter you," I growl through gritted teeth. Rad's face lights up even more when he stares down at me with satisfaction.

"Now you're speaking my language! He's just trying to find his home, Pretty Girl. You hear that, boy? We're almost to where we belong. It's like somewhere over the rainbow, but my pot of gold is your pussy." If I could cover his mouth, I'd slap my palm across his lips. But alas, I'm still stuck and forced to listen to him.

"No, I swear! If your dick gets any closer to me, I will chop it off. You asked me if I still carried my knife. Well, it's still in my damn pocket. Ashton, if you don't get off me, there will be blood," I say, making him laugh. His nose nestles into the crook of my neck, with a happy sigh rocking through him. Every muscle in his body relaxes, and for a few golden seconds, he doesn't utter a word.

"I'm sorry, Pretty Girl." Rad doesn't move when my body stiffens. Oxygen evacuates my lungs, leaving my head a muddled mess.

"You're sorry for what? For dragging me into this wet bed or putting your dick on my leg?" I whisper, with my heart pounding against my chest. I swear it's about to come through my ribs and fall out onto the floor when his glossy eyes find mine.

Rad swallows hard, gracefully moving my hair from my face. He examines me with concentration, taking in every aspect of my features. Silently, he shakes his head.

"For all of it, Pretty Girl. For years, I thought the worst about you.

I thought you fucking broke my heart. I've been a different man since we left Central City. I've become someone I'd never wanted to become. But seeing you and Lyric, I see that I missed out. I missed out, Pretty Girl, because I didn't talk to you before I left. So, you ask why I'm sorry? I'm sorry because I was a jackass. No matter what actually happened, even if you did..." He sucks in a breath, closes his eyes, and regains himself as a tear leaks down his cheek. "River, I believe you."

I reel back as if I've been slapped. Just two days ago, he sang a different tune. And now...

"You believe me?" I ask through a shuddering breath, swallowing the emotions drifting up my constricted throat.

Rad slowly nods in confirmation, leaning closer and hovering his face above mine. If he moves another inch, his lips will press into mine, and I don't know how well I'll be able to stop him. Thankfully, he doesn't. He lingers there, examining my eyes as they wildly take him in.

"Yes, I believe you. I just have to figure out what the hell actually happened. Something fucking stinks." He shakes his head in aggravation but doesn't make a move to get off me.

Raw emotions splinter inside of me, cracking open old wounds I thought had festered closed many years before. Seeing Rad and hearing all the feelings behind his words does something to my insides. I've erected walls for so long, trying to keep the pain of what they did to me at bay, that it feels strange to let the dam break. But it doesn't mean anything that he is sorry now.

"You're sorry now?" I whisper through trembling lips, trying to keep my emotions on the inside. I don't have time or the energy to dissect our relationship or lack thereof.

Rad nods again, shakily running his fingers through my hair. If he doesn't stop touching me, I will lose all my composure. If there's one person who can break down the walls I've put in place, it would be him.

"I'm so sorry that I ever doubted you. I was in love with you, River. I wanted so many things with you, and I fucking blew it because I took Asher's word for it. Now I see that not only should I have talked to you first. That I shouldn't have listened to him. But Callum, when he came back from your apartment, he looked so devastated and... I'm sorry, Pretty Girl."

"I believe that you are, Rad." I swallow my tongue when he looks at me again with raw emotions emanating from him. You can practically taste it in the air.

I don't know what happened. Why the hell is he suddenly sorry? Was it our talk from last night that resonated with him, and he finally listened to me? Whatever the case, I feel in my soul that he truly is sorry for what happened back then. It just doesn't make up for what they did. No matter if they didn't sign the restraining orders or if they didn't know about Lyric. They walked away. Endpoint.

"You never signed a restraining order?" I ask, swallowing hard.

"Fuck no. We were hurt, but not that hurt. We would never have done that. How can I make this up to you, Pretty Girl?" he asks with pleading eyes. "How can I show you or tell you that I'm sorry? That I believe every word you said." Rad's grip tightens on me as he lays his forehead against mine and closes his eyes with a deep, heavy sigh. "I lost you once because of my stupidity, but I will make up for it with every fiber of my soul."

With a labored breath, I turn my head forcefully, trying to remove his grip from mine. The warmth of his body wraps me in a hug, and something screams in the back of my mind for me to stay there, stay under him and enjoy his presence. But the hurt I feel bubbling up and wanting to come out in tears has me retreating inside myself. As I stare at the plain white wall, with my ex-lover on top of me, begging me to forgive him for his indiscretions, I shake my head.

"It's too late, Rad," I say in a shaky voice, barely above a whisper. "There's nothing you could do now to make up for what you did. The only reason you will ever stay in my life is because of Lyric. She needs her fathers, and that's all you'll ever be. I don't forgive you," I whisper, holding in the hurt I feel with every word

I say. It's not that I don't believe them. I do. I believe every word I say. "You hurt me too badly."

Our relationship isn't fixable. Asher, Rad, Callum, and Kieran will only be her four fathers. We will co-parent, and we will coexist together for the next six months for the sake of their jobs, but I will never put my heart on the line ever again and have them eviscerate it by walking away. If they did it once, what's stopping them from doing it again?

"I understand, Pretty Girl. But you think I'm going to give up because you said that it will never happen again? Seriously, you don't remember who I am. At all. I am Ashton Radcliffe the Third. And I go after what I want. I will make this up to you. I will follow you to the ends of the earth on my hands and knees and bleed for you until you're back in my arms just like this. Mark my words. One day soon, you, my Pretty Girl, will be mine again. Oh, and also scream my name. But we'll get to the sexy stuff once I prove myself." With reluctance, Rad peels himself off my body and sits back on his heels. With a grin, he lets his naked body hang out without shame.

I groan, covering my eyes and removing myself from the wet sheets. What a bad fucking idea water was. Next time, I'll get more creative with cymbals or something loud and disruptive.

Somehow after our conversation, I feel a little lighter, knowing that Rad believes me. Something in my gut tells me that they were lied to. They had no knowledge of Lyric like that bitch had said. They seemed highly offended when I mentioned restraining orders. Rad is right, something does stink about the situation. But until I know the whole truth, I can't make any sort of judgment.

"Oh, come on, Pretty Girl. You act like you've never seen it before. Just wait. One day soon, when you forgive me, I will make up for everything; you'll be down for the Rad ride." He wiggles his brows with an adorable grin plastered on his face.

"Nope. Never going to happen, Rad," I say, groaning when I stand up on jelly legs, feeling miserable in the wet clothes. "You might want to change your sheets and let your mattress air out." I wave a hand in his direction, only earning myself a chuckle. I feel his eyes burning into me when I turn my back, and his fingers brush across my shoulders, removing the hair from my neck.

"Oh yeah, Pretty Girl. I'll definitely have to air out this mattress. I need to get it ready for all the nasty stuff we're going to do on it. Just you wait," he says, placing a soft kiss on my shoulder and then slowly backing away.

"Oh God, get dressed," I groan again.

"I meant what I said," he says, rifling around in a drawer somewhere in the room. Grunting, the sound of elastic snapping against skin and clothes rustling offers me a reprieve from his naked flesh. Turning, I stare at him as he pulls his tight-fitting black band shirt over his head and grins. "I will fight for you every step of the way." I raise a brow when he wraps his arms around me like he has the damn authority to do so. "Bring on the fight," he whispers, slapping my ass, and then walks away.

"What the hell, Rad!" I yelp, rubbing a hand over my butt cheek. "I am your boss!" I hiss, smacking his shoulder when we exit the room.

"Yes, bossy lady. You sure are. And you're my girlfriend. That ass is mine and..."

"I forgot how annoying you were. Now, go! All of you!" My voice carries through the room, finally getting another response as another door opens.

Kieran steps out with a scowl. "The fuck you wet for?" he grumbles, running a hand through his dark hair.

I blow out a breath, getting ready to open my mouth.

"She was in my bed, that's why!" Rad shouts, quickly moving down the stairs and onto the main floor. Turning slowly from the bottom, he gives me a megawatt grin, seeming happier than he's ever been in my presence since we reunited.

"Rad," I growl in warning, earning a chuckle before he disappears, running downstairs.

"Why're you here?" Kieran grunts. "And already in his bed?"

He raises a stupid judgmental eyebrow, looking me up and down with a wrinkled nose. *Prick.*

"Did no one else remember that Monday, mandatory band practice begins? Was I talking to brick walls?" I ask, crossing my arms over my wet shirt.

"Right," he grunts, shoving away and waltzing down the stairs. "You should know your shirt is see-through," he quips, showing his humor for the first time in my presence.

"I swear by the time this six months is up, I'm going to murder them," I mutter to myself just as their practice starts without me and I head home with the intention of changing out of my wet clothes.

As I re-enter the house with fresh clothes, my phone buzzes, lighting up with one of my other best friends' names. Rocco.

ROCCO
Sushi date? *Winky face*

ME
Sure, and stop winking at me.

ROCCO
Haha. *Wink*

ME
Remind me to slap you when I see you.

ROCCO
How about Cherry Blossoms? Saturday night?

ME
Sounds good.

ROCCO
Wear something sexy...

ME
You are impossible...I swear.

ROCCO

That I am, babe...but I can't wait to hear about this mysterious band you've gotten yourself assigned to. *Winky face*

ME

I hate you. Goodbye...

15
Rad

I SCOWL, discreetly peeking out the blinds with narrowed eyes. There, beneath the streetlights, in River's driveway is a loaded-up, flashy, black sports car. In my girl's driveway, which definitely isn't mine. I fucking wish; it looks sick as hell. But still! Not! Mine!

About ten minutes ago, the loud exhaust of an accelerating vehicle plowing down the driveway caught my attention, dragging me to this spying chair and magically splitting the blinds for me to watch. With a rapidly beating heart, I focused my gaze on a tall man with dark hair and a fancy suit walking straight into River's house without knocking. A man! In her house! That isn't me!

Jealousy rages through my system at the thought of another man not currently in this house laying a finger on her. River West is mine to win back. Not Mr. Fancy Pants, who better keep his hands firmly to himself. I nibble my bottom lip, watching with rapt attention for any movement outside the house.

A few nights ago, after kicking the shit out of my bike and clearing my head, a light bulb went off inside my brain. An important, life-altering decision came to me like a damn epiphany. Within two seconds of my ah-ha moment, I erased the past with a flick of a switch and decided to bury everything that happened. There is no past between us; there is only the future. That I will absolutely be in.

After our short, intense talk and seeing the raw emotions simmering behind her gorgeous eyes, I knew everything she said held nothing but the truth. Sure, a few more incidents need to be investigated. But I'm all in again.

And if I'm being real, I never really got over her. I'm ready to prove that I'm up to the task of being her boyfriend. More importantly, I'm ready to be a father to the little girl who bandaged my face and made me feel something for the first time in years. Everything seems so damn clear to me now. My Pretty Girl belongs to me. Not Mr. Tall, Dark, and Sexy in a suit with a fancy-ass car.

"What are you doing?" Callum asks, plopping down next to me on the couch. Looking me over with a curious gaze, he raises a brow.

I grit my teeth, glaring out the window. "There's a car in River's driveway," I grumble, wildly gesturing.

"A car?" Callum asks with suspicion, peeking out the blinds. "Who is it?" he asks, nearly growling at the thought. That only fuels me further, making a grin spread across my face.

"You care, don't you?" I ask, studying the darkening of his face when his eyes meet mine. The little shit doesn't have to say anything. For the first time in a long time, I see his transparent feelings shining through. "Callum likes River. Callum wants to FUUUCK her," I sing-song mockingly, earning a slap to the back of my head. "Ouch, Fuckface. That's not very nice." Rubbing the back of my head, I shake off his attack and continue my ninja spying.

He grunts his answer, huffing as he peeks out. "Who is that?" Callum questions with suspicion, eyeing the man who has the audacity to have his arm around River's shoulder.

God damn. My heart drops when she smiles up at him, laughing at whatever he says. It lights up her gorgeous face, highlighting her flawless look. A beautiful teal dress clings to her body, letting the world—me and Callum—see her shapely form. She's definitely not the same girl from Central City. Half of me bets my daughter is the reason she's filled out after all these years. God damn. I bite my damn fist. No matter how big or small or tall or short River West is, she'll always be beautiful. Even with a top knot on her head and mismatched pajamas.

"No idea," I mumble, tracking their movements as he opens the passenger-side door for her. Briefly, she stalls, staring up at him and running a hand down his chest. "Whoever he is, I'm going to bury him." My heart accelerates when they get into the car together, and I jump from the couch, attempting to walk away. Callum catches my arm, studying my face with concern.

"Where are you going?" he asks softly yet demanding me to answer him. Ah, there he is—the Callum I grew up with. Finally, he's coming back, and so am I. Call us the comeback kings of East Point. It's time to reclaim our girl and reclaim ourselves—and cum on her back, of course. It's the greatest comeback of all time!

"To follow them, duh. I thought that was obvious. Grab your cape and black hood; we're going stalking, Cally boy." I grin at his unwavering frown as he stares at me for a few more seconds until the sound of the stupid flashy car roars to life, and he lets me go with a resigned sigh.

"Okay," he says reluctantly, digging into his pocket and pulling out his keys. "But you're riding bitch," he snickers when my face falls.

I purse my lips. "Asshole. Ash has a car we could steal," I mutter, crossing my arms over my chest. "He wouldn't fucking mind."

Since the day we moved in here, we've been cooped up. Well, some of us have. I brought my damn dirt bike but no other forms of transportation like an idiot. The guys, on the other hand, brought their vehicles and stored them in the garage—genius assholes.

"Ride bitch or don't, but I'm following to see. You can sneak up the stairs, steal Ash's keys, and then try to keep up. But they'll be long gone by then." Fuck. Fuckity, shit balls. I hate his stupid logical side.

I scowl even more, huffing at his words. "Fucking fine," I grumble, shoving my feet into my sneakers as he does the same. "But if I get a boner, it's from the vibrations. Not you."

Callum stiffens, stopping dead at the doorway to the garage. "Really? That's the first thing that pops into your head?" Pops up, hell yes, it will.

"Vibrations, dude! It's like..." He holds up his hand, cutting me off.

"I don't want to hear about the vibrations, Rad. Keep those thoughts to yourself. And your fucking dick. If I feel anything stiff behind me..."

"What are you going to do?" I goad, grinning when we walk into the garage. "Stroke me? Cuz yeah, I might like that, baby," I quip, earning a gut punch that knocks the air from my lungs. "Fine, fuck. No need to get violent," I wheeze, bending at the waist. "Your punch is wicked good."

"Get on," Callum demands, patting the seat behind him as he settles his helmet on his head and hands me mine. "They haven't left yet, but they will soon." He raises a brow as the idling car outside starts revving in the driveway. "Now or never," he says, hitting the button to the garage as the car's loud exhaust echoes as they drive off down the long, winding driveway.

"This never gets out," I grumble, straddling the bike. "Like ever." Callum snorts in response, shaking his head.

"Hands on my waist," he says, as the garage door lifts, and he revs the engine, taking off at full speed toward the closing gate.

"Fuuuck!" I shout into the air, clutching Callum's waist with my tight grip. The wind whips around us when he accelerates more, narrowly making it through the closing gate until we're free and on the road. In the distance, I swear I hear River's guard yelling at us to stop or go get the girl. I'll pretend it's the latter, because that's what I'm about to do. Go get the damn girl.

"There they are!" I shout, pointing to the stupid car ahead. "Follow that car!" Shit, I've always wanted to say that.

A sense of joy spears through me for the first time in years; I finally feel fucking alive. No more drowning myself in groupies. No more chasing a high that never fucking came. This entire time, I needed River. I needed her back in my damn arms. This go-around, no matter what, I'm not letting her go. Ever. I'll beg and plead and suck her clit until she forgives me again.

"It's a restaurant," Callum grumbles, bringing the bike to a halt in an alleyway next to the fancy-looking eatery.

"Fucker took my girl out on a date," I huff, jumping off the bike, watching like a hawk as he opens the door for her, and she snorts at him, looking up at him with those big eyes of hers. She is probably batting her eyelashes and flirting and shit. Fuck. I grunt, removing my helmet and smoothing down my curls.

"Your girl?" Callum asks, shoving his helmet off and setting it on the bike with a grunt.

"Yeah. My girl." I shrug, peeking through the big picture window, spying on them through the glass. "Fuck. He's wining and dining her and pulling out all the stops. Look at that shit! I bet it costs thousands of dollars. Shit. He's hot. So, fucking hot, and I'm..." I frown, looking down at my torn jeans and my damn cut-off shirt that splits over my ribs, showing off my tattoos. "Different," I mumble, folding my arms over my chest.

Years ago, she loved this version of me. Watching her now, it seems her tastes have changed from broody, quirky rock stars to stuffy, suit-loving douchebags.

"What's going on?" Callum asks gruffly, running a hand through his blond curls. "Your girl?" His face twists in confusion, and a pained expression takes over. "But she..." My gaze snaps to him, recognizing the war he's fighting inside his mind. Because I was there, too. Fighting with myself on the rights and wrongs of what happened. There's so much we don't know the truth about. But you know what they say? The truth always has a way of coming to light. Sooner or later, we'll fully understand what happened.

"Cal, bro." I lay a hand on his shoulder, squeezing tight.

"How can you... I don't understand," he mutters, squeezing

his eyes shut. Pain flashes across his face in waves until he's sucking in breaths. "She kissed him, and then that video—" I squeeze again, forcing his gaze to meet mine. "I saw it all, Rad. How can you—" He swallows hard, unable to finish his sentence without letting his feelings known.

"We don't have the whole story, man. I feel it right here," I say, pounding my fist into my aching chest. "Look past the hurt and the damn pain from losing her. Use logic, Cal. River West was so annoyed by Van. Why would she go back to him? Why would she willingly get in his backseat again? Why would she willingly kiss him? Tell me because right now, nothing makes sense."

Callum runs a hand down his face in contemplation, staring off into the distance. From here, I visibly see the memories working through his mind, and he shakes his head. "She wouldn't," he murmurs, collapsing back with realization. "She called us for help when he stalked her at the bar. I remember the weariness in her eyes every time he was around. She never asked for help and did with us," he whispers with a cloudy look fogging his eyes. "She trusted us," he finally surmises exactly what I've been saying. I vigorously nod, noting the moment my dear Callum gets on board with my plan.

"You see it, don't you? Yes! Now, all I have to do is figure out what the hell else happened. We know Ash got the video from Van. For whatever reason. Then he was there at the damn apartment when you showed. But why?" I pace the small length in front of us, wracking my damn brain about the entire situation. By the end of it, my brain aches from trying to figure it out. "Why the hell was he there? It's like someone told him to go or something. But how fucked up would that be?"

"It's odd," Callum agrees, scratching at his chin. "I still don't understand. Why would he be at her apartment? I thought he was there like it was a regular thing," he murmurs, blowing out his cheeks and releasing the air. "He was so damn comfortable there."

My pacing takes me back and forth, finally delivering me to my intended target. Stumbling over my feet, I right myself just in time to see my worst fears coming true. God damn it! I can't be too late! She can't get involved with him. She's mine! Unless we become brothers in the dick brigade for River. Now, that could work. But I'm not sure how I feel about another dick when there are four of us. If the others jump on board, that is.

"Motherfucker!" I hiss, peeking through the window, eyeing my damn mission. "He's holding her damn hand from across the table!" I frown, stepping back and checking my reflection in the glass. "I look okay?"

Callum blinks at me several times. "What the hell are you about to do?" His muscles turn rigid, and he cocks his head. "Rad."

"I'm going in there, of course," I say, waving a hand in the direction of the restaurant where my girl sits with another fucking man. "Duh! We didn't stalk her all the way downtown to a fancy restaurant to not interrupt her date." I narrow my eyes looking around the area, noting how empty the streets seem on a Saturday night. "I can't go in there empty-handed, though," I grumble, stepping out of the random alleyway and taking in the shops around me. "Ah-ha! I'll be right back!" I shout, taking off down the road at a full sprint, slamming into the flower shop as Callum shouts my name.

16

TEN MINUTES LATER, I return to the familiar alley with my newly acquired gift in my hands, smiling at Callum's bored expression.

"Okay," I say, breathlessly fanning my face with my free hand. Jesus. I haven't run in years, and I guess it shows. "Now, I'm not empty-handed."

"Rad," he says sternly, stiffening my spine.

"What?"

"You can't just march into the restaurant, hand her a bouquet of tulips, and expect her to forgive you."

Ah, Callum, the cricket on my shoulder whispering logic into my ear. Always full of reason and concern, guiding me on the right path. But not today. I don't need the right path this Saturday evening. No. I need River, a thorough discussion of forgiveness, and her pussy in my mouth. Yeah, everything in that order, too.

"Sorry, bro," I say, clapping him on the shoulder. "There's nothing stopping me from marching in there and winning her back one flower at a time." Callum's face drops in defeat, and his eyes roll toward the star-filled sky with a loud, long-drawn-out groan.

"Christ," Callum curses, knowing he's lost this battle with me. "If you piss her off, it's all on you. Then you can tell the other two why she's making our lives a living hell." He gives me a pointed look, leaning against his bike with interest. He can pretend all day long that he doesn't want me to do this, but I can see it in his eyes. Excitement sparks there for the first time in years.

"You don't want to join?" I wiggle my brows, earning a scoff in return.

"She'll bury us alive. Better you than me," he grumbles, pulling his phone from his pocket.

"I'll be back soon," I say with a confident grin. I straighten out my shirt, double-checking the tulips in my hands and counting all twelve of the pink and white blossoms beaming under the streetlamp above. "Please, let this work," I softly beg, staring at the bright orbs twinkling in the darkened sky above me. It's all I have right now.

Something deep festers inside me, guiding me through the ornate doors of the restaurant with the name Cherry Blossom hovering above the entrance in golden letters. The intense need to sit beside River and soak her presence in has me bursting into the eatery like a bat out of hell.

I heave a breath, glimpsing the intricate decorations adorning the walls. The light atmosphere envelops me in a hug, pushing away the urgency I had waltzing in. Soft music filled with harps and violins floats through the air.

"Sir." I raise a brow, turning to stare at the man beside me with his nose in the air. Wrinkles drag down his cheeks and forehead as he scowls, raking his gaze over my attire, and he scoffs. "You do not meet our dress code. I'm going to have to ask you to leave," he says, pointing toward the door with a haughty attitude I don't quite like.

"Nah, that's okay," I say with a grin, digging into my pockets. "I can't leave yet, bro. I have a girl to win back. You see her over there?" I ask, pointing toward the back of the crowded space where she sits with Mr. Handsy, snacking on delicious-looking sushi. When he should want to snack on my delicious Pretty Girl, looking like a full damn meal in her dress.

God damn. Up close and personal, she looks hotter than from across the street. Back in Central City, my girl would never be caught dead in a tight-fitting dress. Not to mention the makeup. But I guess she has that privilege now that she works for her brothers and has created this entire empire. My Pretty Girl sure has made something phenomenal out of herself, and I couldn't be more damn proud of her. I'll show her in the upcoming weeks that I'm all into this repair and refresh service she's offering. And other things if she wants.

"A tragedy," he mutters under his breath, following my finger. "But you're still not appropriately dressed. Our attire requires suit jackets and closed-toe shoes."

I huff, digging into my back pocket and pulling out my wallet. "I'll pay you five-hundred bucks to turn the other cheek," I say, waving the green under his greedy little nose. Instantly he perks up, watching the money like a pocket watch in front of his face. Yes, doorman, get hypnotized by the green in front of your face. Let me in! I want to beg and plead, but I know in this town money talks.

He peers around at the rest of the crowd, snatching the money from my fingers. "Then, Welcome, Mister..."

"Ashton Radcliffe the Third, my guy," I say, patting his shoulder with an eager clap. "Now, if you don't mind, I'm on a mission to get my girl back." I saunter away without a backward glance, darting toward the quaint little table located in the back. The further I walk through the tables and booths, the dimmer the lights become, and I squint until I get to my destination.

My fingers turn white around the stems of the bouquet when the fucker my girl is with raises his gaze to mine. A cocky smile pulls at his lips when we lock stares, and I'm eager to punch the sureness from his damn body—over and over. He hasn't faced the mighty Rad rage yet, but he's about to meet the bull if he doesn't stop touching my girl. With more confidence than I feel, I wink at him, nodding in greeting.

"I believe you're in my seat," I say, pointing in his direction.

Mr. Tall, Dark, and Handsome has the audacity to laugh at me, waving a hand to the unoccupied chair next to River. Even better. I don't need to sit across from her and play footsie; I need to be beside her, luring her in with my manly musk.

Shit. Discreetly, I sniff myself and recoil. If I had more time to get ready for this stalking adventure, I would have prepared a little better. Earlier, I pounded the drums to beat my damn frustrations away. And unfortunately, it shows with the stench coming from beneath my armpits. No wonder Mr. Doorman didn't want to let me in. I'm ripe as hell.

"Take a seat," he says in a smooth voice full of generosity.

"No! What the fuck!" River hisses at the same time, glaring in the direction of her date. Ha. If he's not careful, I really am going to win her over and steal her away from him. But only after she stabs him in the dick to assert her dominance.

"For you, Pretty Girl," I beam, presenting her with the vibrant tulips, even bowing a little to prove to my queen that she's important.

"Wow! What a gentleman," the man says, folding his hands under his chin with stars in his eyes, watching closely as I take a seat. "So, you must be one of the exes I've heard so many wonderful things about."

"Rocco, I swear to God," River mumbles, taking the flowers with a tight smile and setting them beside her on the table.

"Well, I suppose that's me. Just depends on what you've heard about me. Charming, irresistible..."

"Annoying," River gripes, slapping her palm across my lips. "What exactly are you doing here, Rad?" She raises a brow when I grin beneath her hand, basking in the feel of her flesh against mine. "This is a private dinner. No one invited you." Her glare intensifies tenfold, lighting me from the inside out. Holy hell. I forgot how damn sexy her glares were. I'm going to—fuck, too late. *Not now, Little Rad*, I grumble to myself.

"Fascinating. I'm Rocco, by the way. It's wonderful to meet you." Reaching across the table, we clasp hands and shake in greeting. Rocco's dark, devilish eyes twinkle in the low light with mischief when we separate, and he places his chin in his hand.

"Ashton Radcliffe," I say through the gag over my mouth, grinning wildly when River huffs and pulls her hand away, wiping it on a napkin to remove my spit. "Great to meet you too. So, are you two..." Holding out the last word, I point between the two of them. A stark ray of hope flashes inside me when Rocco chuckles, turning a shade of red.

"Will you excuse us?" River asks sharply, jumping to her feet.

"By all means," I say with a cocky grin, sitting back and expecting him to take the hint and leave the table.

"Idiot," River mumbles.

"Oh God," I yelp when her thin fingers grab the top of my ear and yank me out of my chair. "Pretty Girl," I groan, grabbing hold of her wrist and trying to yank her hand from me.

"Excuse us, Rocco. I need to square some things away with Rad here before we finish our dinner," she says in a sickeningly sweet tone, yanking me forward.

"Take your time, Doll! We've got all night," he calls, waving us along.

"Pretty Girl, I swear!" I groan, hunching over as she drags me through the restaurant with no shame and throws me outside.

"You swear what? Rad!" she shouts, throwing her arms all around.

"I just..."

"You just what?" she shouts, pointing a manicured nail straight into my chest. "What the hell are you doing here? I don't —" Her eyes lock on someone behind me, and she groans. "You, too?"

"In my defense, he-he dragged me into this," Callum stutters, shoving his hands in his pockets.

"Liar," I hiss in his direction between clenched teeth. "Don't let him lie to you, Pretty Girl. He came all on his own with little to no convincing." I raise a brow when Callum flips me off with a grunt, kicking a foot at the ground.

River pinches the bridge of her nose, stepping back from us. "Just explain this to me. Why are you two here?"

"Ask him," Callum says softly, eyeing River with hooded eyes. He watches her every damn move, just like I thought he would.

"Ashton," she hisses my full name, making my heart leap from my chest when she glares at me again.

"Well, fuck! Pretty Girl. I saw that man at your house, and you look like that," I say, waving a hand up and down her body.

"Like what?" she asks through gritted teeth. "And having a man at my house is none of your damn business! None of my life is your fucking business!" she shouts angrily, turning redder and redder by the second. "You lost that right when you left."

Swallowing hard, I take in the rage she exudes. My damn heart hurts when she looks between the two of us. This is not how I saw this going. I guess I should have expected it, though. We're not exactly on good terms right now. I have a lot of making up to do before she'll jump into my arms again.

"I'm sorry, Pretty Girl," I say softly. "I..."

"Just because you're fucking sorry doesn't mean you have the right to follow me out. This is my private time. I've lived without you assfaces for years now. Do you think I'm just going to open my arms and invite you back in?" she asks with moisture blooming in her eyes.

"No." I shake my head. "That's not what I expected at all," I say seriously, taking a step forward. Gripping River's chin between my thumb and forefinger, I force her to stare into my earnest eyes and really see what I'm saying. "I am sorry. I will prove to you how sorry I am over and over again. I will be your damn tail, following you on all your dates and outings. I'm sorry. I'm sorry. I'm so fucking sorry, River. That I left you. That I left our fucking baby. That you had to do all this yourself." Tears burn the back of my eyes when she stares up at me with those wide, moss-green eyes filled to the brim with much-deserved anger. "I'll never give up on you," I whisper. "Not again."

River pulls back, anger twisting her face. "Just leave me alone.

I'm your damn boss. Not your girlfriend. Not your romantic interest," she chokes, bringing a fist to her lips. "I'm going back inside and..."

"Here you go, Doll," Rocco says, emerging from the door with a grim expression. Handing her a Styrofoam box, he kisses the top of her head with affection, keeping his eyes firmly locked on us. "We'll postpone this to another time." Looking between me and Cal he frowns, shaking his head. "Take care of my girl, yeah?" He raises his brow, taking a step away. "Call me later." With one last wave, Rocco disappears into the shadows, leaving the three of us.

"Wait!" River shouts, turning on her heel and groaning when Rocco's sports car speeds down the road, leaving her behind. "Well, there goes my ride. And my phone. And my damn purse. This is just great!" she shouts in frustration, clutching the take-home box.

"Who is h-he, Little Star?" Callum asks softly, bringing her attention back to him. Almost.

Her eyes fall to the ground, and she shakes her head, refusing to look at him. There's something so broken between them, worse than all of us. She can't even stand to be alone with or look at him.

"Come on, Pretty Girl! Spill the beans. Is that your boyfriend, too? Are we adding him to the firehose brigade? There's always more room for cocks, I guess. Is he nice? Is he hung..."

"He's not my fucking boyfriend, you assface!" she shouts, her voice echoing off the surrounding buildings and filling the air with her rage. "Do you think I've had a fucking second to have any sort of relationship these past few years?" Her gorgeous chest heaves when she covers her mouth with her fingers and shakes her head like she didn't mean to yell that. "You think I had any time to date while finishing college, raising a baby, being an intern, and then running my own department?" Pain encases my chest when the first tear falls, and she growls out with frustration, curling her fingers. "I barely had time to think, let alone chase dick."

ALY BECK

"We're-we're sorry," Callum whispers, stepping toward her with a twisted-up expression, dripping with the grief I feel pouring through me.

We weren't there for her. At all. We fucking abandoned her when she needed us most. Not only did she soar through the clouds, she fucking flew higher than the sun and achieved her goals. Just like we did ours. But the worst part about it is we didn't do it together like we had planned. We promised to bring her with us and help her start a new life with us out here. We failed her. Miserably.

"You're sorry?" River asks, shaking her head.

"Yeah, I'm sorry, Pretty Girl. We both are. Aren't we, Callum?" My eyes snap in his direction, catching the emotions building in his gray eyes.

"Yeah-yeah, I am sorry. I've regretted a lot of things in my life, Little Star. But there's one scene that plays in my mind over and over again, riddled with regret. It's the night I came to your apartment and saw him there with you. I couldn't hear anything that was said. But I watched him kiss you. And I ran. I ran so far away that I tried to force the memory of you out of my mind." Callum runs a hand down his face and shakes his head. Grief flashes across his face at the woman that he lost in a moment of fear and misunderstanding. "I've never been able to admit to anyone that I regretted running. I didn't really know what was going on, and it kills me that I never stopped to really think about what was happening right in front of me." Callum's breath shutters in his chest. Quickly, he averts his eyes from her as she silently stands on the sidewalk, clenching and unclenching her fists. "But I see the mistake I made now. If I had just stopped and not let my emotions take over and thought logically about what was happening, I wouldn't have left."

I can't tell if the tears falling down River's face are from anger or sadness. Her body doesn't move, standing stock still watching as Callum continues to war with himself.

Angrily running her tongue over her top teeth, she shakes her head. "Why? Why the fuck are you guys doing this to me now?" River's eyes look between the two of us, searching our faces for the truth that she's heard from us in the past few days. I'm not sure what she sees when she looks at us, but I hope she sees that there's nothing but honesty behind our eyes.

"Because it's time that we set everything straight," I say, stepping forward again and putting my palm on her cheek. Whether she wants to admit it or not, her entire body shudders when our flesh meets. "I think it's time all of us sat down and talked. You know we didn't sign the restraining orders. We had no idea about Lyric. It's time, River. For our future. Whether we return to what we were before and start fresh. Or whether it's too late to fix what we broke. We need to have a discussion and figure out what happened and why it happened the way it did."

Once again, those big green eyes look up at me with continuous amounts of moisture pooling in them and running down her cheeks. I can't tell what's going through my Pretty Girl's head, but I know at some point I'm going to get an ear full. My heart pounds when she gives me a tight smile, stepping back from my embrace.

"Okay," she says with a resigned sigh. "But not tonight. I know we have a lot to talk about. I'm so fucking angry at you guys. But I deserve an explanation from all four of you. For now, can someone take me home?"

"Yeah, Little Star. I'll take you home," Callum says, waving a hand for River to follow him.

"Hey, wait! You're my ride," I say, sprinting after them as Callum hands River my helmet.

A smile blossoms across my face when she stares down at the helmet like it's the bane of her existence. Her nose crinkles, and she shakes her head.

"There's no way in hell you're getting me on this deathtrap." She shakes her head when I advance on her, pulling the helmet from her hands and plopping it over her head, nestling the straps under her chin. Ah, just like old times. "Rad," she warns with a growl, reaching to take the helmet off again.

My fingers wrap around her wrist, stopping her from removing it. "No, Pretty Girl. Do you remember what I said before?" She shakes her head, frowning at me. "It was when you were about to get on my dirt bike. Do you remember that? You didn't want to because you thought I was going to drop you. Callum's got you, babe."

"I won't let-let anything happen to you, Little Star." He eyes her up and down, taking in her trembling fingers and flaring nostrils.

"I swear to God, Callum. If I die on the back of this moving deathtrap, I will come back to haunt you," River says through clenched teeth, glaring down at his motorcycle.

For the first time in a long time, a genuine smile crosses Callum's lips. It's like a breath of fresh air fills his lungs, and he can breathe for the first time in forever.

"Don't worry, Pretty Girl. He's got you. You just have to hang on tight," I say, patting the back seat as Callum climbs on and scoots forward.

River stares down at the empty seat contemplating her options. Moving from foot to foot, she shakes her head and backs away.

I snort at her discomfort. Putting my hands on her hips, I suck in a breath. The feel of her warmth beneath me does funny things to my insides, and butterflies take flight in my stomach. Gently, I help River straddle the bike, biting my lip when her dress rides up her delicious thighs.

"I swear I'm flashing the entire world right now," she grumbles to herself, pulling her tiny dress down. Gently, she places her hands on Callum's shoulders with trembling fingers. "I should've just called a ride."

"Now, now, Pretty Girl. You're going to fall off if you keep your hands on his shoulders. Right here," I say, pointing to Callum's waist, noticing his shoulders bunch when I drag her hands around him and secure them at his front, forcing her chest against his back. "There! Now, you won't fall off. Just stay like that and lean into my boy Callum. And you'll be as good as new."

"You-you ready?" Callum asks, peeking behind him as River tightens her hold on him and nervously nods.

"Hold on to your ass, Pretty Girl. He's about to take off." And with that, Callum and my Pretty Girl ride off into the moonlight, slowly making their way downtown and out toward the mansions we live in.

Shoving my hands into my pockets, I begin the long trek back to the band house. Sure, I could walk a few blocks and make it to my normal house, grab my keys, and drive my car back there. But I decide a nice, long, relaxing walk could do me some good. Besides, it gives Callum time to get over his fear and talk to River a little bit more. Because I have a feeling that in the next week or so, change is on the horizon.

17

Kieran

"KNIGHT!" River's small voice pulls me out of my reprieve as she runs over to me with her arms spread wide.

A small laugh escapes me when she bounds into me, knocking me over into the grass, flat on my back.

"What's up, Blue?" I chuckle, righting us, so we're sitting side-by-side on the hill behind our apartment building.

Something about these stolen moments with my Blue cements my need for her. Nothing on this planet will ever compare to our rendezvous. Not my guitar. Or my favorite chocolate bar. This is it for me; I feel it in my bones.

She giggles, staring at the guitar beside me, and shrugs. "I just missed you today. Where were you?"

Kicked out. My mom didn't want me anywhere near the apartment today but didn't have enough sense to get me on the bus for school. Or even dress me properly before she gave me the boot. In only a T-shirt and jeans, the only other things I had time to grab when she yanked me by my shirt collar were my guitar and a pair of socks. My stomach rumbles violently from missing not only breakfast but lunch. Hours ago, I ventured back to my apartment door and knocked, hoping my mother would at least have enough sense to feed me, but she didn't. That man answered the door with *his shirt off and a scowl, telling me to get lost. I'm sure I'll hear about my indiscretions later.*

"I missed you, too, Blue. Mom has someone important over. She says he might be my new dad soon." I shrug, hoping it's not true. He may have gifted me a guitar, but I see how he looks at me with disdain.

"You won't leave me, will you?" she asks with a quivering lip. Tears pool in her big, green eyes, and I swear my heart breaks from one look.

"Never," I murmur, picking up my guitar. "Want to hear my new song?" I ask, strumming the strings and humming under my breath.

"Yes!" she shrieks with excitement. "Play me a song, Knight."

I grunt, slamming my fists into the hanging bag over and over until my raw knuckles bleed. Red pours down my arms in tiny droplets, but I don't fucking stop. I revel in the pain, washing away the happy memories pouring through the black box I locked them in. My only happy times as a kid were with River on that hill and my guitar on my knee. I didn't know how to play, but the internet was a hell of a teacher. Slowly but surely, I figured it out and played River song after song. Then we left Central City for greener pastures with the man who not only ruined and controlled my life but my mother's, too. Sometimes I wonder why the fuck she jumped into bed with him and stole my fucking life from me.

Fuck. Her. Fuck River. Fuck. This. Fuck. Everything.

Why did it have to be her? Why? It could have been anyone else on the West's payroll, but it just had to be River fucking West. The once love of my damn life, and now...

I shake my head, dispelling the tumultuous thoughts banging around in my mind. The need to walk away from this entire situation sits heavy on my chest as I continue to pound into the bag with all my might, forcing myself to fucking forget everything —even how to breathe.

When I stop my frantic jabs, black spots dance in my vision, numbing the rage and pain eating away at me. Leaning my forehead against the bag, I suck in oxygen, refueling my body until the world returns to focus. Slumping down onto the mat, I lay on my back, staring at the tall ceiling.

Whoever built this house knew exactly what they were doing. A full-sized gym with every piece of equipment possible surrounds me. And in the next room, a full-blown recording studio taunts me, begging me to create new music, and digitally immortalize it for the world to hear. If fucking only.

Not only does my dick refuse to work around other chicks, the moment River numbed my heart—the music fucking died inside me. Like she sucked the spark from my damn soul and stole that shit from me. I curl my aching fingers into fists and snarl at the fucking ceiling for the millionth time in the past week. A helpless feeling of being stuck in the damn mud, unable to take control of my destiny, creeps up my spine.

I huff, turning to my side and forcing myself to stand on my jelly legs. Looking at my smartwatch, I stop the timer at precisely two hours. Blowing out a breath, I bask in the momentary reprieve this session has given me. My mind quiets for one bliss-filled moment, and serenity runs through my veins. Right now, it's as if I never laid eyes on River West and had my soul stomped out, only to return to her years later and have to follow her orders.

"Fuck," I grumble, stumbling toward the white towels dangling from a rack attached to the wall.

Wiping the sweat from my face, I smack my lips, desperately seeking the water I forgot to grab before disappearing. Every inch of me aches deliciously as I trudge up the steps into the brightly lit kitchen heated with the sun's rays. It's like walking out of my damn casket and into the real world. When I entered the basement two hours ago, the sun hadn't even peeked over the horizon. And now, the new day is here—Sunday. A day of nothing but working out and taking it easy before the reality of our new week begins, band practices, and our early morning therapy sessions.

Over the past few days, the guys have already started to fall into her bullshit. Again. They're falling into her fucking honey trap and gravitating toward everything she says, like lost little puppy dogs with big heart eyes. It fucking disgusts me. How can they do that? After everything that she put us through.

Fuck. Despite the grueling work out this morning, my head is still a damn mess. Sure, I momentarily distracted myself from the bullshit happening. But the pain never truly leaves. Every time she walks into the house, she rips open another scab and exposes my wounds.

This entire situation has been one fucked up, long nightmare, and there's no way out. Believe me, I've checked every day. My agent has been searching this entire week, hoping to bring me good updates about another prospect. But nothing has come of it. According to her, I should stick to my contract, even though we could void it by walking out and starting somewhere new.

Stick it out? Yeah right. She has no idea what I'm up against. When I walked away, I walked the fuck away. Endpoint. Nothing was going to bring me back to the woman who crushed my heart in the palm of her hand. So, thanks, cruel world, for plopping me smack dab in the middle of this shipwreck with no lifeboat in sight. I'm fucking drowning in rage, pain, and the constant memories holding me captive. One day, I'll be able to break the surface and breathe again.

Nothing in this world could make me forgive River West for what she did. That fucking video lives in the deep confines of my head, reminding me to never again fuck around with relationships. Women, yes. Well, fuck—kind of. If my dick would fucking cooperate. It's like he's holding out on me for someone I refuse to let him have. Fuck him.

My fingers curl into fists when I step further into the kitchen and rest my head against the cool metal of the fridge. I heave a breath, trying to shove down the emotions River always brings up. I've locked that shit up for so many years with success. Now, here it is again, trying to ooze out of me. I would rather swallow my emotions and let the numbness take me over than feel what I felt for her.

Taking a deep breath, I ground myself to the now. Fuck my brain. Fuck my thoughts. As I listen to the sounds around me, I note the others must still be asleep. Like hell do they get up early and fight invisible demons at the gym like me. Not that I get up fucking early. Ever. But today was different. A calling clawed through my ribs and pulled me toward the gym so early in the goddamn morning.

Thud. Thud.

My face scrunches when a small scratching sound comes from somewhere in the house, followed by a small, strangled cry.

"What the hell?" I mutter, pushing off the fridge and looking around for the source of the sound. "Better not be a goddamn rat," I grumble, cautiously walking toward the sound.

The more I walk away from the kitchen, the louder it gets, seeming to come from the large living room.

"Help!" a little voice calls, making my heart slam in my fucking chest. "Please, Daddies!" It comes again through sobs.

That's when I realize it isn't scratching coming from anywhere. It's light pounding coming from the front door.

A million thoughts race through my mind when I march toward the front door, catching more words from the tiny voice on the other side.

"Help! Mommy is dead!" The tiny voice cracks with emotions, sniffling behind the front door. "Daddy!" the voice calls frantically, sounding more urgent than before. The pounding continuously beats against the wood until I'm standing right in front of it with my brows furrowed in confusion.

Daddy? There's no one's dad here. Unless one of these idiots knocked up some chick and decided not to tell anyone. Fuck. What a dick move that'd be. I don't care who the chick is. I'd never abandon my child like my dad left me high and dry.

"Fuck," I shake my head, throwing the door open, and freeze at the sight of her.

A beautiful little girl with fat tears rolling down her cheeks and a white bunny clutched to her chest shivers outside my front door. Her eyes screwed shut as she sniffles on her bunny's head.

"Hey, little girl. Are you okay?" My hoarse voice falls from my lips in a soothing tone, grabbing her attention.

I swear all the oxygen in my lungs ceases to exist when she looks up at me, cries even harder, and launches herself at me. Her little face buries into my thighs as she sobs harder, clinging to me for dear life.

Panic ensues inside me. What the hell do I do? If this were my little sister, I'd scoop her up and soothe all her pain. But I don't have a fucking clue who this is or why she's at my damn door. Almost instinctively, my protective side roars to the surface, and I run my fingers through her long, dark locks in a soothing manner, getting snagged on the knots.

"Hey, little girl? Are you okay?" My voice softens as I crouch down, pulling her from my leg and cupping her cheeks in my palms. "What's going on?" I ask again, earning a small hiccup in return.

"My mommy. She-she, I-I can't get her to move. My mommy is dead," she wails again, squeezing her eyes shut and trembling beneath my hands.

My heart skips a beat as I take her in, noting the similarities between her and River. Fuck. Her long, dark hair with tiny freckles on the bridge of her nose. Little pajamas hang loosely around her body; hell, she's not even wearing shoes. But where else could she be from? We all know River has a kid, but I never expected to see her standing shoeless outside my front door with tears falling from her eyes.

"Your mommy is River?" I ask as my eyes roam over her face, memorizing the shape of her nose and the pout of her quivering lips.

Time stands still when River's daughter blinks open her moisture-filled eyes, hiccuping in my grip. Oxygen evades me. My fucking head spins. Something primal and deep inside me snaps into place when her eyes connect with mine, full of terror and sadness. She quivers in my grip, nodding vigorously in confirmation.

More tears stream out of her identical mismatched eyes, falling down her small chin and dripping on me. Her wetness coats my flesh as those big, hurt eyes flash with disappointment, taking in every inch of me, too. Dipping down my chest and arms, she silently notes the tattoos etched into my flesh. She doesn't spare a second, gripping my wrist and trying to yank me across the street.

But I'm too stunned to move. Her tiny words don't register in my damn walnut brain as I process the fucking situation. River had a baby four years ago. She wasn't Van's like Gloria had claimed. This beautiful little girl standing before me is one hundred percent my flesh and blood.

This little girl isn't just a spitting image of River. She has my fucking eyes. My. Fucking. Eyes. Something my goddamn dad passed down to me before he bailed to pursue music. How fucking ironic. There's no goddamn way that's some sort of coincidence. You don't just show up with these eyes and not have similar DNA. It's an anomaly. Yet, here she is, looking at me.

There's no goddamn way.

This can't be fucking happening right now.

No.

A tidal wave of guilt crashes over my head, pulling me into the depths of the turbulent waves. My muscles jump under my skin, begging me to make a move. An itchiness spreads across my flesh, stretching too damn thin. I run a hand through my hair, digging into my scalp as the memories of my father resurface.

"Where's Daddy?" I whisper, staring out the window of our home. Longing clings to every inch of me. He's been gone for way too long. He said he had to work. And the sun is down.

Mother scoffs, gripping a beer bottle. "He's never coming back," she mutters coldly, staring at the wall with glossy eyes.

He's never fucking coming back. Is that how my little girl felt?

Does that run through her mind, too? Late at night as she stares at the white ceiling with hope dwindling day by day that she'll ever see her father again. If he'll ever walk through the door with a smile, saying he was joking about leaving? That he'd never do that to his family and perpetuate the hurt?

I abandoned my child like my father did to me.

I fucking did that!

Holy fucking shit. The walls close in on me. Oxygen refuses to refill my empty lungs. When did the air become so damn thick? Fuck! When–

"Daddy," she whispers with urgency, knocking me out of my own damning thoughts. "I think my mommy is dead," she says more calmly now, tugging at my wrist again with all her strength. "Please," she begs, yanking again until I'm on my stumbling feet and dumbly following her out onto the step.

"Wait," I struggle to say through the tightening of my throat. "Fuck," I rasp, collapsing to my knees again. My limbs tingle like damn Jell-O has replaced my bones, sending me spiraling to the ground. "You're..." I jerk my hand from her grasp, blindly gripping her cherub cheeks. Moisture burns behind my eyes when I really look her over again. "Mine," I mutter with a heavy tongue. She's too young to confirm or deny my ramblings. It's something I'll have to discuss with the fucking corpse she keeps talking about. Fuck! River.

"Daddy," she wails again, tugging at my arm. I shake my head, trying to knock the fog from my brain, processing all her words.

"Hey, whoa. Lyric!" Rad says, breathlessly running through the open front door with a pale face, falling to his knees beside me. "What are you doing here, Little Pretty Girl? And why are you crying? Did big, mean Kieran make you cry?" Rad asks with a low tone, tinged with unveiled anger.

I swallow hard, watching helplessly as she runs into his arms. Burying her face into the crook of his neck, she cries harder, taking comfort in him. Jealousy rushes through me. I clench my damn jaw, wishing I was the warmth that brought her salvation. Instead of him.

"What did you do?" he hisses, narrowing his eyes at me with such venom I have to shove away all the damn hurt and anger.

Mostly, it's the questions resting on the tip of my numb tongue that beg to come out. I swallow them all, ready to unleash them at the right time. Not now. Not when River is possibly in danger. Adrenaline spikes in my system. I push to my feet, glaring down at him as I march away with determination leading the way.

"What the fuck are you talking about? I didn't do anything. She was pounding on our door..." I shout over my shoulder and curl my fists at my side. "Doesn't fucking matter. Something is wrong with River."

"Fuck!" Rad huffs, climbing to his feet with her in his arms still. "What's wrong with your mommy, Little Pretty Girl?" he huffs, hoisting her further up his body as we quickly walk toward the house that now seems like a damn mile away.

Oh, how I ache to comfort her like a father should and make all the pain leave her. From here on out, I'll give her anything she desires. I'll never be my fucking father, sending a few post cards here and there. But he never really fucking cared. He rode off into the sunset with his guitar strapped to his back and a dream on his mind.

Sounds so damn familiar. God.

"My mommy is dead!" she sniffs again, shaking her head with a renewed sense of sadness clinging to her voice.

"Dead? Tell me what's going on, Little Pretty Girl. Tell daddy what is going on," he says, emphasizing daddy and glaring at me like I have any idea what's happening.

I cock my head to the side when he says the word daddy. Daddy? What in the ever-living fuck is going on in this house? Why is he daddy? My face twists into an unmasked expression, flushing the color from my face.

Something in my spooked expression must give me away as

Rad soothes the little girl, pumping his skinny legs harder toward River's house.

Turning his gaze to me, he cocks his head to the side and gives me a tight grin. "Welcome aboard, Daddy Kieran. Fucking finally. Now, apparently, River is dying, so we should probably go save her," Rad says with urgency, waving me along as I blindly follow right behind him, staring at the little girl in his arms with longing.

It's ridiculous to feel so much toward someone I met two seconds ago on my front step. But it's all there. A ball of feelings formed in my tight chest and squeezed out my breath. So many fucking questions beg to unleash as a sliver of denial hits me square in my stomach.

"Rad, what the hell is going on? Why does she... Who is her..." My heavy tongue is barely able to work as we slam through River's unlocked front door, loudly entering the pristine home. "Tell me what I'm thinking isn't the truth. Tell me that this is..." Because if it's true. Then I'm a piece of fucking shit. I walked out. I left her.

Without ever knowing she existed.

Rad turns sharply on his heel in the middle of the living room with a scowl. The little girl clutches tighter to him, whimpering like she's known him for years. Has he? Fuck. My heart pounds like a drum against my ribs as so many thoughts go through my mind. I knew River had a fucking kid. I knew because of Gloria... Gloria fucking knew and fucked up my entire life. She fucking...

I grip my hair tightly, pulling at the roots. My brain goes in a thousand different directions, leading me back to the same damn conclusion; Gloria somehow lied to me and led me astray. She used my vulnerability against me when I was at my lowest and manipulated me into thinking that, for some reason, River's baby was Van's. Shit. The phone call I received so many years ago plays in my mind on a constant loop.

The beautiful scenery of the large bluffs overlooking the blue ocean, my phone vibrates on my side table. I groan when it displays the name of the last person I ever wanted to speak to again. It's bad enough that growing up she was the world's worst mother, but the second the boys and I won, she called me and begged me for some money. With reluctance, I answer the phone, inwardly groaning at the lecture I'm sure I'm about to receive.

"Hello?"

"Kieran, so lovely to hear your voice again," Gloria sings through the phone with a cheerful hint to her tone.

"Sure, I guess. What's going on?" I ask, getting straight to the damn point.

"Well, I'm fine! Thanks for asking. Everything is settling so well since you boys left. Nigel has been on a business trip for the past week, and it's been so quiet around here. I've missed you so," she says through a wistful sigh. I'm sure not missing my ass at all.

"That's good to hear," I grunt, plopping down on the edge of my new king-sized bed. "So, why the call? It's been a few weeks."

"Well," she huffs out a laugh. "You'll never guess who got herself knocked up!"

"Hopefully not you," I grunt, cringing at the thought.

"Heavens, no! A few days ago, I got a little visit from someone you used to know. You know, that cheating whore you ran from."

I physically recoil from the phone, almost throwing it across the room. My mouth instantly dries as my gut tightens at the news.

"She-she..."

"Yes. She came sniffing around looking for you boys, claiming she was pregnant by one of you. Don't worry, though. I got her to confess it's Van's. Can you believe that? She tried to pin it on you four! What a lying slut she is." Gloria rambles on and on about River until I clear my throat.

"So, she's pregnant by Van?" I ask hoarsely, squeezing my eyes shut. It's bad enough she fucked him behind our backs. But this? Getting pregnant by the dickhead is the ultimate fuck you to us.

"Yes," Gloria sniffs. "It appears so." She talks more, but her words move like sludge through my ears, drowning out her annoying voice.

"Okay, bye," I mumble, not bothering to listen to her goodbye.

Through my stunned daze, my phone slips from my fingers, landing with a thud on the ground. Whatever effect the shocking news has on me knocks me out of my stupor. Uncontrollable rage storms through my system, turning my vision a dark shade of red. My nostrils flare as everything Gloria said settles heavily on my chest, caving it in. Through my fit of anger, I march toward my old guitar leaning against the wall—the same one I wooed River with so many years before. Everything blurs around me. Sound stops. My feelings cease to exist.

Before I know what's happening, my long fingers wrap around the long end of my guitar. The only sound that fills the room besides my pounding heart is splintering wood crashing against the hardwood floors. Over and fucking over, I smash it to pieces, basking in the destruction of my once precious guitar.

I stand tall with a heaving chest, keeping the news of River's pregnancy to myself. No one marches into my room to check on me because the distance between my brothers and I have hit a fever pitch for the past few weeks. A black void has split between us, making us strangers more than brothers. Callum barely talks. Rad is chasing anything with an ass. And Asher has folded in on himself, remaining quiet and calm—nothing like the man I knew two months ago. But I know something is distracting him into silence. I've never seen him like this before.

At that moment, I vow to myself never to fall into the grips of another woman and let her ruin them or me ever again. Pussy, sure. But a full-blown relationship? Fuck that. The last one I had exploded in my face.

I swallow hard, shoving that awful memory into the back of my mind, bringing me back to the situation at hand. River is off somewhere dying, and I've come face to face with our daughter, the little girl who magically resembles us.

A perfect damn mix.

Fucking hell, this can't be real. Is this real? Is this little person with my eyes really standing before me? My heart thumps wildly against my damn ribs.

"This is River's daughter, Lyric." A pained expression crosses Rad's face as he looks down at her and shakes his head. "And by the look on your face, you've already guessed that. You're pale, Bro. Are you finally figuring out that you're a damn dad? That you purposefully... That you goddamn... Fuck." Shaking his head, Rad squeezes his eyes shut. Anger swims across his down-turned features until he blows a breath and smothers it away. "We'll have to talk about this later, so we're not in front of little ears."

"But you swears a lot, Daddy," she murmurs through a sniffle, wiping her nose along Rad's shirt.

Rad stiffens. "Fuck! I mean. You're right, Little Pretty Girl. I'm sorry." She nods, sniffling again.

His words crash into me like a wave, taking me under. Momentarily, it's hard to suck in oxygen, and my lips pop open. Over and over, his words repeatedly play until they finally fucking stick in my brain. I'm a fucking father. A dad. Shit. The walls close around me as my panic rises and sweat glistens over my flesh. My chest fucking tightens like thick rubber bands constricting the oxygen from my body, and I'm only saved by the heady amounts of adrenaline shooting through my system. Deep breaths, idiot. I can't freak out now. There's too much going on to fall down the rabbit hole of realizations. Wiping a hand down my face, I erase everything going haywire in my body and numb it. The time for panic is later, not now.

18
Kieran

"Lyric," I say softly, running a hand through her hair again. "Where is your mommy? And what's wrong with her?"

Lyric sniffles, finally lifting her head from Rad's neck. Her big, mismatched eyes look directly into mine, and she sniffles again, silently pointing down the hall with a hiccup.

"She's dead in the bathroom," she says through a quivering lip and clings tighter to Rad for protection.

"You watch the kid, and I'll go see what's wrong," I say with apprehension, taking a step toward the hallway. "We'll make sure your mommy is okay. Okay?" I swallow hard when she meets my eyes again, and I swear it's like looking in the mirror. A million questions run through my mind when she nods in agreement, still clinging tight to Rad, who soothes a hand down her back and murmurs soft words in her ear. Protectively he stands taller, watching as I exit.

I have a kid, is the only thought that runs through my mind as I make my way down the silent hallway. I perk my ears up, listening for any sound, but nothing comes to me. On quiet steps, I continue down the never-ending hallway and stop at the end as light catches my attention, leading me to a gigantic main bedroom.

A fully made king-sized bed sits in the expansive room, with a glittery purse thrown on the comforter. Everything around me is in pristine condition. No dust. Not even a scrap of clothing on the ground. I walk further into the room and turn to my left, where the light shines on the semi-closed door. I hold my breath as I slowly push the door open, and my heart speeds out of control. When Lyric said her mom was dead, I didn't expect to actually find an unmoved body.

"Shit," I grunt, marching into the bathroom with determination. "River?" Gently I move my fingers through her hair, guiding it off her pale-looking face. Gently I press my fingers into the side of her neck, noting that she still has a heartbeat. Thank fuck. The stench of stomach acid and vomit fills the room. My stomach turns at the putrid smell. God, it reeks like fucking death walked into this bathroom and grabbed River before running away.

River's upper body clings to the porcelain God as she sleeps, pressing her cheek on the open toilet seat. How uncomfortable. But it was probably the only way to simultaneously get some rest and vomit. I cringe at the thought, crouching in front of her and running my finger over her heat-filled cheek.

"River?" I ask again, trying not to shake her.

"Fuck off," she mutters but doesn't move to make me fuck off. In fact, she doesn't move a muscle at all.

I smirk, almost chuckling to myself as the memories once again assault my mind. It's so like River to act like this even when I'm trying to help in such a dire situation.

"Sorry, River Blue, but I can't fuck off. A child was knocking at my door this morning. And I think you and I have some things to discuss." Emotions creep into my voice, taking them hostage and effectively choking me up. Tears burn behind my eyes as new feelings spill through me in her presence. Sure, I'm still pissed the fuck off at her. She cheated on us like we were nothing. But this? This is a child, and I'm sensible enough to realize there's more to this story than just black and white. There's a gray area that needs to be discussed.

River's eyes pop wide and frantic, refocusing on me as I crouch beside her. Her brows furrow with confusion as she takes me and the bathroom in. At that moment, I hear the distinct gurgle of her stomach as panic swallows her, and she heaves over the toilet.

"Oh God," she groans as she spills the contents of her stomach into the toilet. "It won't stop," she heaves again, spitting more chunks into the water.

My goddamn stomach turns at her noises, desperate to empty, too. But I hold it back, turning my head to give her some privacy. Like a gentleman, I grip back her hair despite the growing, conflicting feelings rising inside me. Just an hour ago, I beat the shit out of my hanging bag to her memory. Now here I am, holding back her hair as she's helplessly getting sick.

"I think I have food poisoning," she grumbles, squeezing her eyes shut. "Stupid sushi. Never again." A shiver runs down her spine, eliciting goosebumps when she sets back, heaving a few breaths. Blindly, she feels for the toilet paper, tears off a piece, and wipes her mouth.

"Well, whatever it is, you're definitely sick. And apparently, dying," I grunt, loosening my fingers from her hair as she settles her cheek against the rim of the toilet again. Exhaustion pulls at her features, and she huffs at me.

"Dying?" she grumbles, licking her chapped lips. "Why would I be dying?" she asks softly, flinching away from my touch when I remove some fallen hair strands from her face.

She watches me with suspicion when I plant my ass beside her. My eyes wander across her familiar yet grown-up features. She's still the same girl I knew back in Central City, yet not.

"Is she mine?" My tongue dries out as I wait on pins and needles for her answer. Even though, in my heart, I already know the damn truth.

The realization of having a kid and not knowing she existed breaks me in half. I promised myself a long time ago that if I ever had a child, I would never do to my child what my father did to me. He took off and never looked back. He made something of himself. He may not have been famous, but he took off for greener pastures and left my mother and me all alone. What kind of man does that? How can a man do that?

"Can we talk about this later when I'm not on my deathbed?" River rasps, squeezing her eyes shut with a pained expression crossing her features.

Although it's the last thing I want to do right now, I give River the reprieve she needs. "Yeah, but we will talk about this. And the fact that Rad knew..."

"Yeah," she says, heaving a breath and blowing it out between her lips.

Nervously, I rub my neck. "Do you need any water? I need to fill Rad in on what's happening."

River peeks an eye open, staring at me like I've grown a second head. "Um, sure. I don't think I've moved for at least six hours. Thanks," she says with reluctance, watching my every move like I might poison her water.

"Okay, no problem. I'll get you some water, and... I'll be right back, stay here," I grunt, stumbling my way to my feet, nearly falling over. A tight smile crosses my lips when I give her a little wave before exiting the bathroom.

The awkwardness of the situation presses down on me and doesn't leave until I walk out of the bathroom and down the hall. Running a hand through my hair, I halt in the living room doorway. My brows pull together at the sight of Asher, Callum, and Rad surrounding Lyric and cooing soft words into her ear. There's a familiarity between them that pulls at my damn heartstrings, tugging me in so many damn directions. She's mine. Yet, I don't have that connection with her.

"Is she okay?" Rad asks, jumping to his feet with concern etched onto his face.

My eyes stare from him and Lyric to the rest of the guys sitting there, staring up at me with wide eyes. "Um, yeah, I think she has food poisoning. She's stuck on the toilet and doesn't look very good," I say, scratching at the back of my neck. "But she's definitely not dying," I say confidently, locking eyes with Lyric, who sags with relief in Callum's lap.

"My mommy is going to be okay?" she asks with a quivering lip—more moisture pools in her eyes, threatening to cascade down her cheeks again.

"Yeah," I say, clearing my throat, not sounding as reassuring as I wanted. "She's going to be okay."

"Yeah, Little Pretty Girl. We'll make sure that your mommy is all better. Sounds like she's just got the flu," Rad says, narrowing his eyes at me. What the hell did I do? Shit. I'm trying to make a difference.

Without another word, I walk into the kitchen and search through the cupboards for a glass with Ash on my ass.

"You good?" Asher asks with reluctance, rubbing his fingers over his stubbly jaw.

I grunt, grab a glass from the last cupboard, and slam it down onto the counter. "Define good," I hiss through gritted teeth, filling up the glass. "How long?" Asher's eyes fall to the ground, and he shakes his head.

"I only found out about a week ago." He doesn't elaborate more, but it pisses me off. Rage boils through my veins, and my fists clench at my sides.

"And you didn't fucking tell me?" Stalking up to him, I grab him by the shirt and pull his face into mine, letting him see all the emotions bursting through the surface. "I have a fucking kid, Asher. And you didn't think to tell me that you met her and that she existed?"

"You said you knew," Asher says, aggressively growling in my face, pushing his forehead into mine. "I asked you if you knew River had a kid. And you said you fucking knew. How long, Kieran? How fucking long did you know?" he grunts back, pressing his face harder into mine.

I blink several times, going over our conversation in the limo.

Yeah, I did know she had a kid. Gloria told me that she did, and she also fucking lied through the damn phone.

I grunt, pushing Asher away from me, and pace around the kitchen with my hands clenching at my sides. "Gloria called me. We had just moved into our first apartment together. She told me that River had come to her and told her that she was pregnant with Van's baby." I stare at Asher as the news computes in his mind, and he shakes his head.

"So, you had nothing to do with the restraining orders either?" Rad asks, strolling into the kitchen and giving me the death glare.

I recoil as if I was slapped, and my lips popped open. "Restraining orders? What the hell are you talking about?"

"No, I think that was all Gloria's doing," Asher surmises, darting his eyes around the room and avoiding our curious stares.

Confusion swirls around me as I fall back into the countertop. "Somebody better fucking explain what is going on. Before I lose my shit."

"I think that's a better conversation between you and River," Callum mutters, shuffling into the kitchen and shaking his head.

My eyes drop to Lyric clinging to his hand as her wide eyes take every inch of me in, sizing me up. I swallow the hard lump forming in my throat. She's a fucking mini version of River mixed with my features, too.

In my heart, I know there's no denying who she belongs to. You take one look at her and you know without a doubt, without getting a DNA test, that she belongs to me. And because we walked away, we never got the chance to know her. I never got the chance to watch her walk or talk or crawl. Fuck.

"I'm going to take care of River," I say softly, peering into Lyric's eyes. "I'm going to take care of your mommy until she feels better, okay? And then maybe we can hang out?" I question, raising a brow when she slowly nods in agreement.

My heart seizes in my chest when she pulls away from Callum and slams into me, hugging my thigh. Her strong little grip clings on as she takes several deep breaths and finally peers up at me.

"Thank you, Daddy," she says in a raspy, overused voice.

"You're welcome," I say, as a burning heat rises behind my eyes. My fingers trail through her long dark locks, trying to soothe the worry.

"Yeah, Little Pretty Girl. Why don't we get you dressed and have a fun daddy's day," he says with uncertainty, looking down at her like she's the fucking sun in his sky.

Looking around the room, I examine all their varying expressions. From the looks of it, they've all known for a period of time and haven't said a word to me.

An off-feeling of understanding presses down on me. I fucking get why they didn't talk to me about it, but it still fucking sucks. I was so bitter in the limo when Asher asked.

It fucking hurt so goddamn bad that she would go behind our backs not only sleep with Van but have his baby, too.

Gloria picked on me when my nerves were raw as hell and dropped the news on me at my lowest. Her mothering skills were weak at best, and I don't know why the hell I took her word for it back then.

Rad scoops Lyric into his arms, navigating toward her room like he's tucked her in a million times before. Within ten minutes, Lyric is dressed in a mismatched outfit and a worried expression lining her face.

"My mommy will be okay, right?" she asks in a quiet voice when I crouch in front of her. The back of my fingers brush against her plump cheeks, and I nod.

"Don't worry, Little Blue. I won't let anything happen to your mommy today." And that's a fucking promise. River has to feel better so the five of us can sit down and have a lengthy discussion.

As if my words erase the worry sitting on her shoulders, she gives me a toothy grin. She's melting my fucking heart without doing anything at all. The need to not only protect her but heal her wounds has my fatherly instincts on overdrive. Without another word being said, she wraps her arms around my neck and squeezes me while kissing my cheek.

"Thank you, Daddy."

Those words. They stay in my mind long after they take Lyric across the street and do God knows what with her. Our house isn't exactly childproof.

I silently chastise myself. Grabbing the forgotten glass of water, I silently walk back into the bathroom where I had left River minutes before. River has barely moved from her spot. Except now she leans against the wall with her eyes squeezed shut and her knees at her chest, sucking in air.

"Sorry," I mutter gently, sitting beside her and handing her the glass of water. "I met Lyric. Don't worry about her, though. The guys took her across the street." Her breaths shutter in her chest as she gives a slow nod. Taking the glass of water, she gulps down a few mouthfuls and takes a deep breath.

"Let me guess; you didn't know either." She doesn't bother opening her eyes, instead squeezing them tighter. She grimaces, rubbing a hand across her stomach.

"If I would've known, I wouldn't have stayed away. Even if I fucking despised you for what you did... I would never stay away from my baby." My sentence starts out strong but dissipates by the end, coming out as a breathy whisper.

River doesn't react like I thought she would. I expected a scoff or some form of disagreement, but she simply lays her head against the wall.

"Yeah, I'm getting the distinct hint that nothing I believed is real," she grumbles, finishing off the water in three long swallows.

"Gloria told me that you had a baby. But she said it wasn't mine or the guys; she told me it was Van's."

Running a hand down my face, I relive all the situations that long ago I shoved into a little black box of forgotten memories. From the moment we left Central City to the day we got to East

Point. It all comes back like a tornado, wreaking havoc on my emotions.

"And you believed her," she says defiantly, with anger rising in tinging her voice. If this conversation keeps progressing, we are going to have an all-out brawl of words we can't take back.

"Not now. Let's do this when you're feeling better; then you can bust my lip. Right now, you're sick as shit. And you need to rest before we can hash this shit out." As much as I want to continue the conversation and get to the bottom of what the hell happened, I know my words are true. I want her to get better, and I want to figure this out.

"Fine," she says through a breath. "I'm going to bed. You can go home," she says, trying to get to her feet. River stumbles around a little bit before catching herself against my body. Fuck. The feel of her pressing against me messes with my damn head. Fire brews beneath my skin. Her touch is so right. Yet so wrong at the same time.

"Yeah, I'm not going anywhere. You've been here for six-plus hours. You need help. And that's what I'm going to do. Once you're better, we are all going to sit down and have a nice long conversation." The familiar glare I grew to love years ago stares back at me in defiance.

"You really don't have to stay. I'm a big girl, and I can take care of myself. I didn't ask you to come over here..."

"This isn't a discussion, River Blue." She scowls at me even more, angrily snarling at the nickname I refuse to let go of. "This is me doing what I said I'm going to do. You are going to bed, and I'm going to get you more water. Then when you're feeling a little better, I'll get you some crackers. I'm not leaving until you feel better."

River doesn't say anything else, leading me back to her bedroom. Plopping onto her mattress, her fingers run the length of her forehead, and she groans, refusing to meet my eye.

Today is the day everything changes for us.

19

River

EVERYTHING HURTS, and I'm slowly dying from cramps and constant nausea, turning my damn stomach. I groan when my phone goes off at my bedside, vibrating incessantly until I put it up and view the messages I sent Rocco a few hours before, informing him of my delicate situation. Of course, the bastard retorts with this...

ROCCO

I'd ask if you were pregnant...

You're not, are you?

Is one of them there now? Beside you?

Are you the cheese in the ham and turkey sandwich yet?

The cheese in between the many layers of lasagna?

ME

*middle finger emoji** I'd actually have to have time to fuck to achieve that. I blame you and the sushi.

And no. I'm still a single Pringle with no dick on the horizon.

Now stfu...

ROCCO

Do you need anything, Doll? Christian is making his famous chicken noodle soup right now... *wink*

ME

Consider me interested...

ROCCO

Figured. He says...feel better, babe. I'll be there soon, then. Please don't go into the light...it's not your time yet.

ME

Sometimes I wonder why you're my other bestie...

ROCCO

Because I bring you soup and quick wit...

ME

And poisonous sushi...

ROCCO

Debatable. Just make sure your baby daddies don't murder me. I like my life, and that mullet one at dinner wanted to pin my dick to the wall. Not in a fun way, either.

I snort, rolling my eyes.

ME

They'll behave... They're at home anyway.

ROCCO

Like you can control four dickish rock stars...

ME

Stfu...and bring me soup.

ROCCO
So demanding and bossy...

I groan, forcing myself into the seated position. A rock band plays off-tune inside my head, pounding repeatedly. Peeking an eye open, I stare at the tall glass of water and the note sitting next to it.

River Blue–
I went home to eat. Drink the water. I'll be back soon.
Don't fucking move.
Knight.

"What the fuck?" I hiss, rereading the note. Just a few days ago, he was being an unbearable ass. Now he's leaving me a concerned message demanding I drink water. What in the ever-loving fuck is happening right now? Shit.

I met Lyric. His words ring through my head. That's right. In my haze of sickness, he met his daughter. Shitballs. No wonder he's trying to butter me up. Pinching the bridge of my nose, I head into the bathroom and wash the sickness from my body under a steaming hot shower. By the time I'm out and dressed in my comfy leggings and oversized shirt, I meet Rocco at the front door and lead him into the kitchen where he bustles around like a concerned mother.

"There's my sickly Doll," he greets me with a smile, kissing my forehead. "Christian sends his regards but refuses to step foot in here while you're contagious."

I frown. "I don't have the damn plague. Your husband is ridiculous."

He shrugs, waving his hand. "You know him. He'll give you all the soup you want, but don't you dare invite him to the germs."

"Well, thanks for the soup," I say, making grabby hands at the container he's holding.

Flicking my forehead, he takes the precious container away with a villainous cackle. *Prick.* Marching into the kitchen, he riffles through my cabinets until he finds a large bowl and pours it in.

"Sit," he demands, waving at the stool by the marble-topped island.

"I'm not a dog, you asshole," I grunt, sitting in the chair with a huff. Rocco, ever the smartass, opens his lips to retort, but I stare at him, forcing his mouth shut.

"Fine. I want to make sure my bestie is feeling loads better. Now, eat the soup and spill the tea," he says with a grin, setting the large, steaming bowl of chicken noodle soup in front of my face.

Taking in a large breath, I catalog the delicious scents wafting from the bowl and test how far I can push my stomach. It gurgles as I slurp the first spoonful of broth, protesting until the heat hits. I haven't gotten sick since Kieran held my hair back and embarrassingly watched me puke my soul out.

God. What a fucking day. I'd been over the toilet for what felt like twenty-four hours, puking out the sushi from the night before. Every damn minute, I heaved until I had nothing left. Eventually, I fell asleep with my cheek plastered against the toilet seat. Only waking when Kieran gently nudged me and talked me out of my sick-induced slumber. My cheeks heat at the memory. The last thing I ever wanted was for one of them to see me in such a vulnerable position ever again.

Then I learned sweet Lyric thought I was fucking dead and introduced herself to Kieran, blabbering about my sickly status. Granted, I didn't tell her I was keeled over by the toilet. She just happened to find me, and I wouldn't wake up.

By the way Kieran talked, he had no fucking clue she was his. Or that she existed at all. Heartbreak rested behind his eyes, and my fucking heart tore in two. It was at that moment I knew that, for some reason, Gloria had lied to me about everything when I made my way to Callum's house. I don't understand why she would. Wouldn't she want her potential granddaughter in her life? Not that I'd want her to be, anyway. She was—and probably still is—a big fucking bitch.

"They'll leave you one day, Central Slut," she leans in, *whispering into my ear with a tone of pure evil. "I won't let you drag them down into the depths of poverty. They're better than you and better than this town. One day they'll be fucking stars, and you'll be here. Where you belong." My jaw ticks from the back of the crowd, gathered to watch as Whispered Words plays for the entire cookout, they drug me to. Not only have I had to deal with my stupid, stalker ex, but now I must deal with Gloria sputtering abuse in my ear.*

I catch Asher's eye as he watches us closely, no doubt wanting to know what she said. Too bad I never gave him the satisfaction of knowing what she had to say.

I guess that evil cunt kept her promise, after all. My stomach turns again. Not from the food this time. It's her words playing on repeat like a damn nightmare. I never honestly thought she'd be so damn vindictive enough to pull something so cruel. Apparently, I was wrong.

My fucking head hurts thinking about my current predicament. Constantly warring with my damn self on the rights and wrongs of the situation. I'm still deeply hurt, and that won't change. More than deeply, I'm fucking shattered with deep crevices splitting further inside me the more I'm around them, held together by fucking super glue for the past five years. At the slightest inconvenience, I'll completely crumble. Fuck. I'm ready to move on and heal from my trauma. But I know I won't. Not until I've hashed it out with them—really hash it out. It might be through strong words. I'll have to step out of my boss shoes and into the hurt River shoes and get to the nitty-gritty of what went wrong and why they left.

I take a tentative bite, groaning as the mild flavors hit my desperate tongue. "Tell Christian never to stop cooking," I hum, slowly slurping the broth.

"He wouldn't dream of it," he says with a snort. "So, tell me about these baby daddies you suddenly have hanging around. How's life, Doll?" He raises a brow, ignoring the twisting expression crossing my face.

"There's nothing to tell, Roc." I shove a spoonful of soup into my mouth, distracting myself from the question. I've gone down this spiraling road before. "They're there, and I'm here. I'm their boss, and they're my—the band I'm taking care of. End of story."

"That's why you're avoiding the conversation altogether. Discussions are a healthy part of life. Now, tell me all about them. Have they apologized? Have you found out new information? How is my godchild holding up now that her four daddies are in her life? Spill." His tone accepts no arguments as he glares at me. I nibble on my bottom lip when he raises a brow. "You are afraid," he states, eyeing my face. "Why?" Reaching across the table, he gently squeezes my hand.

Rocco has been my best friend for four years now. Hell, he's one of my damn pillars to lean on. Greater than any partner in the world. We met on the set of a music video I was helping with, and he was the actor they had hired. From there, we hit it off. At one time, I thought he might be interested in me and pursued it. After a fun night, we discovered we were good friends. Several months later, he found this amazing chef named Christian and married his soulmate. Granted, their relationship started off rocky with several toxic breakups, and then, Rocco pulled his head out of his ass.

"It's annoying how well you can read me." Slurping more soup into my mouth, I completely avoid his gaze.

"Like an open book, Doll," he huffs. "It's quite annoying that prying you open is so hard. We've been friends for years. You'd think you'd trust me by opening up and telling me how you're feeling. I know you're strong, but trust me, you'll feel better when you talk about it." He squeezes my hand in support.

I blow out a breath, stabilizing the nerves eating away at my insides. Sometimes it's frightening how well he knows me and can easily peel my layers open one by one. Staring into his dark eyes settles the wrath and pain stirring in me. Sometimes I swear Rocco is my friendship soulmate. The one truly meant for me, but not romantically. And throw in Kaycee, Olivia, and Ode to form my perfect circle of friends. I couldn't live without them. They're all my family in their own way, building me up and supporting me through this whole mess I call life—the after Whispered Words fiasco.

"What if they leave again?" The words leave my lips, barely in a whisper. All the fear swirls like a damn tornado inside me, spiraling my damn mind in so many directions my breath stalls. "They're rock stars. What if this is all a passing phase to them?" I swallow the lump in my throat and ignore the burning behind my eyes. "If they walk away, Roc. If they decide this is too much for them and bail on her. She won't survive. Lyric will burn down the fucking world to get to them now. She's had a taste of their fatherly love. I can't protect her from them like I protect myself." Everything in the room spins from my revelations, and my fingers clutch the edge of the countertop.

"The way I see it, Doll. You're going to have to make a big decision. They're in her life now. You told me over dinner that they didn't know about her or the blasted restraining orders. It seems they were in the dark for a lot of it. Did they leave you? Yes. They knowingly walked away without a goodbye and blocked you. What was the true reason? Only they know. Now, it's up to you whether or not you'll ever truly trust them again. From what I saw of Mullet when he showed up to our dinner, there was a lot of determination and love behind his mischievous eyes." I stiffen at his words, snapping my gaze to him. There's no way in hell he had an ounce of love for me.

"Love?" I scrunch my nose. "There's no way..."

"I'm a love-sick fool, Doll. Christian and I didn't have the greatest start. But I knew when he walked away and right back into my life that the look he gave me when we finally reconnected was a look of admiration. I worked every step of the way to amend my wrongdoings. That look Mullet gave you was the same one Christian gave me. They're not giving up on you. They obviously want to be in Lyric's life. Isn't that what you've always hoped for?"

I nod, nibbling my damn lip again as a headache pounds against my damn skull.

It's all I've ever dreamed of since the moment she was born. It's why I educated her on who they were and familiarized her with them. There's never been a second in her life that she didn't know who helped create her.

My father's existence was hidden from me for so long. My mother refused to talk about him until I snooped, finding more information when I was little. That's when I started writing to him every day, professing my innocent love, and begging him to come back, hence where all my daddy issues stem from.

"I don't trust them. At all. They're going to break her baby heart, and she can't... I can't..." I suck in a breath, squeezing my eyes shut as moisture burns, begging to unleash down my cheeks.

She can't take a first-round heartbreak. Like I can't take another round of them breaking my heart.

Warm, strong arms wrap around me, pulling me into his chest. He kisses my temple like the loving best friend he is. With a deep sigh, Rocco lays it all out for me.

"No one's asking you to fall head over heels for them again. I mean, you could, but it's not a requirement. Feel them out. Get to know them as adults. You're wiser—Co-parent with them. Let them fully into her life. Let them help you through the overzealous schedule you've created for yourself. Now is the time to stop depending on your brothers and start leaning on the men who seem to want to step up," he whispers with sincerity, holding me close to his chest. Comfort surrounds me at the sound of his beating heart thumping a lullaby in my ear.

"I hate you," I mutter through the bubbling emotions tightening my throat.

A deep chuckle vibrates against my arm, and he kisses my temple again. "You love it when I make sense."

"I do. But goddamn, Roc. I'm going to fall apart. They...they broke my heart once, and I..." Haven't let anyone in since *them*. They were my forever, and then my forever ran away and became my never again, leaving me behind.

I've only hooked up with maybe a handful of men since they left and never let anyone in. I haven't dated. I haven't opened the protective cage I had put my heart in for some time. Fuck. And now my child is involved.

Sure, I've versed her with everything I know about the boys. But this is real now. They're here, live and in person. No longer pictures in an album marked: *Daddies*. They're a fixture in her life. She won't forget about them overnight. She'll want more until they're tucking her into bed and staying under our roof. Lyric is persistent as fuck, just like her damn fathers. There's no moving forward without them.

"I'm not telling you to jump into bed with them. Although maybe four dicks would really do you some good. Umph," he grunts when my elbow lands in his gut.

"And we were having such a special moment," I grumble, biting my lip to hide my smile.

"I'll say one last thing. Take it day by day. Don't roll over and forgive them. Make them beg. Make them get on their damn knees and earn your trust back. Let them see Lyric and prove themselves to her and to you. I don't know them very well. In fact, I'd rather rip their testicles out for what they did to you. But I have a feeling there's a lot you don't know. And neither do they. One day at a time, okay?" He raises a brow, pining me with a stern look. "Promise me you'll repair your heart and fix their wrongdoings. No matter what."

"Fine, Dad," I grumble, relaxing when he hugs me again, pulling me into his chest and kissing my head.

"So, do they know about your special visitor?" he asks, squeezing me one last time before stepping back.

"God no," I say, taking another bite. "I'll cross that bridge when..."

"When he kidnaps you, Doll? He's getting brazen. Pictures of Lyric at school." Rocco frowns, concern twisting his features. "I worry about you and her being all on your own out here. First, it's pictures, and then—"

I hold up my hand, shaking my head. "Olivia has it covered. Carter has his eye on things, too. I have security cameras everywhere around here, plus the security company who provides my guards and everything. No one is getting into this house or onto this property without them or me knowing."

He rolls his eyes. "Katrina likes to keep me updated; you know?" I swallow hard. Ugh. My PA Kat and her big ass mouth. Thankfully, she's the best PA I've had in a few years, keeping my office in order when I'm away healing bands. We're not close like some would think, but I know we care about each other in a professional and personal way. The way her eyes tear up whenever my packages come, lets me know she's feeling it, too.

"What happened to boss-personal assistant confidentiality," I grumble, shoving the bowl away and rubbing my temples.

"When it comes to you and me, it doesn't exist. She's extremely worried, too. Your stalker is dangerous. No matter if he's laid low for three years. That's three years of watching you and taking pictures." He shakes his head. "Be extremely careful."

"I know. I will. We've talked about this a million times before," I say, blowing a breath.

The only thing my stalker has done is send me pictures of myself from a distance. No notes. No trying to get at me or kidnap me. I'm worried, yes. But they seem to be resigned to the sidelines and watching from afar.

"Fine. So, is your assistant Kitty Kat single yet?" Rocco grins, leaning his chin on his hand.

"You're despicable," I mumble. "You've both been captivated since meeting her six months ago. Too bad she's still in a relationship with Trevor," I say, sticking my tongue out at him.

He shrugs. "We'll be here when they break up," he says confidently, staring wistfully at the wall. "There's just something about her that connects the three of us. She seems to complete our void—our perfect third. But alas, my elusive Kitty Kat hasn't realized it yet," he pouts, sticking his bottom lip out.

"One day," I say, plucking his lip with a soft laugh. "Thanks, Roc. I'm feeling so much better now."

"You still look like shit," he quips, flicking my forehead again.

"Dick," I huff, sitting straight up as a loud knock sounds at the front door before it flies open.

Almost in slow motion, we turn our attention to the wide-open front door where four rock stars with angry scowls stare at Rocco with untamed jealousy roaring through their systems. Lyric grins in her mismatched outfit, staring up at Rocco with stars in her eyes.

This should be good. Especially when she runs toward him with her arms opened wide, waiting for a hug.

"What the hell is he doing here?" Rad growls, pointing directly at Rocco, who holds his hands up in a placating manner and steps back.

Great. This will be fun.

20
Kieran

"You went out for lunch and brought back that?" Asher's brows furrow as I set the large bag on the counter of our kitchen at the band house, along with the food bags and drinks.

I grunt in response. The tension between the four of us stifles the damn house with its thick fog. It's the giant elephant in the room we've avoided for hours now. The only entity able to break through the thick cloud currently sits on Callum's lap, asking a fresh round of unrelenting questions about his tattoos. The ones she can see crawling up his arms, on his fingers, and wrapping around his neck, she pokes at them.

Ink has been his therapy over the past few years. Rarely does he talk about the miserable night between River and Van, instead throwing himself into complicated riffs on the bass and under the tiny needle. Or in the fight ring, where he risks his life every Saturday, getting the shit knocked out of him.

He and I aren't so different. While I take out my haunted past on the swinging bag until I can't feel anything anymore, he pounds flesh until her memory is beaten away.

Out of the corner of my eye, I watch her with rapt attention, soaking in the presence of this tiny being I helped create. Me. I did that. With the help of River, of course. Somehow, someway, we brought this life into the world. Only I wasn't a part of it. Not entirely. Not at the beginning. I was away living what I thought was my dream. Instead of taking care of the one responsibility unknowingly thrust upon me. Watching her now, I note her familiarity with each of us. Openly calling us daddy and laughing at whatever we say. There's always a smile for us when we talk and a hug when she needs it.

Fuck.

A sharp, painful ache pounds in my chest, desperate to drag all the answers out of this tiny being. River never hid us from Lyric. So, why weren't we allowed to know she existed? The familiar rage I've come to know spikes in my veins like an old familiar friend, but I swallow it down. Now is not the time to lose my shit like I want to. Like I always do.

"That's something we need to talk to River about," Asher informs me when I stomp my way through the house, shouting my anger until the walls bleed and break. After I had left River in her bed, softly snoring her sickness away. The compulsion to beat the answers out of the three men I considered my brothers drove me through the door with a scowl.

"Yeah, bro. We don't have all the answers either. We only found out, too." Rad grimaces as he speaks, rubbing a finger over a scratch on his cheek.

"You need to cool down." Callum gives me a knowing look, discreetly cracking his scarred knuckles in my direction.

Deep down, I know he's eager to pop me in the fucking nose again as retribution for my damn attitude—like always. We've been at each other's throats for years since we left the woman across the street behind. Now, it's hitting a fever pitch. If I don't go, I'll wreck whatever semblance of a relationship we have left and bury it in a grave so deep, it'll never have a fucking chance to resurface and renew.

So, I did. I grabbed my keys and split for fresh air, which led me to the children's store. A place I never thought I'd step foot in.

I wandered around the deserted aisles with my head in the damn clouds, wondering what the hell was happening and how it happened without my knowledge. How could I not have known? How could she not have reached out and told me? She knew. She fucking knew what my dad did to me... What her dad did to her. So, why did she fucking keep this secret from me like I wouldn't fucking care?

"My dad disappeared, too," I mumble, laying back on the grass and staring at the stars.

"We're bastards," Blue mutters with a pout, looking over at me when I burst out laughing.

"Bastards under the moon," I say through a sad smile, keeping the pain of his absence to myself.

"Dear man in the moon," she says, turning on her back and clasping our hands together in the grass for support. "Will we ever meet our fathers again?" I bite my tongue. She may. I'll never find mine. He's long gone, dust in the wind.

I thought my life was spiraling out of control when River walked into the conference room with her head held high. Then came her announcement. Our band manager. Meaning she'd be in our lives for the next six months without pause. We'd see the ghost we'd left behind daily until our contract said otherwise, haunting us for eternity. Well, okay—six months. But six months can change everything. Six months can become a lifetime.

Now this bombshell.

My daughter. A whole fucking, walking, talking child that I didn't have a clue about knocked on our door and called me daddy. *Daddy.* Somehow, she knows who I am, but I don't know who she is. Not yet. I will, though. I will not be Dennis Knight, the man who ran away. I will be Kieran Knight, the best fucking father she's ever seen. No matter the sacrifices I make to ensure my child is cared for. Gloria was a shit excuse for a mom time and time again. The moment my father walked out, so did she. I was never a human being to her. I was just...nothing.

But Lyric is vibrant and full of life and love. Everything inside me melts, thinking about the amazing mother River has become. Lyric is living proof of the love and support she's given her.

I shove all those thoughts away, interrupted by the voice beside me.

"Is that a—" Rad stops dead, glancing at my purchase. A tight smile pulls at his tight lips as he approaches the counter, locking eyes on the tiny brunette pushing her way through.

"Daddy!" My heart fucking stops when she hugs my leg, tugging at my shirt to get a peek at the new gadget I impulse-bought.

"Little Blue," I breathe, hauling her into my arms and securing her to my body. It's so right. I feel it in my fucking bones. She's mine.

"Is it mine?" she asks, curiously looking at the large bag and poking it with her finger. Those eyes find me again, filled with hope; I can only nod. It hasn't even been five hours, and I'm wrapped around her little finger. Forever in her debt and destined to carry out every request she throws my way.

"All yours," I reply in a gravelly voice, thick with emotions.

Every minute I'm in her presence, a rightness clicks inside me. Like I was meant to do this or be here in her company, River promised we'd sit down and talk this over because the number of questions I have could fill up an entire twenty-four-hour period.

Lyric's entire face lights up when I completely unwrap the cotton candy machine, and she squeals with delight, clapping her hands.

"Cotton candy!" she shouts again with a grin. "Can we do it now?" she asks, looking around the room at the four of us with those big, puppy dog eyes she's somehow perfected.

"Of course," I mutter, furrowing my brows as I stare at the box, perplexed by the damn instructions. "But after you eat your burger." With eagerness, she shoves her burger into her mouth and quickly eats her fries without argument.

Like a real family, we all gather around the kitchen island, inhaling our food in silence, keeping our eyes on the ringmaster—

Lyric. She's the only reason we're able to stand being in the same room as each other. It's been years since we've stood side by side without arguing or shouting. Somewhere along the way, my best friends became strangers. Now, it's time to mend our bond. For River and Lyric—the two most important women.

After we've discarded our food bags, we once again settle around the island with our hearts in our throats.

"Let's do this, Little Pretty Girl," Rad says, tearing open the box and setting it up on the countertop. "What flavor should we try first? Cherry? Pink Vanilla? Grape? Blueberry?" With each flavor he reads off, he grabs the bottles from the box and sets them down.

"Blueberry," she says in awe, watching as Callum reads over the instructions and starts setting up the pink machine.

After ten minutes, we manage to wrap the blueberry cotton candy around the tube and grin when Lyric devours it with happy hums of approval. My heart swells ten times bigger at her satisfaction. Her simple happiness is better than fucking music and my guitar. It soars beyond the feeling I get when I'm front and center on the stage, with the spotlights blaring down on my sweat-soaked face with millions of fans chanting my name. Lyric encapsulates that mood just by the smile on her face and the tiny laugh from her throat. She takes away the stress on my shoulders, replacing it with pure joy. I'll hold onto this feeling for the rest of my life.

"What the fuck," Rad hisses, straightening to his full height as the rumble of a loud car roars down the driveway. "It's him!" Rad hisses, widening his eyes. "Dude!" he shouts, marching toward the window. Throwing open the blinds, he watches with rapt attention. "Mr. Sexy-In-Tight-Jeans is sauntering into her house. Again!" I shake my head at his antics but slowly move toward the window when Lyric hustles over, planting herself in his lap.

"Uncle Rocco," Lyric says, taking a big bite of her cotton candy and staring out the window.

We each peer down at her and then at each other with our

brows raised into our hairlines. Rocco? Why do I suddenly feel like a protective monster ready to tear his head off?

"Just your uncle?" Rad asks, swiping some of her hair back from her face. "He's not another daddy, is he?" His brows furrow when she giggles. "Better not be," he mumbles through gritted teeth. I swear he mutters no more dicks under his breath. I haven't seen Rad this pumped up for something since—well—River. I swallow hard as his eyes lock on the house across the street with interest.

Are we really heading down this road again?

"Just Uncle Rocco." She shrugs, leaning her head on Rad's shoulder. "Not my daddy."

I'm not the only one she's got in her grasp. They all look at Lyric the same way, like she's the sun in the sky, shining on their day and warming their hearts. Adding my—our—daughter to the equation brings hope to our situation. Finally, something positive rests on the horizon for Whispered Words. Not just for us as a band; it's for us as a whole. Rad. Callum. Asher. Kieran.

"Uncle?" I ask curiously, raising a brow.

"That fuc–uh, that big tool took River on a date Saturday!" he grits out in a quiet voice, with anger lacing his tone. A possessive light streaks in his eyes. My damn face twists.

"And you?" I question, keeping it as vague as possible.

"Jesus," Callum mumbles, pinching the bridge of his nose. "Stalked her to the restaurant and made his presence known."

Asher and I blink at Rad like he's lost his goddamn mind. Again. He's pulled some stunts in the past. But this? My heart fucking twists at the implications. When Rad wants something, he goes after it in full force without looking back. He's really doing this again without knowing the whole picture. How can he do that?

"Shh, little ears." Rad points down to Lyric in his lap, greedily sucking in the cotton candy as a bluish tint stains her lips and chin, leaving the evidence of her sweet treat behind.

"Avoiding the conversation," Asher notes, crossing his arms over his chest with a huff.

"Does Uncle Rocco spend the night with your mommy?" Rad questions in a gentle tone, brushing her long strands of hair away from the sticky mess.

Lyric snorts, eating the last of her cotton candy. Handing Rad the spit-soaked tube, she nods. "Only when they drink too much grown-up juice." Rad stiffens, narrowing his eyes out the window.

"Time to go," he says, heaving Lyric into his arms. She giggles when he twists her around and puts her on his back. Her tiny arms wrap around his neck, and her legs secure around his middle.

"Go?" I ask with a grimace.

"Are you seriously going to..." I blink several times, talking to Rad's back when he turns, and fucking walks out.

"Yeah, he's gone," Callum grumbles, marching after him out the front door with determination, ready to catch the blazing idiot.

"What the fuck?" My eyes connect with Asher's. He shrugs, grimacing.

"You assholes coming?" Rad shouts from outside, seeming so far away. "We've got some investigating to do!"

"Guess we should?" I ask, motioning toward the door.

Asher and I walk side-by-side, catching up to Rad and Callum in the middle of the road between our houses.

"Anything to stop this train wreck," Asher mumbles, swiping a hand down his face.

Before I can stop anything from happening, Rad practically breaks down River's front door, taking a step inside.

"What the hell is he doing here?" Rad growls, pointing directly at the mysterious man who has sleepovers with River. Innocently, he holds his hands up in a placating manner and steps back.

"Fancy seeing you here, Mullet," the man says with a cocky grin, laughing under his breath when Rad growls in his direction.

"Uncle Rocco!" Lyric squeals, jumping down off Rad's back. Running full force, she jumps into Rocco's arms, wrapping her arms around his neck.

"My monster godchild," he rumbles, squeezing her tight with love. He kisses the side of her temple, eyeing us with an inspecting glare. I recognize the protectiveness he exudes, filling the room with his warning. *Don't fuck with his girls.* "Did you have a good time with your fathers? Oh, what's that?" he questions with a smile, swiping at the blue on her lips.

"Cotton candy," she mumbles shyly with glee.

"Cotton candy?" River questions, weakly raising a brow.

My gaze wanders to her, inspecting the paleness spreading across her flesh. Those moss-green eyes glaze over with sickness, begging her to return to bed and rest some more. Her entire body sags with exhaustion when she rubs her fingers across her forehead.

"She only had one," I amend with a tight smile. "I bought it..."

"You bought it?"

I shrug, rubbing the back of my neck. "Wasn't planned, but we didn't have anything else. She ate lunch before it."

River purses her lips, sighing heavily. "Did you have fun, Ly?" she asks, running a finger down Lyric's leg, getting her attention.

"So much!" she grins, climbing from Rocco's embrace. "We ate cotton candy and hamburgers. Daddy Callum showed me his art. Daddy Rad said bad words." She wrinkles her nose.

I snort when Rad turns beet red and throws his hands up. "Sorry, Little Pretty Girl. Not used to such tiny ears being around all the time." He winks at her, earning a smile.

"Well. It was very nice to meet you, gentlemen. I expect my girls to be in good hands if I take off and return to my husband," Rocco says, scooping up a large, empty container and his car keys. His eyes bounce around to our faces until we're nodding in understanding. He's laid it out clearly to us; he's not a threat to whatever the fuck this is now. "Good. I shall take my leave. Get well, Doll. And remember what I said." He raises a brow, earning the stink eye from River. I can't help the smile that pulls at my lips at her defiance.

"Thanks for the soup. Kiss Christian for me," she mutters when he kisses her temple, much to the unhappy sounds escaping Rad's throat like a possessive idiot.

"You've got it, Doll." Coming to stand right before us, he reaches a hand out and clasps my hand in a gentle handshake. Peering over his shoulder, he confirms River is locked in a deep conversation about cotton candy with Lyric before he speaks next. "It's been a long road for them. You understand? She's endured a lot. My unsolicited advice?" He eyes my face and the other guys who crowd in, reluctantly listening to this strange man in River's house. "Listen to her. Breathe her damn words. Reevaluate whatever is going through each of your minds. Have an open heart. And if this isn't something for you, walk away and never look back. Disappear into the fucking darkness. Go back to where you fucking came from. Once you fully commit to them—to Lyric. There's no walking away. Fix what you broke or forever leave it in shambles so they can repair themselves." He raises a poetic brow, taking his hand back.

We don't say a word when he slips between us. Or when he starts up his car and drives away slowly, leaving us with his parting words.

Fix what you broke.

Determination lifts me in its grasp, choking me without a single thought of leaving this. Lyric is my daughter. My flesh and fucking blood, hidden from me. River was once my best friend— the love of my life. Every action from the past comes back, forcing me to relive our memories in vivid color. My River Blue isn't the same girl I left in Central City. There's an edge to her now. Because we broke her. We walked the fuck away without ever knowing the truth. God. How could I have been so damn stupid to just leave her without uttering a word? I'm confident now that the truth will come to light. It always does. No matter what happened in the past, River is ours now.

Lyric is ours.

21
Kieran

"LAY YOUR HEAD DOWN, PRETTY GIRL," Rad demands, running his hands through River's hair. To her credit, she mumbles her disagreement as he forces her head into his lap.

"Rad," she hisses, squeezing her eyes shut, looking white as a ghost.

"You're making it worse," Callum grumbles, swatting him in the back of the head. Rad shoots him a cutting glare. "You good?" he asks softly, looking down at her where she begrudgingly rests her head on Rad's thighs.

Shaking my head, I rest on the couch opposite them. Nerves prickle beneath my skin. This is our moment. The desperate need for answers hangs in the back of my mind, nagging me to figure it out. We all crowd around her living room, waiting with bated breath for the conversation we've been anticipating.

"I'm fine. I guess," she mumbles, situating herself on the couch better as Callum sits beside her feet. Swallowing hard, he glances up and down her body with a concerned look. His fingers twitch, but he stops himself from touching her.

"It'll be okay, Pretty Girl. We'll care for you and Lyric while you're not feeling good. Do you need any more soup? Crackers? 7-Up? Or—" Rad frowns when she blindly puts her hand over his mouth, effectively shutting him up. Thank God. He babbles when he's fucking nervous, and right now, his voice grates on my nerves.

"I'm fine," she reiterates with a sigh, forcing herself out of Rad's lap. Running a hand through her matted brown locks, she wearily looks around the room, taking the three of us in. "Thanks for today," she mutters. "I appreciate you guys jumping up and helping me with Lyric."

"She came to our door," I say gruffly, taking a deep breath.

All the frustrations boil to the surface after being swallowed for so long. It's getting harder and harder not to show my frustrations physically.

She grimaces. "She knew where you lived."

"And who we are," I grunt, jumping. My fingers grip the roots of my hair as I pace back and forth opposite them. Don't freak the fuck out on her now. You can't be an asshole when you need to stay calm.

"Dude," Rad warns, standing up from the couch with a frown.

"Don't dude me. My daughter knew exactly who I was, but I didn't know about her. I didn't even know she fucking existed," I say in a low voice, gritting my teeth through every word.

The last thing I want to do is rile Lyric up as Asher reads to her just down the hallway, preparing her for bed—something I should have done every night for the last four years of her life. I've missed so much of her growing up, and I don't want to waste another minute without knowing it all.

"We don't have to do this right now. River is sick," Callum says, shaking his head. "We can do this when you feel better," he says, looking directly into River's eyes.

"No," she says, swallowing hard. "Let it all out," she says, waving a hand in my direction.

"Why did she know who we are?" I ask, stopping and towering above her. "Why, River Blue?" All the rage turns to desperation, leaking into my tone. It catches in my tightening throat.

"Because, even after you left, I wanted her to know where she came from. Even after you denied her and..."

"Denied her?" I gape, leaning over her body and forcing her head against the couch. Our eyes lock in an intense battle. "You know me better than that. Or at least you did. I'd never in my fucking life deny my child. Ever," I growl, curling my fists at my side.

River sighs with exhaustion, closing her eyes. The selfless part of me wants to walk away and let her rest more. She's been ill all night and day. But the answers I've been desperate for since the first knock have me prodding further. There's an incessant need gnawing at the back of my mind, desperately searching for an answer.

"That's what we tried to tell her." Rad grimaces in pain, shaking his head. "Tell him, Pretty Girl. Tell him the whole story. Please."

She cracks an eye open, promptly rolling it in his direction. "The whole story?" she rasps. Her jaw tightens, pulling the rest of her face into a tense expression. "Where to begin? Like the fact I ran to Callum's house, only to be greeted by your mother." I tense, jerking back like I've been slapped, but she continues. "You can be pissed off at me all you want, but I've already told the other three the entire story. You knocked me up over the dining room table on our little vacation. Not only did you ghost me after my mom fucking died, but you also left me. You fucking—You fucking promised me that you'd take me with you. That—" Her eyes squeeze shut, holding back the emotions boiling to the surface. Anger roars through her system, twisting her expression until she uses all her strength and climbs to her feet. Her painted red nail pokes into my heaving chest. "You assfaces left me when I needed you the fucking most. My mom died, and where were you? Winning Battle of the fucking Bands. I mean, fucking good for you," she grits out with a bitter laugh. "Good for you for living your dream. But what about me? What about what I needed? You left me like I was nothing more than trash on the curb."

"What the fuck about my mother?" I ask, gripping her finger in my fist, squeezing it gently so she can't back away from me.

"Oh, that bitch," River snaps, trying to yank her hand away from me. "I drove to Callum's with this fucking secret. I needed you—all of you," she cries out, trying harder this time. I eye Rad and Callum as they move to her sides, wrapping their arms around her until she stops fighting me. Angry tears pour down her face, and she shakes her head. "I was pregnant, and all I got were restraining orders and a nice check to 'get rid of the problem.'"

"What?" I breathe, shaking my head. No. No. No. That's not what I would ever fucking want. How could Gloria do all that shit behind my back and not fucking tell me?

"She called you right in front of me. Called you by name. Said you didn't want the baby. You said it was probably Van's," she says through gritted teeth as a fire erupts behind her heated eyes. "Said you wanted me to get rid of it! How could you?" she breathes the last part, staring daggers in my direction.

"I didn't." Words fucking fail me as I stare at the hurt encasing her every movement. "I didn't fucking know, River. I swear to all fucking things holy that I had no clue Lyric existed. Gloria didn't fucking call me. Not then. No, she called me weeks later and told me about you. But she-she said it was Van's baby and that you... That you...." I suck in a breath as the world I've built around me deteriorates. The thick lies that built me crumble in the burning flames of truth, turning to white ash.

"But you still left," she whispers so lightly I have to strain to listen. "You still fucking left me. You left her. You didn't even come and talk to me. You didn't even check on me to see how I was doing." River shakes her head again, shrugging all of us off of her. With a deep breath, she stops a few feet away from us. Her glossy moss-green eyes drag up and down our stunned expressions. "How could you? You were my best friend. You left me once, and I thought maybe it wouldn't happen again. But you left me."

"But Van?" My heart pounds when her face morphs into disgust. "That video. That kiss Callum caught on camera. You-you—" I trail off, losing myself in past events that have haunted me.

"Right. You're convinced I cheated on you. Is that why you turned your back on me?" She crosses her arms across her chest. "Is that really what you believe? I don't know why in the fuck—"

"It was me." The world ceases to turn as those three guilt-ridden words wrap around the four of us arguing in the living room, cutting off our voices.

I blink several times as his words sit heavily on my chest. Turning to Asher, who stands stoically across the room with tears flowing down his pale cheeks, I shake my head.

Asher's been through hell in his life. I've watched Nigel beat the fuck out of him, throw him across the room, and stomp on his ribs. All the while, Asher never made a sound. Tears never came. Not even as an adult. Asher's a fortress, holding his emotions prisoner in those walls.

So, to see the tears welling up and falling down his cheeks like rain cascading down the windows has me flinching back.

"What do you mean?" Every muscle in my body tightens at his words.

"What was you?" Rad asks tersely, balling his hands into white-knuckled fists.

"What the fu-fuck did you do?" Callum shouts brokenly, staring at Asher with wide eyes. He shakes his head several times, stumbling back onto the couch with a ghostly expression like he's figured it out. It only takes a second for reality to take hold of Callum. He stands on silent feet, cracking his knuckles. A deadly expression thunders across his face, and he snarls in Asher's direction with such malice my balls shrivel. "You fucking asshole!" Callum growls through clenched teeth.

"It was me. I did it. I..." He heaves a breath.

"What do you mean?" River asks, taking a tentative step toward him, cautiously approaching like he's a wild animal about to bolt. "You did it? What did you—" her words trail off, staring at him in disbelief.

Wiping a hand down his face, he pushes all the tears dripping down his cheeks away. "River didn't cheat on you. She never touched Van. Even when you went to find her," he says, throwing an arm in Callum's direction.

"What in the ever-living fuck are you talking about?" Rad shouts through clenched teeth.

"You were all so content with staying behind!" he sputters, stumbling back into the wall. Through vigorous head shakes, he finally settles his eyes on the ceiling. "That night at the castle house on the damn lake, you told her you'd stay behind for her. You said you'd drop the Battle of the Bands until she could come with—" His lip trembles until he covers it with his hand. "I couldn't let that happen. This was our destiny, and I was afraid."

"No, you fucking didn't," Rad says through a shallow breath, disbelief pulling his lips open.

"Looking back, it's the stupidest fucking thing I've ever done. And I'm so damn sorry! But I was so goddamn desperate to get away from my father and live our dream. I couldn't stay in Central City. This was it—my only chance. You remember what he was like, right?" Asher's chest heaves when his sorrow-filled eyes connect with mine, but thankfully, he doesn't go into full detail about our abuse at the hands of his father.

"Of fucking course, I remember how he was. But that... That doesn't fucking..."

"What the hell is going on right now?" River mutters, looking around the room, slightly shaking her head. "What exactly are you trying to say?"

"Explain!" I bark, taking a step forward with urgency, slamming into the front of his body. "Explain every fucking thing you did!" My fingers curl on the front of his shirt, pulling him forward so he can't lie to my damn face. "What. Did. You. Do?" I growl, pushing my face into his. "Asher!" I shout again.

"I set it up!" he gasps out, slamming his eyes shut. "The videos were old. River didn't sleep with Van. He sent them to me because I asked him to. I had to convince you guys—" He doesn't get to utter another word when my fist slams straight into the side of his head, knocking him back from me, but I cling on by the scruff of his shirt, keeping him within striking distance.

"You what?" River breathes, going completely still. Her mouth falls open, eyeing Asher as he sways on his feet. If it's humanly possible, all the color drains from her body. A twisted look of betrayal and horror takes over her features, and she shakes her head. "Why would you ask him to send you old sex tapes that I didn't even know existed?" River's words stammer together. Sharp shivers run through her body until she's trembling uncontrollably. Her knees knock together, and her breaths saw in and out of her flaring nostrils.

"Pretty Girl," Rad rushes to her side, throwing an arm over her shoulders. "I got you," he whispers, holding her tightly to his side and kissing her head tenderly.

"Here," Callum grunts through his anger, handing Rad a blanket to drape over her shoulders. Quickly, he drops a kiss on her temple, freezing there for a millisecond before his eyes flash to Asher.

A ringing forms in my ears, cutting off the noise around me. Asher set it all up. He led us to believe a big fucking lie. One that's destroyed every piece of not only us as people but the goddamn band. My gut lurches, threatening to spill my damn dinner. Colors blur around me. Everything swerves out of fucking focus.

"What was real? Was anything you said that night real? Did —" A knot forms in my stomach. "We left her for no reason?" My tongue dries up, sticking to the roof of my mouth. "We left River... My daughter... We left everything..."

My face falls at the realization. All the fucking hate in my heart for the woman I loved was false. I was misled into believing all these radical bullshit lies. I've treated her like utter shit since we reconnected because I was under the assumption she cheated on me and fucking deceived me when the snake in the grass was my own damn brother.

"You fucking snake," I hiss, stumbling back.

"How could you?" Callum says, breaking the silence with a low growl. "We fucking loved her, and you knew it! You fucking knew how we felt, and you...you took that from us!" Callum's fingers ball into fists, and his body vibrates with pent-up anger. "How could you fucking do that to us?" He shudders, stomping forward. Before I can stop him, his fist connects with Asher's nose once and then his ribs. Blood spurts from his face, dribbling down his lips and chin. The more hits that come his way, the less he blocks and takes the pain. "We lost five years with River and our daughter. All her firsts! All her...everything!! Because of you," he grunts, slamming his fist into his cheek and knocking him to the side. "We lost the most precious gift on the planet."

"Stop," I grunt, pulling Cal back before he fucking kills the little snake. Not that I don't want to obliterate him. He deserves every fucking piece of pain doled out to him in retribution.

"I'm sorry," Asher wheezes, clutching his side. His eyes squeeze shut, leaning against the wall for support. "I thought...I was doing the right thing. I thought I was saving us," he says, taking painful puffs of oxygen.

"Saving us?" Rad rasps through his emotions, still clutching River as her eyes glaze over. "How would you be saving us?"

Asher blinks several times through the pain ricocheting through his body. Good. He fucking deserves it. Fucking deserves the pain and resentment and fucking hate we feel.

"I was so fucking stupid," he gasps out, cringing from the pain when he tries to straighten out his spine. "And selfish. I know

I was. I've been carrying this around for years, and it's been killing me."

"That doesn't fucking absolve you of your goddamn crimes," Callum growls, tracing the carnage he left behind with his fierce eyes.

"I can't believe you," I say, shaking my head. "You're a fucking manipulative dickbag!"

"What about the restraining orders?" Rad asks, pulling River's trembling body into his.

"That wasn't me," Asher whimpers, grimacing when he tries to reposition himself. "That was all Gloria."

"Gloria?"

"She started it," he whispers with a voice filled with shame and regret. "She came to me and offered me money. She even told me about Van and the tapes. She...she told me everything."

"Money?" Callum growls.

"How much was your betrayal worth?" I shout, filling the room with my voice.

"Keep it down," Rad chastises, nodding toward the wall separating us from our sleeping daughter.

"How much?" I growl, lowering my voice. No matter how angry I am, I don't want to startle the little girl sleeping just down the hall.

"It wasn't just the money," he wheezes. "It was a way to get us away from Nigel. Away from that fucking house!" he grits out like that justifies his actions.

"How much fucking money did you take to pull your betrayal off?" Callum grits out, flexing his fingers again.

"Five grand and a promise to keep Nigel out of it." His eyes squeeze shut again, sucking in air. "And a promise to leave her behind," he whispers so softly I almost miss the implication.

"You fucking weasel!" I bark, stomping toward him and taking him by the shirt again. "You made a goddamn deal with the devil and lied to us about everything!" My fist tightens again, ready for another round of bashing the asshole who lied.

"Stop," River says, clearing her throat. We all watch as she slowly walks forward, eyeing Asher with apprehension. Standing before him, her lips curl. "Did you send Van to my apartment?" she whispers, almost in shock.

"Yes. I knew they'd go to you, so I had to have a backup plan to leave. I—" Asher's face jerks to the side when River slaps him across the face, leaving behind her handprint.

"River Blue," I whisper, pulling her trembling body into mine. From behind, Callum touches her shoulder with reassurance. A worried look twists his face as he stares at the girl he once deeply loved, so much so that he trusted her with his virginity.

She shakes her head against my chest, burying her face in my shirt before pulling away with flaring nostrils. Anger rests behind her glossy moss-green eyes, ready to burn down the world.

"How could you?" she accuses sharply, balling her fingers into a fist. "How fucking dare you do that to me and send him to my fucking apartment." She shakes her head in disgust, curling her lip back.

"You'll never know how fucking sorry I am," he gasps again. "I was a stupid fucking idiot. Please believe me when I say I'm so fucking sorry. I know—" He cuts off, bending out the waist and crying out in pain. "I know I fucked up so fucking hard." Tears roll down his cheeks in rapid succession. Whether it's from the pain or the deep regret, I don't fucking care. He took everything from us when he went behind our backs and fucked us over. "Please," he whispers, looking at River. "Please don't take her away from me."

"How fucking dare you!" I growl, making a move toward him again.

"Stop," River says, putting a shaking hand on my chest, which I promptly grasp. "No more violence. Not here. Not when she could walk out of here and see this. I'd like you all to leave now."

"Don't fucking come to the band house," Callum growls. "I'll bury you," he promises, curling his lips back and baring his teeth before stomping off and slamming through the front door. Two seconds later, his bike roars to life, accelerating toward the gate.

"Fuck," Rad mumbles, pinching his nose. "He'll be at Ruthless's fucking ring in two seconds." His eyes whip to Asher, who collapses to the floor and leans against the wall. "I love you, Pretty Girl. I've never loved someone as much as I love you. No matter the pain I felt when I thought...thought you hurt me. I'm sorry. I know I've said it before, but I am," Rad mumbles without a second thought, leaning down to kiss her cheek. She startles at his confession but relaxes in his touch. Good. That's a good fucking sign for us. We can make it up to her one day at a time. "I'll leave and take him with me. Call us if you need anything, okay? You're still sick as fuck." He kisses her temple again, reluctantly peeling himself away. As he passes me, he grabs my arm and jerks me back.

"You get the fuck out of here," I spit, trying to advance on Asher.

"I'll take care of it," River says, holding my arm. "Give me some space, okay? I'll see you guys tomorrow for your band practice. We still need to keep up with it."

"Not with him!" I grunt, cupping the side of her face. Searching her eyes, I swallow hard. "I'm sorry, River Blue. I'm so fucking sorry I didn't try hard enough to get to you. I'm so sorry I didn't talk to you. I'm so fucking sorry I walked away. Again. That's on me. Every fucking mistake I made that led here is my fault. But I promise that every day from here on out, I'll be here. For you. And for her. I want to get the chance to be a real dad and someone worthy of you," I whisper through the burning lump in my throat. Leaning forward, I press my lips to her cheek, savoring the feel of her skin beneath mine. She's still as soft and beautiful as I remember. "I'll work my ass off to prove to you that I'm your Knight again."

With those parting words, I let Rad drag me out of the house. Leaving River with my stupid, broken ex-brother. My heart aches from his confession. Rage. Fucking betrayal. Every emotion rushes through me. How fucking could he? He took our blind trust in him and used it against us.

As I lie in bed that night, sleeplessly staring at the ceiling, I make a vow. A vow to be the man I promised River I would be years ago—her worthy Knight.

22

Asher

PRESSING my fist to my lips, I cover up the pain-filled whimpers trying to escape. Leaning my head back against the wall I'm slumped against, I squeeze my eyes shut. The truth finally set me fucking free from the lies I cultivated so damn easily. The guilt that gnawed at me for the past five years ebbs away—no longer sitting heavy on my chest, aching to spill the beans. The burn still sears through me, but it's muted slightly, overturned by the new demand to make the situation right. Driving me to jump head-first into the churning ocean of my betrayal and mend what the fuck I broke. For the first time in years, I can breathe fresh oxygen. Metaphorically, of course.

Pain ricochets through my whole damn body, bouncing around every place; Callum and Kieran's fists pounded into me. Rightfully so. Every punch they rained down on me was penance for my unforgivable sin—my betrayal of the only family I could ever count on.

I'm such a worthless asshole, undeserving of so many things.

I groan, sitting perfectly still inside River's house. At any moment, I know she will kick me to the damn curb. As I deserve, I know that. Who would have sympathy for the likes of me? A traitorous dickbag who couldn't handle a woman coming between his other band members. Definitely not her. Not that I blame her one bit.

But where the hell do I go? I could go back to my townhouse on the other side of the city and sit in my damn misery by my lonesome, letting it swallow me whole. If it comes down to it, that's my only option. Kieran, Callum, and Rad would obliterate me before they let me back in that house. Fuck.

"Here." Peeking an eye open, I stare at the blurry slender hand in front of my face, blinking until it's entirely in focus. "Let's get you on the couch," she says softly, wiggling her fingers. Pain still fills her eyes from my confession, but she's extending a small olive branch despite it all.

"Why?" I grunt, shifting on the floor. "I can leave."

"You could. Or you could take my hand," River snarks, wiggling her fingers again. "It's not that hard, Evil Ash," she murmurs my old nickname with a pained expression.

"Thank you," I mutter, reluctantly grasping her hand and letting her pull me to my aching feet. Violent pain shudders through my body when I stumble up, gasping for air. "Shit," I wheeze again, clutching my ribs with urgency. With every move I make, my ribs splinter like they're about to break and spear me in the lungs. River has the patience of a saint as she slowly leads me to the couch and helps me sit on the edge.

"Let me get you some ice," she says through a heavy sigh, retreating quickly into the kitchen. Coming back, she gently lays a soft ice pack on my swelling eye and hands me two pain pills with a bottle of water.

"Thanks," I rasp. "But I don't understand why you're taking care of me. I expected—" Rage. Hate. Heated words. Anything but the pity in her eyes. Fuck. I want her anger or fists or anything but her kindness because I don't deserve an ounce of understanding.

"For me to kick you out in this state? You look like shit." She raises a brow, settling on an ottoman across from me, leaning her elbows on her knees. Her eyes track my movements as I settle on the couch, trying to get comfortable and not hurt my ribs more.

"After what I did—" I trail off, averting my eyes to my lap in shame. "Why're you helping me now? I screwed you over so fucking royally." Deep remorse once again turns my stomach into knots.

"Yeah, you did," she agrees, running a hand down her face. "You really went behind my back and used my obsessive ex against me. He forced himself on me, Asher. Van marched into my kitchen and took what he wanted."

"Fuck," I heave, squeezing my eyes shut. My stomach rolls at the idea of him waltzing into her house and doing that. She didn't deserve that shit. Not again. "I'm so fucking sorry he did that. I'm sorry I went to him and trusted him to help me." If I could build a time machine, I'd go back in time and kick myself in the balls.

River gives me a blank look, blinking several times. "You forced them to walk away from me." Pain laces every inch of her words like that was the worse offense. Dropping her head back, she stares at the ceiling and releases a breath. "But I can't believe I'm fucking saying this—I get it. I don't know what the hell your home life was like—"

"You see this right here?" I ask, cutting her sentence off and pulling up my pant leg. Drawing her eyes to the thin surgery scar on my ankle, she nods, inspecting it as my finger rubs up and down the raised skin. I take a deep breath, losing myself in the awful memory of my father's rage.

"Stay down there until you learn your lesson!" Tears prickle at *my eyes, staring up the long, dark staircase at my father's massive figure. Agony spears through my twisted ankle, instantly ballooning out. "Worthless," he snarls, shutting the basement door behind him, leaving me with only my pain, tormented thoughts, and pure darkness.*

Goosebumps prickle at my skin. My heart rate accelerates and sweat glistens on my skin from the vivid video-like memory roaring through my mind. Swallowing hard, I shove it all down, trying to forget. What my father put me through was nothing a child should have endured. Yet, I did—we did. Kieran and I have been on the battlefield together, forging our bond through our hellacious trauma. It's why we worked so damn hard to keep him away from Cami. Even if it meant more punches and punishment, she was safe.

"My father had this insane rule of being seen—not heard. I was seven and dropped a glass while trying to get some milk—" My breath shudders, jumping back in time to when I was a scared seven-year-old kid with wide eyes, looking down at the remnants of my glass shattered on the ground. "All I wanted was a little drink before I went to bed, but he heard. Stormed out of his office with this rage-filled face. He scooped me up, yelling profanities in my face, and then—" I swallow hard, squeezing my eyes shut. A slight tremble takes over my fingers, still mindlessly tracing over my scar. "He opened the basement door and threw me down the stairs. I hit every fucking step on the way down and finally landed at the bottom with a twisted foot. The agony was so fucking real. My foot was on fire, and then...he just shut the door and told me I could come out when I learned how to be quiet."

"Jesus fucking Christ," River mumbles, turning a sickly green. My stomach bottoms out when sorrow shines in her wide eyes.

"Yeah," I say, clearing my throat. "I'm not telling you that for any sort of pity. I just want to help you understand why I was so fucking desperate to leave Central City." I lick my lips, taking a big breath. "I passed out on the ground, only waking when he forced me to my damn good foot. He yanked me up the stairs and told my nanny to take me to the hospital. He couldn't be bothered to care for me. After explaining that I had accidentally fallen down the stairs, I had to go to surgery. That hospital was my only reprieve from him. My father was a sick son of a bitch. He took his anger out on Kieran and me for years. He was going to make us follow in his footsteps." I shake my head again, groaning at the pain. "So, he gave our band a year to make it...and I was so fucking determined to get away. I wasn't going to let anything get in my damn way... Not even you," I whisper the last part, firmly shutting my eyes as the tears burn.

"So, that's why you hated me so much," she murmurs, breaking me out of my self-deprecating fog. "I was in your way of getting out of there."

I bark out a humorless laugh, shaking my aching head. "Quite the opposite, Little Brat," I rumble through the pain, cringing when my laugh sends pain through my ribs.

"So you didn't hate me?" she asks, raising a skeptical brow.

"It took me way too long to realize how I felt about you." Biting into my bottom lip, my body sags with the realization I've kept under wraps for so long. "I craved you just as much as the other three. But I fucking fought it. I fought everything about you because you scared me. No one in the history of the damn world, except my mom, had ever made me feel the way you did. So, I did what any asshole would do. I tucked my tail and ran the fuck away."

"But you still..." she trails off, shaking her head.

"Yeah, I still did. My fear led me down that road to do what I did. I was so desperate and scared that I let it get to me. I destroyed something so fucking beautiful because I was a selfish fucking bastard."

River blinks at me a few times, processing my words as silence engulfs us. "You can stay here tonight," she says, getting up and walking toward the freezer again. "Here, take another ice pack so your face doesn't swell too much."

"But why?" I whisper, holding tight to her wrist as she sets the new pack on my eye. "I don't understand."

She gives me a tight smile, takes her hand back, and sighs. "I'm not your karma, Asher. You have to face down what you've done. Do I forgive you for breaking my trust and putting a dangerous guy in my path? No. Not by a long shot. You'll have to earn that.

Somehow... But it's not me you have to get the most forgiveness from. It's them. They were your family—your brothers. But by the look on your face, you already know that. You've probably tortured yourself. Honestly, I don't understand how you've lived with yourself." She shakes her head, crossing her arms over her chest.

I snort. "Not very well. Sleepless nights. The heartburn. My fucking guilt ate away at every inch of me and having to face the guys I deceived so cruelly... Yeah, I fucking hate myself for what I did."

"It's a start," she says with a small shrug, taking a few steps away but stopping abruptly in the doorway. "It's for Lyric." Her tiny voice carries through the room, leaving a crater in my chest. "You're staying because she knows who you are, and I can't drag my kid away from her daddy. She already loves you, and I won't destroy that love by forcing you to leave."

"Thank you," I breathe in relief. "I know I'm a big fucking disappointment, but I want to...I want to be there for her for everything. Now that I know... River, thank you for giving me a chance to prove myself to her."

She nods a few times. "Just don't break her heart like you broke mine," she whispers, leaving the living room altogether.

"I won't," I vow to no one, sinking further into the couch and trying to get comfortable despite the pain pulsating through my body.

From this day forward, I'll be the best version of myself for Lyric. For a chance to fix things with River and the guys. I'll never keep another secret again.

For a chance to prove I'm not the Asher Montgomery from five years ago. No more lies. No more secrets.

Just me.

The following morning, I startle awake at the sound of a sweet little voice in my ear. Her little fingers sweep down my broken face, tracing what I can only assume are bruises darkening my skin.

"Daddy. Oh, no," Lyrics mumbles softly, laying her head on my aching chest. "What happened? Did you get beat up?" her little voice shakes when I finally crack my eyes open and run a hand through her hair.

The darkness of the room greets me with the first hints of the sun rising in the sky. A heavy sigh rocks through me when I look at the clock on the wall, noting it's only six-thirty in the morning. Fuck. Way too damn early to be awake.

"I'm okay," I mumble, bracing her head against my chest in a soft hug. "Why're you up so early?" She hums in response to my question.

"But you're hurt," she mumbles through a crack in her voice. "You got a bruise right here," she says, poking my face and making me flinch away from her touch.

"I do," I say through a breathy laugh. "But I'll be okay," I whisper, kissing her head. Bringing myself into the seated position, I pull her into my lap, wrapping my arms around her. Despite the pain spearing through me, I settle her securely against me until she hugs me back with a relaxed sigh.

"What happened to you, Daddy?" she asks, blinking up at me.

"Just grown-up stuff. It's nothing, Little One," I say with a tight smile. "How are you this morning? Did you have good dreams?" She grins big and nods in response.

"I dreamed of pancakes. Daddy, I want pancakes," she whispers, batting her eyelashes at me. Well, who can deny those puppy dog eyes?

A laugh spills from my lips, and I nod. "Of course. Should we look? See if we have anything to make pancakes?" She beams, jumps off my lap, and drags me into the spacious kitchen.

"Here!" She points to an upper cabinet storing the pancake mix and grins when I pull it down with a pained groan.

"All right let's get to work," I say, smiling down at her beaming face.

Over the next thirty minutes, Lyric helps me mix the batter and oil the pan. She giggles with me, getting the mix all over her face and fingers. Our pancakes morph into weirdly shaped blobs rather than round.

"Taste good?" I ask when we sit together at the island on stools with plates in front of us.

"The bestest," she says, shoving a big piece of pancake into her mouth, sticky syrup hanging from her chin and sticking to her fingers.

"Well, looks like you made a big breakfast," River says, eyeing Lyric affectionately. A smile grows across her lips when she kisses Lyric's head as she walks by.

"Me and Daddy made yummy pancakes!" She giggles around another bite, humming with satisfaction.

Whenever she says Daddy to me, I swear joyous butterflies burst in my damn soul. A smile creeps across my lips when Lyric side-eyes me with a giddy giggle, tearing into another misshapen pancake.

"There's plenty more," I softly say, nodding toward the plate on the stove filled to the brim with pancakes.

River's brows rise as she pulls a plate and coffee cup from the cupboard. "I didn't know you could cook," she says, plopping a few on her plate and pouring some syrup.

I shrug. "I learned to do a lot of things myself as a kid. My father went through a lot of nannies and eventually left me to my own devices at eight. Well, until Gloria came into the picture with Kieran." I swallow hard, finding relief flooding me as all the pent-up childhood memories flood out my mouth unbidden.

"Ly, I think it's about time for you to wash your hands and get dressed for school," River says, scoping up Lyric's empty plate.

"I'm sick," Lyric says, frowning when her mom takes her plate away and sets it in the sink.

River snorts. "I don't think so, missy. Up. Dressed. School.

We have ten minutes." She raises a brow when Lyric stubbornly crosses her arms over her chest and pouts with a little huff of annoyance.

"But I want to stay with Daddy," she grumbles, stomping her feet.

"Better get to it, Little One. Daddy will be around later, okay?" I say, ruffling her ratty dark locks, earning a huff.

"It's a never-ending cycle," River sighs, watching Lyric's retreating back as she scurries down the hall and slams her bedroom door shut with a heavy thud.

"Does she fight it every day?" I grunt, grabbing my plate. Stiffly, I shuffle to the sink and clean our plates off.

"Since the day she started preschool. I've asked her why she dislikes going, but she says she's bored and the youngest one there. I just hope it's nothing like bullying or anything else. She seems happy in the classroom. At least that's what her teacher says. I don't know." She shakes her head, heaving a frustrated sigh. "So, every day, we have this argument," she hums softly, looking toward the hallways as little steps come our way.

"Ready!" Lyric announces through a big grin, marching into the living room ten minutes later, wearing a little frilly blue dress, leggings, and flat black shoes with bows on them. Her once ratty hair is brushed out, and her face is clean of the evidence of our sticky breakfast.

I can't help but smile at her when she proudly beams up at me.

"You look beautiful," I say with pride.

"Thanks, Daddy!" she says, throwing her arms around my waist. "Are you coming to take me to school today?" she asks, batting those damn eyelashes again, wrapping me further around her damn finger. My eyes flick to River, and she nods without reluctance. "Let's get you to school," I whisper, bending and kissing her cheek, reveling in her tightening hug and happy squeal of delight.

I swallow hard when she lets go and takes off, grabbing her

backpack and slinging it over her shoulder. Without waiting for us, she marches out the front door toward River's SUV in the driveway.

"Thanks for letting me tag along," I say, clearing my throat as we step out into the warm morning sunlight beaming down on us. Momentarily, I lift my face toward the sun, soaking in the day's warmth and basking in its refreshing glory. Today is a new damn day, and I am a new man.

After locking her front door, River turns to me, shrugging. "I told you I won't keep her away from you. You're her father as much as the other three are." Her brows furrow when she digs into her pocket and brings her phone out. Tapping a few times, she opens something, and her body freezes. A slight tremble takes over her hands as she scrolls up on her phone and leans in with a horrified look crossing her face. A ghostly white complexion drains the color from her face, and her eyes widen almost in fear as her eyes rapidly move across the screen.

"What's wrong?" I ask sharply, stepping closer and putting a hand on her stiff shoulder. "River?" Gently, I squeeze, coaxing her out of whatever trance she had been put in.

Her eyes widen when she takes me in, realizing she's been stuck on the porch for a solid minute. With a head shake, she brushes off my touch with a tense smile.

"N-nothing," she stammers, unsteadily taking off toward the vehicle. "I'm fine."

I furrow my brows when she shakily gets into the driver's seat, heaving a few breaths until I follow and get into the car. Yeah, fucking right. It's not nothing. Something spooked her, and I'm determined to find the cause. Whether she likes it or not.

As we drive toward the school, worry eats away at me. River doesn't say a word about what happened. She talks back to Lyric, who excitedly chatters away about anything and everything she can think of, avoiding my quizzical gaze. After about ten minutes, we arrive at Lyric's school and drop her off at the drop-off line. As

Lyric exits the car, she grins at me through the window, waving as her teacher takes her hand. I watch with rapt attention when she stands in line by the school door, chatting with a little boy.

"Who is that?" I mumble, pointing to the little boy, throwing his arm around Lyric's shoulders with a grin. He lights up at the sight of her.

River snorts. "That would be her boyfriend. Oh, and that one, too. It seems she's collecting boys."

"Wait! What?" I hiss, staring at the two boys walking Lyric into the building with grins on their faces. "No fucking way," I grunt, attempting to open the door. "River." I narrow my eyes at her, but she scoffs, driving off.

"Nope. Leave her alone. She'll grow out of it. Besides, you'd be a hypocrite." I frown, sit back in the seat, and stare out the window as the horizon blurs by.

"I guess," I murmur, sucking in a breath as I look at the time. "So, will you tell me what freaked you out back home?" I ask, raising a brow when she drives up her long driveway and parks in front of the band house.

"No," is her simple answer as the locks disengage, and she stares over at me expectantly. "It's time to face the music," she says, waving toward the house. "I have an errand to run. I'll be a little late."

"Does it have to do with the text, email, or whatever you got?" Stalling. I'm fucking stalling before I have to walk into that house and face the men I betrayed, too. River may go easy on me because I'm one of the fathers of her child, but they won't fucking care. They'll beat my fucking ass again. Not that I don't deserve it.

Her lips roll in. "Yes," she says reluctantly. "I need to go take care of it. But you all have band practice in an hour. So, might as well tear off that Band-Aid."

I snort, staring up at the looming structure with apprehension. "Yeah. Like a Band-Aid," I mutter, nervously biting into my lip. "If I'm not here when you return, they've buried me somewhere or set me on fire. It's up to them, really," I quip, fighting through the nerves that are begging me to run the fuck away again.

But that's not me anymore. I don't run from the problems I created. I go at them headfirst, even if I'm about to die. Nothing but the truth moving forward.

"I'll make sure your obituary says something about how bullheaded and brave you are," she jokes with an edge to her voice.

"You sure you're—"

"You're stalling, Evil Ash. Get it over with or walk away. Talk to them. Do something other than avoiding the problem. If you leave this house by the time I return, I'll assume it was too much, and Whispered Words will be done with West Records. It's up to you to mend the brotherhood you snapped into pieces." Every word she speaks lights a fire under my ass, motivating me to walk up those stairs and face the guys who hate me more than anything now.

"You're right. Thanks," I say softly, opening the door and stepping out. "But whatever is bothering you, you know we'll help. We're here for you. Even after all this time."

"Thanks." She nods a few times and finally takes off, leaving my traitorous ass in the middle of the driveway.

"Well, well, well. Look what the cat dragged in. A lying, manipulative piece of shit," Kieran says from the porch, sipping a piping hot coffee.

I brace myself for the abuse from my brother and nod. "You're right," I say, lifting my chin. "But if I leave now, she's promised to rip up our contract. Either I'm here as a band member, or we're done as a band forever."

Kieran sits back in a patio chair, taking another sip, contemplating my words. "Don't expect those bruises to fade any time soon."

"Fine." I shrug, ready to take my punishments like a damn man.

"Good," Kieran says through a sadistic grin, standing from his chair. "Watch your back, Asher. You have no friends in this house anymore."

23

River.

"Jesus," Olivia mumbles, pacing alongside Carter's desk, chewing on her perfectly polished black nails. "These are it?" she asks, gesturing toward the screen Carter glares holes at with his vicious stare.

> **You're Mine.**
> **Make them leave.**
> **Or I will.**
> **You'll regret falling back into their arms.**
> **Again.**
> **Remember, I'm watching you, River Blue West.**
> **Always.**

"Just got them this morning." The chilling memory of the email coming through burned into my brain the moment I received them on the porch. It was on the tip of my tongue to tell Asher what was going on, but I knew I had to get to Olivia and Carter at Veritas first. They're my contacts with this whole situation.

"This is nuts," Olivia mumbles in disbelief. "You can't trace it?" She eyes Carter as he grunts, sitting behind his mahogany desk at the Veritas Headquarters, tapping away on his computer.

"No," he growls, scowling at the computer screen. "I don't know why it's doing this shit. It's fucking—"

"What?" Olivia asks, bending over to look at the screen. My heart drops when her eyes widen, but she shakes it off. Olivia can fool many people with her blasé attitude, but she can't fool me. I know her too well to see when she's internally freaking out. Even when her eyes dart to mine, and she locks her feelings up behind a tall brick wall—I know when she's scared. And right now, she's fucking terrified. It sends shivers down my spine and tightens my muscles.

"What? Am I in serious danger?" I ask in a low voice, nervously bouncing my leg.

"Don't fucking panic," Carter grunts, shoving Olivia from the screen.

"Yeah, that's what you tell a victim of stalking," she huffs, rolling her eyes. "Don't panic," she mocks his deep voice with a roll of her eyes.

Carter side-eyes her with an arctic glare, gritting his teeth so hard the veins in his jaw pop out. She doesn't seem to notice, though, probably used to his attitude since they've worked side-by-side for years. Olivia continues pacing the room without a retort, muttering about what an idiot Carter is.

"As I was saying," Carter grumbles, running a hand down his drooping face.

"Then what is it?" I interrupt in a panic, feeling like my heart is about to explode out of my chest.

Carter sighs, running a hand down his face. "Listen, Little West. We were able to trace the email."

"That's good news, right?" I ask with hope filling me.

"In normal circumstances, yes. But it's tracing back to your phone like it's coming directly from it. Like you sent it, and that's not fucking possible." Carter's eyes fill with sympathy, taking me back to the first time I got several Polaroids sent directly to my brothers at West Records. Carter came immediately, taking them from me to examine every inch of them for a clue. One he never found. Whoever they are, they've taken great care in keeping themselves hidden from detection—up until now, though.

"That doesn't make any sense," I breathe, feeling the walls closing in on me from all sides, ready to smother the breaths from my lungs. "There's no way that it could be coming from my phone. I didn't send it to myself." How could they— "Holy mother of fucking shit."

"What?" Olivia asks, crossing her arms.

"My phone... I just... I lost it and had to replace it. You don't think?" I stare at her with my mouth hanging open and thoughts swiftly moving through my brain at hyper speed.

Someone stole my fucking phone and used it against me. If they knew how to get into it, then they probably got into my security app, gained access to my cameras, and even worse—they came to my fucking sanctuary.

So, who the fuck did it? And why? I don't understand this person's obsession with me. I'm no one—just a woman trying to live her life to the fullest and raise my daughter right. It's insane to think someone would follow me, taking my picture from the shadows.

"You mean to fucking tell me you lost your goddamn phone? You have a stalker out there watching every move you make, and you just—"

"Shut the fuck up, Carter," Olivia growls, staring at him like he's the devil's spawn.

But his words. He's fucking right. I've been so naive in thinking my stalker would forever hold back and be happy taking pictures of me for the rest of my life. Stupid fucking idiot. I've watched that show where he follows the girl around, watching from the street through her windows. Jesus, if I end up in a plexiglass room—I'm murdering everyone.

"Listen, they've obviously spoofed your location and your new phone's IP address. We don't know how they're doing it, but we'll find out." Olivia's eyes shine with determination when she finally halts her pacing and slams a hand down onto the desk. "I swear, River. We will find out who has been doing this to you and throw their asses in jail."

I rub a finger over my temple, soothing the headache pounding in my skull. "But why now? It's never escalated like this. It's always been photographs of us in the mail. So, what has changed?" I can't for the life of me figure out what the hell has changed, bringing my stalker out of the woodwork.

"We're not for sure, but we have a theory," Olivia gripes, balling her fingers into a fist. "It seems whoever your stalker is, doesn't like the fact the guys are back in your life. Look at the x's over their faces. It's a clear sign they want them gone and away from you."

"Fuck," I mutter, swallowing the lump forming in my throat.

"Sorry, Little West. I'm keeping a close eye on it. Nothing is going to fucking happen to you. You fucking understand that?" Carter asks through gritted teeth, slowly rising to his feet. He looms over my seated body with a protective spark lighting in his eyes. "Keep vigilant. Lock your doors and keep your cameras on. Don't answer the door for strangers. How's your security holding up? I obviously need to have a fucking talk with the guards stationed at your house." He raises a brow, giving me a no-nonsense look.

I snort. "Yes, Dad. I still have my guard at the gate. I have video surveillance on the inside and outside of my house." I've done everything imaginable to protect Lyric and myself from harm, including building my house with a gate and off the beaten path. Fuck. "But...do you think it's going to get worse?" A thick knot of nerves twists in my stomach when they silently communicate with their eyes.

Finally, Olivia heaves a big breath and shrugs. "This isn't our area of expertise. But from what we've studied, stalkers never just disappear. We can only assume it's going to get worse, River."

"But you fucking have us, Little West. Veritas, your damn brothers, and even those assholes won't let anything happen to you. You've taken every precaution necessary to maintain your safety and Lyric's," Carter adamantly vows. "Besides, when you look over your shoulder now, you'll have a friend every step of the goddamn way. There's no way I'm letting you walk out of this room without a discreet security detail."

"I..."

"You will take my fucking gift, and you will like it. Tom will follow you everywhere. You won't even know he's fucking there half the time. Get the fuck over it. We're here to protect you and my little niece. I actually like your fucking faces. So..." he trails off after growling his words and clenches his fists.

"Okay," I say in agreement.

Olivia rests her hand on my shoulder, squeezing softly. Her comforting gesture does little to calm my rampant nerves running amok inside me. But it's nice knowing I have more people in my corner as this escalates.

"We got you, girl. You are being monitored. You are protected every step of the way; we will find this bastard and throw him in jail once and for all."

"I know you guys do. I appreciate all the help you've given me. Since this started three years ago, it's been hell. Never knowing who it is or if they're watching my every move. I'm just trying to live my damn life." I run my fingers over the crease of my forehead, worry gnawing at the back of my mind, trying to find solutions. "I just want to feel safe," I whisper, desperately seeking a life without the constant threat lurking behind me.

"We're on this twenty-four-seven. We won't rest until this stops. I fucking promise. Besides, your brothers will have my damn balls if I don't figure this out soon," he groans, glaring up at the ceiling.

"You're going to have to tell them," Olivia mutters, twisting her face when I give her the stink eye. "Don't give me that look. They're your neighbors. Your baby daddies, as you've so eloquently put it. She's in danger, too. They deserve to know what's going on."

"You're such a bitch sometimes," I quip with a huff, knowing she's right. It's wrong to keep them in the dark about my stalker, who is apparently stepping up their damn game and directly threatening them. But God, I can only imagine how that conversation will go. Cue the freaking out and demanding me to stick like glue to their sides, especially after our conversation yesterday. Dread fills every molecule inside me. This will fucking suck, but Lyric's safety is my number one priority.

Olivia laughs, settling in a chair beside me. Throwing an arm over my shoulders, she forcefully brings me closer to her as the chair digs into my side. "That's not the first or last time you've called me that."

"Definitely not the last." A grin breaks free for the first time in an hour, and I sigh. "Okay, well, I have to make sure my band is still alive," I mutter, wrinkling my nose at the prospect of entering the tension-filled band house. My imagination has run wild all morning since I dropped Asher off in the driveway. Will I find blood stains? More bruises? A repaired band? Yeah, that last one isn't possible right now. I'll have to give them more time and way more therapy to work through the betrayal that happened. Good thing it starts this week. Even I haven't forgiven any of them yet.

"Afraid they'll tear each other apart after Asher's confession?" Olivia asks, raising a brow in my direction.

After our enormous discussion last night, Olivia was the first person I called when I snuggled into bed. Talking to the guys about everything that happened opened ancient wounds, bringing more tears to my eyes. If it weren't for her, or the other three I call my best friends, I would have cried myself to sleep. Instead, I chatted with her, Ode, then Kaycee, while texting Rocco and snuggled with Lyric after tossing and turning.

"Want me to pound his face in, Little West? I could use an extra punching bag." What I would call a sadistic grin lights up his face at the prospect of beating Asher up.

"Jesus. Calm down, Killer. His ass whooping yesterday was punishment enough," I say, standing from my chair. "Now, I have to figure out how to get them past this. If they ever want to become a band again."

I shake my head, wracking my damn brain on how I can help

them move on from Asher's deceit. Not that it's going to happen easily. Hell, the only reason I didn't kick him to the curb was for Lyric. She's attached to each of them uniquely, and I can't break that bond or her little heart.

Carter deflates and mutters under his breath, finding his way back to his seat. With a grunt, he sits back down and rubs his chin. "Don't be a stranger. If you need a boy band to disappear without alerting the feds, I'm your guy."

Olivia scoffs, throwing a pen in his direction. "We are the feds, you asshole."

"Exactly. We won't be alerted," he quips, chuckling when she throws another pen at him.

"All right. Thanks, guys, for the help. If I get anything else, I'll let you know." Waving goodbye, I stroll out of Veritas' headquarters, making my way across town, hopefully walking into a band practice with little to no blood.

24

Callum

"WHERE'S RIVER?" Kieran asks with accusation, side-eyeing Asher.

Out of the corner of my eye, I watch with fascination as Asher heaves his guitar strap over his shoulder, gritting his teeth through the pain radiating from the wounds I caused him yesterday when we finally found out the truth of our situation.

Violence never used to be the answer to all my frustrations—music was. My bass was my relief. A way to step out of this world, dive straight into the music, to forget I'm a human walking this earth. Forgetting all the pain life has brought me at every damn step. When I lose myself in the music, I'm no longer Callum Rose —airplane crash survivor. I'm simply the bass player, strumming along to the beat of our creations—a no one with nothing stirring inside me but a constant heartbeat.

When I witnessed Van kissing River and what I thought was her reciprocating, I lost that special piece of me to the noise of the world. I let it take me over, becoming a no one without an escape. Every note and string reminded me of her. My River. My Little Star. Her smile. Her laugh. The ghost of my past constantly followed me, threatening to jump out at every corner. Much like my parents, she was dead to me. She may have had a heartbeat pumping blood through her veins, but she was as good as gone.

To push her existence out of my mind, I injected poison into my veins, falling victim to its intoxicating addiction. Once again, I found something to lose myself in for hours at a time, floating above the noisy world. It fogged my mind, subduing my wayward emotions threatening to spill out of me. With every hit I took, the more the edge seemed to loom in the distance, getting closer and closer until the drugs didn't do it for me anymore. I felt more, no matter the amount I took. It was either take more and fuck myself up badly or find something new to take my pain away.

Stumbling across the cage boss, Ruthless, in that empty alleyway outside some random bar was the best mistake I ever made.

"Yo, you're going to fuck up your fists if you keep trying to break the brick," the random voice rings in my ears as I grunt, pummeling my flesh into the scratchy brick, breaking my skin. Blood pours from my wounds, leaving my mark behind on the unforgiving surface. "I said fucking stop," he growls, pulling my fists away from the wall and forcing my back against it. "You wanna fight, Killer? You want to pound into something that will give back as good as you give?"

"Let me the fuck go," I snarl, trying to yank my wrists back.

His grip tightens until I'm stuck between his broad body and the brick behind my back. A large, raised scar runs the distance of the left side of his face, from his forehead, down his eye and cheek, and finally stops before his collarbone.

"Get yourself together. You want to make some money, Killer? Prove to the world you aren't some junky rock star looking for his next damn fix? Hmm?" He raises a brow, pushing off me when my body slumps against the wall.

"You don't know me," I grunt, pulling my shoulders back and squaring my chest. "You don't—"

"Callum Rose. Whispered Words. Rock star extraordinaire," he snorts. "You almost fell off the fucking stage last night in front of thousands. Yeah, I know exactly who you are." He rolls his dark eyes, pulling a cigarette pack from his back pocket. "Listen, I could use a real fighter like you in my octagon. Not only would your pretty boy face bring in a crowd, but by the looks of your punches, you need the

damn release. Are you interested?" Fire illuminates his face as the end of his cigarette blossoms red, and smoke pours from between his lips.

"Sounds tempting." Staring down at the wounds coating my knuckles, I swallow hard. All I wanted was another fix to try and take away the pain rotting my fucking insides and poisoning me day by day. But nothing is working like it should right now.

"Yeah, how's your fucking head right now after beating that wall?" My muscles tense at his question, but it's then I realize...

"I don't feel a single thing," I mumble in awe, breathing fresh oxygen for the first time in months instead of drowning in my own damn sorrow and darkness.

"Yeah. Here's the deal. You ditch the fucking drugs, and then you come to me. I'll set you up with as many damn fights as long as you're healthy. You'll bring more people to the show, and my place will bring you relief."

"Who the fuck are you?" I ask when he hands me a card with an address close to the edge of town on the bluffs.

"They call me Ruthless," he says with a shrug, taking a step back. "See, now we know each other. Come to that address when you're feeling frisky. You scratch my back, and I'll scratch yours." The mystery man marches down the alley and disappears into the darkness, leaving me with a spark of hope.

Fighting became my damn religion, blackening everything and dulling my pain. Pounding flesh became my drug of choice. Spilling blood became my addiction, relieving all the pain festering in the depths of my soul, rotting me from the inside out. For thirty minutes at a time, I was no one—a blank space, circling opponents with one mission in mind—causing pain.

The daily cravings grew less for drugs, going completely extinct without trying. Soon, my mouth watered for the opportunity to jump into the octagon. In a sick way, it knocked her memories away and blanked out my damn mind from the useless noise around me. After pummeling Asher's face, I went to the ring and took on two more opponents, winning each round within five minutes until I wore myself out. Absentmindedly, I rub along the bruise forming under my right eye, reveling in the slight tinge of pain.

Seeing Asher black and blue for his crimes leaves me with a mixed bag of emotions. On one hand, I feel victorious for my swift retribution. Asher got what he deserved and much more. On the other hand, my stomach churns at the thought of what I've become due to my unswallowable pain—a violent monster addicted to cruel bloodshed. The old Callum would vomit at the thought of what I let consume me.

Asher slightly shakes his head, twisting his expression. "I don't know. She didn't exactly say," he mutters, darting his eyes across our faces, scrutinizing our expressions.

Kieran scoffs, hastily marching toward Asher and baring his teeth like a rabid dog on the damn hunt. My body stiffens when Kieran pushes at Asher's shoulder, knocking him back an agonizing step and causing him to cry out in pain. His body pitches forward, slumping over his guitar hanging from his body.

"Fucking hell," he wheezes, taking deep breaths.

"Jesus," Rad groans, rubbing his forehead. "Didn't we just discuss that violence wasn't the answer? Drag your balls across his face or something. Let him smell like cottage cheese dick for a few days. Lesson learned."

I snort at his reasoning. Pure fucking Rad. Pure fucking stupid. There's no getting over what he did or leaving it alone. Asher deserves multiple punishments.

"You'd seriously just forgive him? Just like that?" Kieran snaps, curling his fingers into Asher's shirt and bringing him close again. Asher frowns but doesn't fight him off, letting him growl in his face. "After he fucked not only us but River over?"

"You think I'd let it slide?" Rad asks through clenched teeth, slamming his drumsticks down on his stool. "He deliberately fucked us all in the ass with no lube and a spiked fucking dick. There's no way in hell I'd forgive him with the clap of my ass cheeks." Rad takes a deep breath, pinching the bridge of his nose.

"But we have shit to do. Instruments to play. And a lucky lady to get back into our good graces."

"Her good graces? You think she's going to forgive us?" Kieran asks, dropping Asher back to his feet, forgetting his rage.

"Pfft. I'm not giving her a choice," Rad quips, waving a hand. "Ask Cal about my date." He beams with pride, puffing out his stupid chest.

"Your date?" I scoff. "More like a third wheel no one invited along." I'd never tell Rad how invigorating it was to spy on her while she dined with Rocco. The way her body fit into the dress she wore nearly gave my attraction to her away, even if I was still in denial about it all. Rad was right about everything that night when he slapped his chest and told me nothing felt right.

"That offends me! I bought her flowers—"

"And then she pulled you out of the restaurant by your ear and rode home with me." My eyebrows raise when he frowns, turns his back to me, and mutters to himself.

The warmth of her arms ghosts around my middle, pulling herself closer to me. Discreetly, I hide the heat traveling up my neck and face as I remember how she felt against my back. Like she was meant to be there—like she was mine again. But will she ever be that girl for me again? The one I look for in a crowded room? The girl who holds my aching heart in the palms of her hands? Fuck. Maybe I never belonged to anyone else. I sure haven't touched another woman since her—my one and only.

"Anyway, it was a good date," he quips, twirling his sticks between his fingers. "And I can't wait to do it all over again. It's all about the actions, boys. Do you want River again? You gotta show my Pretty Girl how much you want her. Tell her sorry all you want, but she won't buy it." Rad's smile fades into nothing, swallowed by a darkness clouding his face, plopping on his stool. "Believe me, I tried."

"You tried?" Kieran asks, rubbing his chin. "Even before this asshole admitted to what he did?"

Rad shrugs, twirling his sticks again. "I can't fight this feeling, bro. I almost forgot what I was fighting for. And what I'm fighting for is my lady. All of her. My daughter..."

"Mine," Kieran growls, clenching his fists.

"Lyric is all of ours, you tithead. She doesn't just call you daddy. River made sure Lyric knew who we were."

"But why?" I croak, hanging my head in shame. I've missed everything in Lyric's life.

"I don't know," Rad murmurs. "She knew whose kid she was biologically. Yet, she still introduced Lyric to our faces as her damn fathers."

Silence fills the space. Our thoughts consume each of us with the possibilities of what we missed and what the future holds. At least, that's where my mind travels to. Lyric. Our child. She calls us daddy, looking at us with wide, loving eyes like we didn't put her mother through hell by walking away with our tails tucked. Looking back, I wish I had done so many things differently.

Our story isn't written in pencil. We can't erase the things we've done with a few swipes and move on like nothing ever happened. We'll continue our broken tale on damaged paper riddled with marks and scars, filled with old wounds and betrayals.

Every foundation starts somewhere—built on shifting rocks and unsteady ground. We won't move on until we've patched up our past, talked through our failures, and begin to rebuild on— sturdier terrain.

"Because of her dad," Asher rasps, clearing his throat as he leans against the wall in defeat.

"What?" Kieran snaps again, turning his furious focus on Asher again.

Asher rolls his eyes. "She told me that her mother never let her know her father. So, she gave Lyric a chance to get to know us. We are her fathers." He hesitates another moment, sucking in a breath. "We can't break Lyric's heart. She comes first through everything."

"No. I don't fucking plan on being without my daughter for

another damn moment. I won't break her fucking heart, but you're pretty damn good at manipulating and breaking hearts. Aren't you? Fucking prick. Stay away from her." Kieran narrows his eyes at Asher, who doesn't move. But I see it in his determined gaze. There's no way in fucking hell he will back off from knowing Lyric. Somehow, he's known her the longest.

"No," I say, squeezing my eyes shut. "River told Lyric we were her fathers for a reason. Lyric expects all of us to be in her life."

"Fuck! Even him?" Kieran grunts, pacing the length of the practice room, pulling at the ends of his dark locks.

"Even him, asshole," Rad grumbles, shaking his head. "I know he royally fucked us over, but Lyric is four, bro. She wouldn't understand why he stopped showing up."

"It would break her heart," Asher whispers, licking his lips. "And mine."

"Then we need to make a pact," I say, turning to look at each of them, letting them see the seriousness of my expression.

"What kind of pact?" My eyes drag to Asher's ghostly pale face as he slumps to the floor, cradling his guitar to his chest.

"For our daughter," Rad agrees without a second thought.

"It's for Lyric. Right here. Right now. We promise each other that no matter what shit happened in the past, we don't show it in front of Lyric. She's our priority, but so is River."

Wild plans of groveling run through my mind. I'll get on my knees for hours on end until she looks me in the eyes and tells me she forgives me for my misdeeds. I failed River in so many fucking ways, and it eats away at me. I'm the reason we fucking left. I confirmed what I saw. Hell, I took a picture of his lips on hers. I'm the reason we all got into that SUV and drove away with nothing more than bitterness and our thoughts guiding us into the future.

And I'll never forgive myself for what I did.

"We will not be my fucking parents," Rad proclaims. "Fuck them."

Though he doesn't show it often, his parents' neglect wears

him down, even after years of being out of their grasp. Sure, they fed him, housed him, and clothed him. But their cold stares and constant need to control his every move drove him away from them in the form of rebellion. It's something they've never forgiven him for. As for Rad, he'll never forget their words, actions, and the catalyst of it all—when they kicked him out.

Pain envelops my heart. My parents were fucking saints through everything, taking in Rad when he needed someone most. They nurtured us with love and support, letting us explore our passion for music and never tearing it down like Rad's parents insisted. I was the lucky one. The others didn't fare well in the parents' department and look at where it got us. Deep down, it isn't that big of a surprise that Asher let his desperation drag him down the road of betrayal in hopes of leaving his father's grasp.

"Hell no," Kieran agrees, stopping right before all of us. "Fuck our piece of shit parents."

"Lyric comes first," Asher agrees from the ground, staring up at the ceiling with a pained expression.

Kieran blows out a breath, and his face falls. "We'll be the parents we never had." Running a hand down his face, he turns his icy stare in Asher's direction. "But you stay the fuck away from River. No canoodling or trying to prove yourself. Your story with River is fucking done."

Asher lets out a humorless laugh. "You think she'd have me after what I did? I know it doesn't mean shit, but I am sorry. I was a—"

"Selfish fucking prick?" Rad quips without an ounce of humor lining his tone.

"That," Asher agrees, pointing a finger toward Rad. "More than a fucking prick. Listen, we can disagree as much as we want..." he trails off, taking a deep breath. "But if we want this to work, we need to work together to achieve this band shit...and with Lyric." He swallows hard. "I'll be the best dad I can be. I won't interfere with anything. But I will continue to make it up to River in any way I know how so she sees how fucking sorry I am. I just—"

"I get it," I say, surprising myself with my admission. He may be a prick, but I can see it in the desperate expression he's sending our way. He needs Lyric in his life as much as she needs him. He loves her and has a strong connection with her in just a short time. "Lyric is all of ours. River has made that clear."

Kieran silently broods, deep in thought, rubbing a hand over his jaw. "Fine," he concedes with a nod. "We do this together. Even if I can't stand to be in the same fucking room as you. We do this band shit, go to the therapy she insists on, and try our fucking best. At the end of the day, we step up and help with Lyric. Whatever River needs, we need to be available for her. We need —"

"To let her know how sorry we are," I say softly, earning a nod of appreciation from Kieran.

"Yes," he whispers, taking a deep breath and swallowing the emotions I know he's feeling.

"Here, here!" Rad shouts, tapping out a light rhythm on the snare drum, adding a few light crashes of the cymbals. "Here's to our new future, bros!" he shouts before jumping into our first song, sounding more confident and crisper than he has in months.

We'll make it through no matter the heartache or the trials before us. One day at a time. One steppingstone at a time. The boys and I have been through hell, but now it's time for us to pull our heads out of our asses, swallow our hurt and rage, and let River know we're here for good.

There's no getting rid of us.

25

Callum

THE SUN BEAMS warmth across my face and bare chest when I step out the front door of the band house into the fresh early evening air. Every ounce of tension from our two-hour band practice, and the rest of the day's tension with the new therapist melts away with the sun's unforgiving rays, evaporating into dust.

Finally, I can breathe. My jaw loosens, and my muscles sag.

After practice, the boys and I decided to cool off in our respective rooms. Alone. Hours of side-eyeing, snarking, and undermining each other had put a real damper on our attitudes. We set our egos aside for River and Lyric and did what we had to do until it became too much to handle. Without a word, we trudged to our rooms, shut the doors, and fucking locked them, trying to catch our breaths.

Or, we tried to, at least. Nothing says piling on more stress like an unexpected knock on your front door. Five minutes. That's all the reprieve I got. I barely sat on the edge of my bed, running a hand down my face when it happened.

Knock. Knock. Knock. Who knew something so simple could echo through an entire house, pulling us from our rooms? It was comical, really. Each of us stuck our heads out our doors with frowns, looking at one another like they were the culprits.

"Who the hell is it?" Rad grumbles, wiping the sweat from his

wrinkled forehead sans pants and shirt, barely fitting into his tiny briefs.

"No one should be here..." my words trail off as we step into the kitchen, eyeing each other with suspicion, ready to tear each other's heads off.

"It's the therapist," Asher declares with his know-it-all attitude, shoving his chin in the air. I don't miss the wicked wince he gives when he pulls a piece of paper off the fridge, reading the words. Hobbling toward us, he grunts when he holds it up for all of us to see. "River left this here for us. It's our schedule."

Right. Although we've seen her a few times without a schedule, it's time for more structure.

Kieran snatches the paper from Asher's hand and turns his back to him. "Lucy Steadman Ph.D.—noon on Mondays and Fridays," he says, looking over the paper.

"Ah, man, I don't want to talk to some stranger about my damn problems again. It was already awkward the first time," Rad grumbles as the hand pounds against the front door again.

"Remember the pact," I say, raising a brow when he puffs out his bottom lip. "We promised."

"Fuck, I know. All in. All for our girls. I'll tell this lady everything on my mind. But fuck—" His cheeks turn red, and he looks away, avoiding our stares. "I'm just scared to do it, I guess." He shrugs nonchalantly, but I note the tension lining his shoulders and the clench of his teeth.

Truth be told, I'm scared shitless to unleash my past on a stranger. Digging up old wounds won't be easy. Reliving my nightmares repeatedly and telling them to some woman with a certificate makes my stomach turn. I want to fucking vomit at the thought. Hell, my doctors tried this after my family's untimely death. They swore up and down it'd help me cope with the ghosts haunting my dreams. Back then, I refused. But I'll do it for the brighter future ahead of us.

"For the pact," I say, staring between Asher, Rad, and Kieran, standing a distance apart from each other. They each nod in

confirmation before I open the door and let Lucy in to evaluate us one by one.

Over the next few hours, she takes each of us aside in a private office off the living room, effortlessly discussing our lives. The conversation between her and me flows easily. An odd sense of familiarity sparks between us, and I find myself revealing more about myself than I have for anyone.

The only thing that fuels my eagerness to spill my demons is the two girls across the street.

The road separating our house from River's burns beneath my bare feet as I make my way across the street toward the soft sound of the waves crashing against the beach. Briefly, a few days ago, I caught a glimpse of the paradise River has built for herself.

Something I know she's always wanted.

"I want to bury my feet in the sand and stand on the beach when we get to California," she confesses, burying her face in my neck. My arms tighten around her, pulling her body against mine. As we lie side by side on her bed under the glowing stars glued to her ceiling, filling the small space with neon light. "I'd live by the water if I got the chance."

"Anything for you, Little Star," I murmur, running my fingers through her long strands.

The blue sky, mixing with fluffy white clouds, looms above me as I draw in the fresh salt-scented air. Waves crash against the beach like a steady chorus. Peace washes over me—consuming me for the first time today. The hot sand cushions my feet as I make my way down the small hill, only stopping when a small voice calls out to me from a distance.

"Daddy!"

My body stiffens when her little voice carries from the water's edge. Small hands wave frantically in my direction, drawing my eyes to her. Not that you could miss her. A bright, neon green bathing suit covers her tiny body like the stars in her mother's old bedroom.

"Daddy! You're here!"

Sand kicks up behind her tiny feet as she rushes toward me with a massive grin on her reddened face. With her arms wide open, she slams into my legs, hugging me tight.

"Lyric," I breathe, momentarily stunned when her head tips back, and she looks up at me with down-turned lips.

"Daddy," she whines with a wobbly lip, examining every inch of my face and chest. "You've got a boo-boo just like Daddy Asher." My heart sinks when the waterworks start, breaking it into tiny pieces. Dropping to my knees, I quickly wipe away the fat tears falling down her cheeks, desperate to eliminate the sadness. "Why are you hurt?" she sniffles, tracing the bruises under my right eye with her little finger.

Panic grips me tight in a vise, squeezing my chest. My daughter is crying. Fuck, and I'm the cause of all her pain. How do I explain to a four-year-old that I intentionally let another man put his fists into my face?

Frantically, my eyes dart around the beach, catching a glimpse of River sitting on a towel in a red one-piece suit. Those long, filled-out legs stretch before her, soaking up the heated evening sun. A slight breeze blows her long strands back past her shoulders as my eyes eat away at her appearance, taking in every ounce of the woman I once thought was mine forever.

Lava pools in my belly, reactivating the attraction and pulling me to River. No matter how angry I was at her. Or how betrayed I felt. Her flawless beauty always draws me like a moth to a flame, searing me. Last time, I burned to ash. This time, after learning the truth, I sink fully into the flames of my doom. Or resurrection. However, this turns out. One day I'll prove to River how fucking sorry I am that I walked away without talking to her. How fucking stupid could I have been? The guilt of my ignorance will haunt me for the rest of my fucking life.

Swallowing hard, I avert my eyes when fiery heat envelops my cheeks. Those laser moss-green eyes latch onto our movements, slightly narrowing in on my hands, combing through Lyric's wet strands as I attempt to soothe the hurt bubbling out of her eyes. I breathe when she tips her head in my direction, not uttering a word about my perusal of her body. Thank fuck.

"I'm okay, Ladybug." Her face softens when I speak. "It was just an accident, but I'm okay now. You don't have to cry for me," I whisper, catching her tears as they fall out of her eyes. "So, what are you doing on the beach today?" I ask, trying to divert the conversation to something better than the bruises lining my flesh.

"Sandcastle," she whispers, pointing toward where she was sitting. Sure enough, a few small buckets, shovels, and a mound of sand sit, waiting for her to continue.

"Does it have a moat?"

Lyric immediately grabs my hand and yanks me toward the direction of the sandcastle.

"It can!" she squeals, pulling me forward.

"Give me just a second, okay? Let me ask your mommy if this is okay, all right?" Lyric's eyes whip to River and then back to me as she nods.

"Okay. I can't wait to build the biggest castle with you, Daddy!" she shrieks with a grin, wrapping her arms around my neck again. "I can't wait," she whispers, kissing my bruised cheek with so much love I choke on it.

Climbing to my feet, I watch with stars in my eyes as she runs back to her creation near the water. Plopping down in the sand, she grins up at me as she fills a bucket, continuing to build up the castle.

"Hey," I say, clearing my throat and dropping beside River.

"Hi," she says softly, keeping her eyes on Lyric, who dances at the water's edge with a grin.

"I–I didn't know you guys would be here. I-um just wanted to take a swim and walk. But—"

River snorts, waving a hand. "Thanks for asking permission. You're more than allowed to hang out with her." Her eyes cut to mine from beneath her lashes. My breath catches when she examines the tattoos lining my chest. More specifically, the one for her.

Ask me. Ask me about it, Little Star. Please.

Before she can utter a word, she rips her gaze away from the art etched into my flesh.

"Oh-oh, okay," I stammer, reverting back to the mess I was when I first encountered River.

I'd like to think I've grown these past five years. Nerves no longer prickle at my skin when I'm in front of a crowd on stage, and meeting new people is a breeze. I'm no longer stumbling over my own two feet.

There's something about River that makes my heart skip a damn beat and weighs down my tongue as if concrete encases it. She drives me back to the nervous boy I used to be. And a part of me clings to the old Callum resurfacing because that's the man I want to be. Should be.

For her. For Lyric.

"Thanks. I'd really like that," I say, clearing my throat.

"Daddy! Come on! Our castle needs lots of work!" Lyric shouts over the roar of the waves and light breeze blowing through the little paradise.

A small smile pulls at the edge of River's lips. "You'd better get going. She's a very persistent little girl."

I snort. "I've noticed," I quip, locking my eyes on the little girl excitedly jumping up and down in the sand, waving me over.

"Cal," River whispers, resting a hand on my arm, stopping me from getting up.

My heart beats double time when the warmth of her hand seeps into my flesh, stopping my movements. Shit. The world swims in front of my eyes, swirling together in a mass of colors. My body weaves. All from one simple, electrifying touch. And I think I might pass out.

Swallowing the lump in my throat, I stare at where we're connected and get myself under control. "Y-yeah?" I croak when she gently squeezes my arm.

"Lyric likes to come out here every day after school. It's the first thing she does when she throws her backpack in her room, she gets her suit on and plays in the waves and sand. Sometimes she likes to swim, but most times, she likes to sit right there and watch the waves or build a castle." She squeezes one last time and drops her hand from my arm.

Immediately, I miss the way her hand felt on my skin. My vision clears, and my head returns to its usual messy self.

"Thank you," I whisper, earning a nod in return.

"I'm not here to keep her from you. You know that, right?" She swallows hard, gazing at the blue horizon where the sea meets the skyline in the distance. Away from me and the noise bubbling in my throat.

"I-I don't believe you'd keep her from us. That isn't like you." I shake my head, rolling my lips together as the anger from Asher's betrayal stabs me in the back once again.

There are some wounds you never heal from. They cut deep —to the bone—flaying your soul open. This is one of them. Sure, it may superficially mend back together out of necessity, but deep down, the pain, anger, and pent-up rage will always be in the background, reminding me of what he did. There's no getting away from Asher now. We're in too deep unless we tuck tail and leave the band and go our separate ways.

After today's session with Lucy, I'm thinking we might make it out of this alive. If we band together and really sink into our feelings, we'll get through this and make it to the other side. We may have bruises and scrapes, but we'll heal. Once and for all.

"That was Asher and Gloria's fault that we've been apart for so long," I say, watching Lyric closely as she dips her bucket into the water. "I'm just sorry I missed so much," I whisper longingly, staring at the daughter whose childhood I missed out on. But no more.

Callum is here to stay. To make memories full of laughter and love. I'll be here until the end. No matter what.

Happiness fills every molecule of my body. I'm floating above the damn clouds with a smile etched onto my face. A deep laugh vibrates through my chest when I throw Lyric's squirming body over my shoulder, much to her protests. Her loud giggles fill the dusky air as she pounds a fist into my back, begging me to release her.

"Daddy!" Lyric laughs, hitting me a few times. "Put me down! I need to pick up my buckets!" she squeals again, stopping me in my tracks. "Pleaseeeee!" she begs again until I bring her face right in front of mine.

Her freckles pop over the bridge of her nose, dusting lightly over her sun-kissed cheeks. Her toothy grin lights up my damn life as she examines my face. No longer pouting over the dark bruises.

My blood may not run through her veins, but that's the thing about family, isn't it? You're not always born together. You're brought together by circumstances out of your control, crashing into each other much like the waves of the sea. Lyric crashed into our lives like a tiny hurricane. She's shaking the foundation of everything we've known and believed, and I, for one, am ecstatic to have this little human in my life.

"Okay. But I'll give you two seconds, and then we'll race to the house. Your mom looks like she's about to come and get you." I raise a brow when Lyric wiggles out of my arms and dashes off to get her things. With another loud giggle, she races past me, clinging to her buckets.

River stands on her back porch, leaning against the railing and watching Lyric with a smile that lights up her face. A red towel sits snug around River's body, warming her as the sun slowly sinks in the sky, turning it a bright hue of pink.

"Straight to the shower, you sand monster," River says through a big grin, lightly smacking Lyric on the butt.

"But, Mommy! Daddy..." Lyric points to me with a pout, waving her arms all around. "Can he read to me tonight? I wants Daddy to read to me!" she says again, folding her hands together and silently begging her mom.

River looks at me with uncertainty but nods. "If that's what Daddy wants to do."

Butterflies burst in my stomach, and I nod before I can even think about another response. "Of course, I'll read to you."

One of the happiest memories is when my mom and dad would lay on either side of me and take turns reading lines from all my favorite books. Their voices changed with each new character, and they'd stay there until my eyes fluttered shut. I never thought I'd get to experience that warm feeling again. Only this time, I'll be reading from the book and watching as she falls asleep with my heart in my throat.

"Now, off to the shower! Then we'll have some sandwiches," River says again, shooing Lyric toward the bathroom down the hall until she marches into the bathroom, slamming it shut. "And don't slam the door," River mutters too late.

"Little-Little Star."

I swallow hard when she connects her gaze with mine. Reaching out, I bravely wrap my fingers around her wrist, holding her hostage. Please don't walk away from me now. A familiar feeling bursts inside me as I look deep into her eyes. It's something I haven't felt since I walked away from her. Electricity bristles. My hair stands on end. And a deep, gut-wrenching ache forms, begging me never to let go of her.

"She's amazing. I'm sorry I wasn't here, but thank you for allowing me to be here now. I—" I roll my lips together as the heat behind my eyes intensifies. Guilt tears through me like it has since I found out the truth from Asher's lips. We left because of what I saw. I sealed our separation with a picture, not bothering to ask questions or dig further.

River swallows hard, shaking off my grip. "Well, as long as you're here now."

Not fucking good enough.

"So, she's always known about us?" I ask, stuffing my hands into the pockets of my swim shorts to keep from touching her again—the only thing I want to do right now. Well, beyond a simple touch.

Licking her lips, River nods. "Eventually, Lyric would know where she came from and who her father was. In the beginning, I wasn't positive about who she belonged to. Then she opened her eyes... And I... Couldn't deny her the reality of our situation. So, I did the next best thing. I told her the truth. And wouldn't you know it? She latched on."

"She didn't know about...what happened and why we were apart?"

"No. And she won't either," she says. "I will not break my daughter's heart, nor will you. She's—" She takes a deep breath, rubbing her temples. "Lyric is finally at peace. It's like she needed to touch you all. Don't ruin her peace." Her eyes plead with me until I nod at her request.

"I'd never do that to her. It's only been a short time, but I already love her," I admit quietly as my cheeks heat.

"Come here," River says, waving a hand for me to follow as the sound of water slapping into the tub suddenly turns off. "Here," River says, taking a large photo album off a bookshelf and handing it to me.

My eyes bug out as I flip through the pictures. Page by page, River has organized everything into neat little sections. From her first birthday to her fourth. And every holiday in between. Glorious snapshots of Lyric as a baby, learning to crawl and taking her first bites of ravioli. Her red-stained face smiles up at the camera from her highchair with the remnants of her meal squished before her. Mischief lives in those mismatched eyes—much like now.

Without the perseverance to hold them back any longer, I unleash my emotions. Tears stream down my cheeks. Embarrassing sobs choke my throat. Fuck. I'm a goddamn mess at the sight of my baby girl, who grew up without me. I cry from the anger of missing out, for walking away, and for everything in between. I let it out into the world, letting River see and feel how fucking sorry and fucked up I am over this.

"She was a good baby," River murmurs, turning the page and running her manicured finger over a picture of Lyric's toothless grin, staring up at the camera with cake all over her face. "That was her first birthday. It was our first month in this house." Her eyes dart around the living room, stopping near the entrance of the open-concept kitchen.

"And I missed it all. Fuck," I heave a breath, losing my grip as the photo album thunks to the ground. "River," I breathe, turning to her as she tilts her head, not giving me an ounce of emotion.

She's a goddamn wall of nothing, staring at me and refusing to open up. One day I'll peel back those layers of forgiveness. But for now, I know I have my work cut out for me. We all do.

"I truly am sorry you missed it all, Cal. She would have loved for you to be here this whole time. But the important part is, you're here now. Make the most of it while you can."

I nod, wiping away the remnants of my emotions off my cheeks. "I will," I proclaim, holding her gaze with mine. God, I could get lost in the depths of her eyes and swim in her damn soul. "For you, too," I whisper, drifting a finger across her silken cheek.

The warmth of her skin sends goosebumps pimple down my arms. Tiny hairs stand on end. Electricity runs between us in an undeniable force, pulling me into her. My lips tingle, begging to kiss the last pair I ever touched with my own.

"Words don't mean much, Little Star. Not with you. I could look you in the eyes and promise you a million and one things. But they're just words—-empty promises. From here on out, I will prove who I am and what you mean to me. We may have had time apart, but we're grown up now. No longer the kids running around Central City. You've changed. I've changed. Some for the worst. Some for the better," I whisper, rubbing my thumb against her cheek. Her brows wrinkle as she takes in my words, but I'm not done yet. "I deeply apologize for walking away from you. The moment I saw Van kiss you, I should have known better. Asher had just dismantled my entire world with those fake videos, and then when I saw what I did, I ran without even questioning it. That's on me. I was an idiot...probably still am. Every day and night, I'll show up here and be present. That's my promise to you, Little Star. Because the way I see it now, you're my whole damn galaxy, and I can't stand to be away from you and her any longer."

River shudders as I breathlessly finish my speech, getting lost in her presence. Clarity has completely taken hold. I was an idiot for ever thinking River would turn her back on us. River was better than that—still is. I'm not fucking worthy of her.

River sniffles, slightly leaning into my hand. "She's going to want you to stop doing that," she whispers, running the tip of her finger over the bruises on my face. "She thought you were hurt, and it upset her. She will know something is wrong if you keep showing up with those bruises." She licks her lips before dropping her hand. My body misses her touch when she steps away from my hand.

"Okay," I agree, nodding. "I won't fight anymore." Music will be what I live and breathe from this moment forward. I'll pour my damn soul straight into my bass. For them.

"Why did you?" she blurts before she can stop herself, widening her eyes. "It just...doesn't seem like you, Callum. You were so peaceful and quiet." Still am. Only around you, though.

I shrug. "It was better than the drugs," I whisper through a crack in my voice. "Truth?" She nods, eager to hear my response. "It was the only thing that could knock the joyous memories of you out of my head. For just a second, I wasn't drowning in my misery. I—" I blow out a breath, preparing myself for the conversation ahead of me. "I loved you a lot, Little Star. So much so that I didn't realize how I truly felt until you were gone. But I failed you in so many ways. Will you take this healing journey with me?" I ask, licking my lips. "I want to mend us."

"And what if I... I can't?" she questions, taking another step back. "You did fail me...you all did. You walked away from us. What would have happened if I hadn't made it here? Would I still be in Central City with Ly alone?" She crosses her arms over her chest. "I want to heal, too," she finally whispers, squeezing her eyes shut. "But just give me time, okay? Be present. And I'll—"

"You don't owe me anything," I mutter, stepping forward and taking her into my arms. Stiffly, she rests her forehead against my chest as I soak in her presence. "One day at a time, Little Star. Okay?"

"One day at a time," she whispers with confirmation, and I know that's as good as it's going to get right now. River isn't mine or ours. Not yet. But we'll get there. I know we'll all prove to her that we're serious about this.

My eyes fall shut when the warmth of her fingers glides over my bare chest with curiosity. She doesn't step out of my arms, which I'm thankful for. I want to revel in her body heat for a moment longer until we're pulled apart.

"These weren't here before," she barely whispers, tracing the shapes repeatedly.

"They weren't."

Lifting her head, her red-rimmed eyes lock on mine. "They're over your heart, Cal."

I lick my lips. "That they are." My breaths pass over her face, traveling down her neck. The persistent urge to hold her tongue hostage with mine gnaws at my brain. Not the right time, damnit.

"You got neon stars over your heart," she whispers with an edge, emotions creeping in and ruffling her hardened, emotionless exterior.

I see you, Little Star.

"Truth?" She nods, eagerly awaiting my answer. "I may have wanted to erase the memories from my mind, but there was one place I felt whole." Without a thought, my fingers capture hers over my heart and rest them there. "It was with you, under the neon stars illuminating your bedroom as we lay together, hidden away in your space."

"Oh, Cal," she murmurs, choking out my name like a sin. Her fist clutches near her mouth when she takes a step away from me, refusing herself the comfort of my arms.

Fuck.

"Just remember, I'm not going anywhere," I whisper, stepping up to her again and invading her space. "Ever again. If there's one promise you should take to heart. It's this one."

The old Callum would cower away from her—hide his face from the world. But the new Callum craves her with every ounce of his being like a damn drug or fighting. My body jolts when a little person stares at us from a few feet away, sleepily rubbing at her eyes. Deep blue star pajamas line her frame. Long dark strands of wet hair drip on the hardwood as she eyes the two of us with suspicion.

"Daddy, will you read to me now?" Lyric yawns, stretching her tiny arms above her head.

"I'll get some sandwiches ready," River murmurs, scurrying as far away from me as she can.

You can run, and you can hide, Little Star, but we'll bulldoze through the thick walls you've erected around us. All in due time, of course. Mending our broken relationship and betrayal comes first.

"Of course. What are we reading tonight?" Lyric grins, suddenly looking more awake than she had ten seconds ago, watching me with the biggest eyes I've ever seen. Excitement thrums through her veins when she bounces on her toes.

"Well, it's about this girl who gets picked to compete in this crazy ring. She has a bow and arrow and two boyfriends. Like me!" She giggles when I stiffen, side-eyeing River, who shrugs from the kitchen and hides her smile. Somehow, I feel like I'm missing something vital. "Come on! Come on! I'm ready!"

My brows furrow. "What kind of book is she reading?" I hiss in her direction.

River snorts, patting me on the shoulder. "You'll see," is all she says before she kisses Lyric's head and walks away, leaving me with an eager four-year-old who promptly grabs my hand and yanks me down the hall to her room.

"Your room is so pretty," I awkwardly say, rubbing at my bare chest. Thankfully, my swim trunks have dried since we were outside, but I still feel the sand shifting in places it shouldn't be.

"Mommy helped me pick out all the purple. I'm afraid of the dark, Daddy," she murmurs, climbing into her bed and patting the place beside her.

"Is that why you have a lot of lights shining down on you?" I question as she snuggles into my side, looking up at me with those big, blue eyes.

"Mhhmm. There's a ghost in here," she whispers with a slight hint of fear jumping into her tone. Her eyes dart toward the window above her bed, and she shudders.

"Ghosts? Well, I'm here now, Ladybug. Let's scare them away." She nods in agreement, handing over a large, used book with a bookmark in the middle.

"She marched forward with her bow at the ready, aiming to take down the enemy," I say in a deep voice, only raising it when the character speaks her line. "You will step away from her before I put this through your hands and mince your fingers for dinner." Jesus. What is my child reading before bedtime? Looking down, Lyric looks up at me expectantly, silently egging me on to continue. And so, I do. River meanders in, leaves sandwiches in the middle of the bed, and walks out before I can say a word.

Over the next hour, I lay beside my daughter, nibbling sandwiches and reading about a strong, independent woman who kicks ass and takes names like nobody's business. Also, she shows great interest in the two leading male characters. Many times, I turn to the blurb on the back, making sure I'm not about to read some crazy romance story to my four-year-old. As the clock ticks by, my eyes grow heavy until the thick book lands on my chest, and the world around me is darkness as my eyes close.

"Night, Daddy," she whispers, snuggling further into my side.

"Night, Ladybug," I murmur, falling victim to the perfect night's sleep.

26

Rad

I THINK my girlfriend is slowly trying to murder me. Not with a knife or poison. Nope! She's slowly draining me dry, and I don't know if I can make it any longer. And not the good kind of draining me either. I mean, she can drain my dick as much as she wants. If I had the energy for it, that is. I'm like a damn sack of potatoes heaving myself into bed each weekend.

It's been two goddamn weeks of this. I think I'll put an obituary in the paper and just announce my death ahead of time.

Here lies Rad. Gone too soon at the hands of his Pretty Girl, who overworked him night after night on stage.

When River said we'd have to perform every Saturday per our contract, I didn't think it'd be like this. Hashtag–Radisdead. Hashtag–someonesaveme.

It's all for the pact. Every one of her demands, we follow like good little boys. Now, if she'd only throw me a bone and reward me for my good behavior.

"Should I cut off my balls and put them in River's purse now or later? I can't decide," I wheeze, lying flat on the ground, soaking up the cold tiles. It's like running ice cubes all over my flesh, and it's refreshing as fuck.

Kieran grunts in agreement or disagreement; I can't fucking tell. Splashing water on his red face, he sits back on the leather couch, shaking his head. "I don't know, but I think she's trying to kill us."

"More like punish us," Callum murmurs with a pained groan, resting on the leather couch beside Kieran with ease.

"Why are your clothes off?" Kieran asks, raising a brow like he hasn't known me since middle school.

Hello, being naked is like my damn calling card. Naked Rad has a ring to it, right? I can't help myself. The moment I get on stage and the suffocating heat hits me, I need to take everything off. Fuck clothes. I'd rather live in a community where clothes were banished. Welcome to the Radalicious Naked Compound. Population: 5. Just me, the guys, and my Pretty Girl... And shit... we can't be naked all the time. Oh, the sacrifices we make for our Little Pretty Girl and future babies. Because yeah, the second I get back inside of my woman, that's all I want. Little me's. Little them's. Another little her. God. My dick springs to life at the thought, which is terrible, because I'm barely dressed. Not like they haven't seen my dick flag fly.

"It's hot as fuck. Fuck pants. Fuck shirts and socks. You're lucky I still have my boxers on." I lift my middle finger into the air, saluting the boys in more than one way. Oops. "If she keeps this up, she might," I grunt, searching for a fan. "You guys see a fan anywhere? I need cool air on my dick like yesterday."

If I don't cool my nuts off soon, they will pop right off in protest and wander away, taking my dick with them. I swear they're boiling inside my damn boxers.

"Do you think this is payback?" Callum murmurs, wiping the sweat from his face.

Kieran snorts. "It's not like she can avoid us or get some sort of revenge for what we did." His eyes cut to Asher sitting across the room under the ceiling fan. He hasn't moved an inch since we got off stage and hasn't spoken.

He's retreating inside himself again like he did when we came to California. Back then, he focused on the music to escape her memory. And now, he's doing the same and withering away right before our eyes. He may be an asshole, but it hurts to see him so beat down all the time. The good news is he's moved back into his room at the band house. Since the moment we made the pact two weeks ago, we've been civil with him. We've had to be. He's important to Lyric, and River to an extent. I will not jeopardize my future with my girls. Not one bit. So, If I have to be the nice guy, then I'll be the nice guy. Besides, between therapy and group sessions, we're really starting to hash some shit out and get back to the family we used to be.

Kieran's rage has settled to nothing. He's giving it his all and smiling more, especially when it comes to Lyric. Callum stopped fighting cold turkey and hasn't had a bruise in two whole weeks. It's odd to see him without the discoloration on his face or body, but I'm glad he stopped.

More often than not these days, Callum sneaks out around three and comes back at six covered in sand, with a goofy smile lighting up his face. I was starting to worry about my damn brother all the time. I knew one day I'd find him dead in an alleyway after mouthing off to some asshole on the street. Thankfully, it never happened. So, I can rest easy now.

"At least you bitches just get to sway and look pretty. I'm pounding my shit into the drums as hard as I can. God, I think I'm fucking dying." I wave my hand in front of my face, trying to get cool air across my overheated skin. What I wouldn't give for one of those glorious ice baths.

Ahh, yeah. Dip my nuts into the ice until they're scurrying back inside me instead of trying to melt off. A guy can dream.

I love my Pretty Girl. I really fucking do. With my whole goddamn heart and body, I also know what she's up to. She doesn't think I do. Probably doesn't think I'm as quick as I am. But I know she's trying to get us back into shape. I'm an intelligent guy when I want to be.

But something has to give. It's been like this since everything came to a head, and we made our pact to not fuck anything else up.

And this last stint of torture has been three long ass days.

Yesterday, we were kidnapped and taken to a county fair four hours away. Don't get me wrong, being on stage again felt glorious. It's been months since we've been on tour and getting back up there playing our music in sync was fucking beautiful. Sure, we've played a few shows per the rules of our contract with River. But it wasn't like this. This is fucking brutal.

Then, after our orgasmic performance. Because yeah, I may have cum a little during because I knew my Pretty Girl was right in my sights, watching my every move. I could have used Little Rad as a fucking drumstick. Scratch that. That wouldn't have felt very good unless it was a pussy drum attached to my girl.

Then after that performance, we were ushered home to the band house, where she ripped each of our testicles off and made a damn necklace. With pride, too. Her smile may have lit up the room, but it put the fear of God in our souls. I mean, she's hot with nuts all around her face. Or nuts on her face. But not at that moment. Abso-fucking-lutely not.

"I want you boys to look this over," she says, handing Kieran a piece of paper.

"What is it?" Kieran asks, taking the paper from her outstretched hand. As his eyes gaze at the report, they widen in surprise. His body stiffens, and he sucks in a breath.

"This is a list of everything I noticed that could be improved during your shows. I want you guys to look over this carefully. This will help you be aware of what I'm looking at and what you can adjust. This is your homework for tonight. We have two more shows tomorrow."

"Two?" I choke on my water, letting it dribble down my chin. "Tomorrow?" I squeak pathetically, clinging to the couch. Please don't let it be true. I don't know If I can survive another two rounds of performances.

"Two," she says, giving me that oh-so-pleased smile she's perfected lately.

Evil Pretty Girl is hot as fuck, but goddamn, I need a break. My body might give out on me if I have to drum again.

Yup. This is fucking torture. It's our goddamn penance for being little shits and walking away from her instead of being big boys and having a conversation. Oh, if I could go back in time and pull my dick up—we'd all be in a better place. Maybe we wouldn't be rock stars in the prime of our lives. But nowadays, that doesn't seem as important as River and Lyric.

"There's like twenty things here, River Blue. Were we really that bad?" Kieran asks, rubbing a tired hand down his weary face.

"Not terrible. But not good either."

Well, ouch. Spank my ass and call me Ashton because this woman is bending us over and telling us exactly how it is. Add in a spiky cactus up our asses without the necessary lube. I shudder. Damn, my butthole puckers at the stern look she gives each of us. Would she be offended if I called her Mommy and sucked her tit? Probably. Then we'd be in even more trouble, and she'd probably add another thousand shows to torture us with.

"When I watched you guys before you played as one, you moved around and commanded the stage, forcing everyone to have their eyes on you. You were electric, enthralling, and now, you're like watching paint dry. You're as stiff as boards up there, eyeing each other like you're ready to pounce and rip your heads off. You don't smile anymore; you don't even act like you like music. So, I'm curious, do you guys still enjoy playing, or is this a chore?"

Talk about a slap in the dick. She accused us—Whispered Words—of not enjoying our passion. The audacity! But wait, do we enjoy our passion anymore? Reaching deep inside myself, I try to pull out the magical feeling. Shit. It doesn't come. Where's the giddiness and eagerness I always felt before shows? It's...empty. The well is dry. I frown, staring around the room at the other guys, oblivious to the pain ricocheting through me.

"Just think about it. I'll see you in the morning. We have a show at noon and a show at the KC Club in the evening. Get some rest, boys," she coos, strolling out of the room, sashaying that curvy ass that I want to paint red with my palm. But I'm a good boy. I stay planted in my seat, blinking rapidly, and trying to digest what the fuck just happened. Also, I'm too tired to fucking move.

"Did that just really happen?" I frown, saying my thoughts aloud.

"Yeah," Kieran grunts, staring over the paper. "Looks like we have fucking homework."

"For the pact," Callum murmurs, leaning over to peek at the paper.

"For the pact," I reluctantly say.

I'd much rather sleep it off in my bed than look over my critique. *All for the Pretty Girl*, I repeat in my head, cringing at her words.

"For the pact," Asher agrees.

When River leaves us sitting in our self-deprecating juices, we discuss how we want to move forward with this. We have to prove to my Pretty Girl that this is it for us, we want this, and there's no other way around it. Music is our damn lives. Always has been and always will be. Maybe.

"So, I had an idea."

All our eyes turn to Ash, who grabs his guitar, strumming a few chords. His brows furrow as a soft melody picks up. Over and over, he plays it until it sounds like a solid chorus.

"What is it?" Kieran asks, jumping to his feet. Never taking his gaze off Asher, who closes his eyes and sways with the tune.

"We haven't written in forever," Asher says with a hint of sadness. "Let's build off this. It came to me last night in the shower, and it's been stuck in my head ever since. I want to do something for Ly." A deep, red blush takes over his cheeks when he looks around the room at our eager faces.

"A song for Ly?" Callum asks, rubbing his chin and nodding. "Fuck yeah."

"That would be a perfect way to show our girl how serious we are!" I whoop, jumping to my feet.

"Lyrics come from the heart," Callum murmurs, scrunching his brows.

"Wait, what?" I ask with a renewed energy taking me over.

"You said it once when we were in bed with River. Lyrics came to you, and you said..."

"Lyrics come from the heart and out of nowhere. They're unexpected..." Callum trails off with his eyes widening. "You don't think she..."

My heart beats double time. "That she named Lyric that because she was unexpected?" I will not cry in front of the guys. I will absolutely bawl into my pillow tonight. No tears here. Nope.

It isn't until that night, when I'm staring up at the ceiling do I let my tears fall. If what Cal remembers is correct, he's usually spot on and all. Hello, photographic memory. Then my girl named my baby girl after something I said. One day, I'll bring it up to her. For now, I'll savor it in the palm of my hand and keep the knowledge to myself.

"Yo dummy, are you putting a fan on your shit?" Kieran grunts, throwing a water bottle at me and knocking me out of my thoughts.

I furrow my brows, realizing I'm dangling a massive box fan above my junk. On fucking high. Huh. No wonder I'm starting to cool off. But also, there are enormous fan blades inches from my crotch. Geez, that was close. I could have cut the boys.

"Yeah," I murmur, setting the fan beside me so it still blows the cool air across my flesh. "I think this is a punishment." Definitely a way to get back at us for being dicks. Rightfully so. We were major fuckers.

Here I thought we were on the right track to forgiveness. Maybe we aren't doing enough to prove ourselves. Shit. We need to step up our game and get it together.

We've already been on a date. Well, I mean, I joined her and Rocco again because you can't get rid of me. I'm Rad, the never-ending rash that sticks to you even when you put ointment on me. Can't get rid of me! At least she didn't kick me out this time. I was allowed to sit at the table and eat my Italian food like a good boy.

Take that, Pretty Girl. I'll never give up until you're completely mine.

Like an angel in six-inch red heels, River burst through the backstage door with an adorning smile.

"Did we do good, Pretty Girl?" I ask, lifting my head off the cold ground and giving her my best puppy dog eyes.

"Color me impressed, boys," she says, giving us a little clap. "You put in the work out there. I felt more included in the performance. Kieran, your voice was on point. Rad, your drumming and smiling brought the crowd out. Asher and Callum, you guys did good, too."

I beam under her compliment, peeling myself off the sticky tile floor. "Thanks, Pretty Girl. We're always here to impress." I grin when she snorts.

"Right. Well, you might want to put your clothes on. You have a line of rabid fans begging for autographs and pictures."

"We don't really do autographs," Kieran grumbles with displeasure.

"Oh, but now you do, Knight. I expect you by the bar in five minutes! Look alive, boys!" she shouts, clapping her hands again.

"This is a goddamn test," I hiss, finding my pants crumpled in the corner. "Avoid the titties and ass signatures as much as fucking possible! No flesh." I grumble in disgust when my wet T-shirt sticks to every inch of my upper body. Usually, I waltz out of here half-naked, not caring who sees me nude. Not now! My Pretty Girl is watching our every move. I will not fuck this up.

My body is River's fucking temple. She's the only one who can worship me now: no more ogling eyes or touchy hands from fans. I am a one-woman man. Forever. No matter what.

"She wants to watch us with the fans," Callum surmises, rubbing his chin.

"You think she's trying to see how we handle the girls?" Asher asks with uncertainty.

"My bet? Yeah, she fucking does." Kieran smirks when he stands, running his hands down his ripped jeans. "Our girl is secretly jealous. So, let's show her we can be as professional as her. We sign autographs but stay close to her."

Ohhh, I like secretly jealous Pretty Girl. She gets all stabby and punchy. It makes my dick hard just thinking about it.

"Let's do this. Operation prove ourselves commences," I say, throwing a fist into the air with a whoop.

27

River.

"HAVE A GOOD NIGHT, BOYS," I say, sauntering out of the band house at midnight with my head held high.

Three days of running them through the wringer has every muscle in my body wound tighter than a damn spring. Ready to unload.

Three days of watching their asses sway on stage.

Sexy, stupid bastards. Why do they have to look so damn good and delicious in their natural habitat?

Three days of watching the sweat drip down their bare chests as they move with grins on their faces. Three goddamn miserable days of watching girls flock to their sides, pawing at them, and helplessly watching as I kept my shit together with gritted teeth and fake smiles.

Now, I'm free from them for a few days. I don't know why I thought this torture would be good for them. They flew through my rigorous training exercise with ease.

Bastards.

Sure, the first concert was like watching a cactus soak in the sun. They were stiff pricks, avoiding eye contact with each other, including the roaring crowd. After that, they took my critical notes and ran with them like wild animals. Everything I laid down, they took it like champs.

I had to get creative by torturing their asses somehow and enact a little revenge of my own. I can't exactly burn the house down with them inside to get some retribution, so... I may have overextended their abilities on stage.

Just a little. Three shows in a thirty-hour period isn't too horrible. They survived. Maybe on fumes.

Okay, maybe it was just a little too much.

So, fucking sue me.

If I had it my way, I would have shoved them on a boat, duct taped and unconscious, and driven them out to sea. Sleep with the fishes now, boys.

Fuck. Not really. I couldn't do that. They've been—

Great.

So, fucking wonderful with Ly. They've been here for me, too. Every step of the way. They aren't fighting me on the demands I'm putting them through.

Asher makes her fucking breakfast every morning and brings it over. Even though looking at him simultaneously breaks my heart and hardens it. He's still so bruised from their punches. And so damn subdued and polite.

It's hard to hate a man who isn't the same person he was years before when he pulled this stunt. He may wear the same face, but the demon that once sat on his shoulders disappeared the moment he confessed. Maybe my exorcisms really worked.

See? So damn conflicted.

Callum reads her bedtime stories, and sometimes Rad joins in for comedic relief.

Kieran spends as much time as possible with her on the beach with his guitar in his hand and her on his lap, teaching her the notes.

They've been fucking great. It both pleases the piss out of me and irritates me to no end.

Why couldn't they be bastards so I could continue to hate them?

But no. That's not what I want either.

Goddamn, my head aches with all the different opinions rattling through my head. I try to remember what Rocco and I talked about when he dropped soup off a few weeks ago and live by that mantra. I can't fault these men for trying their hardest. Even when they fucked up in the worst possible way. *Take it day by day. Don't roll over and forgive them. Make them beg. Make them get on their damn knees and earn your trust back. Let them see Lyric and prove themselves to her and to you.* And I've done that. I haven't rolled over. Or forgiven them. It may be on the horizon. Sometime in the close future. But not yet. They still deserve more shit from me.

I slam through the front door of the band house and beeline it toward the beach behind my home. Nothing says refreshing like yelling at the ocean at midnight until your throat is raspy and your emotions are spent. It's the remedy to my problems. For now, at least.

As soon as the warm night air hits my skin, everything crumbles. My facade. My walls. My fucking hormones. I'm in shambles. Reeling from the effects of being in their presence. How can four men wreck me so damn hard without even trying to?

Who said being a badass HBIC was easy? Commanding Whispered Words on what to do while performing on stage is hard as fuck. I'm feeling the after-effects of watching them for hours.

Vivid memories of their hands running down their bare chests as they whipped their shirts off and tossed them in my direction. Always at me. Never the screaming girls. Whether I was standing just off stage or in the front row, they made sure their shirts were mine. Sweat-soaked and all.

God fucking damn it. My head spins, weaving a mess of webs in my mind. Should I jump in headfirst, or should I just let them be fathers? It rattles around in my messed-up brain, pushing me further down the rabbit hole.

My broken heart is slowly stitching together piece by piece.

They're the menders of my soul. How fucking ironic, huh? The men who broke it are now fixing it with the little things. It's always the fucking little things.

We've talked. Cried. Yelled. Argued. Raised our voices. Every bit of healing conversation has been present. The sorrys and stepping up are all there. They're taking therapy extra seriously, too, which surprised the hell out of me. I never expected the guys to willingly talk to a stranger. I knew it would benefit them, especially after learning about their upbringing. Hell, Asher even goes into her office an additional time each week, and Kieran tags along.

Yet, I remember the way I felt when they walked away. They fucking eviscerated me. My heart literally shattered in my chest, turning into tiny fragments of what I once was and numbing me for so long. I tried every day to forget their existence. Whispered Words, who? But it never worked. Every time I felt Lyric kick inside me, I was reminded of who helped put her there. And the moment I finally saw her eyes, I fucking broke in half.

Three of them had no clue what trap they were falling into. Only one knew the truth this whole time. He's the man suffering the most with the remnants of his bruises and the alienation.

He's also trying, too.

How can I be so damn conflicted on something so simple? Do I trust them again, or do I take my chances? Do I drown them in the sea, or keep them afloat?

"Fuckkkkkkkkk!" I shout into the night sky as I stand at the edge of the sea. "Give me a damn sign. Give me something!" I roar at the sparkling stars. They give nothing back. "I just don't know what to do or how to feel—" I trail off, sinking my teeth into my lip. "I just want to know what to do with the future."

Stepping forward, I sigh when the cool water soaks through my shoes. Shivers burst up my spine the moment the water retreats and then splashes me again.

My head falls back, and I groan, counting the dots in the sky.

It's times like these that I'm thankful for my family. They may have come later in life, but I feel more loved and adored than I did throughout my entire childhood.

Kaycee let Lyric come over for a three-day sleepover so I could take care of business with the boys. Not only did it give me free time to reflect on all this bullshit, but I didn't have to worry about Ly. She's safe with her cousins, aunt, and uncles.

And I'm here. Horny and miserable. How could my life get any worse?

Looking out into the soft waves of the dark ocean, I take a deep breath. I've got this. Tits up and all that good badass girl shit. I'll navigate through these muddy waters as best I can. After I change my now wet shoes and pants, that is. As therapeutic as screaming at the sky was, it doesn't solve a damn thing.

I huff, walking up the beach toward my house, getting sand in and on my damn shoes. With a grunt, I toss them on the back porch with a mental note to clean them later.

After securing my home and taking a hot shower, I grab a tall glass of white wine, open my window, and stand in the middle of my bed naked.

The beautiful sound of the waves crashing against the sand filters through my room, relaxing every inch of my body.

The soft, warm breeze brushes against my bare skin as I close the curtains and secure the wedge so no one can push the window open further. You know, like my stalker who looms in the back of my mind. Always there. Every step I take, I swear he's behind me, watching my every move and taking pictures. I shudder at the thought but try not to let him rule my life. I'm vigilant with everything I do. House alarm. Locking my doors. Having a guard at the end of the drive. I know he's been in here before, invading my damn privacy. But I won't allow some pussy coward, who hangs in the shadows, to steal my peace from me. This is my home. My haven.

I nibble my lip. At some point, I'm going to have to clue the guys in on what's been happening to me. I have a stalker. He takes pictures of me. Follows me around like a lost puppy dog but never shows his damn face. Fuck. How can I tell them? Do I sit them down for a meeting and casually throw it out there? No. I can't. It'll change everything once they find out. They'll look at me differently and... I'm not ready for that.

I groan at the pent-up tension coiling in the pit of my stomach, begging me to unleash the feeling. My thighs tighten, and my breaths pick up as I imagine laying back in bed and relieving myself to the images of the boys across the street.

I chug the last of my wine, setting the glass down on my end table. Plopping on my bed, I reach over and open the drawer beside me with a grin. Oh yes, this will do.

"There you are," I murmur, pulling my rose-shaped vibrator out. Energy hums through me, prepping my body for the orgasm I'm about to bless it with. "I've missed you," I murmur, aching to kiss it in relief.

Lying back on the bed, I settle myself on my pillows with a loud sigh. The cool sheets encase me in their grasp as my eyes flutter shut.

My imagination ignites into naughty fantasies as the little rose rapidly thumps against my aching clit, begging for sweet relief. Bring on the orgasm that's been building for the past three days.

Fire roars through my veins as images pour through my mind at a rapid pace. A moan slips from my lips as I reach down and plunge my fingers into my pussy, pumping them in and out.

The vibrations around my clit send liquid lust straight through me. My back bows when my head falls back into the pillow. Moan after moan fills the room, and I'm panting, mentally begging for the real thing. Loud, thumping footfalls stop me in my tracks just outside my window. My heart plummets into my ass. My worst fears are coming true. Visions of my stalker standing outside my window, listening to me getting myself off have me recoiling. Until I hear my stalker's voice just outside my window...

"Shh, fuckers. Did you hear that?"

Relief slams through me as I hold my breath at the sound of Rad's voice. It's so close. Like he's whispering dirty words straight into my ear. Shit! My pussy flutters around my fingers. A moan bubbles up my throat. My teeth sink into my bottom lip, suppressing the noise when my fingers curl inside myself.

"It sounded like screaming," Kieran remarks.

"I'm sure it was an animal," Callum murmurs.

"Now, shut the fuck up. We're going for a swim, and that's it," Kieran urges them on with his commanding voice.

"Fucking finally. You think my Pretty Girl is still awake?" No! I'm not awake. Don't you fucking dare, Ashton.

"All the lights are off. What are you doing?" Callum grumbles as footsteps approach near the window above my head.

If he peeks in, he's going to get a full view of my fingers in my cunt and my vibe against my clit.

"Don't you fucking look in the window, you creep. She'd remove your balls and feed them to you."

Well, he's not wrong.

Time to have a little fun with those assholes who drive me insane. Time for another goddamn punishment.

A thrill shoots through me, tingling through my limbs as my orgasm builds. Something about them being outside my window, able to hear what's going on, heightens my desire.

"Fuck," I moan as loud as I can, gasping for breath.

"Don't cum yet, Pretty Girl," he wheezes outside the window. "Don't do it. Wait for me!"

"But I'm so close," I grit out. "And this is my damn show. I do what I want. You don't get to cum."

"Jesus fucking Christ. Tell me she's not..." A rustling happens, and I grin when I feel his gaze wandering over my naked body sprawled out on the bed. "Yup. She is."

"What?" Callum asks with desperation.

More rustling happens until they're all standing in my window, watching me as I'm about to unravel.

I huff when Kieran groans beside Rad in the window. But I refuse to look at them.

"Shut up and watch. No cumming," I demand, working my

fingers harder inside myself. "Fuck," I moan in a raspy voice, throwing my head back. My heart thumps wildly in my chest.

"This is torture," Rad groans.

Yeah, that's the point. It's what I want. They deserve to suffer after teasing me for so many days.

"You're going to cum, River Blue. Cum right now!" Kieran demands, growling through the screen with such force I fucking combust.

His voice carries me through the most explosive orgasm I've felt in years. It's like I needed them to bear witness to my final crumble.

Blowing out a breath, I throw my rose back into her drawer. I'll just clean her later. "Okay, boys. Go home," I say, making a shooing motion with my hand.

"Go?" Rad all but shouts in hysterics. "My dick is currently saluting and applauding your performance. I can't leave. He needs to show you how much he loved it!"

I snort, staring up at the window with no shame. Thank God for liquid courage. I may regret this in the morning. Or not. I got a damn orgasm and showed these assfaces that I don't need no man to get me off. It'd be nice, don't get me wrong. But that's not the point I'm trying to prove. I could have walked into Rad's room, demanded he strips, and then went to pound town. But I didn't. I did it all on my own.

"Go stroke your dick to the memory of me, assfaces. Because this is all you're getting," I say, throwing a long T-shirt on, covering my naked body.

"Little Star," Callum mumbles through the screen with desperation in his eyes.

"Sorry, boys. I'm all relaxed and sleepy now. Have a good night!" I say, jumping up onto the middle of my bed, bringing me face to face with my peeping toms.

"Fine," Kieran grumbles, glaring at me with lust filling his eyes.

"See you later, Pretty Girl! I'll think of you as I'm stroking my cock in the shower and cum with your name on my lips."

I shudder at the imagery, eliciting a grin from Rad.

As soon as they're walking away, I shut my window and curtains with a sense of pride puffing out my chest.

They can look all they want. But I won't let them touch me until they've proven themselves more.

I grin more when my phone buzzes. Swiping it off my end table, I swipe it open and fucking freeze.

UNKNOWN NUMBER

I heard what you did.

You're more beautiful than I remember. Next time you'll cum with my name on your lips— Not theirs.

You're MINE, goddamn it!!

It's about time you realized it.

My breaths heave when I forward the messages to Olivia and Carter, who get back to me right away.

OLIVIA

I'm on it, babe. Don't worry.

CARTER

Get the fuck over here...

28

Nothing says get the fuck out of your house faster than a text letting you know your stalker heard every single fucking thing you did in your bedroom.

Everything.

The moans. The buzzing. My fucking pleasure.

He stole it from me by listening through my own camera system. The very same security that's in place to keep me safe.

Fuck.

I heave a shuddering sigh, staring up at the white ceiling above me. One that isn't my own. After getting that bullshit text, I threw on some pants and scurried to my brothers' house with fear running rampant through my damn veins. I didn't even grab a fucking bra in my panic. Let alone underwear.

My first thought was seeking sanctuary with Carter. He's Veritas, after all.

I didn't have time for anything. My mind went into overdrive, shoving me out the door before I had time to process what the hell happened. He heard me. He listened in on my most intimate moment. It was different when the boys watched me through the window. I wanted them to see what they had missed out on. But this stalker? He can fuck right off.

My privacy is officially blown. According to Carter, who

collected my messy ass at the front door last night, he's escalated everything in terms of my safety.

"I'll fucking figure this out. Understand? Don't you fucking fret over this shit. That's what me and Liv are for. Now, go the fuck to bed and stop freaking out. I'm going to tap into your camera and track down every goddamn IP address attached to your files. I'll track that bitch. He can't hide from me."

I swallow hard when my phone buzzes on the nightstand next to me. Flashes of the messages my stalker sent me race through my mind.

Is it him again? Is he somehow watching my every move?

My eyes dart around the room. No. There are no cameras in here. I'm secure. This entire mansion is behind a thick fence and beefed-up security. After their scare with the crazy cult years ago, they've never let their guard down. It's half the reason Carter went into Veritas.

Fuck. My stomach somersaults, and my adrenaline spikes. It's not him...

> **ASHER**
>
> I'm bringing breakfast for Lyric. Hope that's okay?
>
> If not...it's okay...just wanted to see her this morning before school...
>
> I can stop by...say hi, and then leave...
>
> Fuck, I sound like a stalker...

Stalker. I squeeze my eyes shut, blowing out a big breath. He doesn't know what he's saying. They don't even know I've been dealing with this for so damn long. When will I tell them? When it escalates too much? My skin crawls, begging me to scratch through it and relieve the persistent itch just out of reach.

What the fuck am I supposed to say? Stay the fuck away? You ruined my damn life? Fuck you, Asher Montgomery? I should say all those things and more. But I can't. Asher isn't stepping into my life for me. He's here for Ly and genuinely putting forth the effort like a good father should.

I'm so damn torn. He's the cause of all my problems. The man who put everything in motion. I hate him. But yet, I don't. Not really. Why can't I? Because I get it. His reasoning, that is. But it doesn't excuse his behavior. Not one bit.

They left me behind because he was a coward. And now, he's putting forth actual effort toward forgiveness.

My damn head throbs as I make my way out of the bedroom. Coffee, small whispers, and food greet my senses. Coffee. I need all the damn coffee in the world to make it through today like nothing happened last night. Or maybe it's time to reveal to the boys what's been going on. It's not just my safety that's at stake. It's Ly's and theirs, too. That maniac has only ramped up since they've come into the picture. Who knows what he'll do to them?

Fuckkk. My head pounds even harder. Why is being an adult so damn hard?

ME

Breakfast is fine. But we aren't home right now... Maybe in an hour? We can meet you there.

ASHER

An hour is perfect...gives me time to make some stops... And coffee? Your usual?

My cheeks heat. Fuck. He'd really go to creepy Nathan, the ever-smiling barista with a knack for staring at me with lust-filled eyes, all for my perfect cup of coffee?

ME

If you insist.

Like fuck am I going to stop him. If this is Asher's way of buttering me up in hopes of a sliver of forgiveness. Then so be it. But let it be known; I'm not persuaded by coffee, enticing words, or damn tattoos... Nope. I need something concrete to cling to before I even think about forgiving them for their transgressions. If I ever do.

ASHER

Are...you guys okay?

I lick my lips, silently going through the list of shit they did to me and convincing myself that I shouldn't fall for their traps again. Nope. Never will I jump headfirst into the deep end named Whispered Words. Not gonna happen.

Liar.

ME

I've been better...

Looks like we're having a talk later, after all. Fuck being an adult.

Huffing a breath, I waltz down the stairs and into the sparse kitchen filled to the brim with children and half-naked men.

"Oh God, my eyes," I hiss, playfully covering them as Kaycee snickers in her seat. "Put some clothes on!"

"Shut it," Seger quips, rubbing at his stomach when I finally open my eyes. "You're in our domain. And in this house, we don't wear shirts."

This isn't the first or last time I've seen my brothers and their husband-in-laws—as Chase makes me say—half naked. It's always in the morning when I've stayed over after drinking just a little too much wine on girls' nights. Sometimes, like before, they happily drive me home. Or Liv and I crash in the bedroom upstairs.

"Good morning to you, too." Chase grins as he flips over a pancake, humming a tune. His shaggy blond hair flaps around as he dances along to the music playing on his phone. "Want some pancakes?"

"They're pretty good," Zepp says, taking a large bite.

"See! I told you I could cook, Grumpy," Chase gripes, glaring at Carter, who scoffs in his direction, not even bothering to make a response.

"Morning. I need lots of coffee, and then Ly and I have to head home..." I trail off at the thought of going home. Dread builds in the pits of my stomach. Home. Am I safe there anymore? Will the same thing keep happening until this asshole has enough and takes me as his own? Shit. I suck in a breath and squeeze my eyes shut. This is the second meltdown I've had this morning. Understandably so. I guess. Fuck. I need to pull myself together, so Ly doesn't sense anything really being wrong.

"Ah, you're getting pancakes from the douchebags living across the street, aren't you?" Seger asks, settling on a stool with a plate loaded with food in front of him. "I'm shocked you haven't murdered them yet."

I wrinkle my nose, falling down the rabbit hole of what-ifs and my family's safety. "They're being punished," I grumble, swallowing the razor blades in my throat.

Carter's eyes dart to mine with suspicion. He nods his head to the side, clearing his throat. "A word?"

I nod, licking my lips, following behind. As I pass Kaycee, she gently hands me a piping hot cup of coffee without a word. Bless her soul.

"You look like you're fucking terrified," Carter remarks, eyeing me as he leans against the wall. He crosses his arms over his chest.

"You think, Sherlock?" I grumble, taking a sip of my coffee.

Ah, the sweet nectar of the Gods. It'll perk me right out of this shitty funk. Soon, I'll be ready to face my stalker head-on. Just give me thirty minutes and more coffee.

"I'll forgive you for that. I was just stating the fucking obvious. You're terrified to go home."

"As I should be, right? That asshole listened to me...me..." I trail off, my cheeks heating.

"Oh, well, that ought to be fucking good. Want to enlighten

me on what you were doing?" He grins wide with a mischievous glint sparking in his eyes.

"Fuck off. Nope. No way." I'm definitely not telling him I was getting myself off as my former boyfriends watched and listened, begging to come inside.

"On a serious note, Little West. We've been working all night to secure your camera system. No one else can view it. We scoured the damn server looking for whoever was in there too and booted them. Unfortunately, we couldn't track them to their location. Only the security company you hired. But we were able to make sure no one else but Veritas has access now."

I swallow hard. Someone was using my cameras to look at me. Hear me. Fucking watched me. And my child. My poor fucking baby has had someone's strange eyes set on her. My stomach drops. How could someone do that? Who even knows how? This is absolutely ridiculous. Our safety is my number one priority. I'm just so damn fed up with watching my back and over my shoulder. I want my safe space back.

"Thanks for looking out for us. Um... Is it safe to go back home?" Despite the intrusion, I want to sink into my bed and never get up. That place was built just for me and Ly. It's my damn sanctuary. I won't allow some desperate asshole to take over my life.

"You're good to go home. Just know, I'll be keeping an eye on you. So, keep your clothes on." He raises a brow, smirking when I flip him off.

"You're an asshole. I don't know how my angel sister-in-law puts up with you," I scoff, faking my anger as he laughs.

"She tamed me," he whispers with affection, eyeing the space near the entrance of the kitchen where Kaycee walks around, kissing her children on the head and handing them their breakfast.

"Okay, well... I'll be heading out then. Anything else I need to know?"

"Keep vigilant. Carry your damn knife... Or that gun Liv gave you a year ago for protection. You remember how to shoot it, don't you?"

"Yes. She forces me to go to the range at least once a month. I'll never forget how to shoot," I grumble into my coffee, taking another long swig.

"I know you don't like it. But knowing how to point, aim, and shoot will be useful if you're ever in a situation with that deranged fuckhead. Got it?" His tone brokers no room for argument. Much like a damn dad's voice.

"Yeah. Yeah. I'll dig it out from my closet and—"

"Load it, River. Load it the fuck up. Put the safety on and put it beside your fucking girly toys in your drawer. Have it available. If he was watching through the fucking cameras... What's stopping him from jumping through your windows? Set your fucking alarm. Load your gun and protect yourself," he growls, inching closer to me. A tic forms in his jaw as his eyes assess the fear on my face and paling skin. Blowing out a breath, he wipes a hand down his face. "I'm not trying to fucking scare you. I'm trying to make you understand. Right now, you're safe. We're doing everything in our power to prevent this from escalating. I have some agents surveying your property and watching for anything serious."

"Okay," I say, swallowing hard again. "Thanks, Carter."

"You're in safe hands, Little West. You just gotta take the fucking precautions yourself, too. That's all."

With that, I finish my coffee slowly, preparing myself for the inevitable. My skin crawls when Ly and I climb into my car. As I buckle her in, I kiss her cheek as she waves to all her cousins, watching us go.

"Are you ready to go home? Your Daddy Asher promised breakfast again." My voice croaks at the word home, but I shake it off. Carter assured me we were safe. There are agents wandering around my property. And Asher is going to meet us there.

We're in good damn hands. I just can't shake this nagging feeling something is about to pop up and throw me off my axis.

Lyric grins. Everything about her lights the fuck up at the mention of them bringing her breakfast.

"Pancakes?" she whispers with big, pleading eyes. She had a few an hour ago, but my child is always down to eat.

I shrug, watching the light in her eyes sparkle brighter. My heart pounds. This is so damn new for us. Slick sweat coats my palms as I slide into the driver's seat, giving one last wave to my family. All the shitty what-ifs bounce around my skull like an unpleasant smell. What if they leave again? What if they break her heart? Or yours?

No.

Scratch that last one. River's barely mended heart is currently locked beneath thick steel and razor blades. It's impenetrable. Maybe bulletproof. More importantly, Whispered Words proof. They can show up as dads. That's it. Nothing less. Nothing more.

Keep telling yourself that.

"He didn't specify," I murmur, driving away from the only family that has ever given a shit about me.

It's odd. Years ago, I hated Seger and Zeppelin for what they had. Dad's love. His money. Everything under the sun while I barely survived on food stamps, two jobs, and a dream. It wasn't until they came to me that I understood what they didn't have either. They may have had a swimming pool with a cave and waterfall, money galore, and twenty cars, but they didn't have love either. They only had each other. Well, and Kaycee, Chase, and Carter, too. They made their own family. Just like I did.

Not until we formed our own bond. I mean, the twenty-million dollars helped out a lot. But money can only buy so many things.

"I hope it's pancakes! Or French toast!" She giggles behind her hands, watching out the window as we drive past all the familiar spots on our way home.

"I should have named you Maple," I quip when she wiggles in her seat with an excited giggle.

No one should be this cheerful in the morning. I need to siphon off some of her energy.

"I like syrup, Mommy," she murmurs, plastering her little face against the glass, leaving marks behind as we pull through the gate of our driveway.

My eyes pass over the guard, sitting at attention in the hut. He eyes me with concern but waves me on. From the looks of it, he's on high alert after last night's incident. I'm sure Carter and his crew filled him in on what fuckery could be on the horizon.

As I pull into the driveway, my brows furrow. There, standing with a tray of coffee in his hand and a large plastic bag, is Asher. His back is turned to me as he stares off toward the house.

"Weird," I mumble, throwing the car into park and turning to look at Lyric, who is scrambling to undo her seat belt. I jump when Asher's worried expression peers through the window as he taps. "What's up?" I ask, raising a brow when I roll the window down.

His eyes dart to Ly in the backseat. "Um, could I talk to you outside? Leave her in here," he whispers.

"Ly, stay here for a second. Daddy needs a word. Okay?" I raise a brow when she crosses her arms and throws herself back into her booster seat.

"Fine," she grumbles dramatically.

"What's wrong?" I ask, stepping out of the car after rolling up the window so Lyric can't spy on us like she loves to do. Sometimes I think my kid is way too observant for her own damn good.

"I don't want to freak you out—"

"You're already freaking me out." My heart pounds out of control when he swallows hard, looking over his shoulder.

"There's a package for you on the porch. And it's—covered in what looks like blood."

I blink rapidly. My breath catches in my damn throat, closing in on me.

"What?" I croak.

"Let's just go through the back and go inside, okay? Then we can look at it. I just want to make sure Ly doesn't see it." I nod without thinking, letting Evil Ash take control of the situation.

My mind doesn't allow me to peek at the porch when he ushers us in through the back sliding glass door.

Once we're inside, he sets the coffee and food down on the counter, spreading it out as a distraction, and puts it onto plates.

"You did bring pancakes, Daddy! I love them!" Lyric squeals in delight as she shoves a piece of sausage link, smothered in syrup, into her mouth with a hum of delight.

"Let me look, okay?" His hand clamps down on my shoulder, drawing my attention to his deeply concerned hazel eyes.

Like hell. "I'm coming with you," I say, lifting my chin. If this is something my stalker did, then I'm going to face it head-on. Fuck his games.

"Your hard-headedness hasn't changed a fucking bit," he grumbles, shaking his head. "Let's look then."

I quickly type out a text to Carter as we walk through the house. My heartbeat echoes in my ears as we slowly make our way toward the front door.

ME

I got a package this morning... It's on my porch...

CARTER

What the hell? Don't touch it! I'll be over soon!
Fucking incompetent agents...

Asher puts a hand across my chest when he swings the door open and nearly gags, stumbling back.

"Don't fucking look..."

Again. Like fuck.

I peek over his shoulder, almost wishing I hadn't. My heart sinks into my ass. All the blood runs from my face as I stare, transfixed by the red mess on my porch. Blood. It's fucking blood. Pooling. Dripping. Smeared over every surface of the concrete, staining it. It wasn't just a box like we thought from the driveway. It's a plethora of pictures and crushed fucking flowers.

Mine.

It says mine amongst the carnage. Photos scattered around of my face. My naked body. My privacy soiled. Fucking again! It's bad enough he heard me through my cameras last night, but this seals the fucking deal.

"Lyric, I want you to look at me right now!" Asher demands, turning around at the sound of her frantic screams coming from right behind us.

Lyric shivers. I'm fucking glued to the ground, listening to my child's cries of horror.

"What the hell?" Callum's voice booms through the house, knocking me out of my stupor. He collects Lyric into his arms, bringing her face against his bare chest. Her sobs echo through the living room.

Where the fuck did he come from? A breeze wafts through the house, coming from the sliding glass doors we came through. Eyeing Callum, he's in his running shorts, dripping sweat from head to toe, panting like he just ran a mile. Fuck.

Asher invades my home with his authority, quickly shutting the fucking door in our faces. Fuck. Blood. It seeps into my mind. It's everywhere all at once.

"It's okay," Asher murmurs, pulling me against his chest. His warm embrace soothes the ache pulling at my lungs. "I have you, River. Okay?" His deep voice rattles through my brain, dragging me from the deep fog surrounding my stupor.

"Little Star?" Callum whispers, putting a hand on my shoulder, gently squeezing until my mind flips back online.

"I have to see it again," I murmur, reluctantly pushing away from Asher. Why did he have to feel so damn good in a moment of crisis?

I shake my head, barely opening the front door again. Photos. Blood. Mine. My eyes dart around the disgusting display.

"You need to come to River's now. Wake up Rad, and get your asses... This isn't for me. This is for River. Something... You're a real dick right now, which I'll let slide. Fucking idiot."

They say when someone dies, you grieve in steps. Denial. Bargaining. Depression. In my case, no one has died. Not yet, at least. But I'm jumping from completely shocked to straight-up rage. It boils through my veins like lava bubbling, ready to spew. I'm so fucking tired of letting this asshole run in the shadows. It's time to bring him out into the sunlight and let him burn.

"The audacity of this motherfucker," I hiss, slamming the door shut. My teeth grind to dust as I march through the house with purpose, only stopping when the incessant sound of my phone dinging nonstop hits my ears.

"What the hell is happening? What's that shit?" Kieran's deep, confused voice travels down the hall, rising above the sound of my phone, getting louder and louder as I step into my room.

"Pretty Girl." Warm arms wrap around me, pulling my back into his chest.

"I need to call Olivia," I mutter, reaching for my phone.

CARTER

I'm on the way... Stay the fuck put.

"What's happening?" Rad murmurs, looking over my shoulder. His entire body stiffens against mine, pulling me impossibly closer.

As I look down at my phone, several more messages come through, displaying the same thing the bloody carnage from outside does.

UNKNOWN

You're mine.

YOU'RE MINE!

You're mine, River West.

No one else's.

Make them leave.

Or I will!

"Jesus fucking Christ," Rad murmurs, holding my shivering body.

"Olivia," I croak into the phone, ignoring the constant messages coming through.

"You never call me..." she trails off in a soft voice.

"My stalker left me some presents. More than pictures...more than..." My voice croaks to a dead stop when the images return, running through my brain at top speed.

"Fucking stalker?" Asher hisses from behind us. He blinks several times, processing my words, and scowls when I turn my back to him and shake Rad's embrace off.

"There are more pictures...and blood, lots of blood." I swallow hard as the images flashes behind my eyelids in rapid-fire succession. "Lots of fucking blood," I murmur again, squeezing my eyes shut. Red. It's everywhere. Infecting me. Invading my damn senses.

"Hold the fuck up, River. You said blood? Are you—" she trails off, emotions building in her always professional tone.

"Not hurt. It's on the porch with some questionable pictures. Every few seconds, I'm getting messages. It's—"

"Escalated to the point of no return. Get the fuck out of that house. Don't touch anything. Get to your boy toys' house and—"

"I'm fucking here!" Carter growls, slamming through the front door with gritted teeth.

"Oh good, he's there," Olivia says, blowing out a breath. "Get. Out. Riv. Leave." She grunts as the sound of fabric rustles. "I'm on my way. Go across the damn street. Protect yourself and my godchild!" I blow out a breath when Olivia hangs up on me, and I stare at the lit-up screen.

"Do what she fucking says," Carter grunts, pacing the tiny space of my living room, looking around at every little corner. "We'll have a lot to discuss."

When I turn around, a wall of men greets me with frowns. Callum clings to Lyric, who's still in his arms, holding onto him as she sniffles.

"Seems like we have a few things to talk about," Kieran growls, crossing his arms.

Fuck. Yeah. Seems like we do.

29

River.

"HOW LONG?" Kieran demands in a low voice, snuggling Lyric close to his chest as we all sit in the tension-filled band house. Far the fuck away from the blood bath currently being investigated.

There, nestled in his lap, is my quiet daughter, sucking her thumb for reassurance. Her other hand clings to Asher's with a death grip. He swallows hard, stiffly sitting shoulder-to-shoulder with Kieran. Unease pulls at his muscles, nestled so close to the same man who vowed to put his fists through his ribs not long ago. For Lyric's sake, he doesn't move an inch.

"Yeah, River. Inform them," Olivia barks, ping-ponging in front of me at a quick pace.

Back and forth she goes, nibbling on her thumbnail like her nerves are eating her alive. She will cut into the wood with her sharp heels if she keeps up the intense pace she's set for herself.

I narrow my eyes at her when she huffs. "Three years," I breathe, nervously running a hand through my hair, not bothering to say anything else.

Blood drips in the back of my mind, spelling out the dreaded word. *Mine.* My head spins, and colors swirl together. Shutting my eyes tight, I breathe through the panic running rampant. When did this sicko go from taking simple pictures of our outings to this? Spying on me inside my home—my fucking sanctuary—

as I undress and go about my life. Vomit soars up my esophagus, ready to spew at the mere thought of what they've seen through their camera lens. Everything. That's what.

"Three. Years?" Kieran growls quietly, keeping his anger at bay.

Barely. Kieran's like an unstable volcano, ready to spew his lava everywhere when the pressure gets too much. If we're not careful, we'll all burn under his intensity. Hell, I could probably stick nickels in his flaring nostrils right now. One false move, and we're all dead. Me, especially.

I sigh. The jig is up, and I'm backed into a corner. The last thing I wanted to speak of or acknowledge was the man following me around like a lunatic. "Yes. Three years of having some stranger following me and taking pictures. It's never been an issue —"

"Don't let her play it off as nothing. He takes fucking pictures of her and Lyric. Up until recently, that's all it's been. Then you chuckleheads came into the picture, pissing the little bastard off. Hence the cow blood on the porch," Carter's gruff voice echoes through the house with authority. Plopping down, he yanks his laptop open and taps a few keys.

"What the hell, Pretty Girl?" Sitting beside me, Rad pulls my hand into his, gently squeezing. "I know we're not in a good place or haven't spoken, but your life is in danger. How could you not tell us? You could have come to us, no matter what." Hurt lines his expression more than the concern etching into his face.

"I'm sorry. I—" I swallow my words. I shouldn't have to apologize. They're the ones that walked away. Not me.

What the hell can I say? *Sorry for not telling you right away that some creep has been following me around. Sorry you weren't here for the past three years to know what was happening. Let's not pretend we're some happy family now. Because of Asher, we were separated and could have done nothing about it.*

"Whoever the fuck this is has a knack for computers. Your cameras have been compromised. Inside and fucking out. Fucking manipulated, too. This fucker took out footage and replaced it with a damn loop," Carter grumbles, staring at the screen with his lips peeled back.

"So, whoever it is—"

"Made themselves fucking invisible." My face falls at his words. "But don't fucking worry, Little West. I'm not the owner and operator of CC Tech for nothing."

"Plus, a Veritas consultant," Olivia adds, snapping her fingers.

My muscles tense at his words. Concealed. Undetectable. Fucking invisible like always, hiding in the damn shadows. Fucking coward! How someone could walk onto my damn property with a security guard and cameras and not get caught is a goddamn mystery. It's like they knew exactly what they were doing and planned it all out.

I've ignored their presence for years, refusing to look over my shoulders. Like hell, would I allow them to see the fear in my eyes. Or the shudder of my nerves when the wind blew just right, and I felt eyes searing through my flesh.

I'm not a raging idiot. I knew they were hiding in the distance with a camera attached to their hands, probably jacking their tiny penis to my image. Denial is a hell of a drug to suffocate yourself in. It convinced me many times that I was okay and that they wouldn't harm us. Until the pictures arrived more frequently. And now this.

"What are we going to do?" Rad asks, squeezing my hand again, comforting me in unexpected ways.

We. Not you. Or her. He's including himself, maybe all of them, into this equation. Something stupid flutters in my chest. Maybe it's the hope of reconciliation. Or perhaps it's the same foolish organ that got me into this situation in the first place.

"Run and fucking hide," Carter suggests without peering at us. A permanent scowl etched onto his face, but I'm used to it by now. He only smiles for violence and my sister-in-law, Kaycee.

Olivia side-eyes him. "Thanks for being subtle like we discussed." He waves a hand, ignoring her presence altogether.

"What do you mean?" Don't say it. Don't fucking say the most rational thing that's about to fall out of your mouth. Please don't. I'm not prepared for this.

"River," she says sincerely, dropping into a chair across from me. "You're more than my friend, babe. I love you and Lyric. I want to protect you both more than I have in the past. It's never been this bad."

"I know." Razor blades slide down my throat at her implication. My mind whirls in so many different directions. I swear I'm giving myself whiplash.

"Then don't hate me when I suggest our safe house in Maine. It's the farthest place away from here. Away from that asshole who won't leave you alone."

Fuck me running, sideways, and up the damn stairs. Maine? Shit. My heart crashes into the waves of my volatile stomach. It's either fly across the country or die at the hands of my crazy stalker. And I like my damn life.

"In the meantime, I'll scour this footage and unscramble what this dickhead did. I'll find this bastard if it's the last thing I do, Little West."

"Maine?" I ask, shaking my head. "I can't go to Maine. Liv, I have a life here... I can't run just because of some weirdo. I'm braver than that."

Fingers squeeze mine in support as my mind jumps off a damn cliff into the what ifs. My calendar flies by in my swirling mind reminding me of my obligations coming in the next few months. The boys need me. They have gigs to rock and mental hurdles to overcome.

"I'm sorry, Riv. I can't give you a choice in this. At midnight we're extracting you. Whether you like it or not, babe. This is for your safety and hers. This is non-negotiable." She rubs a finger along her forehead, nervously watching my blank reaction. "You trusted me with your safety three years ago when Carter introduced us. And I'm saying all of this for your damn safety."

"It'll be for the best, Pretty Girl," Rad whispers with an

aching sadness squeezing his voice, running a finger along my chin, and bringing my gaze to his. "I don't know much about the situation. But we need you safe."

"You'll be safe. That's the only thing that matters," Callum says, sidling up to my other side. "You two are too important to lose." He swallows hard, keeping his eyes locked on mine.

"Why Maine?" I mutter.

"It's on the other side of this place. So far away that your little stalker will have no way of getting to you," Olivia says, raising a sharp brow. "We've been trying to nail this fucker for years. Now, we'll finally have the opportunity."

"What are you going to do?" An evil glint appears in Olivia's eyes, cluing me into her nefarious plans in my absence.

"Whatever we need to do to bring this fucker down."

"What she means is, we'll camp out on your property. Get a little look alike to parade around and act like you while you're away. We'll get this asshole," Carter says, shaking his head. "I'm going to have to take this shit back to the lab and let them work on it." Snapping the laptop shut, he throws it to the side with a worried expression.

"What about—"

"Shh," Olivia interrupts, shoving a finger over my lips. "Think of this as a much-needed vacation. How long has it been since you could not focus on work and live your life to the fullest? Nope, don't answer that. You'll tell me you don't have time, that you're building your damn empire."

"I love you, but I hate you sometimes," I mumble through her finger secured over my lips.

"I'd say pack a bag, but you're under house arrest until we leave tonight. No stepping outside. No going home. You get the picture. There's a team discreetly at your house right now cataloging the weird mess left for you."

"You mean the naked pictures they took of her?" Kieran asks, putting his large mitt over Lyric's ear.

Olivia's lips roll in, and she nods. "Looks like whoever they are, they've been busy."

Carter sighs, rubbing his forehead. "I know how they did that."

"How?" I ask, swallowing hard.

Do I want to know the answer? How they've been getting pictures without my consent and looking at me in my most private moments. No. I'd rather stay ignorant. That's bliss, after all. But I give in like a curious cat for my sanity's sake and the urge to protect my daughter from everything harmful. She doesn't have a clue that a psycho lives on the fringes of our life, snapping photographs of our every move.

Carter locks his gaze on mine, licking his lips like he's nervous for once in his grumpy life. "Not only did they manipulate your cameras, Little West. They hacked into them. They've been fucking watching your every move. Inside and out. Wherever you have a camera, they've been following. Creepy fuckers," he grumbles the last part with a grimace. "Thankfully, you don't have cameras here to compromise us further."

"No, but I have security measures that obviously meant nothing. Fuck. Where was the guard? They're on twenty-four-hour duty." There are four of them for various shifts. Someone should have seen something odd and flagged it for the police to check up on.

Years before, when I got my first piece of mail from my stalker, I invested in a security firm. From there, they sent four guards who watched my place day and night. My cameras also came from them with a live stream sent directly to their database where someone watches for anything suspicious. Window alarms, door alarms, and anything in between secures my home.

"He was there all night. We checked with him. Carter even gave him his scary look, almost making him piss himself. It'd be funny—" Olivia trails off with a huff, and another worried look crosses her face.

Carter chuckles. "Yeah, he was there all night. Believe me. He wasn't lying. Says he didn't hear or see a damn thing. I also checked with your security people, who gave the same answer. Useless fucks if you ask me."

"Great. What good is a security guard if he doesn't see anything?" I shake my head, looking toward the front door as it quietly opens, and Olivia's long-time partner saunters in with a grin.

"Oh, River. You really got yourself into a pickle now, didn't you?" Jordy remarks, twirling his keys in his hand.

"Nice to see you, too," I quip to the Veritas agent I've gotten to know over the past few years.

By looking at his grinning face and easy facade, you'd think he'd be easy to read. He's not. Over the years since he and Olivia took over the Veritas, he's perfected his calm demeanor, even when raging on the inside. With his small-town hunk looks—curly blond hair, boy next door face, and sparkling blue eyes—you'd never guess that he's a full-blown killing machine, taking down the enemy without blinking. Yeah, I'm always happy to have him on my side. He'd put my stalker down in a nanosecond. If we could catch the fucker first.

"Maine is out," Jordy grimaces when Olivia shoots him a look, and he shrugs. "Don't give me that look, *Espie.* There was a storm, and it disabled the house, making it unsecure. You need a new plan."

"How many times do I have to remind you it's Olivia," she growls, narrowing her eyes at his full-blown grin. He shrugs, twirling his keys again, loving the way he's egging her on.

For a time in Olivia's weird and complicated life, she went by another name in the field. It was the name her uncle gave her after the murder of her parents and sister. Or so she thought. As I said, her history is complex and hurts my brain. Since reuniting with her old friends and discovering who murdered her parents, she's returned to her birth name—Olivia.

"We need something now. Everywhere else is occupied." She waves a hand in Jordy's direction.

"I can hide her in my basement," Jordy jokes, grunting when Olivia pushes him away. "Cool your tits, Liv. Sheesh," he grumbles, stumbling over his feet. "Anywhere is better than here. I can hear Riv's phone from a mile away." His nose wrinkles in disgust, staring at the object lighting up on the table in front of us.

He's not wrong. Message after message. Email after fucking email, lighting my phone up like a damned Christmas tree. My stomach twists into a million knots. Whoever is stalking me has finally snapped into a miserable person, hellbent on making my life hell on earth. As long as I'm around my phone witnessing their increasingly aggressive messages, I'll never sleep. Or eat. Or function, for that matter.

"I might have somewhere we can all lay low." Every eye in the room snaps toward Callum as he rises from beside me. Uncertainty twists his face, but he continues before anyone can say anything. "I have a house in a small town. I have a security system and privacy fences. It's completely secure in the middle of nowhere."

"So was this compound River has built up for herself," Jordy remarks, lifting a brow. "You sure some Podunk house will facilitate River and Lyric, and nothing will happen to them? Are you confident?"

Callum stiffens, crossing his arms over his chest. "Yes. It's secure. I built it myself with my fame in mind. It's completely secure. No one knows it's there."

"Where is it?" Olivia asks, slapping a hand over Jordy's mouth. You'd think they were in some ill-fated relationship by the insane chemistry they exude. I told her as much one drunken night, and she laughed. They're friends—nothing more and nothing less. Besides, Jordy has somehow fallen in with my long-lost sister Zandt's grasp. But she's a whole other story. "I need more information before I send my best friend to some ill-equipped house in the middle of nowhere."

He nods, side-eyeing me. "It's in Central City, Illinois. Besides, who said River and Lyric were going by themselves?"

Olivia blinks at him, releasing her hand from Jordy's mouth. "You're willing to go with them? Keep them safe? That's a big task for little boys." Oh, ouch. The boys physically recoil from her remark, tightening their expressions.

"There's no willing about it," Rad pipes up, rubbing his hands together.

"We'll go with them," Asher says for the first time, still clinging to Lyric's hand, despite her tiny snores filling the room as she lies on Kieran's chest.

A satisfied sigh rocks through Asher as his weightless gaze locks on the beauty clinging to his hand. A sparkle flashes in his eyes, relaxing his body on the couch. Asher looks at peace for the first time since our big blowout, where secrets filled the room and choked us. His eyes stare down at her with admiration, filling the holes once left in my soul. How he looks at her is how he looked at me once upon a time when he didn't know I was looking.

"We'll never leave them alone again." His words pierce the room with authority, leaving no room for arguments.

Olivia nods, biting back the grin of *I told you so*. "Good! This is good! The six of you will be extracted from here at midnight. I'll have a local team prepare your house. You say it's secure? Let's go over some details."

And that they do. Thoroughly.

As they make plans, I make my own. Calling the important people in my life about where I'll be, knowing they won't tell a soul. My brothers freak the fuck out. But they knew something was up when Carter took off and came here after I got my package.

"Hey, Kat," I say, pacing around the kitchen as Asher watches me with a close eye.

"Miss West," she says with a surprised tone. "Is something the matter?"

I swallow hard, rubbing my forehead. "Hey, yeah. I'm going

to be out of town for a little while. My stalker paid my house a visit last night, and I need to go into hiding, basically. It's for my safety and Ly's."

"Oh my god! Your stalker? Where are you going?" she asks with concern, breathing heavily into the phone. Soft murmurs come from the other end from a low, deep voice, and my brows raise.

"Uh, Central City. Back to my home. We've got a secured house there." I won't tell her anything else when someone is obviously sitting close to her.

"Got it! I'll keep everything running smoothly in the department. Is there a way for me to get ahold of you? Or should I go through the bosses?"

"My brothers, yeah. Just talk to them about anything you need. I'll be unreachable for however long this takes. Thanks, Kat."

We say our goodbyes and hang up. Worry slams through me at what we're about to do.

The day goes by in a blur as they hash out the details of our extraction and new living situation. After hours of research and ground teams inspecting Callum's house, they clear it for our use.

Under the camouflage of night, Olivia disappears across the street, sneaking around and gathering Lyric and me some essentials for the trip and subsequent never-ending vacation. Only coming back when several bags are filled with our clothes and other items, we may need for weeks to come.

How long would I be away? From my job? From my damn home? Olivia wouldn't give me a direct answer, simply shrugging and telling me to enjoy the dick I was about to receive.

If I wasn't so panicked, I might have killed her. Dick is so not happening.

"I know none of this is glamorous. But if they've hacked into your camera system, they're probably tracking your phone somehow. So, we'll keep that here. We're going to use it to our advantage if they are. We'll start by trying to lure them out and grab them when we can." Her eyes dart to the floor, and she worries her lip.

"I trust you, Liv. You've kept me functioning and safe these last three years. You'll get him. Just...keep me updated or something?" She nods, curling my fingers around the new cell phone, before going to each of the guys and retrieving theirs.

"Sorry, boys, it's a safety precaution." Without a fight, the boys turn in their phones. "Also, Riv. I'll let Rocco know what's up."

"Thank you. He'll worry," I mumble, chewing on my bottom lip.

Before we know it, we're loaded into a blacked-out SUV at midnight and escorted to a private airfield on Veritas' property.

Kieran carries a sleeping Lyric onto the plane, sitting her beside him and buckling her in. He smiles at me, informing me he has her, and urges me to get some rest.

Fat chance.

Murmurs vibrate around me in muted conversations. Some snores ring out. But not mine. I'm left begging for sleep and staring out the darkened window, wondering how my life ended up like this.

Away we go, back to the city that started it all. Our beginning. Our love. Our brutal fucking ending.

For so long, I've held onto this grudge, letting it infect me with the need for revenge. Suddenly, I'm not feeling so vengeful. Day by day, though, they're breaking down the walls I've put in place.

Forgiveness is on the horizon, but there's still so much work to be done to earn my trust and prove their loyalty.

30

River.

Do you ever feel like you're falling down the deep, dark rabbit hole of déjà vu? One second, your life is going according to plan. Work. Kiddo in school. And a nameless band across the street eager to improve under your direction.

The next? There's a stalker on your ass, and you're being whisked away on a not-so-vacation with the four guys you'd rather bury in the sand than spend more quality time with.

Liar!

I frown at my thoughts. Shut it, brain. There's no room for your intrusive thoughts right now. We have more important things to worry about. Like stalkers, security, and whether or not I can fucking sleep tonight.

Besides, if these men want to make up for what they did to me as boys, then bring it on. I'm all for their redemption if they're eager to prove themselves to not only me but Lyric. They can fall to their knees, beg for mercy, crawl over glass shards, and scrape their knees. There's so much they can do to make me truly believe they're sorry for their actions.

Speaking of, they've already achieved step number one...

"Daddy! This is so cool." Lyric's voice echoes through the fucking mansion on a hill smack dab in the middle of a field on

the outskirts of Central City near their old stomping grounds—
Lakeview.

From my spot on the driveway, I can see nothing outside the
tall fence protecting the property all the way around, with
cameras sitting everywhere. Callum wasn't kidding when he said
this place was a fortress.

The only question that remains is why? Why Central City
again? Didn't they run away from this place with the intention of
never returning?

It's fitting, though, sitting here in the familiar early September
heat, sweating my ass off and wishing for the AC. Only this time,
I don't have to walk a mile to work or worry about my computer
taking a shit on me for class. My only obstacles are four men, a
stalker, and a child to protect.

"Are you coming, Pretty Girl?" Rad's hand slides to my lower
back, fitting there as he waits patiently.

His brows dip when I nod, looking around the semi-familiar
space.

"Yeah," I say, clearing my throat through the mess of
emotions bubbling to the surface.

"Okay, now that everyone is here," Jordy says with a pleased
grin, clapping his hands. "Let's go over some rules and whatnot."

I plop on the oversized couch in the spacious, modern living
room, sinking into the fabric. Rad does the same, staying insanely
close to me. Since this morning, he's refused to leave my side,
plastering himself to me. His fingers seek mine, and I let him grip
my hand in his without protest. If he asked, I'd deny the
immediate ease wrapping around my soul like a blanket on a cold
winter's night. Finally, I can breathe. If even for a moment.

"All righty. Callum, I'm impressed. A few of our Illinois
agents looked this place over from top to bottom, and I gotta say,
bro, it's like you were expecting this. No one could trace this back
to you, even if they tried. You don't have any stalking tendencies
to confess to, do you?" Jordy raises a playful brow, grinning at
Callum, who stiffens on my other side.

"No." He blanches.

"Glad we have that settled. There are cameras everywhere, which we've commandeered to our feeds. I'd highly suggest not strutting around naked outside because I'll see what you're packing. Speaking of the outdoors, do that as little as possible. Consider yourselves under house arrest. No sunlight. No midnight ice cream runs."

"No ice cream?" Lyric pouts, climbing into Asher's lap.

Jordy snorts. "That's where I come in, Ly. You tell Mommy to text me, and Uncle Jordy will bring you all the ice cream you need. Only if you stay inside, capiche?"

"Okay," she says, settling back onto Asher, who wraps an arm around her and whispers something in her ear, causing her to grin. My heart melts when she lays her head on his shoulder and sags with relief in his arms.

"A house phone has been placed in the kitchen, and you also have the flip phone in River's possession. That's your tool to the outside world. If you need anything, give me a ring. Food. Toilet paper. Hell, I'll even buy you some micro condoms." He snorts at his own joke, earning glares from the rest of the guys.

"Tool," Rad mutters under his breath, bringing Jordy's grin back in full force.

"Anywho, I'll be here in ten seconds flat. You're completely secure in this giant-ass house in the middle of nowhere."

"You'll keep me updated, right? If you catch him or whatever?" I question timidly, picking at my nails.

"Every step of the way, River. Liv is working hard at your property, trying to lure that asshole out. We checked and double-checked during extraction; whoever they are, they weren't aware you left. Leave this to us. We've got you." He seems so damn earnest when he breaks through his grinning exterior, leaving me feeling settled and secure. "Now, any questions?" he asks, studying each of us as we shake our heads. "Then I bid you good day. Take care of yourselves. Call if you need me. Yaddy...Yaddy... ya. Oh, and set the goddamn alarm!" He rolls his wrist as he exits, lightly shutting the front door and leaving the six of us in a chilling silence.

"So," Kieran mutters, looking around as he stands from the couch. "When did you build this?"

"And why all the crazy ass security, man? This seems over the fucking top," Rad adds.

My eyes snap to Callum, watching intently as he shrugs. "A few years ago. I wanted somewhere to go, and no one would bother me. Especially our fans. You-you know how they can get," he whispers, rubbing his neck.

"This is where you used to disappear to, huh?" Rad asks.

A red tint envelops Callum's cheeks. "Yeah. Whenever I needed to get away, it was like a paradise. No one knows about it. I like to come and see my parents and Jenny."

Ah. That makes sense. He's never really come to terms with the death of his entire family after that crazy plane crash. I don't blame him. I've missed the hell out of my mom since I've been away. Once a week, I visited her grave before I left, leaving her flowers and mementos.

"We literally had the ocean in our backyard, bro. What happened to surfing? The sunshine?" Rad quips.

"Surfing wasn't for me. No coordination on the board," Callum mutters, rising to his feet and setting the alarm through the panel near the front door. When the alarm system rings out that we're protected from danger, I lean back further, closing my eyes.

Sleep was not my friend last night. Not that I could have gotten a wink on the stuffy plane filled with all my ex-boyfriends and worry that my stalker was in the cargo hold, ready to murder me.

It baffles me that one person would follow me around for so long. I'm not that exciting of an individual. Hell, the first two years I lived in East Point, I did nothing but mom, work, and run all over the place. My schedule only settled down when I walked across CaliState's stage with my diploma in hand, if you call my schedule slowing down. Ah, the simple days.

Now, here I am, smack dab in the middle of some shitty joke with no punchline. One girl walks into a house she can't leave with four men who used to put their dicks in her... What could go wrong? Everything, that's what. Fuck. What am I doing? Why did I decide to do this?

Because you sort of had to—yeah, that, I guess. For Lyric. For our safety. Besides, they weren't too keen on walking away from us and letting us go at this alone, which shows how determined they are to earn my forgiveness and make amends.

It's more than absolution, though. I see it in their movements and possessive gazes. Since we cleared the air and freed our sins, their motivations have been strictly pure. No malice or manipulation—they're sincerely trying to prove themselves to Lyric and me.

"You're tired," Callum murmurs from my left, somehow getting there without me noticing. Trembling fingers shift the hair from my face, tucking it behind my ears.

God, his touch does something funny to my insides. All gentle and so full of care. It's a stark difference from the man in the octagon, beating the shit out of his opponent. I shiver at the thought. Memories of his bloodbath come forward. I'd never tell him how much I enjoyed silently cheering him on as he bashed the other guy's brains in.

"Mhhmm," I mutter, heaving a breath.

"I can show you to a room," Callum whispers.

"I have a better idea," I say, peeking open an eye. A loopy grin spreads across my face. "Got any wine?" Because God knows I need some wine to settle my nerves and get through this undetermined number of days stuck in this house with an eager four-year-old and four men who look at me like I'm the light of their life.

"Now you're talking, Pretty Girl. How about some tequila shots off..."

"What's tequila?" Rad stops dead, snapping his mouth shut when Lyric cocks her head with curiosity, awaiting his answer.

"Grown-up juice," Asher says, hiding his smile when she pouts.

"But I want the tequilas. And shots! Shots! Shots!" she shouts, pumping her arm in the air.

"Be better," Kieran rumbles protectively, narrowing his eyes at Rad. "You can't say that shit around kids."

"Shit. Shit. Shit," Ly murmurs.

"Ly," I grumble. "You know that's a grown-up word. Save it until you're eighteen." She pouts more, crossing her arms over her chest.

"Sorry," Rad mutters, putting his hands in the air in defeat, looking guilty as hell.

"Ly, where did you learn to say shots, shots, shots?" I groan, lazily looking her over as she pouts more.

She shrugs. "TV."

"What kind of TV do you watch?" Lyric grins at Kieran when he asks the question that opens Pandora's box of questions.

Lyric's brows furrow. "I saw you on TV, Daddy," she says with furrowed brows. "You won't be a ho anymore, will you?"

"A... A ho?" Rad cackles, falling back into the couch and clutching his stomach.

"What the hell, River Blue?" Kieran hisses when I snort. "What have you been letting her watch?"

I wave a hand, sinking my teeth into my cheek. "Nope! Nu-huh! This is your bed; you lie in it." A laugh bursts from my lips, unable to hold it back any longer.

"Daddy, I saw you with..." Lyric stops abruptly, counting on all ten of her fingers, muttering numbers to herself. "A hundred girls on TV. Did you kiss them? Maggie says that makes you a ho, cuz it was lots of girls." She cocks her head again when Kieran's eyes bug out of his head.

"I am not a ho! And for God's sake, Little Blue. Stop saying ho!" he sputters, standing from his spot. "River! Tell our child I'm not a goddamn ho."

"Your daddy is a ho," Rad sputters, singsonging, unable to contain himself again. "God, Little Pretty Girl. I'm going to bottle you up and keep you forever!" he howls.

"You were in front of the camera a lot with the ladies," I cackle, feeling the effects of my lack of sleep. "She just happened to see you in the aftermath."

Kieran blinks several times at me and huffs, stomping toward me. Standing tall in front of my seated position, he hovers above me, bringing his face to mine. All the laughter leaves me breathless, staring into the intense eyes of the boy I once loved.

"You wanna know something, River Blue?" he whispers, getting in my face.

"Sure." My breath hitches when he inches closer, brushing his cheek against mine.

I shudder when the tip of his tongue brushes against my ear, removing any trace of oxygen from my body. My eyes squeeze shut, and my long-forgotten vagina wets her lips in greeting. Oh, what I wouldn't give to get dicked down. In better circumstances, of course. But fuck. I'm too muddled and exhausted to have any sort of rational thoughts. If I'm not careful, I'll ride them like a cowboy screaming Yeehaw. Yeah, I need wine and a long nap resembling a coma.

"I couldn't get it up." Nothing more. Nothing less. Just a goddamn cocky look with redness spreading over his cheeks.

"What?" I squeak when he chuckles in my ear.

"Did you watch it with her as I walked outside the hotels with my arm around a woman?" I nod. "Mmmm. My dick doesn't like to work for anyone but you. Even when I hated you, he knew the truth. I have over twenty NDAs signed and locked away with their signatures stating they'll never talk about my lack of performance. Couldn't get it up because it wasn't the pussy I needed," he whispers, brushing his lips against my cheek for longer than necessary. "Unlike now," he growls against my flesh, fighting off a groan. "Thicker than steel in my jeans."

"Jesus," I croak, pushing at his chest until he stumbles away with lust dripping from his stare.

Don't look. Don't fucking look. Shit! My eyes dart to his dick straining in his jeans until he discreetly turns his back to Lyric and walks toward the kitchen. Not before sending me a smirk over his shoulder, knowing exactly what he fucking did to me.

"Oh, yeah. This will be the best damn vacation of our lives," Rad whoops. "Now, how about that wine, Cally Boy? I know you have a basement in this monstrosity."

Callum's grin lights up the room. "Yeah. There's, um, a wine cellar and a practice room."

Rad lights up. "Tell me you didn't. Tell meeeee!" he says, slapping his knees.

"It's all downstairs," Callum says through a breath. "Every piece we used to play on before we moved."

"Yes! You saved it all!" Rad whoops. "Come on, Little Pretty Girl! It's time Daddy Rad teaches you how to beat the drums!" Rad grins, holding out his hand. Lyric grins, jumping from Asher's lap and taking it. "Let's go have some fun," he says with a manic grin, leading her to the stairs and disappearing to the basement.

"What kind of wine do you want, Little Star? White? Red?" Callum's body heat pours through my side when he shifts closer.

"Bubbly?"

"Bubbly it is. Anything you want, it's there. I've been collecting them for years. Pink Moscato?" I nod immediately, licking my lips.

"You're the best."

"I'll keep proving it to you every day," he whispers, eyeing my lips until he shakes his head. "I'll be right back."

"How about food?" Asher asks softly from the opposite sofa, staring at me hopefully. I nod in agreement, refusing to move from my spot as the sound of uneven drumbeats and soft laughter echoes up from the basement.

"It's fully stocked," Kieran says, rubbing his hand along his neck.

Asher nods, climbing to his feet. "I'll see what we got, and then we can decide?" Nervously he stands before me, and I nod.

"I'll—uh, help," Kieran mutters, following Asher out of the room.

As everyone leaves the room, my eyes slowly fall shut, succumbing to the much-needed rest I've been craving. The last thing that goes through my mind when the noises around me cease to exist is...

This is what life would have been like if they had been there from the beginning. One to watch her. Two to cook. And one to gather the necessary wine.

31

THE FIRST THING I notice when my mind comes back to the land of the living is... I'm not on the couch anymore. A softness cradles every inch of my body like a floating cloud. The only thing missing is the blissful winds cooling me as I slumber.

The second thing I notice is the burning heat searing through two sides of my body. Front and back. Oh, and the hands in places they shouldn't be, petting my skin in soft circles.

My eyes fly open, greeting the dark world. Only the outline of one mullet-headed, determined man snuggling his face into my neck greets my waking mind.

"What the hell?" I croak, trying to remove Rad's face from burrowing further into the crook of my neck.

"Brings back memories, doesn't it, Pretty Girl? You, me, and Callum snuggled close." His warm breath brushes against my neck, sending delightful shivers. "I didn't even have to sneak into your room this time."

But also...what the fuck?

"Rad," I grumble, trying to bring my hands to his chest.

Instead, the stupid covers hold me hostage, tying them together. Not that I'm complaining. Every girl deserves a little nookie. Right? It's scientifically proven that sex reduces stress. Orgasms bring relief and chase everything else away. Am I convincing myself that what I'm doing is okay? Yeah, probably. I've avoided these feelings with them for days now. And suddenly, I'm falling headfirst into them without stopping myself.

Besides, I don't have the heart to move. For some fucked up reason, my body sags into them. My comfort. My damn home between their bodies. Memories float to the surface of our time together beneath the sheets of my bed in my old bedroom.

"Don't sweat it, Pretty Girl. It's early. We don't have shit to do. Rest with us," he mumbles convincingly, holding me closer. "Just stay here in our arms for a little while."

I sigh. Defeat washes over me. Not that I fought to remove their hands from wandering over my bare...

"Rad! Where are my pants?" I hiss, wiggling my bare toes. "And socks? Shoes?" I swear, before I came in here, I had all the necessary clothes covering my body. And now? Poof! They're missing.

"You, uh...kicked everything off when we helped you to bed," Callum rasps, resting his large, lethal hand on my barely covered ass under the damn blankets. "We tried to stop you, but you told us..."

"You're a bunch of assfaces. Let me get naked for you and rub my titties all over you," Rad mocks with a high-pitched voice, chuckling through the entire sentence.

"Something like that," Callum mutters with a huff.

"I did not." My cheeks heat at the thought. Why the fuck can't I remember? I didn't even drink the wine. Did I?

"You didn't even stay awake for the pork chops Asher cooked. That asshole is getting more and more domestic. Lyric tore into the meat like a rabid dog," Rad chuckles, silently reminiscing about the dinner I missed.

My heart sinks. I left her without a second thought, falling asleep the moment I sat on the couch. Granted, it was a long ass night of hopping on a plane and making it to Illinois so damn early. Then, the trip to Callum's house took hours from the nearest airport. By the time we settled in, it was evening. Guilt churns through me. How could I do that to her? She's probably frightened by the sudden change and not to mention the damn blood that was on our porch. Whenever I close my eyes, the evil word—mine—shines bright red behind my eyelids, haunting me. I can only imagine what it's doing to my four-year-old.

"She was brutal," Callum murmurs. "I think she almost bit Kieran's finger off." A deep, vibrating laugh rattles through my back. Callum takes several deep breaths, burying his nose in the depths of my hair. A deep, relaxed sigh rocks through him when he finally settles against me.

"Where is she? I didn't... God, I'm a terrible mother," I mumble, squeezing my eyes shut and making a move to peel myself away from them. Heavy hands hold me down, refusing my efforts to escape.

I've been so damn consumed with everything happening that I haven't checked in with Ly again to make sure she's okay. She sat between Rad and Kieran throughout the plane ride, entertaining them with her wild stories. She seemed okay—happy, even.

"She's fine, Little Star."

"You're not a terrible mother, Pretty Girl. I'm fucking positive you're the best I've ever seen. You raised a spectacular human being." Taking a deep breath, Rad brushes his lips against my neck without hesitation.

Fuck. Fire devours my insides. My teeth sink into my tongue, refusing to let the moan billow from behind my lips. If he keeps that up, I'm a goner, falling deeper and deeper into them. And it's always them, isn't it? Rad and Callum together have this way of unraveling every inch of me until I'm theirs.

"Thank you for being there for her. You're a goddamn amazing mom, and I feel so fucking honored you included me in the dad category," Rad murmurs, kissing up my neck.

And wouldn't you know, my traitorous body melts under his touch. My neck elongates, allowing him access. And that damn moan I hid softly leaks out, filling the room.

"I-I never wanted her to feel like she didn't have a father..."

My breath shudders in my chest. "Fuck," I moan when Callum swivels his hips. A hard, long object pokes my ass, and his sexy-assin, low moans fill my ears. One after the other, igniting my entire body into an inferno of need.

"You say the word, Pretty Girl, and I'll oh-so-reluctantly stop kissing you. But I've been dreaming of this for weeks."

I could stop this.

I could tell them I hated them for their actions and that I would never forgive them. Ever. There is no way in hell I'll ever be intimate with them again, not after what they did to me. Not to mention Lyric. They left us—walked the fuck away without a backward glance.

After all that, I shouldn't give in to my wild whims. My mind screams at me to get up and walk away. To keep my interactions with them purely professional and not dip my toes in the same waters that fucked me over years before.

But when have I ever listened to reason? Especially when my body demands their hands glide over my flesh at an infuriatingly slow rate.

I fucking need this release. I'm no longer interested in holding a grudge against men who are proving themselves over and over again. Consequences be damned. Asher betrayed us. Yes. It happened. He fucked up. Majorly. But from what I can see, he's stepping up and taking charge of his mistakes by paying for them. He's there for Ly. They all are. They're finally the fathers I've dreamed of since I pushed Lyric from my body, hoping they'd return to my side.

And here they are.

"Don't you dare stop," I moan, leaning into Callum's embrace and aching for the friction.

"Your wish is my command, Pretty Girl."

"We'll take this slow, Little Star."

"Just like old times." I don't need my eyes to hear the grin of excitement on Rad's face. "Lift her leg, Cally Boy. Teamwork makes the dream work," he chuckles, kissing down my jaw until his tongue invades my mouth and takes me prisoner.

Thick fingers wrap around my throat from behind, holding me still as Rad takes everything he's been craving. My soul. My damn breath. My every fucking thing escapes me. Becoming Rad's—theirs.

Every inch of me vibrates. The fire-hot need presses down on me, suffocating me in the incessant tingling, begging to break free. It's been so damn long since someone else has touched me. I'm practically coming when his fingers brush against my stomach, slowly falling to the elastic of my panties.

"Fuck, Pretty Girl," Rad groans when his fingers disappear beneath my panties, gliding through my wet folds. "You're so wet for us," he whimpers, thrusting two fingers inside.

The world disappears, falling away into nothing but the pumping of Rad's fingers going in and out of me. I think I meet God himself when I float into the clouds of pleasure I haven't felt in so damn long. Fuck. White bursts behind my eyes like fireworks blasting off and taking over my damn vision. Explosive moans leak from my throat, resembling their names, when my orgasm finally hits its peak and throws me over the damn edge.

"Oh, Little Star," Callum groans in my ear, stopping his movements and stiffening behind me. One long, drawn-out moan breaks me from my fog. "You made me cum in my damn pants," he murmurs into my neck. A breath shudders through me, and heat forms over my cheeks.

"That was hot as fuck," Rad groans, flopping on his back and admiring his glistening fingers in the pale moonlight slipping through the blinds. "Eyes on me, Pretty Girl," he whispers, releasing his dick from his boxers. When the hell did all his clothes come off, too? "Watch as I cum to the memory of you."

My eyes lock on how he thrusts into his hand, using my cum on his fingers to coat himself. His eyes roll into the back of his head as large streams of cum jet from his dick, landing on his stomach, painting his flesh with his own release.

"Holy fucking hell," Rad heaves.

Those large, brown eyes gaze straight into my soul. Satisfaction sparkles through him, and he grins, leaning over and gently placing his lips on mine. Instantly my eyes close, losing myself in the softness of his mouth and the warmth of his probing tongue.

"Oh, Pretty Girl," he whispers, running his lips down my jaw, only stopping when his face snuggles into the crook of my neck. "You're my home. My everything. I'm going nowhere. I'm stuck on you like my cum has dried and glued us together." He sighs like his words are the epitome of a romantic gesture.

But so, so Rad.

"Never again will we leave your side, Little Star," Callum whispers, shifting slightly behind me. "You can push us away. Light us on fire. Yell at us... But we'll always come back for more. We're in this together from now on. And so fucking sorry for letting Asher talk us into leaving."

"Or believing anything he had to fucking say," Rad gripes with a huff. "I can't believe he fooled us for so long."

I suck in a breath, basking in the moment of declarations. Words are cheap. Meaningless, even. But their actions. They've been proving themselves to me. Callum offered this house as a refuge, and they followed me here. They're protecting us from the person stalking my every move. The guys are just more than empty words and promises.

Their grips tighten on me as they pledge their futures. Promising me things they've broken before. *We'll never leave you behind. We'll take you to California with us.* I've heard that one before. Am I crazy to believe them this time around? Have they changed their ways? So many possibilities run through my mind now that I'm post-climax. They could leave again. They're in a band, after all. What happens in six months when they kick this program's ass and go on tour? I'll be here. Ly will be here.

Fuck. Stay in the present. Yeah, that's what got you here in the first place.

"Don't answer," Callum whispers, running a hand over the curve of my bare ass, letting it rest. "You have every right to overthink this and question our motives."

"I'd marry you tomorrow, Pretty Girl. I'd give you the Radcliffe name in a heartbeat. But it's not up to us. It's up to you. We're all trying here. Even that dickbag Asher. I see it in the way he looks at you and Ly. We're all here for you."

Pfft. River Radcliffe, my ass. This is my damn show. "If anything, you're taking my name. We'll be the West family," I murmur with a grin.

"Mr. Ashton West." He nods a few times, scratching his chin. "Hell yeah, Pretty Girl! I'll take your last name. Fuck my parents and fuck the asshole I was named after. I'm Ashton West from now on. I'll make it official, too."

"Take all the time you need. We still have a lot more to prove to you that you're our end game..."

"You always were, and we were dumb fucking idiots," Rad grumbles, kissing my cheek before he pulls away. Cradling my face in his palm, a slight grin tugs at his lips. "Mrs. Radcliffe has a nice ring to it. Doesn't it? You like it, don't you, Pretty Girl?" His brows wiggle when I whack him in the chest and snort. Those big, expressive eyes of his cloud over with worry as his easy-going expression falls away.

"What's wrong?" Worry takes hold as the serious expression my funny guy usually wears disappears.

He blows out a breath. "If anyone's the ho, it's me, Pretty Girl. I..." He shakes his head, cursing under his breath. "I didn't wait for you like all the others. I..." I place my hand on him, resting it there until he continues. "After we left, a hole opened in my damn chest. There was nothing I could give anyone else except music. No one owned my heart like you did—still do. It was always with you, sitting in your palm. But I... I slept with a few girls here and there. It was never anything serious. I just drowned myself in their existence to rid the pain of what I thought happened."

"We were apart," I whisper, squeezing his hand. "I never would have expected you to." Who would? This is reality. They thought I betrayed them. So, why not enjoy themselves? Move on. As much as it pains me to think of them with other women, they were free of me. Not tied down.

"I know. We were done. Broken and over. But, Pretty Girl. I've felt so damn guilty since we came back together. And since... You didn't with Van. And I..." he trails off again with a heavy sigh. His shoulders slump, and defeat crosses his expression.

"You think I was celibate the entire five years?" I raise a brow when his gaze whips to mine in alarm.

"Of course not," he says, scrunching his face. "Although that's a punch to the damn heart. You and other guys? Fuck. But no, I can't judge you. We were apart..."

"And now we're together." It slips before I can think about the implications of my words.

Together. As in, we're in a relationship. Maybe? No. Ugh. I swallow the razor blades in my throat. There's no time to take back the words now out in the open. Free for their interpretation. Only a few weeks ago, the truth came out about Asher's betrayal. And now, a deep need plows through me. It's more than sexual. It's the connection I've always had with each of them. I want this. Despite everything I went through. I deserve to be happy, right? And so does Ly. Why should I hold back from them when they show me daily how much they care and want to make amends?

Rad blinks at me several times before a sly grin explodes. "I knew you'd come around to being my girlfriend. It was only a matter of time!" he chuckles, resting his head on the pillow.

"Slowly," I whisper with apprehension.

"You're still hurt," Callum says in a soothing voice.

"One day at a time, Pretty Girl," he murmurs, brushing his lips against mine. "But I'll still call you my girlfriend." He snickers when I roll my eyes.

"How about you?" I ask, looking over my shoulder. "Any dirty deets in the sheets?"

If the darkness hadn't covered Callum's face, I'm sure I'd see the redness seeping up his neck.

"You were my first and my last," he murmurs, squeezing my ass with his large palm.

"Well, Jesus, Cal. Way to make me look horrible. Kieran can't get lil Kier to work in the presence of another woman. You haven't touched anyone but our girl. And Asher...well, I don't know about that dickbag... Pretty sure he locked himself up and threw away the key. The only thing that bastard was interested in was music..." he trails off, scrunching his face. "Then there's me, Ashton, the asshole man-whore."

I snort. "You're not a man-whore. Shush," I murmur, feeling the ache of exhaustion pull at my limbs. A tingling starts at my toes, slowly working its way up both legs until I'm on the verge of sleeping again. "You're just fine."

"Night, Pretty Girl. We'll be here when your eyes open." Rad's lips rest on my forehead.

"Night, Little Star. We'll watch over you," Callum murmurs, brushing his lips against my nape.

"Night," I mutter through a heavy tongue, falling into a dreamless slumber.

32

Kieran

By the smiles on Rad and Callum's faces this morning, I can tell something happened between the three of them. Something monumental. Something I want. Fuck.

"You're grinning," I grumble, side-eyeing Rad.

Rad rifles through the fridge with nothing but his boxers on, shaking his ass as he walks. He softly hums a tune under his breath, brimming with joy.

And it makes me fucking sick. My stomach turns at his happy movements. What did he get to do with her? Why is he so goddamn happy? And why wasn't it me?

"I don't kiss and tell," he replies, sticking his head in the fridge. He grins more when he pulls out the coffee creamer and goes to the Keurig. "You have to make your own way."

Running a hand down my face, I blow out a long breath. My own way? How can I show River how sorry I am? Dates? Food? Music? Shit. I've got nothing brewing in my idiotic brain but jealousy and wanting to wring Rad's neck.

"You, too?" I raise a brow when Callum snorts, hiding his blush from me.

Prick.

"Actions, not words," Rad says, plopping beside me with a

steamy cup of coffee. "Lots and lots of action." He wiggles his brows, slumping back into the seat.

"A child lives here, too. Don't you think wearing some pants and a shirt would be smart?" I ask, flicking the metal pierced through his nipple.

"Fucker," he yelps, backing away from me and holding his nipple, giving me a hate-filled look. "How dare you touch my mighty nipple with your fat fingers. Asshole."

"Your mighty nipple?" Callum scoffs, sitting opposite of us on the fluffy loveseat.

"Leave Stanley alone," Rad gripes, rubbing at the metal speared through his nipple and...

"Please don't tell me you named your nipple."

Rad scoffs at my words, continuing his soothing circles. He acts like I cut it off with a knife. I fucking could if he wanted me to. Maybe then he'd shut up. Great. Now, he's pouting at me and sipping his coffee like a baby.

Sometimes it's hard to believe that there was an open rift between the four of us, threatening to swallow everything we'd worked so hard for. Since Asher's admission, the tension has settled. We've drifted into a neutral area where we all have an understanding. Everything we do is for them—Lyric and River. Whether we hate each other or don't get along, we try. For them.

"Doesn't everyone? This is poor Stanley, who is now red and irritated. No thanks to you," he says, throwing nasty looks my way.

"For fuck's sake," I grumble, shaking my head.

"I'm curious what the other one is called," Callum says, further provoking his stupidity with a smirk.

"Don't rile him up." I side-eye Cal, who shrugs, sipping more of his coffee.

"Well, this is Stanley, and this is Shirley. They're married."

"Nipples can't marry, asshat," I gripe, throwing my arms in the air. "This is the weirdest shit I've ever been a part of."

"You pretend like you haven't known me since middle school,

K. It's rude as hell. Leave S and S alone." Rad rolls his eyes in complete seriousness.

What ring of hell do I live in?

God, sometimes Rad drives me up a wall. But he's been my brother for far longer than I can remember. He was the first person to pull me into his orbit in middle school. The first person to make me laugh after falling into my miserable life with Nigel and Gloria.

Sure, he annoys the hell out of me. Sometimes. Other times I want to punch him in the face. Or hug him. The thing about Rad is, even when we were falling apart at the seams, I still loved him like a brother. I don't know how I could have gotten through life without his crazy ass.

River's bootcamp has shown us what we had lost. Why did I fight everything so hard? She's always been the answer both personally and professionally. Here in Central City, she helped us build our band and brand, and now we are back, and she's doing the exact same thing. It's not social media and recording our EP this time, it's family and brotherhood.

"He's got a point," Callum quips.

My eyes snag in the doorway where a very disheveled Lyric stands, yawning. Her tiny fists rub at her eyes as she stands in a long white t-shirt I recognize as Asher's. Her dark locks stick up in every direction as she squints, looking around the room.

My heart aches when my green monster reactivates. Last night, after River passed out from exhaustion, we tended to Lyric. Together we ate dinner, watched a little TV, and hung out. It felt nice having all four of us in the same room without fighting one another. And Lyric, of course.

Am I still pissed as fuck at Asher for what he did? Uh, fuck yeah. He can swallow glass for how he manipulated us into leaving. But for Lyric's sake, I'm trying to keep an open mind and swallow my anger as best as possible. What would she think if her dads always fought in front of her? How could we protect them both if we weren't in sync? Besides, the longer I'm around him, the less rage I feel. Asher did a fucked-up thing, but I'm slowly forgiving him for what he did. Because I get it. To an extent, I understand his reasoning. Albeit fucked up, I get it.

Besides, last night when Lyric was sleepy, she curled up in Asher's lap and begged him to snuggle her in bed and read a story. So, I compromised, even when we locked eyes, and he asked permission with his dopey stare.

Something has changed in Asher in the past few weeks, and it seems to be for the fucking better. He's rounding out, seeming less stressed. It makes sense with the massive secret he was holding in for so long. I'd never admit it to Asher, but seeing the man he should have been peeking out after hiding for so long is nice. For so long, we were under his father's iron fist, facing his wrath daily. We were in survival mode. Now, we're not. Especially him.

"Daddies," she says softly, shuffling her feet as she approaches.

"Sleep well, Little Blue?" I rasp, reaching for her the moment she's within grabbing distance. I drag her onto my lap and place my arms securely around her, wanting to keep her there forever.

"Daddy snores," she mumbles, rubbing her face along my shirt. Her tiny body sags into mine with relief.

I marvel at her when I brush my fingers through her hair. A sense of peace washes through me with her in my presence. This is all I've needed these past few years. I've been angrily stumbling along in life, blindly feeling for my next move. She was it all along. Her and River. The beacons I've begged for, dragging me out of the miserable fog I was in. Finally, the veil has been lifted. I'm seeing clearly for the first time.

"Sorry, Little One," Asher rasps, smoothing down his hair as he walks into the living room, awkwardly looking around. "But you weren't too innocent yourself. You kick like a donkey. Did you have dreams?"

I try to hold in my snort, but it doesn't work when she frowns at me and gasps. "I do not kick! I sleep like a log, ask Mommy. That's what she says." She pouts a little, crossing her arms. "No

dreams. Not like at home when the ghosts tap on my windows."
My brows raise at her admission.

"The ghosts tap?" I ask carefully, and she nods, blowing out a
breath.

Asher shakes his head, rubbing at the bruises lining his ribs
with a wince. "You're a little ninja when you sleep, Little One," he
says, giving her a genuine smile as she stares up at him with a grin.
"You hungry?" he asks her until she nods.

"I want ice cream!" This time she directs those big,
mismatched eyes in my direction, batting her eyelashes.

"No ice cream," I mutter. "That's not breakfast."

"How about some pancakes? I think I saw some ingredients in
there." Lyric immediately perks up, nodding with excitement.
"Okay. Pancakes it is. Um, anyone else?" Asher asks, clearing his
throat as he looks around the room, rubbing the back of his neck.

"Make a stack, but serve me coffee first," River grumbles,
stumbling into the room, squinting her eyes. "When did the sun
get so damn bright?" With a sigh, she sits down next to Rad and
me, closing her eyes with a groan. "Fuck morning," she grumbles
again, slumping into the couch.

"My sentiments exactly, Pretty Girl. Fuck today. Let's just go
back to bed." Leaning in, he brushes his lips against her cheek.
"So, I can lick you all over. Again." He grins when my brows raise
into my hairline.

"Coffee first, licking later," she mumbles, blindly taking a
coffee cup from Asher, smirking at her words. "You're my savior,
Asher. Today, at least." His entire face lights up, displaying how
fucking pleased he is with himself.

My heart pounds at her words. Him? Her fucking savior?
He's the reason we left. It's all his goddamn fault. Everything is.
Has she already forgotten in the midst of the chaos? Fuck. I glare
at him, telling him with my eyes to back the fuck up. He has no
claims over her right now. If he wants her, he'll have to beg for
her. Just like I'm going to do. At some point, when I figure out
how.

"Daddy," Lyric murmurs, looking up at me with a frown. "Your face is tight."

Right. I can't be hostile—the pact. We're in this together and getting along for the girls, especially for Lyric. She can't see the four guys she calls daddy arguing or hating each other. So, I suck up my pride and relax my facial expressions, letting all my rage go.

"I'm fine," I say soothingly, rubbing a hand down her back.

"I call dibs on coffee tomorrow," Rad declares, eyeing everyone around the room. "Then we can let the licking commence." He cracks a grin until my fist meets his gut.

"Little ears," I growl, nodding toward Lyric, who frowns as I put my hands over her ears.

"Dude!" he wheezes, clutching his stomach with a frown.

"Are they little?" Lyric asks earnestly, pouting a lip.

"He means your daddy is saying grown-up things around you, Ly. And he doesn't want Daddy Rad to say anything bad." River sips her coffee, humming under her breath. "Your ears are perfect for your noggin."

"Oh," Lyric says, removing her hand. "Okay."

"Sorry, Little Pretty Girl. I've got to get better at not saying naughty things," he says, touching the end of her nose with a grin. "Will you forgive me?"

She taps her chin like she's thinking about it, letting a little grin slip through. "Maybe. I like ice cream," she says, shrugging.

River snorts. "She also drives a hard bargain. Good luck."

"Well played," I murmur in her ear as she giggles, looking at me with the hope I'll give in and give her the ice cream she's been craving.

River shifts in her seat, heaving a breath. "Despite where we are, I'd like to resume with band practices and my procedures."

"I want to watch daddies play!" Lyric shouts with wide eyes. "Can I?"

My heart swells. "Of course." I grin when she excitedly claps her hands.

"Oh good! You're all dressed!" We all jerk toward the front door as it's thrown open, and the alarm blares through the house.

Seemingly on instinct, Callum rushes to his feet in a flash, squaring up in front of Jordy, who is grinning like an idiot in the face of danger. I've seen what Callum can do with his fists. He's a goddamn deadly weapon these days.

"Aw, how cute, Fighter," Jordy quips, tapping Callum's shoulder condescendingly. "But you can put your dukes away and shut off that alarm." He shoos Callum away with the flick of his wrist.

"Jordy, be nice," River chastises him, narrowing her eyes with familiarity. My spine stiffens at their camaraderie. What does she have with him? Have they known each other for long?

"Me? Not nice? I'm always a joy." I snort at his words, earning a stare. "Anywho, got some updates, Dollface. But first," he grins, holding up a pink tablet.

"My tablet!" Lyric shrieks, abandoning me for the piece of technology and snatching it out of Jordy's hands. "Thank you, Uncle J." She grins up at him as he pats her head.

"No problem, kiddo. Now, do Uncle J a solid and go rest in your bed and watch some TV. I even have your favorite all geared up and ready for you. I need to have a big discussion with your parents—all of them." His eyes roam around the room when he says those words.

"Okay," Lyric says without a fight, skipping off into one of the back bedrooms and disappearing from view.

"All right, kiddies. Time for a discussion. And uh, pants are mandatory," he says, gesturing to Rad, who still only has his boxers on.

"Pants lovers," he grumbles, disappearing into the hall and returning with sweatpants as we approach the kitchen island.

"What's going on?" River asks with a pinched expression. "You've got that serious constipated look about you." I don't see it, but she obviously knows him better than I do.

Fuck.

I wonder if they've ever slept together or...

"Right. It is serious," Jordy sighs, bringing out another tablet. "The lab worked all night unscrambling the mess your little stalker made with the cameras. We were able to scrub some manipulation away and get a visual of the asshole who painted your porch in real blood," he says, cringing when he clicks a few times and stares at the screen. "Cow's blood, before you all ask."

"Do you know who it was?" Asher asks, leaning against the cabinet near the stove as the pancakes he promised to cook are on the griddle.

Jordy's eyes drift to Asher with a grim expression pulling at his features. "We got a look, but it's not perfect..."

"Can I see?" River asks as Jordy turns the screen toward her. "No... I... How?" she stutters through her words. A despondent look takes over her face, glazing over her eyes. Like she's losing herself in the abyss of no return.

"Pretty Girl. It's okay. We got you both. Okay?" Rad mumbles, wrapping an arm around her shoulders. Her nose scrunches when he forces her head to lean against his, but she doesn't push him away.

It's progress.

"Sorry, Dollface. I know it's fucked up to think that someone was lurking around outside your house. Here, I have the footage," he says grimly. "It's not perfect. There's still some static over the picture, and it jumps with lines. But It's the best we could do."

"Okay," River says, clearing her throat.

Jordy sets the tablet out on a stand and presses play. Collectively we hold our breath as someone walks onto the distorted video, huddling near the front door with supplies in his hands. He keeps his ball cap pulled low over his eyes, hiding his face from the cameras.

As he maneuvers around the porch, he carefully lays out the scandalous photos. Vomit rests in my throat as my eyes flick to a paling River, frozen as she watches. If I could scoop her up and protect her from everything, I would. But this seems to be the one thing I can't handle here. Except by being here in this house and ensuring no one but this asshole agent enters.

"Wait." Callum reaches for the tablet with urgency, holding it close to his face. "I know this guy," he says, pointing to the larger-statured man, positioning photos on the porch and throwing blood from a bucket everywhere.

He snarls, looking around River's property in the dead of night. Only illuminated by the night vision, highlighting his pockmarked face.

"Seriously, Genius?" Jordy quips in awe with wide eyes.

Callum glares in his direction but nods. "I remember his face. He's the one who knocked River down at the fights," he says, elbowing Rad, who stares at the screen, blinking rapidly. "He came every weekend with a group, always in the shadows. Ruthless told me once his name was Adrian Spencer." His brows furrow.

"Holy hell. That's the giant who looked like he would eat us for dinner. And not in a sexy way, either," Rad says.

"I remember that," River grumbles. "Knocked me right on my ass, and then I lost my phone that night. You almost got into a fight with him."

"Wait," Jordy says, holding up a finger. "You lost a phone? Liv never tells me anything."

"Yeah. I don't know where it went, but it disappeared after he knocked me over."

"It's possible he stole it. In my book, there's no such thing as coincidences. I'll relay this back to Liv and see what she says," Jordy says, clicking on the screen a few times and then turning it around. "Adrian Spencer. He's been nothing but trouble in the East Point underground for a few years." He shakes his head, scrolling through the contents. "Burglary, arson...looks like anything his boss tells him to do, he does."

"Who does he work for? You said his boss, so he must work for someone?" I question, tapping my finger along the marble countertop.

"You'd be correct," Jordy says, rolling his lips together. "Adrian is the muscle in the local gang we've been keeping an eye on."

"Why is he stalking me?" River whispers with a horrified expression.

"That we don't know. Liv and the gang back home are searching for him to question him as we speak." Reaching over, Jordy puts a protective hand on River's, earning several threatening growls. Jordy smirks, tapping her arm. "It'll be okay. You know we're the best, and we finally have some answers. Your safety is number one. But you still can't leave this place, and we're keeping you under lock and key. Just in case this person was hired for this. We don't have definitive answers. So, stay vigilant."

"Thank you, Jordy," she says through a breath.

"Also, you dickheads should know I have my own girl. River's great and all, but I like her sister more." He winks in our direction and steps away, tucking the iPad into a sleeve. "We'll be in touch." Saluting us with two fingers, he makes his way to the door. Before I can even think about it, I follow him out into the warm September day.

"Hey, man," I say. "Could I...um...ask you a favor?" I rub a hand over the back of my neck as nerves take over me.

"What's up?" he asks, folding his arms over his chest.

"I want to do something special for River and kind of...make amends and shit for..."

"Walking away? Leaving her with a baby? I know all the deets, douche. You're lucky I'm a professional." With a frown, he brings his fingers to his ear and scoffs. "According to Agent Asshole in my ear, I am not being professional. Yeah, yeah, shut it..." He shakes his head, blowing out a breath. "What do you need?"

Anger heats my face. Who is he to judge what we did? It wasn't our fault we were misled by our damn brother. "Listen, I know we fucked up, but there were other things happening that made it happen..."

"Like your brother, the pancake-maker, manipulating you all into thinking she cheated?"

"How the hell do you know so much about our lives?" I growl, growing tired of his cocky smirk.

He shrugs. "Hello, I'm a super-secret agent in a company that doesn't exist on paper. I know things. Lots of things. So, what do you want?"

"Okay, so..." And I tell him every detail of the date I've had brewing in my mind since we stepped back into Central City.

33
Kieran

MOISTURE LEAKS from every surface of my body, pouring like a damn waterfall. It stains my pits, and slickness coats my palms, making it hard to hold the flower in my damn hand. I bounce on my toes on the concrete patio just outside the back sliding glass doors leading to the beautiful backyard.

Calm down, dickbag. It's just a date. With a beautiful girl. You used to be in love with her and fucking tore her heart out. Shit. That's not the pep talk I needed to have with myself.

Tonight is the night I prove myself worthy to River with no expectations.

Noise from beneath me echoes through the glass doors, making me smile. Ever so slightly, my nerves die off when pride puffs out my chest.

First, it's the random banging of Rad's drums. Then comes the loud screeches of Asher's guitar. Finally, like music to my ears, Lyric's loud screech through the speakers fills the house, followed by deep laughs and applause.

I blow out a breath. This is it—the moment I've been planning for the past few days with the help of Jordy. When I mentioned my idea, he seemed impressed. Well, kind of. I'm unsure how to make that man believe I'm sorry for what I did.

"It's a fucking start, dickbag. I'll see what the team and I can come up with. But my advice?" He raises his brow.

"Yeah?" I reluctantly ask, anticipating his wicked words.

"Don't fuck it up again, fuck boy. River West doesn't need you. She's only letting you close because Lyric means everything to her. You walk away again for any reason. I'll cut your dick and balls off myself and feed it to you." I swallow hard at the disturbing imagery.

"No dick-cutting necessary. We fucked up. I fucked up. I want to make it up to her."

"Might work," Jordy says with a shrug. "Now, if you're done planning your romantic date. I have a stalker to catch, so we can all go home."

For a split second, I thought he would blow me off and not pull through. But this morning, he discreetly showed up when River was in the shower and threw boxes filled with my requests at me.

"Good luck. You'll fucking need it," Jordy mumbles, silently slipping out the door.

"What's that?" Asher asks, stirring something in a skillet on the stove. Lyric rests on the stool with her nose in her tablet, laughing at a random video, patiently waiting for Asher's promised lunch.

"I'm taking River out on a date," I say, clearing my throat from the emotions trying to bubble up.

He nods. "I bet that will be fun." His eyes drift to Lyric, who is so lost in her tablet that she doesn't realize I'm standing beside her with four large boxes in my hands. "I'll watch her so you guys can have some privacy. Any time you guys want a date."

I blink several times when he shrugs, returning to cooking. "That's—uh, great, man. Thanks."

"I won't interfere," he says softly, not bothering to look at me. "I don't fucking deserve her, anyway."

No, you don't—is what I want to say, but I bite my tongue. Asher is already hurting so much, and I can see that now. Hell, he's been hurting for years, and I never bothered to pay attention. Was it his fault he was in this mess? Yes. We all fuck up, though, don't we? We all make major mistakes when it comes to the people we love. Not once has he stuck his nose in the air and denied the facts since he spilled the secret. I'm still fucking pissed at him. A little sliver of that anger will probably permanently hide away inside me.

But I want to let go. For my fucking sanity.

Therapy has helped so damn much to come to terms with what happened. Without that, I wouldn't be here with a clearer mind. Asher and I have talked it through in the presence of the therapist, and she's helped us really talk everything out. Every mistake. Every word said. We've discussed it at great length. Slowly but surely, we're getting through this as a team again. A family unit. Our next session, though. I want to talk to him about what he thinks he deserves versus what he actually deserves. He'll live with these mistakes for the rest of his life, but he shouldn't keep punishing himself. The way he is with Ly proves to me he loves River more than anything, too. His actions speak volumes. And it's time they get recognized.

So, now I wait for the woman of the hour on pins and needles, nervously pacing. I pull at my collar, marveling at the suit Jordy picked up for me. Somehow, it fit me perfectly from neck to ankles. I'm almost afraid to ask how he managed to get my measurements and make this happen.

The stars above twinkle on the warm September night, overlooking the beautiful setup on the back porch. For one night only, I'll have River all to myself. Uninterrupted. Mine. And no one else's.

And I can't fucking wait.

"River Blue," *I whisper, stopping her as everyone drifts to the kitchen for the meal Asher and Rad made together.*

"Kieran," *she says playfully, raising a brow.*

"I, umm..." *My tongue sticks to the roof of my mouth. Fuck. Nerves eat away at me. Why am I having such a hard time asking her? This should be simple.*

River, go out with me. River, forgive me for being a dumbass.

"You're sweating," Rad quips as he passes by with a steamy plate of food, grinning as Lyric follows, begging for the meal. "At the table, Little Pretty Girl. I'll cut up your steak as your Daddy Kieran tries to woo your mommy."

River's gaze whips to mine. "Woo me?" she asks, wrinkling her nose.

Rad smirks in victory. "Do it," he mouths.

"Will you go out on a date with me?" I ask, clearing my throat. Silently, I flip Rad off. The bastard. He's still smirking as he cuts Lyric's steak into pieces. Leaning in, he whispers something into Lyric's ear that makes her spine snap straight.

"Do it, Mommy," she says, batting her eyelashes. "Daddy wants to eat you."

"With you!" Rad laughs.

"Daddy wants to eat with you." Lyric nods, shoving a small piece of steak into her mouth.

"Please?"

River's eyebrows raise. "Where?"

"I have a plan."

"He has a plan!" Rad announces over-dramatically, throwing his arms around. "You think it's a good one?" He leans into Lyric as she nods, chewing on her food.

"Daddy always has good plans," she says confidently, lifting her chin.

I snort, the tightness in my chest loosening when River smirks.

"Sure." She shrugs, looking me over. "But you had better show me a good time, Knight."

Knight.

Her Knight.

Relief flies through me at the sound of that simple nickname. Something I've longed to hear for years, even through my hatred.

A grin breaks free as I cup her jaw in my palm. "I got it all covered. Tomorrow night, outside on the patio. Under the stars. Just you and me." She shudders from my intensity and nods.

"If you say so."

"Well, well, Mr. Knight. You clean up well," she quips from behind me.

Fuck! When the hell did she make it out here? I didn't even hear the sliding glass door open or close. My heart leaps out of my chest at her sudden appearance.

Almost in slow motion, I turn to face her. My eyes bulge out of my head at the sight of her standing before me in the most beautiful outfit I've ever seen her in.

"Holy fucking fuck," I mutter, taking her in with heat filling my cheeks and blood rushing to inappropriate areas, especially for a first do-over date.

"Did Jordy have anything to do with this?" she asks, gesturing to the long evening gown dragging along the concrete. Its deep red color accentuates the blood-red lipstick lining her lips, making her look red-carpet-ready as opposed to having a meal under the sparkling night sky.

Fuck. Her lips. I wish I could claim them with my own and make her mine again. Or with my dick. No. Not that. Shit. I have to stop thinking with my cock. It's too damn soon to expect any sort of physical relationship with her. I want to prove myself to her every step of the way and make up for all the wrongdoings from our past. Including the temper tantrums I pulled at the sight of her in the conference room.

"You look beautiful," I breathe, marveling at her in awe as she rolls her eyes.

"So, this is your idea?" she asks, pointing to the fairy lights sparkling along the pergola extending over the concrete patio.

My cheeks heat. "I...yeah. I wanted to have some time with you," I murmur with uncertainty. "Alone time, away from the other guys."

"And the dress and tux?" I shiver when her eyes trail up and down my body, taking in the dark suit with a red bowtie to match.

"All Jordy's idea," I mumble, blushing more under her scrutiny. "Um, I've got a table set up over here," I say, stumbling over my words. "Oh, and I got this for you." Without stumbling, I hand her the single red rose with my heart in my throat. That beautiful smile crosses her lips when she brings it to her nose and inhales.

"It's beautiful," she murmurs with a twinkle in her eyes, looking me over again. Taking her hand, I lead her toward the table and stop before it. "Kieran," she whispers, running a finger over the white tablecloth, only stopping at the dozen roses acting as the centerpiece. "Your doing?" she asks, leaning in to smell the rest of the flowers from the two-dozen-piece bouquet.

When Jordy said he'd lend a hand and get me everything I needed, he didn't skimp a dime.

"Yes. That I take credit for," I say confidently this time, erasing every ounce of nerves shaking my body. "They're for you," I murmur, taking another rose and placing it in her hands, careful so the thorns don't puncture her skin. "You're so strong, River Blue. You always have been. With everything life has handed you, you've always come out on the other side stronger. So, here's a flower as beautiful and as fierce as you. You're a damn rock." My eyes mist over when she shudders, staring down at the flower with an unreadable expression. I'd like to think she's taking my words to heart. Because every ounce of what I've said is true. She's the only person I've ever known who walks through life with her head held high, even when shit hits the fan.

"Well, it's beautiful," she murmurs, staring intently at the flowers. "Thank you, Knight." My heart catches in my throat at the name she used to call me under the stars at our old apartment building.

"Here," I say, stumbling around her chair and pulling it out. "Please sit. I have dinner ready for us. And some bubbly wine." I grin when she arches her brow but sits in the chair.

We're not the only people who have changed since we left this place. Before, River was the skinny girl in short shorts, tight shirts, and beat-up sneakers. Now, she's an elegant lady wrapped in satin, creating her brand in the music business world.

I'm honestly surprised I never knew what she had been up to. Perhaps I was so blinded by the need to collapse into music and forget about what happened that I didn't even try.

River has been in front of me the entire time, and I'm only now seeing her.

I swallow hard when I pour her a tall glass of wine, not stopping until it's at the brim.

"Trying to get me drunk?" she asks, leaning in to take a sip. Her eyes follow me as I bring over a deep aluminum tray filled with the best foods in town.

"Will it work?" I quip, setting the tray between our two plates, grinning when she snorts.

"Maybe." A crooked grin greets me when she takes a large swig, humming under her breath. Once she sets the half-empty glass down, she stares at the covered food tray with big eyes. "What's that?"

A deep chuckle vibrates through my chest as I sit opposite her and pour my glass of bubbly pink wine. "Do you remember that barbecue you came to?"

"You mean that awful one you kidnapped me to?"

"We did not kidnap you," I laugh, shaking my head. "We said there'd be food, and you practically climbed me!" I chuckle when her face falls.

"You literally met me at school, put me over your shoulder, and manhandled me into the back of your vehicle. Say it with me, Knight. Kidnapping. You assfaces wouldn't take no for an answer. I had no choice in the matter."

I grin at her. "I like that," I whisper, reaching over and brushing my fingers against hers.

"Like what?" she murmurs, staring at my fingers rubbing over hers.

"How you still call me Knight..." I trail off, clutching her hand. "Thanks for giving me a chance again, River Blue. I know I have a lot to make up for, and one dinner isn't going to cut it. I just—" I suck in a breath when she squeezes my fingers in understanding.

"But you're trying," she says, nodding. "It won't be easy. You know? You were the world's biggest brat a few weeks ago."

I cringe. "Sorry. God. That was the fucking anger talking. I've bottled it up for so damn long and put it into my music that I... I went off the rails. I'm sorry I ruined our first meeting. But I'm more sorry that I walked away in the first place. I should have known Asher was full of shit." I shake my head, running my free hand down my face. "I was the biggest, most gullible dumbass ever, River Blue. Will you ever find it in your heart to forgive me?" My eyes fall to the table when she squeezes my hand again.

"Maybe. But first, you have to show me what's under the lid. It smells familiar...and delicious," she murmurs, pulling me from the morbid thoughts of no forgiveness overtaking me.

I was wracking my brain for days on how I could show my River Blue how much I cherished her, especially within the confines of this house. I couldn't take her out without risking her safety. And I'd never fucking do that.

Then it hit me as I laid in bed, staring up at the ceiling. The moment I fell in love with her the second time. Our neighborhood barbecue. The time we forced her to come with us and endure our families, all in the name of unity.

It was the way she didn't give a fuck half the people there were looking at her like she had grown a second head. She ate, laughed, and was fucking merry, surrounded by us. That moment in our history will forever live in the back of my mind as the moment River Blue became the one. With everything that's happened in the past few days, I wanted to give her the comfort of something she loved. I wanted to relive that moment with her. Just the two of us.

"Right," I say with a shuddering breath. "Right. It's, um... Well. You remember the cookout."

"I do," she confirms, watching me with big eyes. Reaching over, I peel off the aluminum lid and reveal the goodies I ordered just for her. Or, well—Jordy ordered and delivered them thirty minutes ago, so it was still nice and hot.

"I remember you liked the barbecue we had. The ribs, especially. They had it catered from a small restaurant in town. And I thought maybe we could enjoy them again. Together."

Her fucking eyes light up when the ribs and chicken wings appear with steam rolling off them and dancing in the air. Immediately the smell of sweet barbecue hits my senses and my damn stomach gurgles. But I'm more focused on her reaction to care about my body right now.

Her tongue pokes out, licking her lips. "Dear God, Kieran," she murmurs, reaching in and taking a gigantic bite of ribs. "They're even better than I fucking remember. Oh. My. God," she hums, closing her eyes. "I think I've died and gone to heaven. You know, this is what I craved when I was pregnant with Ly. All she wanted was ribs, mashed potatoes, and some thick chicken and noodles. I went by Loretta's and got it a few times. But fuck —" she trails off, finishing the piece of meat and setting the bone down on her plate.

"Was it an easy pregnancy?" I breathe. Pain envelops my heart at the thought of pregnant River being all alone without me— us.

Who took care of her? Who helped her get to the doctor... Shit! She had no fucking car to get back and forth. How in the hell did she manage before her brothers found her and brought her to California? Guilt eats away at me more, chewing on my insides and swirling them. I wasn't there to protect her from anything. After everything that happened in the alleyway when she was attacked by that fucking dickbag Bradley. And now this with her stalker.

I'm here now. That's what matters. I'll protect her and Lyric to the ends of the world.

She shrugs. "It was. Everything went great. She was huge, though. Nine friggin pounds and some change. It took me so many hours to push her out," she whispers, tilting her head to the side. "But she was the happiest baby I ever met and came right at the end of September."

September? Hell, that's this month. "When is her birthday?" I ask, swallowing hard as another exciting scheme forms in my mind. Only this time, I'll bring the guys in on my plans and not leave them out.

"September 29th," she says, ripping into another piece of meat.

Duly fucking noted. I won't miss another birthday. I've missed four already, and we'll make sure turning five is epic.

"I'm sorry I wasn't there to hold your hand or cut the cord. Or do any of the things I would have done if I had known, River Blue." I shake my head as the shame of my actions consumes me once again. It pulls me deep into the raging waters of guilt, swallowing me whole. I'm drowning in the shame of what I did. I won't resurface until I've made every ounce of my wrongdoings up to her. "What Gloria did...is unforgivable. When we return to East Point, I will speak with her."

River drops the next piece of bone on her plate, not stopping when she shoves more meat into her mouth. God, why is she so fucking hot when she eats and gets barbecue all over her lips and cheeks? I'm mesmerized when she tears into more meat, humming.

"Don't let her near me," River says, wrinkling her nose. "I have some not so fucking nice words for her. In fact, she and I have a lot of shit to discuss. Do you think she'd screech if I put my fist through her nose?"

Yeah, she'd scream a lot. Probably call the cops, too. But it'd be so fucking worth seeing her fall on her ass, getting what she deserved.

"That can be arranged. Do you want to tell her off? I'll let you come with me when I do the same. There's no excuse for what the bitch did and took away from me." I blow out a breath.

After learning everything Asher did to get us to abandon River, I have no doubts Gloria planted the seeds. Her role in the entire plot was way too evident after I sat down and stewed on the information. My mother may act like a stuck-up suburban mom, but she's no dummy. Not at all. She's the key to this entire situation. If it wasn't for her meddling and dangling money in front of Asher's desperate face, this wouldn't have happened. She's the reason we left River. She's the devil in disguise, using people however she wants. And that person she molded like clay was Asher. She took his desperation and used it against him. Fuck. It's her goddamn fault. I shake my head at myself. I've been so blinded by my rage toward Asher, that I didn't stop to think about the situation as a whole.

But that stops now.

My next move is removing Gloria from the cushy apartment she's been gifted by Asher and me. She doesn't deserve to have a nice place to stay when she took my fucking kid from me before I even had a chance to know her.

And then, I'm going to look Asher in the eyes and forgive him.

"Deal," she says, biting into a chicken wing and groaning. "Seriously, Knight. This is the best thing ever. I swear I've died, gone to heaven, and now I have an endless supply of delicious barbecue to hold me over. This is better than sex."

I blanch. "Better than sex?" I gasp in mock horror, earning a toothy grin.

She shrugs. "Maybe," is all she says as she continues to devour our dinner and finishes off her glass of wine. "So, you really couldn't get your dick to work around other girls?"

Just as I'm about to swallow my bite of ribs, I choke on my food at the sound of her words. "Fuck. River Blue, you can't ask that shit when I'm eating," I hack, coughing into my hand. Taking a big gulp of wine, I settle back into my seat. She patiently waits with an expectant look that says: well, do tell.

I lick my lips. "Fine. If you need to know. Yeah, I couldn't get him to pop up. And believe me. I had plenty of opportunities to do so." I shake my head. "He just...wouldn't rise to the occasion."

Unlike now, where he's fully rising to the occasion. Awake and alert all because of her in that red dress with those pleading eyes and luscious lips. Even the barbecue sauce makes her the most beautiful woman on the planet. No wonder my cock never cooperated with me. He knew where his home was this entire time. And dummy me didn't.

"So sad for you," she snickers at my pain, taking a small bite of mashed potatoes.

I groan at her comment, washing my hands on the little wipes provided by the restaurant, making sure the sauce is completely off my skin.

"Yeah, yeah. It was a terrible time for me." I shake my head. "I thought I lost the woman I loved." That makes her eyes snap to mine, and the smile fades away into sadness. "I'm ashamed of how our past is tainted with so much fucked up shit. But I did—do—love you, River Blue. I'm sorry I wasn't there for your pregnancy or her birth. Fuck, do I wish I could have seen her. She's the most amazing little human I've ever encountered. I don't know how I won the lottery with her but thank you. Fuck, thank you."

Without warning, she jumps up and plants her barbecue lips on mine, sealing the rest of my words in my throat. The slightest hint of our dinner invades my mouth when she pokes her tongue between my lips, forcing her way in. Fuck I don't even care what she tastes like. It's goddamn heaven to me. I groan into her mouth, plunging my tongue against hers in a slow dance of passion.

"River Blue," I groan, pulling her into my lap. My fingers weave through her long locks, holding her against me. "What was that for?" I examine her darkening eyes, filling to the brim with lust.

Biting into her bottom lip, she squeezes her eyes shut. "I'm sorry you weren't there, either. I promise I kept you alive in Lyric's eyes. That's why she knows who you all are. I never wanted to keep her from you. I just thought—"

"I know," I whisper, pressing my lips against her cheek.

I groan when she shifts in my lap, stiffening in my grip. Her moss-green eyes fly open, connecting with mine in question. I can't help the sly smirk pulling at my lips. Well, until she shifts again, forcing another groan.

"You don't seem to have a problem getting it up now," she whispers, leaning in to press her lips against mine.

My cheeks fill with warmth when she shifts again. The friction between us sends heat straight to my pulsating dick, begging to thrust deep inside her until she's moaning my name for the world to hear. If she's not fucking careful, I'll cum in my pants or take her right here against the table.

As much as I want to fuck her into oblivion and regain my Blue, I lean away, stopping her movements.

"Fuck," I grunt, gripping her waist. "If you keep that up, I won't be able to contain myself." Besides, I have more plans than this. I need to keep my wits about me instead of letting my dick take the lead.

She chuckles, swiveling her hips again. "No," she whispers, leaning in and resting her lips against my cheek. "I won't stop. And you won't cum in your pants like an inexperienced assface. Hold your cum, Kieran." Fuck. Fuck. Shit!

No! I can't do it. I'll explode before she even has the chance to swivel her hips again.

"Can't," I gasp when my eyes roll into the back of my head. "River Blue," I groan when she picks up speed and swivels her hips more. "I have more planned." I grunt in relief when she stops. Lifting her head, she gazes into my eyes with a mischievous look, having no intention of stopping this madness.

"More planned?" she hums, resting her forehead against my shoulder.

"Yeah," I grunt, lifting her into my arms as I stand. "As much as I wanted to continue that, I have more to show you."

34

Kieran

"Kieran," she mutters when I take a few steps into the night, letting the stars shine above us. There's a hint of storm on the horizon, but that only reminds me of the woman sitting next to me.

"River Blue," I hum in return, settling us onto a blanket in the grass and holding her close. "I dreamed of you for five years. I was so mad at you. So fucking hurt that—" I shake my head. "That doesn't matter anymore. I want to restart with you, Blue." I swallow hard, looking directly at her. "I want to make up for my absence. Be there for you and Lyric. Can we restart?"

"One day at a time?" she breathes, brushing her lips against the edge of mine. My fingers work through her hair, massaging her scalp.

"Yeah, Blue. One day at a time," I whisper, kissing her lips. I pull back. "But I have something I want to sing to you. Just a little something that came to me on the plane."

River's smile lights up my entire being when she flashes it my way with enthusiasm.

"Okay."

"Okay," I retort, gently setting her beside me.

I lay my acoustic guitar, which was set up beside the blanket, over my lap, strumming a few notes, letting them infect me with their melody. It's been a long time since I picked up my guitar and felt inspired to write. For years it's been someone else handling all our music. Sure, we performed it with ease, but we were never the ones to write it. Not after we came to East Point.

This is different. River's different. Fuck. Everything is so different now, and I fucking love it.

As I strum and sing the rough words, she sways in tune. Those big moss-green eyes fill with happiness and disbelief.

"I never knew heartbreak until I walked away," I sing softly, strumming lightly. "So, broken. Empty. Unloved. Second chances come and go. Third chances take your breath away. I'm on my third opportunity to make you mine. And I'll continue to show you all my pieces. Mend me, baby. Make our puzzle one. No longer broken. I'm filled with third chances and love. Mend me, baby."

"Oh, Kieran," she mumbles with tears in her eyes. Gently she clasps my cheeks and pulls me down on top of her. I grunt, discarding the guitar to the side.

"You were my first heartbreak and my second. But never again will I walk away. Ever. You're my forever girl," I murmur in between manic kisses. "My fucking forever."

"You're a jackass," she whispers, laughing when I pull away.

"That's rude, Blue." I raise a brow, staring down at her heaving chest and marveling at her breasts, begging to spill out and have my mouth on them. "God, I missed you."

"Me or them?" she quips, gesturing to her tits as I run my fingers lightly over the swell. Goosebumps rise on her flesh as I trace my fingers between them, reveling in the plush, smooth skin beneath my fingertips.

"Both," I say, grinning up at her when she groans, rolling her eyes.

I swallow hard, aching to sink my teeth into her. My brain screams at me to lift her dress and expose every inch I want to ravage with my tongue and dick. I'm practically drooling when I throw caution to the wind and get the first taste of my girl.

Leaning down, I run my tongue over her neck, nibbling her flesh between my teeth. Her soft moans fill the night air. Bravely, I run my hand over her breast, pulling the material down inch by inch until both pop from the confines of her tight dress. Fuck. They're more fucking gorgeous than I remember. Bigger than I remember.

As my eyes eagerly take in her form, I marvel at the white scars stretching across her flesh, softly kissing every inch of them. These marks represent the human life she grew in her body. I'll worship every inch of her stretch marks. I'll show my devotion on my knees until she understands that I'm in love with whatever body she has.

"You're more beautiful than you were the day I met you," I whisper, running my tongue over her erect nipple and softly blowing on it, causing shivers to run through her body under my touch.

"When did you become such a sweet talker?" she murmurs, running her fingers roughly through my hair. I chuckle, sucking her nipple into my mouth again until she rolls her hips against mine. "Oh fuck, Knight," she moans, holding my face against her tit.

"Never," I quip, tugging on it with my teeth.

River's breaths shudder in her chest, rapidly moving with her breasts until it pops out of my mouth, giving me a chance to take in her flushed expression. Lust drips from every ounce of her body, calling to me like a siren at sea. I ache to do so many bad things to her, but I intend to hold myself back.

For now, at least. Not until she's ready for my cock. And me.

Once I thrust myself deep inside her and paint her with my cum, there's no going back.

"Are you wet for me, Blue?" I murmur against her glistening nipple, running my tongue along the hardened flesh.

Pre-cum drips from my dick, soaking my boxers when I tweak her between my fingers, collecting my saliva on my fingertips.

Repeatedly, I twist it between my fingers as she squirms beneath me, breathily panting.

"Maybe," she moans when I tug it a little too hard, and her body fucking stiffens beneath me.

"Let's see." Her moans are music to my ears, filling me with every ounce of her pleasure.

My balls throb with need, begging for more friction. My damn brain begs to fuck her right here and now. How I ache to feel her wrapped around my cock. God, fucking damnit. Years of not being able to cum in the presence of a woman has royally fucked my brain into a scramble.

Stay focused, dickbag.

My fingers slowly drift up her bare leg from underneath her dress. Swirling around her bent knee and onto her silky thigh, basking in the feel of her under my fingertips, once again. Anticipation for what's about to come holds my oxygen captive inside my chest. "Fuck. I can't wait to worship every inch of your body. You're a goddamn queen, River Blue. I'll kneel for you every chance I get," I murmur. Pulling her silky panties to the side, I work my fingers up and down her slit until I'm thrusting them home with a loud groan escaping my lips.

"Jesus," she moans, throwing her head back into the blanket.

"No," I rumble, slowly pumping my fingers into her wetness, basking in the sounds she makes as she arches her back into my touch. "Knight. Call me Knight, River Blue."

"Knight," she gasps again on the cusp of letting go.

My fingers pump harder until she clamps down on them and pulls them further into herself, spreading her cum all over my fingers. Her moans break through the night air, letting the world know...she's mine. Fucking mine! Never again will I walk away from her. Or leave her side. Or do anything to jeopardize the best fucking thing I've ever had.

River West carved her name in my heart when I was seven, claiming ownership over my being. I just never realized it until now. I am hers. Forever and always. No matter what happened in the past. Or what our future holds, she's mine. Until the day comes, and I take my last breath, and my heart stops pumping; she's mine.

"Good girl," I murmur, diving my tongue into her mouth, twisting with hers. She pants when I pull back, looking up at me with lust-filled eyes.

"And what about you?" she asks, cocking a brow.

I snort. "I'll fuck my hand until I'm worthy of your pussy." River flushes further, licking her lips. "Until then, we'll meet your needs. Then, when you're ready, I'll get on my knees and wait for you."

Always.

"You'll wait for me?"

"We tore you apart when we left. It's only been a few weeks. We can't just jump in with both feet and expect not to fall. Starting over, remember?" She nods a few times, staring up at the stars above. Heaving a sigh, she runs her fingers through my hair as I fall to the side of her and fix her dress, so she's no longer exposed to the elements.

"This was amazing," she whispers. "Thank you for tonight. For the barbecue and the song. It reminded me of all the times we sat on the hill and just...were."

"Those were the simpler days," I mumble, resting my head on the blanket, continuing to stare at the rise and fall of her chest and the peace washing over her expression.

"We were just kids trying to make it through."

"I'm sorry about your mom," I murmur, resting my hand on her stomach. "I'm sorry I wasn't there at the funeral."

"It was beautiful. She would have loved all the people coming to see her," she whispers, sadness clutching her voice.

"I'm sure she would have, River Blue," I murmur, sweeping my fingers through her long brown strands. "She would have greeted each of them with a smile."

Stella was never as terrible as my mother, but she still had her faults. As a kid, River often met me in the dead of night to listen to me learn songs on the guitar behind our worn-out apartment building. Her biggest fault was ignoring River when she needed her most, and that's where I came in. Well, until my mother married a psychopath. Then we moved far away, forcing me to leave my girl behind. Somehow Nigel's crazy ass made me forget all about her. For her protection, of course.

I swallow hard when lightning illuminates the sky, highlighting the darkening clouds closing in on us from a distance.

"Looks like rain, Knight," she mumbles tiredly, gluing her eyes to the incoming storm.

"Maybe we should head inside."

"Okay," she murmurs as we slowly rise to our feet.

Tiny droplets pelt our skin as we gather our things. The wind howls all around us, blowing our hair in different directions. At the last second, before we're safely nestled in Callum's secret house, River captures my lips one last time, silently thanking me with one last heated kiss. In our finest clothes, the rain beats down on us, soaking us to the bone. The only warmth we feel is the heat between the two of us. She presses into me, shivering when I wrap my hands in her wet strands, holding her there. I never want this moment to cease. I'm never letting her go. When we finally pull back breathlessly examining each other, I notice the flowers floating in tiny puddles all around us, surrounding us in their beauty. It's a picture from a magazine, something perfect to forever remember.

Lyric may be the hurricane that stormed into my life. But River is the tornado swirling around me, sucking up my feelings and love.

"Thank you," she whispers, taking my hand as we enter through the back sliding glass door into the warmth of Callum's house.

It blows my mind that the man ran away to Central City so many times and never told us. Granted, we weren't exactly on speaking terms for the past few years. I can look back now and realize that it was, in part, due to my anger and all the tension bubbling between us that drove a wedge in our friendship. We were so damn close at one time, but now, we're slowly rebuilding ourselves, too.

We stop dead in the living room, dropping the wet blanket and supplies near the backdoor. River smiles at the sight in front of us, fondly looking Asher over as he clings to Lyric's sleeping body on his lap. Together, they're in dreamland with their eyes closed and breaths even.

"Will you stay with me tonight?" I whisper, catching her arm before she scoops Lyric up and settles her down.

River bites her lip, staring between us, and nods. "Yeah. She'll probably want in on the snuggles, though." She grins, pointing to Lyric, who still hasn't stirred.

"You take her and get settled. I'm in the back bedroom." Thankfully, the bedroom had a big enough bed for us to share.

When I promised River about waiting for her, I meant it. It might be a year from now until she can fully forgive us, or it could be tomorrow. No matter the wait, I'm here for them. I may not have done the manipulating myself, but I was compliant in leaving her alone.

As only a mother could, River lifts Lyric into her arms without waking her. She sends me a soft smile and leaves the room.

"Good date?" Asher rasps, peeking an eye open.

"Good date," I confirm with a nod, eyeing the multitude of healing bruises lining his chest and ribs.

Some are tinged green, and some are already yellowing and entering the healing stage. Finally, Guilt slams into me. He may have fucked up so royally and deserved our fists, but violence, to me, is never the answer—unless genuinely called for. Like that time Van and I had a discussion with our fists. The fucker deserved it. But Asher? He's my brother. We've been through a war together on the home front, fighting Nigel off and taking his blows. We've been through so much together. He's more family than I ever had. And Gloria fucking ruined that by pitting us against each other. She just had to stick her nose in something that was none of her business and contort the situation in her favor. She knew what she was doing every step of the way, and that includes playing Asher like a lost little puppet.

"Sorry about your face, bro," I say, running a hand through my wet strands. "I shouldn't have hit you like that. It was just... I couldn't stop the feelings."

Asher's brows raise. "No need to be sorry. I needed it."

"Nah, man. You fucked up. Like so thoroughly fucked up. But we all did, too. You may have led us to leave and manipulated us into believing lies, but Gloria was the man behind the mask. It's her fault, too." I shake my head, hammering the point home that Asher alone isn't at fault. This wasn't totally his doing. "She did this to us. But I want to put it behind us. For them. For us. For everything. What do you say? Can we move past this together?"

Asher blinks several times when I reach a hand out, wiggling my fingers. Hesitantly, he grabs on, and I pull him to his feet, shaking his hand. He swallows hard, shame tightening his face.

"Thanks," he croaks. "I don't really deserve it."

"Yes, you do," I say without hesitation. "But you did what you did. And I get it after thinking about everything that happened. This isn't solely on you, Ash. You were fucking used." It's true. I get why he was so damn desperate to leave. I was, too. But not at the expense of River. That's the part that fucks me up the most. That we left River without even knowing about Lyric.

"If we would have stayed, we would have been stuck with Nigel and then...probably gone to jail with him." Yeah, he would have lifted us in his company to the highest regard and then sent us to the slammer in his stead after all that shit the FBI found out. I'm thankful we skipped town. "I was desperate and obviously not thinking." His eyes fall to the floor, and he heaves a breath. "I'll say I'm sorry a million times."

"I get it. Fuck, do I get it. I didn't really want to stay behind. I just wanted to be with her. Imagine where our life would have been..." I trail off as several scenes rush through my mind. Lyric being born. Hell, River confiding in us that she was pregnant. The baby shower. Moving her in with us at Callum's because that's where we would have been despite Nigel's iron fist. So many possibilities. And yet, here we are.

"We would have survived," Asher says, squeezing my hand.

"Like we always did, brother," I murmur, squeezing back.

Finally, our hands drop to our sides.

"I bet Callum has some cream for those bruises somewhere in this place. It will help take some of the pain away if you still have any."

He shrugs, rubbing the back of his neck.

I know what he's thinking by the sadness clouding his eyes. He doesn't want it. He wants to suffer because he wants the remnants of what we did to him to remind him every day that he fucked up.

"Don't worry about it," he says, waving a hand. "Have a good night. I'm heading back to bed."

"Thanks for taking such good care of Ly," I say, catching him before he leaves the room. "You're not a bad guy, Asher. You just made a shit decision."

He gives a humorless laugh. "Yeah. I am a bad guy, though. That's the problem."

"But you wouldn't do it again, right?"

His shoulders stiffen, and he shakes his head. "Fuck no. Never again." He scratches his neck. "I've felt empty as fuck, and I finally feel full again just being around them. Being with Ly and having her call me daddy. It's bringing me back from the grave I put myself into." He heaves a breath as his watery eyes meet mine.

"You and me both. I love ya, Ash. I know we still have a lot to work out," I say, giving him a respectful nod and heading to my bedroom.

When I enter, I stop dead at the dress pooled on the ground and River sitting on the edge of the bed in my oversized T-shirt.

How the fuck am I supposed to keep my hands to myself all night long?

My heart fills with so much love when I change into my sweats and climb into bed. Lyric's sleeping form rests between us, snoring.

"Should I tell her she snores, too?" I murmur, marveling at her little face.

River snorts, snuggling close to Ly. "She'll fight you tooth and nail," she murmurs, giggling. "Like father, like daughter." I swear my chest puffs out a million times more at the thought of Lyric gaining my stubborn streak.

"Night, River Blue."

"Night, Knight," she whispers with a whimsical smile crossing her lips. "See you in the morning."

35

WHAT THE HELL is going on with me? I promised I wouldn't cave, but goddamn, I'm falling into the darkness with only them as my guides. Again! It's so easy falling back into their arms. It's like time never slipped away from us.

Even as I sit in the basement, remarkably similar to Callum's old house, watching the boys jam out with smiles on their faces. For the first damn time, joy ignites in them. Completely different from a few weeks ago.

Lyric dances before me, lip-syncing the lyrics to the song she's memorized from years before.

"Again!" she yelps, stomping impatiently, staring at me until I relent.

The last thing I want to do is subject myself to Kieran's sultry voice. But I can't deny those big, weeping eyes staring daggers into me.

"If you say please," I murmur, hovering my finger above the first song of their new album.

"Pwease, Mommy. I want to listen to daddies sing!" Yup. I'm whipped despite hating the voices blasting through the speakers of our home.

"Okay, one more time." Let the record show it wasn't one more time. It was twelve more times that day and beyond. Every

day from then on out, Lyric demanded Whispered Words on repeat. I tuned it out as best I could, but you can only do it for so long.

"Hold on," Kieran says, raising a hand. The loud music dies down as the guys watch him with curious gazes. "Come here, Little Blue," he says with a grin, curling a finger in her direction. She doesn't hesitate a second, barreling into Kieran's legs with a squeal. "I see you're singing. Do you know all the words to this one?"

"Every song, Daddy," she says with a huge grin and a clap. Kieran quirks a brow in my direction. I nod, biting the inside of my cheek. No way in hell am I admitting our spawn forced me to listen to them every damn day until I fell asleep to their voices rattling inside my brain. Nope. Not gonna happen. "I listened to them every day!" she whispers directly into the microphone, letting everyone hear our dirty little secret.

My cheeks heat when all their eyes fall on me. Can the ground please swallow me up, I'll never hear the end of this shit. Not until I'm six feet deep with flowers blooming above my decaying body.

"Every day?" Rad grins, wiping the sweat from his forehead.

Fucker.

"Every day!" she squeals in confirmation when Kieran hands her the microphone.

Rad smirks in my direction. "I see you, Pretty Girl," he quips, settling back on his stool.

"Why don't you help us practice then, Little Blue? Sing with me?" He questions with pride, lighting up his eyes at the prospect of singing with his daughter.

Lyric frantically nods, screeching joyfully when Kieran pulls her into his arms.

"This one's for you," he says in a low voice, locking eyes with me, sending shivers down my spine at the intensity of his gaze. Fuck me. It's the same look he gave me last night when he rested above me, with his fingers settled deep inside my aching core. My pussy clenches at the memory. I'm such a fucking goner. I need

Ode's advice before I jump in headfirst and drown in them. "How about River's song? Rushing River?"

Double fuck.

Rad snorts, whooping. "Let's do this! Get ready, Pretty Girl. I'm about to serenade your panties off."

"Panties?!" Lyric giggles into the microphone, making everyone else chuckle.

"Cal?" Kieran asks, locking eyes with the silent bassist.

A grin tugs at Cal's lip, lighting up his face. "It's been a while," he says, plucking two strings on his bass.

"Ash?" Kieran asks with a broken voice, catching the guitarist off guard.

Licking his lips, Ash gives an unsure nod. "Yeah, man. River's song."

And with that, Lyric belts out the song she shouldn't know. The song they only played at the Battle of the Bands winning celebration and recorded for their demo became a short-lived radio hit. The song they swore—because I happened to catch an interview—that they'd never publicly play again. I heard it everywhere I went. It followed me like their betrayal clung on. The day I had lunch with Seger and Zeppelin at that shitty diner, this song buried knives in my back, forcing me to relive what they did to me. Over and fucking over. And for some strange reason, my fucking daughter loved the shit out of it, making me suffer further.

Here it is again. The words are the same. About a roaring River, breaking through and making a life for themself. It's about strength and perseverance. Before, Kieran snarled every word until he refused to play it again. Now, their tone is different. Happier. Joyful. Full of life. And dare I say, love.

Their smiles light up the room when Lyric perfectly duets Kieran, matching his pitch changes. Sometimes she goes higher. Occasionally she dips lower. Together, they're creating an out-of-this-world sound. Almost like this is their destiny, like they belong together.

"Holy fucking shit!" Rad shouts, jumping from his stool. "Little Pretty Girl, you've got some pipes on you!" Kissing her hair, she giggles at his words, thanking him with a big hug.

"You sounded amazing, Little One," Asher marvels, staring at her with stars in his eyes.

"So damn good. Shall we go again?" Kieran asks, earning a yes from her.

"Again!" she screams like she used to, begging to continue.

I watch in awe for the next several hours as my daughter commands the makeshift stage. She prances around with the microphone, throwing out some ballet moves. She screams. She wails. And dear God, she sings, carrying the tune like a damn pro.

"When did that happen?" Kieran asks, sitting beside me on the couch after calling it quits for the night when Lyric showed signs of slowing down.

Do not look at his shirtless chest. Or his tight jeans. In fact, don't look at any fucking thing regarding him, or you'll jump his bones. There's a child in the room, for God's sake.

He guzzles a water bottle in two seconds flat before wiping his mouth after he's done. Why something so simple sends shivers directly to my pussy, has me questioning my sanity. I've gone without sex for so long without a thought. Now my body has reawakened, begging for more orgasms. Stupid body. It's been two nights of orgasms, and suddenly, I want more.

I swallow hard, averting my eyes to my sleeping child snuggled beside me after too much activity. And stealthily avoid the half-naked man. If I don't look at him, he'll disappear, right? Before I do something stupid.

"When did what happen?" I ask, clearing my damn throat from all the lustful thoughts trying to break free and fulfill my damn fantasies.

Make it more obvious, would ya?

They're already starting to cloud my thoughts with their manly scents, heated touches, and sinful looks. My stalker better be behind bars before long, or I'll lose myself to them. Again.

God, they're like a fucking drug I can't escape, infecting me with their beings.

I'm so fucking screwed, aren't I?

I want to take it glacially slow and build something meaningful. Before I stupidly jump into the sack with them like I did before. Sure, sex sounds so wonderful now, but I want to be sure they're in it for the long haul.

"Her singing."

With so much affection, Kieran stares at Lyric, too, gazing at her sleeping form. She doesn't move an inch when my fingers touch her tiny, red ears—barely stirring when my fingers weave through her hair and straighten it out.

"She's a natural talent," I murmur.

"Good news, everyone!" Jordy shouts from the basement stairs with a grin, throwing his arms out wide.

Dressed in his usual black attire with guns hanging off holsters, he strolls in like he owns the place. Typical fucking Jordy. A cocky smirk plays on his lips until he's at the center of the room. Everyone eyes him when he untucks a file folder from beneath his arms and takes us in.

"How do you keep sneaking into my house?" Callum asks with a tic forming in his jaw. Agitation sparkles in his eyes like he's ten seconds away from laying Jordy out flat. A fact I don't doubt when he puts his bass down and cracks his knuckles.

"Special agent, duh," he quips, affectionately eyeing Lyric as she rests beside me.

"What's up, Professor?" I say jokingly, making him snort. "Anything good?"

Jordy nods, tapping the file folder and handing it to me with a grim expression. "Adrian was caught last night," he says as I flip open to a picture of a messy apartment littered with trash and debris. How anyone lived there is beyond me. Dirt and grime make up the walls and the furniture.

"Is he in jail?" Kieran asks, straightening his spine.

"Better," Jordy says, helping me flip to another page. "Adrian was such a pussy about getting caught that he ended everything before we could question him." He rolls his lips together. "Sorry, we didn't get you any clear answers, Riv." Shaking his head, he points to the report, stating Adrian shot himself in bed. "But it's over, at least."

"No notes or anything?"

Jordy snorts, scratching the back of his head. "We're still investigating his apartment. But we found your old phone, a camera, and a shit ton of pictures of you. From errr...your house, the beach, and anywhere this sick fuck could get into. Basically, it's all pointing to this asshole 100 percent."

My damn heart drops. Right. That asshole had access to my house. "Fuck. He saved them from my house?"

Jordy squats down, making eye contact with me, and gives me a reassuring look. "From what we could tell from your old phone, he was able to gain access to your cameras." I blanch, bringing a hand to my chest, trying to calm my rapidly beating heart. Another hand grasps mine, squeezing in support as I get the full picture of my stalker's activities.

"You'll let me know if you find a connection? I don't understand why someone I don't even know would follow me around."

It's always blown my fucking mind that someone would want to follow me around. I'm so damn dull and do the same shit every day. Go to work. Take care of Ly. The list goes on and on. I'm never in the same spot for too long and always taking care of others. So, why in the hell would some asshole want pictures of my boring life? I'll never fucking understand.

"Always, Dollface. I'll keep you updated on anything new. So far, all we have is what we've investigated. Stalkers tend to latch on to a person who fits an idea rather than the person themselves. Our running theory after checking into his background is Adrian had an ex who passed four years ago, who was around your age, build, and height. So, we think somewhere along the way, the two of you crossed paths, and he latched on to you. And as soon as these assholes came into the picture, something flipped in him. Maybe it was meeting you again in real life at the fight, but we're not totally sure. But we're pretty damn confident he's our guy." He claps his hands with confidence, shutting the door on my entire stalker situation.

I should feel relieved that this whole thing is over, and I can rest easy now, but something nags at the back of my mind. From here on out, I'll be looking over my shoulder. No matter what.

"Liv will keep you updated, too. Since she's your go to and all. Which is hurtful by the way. I thought we were pretty tight. She'll be thrilled to have you under her nose again. She's been a damn beast since she sent you away." He scrunches his nose. "Please come home soon," he quips, flicking my nose like the annoying gnat he is.

Fucker.

"Bastard," I grunt as the others tense at his actions. Gently, I run my fingers over the soreness on my nose.

"When can we?" Rad asks, running a towel through his sweaty mullet.

"Whenever you want," Jordy says. "We see zero threats from here on out. All of our intel suggests it was him, and with the evidence...Liv has officially declared you free to leave your sex house."

"What's a sex house?" Lyric asks in a tired rasp, scratching at her eyes.

"It's how your little brother or sister gets produced," Jordy says, earning a glare from me and everyone else in the room.

Oh hell no. I've had an IUD secured for four years now. Since the moment Ly blessed me with her presence, I wasn't taking any chances.

"Not cool, asshole," Rad mutters, shaking his head.

"Brother? Sister?" she squeals, sitting up with big eyes, looking at all of us with hope. It's the one thing she's begged me for since she was three—siblings.

"Maybe one day, Little Pretty Girl," Rad says, giving her a lopsided grin and winking in my direction.

"Nope!" I croak, turning to Ly. "They're using adult words again. Something you shouldn't repeat." She blinks several times at me and nods.

"Okay," she says with a shrug.

"Okay, here are all your phones," Jordy says, reaching into his pocket and pulling out four phones. "Both of yours are still in evidence."

I cringe. "Will you keep it forever?"

"Believe me. There's nothing on there you want right now." Jordy shakes his head, giving me a look. "All right, kiddies, especially you," he says, grinning at Lyric. "We're leaving our post. You're free to leave. Our private jet is waiting for you all to decide. So, call me! I've put my number in each of your phones. I know we have this intense bond now," he quips, walking backward and pointing finger guns in our direction.

"Bye, Uncle J!" Lyric waves as he disappears up the stairs and presumably leaves the house.

"We'll get you a new phone," Kieran says, squeezing my hand.

I snort. "I can buy my own these days."

Memories of the phone they gave me run through my mind on repeat. They had been so thoughtful when they did it, and it helped so much to finally have a working phone that didn't abruptly end calls or have a cracked screen.

"I know," Kieran smirks, looking down at his phone and scrolling through his messages. Without warning, the joyous look he has falls away into annoyance. "Fuck," he grunts, scrolling through message after message.

"Everything okay?"

Kieran sighs, showing me his screen. "It's never-ending."

GLORIA

I need money....

I'm almost out of coffee, Kieran!

Kieran! Where are you?

Kieran! Please!

KIERAN!

Kieran rubs his temple with a pained expression. "I've been paying her way," he mutters. "I was trying to look out for my sister, and I had to take care of her. But if I would have known what she pulled, she never would have been given a penthouse and princess treatment," he growls through clenched teeth, glaring a hole through the floor.

I pat his arm. "You didn't know. Plus, she's your mom."

"A mom who went behind my back and filed a restraining order without my knowledge. She knew what she was doing. Now, I just have to figure out how to punish her," he says, squeezing his fingers into fists.

"I'll help," Rad says with fire in his eyes. "You're not the only one she fucked over with her scheme. I'll put a boot in her stuck-up ass and throw her out onto the streets. Where she belongs."

"I helped you get her into the mess. I'll help you evict her," Asher says, sitting on the edge of a chair with his brows furrowed.

"Okay," Kieran says with a nod. "You can all help. But we'll have to come up with a plan."

GLORIA

You know what? I just found some. I'll talk to
you later, K. :)

His nose wrinkles at her message before he darkens his screen and shoves it into his pocket.

"I'll deal with her later," he grumbles, putting his hand on my knee.

We sit and talk for a few more hours, reminding me of the old times when we hung out at Callum's and did exactly this. We don't discuss anything important. But they make me laugh more times than I can count.

And that night, when I slip into bed, two more bodies follow, helping me drift off to dreamland. Getting the best night's sleep I've had in ages. The overwhelming feeling of rightness settles over me. No matter my reservations, they will always have a piece of my damn heart.

They're my damn kryptonite.

"Night, Pretty Girl."

"Night, Little Star."

"Night," I sigh, snuggled between them without any mom guilt, knowing Ly is safely tucked away in a bed down the hall.

The moment we came upstairs, Lyric clung to Kieran and asked him to read her a bedtime story and stayed with him for the rest of the night.

36

[Chapter title decorative: "River" in script, with audio waveform and playback controls]

River.

1:49   4:10

⤬ ◄◄ ▶ ►► ⇄

COMING HOME IS WEIRD, especially when it's in the city that made you. It twists my stomach into knots. Everywhere I look, memories sink their claws deep into my psyche. In the front seat of Callum's modest SUV, I twiddle my thumbs as the world flashes by. Discreetly, I peek at Lyric, sitting the same way in her booster seat, which Jordy procured before he left. Her tiny blue eyes take in the colors flashing by with interest.

"Are you going to be okay?" Asher asks from the driver's seat, nervously shifting.

"I'll be fine. Thanks for driving me here." Not exactly sure why he thought he needed to be my chauffeur, but I'm not complaining. I'm in no mood to drive across town by myself. My head is in the clouds and stuffed full of cotton balls. After everything I've endured with the shock of my stalker and my forced visit here—I'm exhausted.

I'm so fucking tired of fighting myself on what is right and what's wrong. I'm so fucking tired of fighting these feelings festering inside and begging to reemerge. Hopefully, my talk with Ode will wield some insight into what I should do. She was always the one to give me a little nudge here and there.

"No problem," he says softly. "They were your family, too." Understanding oozes from his eyes when he sends me a smile, lighting up his face. The bruises continue to disappear, especially since Callum handed him a tiny bottle of cream and instructed him to use it.

I side-eye Ash as we travel through the center of Central City —the heart of my hometown. Down these streets is where I walked daily to and from work, heaving a heavy backpack with determination forcing me forward. This place molded me into the woman I am. Breathing the same air I left is so fucking surreal. I've intended to return for years, promising Ode I'd come to visit her and the family but work always held me back.

As we pass the old record store I once worked at, I smile. Every once in a while, Booker texts me updates on his life. After I paid off all his bills, including his loans, he could relax instead of drowning in debt. He was always the father I never had, taking me under his wing and providing me with jobs. I worked my ass off for him to prove to the world I could succeed. And in turn, he always believed in me. No matter what.

Before I know it, I'm pointing Asher in the right direction, down a long, winding path toward the beautiful farmhouse in the middle of three acres of grassland. Corn and bean fields lie around the edges, cutting the property off from the rest of the world. Giving the seclusion, they always dreamed about.

"Where would you live if you could ever get away?" I ask, *sipping Korrine's sweet tea at her dining room table after a long school day.*

Korrine smiles, stirring the pot soup she started for dinner. "Long time ago, baby, my mama and papa had a beautiful farmhouse out on Route 36. It was two stories, surrounded by fields. The best sound was the cicadas as the sun set and painted the sky pink." A nostalgic look overtakes her.

"What happened to it?"

"My brother inherited the property and tore it down. It was unlivable," she says sadly, looking at the murky soup on the stove. "One day, I'd love to relive that. Sitting on the porch, drinking my

sun tea without a care in the world. But that's just a dream some old woman thought up."

"This place is huge," Asher mumbles as he pulls the car to a stop near the side of the house.

I grin, pride puffing my chest. As the house was being built under the constant supervision of a contractor, Ode sent me daily pictures.

"It was her dream house. Thanks for coming with me. This might be—"

He snorts. "A little awkward? I'm about to face the wrath of your best friend. All deserved, I suppose." His hazel eyes look upward, cataloging every inch of the house with a grin. "It's beautiful."

"You'll live," I say, patting his thigh without thinking.

The instant my hand comes into contact with him, a buzz zings through my arm, and heat forms on my cheeks. I clear my throat, turning away from his curious gaze. Oh, and I also removed my hand. As quickly as fucking possible before I do something stupid. Like squeeze it. Or lick it or something. God, I need more sleep.

I clear my throat, refusing to look at the man I know is staring at me in question. Not falling into that trap again. No way in fucking hell.

"Ly, are you ready to see Aunt Ode again?" I ask, turning to my quiet child, who hasn't spoken since we got into the vehicle. Saying that's odd is an understatement. Lyric must be feeling the same effects I am.

"Yes," she says with a grin. "Is Daddy meeting Aunt Ode?"

Asher's eyes dart to Ly through the rearview mirror, and he grins. "Yes," he answers, not bothering to explain he met her years before at the bar, knowing exactly who he is facing in about two seconds.

We all pile out, Ly a little more enthusiastically than Asher, who hangs back a step with his hands in his pockets. Now and again, his eyes drift back to the car, probably contemplating driving away and leaving us here, so he doesn't get his ass handed to him. Once Ode sees Asher, she will lose her damn mind and probably try to beat his ass with a broom. It wouldn't be the first or last time she's pulled something like that.

God, I love my best friend.

"My, my... Do my eyes deceive me?" A single rocking chair squeaks against the wooden wrap-around porch, swaying as the owner slowly rocks herself.

Her smile immediately greets me when she comes into view, and I halt as the nostalgia hits me square in the chest. Immediate longing to have her motherly arms wrapped around me has me itching to run up the stairs and bury my face in her neck.

Pure joy soars through me at the sound of her voice. I've missed hearing it in person after all these years. It may not be as strong as it was when I was a kid, but she's still the same Mama Korrine. The woman who helped raise me when my Ma worked overnight. Her home became my home. She was my unofficial second mother, and I couldn't have asked for anyone better.

"Grandma!" Ly squeals, breaking away from us with excitement.

"Ly, careful!" I warn as she charges up the porch stairs and throws herself into Korrine's awaiting arms.

My breath hitches. Korrine has been through the wringer with her cancer treatments but always seems to come out on top. So far, she's had several rounds with success. But by the look in her weary eyes and shaking hands, it's wearing her down to the bone.

"Oh, my baby," she coos, kissing the top of her hair and squeezing her arms around her. Gingerly, she pulls Ly into her lap. "Now, let me get a good look at you." A warm smile crosses her face when her dark eyes take Lyric's features in. "My, how you've grown. I think you got more freckles than before."

"Mommy says it's angel kisses, and Grammy Stella is sending me loves." Lyric's grin expands as she explains, tracing her fingers over the freckles continually popping up over the bridge of her nose and cheeks.

"I think your mama is right. Grammy Stella has lots of love to give you from Heaven," Korrine says, booping a trembling finger on her nose. "Now, are you gonna stand there all day? Or are you going to come and give me some sugar? I've missed you both so much," Korrine rasps, waving a hand in my direction.

I don't need any further instructions. I march up the stairs with burning tears and settle my weary bones in her embrace, letting her warmth envelop me and soaking in the motherly hug she always gives me. It's one of those hugs you don't realize you've missed until your mother is gone. No one prepares you for the mediocre hugs that can't even compare to the last one you gave to your mother. Ever. But Korrine's do. And today of all days, after finally becoming free, I needed this.

"We've missed you too," I whisper, kissing her cheek and sniffling.

"No crying now," she murmurs, brushing my tears away with the pad of her thumb. "Hmmm. And who is this?" She gestures to Asher as he stands at the bottom of the stairs, scratching his neck.

"That's my daddy, Grandma! Or...one of them. I've gots four. And they're so cool." Korrine's brows raise, but she doesn't utter a word as Lyric recounts her mini vacation trapped in the house with all of them and what we've been doing.

"Well, don't be shy, Boy. Come on up and introduce yourself. I don't believe we've had the privilege of meeting." Korrine's tone leaves no room for arguments, coming out stronger than I've heard her in months through our many phone calls.

"I'm Asher," he says softly, extending his hand as he sways in front of us with a look of pure terror.

Huh. Who knew? The way to scare these boys straight was in front of me all along. Now, I need to get the rest of them out here because Asher's so pale; he looks like he's about to shit his pants.

"One of them?" she asks, taking his hand in a firm grip.

"Yes?" he questions, gazing at me with wide eyes.

Internally I laugh at his pain, biting the inside of my cheek when his terror turns into slight trembles.

"Yes," I say, clearing my throat.

Korrine purses her lips. "Nice to finally have you on board."

"Mama! Who are you talking—" Ode, my best fucking friend, stops at the threshold of the front door, turning pale when she looks me over.

More tears burn the back of my eyes at the sight of her with her mouth agape and her body frozen in the doorway. My heart pounds wildly in my chest. A sense of home settles deep in my soul, unlocking all the turmoil I've faced in the years, months, and weeks leading up to this.

I'm finally where I need to be. If only for a little while.

Her dark eyes widen, and she drops the glass in her hand. It shatters against the wood, hurling glass everywhere. "Either I'm too sleep-deprived from that baby trying to eat every piece of lint off the floor or—"

I wrinkle my nose. "I'm really here."

"You dirty bitch!" she squeals, running toward me. Her arms fly around me as we laugh, hugging each other. "God damnit, River West. You bitch," she cries into my shoulder, snotting everywhere. But I don't give a shit. "If I had known you were coming, I would have laid out the red carpet."

"No, you wouldn't have," I choke, clutching her tight.

"You're right!" she cries, sniffling on my shoulder. "But I would have at least cleaned my house. Alma and Anni have flipped my damn house upside down." Sniffling, she pulls away, clapping a hand on my cheek. "But I've missed you and—" Her brows furrow. "What are you doing here? Last time we talked to you—" Her eyes widen on Asher, who awkwardly stands beside Korrine, softly talking to her and Lyric.

"Um, yeah," I say, clearing my throat.

"Yo, Ricky!" she shouts her husband's name. "Grab the gun. We've got a snake to fill with pellets!"

"Um, maybe I should just wait in the car," Asher says, gesturing toward the SUV with horror lining his face. If he thought meeting Korrine was terrible, he's now facing the wrath of my best friend, who openly glares at him with hostility.

"Oh, no, you won't. You and I are going to enjoy some sweet tea on the porch." I suppress my snort when Korrine gives him a *I'm not taking no for an answer* look.

"Oh, shit. She's breaking out the sweet tea," Ode hisses, pulling on my arm. "We better get before she breaks out the vanilla wafers and wants to have the sex talk again." Ode snickers under her breath when Korrine side-eyes us with a knowing smirk.

Yeah. I don't want to have that talk again.

"Y'all go inside. Asher and I will sit out here and enjoy the sun and conversation." Asher's eyes scream for help, silently begging me not to leave him in the clutches of Korrine.

"Okay. Have fun," I snort when Asher swallows hard, sitting beside Korrine in a second rocking chair.

"All right, you're coming with me. We've got lots of tea to devour ourselves." Ode grins at me, pulling me along. "Come inside, Lyric, my love! Alma would love to play!"

"Okay, Auntie Ode," she says, hopping off Korrine's lap and running inside without looking back.

"Is he going to be okay?" I murmur as she pulls me through the large living room littered with toys. The TV screams, but not over the squeals of Lyric and Alma, Ode's three-year-old daughter and Ly's long-distance best friend, hugging amid chaos.

"Bitch, please. Mama is going to eat him alive. Maybe he'll be a changed man by the time she's done with him. Converted and everything," she snorts, plopping my ass in front of the dining room table. "Now, how about some drinks?" she asks, setting down a large bottle of tequila in front of me.

"Ew. Why tequila? And it's only like eleven."

"Pfft. Bitch, this is the only alcohol that makes you talk. And it's five o'clock somewhere. Now, explain why douchebag number one is sitting on my porch like a domesticated dog," she says, pouring a tall shot of tequila.

"No lime? Salt?"

"No fucking lime for you, Missy. Take your shot and tell your bestie everything," she demands, pointing to the shot with her brow raised.

"Fine," I grimace, tossing back the shot. "Jesus," I croak through the burning sensation tingling down my throat.

"Out with it!" Ode says, pouring another shot. "I need all the dirty deets."

So, I tell her everything that's happened since we last spoke on the phone, starting with the fights, the revelations, and everything in between. I've texted her updates here and there in our daily messages but being in her presence hits differently.

"I just...don't know how I feel about it, Ode. I'm so fucking conflicted about everything," I murmur at the last of it, drowning myself in another shot of tequila.

"Wow," Ode says, drinking a shot, too.

"Yeah..."

"So, they volunteered to follow you here to protect you and Lyric. They've stepped up."

"Massively. Asher makes her breakfast every morning, even before all this. He wants to be her father. Rad's teaching her the drums. Callum tries to read to her every night. And Kieran is bonding with her like he never left her side. They're all trying as dads and—" I look out the window, examining the bright blue, cloudless sky as I gather my thoughts.

"And with you?" she asks, pouring two more shots for each of us.

I lick my lips. "That's the part that scares me, Ode. What if..."

"What if they break your heart? What if they walk away? What if... What if..." she trails off, shaking her head. "I saw how much it broke your heart when they fucked you over like that. Seeing you so damn sad and mad at the entire world broke my heart, too. You were ready to burn their entire existence down.

But hearing that bitch Gloria was the one who did most of it."

She grimaces as she downs another shot, sticking her tongue out and making a face when she sets the glass down.

"But Asher orchestrated it with her help. He made this entire thing happen."

"Yeah? And what's he doing now, bitch? He's sitting on the porch with Mama, probably getting ripped into through polite words. He drove you here?"

"He insisted."

Ode nods wistfully, taking another shot. "This could be the tequila fogging my thinking skills. When I saw him outside my house, I wanted to slice his balls open and shove them up his ass. The fucker deserved it. But the way I see it and from what you've told me, they're trying. With you. With her. With every fucking thing. Three of them walked away because they thought you broke their heart. One walked away because his fucking dreams depended on it. They were fucking idiots. So fucking stupid. God! Who put these men on this earth?" she slurs, covering her mouth.

"Way beyond idiots," I snort, taking a deep breath after I force another burning shot down my gullet. "Am I fucking crazy for even contemplating this?"

"Were you contemplating it when Kieran's fingers were in your–" I grunt, slamming a hand over her mouth.

"You get awfully vulgar when you've had tequila." She grins behind my hand, licking my palm.

"Well, I'm just saying... What's the worst that could happen?"

I blow out a breath. "They could leave us again. They are in a band. What happens when they go on tours? They'll leave for months at a time. What about Ly? How the hell is this all going to work out into a happy ending, Ode?"

"No one knows, babe. That's the beauty of life. You don't know the ending. Remember before? You thought you were going to travel the world with them. Maybe you were presented with this second chance for a reason." She shrugs, putting the lid back onto the now half-empty bottle of tequila, and hiccups. "No more day drinking for us, bitch." She giggles, thrusting a finger into the air as a lightbulb illuminates above her head like it always does before she has a brilliant idea. "Okay, so hear me out. I've got two ideas. You have enough money. Why don't you go on tour with them? Be their HBIC all over the world or some shit?" she asks like it's that fucking simple to drop my day job and go off with them on tour.

"I may have the money, but I like my job. And Ly loves her school... We could survive tours, right? We could—" Ode gives me an all-knowing smile.

"You have your answer. You didn't need me and the tequila to decide you wanted them. For some reason, they're your ones. You're meant to fucking be. You just had to go through some trials to get here."

I nibble my bottom lip. "Maybe you're right... But what is your second idea?" I ask, putting my elbows on the table as Lyric, Alma, and baby Anni toddle through the kitchen, singing at the top of their lungs.

"Okay, so... Here's my idea..." Ode says, spilling her idea with a grin on her face. Butterflies burst in my gut, and I nod in agreement. "Come to Dead End tonight with the boys and have them put on a show. You know, like old times. God, it would be great!"

"Holy shit. That's brilliant," I giggle, taking another sip of my shot, much to Ode's raised brows. She'd rather I knock it back, but my head is already swimming in an ocean of tequila. "I'll make a big announcement on their socials later and get the biggest crowd we can. No cover charge or anything. I'll pay for it all."

"Well, then there you go." Ode grins, pouring us one last shot. "To Whispered Words!" she says, slamming her glass into mine before we empty them down our throats.

37

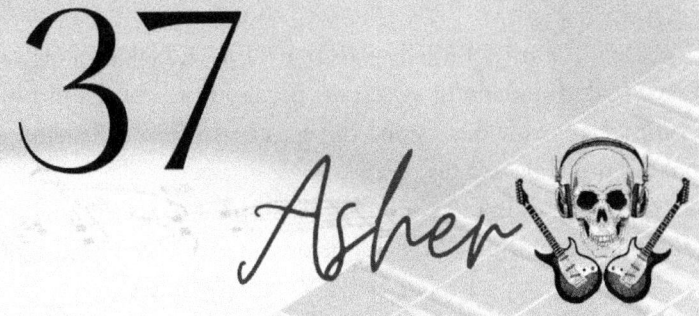

Asher

Gazing at the grassy fields surrounding the farmhouse, I contemplate my life choices. Korrine hasn't said a word since the girls excused themselves and went inside to catch up. I had no idea our visit would entail this, or I would have tucked tail and stayed with the guys.

"You know, I've always been curious. Which one of you fixed River's car after you left?"

My eyes whip to her in surprise, widening as she softly smiles. Somehow, I think she knew the answer before she even asked.

"Did she take it?" I ask, hoping River took the much-needed gift without protest. Knowing her, she scowled and cursed at whoever fixed the car but eventually took it because she knew she needed a vehicle to get her around without us there.

The moment we left; the guilt started scorching me from the inside out. The flames of my stomach were impossible to douse. Any remedy to tamp down my heartburn never worked until the antacids. Now, I eat them like candy, popping them six to eight times a day, trying to find some damn relief. Or I did. Since I confessed my wrongdoings, my stomach has been less volatile, ridding me of the constant acid reflux. And to me, that's a win. It still aches here and there as I swim through unfamiliar waters with

River, working to earn her forgiveness. But the pain is worth it in the end.

"All the time," Korrine chuckles, pouring us a glass of ice-cold sweet tea.

"Good," I say, lifting the glass to my lips and taking a big swig. The wonderful blend of sweetness fills my taste buds, and I hum in appreciation. If there's one thing I can say about Korrine, she makes a mean glass of tea.

"Boy, you didn't answer my question," she says sharply, again gaining my attention. "Which one of you gentlemen fixed River's car?"

"I did," I murmur in confirmation, letting the comfortable silence envelop us.

The warm September breeze blows through the porch, bringing a sweet, familiar laugh on its tails. Hearing a hint of happiness sputtering out of River brings a smile to my face and joy to my galloping heart.

Through the open window, Odette and River softly discuss our entire situation. In explicit detail, too. I side-eye Korrine, who nods with a knowing grin and doesn't say another word. It's as if she planned all this.

I sigh, sitting back in the rocking chair and letting its soft sways lull me into a once joyful memory, now tainted by every action I took to get us there.

"And the winner is," Seger says into the microphone, standing tall on stage with all the hopefuls clumping together behind him. The crowd beyond extends for miles, staying silent in anticipation humming through the entire venue. The spotlights above dance across everyone's heads in a multitude of colors, counting down until Seger opens his mouth once again. "Whispered Words!" he shouts, turning to look at us as pinks, blues, and reds dance across us.

"Holy Fuck!" Rad shouts, jumping up and down. His fists pump the air before he turns to us and pulls us into a massive group hug.

"We fucking did it!" I shout with a laugh, hugging everyone tight. Pride spears through me at how fucking far we've come since

Callum's basement. If it wasn't for our dedication and... My face falls a mile when a second thought roars in my mind.

We were Whispered Words before we met River. We did fine obtaining gigs and getting there. But we were a different Whispered Words after we met her. She changed our entire life... And she's nowhere to be found to enjoy this win with us.

"Congrats, guys!" Seger says through the microphone again and slaps each of us on the shoulder in congratulation.

We won. We fucking won the Battle of the Bands! My heart pounds against my chest as the words ring through my mind repeatedly. We're a signed fucking band! No more scrounging or praying for a better future. We've done it.

"Holy fucking shit!" Kieran roars out over the crowd's rampant cheering. "We fucking did it!"

We fucking did it...

My brothers and I look around, sweaty and smiling, staring at the adoring crowd as they cheer so loud it sounds like the roof is about to collapse. Not only did we receive the gold microphone as a trophy. We also received a one-million-dollar paycheck and a giant ass record deal.

This can't be fucking real. I pinch myself with a shuddering breath. Nope. I'm not fucking dreaming.

Our dreams are finally coming to life after so fucking long of hoping and praying for a break.

The work will be hard. So fucking hard. This is what we've always wanted. Right? This is everything we've worked for. Everything we've talked about in Callum's basement with stars in our eyes and determination in our guts. It's fucking everything...

So why do I feel so goddamn empty?

As we walk off the stage, shaking hands with everybody who came out to see the contest, something breaks inside me. With desperation, I look around with longing deep in my soul, hoping to see the familiar girl with moss-green eyes smiling in our direction. I ache to see her pushing through the crowd with excitement thrumming through her veins, shouting congratulations in our faces.

She'd jump in my arms, wrap her gorgeous, long legs around my torso and fervently kiss my lips. Without hesitation, she'd jump to Callum, Rad, and then Kieran, pouncing on them happily.

My heart cracks when we finally walk into the night air, whooping and hollering—all but me. I hang back as they jump up and down around our SUV, cackling and singing our praises. They don't notice when I shove my hands in my jeans and slowly walk away from the commotion. They don't see me when I slump against the club, crying out in frustration. Or the tears glistening down my cheeks under the glow of the light post. No. They don't seem to notice anything but our win.

"I'm so fucking sorry, Little Brat," I mumble with a quivering voice. Leaning my head against the scratchy brick, I glare at the twinkling stars, not drowned out by the city's lights. "I'm so fucking sorry I ran away from you." There's nothing I can do about it now. I'll keep pushing forward with her on my mind. I'll never forget what I did, the sacrifices I made to get us away from Nigel and Gloria.

As the guys continue their loud celebration across the parking lot, my mind wanders, concocting wild ideas to ease the shame of what I've done. As the night goes on and the celebration gets bigger, I realize there is something I can do for River to ease the pain of our departure.

"Yeah, it's stuck in the parking lot of the Dead End bar in Central City," I say, silently pacing my room at 8:00 a.m. the following day. The boys are still sound asleep after a wild night out, drinking anything they could get their hands on. So, as soon as they passed out, I researched the best shops in Central Illinois hoping to get River's car in.

"Yeah, sure, Asher. I can pick that up today. If you want me to take it to the shop?" he questions gruffly through the phone.

"Uh...yeah, Man, just to fix whatever is wrong with it. Just send me the bill or whatever you need me to do." I rub my temples as a headache forms, pounding against my skull.

Fuck. I didn't even drink that much last night. Not with the *way I felt. I couldn't touch more than two drinks without wanting to throw up.*

"No problem, man. I'll get it taken care of and send you updates. *Anything else?*" *he asks as I plop into bed and lay back, staring at the dull white ceiling.*

"Fix it. Clean it. And then send me everything. *But make sure you put it back where you got it from; I'll be in town in about a week to pay.*"

"*Sounds good. I'll see you when you get into town.*"

"I just wanted her to have a way to get around," I say softly, chuckling when I remember the note I left on her windshield.

Stop fucking walking.

As I stand in the empty parking lot of Dead End at 3:00 a.m., an emptiness engulfs my entire being. My stomach churns, sending acid up my throat as I set the note beneath the windshield of her car. I don't have a clue when she'll come back to it or even see this, but it'll give me plenty of time to sneak away without being noticed. I swallow hard, staring at the piece of shit she drives around. If I was a better man, I would buy her something new so she's able to get to work and school without worry.

But I'm not a better man. I'm the piece of shit under her shoe. So, this is the best I can fucking do for now. Maybe in the future, when we're in a better place as a band, I'll tell them what happened.

"Mmm. She used it, too. Every day until her brothers came into her life. You fixed it up real good, son." Reaching over, she lays a weary hand on my arm, gently squeezing. "You did a damn good thing for her."

I scoff, shaking my head. "I would have been a better man if I could have just let things be and let her come. If I hadn't meddled in our relationship and—"

"Now, now," Korrine chastises, squeezing my arm again before pulling away. "How many years have you put yourself through the wringer?" She raises a brow when I blow out a breath, willing the stupid tears to melt away.

"Since the moment I left," I mumble.

"And she knows it?" she asks as we both take sips of tea. "You've explained and said your sorrys?"

"Of course." I set my glass back down on the tiny table between us, staring at the miles of nothing again, getting lost in the blissful breeze and the sounds of insects. "I'll say I'm sorry forever until I'm blue in the damn face and have bruises on my knees. Even if she forgives me, I'll remember what I did and how it affected everyone. I don't expect anyone in this situation to forgive me, though. I know I wouldn't."

"There's a blessing with forgiveness. Humans never forget what happened but find it in their hearts to forgive, anyway. Some way, somehow, it happens. Not many people know, not even my own children, but the love of my life left me after one year of marriage. Said he couldn't do it anymore and disappeared for a week."

"Why?" I ask, swallowing hard.

"Who knew with that man? We were young and in love, moving through this world at warp speed." She shakes her head.

"He came back?"

"On his hands and knees, begging me to forgive him for being the biggest dummy in history." She sniffles a little, folding her hands on her lap. "He just needed to sow his wild oats one last time before settling down. The week he came back, well... Leon came nine months later. It wasn't as blissful as a marriage like Hallmark would lead you to believe, but we managed. We loved hard. Played hard. Life is full of ups and downs, betrayals, and misfortune. But as long as you keep getting back on your feet and showing that woman how much you care. Then you're on the right path, Asher Montgomery."

I swallow my tears. "Thank you," I murmur as the quiet envelops us again. The only sounds are nature, and the girls getting louder and louder with their conversation through the open window.

My heart beats double time when River's voice floats through the air again, confiding in Ode about her concerns about the future, but the one line filled with so much despair has my breaths coming in short pants and sweat breaking across my skin.

"They could leave us again. They are in a band. What happens when they go on tours? They'll leave for months at a time. What about Ly? How the hell is this all going to work out into a happy ending, Ode?"

"So, now you know what you have to do," Korrine says cryptically, staring at the leaves ruffling in the wind. "Make it happen, or all your pain and suffering will be for nothing. You'll lose her again, before you have a chance to keep her." With that, she gets up from her rocking chair on unsteady legs and enters the house, leaving me to stew in my thoughts.

Yeah. I know exactly what I need to do so River never has to worry about if we're leaving or staying.

I'll make the ultimate sacrifice for her and Lyric. And hopefully, the others will, too.

38

I'M NEVER DRINKING FUCKING tequila in the middle of the day. Ever again. Even if Ode convinces me, it's a good idea. It's not. Or maybe it was.

Talking to Ode is like walking through the front door of my house. She's warm and inviting and always knows the right thing to say. I'm still surprised she gave me the green light to follow my weary heart into the ultimate make-or-break situation.

I'm so tired of fighting with myself. With the thoughts rumbling in the back of my mind, screaming at me to fall into their familiar arms. They're my home, too. For some strange, out-of-this-world reason, my heart aches for them.

I take a deep breath, grounding myself in the present. Forgiveness is my new state of mind. The mantra I'm going to live and die by when I sit the boys down tonight and tell them all is forgiven in my eyes. Peace washes through me, relaxing every muscle in my body. Just at the simple thought of no longer holding the hostility inside my warring mind.

My burning anger sizzles into ashes. And it's gone...

Korrine and Ode lean against the white railing of the wrap-around porch. Asher, bless his heart, stands beneath them on the ground with his back to me. The women nod a few times as he shoves his hands into his pockets. His shoulders deflate.

I yearn to see the expression on his face. *Look at me, damnit.* What is going through your head? I'm so desperate to hear what they're discussing.

"Auntie Ode doesn't like Daddy," Lyric says with a little yawn in the back seat, staring in their direction.

Yeah, because your daddy did some fucked up things in the past. But the past is the past. My forgiveness shouts, reminding me.

"She has her grown-up reasons for it," I say, leaning my head against the cool glass window, letting it soak into my drunk-ass brain.

There's no way I'm getting into this discussion with a four-year-old who repeats everything word for word. If she found out what her daddy did all those years ago, she'd hate him forever. Or be so hurt she wouldn't know how to act. Ly takes everything to heart, and I can't break hers because of him.

To Lyric, her fathers are the saints on her walls. The music in her speakers. And the blood running through her veins. If I wanted to spoil their image, I would have done it years ago.

Sure, Asher manipulated the situation and fucked us all over, but he's grown up. He's making up for what he did. Owning up to his faults. He's trying to make this right every day. I see it. The guys see it.

"Sorry," Asher says, climbing into the driver's seat out of breath, wearily staring at the two women standing on the porch. "I was discussing a few things with Korrine."

Nothing says suspicious like avoiding eye contact. Even when he starts the car and slowly backs out of their little driveway, he avoids me at all costs.

Ode grins on the steps, shaking her head almost in disbelief. Something odd sparkles in her eyes. Even from here, I can see it. I know when my best friend has something up her sleeve. What the hell is going through her head? She grins more, waving as we ease away down the long lane leading toward the main road.

"What was that about?" Please! Give me something. I need to know what you all discussed, or it will drive me nuts.

Asher shrugs at my question, still not bothering to look in my direction. I narrow my eyes on his guilty behavior. He's suspect as fuck, and I can't put my finger on what he's up to. Maybe it's the tequila taking over my brain, but I kinda want to torture the information out of him.

"It was nothing," he says, giving me a tight smile. "I was just... getting some advice. That's all."

Yeah, because that's not suspicious one-bit, Evil Ash. You can keep your secrets. Best believe, I'll find out soon enough. Ode tells me everything. At least, I think she does. My eyes narrow when I pull out my phone and shoot a quick text, earning only a devil emoji in return.

Traitor.

And I tell her so.

"Right. Advice..." I trail off as we head down the main road toward Central City again. "What exactly did they say to you?"

He shakes his head again, chuckling at my curiosity that will one day get me killed.

"Can I—" Asher hesitates a moment, his lips flapping like a fish out of water. "Um, can I take you to meet someone?" I blink several times through his rushed words, leaving him breathless beside me. "I mean, if you want to. I'd really like to introduce you to someone important to me," he murmurs with uncertainty.

"Meet someone?" I ask, raising a brow of suspicion.

"Yeah. It won't take too long, I wanted to stop by before we left town to say hi to her. I, um, haven't seen her since I left." He swallows hard, with a glossy sheen taking over his hazel eyes. "I want her to meet Lyric," he whispers, sinking his teeth into his bottom lip, stopping the sudden quivering.

"I want to meet her! Who's her?" Lyric chirps, leaning forward, clutching the new white bunny Ode gave her as an early birthday present.

From the once dismal expression to something only the sun

could conjure, Asher's entire face lights up with a wide grin, exposing his teeth. For the first time in a long time, I see the delight written in his expression and fluid movements.

Whatever we're about to do, lifts the weight of everything off Asher's shoulders, making him whole.

"First, we need some flowers," he says softly. "Then, we can meet her. I promise."

"Flowers?" she questions, furrowing her brows. "I love flowers," she says, cocking her head with curiosity as the car zooms down the empty road on our way back to the city that made us.

"Flowers," he confirms, pulling off the main road and into a tiny gravel parking lot.

A few older model cars rest around us, unoccupied. One license plate reads—flowers2233, attached to a large van with the Central Florist Shop logo painted on the side with beautifully crafted purple, pink, blue, red, and white flowers decorating the entire van. Even the hubcaps have been touched by the bright and cheery colors.

My head pounds as I rest it against the window, staring at my surroundings. "A florist shop," I surmise, glancing over at Asher, who nods.

"She loved this place." He doesn't take his eyes off the front of the shop, directly in front of us. "Her favorites are in there. Roses," he says cryptically, not bothering to mention the name of the woman we're speaking about, which, again, kills my curiosity.

I'm so damn desperate to understand what's going on, but something about the way Asher peacefully stares at the shop eases all my wonderings.

"You can stay here if you'd like," he murmurs, side-eying me until I nod. This seems like something he needs to do all on his own. "But can I take her to help?"

My heart explodes when he stares at me earnestly until I nod. "Of course. Ly, you want to help Daddy pick out flowers?"

"Yes!" she gasps, hurriedly undoing herself from her booster seat.

"Thank you," he breathes, reaching over to squeeze my hand. "We'll be right back."

"Of course," I murmur, gluing my eyes to his loose movements as he removes himself from the car with a smile pulling at his lips.

Who is this Asher? He's a completely changed man from even a month ago. I'm not complaining one bit. The old Asher was a rigid asshole who put me through the damn ringer with his attitude. This is the same Asher who manipulated everyone around him to achieve his dream and leave his abusive father.

But this new Asher. Dear God... I could see myself falling, madly, deeply, head-over-heels, in love with him.

Something weird happens inside my body, like my ovaries exploding, when he gently helps her out of the car with that grin plastered on his face. Light captures his hazel eyes when he bends down, coming eye level with her. His long fingers run through her hair, tucking it behind her ears with a chuckle as they whisper things to one another.

"Have fun," I rasp, waving my goodbye as they set off on their little adventure.

Butterflies burst in my stomach when he takes her tiny hand in his, swinging their grip back and forth. I touch a hand to my lips, watching Lyric's mouth move a million miles a minute. Every ounce of darkness flees from her face like there isn't a worry in the entire universe. Right now, her world is Asher Montgomery.

Asher's shoulders relax as he clutches her tiny hand, nodding his head to whatever she's saying. He grins more, opens the door for her, and follows her inside. It's like they've had these outings a million times before. This is our new normal.

The moment they disappear, tears burn the back of my eyes. I squeeze them shut, refusing to let any tears fall down my cheeks. Happy or sad. It doesn't matter. Despite the need to purge my emotions, a warmth spreads across my chest. Tingling courses through my veins, and a weightless feeling lifts me.

All I ever wanted was Ly and her dads. Them taking her places. Wanting to be there for her and listen to her when she needs them. She's always wanted them by her side; now, she's getting her wish.

I blow out a breath when they leave the store side by side. Ly clutches two small bouquets of dark pink, light pink, and white flowers—one in each hand and a shit-eating grin taking over her lips. Once again, Asher helps Ly get into her new booster seat, carefully strapping her in with furrowed brows.

"Mommy, I picked out the most beautiful flowers! Here, smell," she squeals, bouncing in her seat before shoving the flowers directly into my face.

I flinch back from the petals hitting me in the face. The wonderful scent of roses hits my nose when I inhale, reminding me of the night I spent with Kieran in the rain with roses floating all around us. "They're beautiful, Ly," I chuckle, lightly shoving them away from my face. "You did a good job, baby."

Setting back in her seat, Asher finally straps her in with success as she babbles until he kisses her forehead. "I love you, Daddy." Her big eyes stare at him like he hung the moon for her.

Yup. There goes my heart. It's a melty puddle in my chest, beating rapidly when he beams.

"I love you too," he murmurs, softly shutting the door.

She preens, pulling the flowers into her nose and taking a big whiff. "Mmm, I think Grandma will like them. Do you think Grandma will like them, Mommy?"

"I'm sure Grandma will," I rasp, side-eyeing Asher again when he settles into the front seat, unable to look at me.

"Flowers for grandma?" I murmur, resting a hand on his forearm and gently squeezing until his eyes snap to mine, dilating the littlest bit from the warm contact. Electricity zaps through my fingertips, running straight to my toes from the slightest touch of his flesh. My hairs stand on end when his eyes fall on our connecting flesh, and he swallows hard.

He shudders at the contact, the briefest hint of a blush pinkening his cheeks. "Flowers for both grandmas," he murmurs. "Our mothers are both at the same cemetery."

The world stops moving. I freeze in place, letting his words knock around inside my brain. My mother. His mother. They're in the same damn place?

"Oh, Asher," I breathe, pressing my fingers to my trembling lips. "The cemetery?" I lamely ask with a rock stuck in my throat.

"We weren't there for you when it happened. I feel—" His grip tightens on the steering wheel as his chest expands. Heavy breaths pour from between his parted lips as his body loosens more. "I feel so fucking responsible for you not having the support you deserved. It was me. I did that. We should have been there for you and held you. Let you cry on our shoulders. Rad could have made some ridiculous apple pie and any comfort food you needed. And...and...we weren't there." Asher blows out a shaky breath. "It may be a little late, but that's what we're doing now."

"Yay! Grandma gets flowers!" Lyric sings, swaying in her seat. "I can't wait to give them to her." She continues babbling, not comprehending what we're about to do.

I've had this talk with her before. She constantly questions where my mommy is and why she's not here. I've explained to her by pointing to the bright orb hanging out in the darkened sky that she's with the man on the moon. She left this world because she was sick, and now she watches us with a smile. Sometimes it's hard to explain to a four-year-old that my mom is never coming back to meet her.

"Jesus Christ," I rasp through the razor blades sitting in my throat every time I swallow.

"That's okay, right?" Asher asks, pulling out of the parking lot with concern twisting his face. "I can just take you back to Cal's, and you can do it privately if you want. Take the flowers and do what you want with them. I'll call the boys and tell them you need this time to yourself."

"Please take me there, Asher," I whisper through the tears heating the backs of my eyes. "I want to do this with you."

And I do. Every molecule in my body settles at the thought of visiting these graves with him.

It's been five years since I faced my mother. The moment they lowered her into the ground was the hardest day of my life. I had my found family with me that day. I cried on their shoulders. But when I went home all by myself with no one to pick up the pieces, I fell hard.

When I was pregnant, I made a vow to visit my mother any chance I could. I'd sit in the sun and talk to her, letting her know about Ly and what was happening. I've celebrated her life from far away for too long. It's time to face her again and tell her everything that's happened while she's been away.

39

As we travel closer to the cemetery, I can't look away from the man I once saw as a monster. My enemy. The man who took everything away from me with one little lie. He's no longer the man he once was. Not at all.

My gaze eats him alive, taking in every inch of his profile and memorizing them. My eyes trace the tired lines, old bruises, and scrapes I had missed. A few scars line his cheeks and neck, falling beneath his tight black T-shirt.

Were those there before? From his father? From something else?

"Wow!" Lyric proclaims, knocking me out of my thoughts as we travel beneath the iron banner, welcoming us to the last place I ever thought I'd be.

Central Cemetery hasn't changed much since I was here last. Gray stones peek above the trimmed grass. Bright flowers sit all around in memoriam for loved ones lost. Tall mausoleums with last names carved into stone sit on the horizon in various spots.

"Is this where the dead people are?" Lyric asks, swallowing a lump in her throat. Her curious eyes dart across the stones passing by in slow motion.

"Buried here, yes." I watch her shuddered expression closely as she nods.

"No zombies, Mommy?" she whispers frantically, searching her surroundings. "Daddy Rad and me watched zombies, they eat people's brains."

"Did he?" Asher asks with a disappointed head shake. "Idiot," he murmurs quietly, enough so she doesn't hear.

"We're going to have to give your daddy a parenting class on what four-year-olds should watch," I say, shaking my head in disbelief. One dad always throws on a horror movie for a child who shouldn't be watching it, and that dad is Rad.

"And say," Asher chuckles, unclenching his fists.

My heart pounds when the car stops near the row my mother is buried in. I eye the names etched into the marble with interest, bouncing from one to the other.

Baker. Jones. Hogan. West. Montgomery.

Right there, under the dirt, rests her corpse. Still dressed in the same outfit Korrine and Ode helped me pick out—a dress she loved to wear in the sunshine. A simple headstone poking out of the ground with her name, date of birth, and inscription indicates where she rests eternally.

Loving mother and friend. Gone too soon.

What an understatement that is. If it weren't for her autoimmune disease, she'd still be around, watching Lyric grow.

It's odd that I vaguely remember the day I stood in the sunshine, watching for the last time as my mother's body rested above ground. Her old and new friends gathered around, taking flowers from a large bouquet on her oak casket. Tears fell. Laughs echoed through the large cemetery in her memory. Some good. Some bad. Everyone remembered my mother in a positive light.

As for me? I was utterly frozen, running my fingers over the smooth wood, begging her to come back for one more day, just for a few more hours. There were so many unsaid words and declarations.

My brain was fogging in chaos, trying to digest what had happened. My mother fucking died. The boys left me without a word or goodbye. And I was carrying their child. To say my thoughts weren't in the present was the understatement of the century.

I was a million miles away, but my feet were still in the same spot.

I knew she was in a better place. Or so they say. Her MS wouldn't bother her anymore. She would be free from the complications of life. But it didn't stop me from aching for one more hug. One more kiss on the temple. One more, 'You did good, Riv.' Just a single chance to tell her that I loved her and wished her well.

Fuck. I miss my mom.

My mother may not have been the best human being on the planet. She worked hard when I was a kid—left me to my own damn devices. But I still loved her. Always will. I reread the names, going down the line until my heart plummets into my ass at the realization.

Baker. Jones. Hogan. West. Montgomery.

I blanch, turning to look at Asher. He stares out my window, locking on the tallest headstone at the end of the row. Shade trees block out the sun, blanketing our moms in beautiful darkness.

"They're..." I swallow hard, shaking my head.

"I can't afford this," I whisper to the funeral home director. "I can't."

"You don't need to, Miss West," he says softly, eyes brimming with understanding.

"I don't understand. Why was she brought here? I told them... I..." I squeeze my eyes shut, leaning back in the chair across from him at his mahogany desk.

"It's all been taken care of. An anonymous donor donated the plot, and the funds have been raised for the funeral. It's just enough," he says, sliding a piece of paper across the desk.

"But why would—"

"It was you, wasn't it?" I whisper with tears streaming down my face. I swear, since I had a child, I have cried like a baby at everything. It doesn't fucking matter the circumstance. "The donated plot? The funds for the funeral?"

"You asked for space, and I used that against you..." he trails off, looking over his shoulder at Ly playing with the flowers and lightly humming.

"Asher," I breathe. The roughness of his fingers beneath mine has me gasping for air when I clutch his hand. "You did all that for me? But why?" Why would he leave me and do something nice for me in return? Why would he do that?

"That was my plot. My father bought it in anticipation of my early demise. I... As much as I wanted to be buried next to my mother for eternity, I wanted to give it to someone who could use it more than me. Someone who deserved it. And that person was Stella. I raised funds for her funeral through Rad's parents. I... went to them for help, and the church stepped up. I just... What I did is inexcusable, and I made it up with everything I did. Your car —"

"Jesus, Asher. My car?" I gasp, clutching my shirt over my chest.

Stop. Fucking. Walking.

I remember the moment I walked outside as the snow started falling. Ode handed me her keys and told me to track down the guys using her vehicle. I had been walking since they fucking left me. Then, out of nowhere, I found my car with a wet note attached under the windshield wipers from an unknown person. I should have fucking known, but I didn't question it. It was a gift from someone anonymous.

And I used it every day after that.

"It never gave me problems after that, Asher. What did you have fixed?" I murmur through more tears, trying to hold them back. My goddamn emotions are everywhere lately. It all has to do with the four men who have, once again, broken down my carefully constructed walls. They're the damn masters of destruction and rebuilding.

Redness takes over his cheeks. "I did what any person would

do, Little Brat. I fixed everything so you could have something reliable. And I'm glad I did. If you wouldn't have had that for Lyric..."

"But I did," I whisper. "It was the greatest gift you could have given me while I was pregnant."

"Why don't we take a walk," he whispers, nodding out the window toward the headstones. "Lyric, you want to put those flowers in both your grandmas' vases?" He clutches my hand as he speaks softly to Ly.

"Yes!" she squeals, scrambling to remove herself from her booster seat.

The warm sun heats my skin the moment I step out of the car, helping Lyric jump from the vehicle. She giggles as she clutches the flowers, one bouquet in each hand.

"I can't wait to give these to my grandmas!" Her grin brings more tears to my eyes.

"You understand, don't you, baby? That your grandmas aren't living. That they're somewhere different than Earth?" I ask, crouching down in front of her. "Sometimes humans get sick and only get better when they leave Earth for better places."

Bloated tears gloss Lyric's eyes when she nods in understanding.

"Daddy told me." She sniffles, staring into the bright colors of the flowers. "But Daddy said both grandmas were smiling down from the sky, watching me. So, I wants to talk to them." She gives a firm nod, full of four-year-old determination. "I wants to give them flowers and kiss their stones. Daddy said they'd like that lots."

"They would, baby," I whisper, tucking a piece of her dark locks behind her ear. "They really would." I kiss her forehead before I stand tall.

"Lead the way," I quietly say to Asher, who nods, putting a hand on Ly's shoulder, and leads the way toward the graves we haven't been to in years.

It's funny that Mrs. Montgomery was here as I mourned my

mother. How many times did Asher stand in this exact spot with tears in his eyes?

"You can put them in here," Asher murmurs, directing the flowers to the tiny vases connected to the base of each headstone.

"And grandmas will get them where they are?" she asks, kneeling before my mother's grave, clinging to both bouquets.

"Yes, Ly," I softly say, kneeling beside her. "You remember Grandma Stella, right? She was my mommy, and she died when she got really sick. Her body couldn't take it anymore, so she went to meet her maker." I kiss her head when she sniffles again, placing the first flower bundle into the vase.

"What about your mommy?" Lyric looks up at Asher with those big puppy dog eyes as he rests beside her, leaning against his mother's headstone a touch away.

He smiles. "Kathryn Montgomery. She was the best cook," he chuckles, rubbing a hand along his chest. "I got my hair from my mommy, just like you did yours."

Ly wrinkles her nose. "Mommy says I gots daddy's hair," she murmurs, running her hand through her hair.

"Every morning, my mom got up early and made pancakes. Sometimes, I'd sneak in and help. We'd add anything we wanted. Blueberries, chocolate chips, and caramel chips. She loved cooking and playing with me." His eyes drift upwards, examining the fluffy clouds blowing in the wind.

"What happened to your mommy?" Ly whispers, shuffling toward Asher with the flowers outstretched.

Emotions choke my throat at her simple question. She's been desperate to know all about them, and finally, she's getting the answers she's been seeking.

Asher pulls her into his lap, leaning against his mother's headstone together. Running a hand through her long hair, he kisses her cheek.

"My mommy was very sad," he whispers with a tortured expression twisting his face. But he doesn't show it to her. He keeps all his emotions hidden from her inquisitive eyes, except for the tears. "She got very sick, too. For some reason, she left this earth. But I know she loved me."

I'm frozen with a heavy tongue. Unable to utter a word as I watch them together.

"I'll give her flowers now," Ly sniffles again, crawling off his lap and planting herself in the grass. Reaching over, she places the last bouquet into the vase with a tiny smile. "Hope you like your flowers, Grandma," she murmurs, kissing the granite.

"I think she will, Little One," he says, leaning forward to kiss her cheek until she grins.

Warmth fills every molecule in my body as they continue to converse one-on-one. Lyric watches him intently, absorbing every word he utters about his mother and the stories he tells.

The sound of crunching rocks pulls my attention away from them and onto another car stopping behind ours. One by one, the other guys get out with suits plastered to their bodies and flowers in their hands.

My fucking heart stops at the sight of them slowly walking toward us with varying expressions.

"Oh, Pretty Girl," Rad murmurs, sitting beside me in the grass, not bothering to keep his new suit clean from stains. "I'm so sorry you had to come and do this all by yourself. I fucking loved Stella. She was so damn bossy," he tsks the last part jokingly.

His fingers brush against my jaw, sending shivers down my spine. Without hesitation, I brush my lips against his, capturing him in a simple kiss, trying to convey my thanks.

"I think she liked you guys, too. She even called you 'good guys,'" I chuckle, pulling back with admiration in my heart. "Thank you all for being here. This... It means a lot to have you here."

Kieran sighs, sitting on my other side, tossing an arm over my shoulder. The tips of his fingers brush up and down my upper arm, eliciting goosebumps over every inch of my flesh.

"She was a good lady," Kieran says solemnly, staring at her

name etched into the granite with his brows furrowed. "She tried her hardest."

"Yeah," I murmur, leaning my head on his shoulder. "She tried the best she could." And that's all that matters to me. She was there. Sometimes. Whenever she could be, at least. I had a roof over my head, food in my belly, and determination in my veins. If there's anything my mom did for me, it was to prepare me to work hard.

Life isn't roses and rainbows with pretty sparkles. It's muted grays, blacks, and whites with struggles.

"Here, Little Star. These are for you," Callum murmurs, falling to his knees to complete our little circle.

I smile, reaching for the pretty white roses bundled together. Inhaling deeply, I catch their scent and hum.

"Thank you," I whisper into the petals, squeezing my eyes shut.

"I've prepared some words," Rad says, clearing his throat. I peek an eye open when his tongue pokes out as he searches through his suit pockets. "Ah-ha," he murmurs, pulling out a white piece of paper with scribbles. "Pretty Gir... River," he says, choking back tears as he takes my hand. "Stella was the most magnificent woman, besides you, of course."

"And me, Daddy?" Lyric asks with a tiny voice.

"Of course! You, too, Little Pretty Girl. You're the most important girls in my life!" he proclaims with a grin, staring between us. "And I wouldn't give you up for anything."

"Even unicorn ice cream?" Lyric whispers, leaning in. "Cuz I love unicorn ice cream."

"I love it, too," he says, grinning from ear to ear. "But I'd give up everything to be by your side, Little Pretty Girl. And your mommy's, too."

Be still my beating heart.

"I really only knew Stella as a kid," Kieran says, squeezing my shoulder. "If it wasn't for her, I wouldn't have had you. Those days and nights on the hill, strumming my guitar with you at my side. They meant the world to me. Stella worked hard. She was nice as hell, giving the shirt off her back. That one time when she fell and hurt herself in the bathroom, I was so shaken up thinking that she was dead. My heart hurt for her and you," he murmurs, kissing my cheek. "It's a shame that she had to leave this world."

"That shit was scary," Rad murmurs, shaking his head. "I think my heart fell out of my chest when we found you crying at your front door. Stella was so hurt, and I knew I had to call my mom to get her some help."

"You talked to her lately?" I ask, squeezing his hand.

"Nah. Haven't talked in a while. She disapproves of the rock star lifestyle. It is what it is. I don't need a negative Nancy in my life, anyway. Besides, I already have a family."

"You do," I whisper, leaning forward to kiss his lips again. "We're a family," I murmur. He grins against my lips until I'm ripped away by Kieran, who pulls me back into him.

"She knew I snuck into your room every night," Callum murmurs with a hint of a grin, pulling at his lips. "Caught me one night," he chuckles.

"She did?" I ask, raising a brow.

"Yeah," he breathes. "I had to go to the bathroom, and she was out in the hall with her arms crossed. She asked me if I was one of the boys making you happy?"

"What did you say?" I ask, staring into the depths of his gray eyes.

"I said... Yes, but the feeling was mutual. You made me so damn happy. So, she nodded and walked away from me toward the living room."

"She was always really nice to me," Asher mumbles, scratching across his chest. "I don't think I was over there as much as you guys, but she always smiled at me when I was by." He swallows hard, looking deep into my eyes. "I'm so sorry you lost her like you did. Especially after being away with us at the Castle house."

"Castle house? I wanna go to a castle!" Lyric pipes up, reminding us of what happened at that damn house.

Her.

Kieran chuckles. "Maybe we can vacation to an actual castle sometime soon. Okay?"

"Yes, Daddy! I want swords and armor! I want to sleep in a castle like a princess." She grins when he chuckles, ruffling her hair.

"Of course, Little Blue. Anything for you."

"Thanks, guys. For coming here with us and for bringing flowers. It means a lot you're here now," I whisper as more tears well in my eyes.

"We missed it the first time, Pretty Girl. So, here we are now. We wanted to celebrate Stella's life."

"And Katy's," Kieran murmurs, locking eyes with Asher, who stiffens.

"Thanks, man," Asher murmurs, rubbing a hand across his chest. "Means a lot."

"She was your mom, bro. I never knew Katy, but I'm sure she was the bomb," Rad proclaims.

"She made daddy pancakes, too!" Lyric giggles. "Just like daddy makes me." She beams when he grins.

"All right, River Blue. How about we all go out for a nice dinner?" Kieran asks, looking around at the boys, who nod.

"Pizza?" Lyric asks with hope.

"If that's what you want, Little Blue. We can go to Tuscany. They've got it all. Pizza, pasta... Whatever your heart desires."

"Yay! Let's go!" she shouts, jumping up as we all rise. Grabbing hold of Kieran's hand, she drags him back to his car as the others follow.

"Asher," I whisper, clinging to his arm as he stops dead.

"What's up?" he questions, swallowing hard.

"I want you to know something," I whisper, moving into his space. We stand chest to chest. Our breaths hitch together.

"What is it?" he questions with furrowed brows. "Are you

okay? Did I cross a line? I didn't mean—" The moment my lips touch his, he shuts up, staring at me with wide eyes until he relaxes. His fingers brush through my hair, desperately holding me close.

"I forgive you," I whisper against his lips. "Don't beat yourself up anymore. What you did is in the past. I'll remember it forever, Evil Ash. I'll remember how it made me feel. But I don't want to hold a grudge against you anymore. What you did sucked, but you're... You're so different, and I forgive you for what you did. I want to move forward with this relationship. You're so important to Ly... And to me." I swallow hard when his grip tightens in my hair, and a whine slips through his lips.

"Oh, Little Brat," he chokes out. "I really don't deserve that, baby," he whispers. "I fucked up so hard. I'm...so fucking sorry for what I did. I don't—"

"You deserve forgiveness, Asher. You did a bad thing. But it doesn't mean you're an evil guy. You were desperate. Your abusive father and stepmother were going to force you into something you didn't want to do. Could you have done it differently and talked to me? Yes. You could have. But, Ash. I'm ready to forgive. I feel it in my heart," I murmur, thumping a fist against my chest. "Are you ready to forgive yourself?" I whisper, putting my palm against his rapidly beating heart.

"Little Brat," he whispers with tears falling down his cheeks. "Yes. If that's what you want, I'm ready to move forward. But just know, I'll forever prove to you that what I did was the biggest mistake of my life," he whispers, cupping my jaw in his palms. "The biggest regret I'll ever have is leaving you behind. It was the dumbest thing anyone ever could have done."

"I believe you," I whisper, wiping away the tears on my cheeks. "Now, let's get some Italian food and continue going forward."

"One day at a time," he whispers, leaning in to brush his lips against mine again in a soft embrace.

"One day at a time," I whisper my declaration when he takes my hand, pulling me toward the cars.

The other three guys watch us with neutral expressions. Their arms are resting across their chest, taking us in as we walk up hand in hand.

"I forgive you all," I say softly. "I don't want this grudge to come between us anymore. I know it's only been a short time. Our time here on Earth is never promised. I don't want to go to sleep anymore with this anger I've held."

"We'll continue to support you both," Callum says, marching to me. "Every day, we'll fight the wrongs we put you through." Without a moment to second guess himself, he pushes his lips onto mine in an eager kiss. He hums, swirling his tongue against mine in desperation. "My first and last," he murmurs when we finally break apart. "My forever."

"We'll always show you, River Blue. We'll be here every day," Kieran chokes out, moving forward to capture my lips with his in a soft, dominating embrace.

"There's no getting rid of us, Pretty Girl. You can put a collar around my neck with your name as my girl. Forever and ever..." He kisses my cheek, grinning when Lyric makes a face.

"Gross," she says, wrinkling her nose.

"All right, how about some pizza?" Kieran asks Lyric, bringing her into his arms.

"Pizza! Pizza! Pizza!" she proclaims loudly, thrusting her tiny fist into the air with a giggle.

"And then after pizza, you're going to spend the night with Alma and Anni," I say, grinning when she whips her gaze toward me.

"Really?" she squeals.

"Really," I confirm with a nod as she wiggles excitedly in Kieran's arms.

"Really?" Rad asks with suspicion, narrowing his eyes.

"Yes. Because your daddies have a show, we'll be out soooo late!" I say, pinching her cheeks.

"What show?" Callum asks, tilting his head to the side as a slow smile spreads across his lips. "We do have the instruments."

"What? Where?" Rad begs, jumping on his toes.

"Where else would we go?" Asher snorts. "We're in Central City. There's only one place with our names carved into it." He smiles, chuckling.

"Fuck yes!" Rad whoops.

"Daddy, I think it's time you owe me money with every bad word you say. That'll be thirty-thousand dollars," Lyric says, holding her hand with an expectant look.

I snort. "Yeah, Daddy. Pay up..."

"But... But... Little Pretty Girl! That's a lot of money."

"Pay up, Daddy." She sticks her nose in the air, wiggling her fingers like he'll pay her right here and now.

"I'll add it to your college fund," he grumbles, high-fiving her hand.

I snort. "Responsible parenting," I commend, earning a grin. "All right, Whispered Words. Let's get some dinner and then—."

"Show time," Rad interrupts with jazz hands.

40

"OH MY GOD, BITCH," Ode breathes, staring out at the sea of people chanting below the stage. Her hands slap at my shoulders over and over, leaving a slight burn behind her hits.

"Stop," I cackle, lightly pushing her away from my side.

"But bitch!" she hisses, hitting my shoulder. "My bar." She shakes her head in disbelief as her dark eyes continually dart around. I swear tears form in her eyes as she chokes back a small sob.

Dead End is still an active place. It's a bar. People come from all over town to eat Leon's spectacular dishes, drink beer, and talk with friends. Even with my help in getting small bands to play every weekend—because yeah, this is my home. I can't leave them down and out with no options. From afar, no matter where I am, I'll always help out the place that gave me every chance under the sun. Still, they haven't been this packed since Whispered Words left the area.

But here they are in all their glory, slowly setting up their equipment in front of the large, cheering crowd. The volume rises with every person who enters with excitement running through their veins. Nothing beats a free pop-up show with no cover charge. Luckily for Leon and Ode, I'm footing the bill. And I wouldn't have it any other way. Besides, this was all Ode's idea.

"I think we might be over capacity," Ode murmurs in awe.

"You mean my bar," Leon chortles, handing me the biggest plate of chicken nachos I've ever seen.

"Yes...yes, his bar!" I quip, salivating at the plate steaming in front of my face.

"I will snatch those nachos away, you traitor!" Ode quips, coming in for my precious chips slathered in melted queso cheese, calling my damn name.

I haven't eaten since we went to an Italian restaurant a few hours ago. The food was amazing. Like out of this world orgasmic. Especially for Central City. Granted, it was on the edge of town near their old stomping grounds. People stared and pointed as the boys walked in. And even more when I trailed behind them, scrunching my nose.

I've never been the type of person to care what others think about me. Where the hell would that get me? Nowhere. I am who I am. And my roots started in this very city. I'll always give back to the people and places that raised me from the ashes of my demise.

But Leon's nachos? Nothing beats them. Not even a five-layer lasagna with extra cheese and garlic bread at a snooty five-star restaurant. Especially when he adds creamy cheese on top with shredded bits of cheddar below, leaving it a melting pot of cheese, meat, and lettuce on top. It's his specialty he loves to call...

"You love my cheese-on-cheese!" he says, grinning as he leans against the bar, placing his elbows on the top. "This is so surreal, Riv. You. Them. All here again." He blinks several times, staring up at the now empty stage, devoid of human life. The only sign they were there is the instruments glistening in the blue and yellow spotlights. "They treating you right, baby girl?" he asks, raising a brow.

I shove a chip into my mouth, stuffing my cheeks. Nope. Nu-huh. Don't want to have this conversation again.

"She's afraid they'll leave her again," Ode, the loudest traitor, says. "Which I get, by the way. They were jackasses to the extreme. I still don't want to trust them."

Can't she see I'm stuffing my face and don't want to talk about this again?

"Give her some tequila; she'll spill everything," Ode, my former best friend, says with a menacing grin. I snort when she walks behind the bar, standing beside her brother. Reaching behind her, she grabs the most expensive tequila they have and slams it on the bar.

"Mmhmm," Leon hums, grabbing three shot glasses and filling them with tequila. "Take your shot." Sliding the small shot glass in front of me, he watches intently as I swallow my bite.

"Remind me why I call you family?" I quip, tapping a finger on the tiny glass filled to the brim with the devil's golden liquid.

"You love us," Ode says with a grin, holding up her shot glass. "Let's toast!"

"To my sister from another mister fighting for love and happiness," Leon says, grinning when we clink our glasses together.

"Weak toast," Ode grumbles, bumping her elbow into his ribs.

"It was perfect. Thanks, guys," I laugh, downing my shot.

It's time to let go of everything. My hurt. Anger. Resentment. I wash it away with the burning liquid scorching my throat. This is a new adventure. Our past may guide us into the future. But I'm so tired of looking back and remembering how I felt when they left without a word. I'm ready to forgive and move on.

Reaching across the bar, I grab the bottle of tequila and refill our glasses with a grin.

"Oh, Riv's getting wasted," Ode laughs, grabbing her filled glass again.

"This is to new beginnings. New adventures. The door to the past is closed, and I'm ready to open the new door to my future. Here's to us," I say, clinking my glass against theirs. Tossing my head back, I down the shot again, groaning at the slight burn.

"You got this, baby girl," Leon says, squeezing my hand. "Or

I'll hide them in my basement." He grins, staring behind me as the crowd goes wild.

Butterflies fill my stomach when Rad pushes through the crowd. His grin lights up the room as he takes pictures with every person who asks him with joy until he gets to me. Those molten lava eyes catch mine, and he winks. He fucking winks, and my insides melt.

I blame the tequila.

"Is that nachos?" Rad asks, settling next to me on a bar stool with hearts in his eyes. "I love your damn nachos..." he trails off when he reaches for a piece. It's the hand slap heard across the world. Or that's what it seems like when he gasps. "Ouch, Pretty Girl. Sharing is caring!" he shouts with mock horror, putting a hand to his chest. "I swear we've had this discussion before. What's yours is mine, and what's mine is yours." He waggles his brows at the implication.

Where's that tequila? Because at this rate, I'm going to need the entire bottle to make it through tonight without doing something stupid. Like jumping their bones in the bathroom. Or reclaiming my office.

Calm your tits. No boning. Not right now. We're just now working on us and becoming an us again. Sex complicates everything.

Or makes you feel better.

Fuck my life. I blame this entire day on the amber liquid sloshing around in my stomach. It's always the tequila's fault.

"Yeah. It is. But I don't share my cheese-on-cheese nachos. Get your own." I give him my best stink eye, and he grins, rubbing his hands together.

"Yo, barkeep! I want some nachos," he says, playfully pounding a fist onto the counter.

Leon frowns, leaning forward with a sour huff. "I'm not your damn barkeep, Mullet. How many times do I need to tell you that?"

Rad pouts, batting his eyelashes. "My girlfriend is stingy and won't share. Won't you help a guy out and make—"

"An extra-large plate," Kieran says, sauntering up with a hungry look taking over his face. And not for me, either. His eyes fall to my plate, practically salivating over my damn food. "Smells delicious." He grins, swiping a loaded chip from my plate, and throws it into his mouth.

"Thief," I grumble, shoving another piece into my mouth and humming at the spicy nacho taste.

I could live on these damn nachos. All I have to do is pack Leon up—aka kidnap him—and take him with me so he'll make food every day.

"Oh my God, it's Kieran!" someone suspiciously familiar in the crowd shouts.

I stiffen at the sound of her voice. That scratchy, shrilly, annoying voice haunts my damn memories. Oh, snap. It couldn't be. Could it? My eyes dart around, searching for her mop of blonde hair. Several catches my eye, but none resemble her. Yet. If she thinks she has a chance, well, I'll show her my damn territorial side and claw her precious little eyes out.

My hands feel around the pocket of my jeans, and I grin when my knife sits snugly against my thigh. Yeah, come at me, Tessa Boo. I have a three-inch treat in my pocket, ready to drive you away.

Rad blinks several times. A look of horror opens his mouth into the shape of an O. He claps a hand on Kieran's shoulder, chuckling wildly.

"Sounds like you know who from high school..." he trails off, grunting when I suck cheese off my fingertips. "Pretty Girl. If I slather cheese on my cock, would you lick it off slowly?" He groans in a low voice, leaning forward to lick a line of cheese off the corner of my mouth. His moan vibrates against me, going straight to my pussy. Who flutters in anticipation. Fuck me. I need to push him away.

"I bite," I hum with satisfaction when he kisses the same spot again, working his way toward my cheese-lathered lips.

"It's okay, big man," Rad mumbles, adjusting himself. "She doesn't mean it." He taps his dick softly several times like he's petting a dog, giving me a lopsided grin.

"I do mean it," I quip, leaning toward him with my face toward his crotch. "But maybe I could slather him in cheese and —" A large hand slaps across my lips with a grunt.

"Shhh," Kieran grumbles. "Before you awaken more beasts." His eyes trail down his own front with a wicked grin. "I might like that, though," he whispers, flicking his tongue across my ear lobe as shivers roll through my body. "I could lay out as you slather my entire body in cheese and slowly lick it off." He groans, heaving in a breath. "Have I proven myself yet, River Blue? Have I made it clear that I'm the only worthy knight for you? Because I'm getting desperate here," he murmurs against my ear as his warm breaths cascade across my heated flesh.

Fuck. Me. Fuck. Tequila.

"You'll always be my knight," I murmur just loud enough for him to hear. "But getting on your knees for me again wouldn't hurt." I shrug when his eyes dilate.

"Good girl," he whispers, kissing my cheek. "I'll always get on my knees for you. Bloodied and bruised with lust in my eyes. You're my forever girl. I just wish I had realized that years ago." I swallow hard when his lips crash down on mine, shoving his tongue deep into my mouth. I have no choice but to moan into his mouth and pull him closer.

"God damn, that's hot," Rad murmurs, squeezing my knee.

"Don't make me get the damn hose," Leon grumbles. "I will spray you both and throw you outside. No sex in my bar."

I pull away from Kieran breathlessly, looking around. He pulls my head against his chest, cradling me there. Where I'm meant to be. In his arms and surrounded by him.

Kieran and I have always been in the fates. No matter who was there to tear us apart. We'll always find each other again. I feel it in the way my soul calls out to him. The way my heart attempts to push out of my chest when he's nearby.

Fuck. I think I'm in love all over again.

"No sex? You weren't here that night, we—" I slap a hand over Rad's mouth. His laugh vibrates against my skin.

"Unfortunately," Leon mumbles, scrunching up his face. "These walls are thin, is all I'm saying." He eyes each of us before making his way down the bar to help more patrons who wave money in his face.

"Well, duty calls. Love you, bitch. Play good tonight, boys. Maybe I can convince my stingy brother to cough up some extra nachos to go." She winks at us, sauntering away to help her brother man the bar. Along with the other servers meandering about and taking orders.

It's a busy ass night.

"Better cool it," Callum says, leaning in and stealing my food.

"I'm going to stab each of you with a fork," I hiss, missing his hand with my slap. He chuckles, slowly putting the cheese-soaked chip into his mouth.

Eating nachos shouldn't look so damn sexual. But here we are. I'm panting like a bitch in heat at the sight of the gooey cheese rolling over Callum's lips and onto his chin.

Don't lick it off. Don't lick it off. Fuck.

I reach up, rolling my tongue across his chin and onto his lips. He startles, gripping my waist hard.

"Little Star," he murmurs with lust-filled eyes dilating his pupils to the max.

"I dunno, Pretty Girl. I might like that. Or, and hear me out —I could stab you. With my dick. He's incredibly hard right now. You won't make me go on stage like this, will you?" He bats his eyelashes at me with a grin.

"Shut up," Asher laughs, reaching across and grabbing another chip.

"You are a buzzkill!" Rad proclaims, eating a bite of my nachos.

"I guess this is a communal plate," I grumble, taking another bite, no longer fighting their grabby hands.

"We have to fuel up," Kieran says with a smirk, taking another bite.

"We do have a big show ahead of us," Asher surmises, sitting next to Rad.

"The biggest one yet." Callum smiles, kissing me again. "I can't get over this," he murmurs against my lips. My fingers play with the shaggy blond strands at the back of his neck.

"Over what?"

"That I get to kiss you whenever I want now. No more dreaming of having my lips on yours and wondering if it feels the same."

"Well, does it?" I ask, raising a brow.

"Does it what?"

"Feel the same?"

"Better," he whispers, kissing my lips again, lingering for longer than necessary as the world disappears. It's only me and him standing amid the crowded bar. His warm hand wraps around the back of my neck, locking me in his grip. Not that I'd want to escape. "Kissing you is coming home. It's my peace in the darkness of chaos. You ground me and make me better."

"Marry them!" Ode says in passing, passing drinks to the guys.

"I agree, Pretty Girl. Marry us!" Rad waggles his brows.

"Maybe someday," I quip, shoving the last nacho into my mouth.

Fuckers ate all my damn food. I side-eye their oblivious asses with disdain.

"Later," Leon says with a grin, pointing to my plate as he takes it from the bar and hands it to another worker.

"Someday?" Rad asks with wide eyes, sitting rigid in his chair. "I'll ask again tomorrow and the next day and the next day after that. I won't stop begging until you become my wife."

"Our wife," Kieran mutters, reaching for a nacho and sighing. "We ate them all," he grumbles.

"Yeah, you assholes ate all the good nachos. That's grounds for divorce. Now, don't you have a show to do?" I ask, playfully folding my arms across my chest.

A lightness takes me over as we grin at one another. It's as if the past didn't happen. And we're back to where we started, like a full-circle adventure.

We'll build and build until our future is secured on trust and love—a steady foundation.

We'll never be perfect. We'll fight. Shout. And make-up again. For some reason, I can't ever get these four men off my mind.

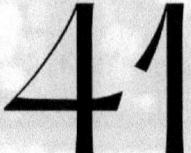

MY EARS BLEED with the crowd's enthusiastic screams as the boys take the stage.

"Hello, Central City!" Kieran shouts through the microphone, heaving a breath.

I won't mention the way his tight T-shirt clings to his sweaty chest, highlighting his delicious and defined pecs. Or, you know, the way his tight jeans outline the package he's smuggling. Nope. I won't mention it at all. My lips are sealed...

"You want more tequila, horndog?" Ode asks, slapping my shoulder with a giggle, knocking me out of my horny thoughts.

My face heats, creeping down my neck. I'm sure I look like Rudolph, the red-faced whore, by now. I grunt, covering my face with my hands.

Again, I blame the tequila.

"Who are you calling horndog?" I ask, pushing my shot glass toward her as the boys continue speaking to the crowd with excitement.

More screams and shouts, chanting their band name over and over again.

"We're happy to be back where all the magic started!" Rad chimes in, kicking his bass drum with excitement.

"You all are in for a treat tonight. We've been working on

some new pieces." Wait, what? I turn on my stool, staring at the man grinning on stage. He sends me a goddamn wink as he saunters around, hyping up the crowd even more. That's the Kieran I remember.

"They have new music?" Ode asks over the shouting.

I shrug. "I—"

"You had no idea," she surmises, pouring me another shot. "Well, here's to bigger and better things from those dick faces." She clinks her glass against mine again.

"Bigger and better," I giggle, letting all my inhibitions go as Kieran belts out the first note of the first song he ever sang under this roof.

Twirling in my chair, nostalgia presses heavily on my chest. The first time I saw Kieran after high school was on that very stage. He sauntered, eating up the attention of their growing fanbase.

Like now.

He eats it up, smiling at them, soaking up their screams. I swivel my eyes toward the door girl sitting in her seat, staring at the men on stage with raw hunger.

Yeah, they're fucking hot. And fucking mine.

That was the same spot all those years ago. Where I sat and watched with my heart in my throat, begging Kieran to recognize me. Just once. I wanted to hear him call me Blue and kiss me and tell me he missed me.

Dead End is where it all started for us. From the moment I sent that email asking them to play, I sealed my fate. From the frantic fucking against Booker's desk with an audience behind us. To that moment we walked into the Castle house on the lake in Missouri and left changed people, leaving me with a little present I'd come to love. Never regret.

Our story isn't a short book. It's long. Fucking tragic. Filled to the brim with angst and betrayal. It's four hundred thousand words of our start, our middle, our tumultuous end. Bringing us to the unexpected reunion. The tears, shouts, fights, and finally—our new beginning.

We've come full circle.

In the very place that started us. This is the story of Whispered Words and the girl they so desperately loved, forgot, ruined, and pieced back together. Only this time, I'm getting my happy ending.

No matter what.

Fuck. Tequila makes me horny and sappy. I need another goddamn drink before I shed some tears.

"Another," I rasp, turning back to Ode, who grins, watching my misty eyes with fascination.

"You've got it so bad, girl," she says, leaning in so only I can hear her. "Make them make it count this time. If they fuck up..."

"They won't." At least, I hope not.

"No," she says, filling my shot glass. "They wouldn't dare fuck it up again. You know why? Because they've got it bad, too. Even worse than before."

I nod in agreement.

Taking another shot, I watch with hearts in my eyes as they continue their set into two more familiar songs. The crowd waves their hands in the air. Phones come out of pockets, recording their free show. People shout their names individually, gaining their smiles.

Kieran huffs breathlessly into the microphone, wiping the rogue beads of sweat dripping down his forehead.

"Central City! You guys are amazing! You enjoying the show?" he shouts, earning yells of approval. "Good! It's so damn good to be back here!" He grins more, showing off his pearly whites. "You all know this is where we started. Right on this stage."

"Hell yeah!"

"You're amazing, Kieran!" that annoying, familiar voice shouts again. I swear if she shows her tits, the new door girl is going to have to walk her out before I beat her eyeballs in.

"Careful, Green Monster," Leon quips, squeezing my shoulder. "I can kick her out if you want. But this is probably the most exciting thing that's happened to her since she had kids."

I wrinkle my nose, finally glimpsing Tessa in her short shorts and tube top. She looks the exact same as back in the day. Blonde hair. Pearls. Lean body. And a beautiful snarl twisting her face.

"Someone mated with her?" I snort.

"Jesus, how drunk are you?" Ode asks, passing by with drinks in her hands.

"Little," I giggle, holding my fingers together.

"Yeah, she has three little spawns running around. She got married to some old, rich prick four years back," Leon says with a shrug. "Take care of yourself, baby girl. Maybe no more tequila for you."

"Tequila lets my girl live the damn life she's craving. Let her drink more so she can go home and get dicked down in the darkness by four hunky rock stars who look like they want to eat her alive," Ode says, sliding the entire bottle of tequila in my direction. "Have at it, bitch. Drink all the drinks. But don't regret a damn thing in the morning."

"No regrets," I say, lifting the bottle to my mouth and down a mouthful.

"That's my bitch," Ode chortles, running off to more patrons.

"River West!" I startle when the sound of my name rings through the entire fucking bar over the speakers.

Oh, no, he didn't.

"Yeah, you, Pretty Girl," Rad cuts in with a grin, waggling his long finger at me.

"Make way," Callum says softly into the microphone, echoing his timid voice through the bar.

The crowd hushes. Their eyes dart around, searching for the person they're calling. Meanwhile, I'm trying to find a cool new place to hide so they can't find me.

"Come on, River. Don't be shy now," Kieran's deep voice pulls me to my feet.

"Fucking hell," I grumble, thrusting my bottle of tequila into the unsuspecting bartender's hands. "Don't let anyone drink that."

"You're River West," she blanches, looking me up and down with wide eyes. "You're a goddamn legend around here."

Legend. Huh. I kind of like that. I thrust my shoulders back and put my chin in the air. I'd look smooth if I didn't trip over my damn feet two steps away from my stool. The room spins. It's either from the copious amounts of tequila I've been drinking. Or...it's the four heated eyes staring at me from the stage. Incinerate me now. Fuck.

Asher holds up a finger, placing his guitar down. "I got her," he says in a smooth voice, earning a grin from Kieran.

Somewhere along the way, the boys not only mended our relationship, but theirs, too. Maybe it was the extra therapy they've been diving into. Or maybe, they're finally healing something within themselves.

The crowd parts when Asher jumps down, making his way toward me with determination.

"How much tequila have you had, Little Brat?" he murmurs, hoisting me into his arms. My legs instinctively go around his waist, where I tighten them, bringing our centers together.

I squeal, clinging to his neck. "Not enough, Daddy," I whisper, blowing into his ear as he groans.

"I'll spank you if you keep that up. I can't go on stage saluting everyone. They'll know I have it bad for you." I shiver at his words, flicking my tongue against his earlobe.

"And do you have it bad for me?"

"So goddamn bad it fucking hurts. Now, stop squirming and be a good brat so we can play you a new song."

"A new song?" I ask, pulling back to stare into his eyes.

"Just for you," he says with a smile, stopping right before the stage. "Climb onto the stage, baby."

I swallow hard, letting go of my anchor, and drunkenly climb onto the stage. Somehow, I fall over my damn feet, straight into Kieran's waiting arms.

"No more tequila," he huffs at my flushed face, kissing my nose.

"But tequila—" I'm cut off when he places his lips on mine, stopping my words. Pulling back, a sparkle in his eyes has butterflies flapping and taking flight inside my damn stomach.

Hoots and hollers bring me back to the present after the world had completely disappeared. I swear, in this heightened state of drunkenness, their touches are unraveling every thread inside my body. Inch by inch. They'll pull and pull until I'm completely raw and naked before them.

"I want you all to meet someone special to us." Kieran's eyes don't drift from mine when the others close in on us.

Four hands touch my flesh. I'm done for. Absolutely fucking unraveled.

"This is the mother of our child," Rad says with a grin, pulling the microphone in front of his lips. "I know! We're daddies!" he says with a whoop.

"That's where we've been for the past month," Kieran says, putting his fingers beneath my chin. "We made a big mistake five years ago in letting this girl go. Something happened that tore us apart."

"Something that will never happen again," Asher says, kissing my cheek. "Never fucking ever again."

"So, this is our official notice," Rad pipes up. "We're officially off the market."

"And committed to one girl only."

"Two," Rad corrects. "Our woman and our baby girl."

Deceased. I swear to fucking hell. I melt into a tiny tequila puddle right there on stage as they take turns kissing my lips after their very public proclamation. Their PR teams are going to have a fucking fit. My brothers will surely hear about this. Not that they'd care. But everyone in the world will now know, Whispered Words is mine.

And I am theirs.

"Here," Kieran whispers, pointing to a chair Ode drags to the middle of the stage.

"You bitch," I murmur, sitting my ass down. "Were you in on this?"

"What? Operation distract River with tequila so the boys could plan this epic humiliation. Yes, yes, I was," she laughs, sticking her tongue out at me. "Don't worry, though. I did my best friend duties. I've thoroughly threatened their balls. For real, this time. I even gave a demonstration. They turned a pretty shade of green." I snort when she strolls off stage, sneaking looks over her shoulder.

"All right, Central City. We want to play you something new. It's something we've been toying with for the last few weeks of practice."

I blanch. What? They've been writing music right under my nose? And I had no idea. I've been too consumed with my own shit that I didn't notice what they were doing.

"Want to count us in, man?" Kieran asks, looking over his shoulder at Rad, who taps out a softer beat than their normal material.

Asher joins with a quiet, slow guitar riff, reminding me of a lullaby. Callum's bass pipes in a second later with the same laid-back, softer tune.

You burst out of nowhere
Like a hurricane beating down my door.
Your tears.
Your laughs.
They're mine forever more.
There's no looking back, Babe.
Tiny lyrics come from the heart.
Out of nowhere
With no design.
Tiny lyrics seep through our souls.

Ride us a mile high.
The end is nowhere near.
The beginning is somewhere we'll start.
You see, Babe...
There's nothing tearing us apart
With lyrics in our veins.
In our walls.
In our fucking songs.
Lyrics is where we'll stay.
The end is nowhere near.
This is just our beginning
Becoming crystal clear.

Am I crying? Are those tears pouring down my damn face? No. My damn eyeballs are sweating in front of hundreds of people. Good God. I can't stop them. Callum reaches down, pulling my face into his neck as I sob my fucking heart out.

I fucking hate tequila.

"Fucking hell, Little Star. My goddamn galaxy," he whispers, holding me close to his sweaty as-hell body. "I love you," he murmurs. "To the damn moon and back."

"I love you, too," I sob like an idiot. "But I'm never drinking again." His chuckles vibrate against me as I cling to him.

Kieran stops, breathing heavily into the microphone.

"So?" He eyes the silent crowd as they break out into hysterics, screaming his name. "It's a work in progress. We'll keep you posted on how it's going in the weeks to come when we get back to our roots and start this music thing over."

When I finally lift my head from Callum's neck, he stares into my eyes. Gently, his fingers wipe away the makeup, I'm sure I smeared everywhere from my emotional outburst.

Callum's grin lights up my world. Those gray eyes I could get lost in steal every ounce of oxygen from my lungs.

These boys drown me in the best damn way.

After another round of hot kisses in front of the crowd, I walk off stage, using the back exit to cool down. My thoughts race a million miles a minute as I pace the backstage area, heaving in several breaths.

This is real.

This is fucking happening again. I'm letting them consume every part of me. I'm fucking terrified in the best and worst ways. This could go sour. But as my chest caves in from the chaotic thoughts, I know I'm heading in the right direction with them. More than before. We were right for each other, but the timing was shit. We needed room to grow into the people we are now.

After I gather myself, my feet drag me down the hallway with more tequila on my mind. What? Don't judge me. I know I swore off alcohol before, but I left my bottle half empty in the arms of a bartender. It's calling my name. Especially after that song. Those kisses. Those fucking words Kieran belted out. Jesus, I'm a goner.

As I make my way down the darkened hallway, I grunt, running straight into a damn brick wall. "Jesus, sorry," I grumble, pushing my hair out of my flushed face.

I blink several times. My heart falls into my stomach. And not in the good way.

"Rivey, hey," he says with that same slimy grin plastered on his face. His eyes take me in from head to toe. Somehow, his hands are on my shoulders, steadying me from falling over. Gently, he squeezes, something brightening in his eyes at my proximity. Fuck. Cold shivers break out through me.

"Van?" I question, wrinkling my nose. "I thought you were in Europe or some shit," I blurt.

Alarm bells ring in my head for whatever reason when he shifts, shrugging nonchalantly.

"Mom is sick, so I came home for a visit. I saw a post online that Whispered Words was going to be here, so I thought I'd come to see the show. Didn't expect to see you, Miss California," he says with a big goofy grin, finally letting go of my shoulders when I bat him away.

An uneasy feeling floats around in my sloshing stomach. It's either the booze revolting against my stomach, or it's the creep standing before me.

Not much has changed since I left him all those years ago. Same hair. Same stupid face—as if he could change that. Not to mention that sickening grin I once thought was the best thing on the planet makes my stomach knot. How in the hell did I fall for this jackass when I was a teenager? Was it the thought of dangerous dating?

The last words he ever said to me before he fucked right off have haunted me since the moment he walked out of the record store I used to work at.

"I have every arsenal in my pocket for us to have a better future. You, me, and the baby..."

It's like I'm back in that record store, listening to him tell me all that bullshit about him going to Europe for an internship. And how delusional he was in thinking that Lyric was his.

"I just wanted to say how sorry I was for all the things I said and did. You know, back then," he grimaces, obviously still talking as I silently freak out. What else has he said since I've drunkenly stared at him with a blank look, lost in my thoughts? "I was a real creep, and I...just never got over you, I guess. I saw everything as an opportunity to get the girl I loved back. But I went about it all wrong. Sorry, I was such a fucking chump."

Chump doesn't even begin to describe what I feel for him. "Um... Yeah, sure. Nice to see you, but I've got a date with a bottle," I grumble, shoving past him.

"Nice bumping into you, Rivey," he says in passing, waving as he walks away from me without fanfare.

"So not nice bumping into you," I mutter under my breath, watching his every move. He stands at the back of the crowd with no expression lining his face as the guys continue their performance. He doesn't sway. He doesn't fucking move. He's a goddamn statue. Tension lies in the backs of his beady little eyes, raising the tiny hairs all over my body.

ALY BECK

"The fuck is Donavan Drake doing here?" Ode asks in alarm, guiding me to the bar by the elbow.

"Being a creep as usual," I grumble, staring over at the place he stood and startling. "He's gone," I say with a shrug, blowing out a breath.

That was a close one. Shit. That's the last person I ever wanted to come face to face with, especially in this condition. I'm liable to say whatever the hell is on my mind. Like, fuck off, Van. Eat a snake, Van. Or my favorite, drop dead, Van. In fact, I should race over there and say that to him. He distributed our damn sex tape like it was a movie. Fucker.

"I'm going to sue his ass," I mutter under my breath.

"I haven't seen that asshole since he left Central City for work. Wherever that was," she says, shaking her head.

"In Europe, right? Veritas has been tracking his ass since my whole stalker fiasco started."

Her brows furrow. The color slightly drains from her face at the thought of my stalker. Thank fuck, that dickbag is dead and gone. I no longer have to look over my shoulder, wondering if some sicko is taking pictures of my every move.

"Yeah, I think so for the first year or so. Not sure what he did after that, but he got a job with his company. I think he travels or something. Fuck, I don't know. As long as he's not around here," she says with a shrug, handing me my bottle.

"Thanks," I say, taking another swig of the burning tequila, drinking the memory of Van away.

He's here doing his own thing. He can't hurt me anymore. Not when I'm living for the future. Not the stupid past.

Damn the consequences. I'll deal with them later. Naked. And freshly fucked. Because any man who writes a song clearly dedicated to me and their daughter deserves a little love between the sheets. A reward, if you will. And then, I'll get a nice reward.

42

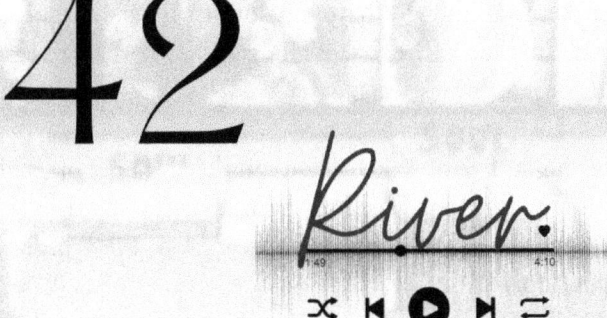

River

"IT'S GOING TO RAIN," I whisper, staring out the dark window of our SUV, traveling down the road near Callum's home.

It's in the air. The smell of sweet rain floats through the breeze, infiltrating all my senses. My hair stands on end. My aching heart pounds rapidly against my ribs. All in tune with the weather changing at the drop of a hat. My eyes widen in awe as the wicked sky lights up, showing off the darkened clouds miles away, heading straight for us. There's nothing that compares to a Midwest storm on the horizon.

Soon we'll be soaked.

My head leans lazily on Callum's shoulder with his hand clutched tightly in mine. Every so often, he gently squeezes my fingers with his. Three times. Over and over. Conveying a message unlike any other—he loves me.

There's no denying the love we have for each other. All five of us. In some weird and twisted way, we care for and deeply love one another. Like we're meant for each other. No matter what we went through in the past. No matter how long we were apart, basking in our hate for one another.

This was always meant to be.

Some would say, it's way too quick. Way too soon to shout it from the rooftops. I'm so damn tired of living in the past and reliving the hurt I experienced. It changed me for the better. Helped me grow into the woman I am today. I'll never forget the way their betrayal hurt. I'll have my doubts. I'll cry and question them until I'm blue in the face. As long as they're there to ease the pain and constantly reassure me that we'll be okay, then I'll believe them.

But tonight, I want to live. Dance in the icy rain. Forget all my inhibitions for freedom. Freedom from my crippling thoughts of doubt. From the pain. From my stalker. From every little thing bogging me down.

Tonight, I want to fall into the arms of the men redeeming themselves for me. The ones who wrote that song. Who pulled me on stage, kissed the oxygen from my lungs, and told the world I was theirs.

I need this.

Rad's fingers trace up and down my jean-clad leg from my other side, bringing me out of my swirling thoughts. Judging by the trembling of his fingers, he's eager to lock me inside the house. How do I know? As soon as we left Dead End, he told me.

"I want to lock you in Callum's house for a month straight to get reacquainted with every inch of your curves. My tongue will own every piece of flesh... inside and out. I'm serious, Pretty Girl! Don't drunkenly giggle at me. Little Rad is going to punch a hole through my jeans if he doesn't get a taste of his obsession," he murmurs with a soft whine in my ear as we walk out into the night toward the SUV. The boys stand near the trunk, lifting their equipment in and securing it in place.

"Show me how much you missed me," I murmur, kissing his cheek. I saunter off toward the others, who watch me with heated expressions. Even in a T-shirt and jeans, they look at me like I'm completely naked and spread out.

Once again, mother nature shows off, illuminating everything outside in a quick flash. Ten seconds later, thunder rumbles, vibrating the car as we pull into the driveway of Callum's house in the middle of nowhere.

The dark trees swish in the wind, picking up speed ahead of the rain blowing in from the west. Rainy September days always mean the changing of the season is upon Illinois.

Thankfully, we're heading home tomorrow evening. Home. What a strange sentiment. Our home is no longer in this town. Central City is just another city. Another stop along the way. No. Our home is nestled in East Point. Somewhere. They'll still work on themselves in the band house for another five months. And I'll be across the street with Ly. At some point, we'll have to figure out living arrangements. I never intended anyone else but Lyric and I living in my home. It'll burst at the seams with all six of us living there.

The future is unavoidable. Scary, even. Will things stay like this? With each of them looking at me like I'm that plate of nachos? Or will we fall into a weird pattern once the forced proximity implemented on us vanishes? Only time will tell where our adventure truly ends.

I take a deep breath.

Fuck the future. Live in the now.

And right now?

It's just the five of us. Ly is at a sleepover until tomorrow morning.

Stay in the now. It's something I've repeatedly told myself through the years after falling victim to memories assaulting my mind.

Water softly pelts against the glass when Kieran throws the car into park in Callum's driveway, instead of pulling into the two-car garage. The dark house looms before us in all its empty glory.

"We'll load everything in tomorrow," Asher says, looking around the car for approval. "That way our things don't get soaked. It's coming down out there." He eyes the heavy droplets dripping down his window with furrowed brows.

He rubs his chin in that calculating way I'm used to seeing on him. Except now, Asher isn't using it against us to tear us apart. He's using his brain to unite us as one.

"Sounds good," Kieran agrees. "How are you feeling, River Blue?"

How am I feeling? I've drank my weight in tequila. Saw a boy from my past. Had a song dedicated to Lyric and me. Also, I sobbed in front of people. God, how embarrassing. I bet someone filmed it, too. My beautiful, snot-caked, tear-stained face will be on all the gossip sites by tomorrow. I can see it now.

River West fucking an entire band! Love declarations! How long will it last?

So, you know. Just fucking peachy. But instead of telling him the truth of how chaotic my emotions are whirling around inside of me. I simply say the first thing I imagined when the rain started falling from the sky.

"Like a dance in the rain," I say, mesmerized by the brisk rain drenching every inch of the earth outside, puddling on the grass.

The rain comes down so thickly it's like staring through static, unable to see your hand in front of your face.

"Must still be drunk," Kieran quips with a smirk.

Assface.

I wrinkle my nose. "You know what they say about people who assume things..."

"Makes an ass out of you and me," Callum snorts, completing my sentence.

Good boy.

"Exactly. So, no. I'm not drunk. I'm stone-cold sober," I grunt, extracting myself from between Callum and a reluctant, clingy Rad.

"Pretty Girl, come back," Rad whines, reaching for me as I plop on Callum's lap and open the door. "I need to feel your skin against mine." I raise a brow when he folds his hands together pleadingly. He even goes as far as pouting his bottom lip with a soft whine, trying to entice me back into the vehicle and near him.

"Calm down, psycho," Callum murmurs jokingly, intently watching as I waver at the open door. I may be perched on his lap, but he doesn't stop me when I look out into the wet world with wonder.

Little sprinkles mist, wetting my hand as I reach out, letting the cool rain soak my fingertips. Goosebumps rise across my flesh, and shivers run through me at the icy feeling crawling across my skin.

The beautiful sound of the rain pounding into the grass greets my ears like a symphony playing through the speakers, begging me to come and play. I extract myself from the car with a serene smile stretching my lips. Heavy droplets pound against my skull, dropping down my hair and soaking every inch of me. Tentatively, I take a few steps, letting mother nature thoroughly soak through my clothes. Through my joy, I swirl with my arms stretched wide, capturing the moment.

"Little Star. What are you doing?" Callum asks in a raised voice, clutching his seat.

I chuckle, throwing my head back. The bitter rain beats down on my face when I stick my tongue out and collect the drops in my mouth, swallowing mouthfuls of fresh water. This is living. Feeling. This is fucking breathing for the first time in so damn long. There's no work bogging me down. No heartbreak at the corners of my mind, haunting me.

I'm free.

My clothing clings to every inch of me, winding around my flesh like a second skin, stretching too tight and restricting my movements. My chest heaves. My fingers beg to tear into the fabric and remove it from the situation.

"Have you ever danced in the rain, boys?" I ask, lifting my T-shirt over my head with a grin, shivering when the ice-cold water pelts my bra-covered chest.

Water drips down my abdomen, making my stomach suck in from the chill spreading through me. No doubt I'll need a hot, steamy bath with four hunky rock stars after this. Maybe some hot coffee to ward off the chill. And then, a cuddle pile to end the night.

ALY BECK

Without hesitation, I do the same with my socks, shoes, and my jeans. Leaving them in a heap in the muddy grass as I take a few steps back in nothing but my bra and thong.

I do a twirl with my arms out wide. This is what true freedom feels like. It's so damn liberating. Here I am in the middle of nowhere, nearly naked, with four sets of eyes glued to my every move. I swear, even through the sheets of rain, I see their eyes dilate with thick amounts of lust.

"I have," Kieran remarks through the commotion.

I stop my spin, grinning at his memory. It's funny how he forgot so much about me and our early childhood. Thanks to Nigel, Asher's father. Yet, in times like this, his memories sneak up on him and slap him upside the head, reminding him of the ghost he left behind in the apartments.

I grin. "It was summertime. A random warm rain had just come through. We were on the hill behind our apartment building. It was either we stay dry..."

"Or my guitar does," he marvels, scratching at his chin with a little chuckle.

"So, we chose your guitar to leave under the secret spot."

"Then you grabbed my hand and led me out into the rain," he says, blinking several times and watching me, curling my fingers in their direction.

"So. What do you say? Do you guys fancy a cold dance in the rain on our last night before we return to East Point?" I ask, moving to the center of the front yard with my arms stretched out wide. Leaning my head back, I take a deep breath.

A drum booms in my chest, knocking against my ribs when they sit in the car, darting their eyes at one another. After a few agonizing seconds, they slowly climb out, shutting the doors behind them with predatory intent in their eyes. One by one, they take their shirts, shoes, and pants off. Together, they collect my clothes and shut them in the SUV.

I suck in a breath at their unholy, ripped bodies on display for me and only me. Oxygen refuses to fill my lungs when they walk in unison toward me. No, not walking. They're stalking toward me with hooded eyes. Each of them looks like they're about to sink their teeth into my flesh and mark me as theirs. Fuck. Maybe that's what I want. You know, a wall of man meat decked out in muscles and tattoos. And they're all fucking mine.

Their feet squish in the grass, squelching with every step they take with vicious smirks lining their lips and eyeing each other when they finally stop before me. All their gazes fall on me, taking me in. Inch by miserable inch, flames lick at my flesh from the intensity of their stares. I no longer feel the icy burn of the rain—just the deep heat blossoming in my guts.

"This is for you, River Blue," Kieran says over the noise. "Everything from here on out is for you. For Lyric."

"We all agree," Asher says, blinking rapidly as raindrops collect on his eyelashes.

"Everything we do is for you, Pretty Girl."

"Never again will you wonder if we're in this," Callum says, licking his lips.

"We're all in, River Blue. And you'll never get rid of us now," he says, discreetly eyeing the other boys. They nod in unison.

The entire world flips on its axis and stops spinning. One by one, they fall to their knees in worship, staring at me with lust dripping from their eyes. More than lust. It's dedication. Once again, they're proving to me that they'll drop everything for me. Even to their knees in a time of uncertainty and chaos.

Fuck. My heart stops working. I'm a dead woman walking as I stare at them.

"What the hell are you doing?" I breathe, putting a hand on my chest.

"Kneeling before our queen," Kieran says, grinning when he sees my expression.

"Long live our queen!" Rad hoots, tossing his fist into the soaked air.

"What the fuck," I mutter. "You guys don't have to do that."

Although I had envisioned it a long time ago—them on their

knees, begging me to forgive them for what they did. Only in that scenario, I turned my back on them with a humph. Back then, these boys could have done nothing to earn my forgiveness.

Oh, how the times have changed since they sauntered back into my life with cocky attitudes. They've proven themselves to me over and over again. There's no way I could turn my back on them. Not after everything we've been through.

Our tale is fucked up, but it's the kind of fucked up I never want to give up. No relationship is perfect, and we're the prime example. Not only because there are four of them and one of me, but because of the past.

Callum smiles, shifting his weight. "We told you we'd get on our knees for you." Wait…I don't recall this conversation. How drunk was I before? Shit. Did I demand this of them? "And you said you better, Little Star."

"Facts," Rad agrees with a grin.

Well, shit. Maybe I was drunker than I thought after the show. I slightly recall asking them to kneel in the back room. But that was for a completely different reason.

"This is our devotion," Asher says, clearing his throat. "We know you'll have doubts, Little Brat. We know you'll fall and break and cry. But we'll always be here to pick you up when necessary. We're your nets when you fall."

Be still my beating heart.

I blink several times, letting my stupid tears mix with the rain. "All in?" I croak, watching them as they nod in agreement. "You're seriously just… Wanting to dive back into this? Aren't you scared?"

"Absolutely frightened," Callum says, climbing to his feet. "You're not the only one terrified. I know you remember how it felt to have us leave you. And how it tore you apart to have those restraining orders handed to you. But I remember, too, Little Star. I remember how Van kissed you and how it broke me in two. I know he did it. Not you. You weren't to blame. But I'm working through that. I meant what I said on stage. You're my first and last. My one and only. I'll never look at another woman the way I look at you. My light in the darkness. My bright galaxy in this dismal universe," he mutters, capturing my face between his palms. The warmth of his body soaks through the coldness seeping into my aching bones.

"All in," I confirm, even when my gut squeezes with anxiety.

"All fucking in," Rad says from behind me, putting his warm hands on my hips. "The only Pretty Girl I see."

"Better than your groupies?" I hum in ecstasy when Callum's lips press against the side of my mouth.

"No one compares to you, Pretty Girl. Callum had his fighting. Asher had his music. Kieran had...his anger. I had them to try to forget about you. It never fucking worked. You're my girl. You always have been and always will be. I'm just so fucking sorry I sought—"

"No," I interrupt, turning in Callum's embrace to face Rad. Sadness pulls down his expression, and hurt flies through his dark eyes. "You don't have to be sorry. We were not together. You thought I cheated on you... That's... It's all in the past, okay? We live for the now." My fingers delicately trace his jawline, holding him in my grasp.

"You're mine," he whispers, devouring my face with his lust-filled eyes, dropping down until they rest on my lips. "I'm going to kiss you now. Then, we're going to take you inside and fuck your brains out. Okay, Pretty Girl?"

"We've been hanging by a thread, River Blue," Kieran murmurs, caressing my cheek.

Shit. When did they all get off their knees and surround me? No matter. My pussy flickers to life at the sound of their promises.

"Is that a promise?" I murmur, darting my eyes to Rad.

His grin lights up the dismal weather, and he snorts. "More than a promise. It's a damn commandment now. Thou shalt pleasure River with tongues, dicks, fingers, and toes."

"Dude, no toes," Callum grumbles, pressing the warmth of

his lips against my exposed neck, licking and sucking at the water still falling on us.

"No toes," I say, wrinkling my nose.

"But the commandment says," Rad whines playfully, gripping my chin between his thumb and pointer finger. "And whatever it says, goes."

"I really don't want toes near my—" My eyes widen when Rad cuts me off, thrusting his tongue into my mouth with a groan.

Rad's soft lips envelop mine, marking me as his when his moans vibrate, mixing with my own. You'd never be able to hear it over the roar of the rain still pounding down on us.

The caresses of his tongue glide against mine in a slow, sensual swirl, sending frantic sparks of desire through my body. Everything lights up inside of me, just like the lighting flashing overhead and sending shocks of electricity through every inch of my body. I melt into Rad like putty in his hands. Simultaneously, leaning into Callum at my back.

My breath quickens as the kiss hits an all new height, taking me fucking captive. My heart threatens to leap out of my chest when Callum grinds his hardness against my ass with a groan. His fingers curl around my waist as his warm breath brushes over my flesh. I nearly die when his teeth sink into the sensitive flesh of my neck, and an orgasm sits at the cusp of letting loose. And they've barely touched me.

When Rad pulls back, I chase his lips, eager for more.

"Let's go inside," Rad whispers, tightening his hold on my face. "Let's get you dried off and then wet all over again. I can't wait to show you my new piercings. You're going to love them, Pretty Girl. They're going to hit all the right spots deep inside your pussy." He grins with his eyes darting south, toward his dick straining against his boxers.

Right. His piercings. Something he's hinted at before. But now? I'm about to take the plunge.

"You're wet for us, aren't you, River Blue?" I gasp when

Kieran's fingers pull my wet panties aside and thrust inside me. There's no running his fingers through my lips or testing it out. He went straight for the gold. And dear god, I flutter around him, yelling at the rain pounding down on me.

"Dude," Rad says when Kieran thrusts again, chuckling.

"Oh, fuck off," I mumble with a heavy tongue. "I haven't gotten laid in years." Orgasms, sure. But getting dicked down beneath the sheets with an actual man? Nah. I haven't had the time.

"Yeah, let's get her inside," Kieran says, kissing my cheek and removing his fingers. "Eyes on me, River Blue." My world collapses into little pieces when he shoves his fingers into his mouth, licking away my cum from his flesh with a groan. "How I've missed the taste of you." Flicking his tongue out again, he makes sure to swallow every piece of evidence glistening on his fingers. His eyes dilate to almost black. And I swallow hard when my eyes fall on his dick, standing at attention.

I yelp when Callum turns me around, picking me up without effort. His hands grip my ass tightly as he marches toward his clothes and digs out his keys. Before I know it, we're in the safety of his home, but he doesn't stop until he deposits me on his king-sized bed.

43

"Unfair," Rad grumbles, walking into the room with a frown. "We should have drawn straws."

"That's not how this works," Asher quips, standing against the wall with his eyes eating away at my laid-out form.

Callum tunes them out as he drops his soaked boxers to the ground and kicks them aside. "I can't fucking wait any longer," he mumbles, stroking himself. "Please, Little Star. Please take off everything." Desperation lines his tone when I sit up straight, staring into the depths of his gray eyes.

You could hear a pin drop in Callum's bedroom when I remove my bra, flinging it aside. The cool air blows past my nipples, hardening them under their stares. I'm at the center of their attention.

"Dibs," Rad quips, scooping it up with a grin. If he had pockets, I'm sure he'd stuff it in there and keep it forever. Luckily for him, I have more than two bras these days.

With shaky fingers, I pull my thong down and take a deep breath. I've been naked in front of them before. Years ago. Multiple times. Weeks ago, they looked through my window, watching as I brought myself to completion. I'm not insecure about what pregnancy did to my body. But sometimes, I wonder if they still look at me the same. Or expect the same girl

I was back then with the tiny waist, average boobs, and tiny butt.

I'm not as thin as I once was. Curves took over my body when Lyric announced herself to the world, enhancing everything. Those new curves brought on the stretch marks pulling at my breasts, butt, stomach, and on the skin around my knees. I've always felt so comfortable inside my skin. I'm me. No one else. No matter the marks lining my body or where the fat situates itself. I'm still River West. Doubt creeps into the back of my mind when silence echoes loudly through the room. Nothing but our breaths. No one moves a muscle or ruffles fabric. They just...stare with heated gazes, zeroing in on my heaving chest.

"So fucking beautiful," Callum whispers, slowly climbing over the edge of the bed until he's hovering just above me. His gray eyes lock on mine with a slight grin, marveling at the artwork before him. "Every inch of you deserves to be worshiped. One day, I'll take my time. But I'm aching, Little Star. I need to be inside of you. I can't wait for a second longer," he murmurs, brushing his lips desperately against mine until his tongue plunges into my mouth.

"Please, Cal," I murmur through heavy breaths. "Please, do it." I can't stand it any longer, squirming beneath him and seeking the friction I crave.

"Yes, Little Star," he rumbles with a gasp. His jaw falls open when the tip of his dick slowly stretches me wide open, settling snuggly against my pulsating walls.

I groan, spreading my legs further to accommodate him more, aching to feel him deep inside me. My mind begs him to move faster—go quicker. He's so goddamn thick and throbbing when he bottoms out, groaning with deep satisfaction.

"Even better than I remember," he murmurs breathlessly. "You're so fucking perfect. You're so fucking mine," he murmurs with a strained expression.

"Fuck, Cal," I moan through shuddering breaths. "Please move. Please."

"You never have to beg me, Little Star. Whatever you want, I'll do it," he whispers, pulling back again and slamming his hips into mine. For an eternity, he stays there, soaking up the feel of me wrapped around him. Only to pull out and slam into me again and again.

I cry out, running my nails down his back with a gasp. He fills me up. Every crevice. Every fucking molecule. I'm so fucking full of him that I can't help but moan his name as the blinding white pleasure snaps across my body.

He grunts, slowly working himself in and out of me until his eyes roll into the back of his head. His taut muscles shudder with exertion as he slams home one last time. My pussy flutters again when a set of fingers moves over my throbbing clit, throwing me into orgasm sent straight from the wicked skies above. My toes curl. My heart pounds and breaths rage out of control. Static takes over my hearing, muffling out the breathless words of the men around me.

"Fuck," Callum grunts, stilling as he places his forehead against mine. "Little Star. I'll fight for you to the moon and back. Through the damn galaxy and beyond. I'll love you until my last dying breath."

I brush my lips against his. "I love you, too," I murmur, warmth spreading through my chest.

In a daze, I barely notice the bed dipping beside me. Rad lies against the thick, wooden headboard, lazily stroking his hard, pierced cock. I don't know when he got naked, but I can only imagine it was the moment he walked into this room. My eyes zero in on the shiny metal at the tip of his dick forming a cross through his mushroom tip.

"You on birth control, Pretty Girl?" Rad asks, lounging beside me with his dick in his hand, slowly pumping it up and down. Glistening pre cum falls from his slit as he spreads it around. "It's okay if you're not," he murmurs with a mischievous grin.

I blink several times at his question when it finally penetrates through the fog. Not like birth control did me any good the last time they knocked me up so damn easily. Although I blame the antibiotics. My idiotic doctor didn't warn me about the consequences of fucking while treating potential infections after my attack. Well, lesson fucking learned.

"I'm on birth control. I have an IUD." I raise my brow when he shrugs.

"Get rid of it then, Pretty Girl. You don't need it anymore. All you need is us." He swallows hard, a vulnerability wrinkling his brows. I'm not exactly sure what's going through his mind. I know it's pulling him into the depths of something and killing his mood. Something is bothering him about the whole situation.

Reaching up, I take his free hand into mine, gently squeezing. "Maybe when I marry you," I say, winking.

"Fuck yes. I can't wait to marry you and use my baby batter to knock you up. I missed it the first time around. I won't miss it again."

Ah, okay. There's the reason Rad's looking like someone kicked his dog. It all makes sense. And I get it. They weren't here for the pregnancy. A part of me is thankful that they didn't get to see me in all my pregnant glory. Because, yeah, sometimes pregnancy isn't glorious. For me, at least. But I wouldn't be opposed if they want that in the long run. But for now, I want to get to know them again.

"I wouldn't mind that," Callum murmurs, kissing my cheek. With great reluctance, Callum pulls out of me with a pained expression. "I miss you already," he whispers in my ear, leaving one last kiss on my jaw before climbing to the side of me.

"Sorry, River Blue," Kieran pants, taking Callum's place on top of me as Rad desperately holds my hand. "I can't take another minute without being inside you." He shakes his head, hovering above me. "It'll be quick," he rasps, pulling my left leg over his shoulder. "But I'm so damn desperate for you."

And with that, Kieran enters me hurriedly. Plunging into the depths of my pussy with one thrust and a grunt of satisfaction. His mouth forms an O as his eyes squeeze shut. All movements stop. Nothing but our ragged breaths echo through the room again.

"You feel like heaven," he murmurs, pulling out and pushing back in torturously slow.

The entire room falls away. All the noise. The lights. Even the guys disappear completely. Leaving only Kieran and me staring deep into each other's eyes. He groans, holding still, cradling my face between his palms. "You're my own fucking paradise. I'm never leaving this again. You're stuck with me forever. My Blue. My girl." His breaths quicken when his lips meet mine, solidifying the bond we've always held.

Something deep clicks inside me as our tongues dance together in an unhurried kiss. He takes his time with me. Never going too fast. Or too slow. It's just the right amount. Kieran doesn't show his love through just words. He never has. It's always been the kisses and the fucking. Hell, even the guitar on the hill. He's showing me now how much I mean to him and savoring every moment of our time together.

"Please, please, please," I moan, swirling my fingers over my clit. "Please fuck me, Knight. I need to cum."

Pulling back, he stares into my eyes with heavy breaths. "Is that what you want?" he murmurs until I'm nodding. "Say it for me, River Blue. Tell me what you want me to do."

"Fuck. Me," I growl, curling my toes when he slams his hips into mine, filling the room with the sharp sound of slapping skin. "Oh, Knight," I moan, meeting him thrust for thrust.

"Cum for me, River Blue. Let's do this together. I'm going to paint your pussy with my cum. It's yours. It belongs to you. Just like I do. Now cum!" He grunts, slamming into me and rocking my body with every damn thrust.

White hot static blares behind my closed eyelids as another orgasm rips me in half. My pussy clenches around Kieran's length, eagerly holding him in place as he releases himself inside me with a loud, satisfied moan with my name on his lips.

"Holy hell, River Blue. You're ours forever now," he breathes, slowly lowering my leg to the bed. "Forever and ever," he whispers, kissing my lips. "I don't think I've cum that hard since I bent you over that dining room table."

"I'm boneless," I groan, still squeezing Rad's hand like a lifeline. "I don't think I can move."

Nope. Can't move a muscle. My bones are Jell-O, and my muscles are mashed potatoes. I'm so dead from all this fucking. And I still have two more dicks to include. Whoever said being a part of a why-choose relationship was a good idea? Those women in books can go for hours. Me? I'm dead after two dick downs. How can I handle four again? They'll kill me before I have another orgasm.

God save me.

"You're going to have to, Pretty Girl," Rad says, tugging my hand so my eyes connect with his. "I've got a seat for you. I've saved it for five years now. Hop aboard."

I blink several times as he wipes his mouth with the back of his hand, grinning at my stunned expression.

"You want me to—"

"Yup! Ride my face, Pretty Girl. Straddle my head so I can lick you from clit to ass. I want to taste everything you've done. You. Them. Consider me the clean-up crew." His pupils dilate to almost black at the idea of me smothering him as I ride out another orgasm.

Shit. Another one? Can I even pull another one out of my body? Will this be death by sex? Prepare my casket. I'm about to die a pleased but worn out girl.

"Jesus," Kieran murmurs, slowly pulling out of me with a deep, vibrating groan.

"The clean-up crew, dude?" Asher barks out a soft laugh, shaking his head with a grin from the end of the bed where he watches everything unfold with rapt attention.

"I forgot what this was like," Callum muses softly from beside us with a satisfied expression.

You and me both, buddy.

"Uh, yeah. And you can act as her gag," Rad says, raising a no-nonsense brow in Asher's direction. "It's time to double-team our girl, or she's going to fall asleep with only half the team inside her. Operation Fill River Up is on." He grins, curling a finger in my direction. "Come on, Pretty Girl." I blow out a breath, lazily rolling to my stomach, and crawl toward him with the last of my energy.

Like a hawk zoning in on his prey, he watches me every step of the way.

"You're ridiculous," I grumble with Jell-O for limbs when he pulls me into his lap, grinning maniacally.

"Rad-iculous, you mean," he quips as a suddenly serious expression passes over his face. He shakes his head, gripping my waist tightly. "I've been dreaming of you for years, Pretty Girl. You're the only one who has ever been on my damn mind. I want to savor everything. I want to lick you clean and then make love to you. I've been ready for weeks. Hell, years. I'll tattoo your name across my cock so everyone knows who he rises for. Every inch of you calls to me. Please indulge me," he says, staring straight into my eyes.

"One more orgasm...such a hardship," I quip, grinning when he leans in and takes my lips captive. No, seriously. It's a fucking hardship. My body shakes with every movement I make.

"Good. Now, ride my damn face. Smother me with your pussy until I suffocate and die. In the best damn way. Just make sure my grave says something sexy like... Here lies Rad, who smothered under his girl's pussy and choked on her cum." A dreamy look crosses over his face when he thinks about what will come. You know, me preferably. If I can manage not to fall over.

With a quick peck to my lips, Rad shimmies his way down the bed, leaving me straddling his bare chest. Those pleading brown eyes stare up at me. "Climb on my face," he demands, digging his fingers into my ass cheeks, encouraging me to scoot forward.

"Okay," I say through a heavy breath, slowly making my way

up his body until my pussy dangles just above his mouth, filled to the brim with my previous encounters with Kieran and Callum.

Excitement hums through Rad when he looks me up and down. "Sit," he whispers, blowing hot air against my lips and sending shivers down my spine. "Asher, dude. Get over here!" he shouts before shoving his tongue into my pussy and back out.

I cry out, looking for leverage to hang onto and find it when Asher's lean body stands at the edge of the bed. His wide, hazel eyes take us in as my hand clamps down on his, begging for something to grip onto. I throw my head back with a groan, nearly coming when Rad's tongue plunges in and out of me. Back and forth. Up and down. Wetting every inch of me from below. Not a spot goes untouched, driving me fucking wild.

"Little Brat," he murmurs, leaning over and kissing my lips. "You're good with this?" he whispers, holding my face in his palms. I nod, moaning at the sensations working through me. "Good. Now, stroke me, baby," he whispers, guiding my hand to his hard-as-steel dick.

Asher's breaths blow out of control when he thrusts into my hand, twitching wildly in my grasp. "You're hard as hell, Evil Ash," I murmur against his lips. "You like this?" I bravely ask, earning a groaned yes in return. "Good. Fuck my hand, Asher. But don't cum yet. Wait until Rad bends me over and fucks me so I can use you as my gag. I want your cum down my throat, not in my palm. Right?" He nods frantically, slowing his pace.

"Yes, Little Brat," he heaves, sucking my tongue into his mouth and getting lost in the sensation.

I moan into Asher's mouth when Rad's fingers creep up my backside and twirl around my ass. "God, yes!" I shiver as another orgasm peeks around the corner.

Fire licks at every fucking nerve, working its way toward my over-sensitive center. The second Rad's thumb enters my tight ass, I come undone, convulsing another orgasm.

"Holy fucking shit," Rad murmurs from beneath me, lifting me off his face. "That's the hottest thing I've ever tasted and done.

You're so fucking amazing, Pretty Girl. Are you ready for the last bit? I'm going to fuck your pussy. Asher's going to cum down your throat. And you're going to like it."

"I sure fucking am," I breathe, pulling my hand away from Asher.

"Get on all fours, Little Brat," Asher demands with a flushed expression creeping up his neck. All his veins protrude beneath his skin, showing me he's holding back.

There's a snark on the tip of my tongue. Naturally, I want to fight back against his demand. Tell him to make me do what he says, but I don't have it in me. I'm horny as hell, ready to take them both. But exhaustion sweeps through me at a demanding rate.

I crawl on my hands and knees to the center of the bed and present myself, sucking in several breaths. Rad's fingertips brush down my spine, tingling as he draws patterns.

"You should see yourself," Rad murmurs, gripping my ass cheeks tightly and pulling them apart to expose me to his gaze. "You're more beautiful than I've ever seen. I'm so madly, deeply in love with you. My chest aches for you. I definitely won't last long, but I want you to know that next time we're chaining you to the bed for a whole night of worship."

"Damn right, we are," Kieran's gruff voice agrees from my other side as he plops down on the bed, leaning on his elbow.

"Hang on, Pretty Girl. This is going to be a bumpy ride," Rad rasps, thrusting deep inside me with one go. "This right here is heaven, boys," he gasps, wildly pumping into me.

"You're good?" Asher asks, clutching my jaw in his hand. I nod, opening my mouth, awaiting the treat I'm about to receive.

"You can finally cum," I murmur, running my tongue over his tip.

"Please, Little Brat."

His gasp echoes through the room when I suck him completely into my mouth, running my tongue over his slit. My cheeks hollow out, swallowing him whole.

"Shit!" Rad pants from behind.

I moan around Asher's length when Rad's hand slaps down on my asscheek, leaving behind a delicious sting.

"You liked that, didn't you, Little Brat?" Asher grunts, breathlessly slamming his hips into my face, using me for his pleasure. His loud moans fill the room when his fingers curl into my hair, holding me in place.

I couldn't answer if I tried.

Rad gently rubs the reddened spot on my ass. Leaning over, his chest presses into my back. As he whispers sweet words into my ear.

"I'm so close, Pretty Girl. You're amazing, you're...mah—" His pace slows until he stills, sinking his teeth into my shoulder. Warm breaths caress my skin when he lays his forehead against my shoulder, panting wildly.

Rad doesn't try to move away, keeping himself buried deep inside me as his cock slowly deflates.

"Never leaving. I'm sleeping with my dick inside you. He's finally home," Rad mutters nonsensically.

"Fuck," Asher pants, throwing his head back when his salty cum jets into my mouth and dribbles down my throat. "Holy hell, Little Brat." Frantically, he pulls out, clasping my jaw between his palms. "You're amazing...I...thank you." Before I can ask him what he's thanking me for, his lips are on mine. Pulling away, raw emotions sparkle in his glossy eyes. I don't know what's going through his head, but something profound rattles around in there.

"Fine, I'll leave," Rad grumbles, pulling himself out of me with a whine.

I fall into the bed face-first with a groan. I'm not as young as I used to be. Even if I'm only twenty-four. Nineteen-year-old River could handle four dicks at a time without blinking an eye. But my body feels like I've been run through the wringer.

"Pretty Girl! Did I kill you with my dick?" Real concern drips from Rad's voice as he moves my hair from my face.

"Yes," I mumble into the comforter. "Just leave me here," I quip when he chuckles.

"How about a hot shower, baby?" Asher whispers from my other side, moving his fingers through my hair. "We'll help."

"You'll help?" I question, raising a brow and turning myself over. Looking up, I watch Asher's soft face when he nods.

"Yeah. We got you into this situation. Now, we'll help you relax afterward."

"Okay, take me to the shower," I say, reaching up like a child until Kieran lifts me off the bed and into his arms.

"We got you, River Blue. We'll clean you up. Have a little snack. And then, we can all go to bed."

After a hot shower, they carry me to the kitchen and make me food. And then, after we've all eaten, they take me back to Callum's bed, where they cuddle me throughout the night.

Just like we used to.

After picking up Ly from her sleepover and saying our goodbyes to Central City the next day, we head home with a new outlook on life. And our relationship.

The trickiest part about our newfound life together will be the reality we're about to step into. They're a band. They'll have to travel at some point. And I still have my work. By tomorrow morning, we'll all be back on track with what our lives used to be, while incorporating our new relationship.

44

"Coffee," I groan for the thousandth time today. Or it feels like it, at least. I've only been awake for thirty minutes, wrangling Lyric into school mode.

I have to get her back into the swing of things after missing so many days from being away. And let's just say she doesn't want to cooperate.

I swear that's all being an adult consists of. Coffee. Work. Zombie mode. Tired. Hungry. Horny. More coffee to feel human. When will this endless cycle stop?

Right. Never.

"Here," Asher chuckles, handing me a large Styrofoam cup of boiling hot nectar from the Gods. "It's your usual." Pride sparkles in his eyes when he looks away, watching with intent as Lyric approaches with a grin.

"Morning, Daddy," she says, reaching a hand out.

"And what do you want, Little One?" he asks, bending at the waist to meet her sparkling eyes.

Her eyes slip to the white bag on the counter containing the treat she's so desperate for. The one thing Asher brings her every morning. Something delicious. Sweet. And will probably rot her damn teeth out.

"My treat," she whispers, pointing toward the bag like it's a secret tucked away.

"What do you say?" I ask, groaning into my coffee like the addict I am. If it wasn't for the caffeine, I think I'd die a slow and painful death.

"Pwetty, please," she whispers, puffing out her bottom lip. Convincingly, might I add. If he hadn't bought it for her, he'd definitely give it to her now.

"Well, who can resist that," he quips, gliding over to the bag and pulling out her treat. "Come sit so you can eat, and then we'll get you to school."

I grin against the lid of my drink, watching him beneath my lashes. Sometimes, I like to watch as they each interact with her, giving away a little piece of their hearts each time.

Every day they fall a little more in love with her. And she with them. Like they never separated, and they've known each other since the moment she screamed her first breath.

Emotions rise in my throat at the love they've shown her in such a short time. And me, too. Even though we knew each other at different times in our lives, it's like we were never apart. But yet, we were. They're so different from who they were.

"So, I'll bring you some lunch today, okay?"

My eyes zone back in on Asher, who eyes me with a little smirk pulling at his lips. I raise my brows. How long have I been staring at him while biting into the damn lid? Fuck. I pull my drink away and clear my throat.

Apparently, long enough. Ly chomps down on the pink-frosted donut with sparkly sprinkles dotting the concoction, devouring it like a little hungry monster. Leaving the remnants behind around her lips.

"Lunch?"

He grins. "Yeah. I figured I could bring something to you since you're going back to the office today."

My cheeks heat. Why is it so hot when a man insists on

feeding me copious amounts of coffee and food? I'm not complaining. Like at all. He can stuff me full with... Well, my mind instantly travels down the deep, dark road of cock and moans, heating my face more.

Apparently, I need to get laid. No matter how hard I tell myself to take it slow, my body has other plans. And well, to hell with it. I've always given my body what it wants.

"Lunch is great," I say with a smile, pretending I'm not thinking about his dick.

Totally not, by the way. Nope. I'm not thinking about the way he gagged me just a few days ago. Or the salty cum that slid down my throat as I swallowed him whole. Nah. Not me.

Fuck. It's only seven or so in the morning, and I'm already horny. It's like their cum was the key to awakening my long-forgotten sex drive hiding inside me. Once they entered me, thrust into me, and came inside me—I was a goner, drowning in them again.

Something I swore I wouldn't do. Just yet. But I'm constantly breaking my promises to myself. Take it slow, I said. But yet, I got dicked down by my four baby daddies in one night.

You see, my body remembers theirs now. Every one of them. And now I'm scared I'm addicted to getting bent over and fucked within an inch of my life. I promised myself I'd take it slow. All in, yes. But I want to get to know them again. And at this rate, I'm only going to be reacquainted with their nether regions.

Shit.

"Great. I can stop by after therapy and practice," he says with ease, leaning over to wipe Lyric's mouth off with a paper towel. "Go wash up for school, or we'll be late."

"I'm sick," she pouts, crossing her messy hands over her chest.

"Lyric," he says in a stern dad voice, even giving her the pointed look that has her turning tail and stomping down the hallway to her room.

I shudder at the strength in his voice. Settle down, you hussy.

He's not bossing you around. Not yet, at least. He will, though. I'll bring back the dominant man who made me hold out my wrist with salt lines on it so he could cut limes.

It's time to bring the old Asher out. He's said sorry multiple times and proven himself over and over again. Now, it's time to release the beast simmering under his flesh until he's pounding into me without mercy.

I'm so fucking screwed.

Or want to be.

"My little sister from another—" Seger twists his expression when I walk into his office.

"That saying doesn't work like that," I say, plopping down onto a leather seat across from his desk.

Zepp snorts, sauntering over from his desk on the other side of the room, and lounges beside me in another chair.

"First-day jitters?" he asks, taking a sip of coffee before placing it on a coaster on Seger's desk.

"Weird to be back, but I have to get back into the swing of things. They're handling practice and therapy without my assistance now. So, I figured I'd stop in and see how Kat was handling things here."

I raise a brow when they exchange a look, doing their freaky twin, silent conversation bullshit with their eyebrows.

"Kaycee and I agree that's annoying as fuck, by the way," I say, pointing between the two of them.

Immediately, both of their moss-green eyes lock me in place.

"You're not allowed to be friends with our wife anymore," Seger sniffs, raising his chin in the air.

"All you two do is conspire against us," Zepp says, pointing in my direction.

"She's like my sister. We're allowed to conspire against you. Get over it," I say, sticking my tongue out.

Zepp sighs, running his fingers over his forehead. "Kat called out today."

I stiffen. "Called out?"

"Yeah. You know, used a sick day today and yesterday," Seger quips like the cocky asshole he is.

Such a goddamn know-it-all. I swear I would have put them six feet deep if we had actually grown up together. I mean, I plot their murders every once in a great while when they're being jackasses.

Like today.

I blink several times. Seger puts his feet on his desk as he leans back in his chair. Secretly, I hope he falls backward. I don't want blood. Well, not much. But a nice bruise would suffice to knock the little attitude out of him.

Ah, siblings. They're a joy to have.

Zepp's jaw tics with irritation as he glares at Seger's dirty shoe on his desk. "Act like a civilized adult, you pig," he mutters, swiftly knocking Seger's feet off his desk and jolting him forward.

Seger grunts, placing his palms on his desk to stop himself from smacking the wood. Damn, too bad.

"Back to the matter at hand. Is she really sick? She hasn't called out in all the months she's worked here."

Finally, they each take a deep breath. Sometimes I think they need a vacation away from each other. But being twins and all, they have a weird bond. Not to mention they share a wife.

I shudder. I hate thinking about what they do in the damn dark of their home. Stupid intrusive thoughts.

Zepp grimaces. "She and her weird boyfriend, Trevor, are having some issues. Um, she just needed some time to straighten it out. Mental health days are classed as sick days here, so we just gave her the go-ahead." Oh good, that means there is work on my desk ready to be completed. Thankfully, I won't have to worry about any anonymous notes landing there again.

"Well, okay then. I'll be off to my office for now unless you need something." Peering at both of them, they shrug. "Good. I'm out."

"Good to have you back, my sister, from the same mister! Ha! I nailed it!" Seger's whoops follow me as I make my way down the long hallway toward my office, which sits a little ways from theirs, giving me the much-needed privacy I crave.

Since Whispered Words is only a couple months into my program, there isn't too much work for me to handle at the office. My sole purpose once a band is put in my hands is to mold them back into best-selling artists. But it's nice to be back here in the peace and quiet I've carved out for myself. My office is my place of Zen—a place no one disturbs anymore.

As I shut my office door behind me, I dig my phone out of my purse.

ME

> Hey, Kat! Just wanted to make sure you were okay. My brothers said you were feeling a little under the weather.

Listen, I am concerned about her well-being. She may not be a close friend, but I like to think Kat and I are on good terms. She may be my employee, but I like to check in on her.

KAT

> Hey:/... I was just having a rough time. Trevor disappeared without saying goodbye, and I didn't know where he went... I was worried until he came back this morning.

Jesus. Who disappears without saying goodbye? I hope he had a damn good reason.

ME

> Just checking to see if he is okay.

KAT

> He's been better. His mom got sick, so he
> went to check on her, and his phone broke
> when he was there. He wasn't able to get
> another one until today. I'm sorry I couldn't
> make it today. There's a stack of mail on your
> desk.

ME

> Family comes first, Kat. I'm just glad that
> you're okay, and he's okay.

KAT

> Thanks, Miss West. I appreciate you checking
> in. Glad you made it back safe and sound,
> too. It must have been terrifying having a
> stalker out there.

Yeah. Beyond terrifying. Having some stranger watching your every move is something no one will understand unless they've lived it. If I would have known it was Adrian, a man I had never actually met. Then I would have put a restraining order on him. In some cases, though. That doesn't do shit. They walk right through those restraining orders without a second thought. Not like me. When Gloria handed me those papers I thought were from the boys, I thought why bother?

ME

> Call me River. And yeah...it was. Stay safe. I'll
> check in tomorrow.

Leaning back in my chair, I stare up at the ceiling reveling in the silence around me. It's odd going from having five other people constantly making noise to just myself. Alone. Just me and my rampant thoughts.

The morning goes by in a rush. I slowly catch up on some paperwork I need to sign regarding past bands and even potential new ones. It's odd I never saw Whispered Word's name come across my desk. Yet, here I am as their new manager. I swear, even though my brothers knew about the past, they made this happen.

"Talk to them again. That restraining order is over," Seger *huffs from behind his desk, slowly nursing a beer he pulled out of somewhere.*

"I don't think I can," I mutter, pinching the bridge of my nose. *"They walked away. Remember? They're the ones who signed that restraining order. Not me."*

"You ever get a funny feeling about it?" Zepp asks, cocking his *head to the side and examining my twisted expression.*

"No." Yes. I did. It always made me feel uneasy and off. *But who was I to question their signatures on the dotted line? Besides that phone call, too. It was pretty damn convincing.*

Well, maybe I should have listened back then. I was so determined that they wanted nothing to do with me that I kept it all together for Lyric. She was my priority. It scared the living hell out of me thinking about dropping her in their laps.

What if they truly didn't want her?

Now I know the entire situation was bullshit. Concocted by some psychopath who hated my guts and twisted Asher into her grips to get what she wanted most. Money.

"Knock, knock."

I nearly pee my pants when I jolt upright, staring at Asher loitering just inside my office door with a grin, shutting it behind him.

"You were deep in concentration," he chuckles, walking toward my desk with a tray consisting of two drinks and a take-out bag from my favorite coffee place. "I got your favorite again. The avocado sandwich I always see you eyeing."

I sweep my papers into a pile on the side of my desk as he sets out our lunch.

"God, Asher. You're a lifesaver," I murmur, biting into my chicken and avocado sandwich.

He chuckles. "Well, I figured you needed to eat, and I just so happened to be getting that anyway." His eyes dart away, refocusing on his sandwich as he takes tentative bites.

"Why're you still holding back?" I ask, setting my food down.

"I'm not," he says, shaking his head.

"You are."

He swallows his bite, chugging his Dr. Pepper. "I'm not meaning to." His teeth sink nervously into the bottom of his lip when he sets his sandwich down and takes a deep breath. "I—"

"It's okay, Evil Ash," I murmur, reaching across my desk to take his hand.

Squeezing my hand in his seems to bring out his bravery a sliver. His hazel eyes stay glued to the ground when he opens his mouth. "I'm all in, Little Brat. I promise I am. I just... I still feel guilty. It sits so damn heavy on my chest. I know you forgave me."

"Completely. You are 100 percent forgiven. I told you that I'll remember forever what it felt like when you left. But I don't dwell on it. Look at you... The old Asher wouldn't have given me the time of day. Not to bring me lunch, at least. He'd only have wanted to jam his cock down my throat."

I smirk when he chokes on his own drink, turning a bright shade of red like he didn't do that exact thing a few nights ago after dancing in the rain.

"Christ," he croaks, shaking his head. "You can't say shit like that."

All the pent-up horniness from before slams into me as I watch him wipe his mouth. This Asher is much more delectable than the old Asher. But there's still one side I miss more than anything.

"Take me," I say, pushing my chair back and slowly rising to my feet.

"Take you?" he asks, lowering his voice into a smooth rumble.

Yes, you idiot. Take me. Fuck me. Make me cum harder than I've ever cum before.

Those hazel eyes latch onto my movements as I begin to slip

my high heels off and kick them under my desk, instantly becoming inches shorter. His gaze doesn't leave my movements even when I start to unbutton my work shirt, leaving it half open and exposing my white silky bra underneath.

"Yeah," I say, shrugging out of my shirt and letting it drop to the ground near my chair. "Fucking take me, Asher. Do what you want to do to me."

His eyes blow wide, darkening with each piece of clothing I remove. Yet, he doesn't utter a command. Simply stares at me like I've grown a third boob he can't wait to devour. Wicked thoughts must travel through his mind when his fingers twitch on top of my desk, desperate to reach out and grab me.

The cool air of the room rushes across my flesh, pebbling goosebumps up and down my body as I remove my pants and toss them across the desk, hitting him in the face.

He jerks back, gripping them in his hands. "Little Brat," he rasps with roaming eyes, staring me up and down as I stand before him in only my bra and underwear. "Fuck, you're so goddamn gorgeous."

"Tell me what to do, Asher." I won't move unless he says so.

I won't cum or moan or curl my toes unless he gives me the go-ahead. This is me taking back the Asher I once knew and giving him back to the Asher 2.0 sitting across from me. Someone needs to take him by the balls and force him to be the dominating man he once was.

He's no longer allowed to stay on the sidelines and wait his turn. It's time for action.

He blinks several times, rubbing his jaw. "Come here," he says with less confidence than I hoped, but it's a start.

"Yes, Daddy Asher," I murmur, sauntering around the edge of my desk.

God. The full-body shudder that works its way through him at the sound of his old nickname has my pussy weeping with delight. If I thought I was horny this morning, this is nothing compared to that.

It's odd having him at my mercy. Or me being at his mercy, I guess. Trying to be, anyway. It brings me back to the night he laid me out on the dining room table at the Castle House and rocked my goddamn world with his demands. Every word he said, I did. Every command he laid out, I fucking followed.

Today will be no different. Today is the day Asher takes me how he wants me.

Asher doesn't reach out for me when I stand before him in my underwear. His fingers may not caress my flesh just yet, but his eyes absolutely ignite with lust, traveling over every inch of my body with a fine tooth comb.

"Fucking hell. You're going to kill me," he murmurs, finally brushing his fingertips over my abdomen and gliding around my belly button.

"How so?" I whisper, leaning into his warm and inviting touch, still refusing to take the reins on this whole endeavor.

Whatever Asher wants to do, it's up to him.

"You're just so fucking beautiful. Then and now." His fingers trail up to the swell of my breast, gliding over the white stretch marks lining my skin. Abruptly standing, he towers over me, still fixated on running his fingers over my boobs.

"This is your show, Daddy Asher," I murmur, pushing my tits into his hand as he cups it through my bra, running his thumb over my pebbling nipple.

"Hmmm," he hums, leaning forward to bite through my bra.

"Fuck," I hiss at the beautiful sting flaring under the intensity of his teeth.

"My show," he murmurs, running his tongue along my bra until he meets my flesh, traveling up my neck and right below my ear.

I nearly cum when he sucks my skin in between his teeth, nibbling around until my lips meet his.

"I want you to bend over, Little Brat," he breathlessly says against my lips, palming my ass.

Fire brews beneath my skin when he watches my reaction with such intensity I feel like flames are licking every inch of me.

"Yes, Sir," I say with a smirk, growing wetter by the second.

Turning around, I place my palms on my desk. My back arches, and when I look over my shoulder, I nearly combust at the sight of him.

Those hazel eyes gaze directly at my ass, trailing toward the wet spot collecting on my panties. All these pent-up hormones run rampant with need, turning me into a begging mess.

"Please, Asher," I moan, wiggling my ass a little.

"Please, what?" he dares to ask, undoing his belt from his jeans and rolling down his zipper. I watch in fascination as his cock springs free, bulging and twitching with need. "What do you want, My Brat? Do you want me to fill you with this cock? Shove it so far up your dripping pussy that you cum?"

Jesus fuck Christ, I've created a dominating, dirty-talking monster.

One that I like.

If he keeps this up, I'll come before he ever fucks me. Or before we finish our damn lunch.

"Yes, Asher." I swallow hard when one finger trails down my ass cheek, slipping beneath the fabric of my panties. Getting closer and closer to the promised land.

I jolt in surprise when the thin fabric of my panties rips in two. My breaths shudder when he holds them in front of my face, displaying the wet patch on the fabric.

"I have been holding back," he admits, pressing his lips to my bare shoulder, trailing kisses up my neck. "I've been trying to respect what we have now. But you make it so fucking hard to respect you when all I want to do is fuck you like you're my fucking little whore. I want to shove my cock down your throat and watch you swallow. Fuck. I've—"

"Then do it. Fuck me like you hate me. Fuck me like you used to."

"But I never truly hated you," he whispers with desperation as his finger finds my clit, turning light circles. "I never ever hated you. I was so fucking madly in love with you that I hated myself. I loathed what I thought about you. What I did to you. Said to you. You're my goddamn angel, River. My Brat. My baby. My salvation into becoming a better man."

"Fuck," I moan, thrusting back into his pelvis. "Asher," I whine, begging for him to fill me.

"I'm going to fuck you now, River. I won't hold back. But you should hold on. I'm going to shove this into your mouth so your brothers don't come running. The last thing we need is visitors when I'm helping you meet Jesus." I swallow hard when he traces the lace of my white panties along my lips, softly tapping them. "Open up, Little Brat." Without hesitation, my lips part, welcoming the panties into my mouth, muffling anything that comes from my throat. "Good girl. Now, wrap your hands over the edge of the desk." My breaths hitch in my throat when I wrap my hands around the edge of the desk so tight my fingers turn white.

That's the last thing he says before he brushes the tip of his throbbing dick at my entrance and thrusts completely inside me.

"Oh fuck me," Asher murmurs. "Goddamn, you're one hundred percent going to be the death of me, and I'm okay with it. I'll die right here," he grunts, slamming into me several times and knocking my hips into my desk.

Whatever bruises I have later will be something I look back on as the moment Asher took back his control.

I groan around my panties as droplets of drool roll down my chin. It does its job, holding back my loud moans so hopefully my brothers don't fucking hear us. The last thing I need is those two idiots interrupting this much-needed fucking.

Asher's pace picks up, slamming into me relentlessly. Without fucking mercy. My desk squeaks with every move, dragging against the floor, surely giving away what we're doing in here.

"I want you to cum around my cock," he demands breathlessly in my ear.

I nod, leaning into the fire eating away at me, and release my fucking orgasm from the Gods, suffocating his dick as I convulse.

"Fuck me," he says, stiffening and releasing himself inside me with a long, drawn out moan of satisfaction.

My forehead rests against the cool wood of my desk as he hovers behind me, rubbing his hands up and down my body. Small words of affirmations are whispered against my neck as he catches his breath.

"Thank you," he whispers with sincerity. "I knew only you could bring me back to who I was but keep me in check."

Spitting out my panties onto my desk, I desperately suck in air. Asher hurriedly hands me my drink, and I gulp it down with him still nestled inside me.

"No, thank you," I rasp, clutching his hand in mine. "Thank you for letting go. Please, don't hold back again. I need both sides of the Asher coin." I swallow hard when he gently pulls out and spins me around.

His palms cup my cheeks as he leans in, suffocating me with his kiss. His tongue darts into my mouth, twisting with mine as he pushes me against my desk.

"Never again will I hold back, Little Brat. I'll be whatever Asher you want."

"A mix of both," I quip with a smirk. "Now, if you don't mind, I need to get back to work."

"I'll wait," he says with a shrug, kissing me one last time. With ease, he puts himself back in his pants and rights his belt.

"You'll wait?" I ask, heaving a breath.

"Yup," he says with a grin, sitting back in his chair and picking up his sandwich. "But why don't you work like that?" He gestures to my bra and the cum dripping out of my pussy and onto my leg.

I smirk, walk around my desk and plop in my seat. "If you insist."

"Oh," he chuckles. "I do."

Until the end of the day, Asher stays with me. He doesn't say anything as he cleans up our lunch mess. He just rests, watching me wade through the paperwork Kat left me until the clock hits 2:00 p.m., and I've run out of things to do.

45

Callum

It's been four days since we went all in, diving head-first back into this little thing we call a relationship.

Well, not little. This is huge. Monumental. Our girl is finally ours again and within our grasp.

It feels damn good to have her back in my arms.

We've all fallen back into our regular routines. Us, as a band, going to morning practices and therapy sessions.

And River, acting as our manager. The boss in charge.

Since our return, it's been a whirlwind of emotions. For me, I realized what I lost when I left her behind. Her. Lyric. All the love we had together.

Now, it's reignited into something bigger and more beautiful.

This is our new normal. Together. All five of us. Plus, our daughter who hasn't stopped smiling since we sat her down and told her we're together now. And she'll be seeing a lot more of us.

My new normal tonight includes taking my daughter to a book reading of some book she's been desperate for me to read. Later, I'll tuck her into bed and kiss her goodnight. Like I do every night.

This is a dream come true. It's my everything. From the time I was a kid, this is everything I always wanted. Family. A wife. And children.

"What book is this again?" I whisper, frantically darting my eyes around the massive crowd gathering outside the downtown library, chatting before they step inside.

River snorts as we walk through the front entrance. I cringe at the mere size of the people huddling together in small groups. Someone is bound to recognize me. Everywhere I look, unfamiliar faces greet me with big smiles and heated cheeks. Their eyes drift over my face, recognizing me from a mile away—the one downside to being famous. I can't walk into a room, especially in this town, without someone pointing at me. Or wanting an autograph.

"My favorite, Daddy," Lyric replies, tugging at my hand with renewed vigor, grunting at me when I don't move quickly enough.

River chuckles, clutching my other hand as we walk further into the large East Point library built to impress. Marble floors. Large ceilings. Hell, it even has tall columns holding up the balconies above our heads.

"Oh, my God! It's Callum Rose!" a woman's voice squeals as I pass by a group of girls huddled together near the entrance. "Callum! Can I get your autograph?" Her voice echoes, following me until I stop and turn with a tight smile, greeting the red-faced woman, clutching a pen and notepad to her chest. "Please?" she whispers, flicking her long brown hair over her shoulder.

"Sure," is my clipped response.

I get it. I really do. They see a celebrity they love and automatically want an autograph. Or a picture together. Or to beg one of us to crawl under the sheets for a good time.

Never happened. Not for me, at least.

But today.

I'm here with my family. Ready to enjoy a reading of Lyric's new favorite series. The last thing I want to do is stop hanging out with my family to sign her notebook.

"But, Daddy! We gots to get good seats," Lyric whines beside me, tugging at my hand with impatience.

My eyes dart to Lyric as her bottom lip puffs out. Little tears glisten in her eyes as she watches me grasp the notebook.

"I know, Ladybug. Give me just a second, okay?"

"It'll be ok, Ly," River whispers, taking Lyric's hand from mine and forcing her to face River. "Daddy just has to do this, and then we'll find our seats." Lyric huffs, crossing her arms over her chest.

"So, it's true," the fan sneers in River's direction with disbelief.

I blink several times, watching the woman's face morph from a smile to a deep frown, forming wrinkles on her forehead.

I don't dignify a response to the fan's question. It's none of her business. In fact, it's no one's business. They can be as upset as they want to be. Just like our PR manager was.

They can all shove it up their asses and keep their opinions to themselves. We're happy, and that's all that matters.

"Here," I grunt, handing her back the notebook with my tiny signature decorating the page.

"Thank you so much!" she giggles, running her finger over my writing. Leaning in as if she's about to whisper something, she says, "If you don't feel like sharing anymore, I'm available. Only whores share." The bold fan sniffs, sticking her nose in the air with a tiny smirk like she's won something over on River, who snorts beside me.

"I'll take that," I grunt, ripping the page from her notebook and shoving it in my pocket.

"What?" she gasps with big eyes, reaching out to take the paper from me. "But you…"

"That was before you insulted my girlfriend. In front of my daughter, might I add. It was nice of me to even stop and sign this for you. I'm trying to have a nice night with my family, but I stopped because…"

I don't know why I stopped. I suppose it's instinct now. I hear my name, and I stop for signatures. Not anymore. Not when I'm with my girls. I'm here to protect them from everything. And that includes the disapproving look she's giving us.

"I stopped because I thought it would be nice. This is the love of my life. So, have a good night." I don't bother giving her another look as she stands there, staring at me with wide, unblinking eyes.

She could be crying. Or giving me dirty looks. Maybe she'll stay there all night glued to the spot, thinking about the day she stopped Callum Rose and was an asshole. I don't care anymore. No one insults my Little Star without consequence. No one.

The fallout of our announcement hasn't gone exactly bad. Well, until tonight. I guess.

But not good either.

The press is having a hay day with our unusual relationship. That's what they call it, at least. Haven't they seen a poly relationship before? Apparently, not. They're always snapping pictures anywhere they can find us. If we leave the house anymore. It's only been a few days, but we're the talk of the nation.

River doesn't seem to give a shit as long as Ly is safe from harm. So, whenever we're out, I try to cover Lyric as best I can. She shouldn't have to endure public life at such a young age because of us.

River clings to my side as she reclaims my hand, gently squeezing. "Poor girl," she hums with sarcasm lacing her tone.

I snort. "Right. Poor thing."

River grins, looking at me from beneath her lashes. "Kinda sexy how you stood up for me."

Fuck. My cheeks heat when she nibbles her bottom lip. I swear my stomach bottoms out, swirling into a mass of lust as she bats her eyelashes in my direction. If she's not careful, I'll salute the entire crowd.

"Stop it, Little Star," I whisper, leaning over so my lips brush against her ear, sending a shiver down her spine. "We're in public," I murmur.

"Have you ever..." she trails off, looking around the large library with a mischievous grin. "You know, they'll let all the kids sit in a circle around the narrator. We could sneak away and give the books a show."

Fuck. Me.

"No," I choke out, kissing her cheek. "Stop it." Little fucking tease. She giggles, shrugging.

And to think, Rad begged to come with us. He wanted in on the action of hanging out with Lyric. But I wanted this time to myself. Them to myself. Like the selfish bastard I am. Now, I'm kind of wishing I wasn't so selfish so he could sit with Lyric, and I could fuck River over a stack of books in the hidden part of the library.

Maybe later.

As we walk further through the loitering crowd, people of all ages hang around the large, open reading room, murmuring to each other. Thankfully, no one else notices who I am.

A single chair rests at the front of the room reserved for the children's librarian giving the people of East Point a treat for tonight.

"You sit here, Daddy!" Lyric says, bouncing on her toes and pointing to two chairs sitting side by side. "Mommy here. Daddy here," she demands.

If there's one thing I've come to know about my daughter, it's that she's a bossy little thing. One day she'll grow up to be the leader of something. A business. A CEO. A band. Hell, she could form her own army, and everyone would listen to her. She has that kind of presence.

All I know is I'm nurturing her bossy side and helping her turn it into something powerful.

"And what about Lyric?" River hums, settling into a plastic chair with a grin. Looking up at me, she pats the spot next to her.

I grin when I sit, and Lyric happily climbs into my lap, situating herself so she's staring at the front.

Ah. That's where she wanted to be.

"This is book three, Daddy. It continues where we left off last night," she squeals, clapping her hands with such glee I can't help myself.

Her joy infects me. Fills me up with her laughter and claps. Watching her light up as the librarian comes out with the third installment nestled beneath her arms has my hair standing on end.

This is my time with her. Our love for this simple book about a murderous archer, who protects the people around her as she gallivants trying to find a cure for her mother's mystery illness, has me in a chokehold.

One day they'll make this into a movie, and I'll be the first in line with Lyric to watch as they hopefully don't butcher it.

Lyric softly snores in my lap, never having made it to the small circle of kids gathered around the librarian.

I chuckle, running a finger down her reddened cheek as she lets out another tiny snore in front of the crowded room, intently listening as the story continues.

She barely lasted twenty minutes.

The snores are something she swears she doesn't do. Mostly, she blames me or one of the others for waking her up. Little does my baby know she's the one responsible for all the noise.

"She's out," I murmur into River's hair as she rests her head on my shoulder.

I could get used to this. Every night having them by my side, snuggling me until they each fall asleep.

"Let's roll," she murmurs softly, gesturing toward the exit.

You don't have to tell me twice. If Lyric is out, then I can tuck her into bed. After that, I'm going to tie my Little Star up and fuck her into oblivion.

Those remarks from earlier sit fresh in my mind, creating fiery ideas. Her. Me. My mouth between her legs, licking the repeated orgasms from her slick pussy. Fuck. I shake the thoughts from my head and save them for later.

As quietly as we can, we exit the reading without disturbing Lyric and successfully put her into her booster seat in the back of River's car.

"It must have felt like bedtime," River chuckles, leaning against the passenger's side door with crossed arms, staring up at the stars beaming down on us.

A cold chill flows with the tiny wisps of wind, blowing the leaves on the trees. Goosebumps pucker at River's skin, but she doesn't pay it any mind.

"Must have," I say, softly closing the door after buckling Lyric in.

"Did you see the way that lady looked at me when we walked out?" she asks, licking her lips. "I think your groupies might claw my eyes out and try to steal you from me."

"Fuck them," I murmur, crowding her against the car with a smirk. "You're the only one who matters, Little Star."

"Hmm. Is that so?" she hums with sass, staring straight into my eyes.

"It is."

Before she can blink, I brush my lips against hers, leaning into her. Mine. All fucking mine.

Butterflies swoop in my belly every time I'm around her like it's the first time all over again. Something that will never go away.

Every time I'm in her vicinity, my internal wounds stitch back together even more than before. She's the balm necessary for my healing.

Even when she used to be the reason I fell. Now, she lifts me.

"You and Ly and the guys are the only family I need," I whisper against her lips with a grin. "Should we get home?" A soft moan falls from her lips when my hips brush against hers, letting her know how desperate I am to get her to bed. "Those little comments from earlier really stirred something up," I murmur, kissing her one last time.

Out of the corner of my eye, something flashes in the distance, repeatedly going off. I sigh. There they are again, following our every move. Even at the library, we're not allowed peace by the paparazzi. They can follow us to the end of the world, though. I'll never stop kissing my girl out in public. This is our life.

"Yeah? And what do you want to do to me?" she rasps, oblivious to the cameras documenting our make out session against her car.

I lick my lips when she challenges me with one look.

"I'll catch you," I whisper directly into her ear. "No matter where you run off to." And that's a goddamn promise. She can run as fast or as far as she wants, but River West will always be caught by me. Or the others.

"Sounds like a fun game," she says with a wink, pushing me away from her playfully. "Take us home now, Cal."

God. I wish she'd say my name like that all the time. All breathy and deep, just begging me to take her right now. If we weren't in public, I'd rail her against the car. Fuck that camera still flashing.

River's brows furrow as alarm widens her eyes, focusing on something behind us. My heart rate kicks into overdrive. Her stalker might be gone, but we've all been on high alert, scanning for any more threats. Who is to say that he was the only one coming after her? He had friends, after all. Three of them, to be exact. What if they're upset that their friend is dead because of River?

Swiveling around, I cover her with my body, facing the person who has somehow snuck up on us.

The man grins, plucking a toothpick from between his teeth. His head nods in greeting as a smirk pulls at his lips.

Fuck. I let out a breath but don't move from in front of River. I'll protect her from anyone. Even if I know who they are.

"Jesus, Ruthless," I shudder, blowing out a breath at my former fight organizer.

"Sorry to interrupt, Kid. Saw you over here with your lady friend and thought I'd stop by and say hello." Ruthless offers us a toothy grin as he holds his hands up in surrender.

"Do you come to the library often?" I quip, shaking off the adrenaline pouring through my veins.

Ruthless snorts, nodding to the little person clinging to his hand. "My kid likes the readings. But something came up." He shrugs. "Haven't seen you around much," he says, twirling the toothpick with his tongue. "The crowds miss you. Want you back." He raises an intimidating brow, prodding me for information.

The moment River told me that Lyric didn't like the marks on my face, I quit. No questions asked. I'd do anything for them. Besides, I couldn't stand to see Lyric cry anymore for me than she had. It broke me to wipe her tears away, knowing I was the reason that I had bruises on my face.

So, much to Ruthless' dismay, I talked to him and let him know I was done. Out. No more.

I know he misses the attention I brought to the ring. The money, too. I was Rock Star. One of his best fighters. And I loved it while I did it. But I'm done with that life now. It's in the past. Just like a slew of other things.

"I've found peace," I say, crossing my arms over my chest. "I don't need to fight anymore."

"Can see that," he says with a shrug. "If you ever change your mind..." he trails off, grinning more at something behind me. "Ah, you're the little lady from the crowd."

River snorts without fear. "Something like that."

"If your man here ever needs to let out some aggression, well. I got him covered," Ruthless's deep voice breaks through the darkness, sending anxious shivers down my spine.

He stares at me like a piece of meat. Like I owe him something. Maybe I do. He saved me from a life of drug consumption. Instead, giving me a way to let it all out in the octagon. I'm forever thankful he stepped in and stopped my self-destruction. But I won't risk making my daughter cry again.

"It was nice seeing you, Ruthless. But I'm out."

His dark eyes assess me, and he nods. "Sure thing, Kid. I'm always around. You know where I'll be."

I nod. "Of course..." I trail off, thinking about the last time I stepped foot into the old school.

I won't. That life is behind me. Just like everything that happened before. It's in the past. The old Callum. I'm new again. With a brand-new outlook on life. I don't need to ram my fists into anyone's skull to feel better. All I need is my girl, my brothers, and my daughter.

End of story.

I nod. "Of course. Thanks for the opportunities, man," I say, holding out my hand.

"You're a good kid," he mumbles, clasping my hand with his, and we shake on it. "Miss seeing you around."

I lick my lips when he walks away, holding tight to his kid. Together, they lean in and have a discussion before disappearing into the parking lot.

"He seems lovely," River quips, watching as he leaves.

"Lovely and him don't mix. He's a solid dude. Good fight coordinator..." And he saved my life. But I won't go into that detail just yet. "How about we get her home?"

River and I get into the car and take a long way home, enjoying the ocean views. Her hand slips into mine over the center console, squeezing as we take several turns, enjoying the silence. And each other's company. Finally, after twenty minutes, we pull into her driveway, and I park the car.

"Want to put her to bed?" she asks, inspecting my face in the shadows of the car.

"I'll put her to bed." A smile grows across my face when I bring our conjoined hands to my lips and lay a gentle kiss along her flesh. "And then I'll put you to bed."

Through the darkness, I only hear a sharp intake of breath before I get out and collect a still-sleeping Lyric. I waste zero time getting this show on the road. My girl needs me. I can practically taste it in the air.

When River unlocks the front door, I follow her all the way back to Lyric's room, where I lay her down on her bed.

"Good night, Ladybug," I murmur, kissing her head as River undoes her shoes.

"Daddy," she says with a groggy voice. "Don't leave." Her tiny hand shoots out with deadly accuracy, grabbing me by the shirt.

"Ly," River sighs, throwing her shoes near her white closet doors.

"It's okay. You go to bed; I'll only be a minute." River raises a brow at my demand, but she does as I say and leaves the room.

"Daddy, the monsters are back," Lyric mumbles, yawning as she snuggles deeper into her bed.

"The monsters?" I question, peeling her fingers away from my shirt. Without a fuss, she lets me pull the purple comforter over her legs and up to her chin.

"Mmhmm. Tap. Tap. Tap," she mumbles as her little eyelashes flutter again.

"I won't let the monsters get you." Leaning forward, I brush another kiss on her cheek.

"Night, Daddy," she mumbles just before the snores start and sleep takes hold.

I could stay like this forever at her bedside. Watching her rest so peacefully is the greatest joy.

But I have other plans to follow through on. In detail. With my tongue. And other things.

On my tippy toes, I sneak out of Lyric's room. Determination takes hold as I march across the hall and walk straight into River's room, stopping dead at the gorgeous sight before me.

My heart rate accelerates, pumping blood straight to my dick and hardening it in an instant. She doesn't have to touch me to have this effect on me.

Fuck. She will be the death of me.

There's my girl lying back on her bed. Completely and utterly fucking naked. Displaying her body for me like a treat I can't wait to savor. Saliva pools in my mouth the moment I visualize my tongue running over every surface of her body, worshiping her like the goddess she is.

My Little Star is mine right now. No one else's. They aren't here to disturb us or join. So, I'll take my time with her. Hours, if I have to.

I lick my lips, reaching behind me, shutting, and locking the door. If Lyric needs any assistance, she can knock. But hopefully, she's sound asleep and will be for the next few hours.

"I heard you wanted to put me to bed," she says in a sultry voice, running her fingertips over the cool sheets of her bed.

"Oh, do I ever, Little Star. Look at you." My eyes travel up and down her body, memorizing it for later. "You're ready for me," I say, taking a deep breath as heat rushes up my neck. "Are you wet for me already?"

Lust dilates her eyes to saucers. Her labored breath pours from between her parted lips. Just as she slowly trails her fingers down her abdomen with deliberate strokes. Forcing my eyes to watch her every move. Leaning back onto the bed, she peels her legs apart, displaying her wet, pink pussy to me.

"I might be," she says on an exhale, keeping her gaze connected with mine.

I sharply inhale as her fingers slowly spread her lips, and her fingers plunge inside her, moving in and out.

"Oh, yeah, Callum," she moans breathily. "I think I am. Why don't you come over here and find out?"

I don't have to be told twice.

As I march toward her, I throw my shirt on the floor, kick my shoes off, and undo my jeans, taking everything off until I'm throbbing and hard, landing on her bed. A primal feeling to take her rushes through me, begging to be where her fingers move in and out.

I watch with rapt attention, barely daring to breathe as she continues her movements. I'm transfixed. By her motions. By the breathy little sounds coming from her throat and softly filling the room. Everything about her draws me in. And it's worse than before. I want to wrap myself in her and never leave.

I throb against her comforter, not daring to make a move. Her toes curl in the sheets, and her body stiffens until I grab her wrist, stopping her movements. She can't get off unless I'm the one making her cum with my name on her lips.

I ache to bring her pleasure.

"My turn," I whisper, slowly bringing her fingers out of her pussy. I groan when her wetness coats them, and then I lick them, savoring the flavor of my girl on my tongue.

My tongue swirls around her fingers until I let them go, letting her hand drop onto the sheets.

"I'm going to eat my dessert now," I whisper, leaning in closer to her pussy until I'm face-to-face with it. My warm breaths blow over her soaked cunt. "Say my name, Little Star."

My name falls from River's lips over and over when I plunge my tongue deep into her pussy, carving my name into her spasming walls. Fuck. She tastes so goddamn good.

Her back practically arches off the bed when I remove my tongue from her pussy and swirl it wildly around her clit. Over and over again, I make circles and thrust my three fingers deep inside her.

"Callum," she gasps, gripping my hair when she comes around my fingers, squeezing them tight.

"You're more delicious than I remember," I murmur, pressing my lips to her pussy one last time. Slowly, I work my lips up her body until I'm hovering above her, lining my dick up with her pussy. "Sometimes I think you were meant for me."

She smiles, running her fingers through my hair and down my jaw, wiping away the moisture pooling on my chin. In unison, we groan when I slowly enter her.

My eyes roll into the back of my head when her softness wraps around me, squeezing when I bottom out.

"Oh, Little Star," I moan, pulling out and slowly working myself back in. "I'm going to take this slow," I murmur, resting my forehead against hers. "Maybe all night."

She moans, bringing her lips to mine, and thrusts her tongue into my mouth. Intertwining together and slowly dancing. Nothing about our connection is hurried. Minutes pass, and an hour ticks by.

She gets on top, riding me with her head thrown back and her tits bouncing with every thrust. Yet, I hang on. I don't blow my load.

Sweat coats every inch of our flesh when I throw her onto her back again, feeling the familiar tingle working down my spine. My balls tighten when I thrust back inside her, working myself in and out at a steady pace.

River moans, throwing her head back when my fingers brush against her clit, turning heavy circles.

"Cum for me, Little Star," I murmur, sucking her nipple into my mouth until she's squeezing around me and calling out my name. "River," I cry out, stopping my thrusts as I cum deep inside her, coating her spasming walls. "You're the best thing that ever happened to me," I whisper, kissing her lips again. "Twice over. I wouldn't give you up for the world."

She smiles, grabbing my hand when I fall to her side, curling myself around her. "I wouldn't give you up, either. We're meant for this life."

"We are. Now, how about we take a hot shower?" I ask, brushing her hair from her face.

A tired grin pulls at her lips. "Okay," she hums with a yawn.

Over the next hour, I take my time washing her body. When I said I'd worship her like she deserves, I meant it. In and out of the bedroom. She'll never wonder again if we're for real. Or if we love her. We do. I do. She's my forever girl, and I tell her so when we fall asleep on fresh sheets after getting cleaned up.

River falls asleep quickly, cuddling her face into my chest. Through the darkness, I watch her bare chest expand and deflate with her breaths. Some would say it's creepy, but I want to memorize what peace looks like drifting over her face when she's lost in dreamland.

I hold her close when her bedroom door opens, revealing a grinning figure standing in the hall.

"Dude," I mutter, shaking my head when Rad waltzes through the room with slumped shoulders.

"Couldn't sleep," he mutters, taking off his layers of clothes, only leaving his boxers.

"You're lucky we unlocked that door," I say with a pointed look as he slips into bed and curls around the backside of her body with a satisfied sigh.

"Yup. Now, I can sleep," he murmurs, kissing her cheek.

"How the hell did you get in here?" she rasps without opening her eyes.

"I have a key."

That makes her peek open an eye. Turning her head, she looks at him with furrowed brows.

"A key? I never gave you a key."

My gaze snaps to him when he chuckles. "You didn't have to give me a key, Pretty Girl. I always find a way in."

"That's creepy, Rad," she grumbles, shaking her head.

He grins more, curling his hand around her waist. "Nah. Not creepy. It's for your protection. What if you needed me, and I couldn't get in? I couldn't let that happen. So, I stole your key and made myself a copy before you even noticed."

River stiffens. "Yeah. Totally not creepy," she mutters with a sigh.

"Besides, I had a brilliant idea come to me. So, I couldn't sleep either. I missed you today. Cal hogged you, and it made me sad."

"Sharing is caring," I say, flicking his ear.

"When did you become so mean?" he whines, covering his ear.

"What's your idea? I'm awake now," River grumbles into my chest.

"Do you have any plans for our baby girl's birthday? Because I have the best damn idea on the fucking planet." Pride leaks into his tone when he grins so bright it's visible in the darkness of the room. "I'm taking your silence as a go-on moment. How about we rent out the East Point Amusement Park? It has that cute little unicorn section for kids and maybe some roller coasters for us adults. What do you think?"

"Not a bad idea," she says. "But let's smooth over the details later. I'm tired again."

46

Kieran

"I HAVE AN IDEA!"

I raise a brow when Rad waltzes into the living room, pointing his finger toward the ceiling.

Great. The brilliant idiot has an idea. Judging by the goofy grin stretching his lips, he thinks it's a good one. I'm going to need a shit load more coffee before this is over. I just fucking know it.

The morning sun blazes in through the windows on our lazy Saturday morning. It's been a week since we returned from Central City, and everything is falling into place after our time together with River.

Like beautiful patches coming together after being blown to bits. We're repairing ourselves one stitch at a time. Not only our relationship with each other, but our relationship with ourselves as individuals.

We came to an agreement with River when we got back about taking things slowly. She's determined to get to know us better again as the men we are now as opposed to who we were back then. AKA—she wants to take things at a glacial pace, which is fine. Totally fine.

Slow and me don't mix anymore. I've had my taste, and now, I need to devour her completely. With all the restraint I have nestled in my body, I'm trying to hold back from tearing every inch of her clothes off whenever she's around.

More than anything, I want to show her I can respect her wishes. And I do. I love that she wants to reacquaint herself with us before we jump into the deep end with each of us. The last thing our new relationship needs is for us to drown before we ever learn to swim together. Despite the paparazzi constantly watching us and photographing our every move, which she doesn't seem to mind, I'm letting my River Blue come to me, like she has the others.

Which immediately took my plans of moving her in with us out the window. If it were up to me, I'd hogtie River and kidnap her, so she'd stay with us twenty-four seven. Her and Ly.

Am I feeling a little territorial about my woman? Yes, yes, I am. I've been away for too long, suffering in an all-consuming rage.

I need her.

She's the light at the end of my darkened tunnel, shining brighter by the day.

"You and great ideas are usually not in the same sentence," Callum quips from the couch, nursing a cup of coffee with one eye open.

Sometimes I wonder how Rad rolls out of bed in the morning with so much pep. It's disgusting.

Rad frowns, stopping short. "I have good ideas. I take offense to that."

I shrug. "Sometimes." More like never.

"Sometimes? Rude," he huffs, plopping down next to me on the couch. "You assholes never change."

"What's your idea?" Asher asks from the recliner, lazily rocking himself.

Rad grins. "I want to throw my Little Pretty Girl a birthday party. She's going to be five soon." His brows furrow, pain twisting his expression.

I know that look. Haunted. Pained. Filled with regret. It's the same one that consumes me every time I think about what we've missed out on.

Instinctively, my eyes dart to Asher, sitting rigidly now. He knows that look, too. It's written on his face. Anguish and utter devastation contort his features, dropping his eyes to the floor where he studies the wood like it's the best thing he's ever seen.

"I'm sorry," Asher says again, licking his lips. "I know we missed a lot of time with her because of me." Guilt drips off every word he utters, thickly laced with a pain I can't even explain. His hand rubs across his chest. No doubt aching from his massive mistake.

I know what he did hurts him, too. It has to. He was an asshole for what happened. But we're moving forward. Together. With the help of therapy and group sessions, we've come to rebuild our relationship as friends. We're a damn brotherhood again. And damn, does it feel good.

"Every birthday. Christmas. Easter. Thanksgiving." Callum murmurs, looking deeply into the swirls of his coffee.

"Every step. Her first words." I shake my head, sinking my teeth into my tongue. "It happened, okay?" My gaze connects with Asher's glossy eyes, and he nods. "You can't take it back. But we're here now. In the present, to be there for Ly. We can talk to the therapist about this more. Okay?"

"Okay." He nods with reluctance, pulling his lips into a tight line.

"So, no more missed birthdays or holidays. We're here for good," Rad says, rubbing his hands together.

"Tell them your idea," Callum huffs, sipping his coffee with a knowing look.

"Four words..." He grins, looking around the room as anticipation builds in the air.

"Go on," I say, rolling my wrist.

"Put us out of our misery," Asher quips with a snort, wiping away the uncomfortable look.

Every so often, I see defeat in his eyes. He's still beating himself up every chance he gets. Even in River's presence, he takes a backseat, offering to care for Ly if we want to go out. Asher did a shitty ass thing when he ripped us apart. But I don't want it to define him anymore.

River forgave him and us. There's no need to keep rehashing what he did. It'd be different if he didn't feel remorse. But he does. He feels it with every step he takes. So, he's off the hook for now.

"East Point Amusement Park." Rad holds his hands out in front of him with a grin. "Huh? What do you think?" His brows waggle with excitement as he looks around the room at our stunned expressions.

I blink several times. "You mean the place off the highway with all the rollercoasters and stuff?"

"Yeah! That's the place." He physically lights up, jumping from his seat to pace the room.

"Why that place?"

East Point Amusement Park is larger than life. Filled to the brim with rollercoasters, arcade games, kiddie rides, special sections, and so much more.

Rad swivels in my direction with a grin. "Because our little girl likes unicorns, and that's the birthplace of her favorite ice cream. Believe me! I researched all night long, looking for the perfect place. Just imagine our baby girl on the unicorn ride holding an ice cream cone and laughing. They even have a whole unicorn adventure inside the park, with kiddie rides, unicorn games, and that damn ice cream. The owner said we could buy out the whole park for a day. Her birthday is next Saturday." He wiggles his brows again, waiting for our excitement to kick up.

"Can confirm. I'm pretty sure he kept River up all night long with his search," Callum says with a groan, finishing off his coffee.

"Well, would you look at that? He does come up with some good ideas," I snark, chuckling when he flips me off.

Poor bastard. He's not sleeping well again. And I know damn well the cause of his ache and the balm to his restlessness—our girl. But apparently, he was with them last night after Cal took Ly to the reading.

"See! I told you! You fuckers didn't believe me." He rolls his eyes in disbelief, shaking his head. "Even my Pretty Girl agrees it's a good idea."

"Book it," I say with a nod. "It can be a big surprise party. We can invite Ly's friends and family."

Excitement thrums through my veins at the prospect of surprising my baby girl with a unicorn-themed party, her favorite ice cream, and plenty of presents. The need to spoil the hell out of my mini-me has me thumbing through my phone on the hunt for the perfect birthday present.

The ultimate unicorn stuffed animal with sparkles and a horn. I grin when it has the option for a voice message. All you have to do is press its hoof, and your voice will come through. And sold.

I furrow my brows when a loud thump comes from the front door, echoing through the house.

"The hell?"

We all look at each other when the sound thumps again, followed by a little voice calling out to her daddies.

My fucking heart drops. Flashbacks of the first time I laid my eyes on Lyric flash through my mind. Her frantic cries. The tears I couldn't wipe away fast enough. Shit.

"River better not be dead again," Rad hisses, running toward the door as we all follow behind with our hearts in our throats.

I grunt when Asher slams into my back as we huddle around the door. Nerves shake my fingers when Rad throws it open, staring down at our little girl.

"Daddies," she says with a big grin, clutching two white bunnies to her chest.

"Little Blue," I say, kneeling down in front of her. "What's wrong?" I frantically check her over, noting the backpack glued to her backside. She smiles so damn wide it's almost blinding.

"Nuffin. I'm staying here tonight. We're having a sleepover! With lots of cotton candy," she says with a shrug, casually pushing me out of the way with her tiny hand. I don't fall on my ass when she shoves by, but I think I could have.

"What the hell?" Rad asks with his eyes glued to the little girl strolling into our house with nothing but a smile, her backpack, and her two stuffed bunnies.

"She wanted a sleepover," River says out of nowhere.

"A sleepover?" Callum blanches.

"Yeah. Good luck!" River says, waving a hand as she turns to leave.

"Whoa! Pretty Girl!" Rad grunts, rushing after her with determination. "What's happening right now?" he asks, clutching her shoulders and stopping her retreat.

"I'll uh...make sure she's settling in okay. Looks like we have a guest for the night." I nod at Asher as he walks away with a grin lining his face. I bet he can't wait to cook and play with her.

Callum sighs. "I'll help him."

"She wanted to stay with you guys," River says, sinking her teeth into her bottom lip. Amusement soars through her sparkling eyes like she finds the prospect of us alone with Ly hysterical.

"Oh, yeah?" Rad asks, lighting up at the idea.

"We don't mind," I say, meandering over to where they're standing at the bottom of our porch. "She's welcome any time. You know we love to spend time with her."

"You could sleep over, too," Rad says in a low voice, smirking when she shudders from his touch.

"That, too," I say, brushing her hair over her shoulder. "You could sneak in after we put her to bed. Then we could play some adult games."

She snorts, batting us away. "Such charmers. Would these adult games include the no pants dance?"

"That could be arranged," Rad says, waggling his eyebrows as he undoes his belt.

"Jesus, keep your pants on," she laughs, shoving him away. "Listen, I couldn't stop her. She just packed a bag and told me she was going. I barely had time to grab shoes when she stormed out the door. For some reason, she was determined to get here. I think —" Her brows furrow. "I think she misses seeing you guys all day, every day."

"We could fix that, River Blue. We could build a big house right over there for the five of us."

I can see it now. Our beautiful forever home rises in the distance with enough room to accommodate all of us, plus more. If we wanted, of course. There's nothing that sounds better than knocking River up ten times more and having kids and pets running around. It's the normal family I've always dreamed of. With an abundance of love pouring through the house to fill the ocean. Our children would never know what it felt like to lie in bed at night, wondering where the next meal or hug would come from.

"Keep dreaming, Romeo," she quips.

I don't miss the way she looks out in the distance to the place I pointed to with dreamy eyes. She's keeping us at arm's length, doing what she needs to do. That's fine. I can tell it's eating her alive not to be by our side. She's aching to fall into our loving arms and ride happily out into the sunset.

"Well, then, Pretty Girl. Enjoy your day all to yourself. Just if you take a hot bath or play with that amazing little rose later, take lots of videos for me. Moan my name a little so I can go to sleep with a smile."

River rolls her eyes, leaning in to kiss his cheek. "Mmmhmm," she hums with mischief.

"Enjoy your day, River Blue. We'll take good care of our baby girl." I kiss her lips before she walks away.

What could go wrong?

"What the hell do we do!?" Rad hisses, panicking as Lyric throws up every fucking thing we've given her tonight.

Cotton candy. Cake. Cookies. Pizza. Shit. We broke our child with junk food.

"Jesus," Callum grunts, pushing a fist to his lips. "Hold her hair or something."

"She's going to need a bath," Asher remarks, standing at the edge of the bathroom with a sickly green tint taking over his complexion, staying as far away from the spewing child as possible.

"My belly hurts," Ly says, sitting near the toilet with her bottom lip puffed out. "Hurts so bad, Daddies."

I turn away, taking a deep breath when she yacks where she sits, spewing chunks of candy, cake, and whatever the hell else Rad engorged her with all down her shirt and onto the floor.

"Oh God, I think I'm going to be sick," Rad groans, clutching his stomach next. "Yeah, I'm going to—" Rad doesn't say another word when he leans over the toilet and empties his stomach into the water.

"Daddy," Ly whines, puking again.

"Jesus Christ, we need an exorcist," Rad moans into the toilet. "Be gone, devils!" he hisses, spitting into the toilet and finally flushing it.

"Fuck," Asher hisses, pressing his hand to his mouth again. "This is like a goddamn puke fest."

"Should we call River?" Callum whispers in hysterics. "We need to call her. She can fix this. Fix this, Kieran!" His wide, gray eyes scan the room frantically, searching for God knows what.

"No!" Rad hisses. "Then she'll never let us have Ly alone again. You won't tell Mommy we fed you too many sweets, will you?" he asks, batting his eyelashes just like she does.

Lyric pouts, rubbing at her stomach. "Nope, Daddy. I won't, I promise—" her little voice trails off when she looks down at her puke-soaked shirt. "Is dirty," she whines, tears coming to her eyes.

First, she has a tummy ache and pukes, and now, she's about

to cry about the stains lining her shirt. Not to mention the stomach acid stench wafting from her body.

"Bath time," I say, kneeling in front of Lyric. "Is it okay if Daddy gives you a bath? We can go to the bathroom in my room. I might have some bubbles."

"I uh, have a bath bomb she could use. It's green, though," Asher chimes in, rubbing the back of his neck.

Her entire face lights up, and she nods. "Bath bomb!!" she squeals like she didn't just projectile vomit all over the room.

Little devil.

"Let's take this shirt off first," Asher says, holding his breath as he pulls it over her little head, muttering unintelligible words resembling fuck and shit. "I'll throw this into the wash and grab the green bath bomb. Little One, you have a fun bath, okay? I'll be up there in a sec."

"I guess I'll clean up the mess." Rad's lips turn down as he surveys the vomit chunks on the floor. "I'll just puke my way through it," he whines, covering his mouth.

Lyric nods with excitement, taking my hand in hers. I hold back the hot acid sitting in the back of my throat when she pulls me out of the bathroom, and we make our way upstairs.

"All right, Little Blue. Let's get you into the bath," I grin, starting to fill up the bath with warm water.

"Here," Asher says, peeking into the bathroom and handing me a green-looking ball.

"You use these?" I ask, holding it up in the air to examine it.

"They smell nice," he mumbles, turning beet red, and walks away before I can say anything else.

Within a few minutes, tiny green bubbles appear in the water, getting bigger as the tub fills. After getting Ly undressed and ensuring she's comfortable, I set her in the water and begin washing her face and shoulders with a washcloth.

"Lean your head back," I murmur, finding a large cup.

"Okay," she says, squeezing her eyes shut.

Emotions bubble in my throat as I gently lean her head back and pour the water over her hair.

"Does your belly feel better now, Little Blue?"

"Mmhmm," she hums softly as my fingers work through her hair, lulling her into serenity as I push shampoo through her strands and repeat the process.

"Do you love Mommy?" she asks, wiping her eyes when I'm finally done washing her hair and body.

Sitting back on the floor, my stomach drops at her question. "I do," I whisper, grabbing a towel to wipe her face off. "I've known your mommy since she was your age. We were best friends."

"Then why didn't you want me?" she whispers, squeezing her little eyes shut. Her little lips quiver, and she sniffles, trying hard to hold back her heavy emotions.

"No," I whisper frantically, clutching her little face between my palms. "I always wanted you. I just didn't know about you as I should have." Fuck. My heart pounds in my chest when she sniffles, slicing through my fucking soul. No child should have to feel such deep, earth-shattering emotions. "I've always wanted you, Little Blue. Even if I didn't know about you. I swear, baby girl. I love you."

"I love you, too, Daddy," she whispers, leaning into my touch.

"How about we get you out of there and into some pajamas? Then you can show me what you watch on your tablet," I murmur with a broken heart until she nods.

"Okay, Daddy," she says softly as I grab a towel and help her out.

Once she's wrapped tight in a towel, I set her on my bed and dig out an old Whispered Words shirt. Much to her delight. It's like the entire night didn't happen when she climbs under my sheets after grabbing her tablet.

Selfishly I keep her to myself in my bedroom, lying in bed together under the blankets. Thankfully, the other guys give me that time to cuddle with my baby. Lyric smiles and laughs, like our conversation in the bathroom hadn't shattered her, as we watch her favorite YouTube videos until she falls asleep with her tablet clutched to her chest.

"I'll never let you down again," I murmur into her wet hair, knowing at some point in her life, I'll disappoint her. I'm not perfect. But I'll try to be for her sake. I'll be the best damn father I can be. Unlike mine. He walked away without regretting a damn thing. But that's not me. I walked away, sure. But I didn't know about her.

At some point in the night, I wake up with my brows furrowing in confusion. Last I knew, Lyric was snuggled beside me. Now, a warm body presses against mine, clutching tightly to my side.

My fingers roam the body beside mine, taking in the curvy figure snuggling into my side. Yeah, that's not Lyric anymore. That's my girl. My River Blue. I don't even have to open my eyes. My fingertips are my looking glass, revealing the woman I'm madly in love with. I'm about to open my mouth and ask her what the hell she's doing here, but she beats me to it.

"She woke up and went to sleep with Asher. She's playing musical beds. By morning she'll be right back to where she started," River murmurs against my bare chest.

I blow out a breath, kissing her forehead. "And now, you're here."

"I didn't want to be alone," she whispers, shifting so her eyes connect with mine. Only a sliver of moonlight through the blinds reveals them to me.

"You're never alone when you have us." Gently, I move a piece of hair out of her face, taking in the beauty of my best friend. My girl. My fucking everything lying beside me. "Did something happen?"

Her brows furrow. "It's stupid."

"It's not stupid. Whatever it is. You just had someone following you around for three years. You're on edge being back here."

"The wind was making the branches tap on my windows. I swear... I just felt..."

"It's okay," I murmur, kissing her forehead again. "You're allowed to feel scared, River Blue. We'll always catch you when you fall."

Her fingers trail over my jaw, and she brings her lips to mine, pressing them softly there in an unhurried kiss.

I'll hold her for infinity. Kiss her until the world burns to ashes. I'll never let her go again.

"So, are you excited for Ly's birthday party?" she asks, throwing me to my back with a sneaky grin.

Fuck. My heart pounds against my ribs when she stares at me like I'm the little prey beneath her, and she's the tiger about to rip my throat out.

Her fingers curl around my biceps, holding me in place as she climbs on top of me and straddles my hips.

The second she's settled, my hands descend on her, feeling every inch of her warmth.

"Our baby girl only turns five once. Five is a number important to all of us. We can't rewrite the past, but we're going make this five-year mark count." My fingers curl in her hair, bringing her eager lips to mine.

I groan when my tongue intertwines with hers, dancing slowly together. Her moans vibrate through my damn soul. Even more when she grinds against my hardening dick, waking him up.

"Ride me, River Blue," I groan, licking down her neck. "Put me inside you. I need you right now."

"Beg," she whispers, digging her fingernails into my scalp. "Beg me, Knight." God. Fuck. I could cum right here in my pants if she keeps breathing against my flesh and pulling my hair.

I'm never too proud to beg my girl for what I want. Only for her will I bend the knee. I'm her Knight, after all.

"Please, River. Please ride me. Fuck me. I need you so damn bad right now. I need to be inside you one more time. Pull my hair. Choke me. Fuck me. Please!" I cry out when she claws her fingernails into my scalp again, yanking at my hair. Leaving behind the delicious burn that lights me up from the inside out. My dick throbs harder. My hips push up, begging for friction. "I need you. So fucking desperately."

River's fingers wrap around my length through my sleep pants, slowly stroking up and down.

Now, we're getting somewhere.

"Please," I gasp when she shimmies down my body and pulls me out of my pants and boxers. Her warm tongue glides over my tip, sucking my pre cum from my slit. My hands fly to her hair, holding her in place when she swallows me whole, taking me into the back of her throat. My balls tighten a fraction as heat swarms in my gut. I'm ten seconds away from exploding in her mouth. "If you keep that up, I'm going to cum down your throat," I gasp, yanking her up until she's face to face with me. "Fuck me, River Blue. Fuck me so hard."

She grins, sitting up and taking off her T-shirt and then her bra. I marvel at her fucking beauty. Reaching up, I caress her soft breasts, pinching her nipples between my fingers.

"Fuck," she gasps, thrusting her chest out. I grin as she squirms on top of me.

"Take it all off, Blue." I don't have to tell her twice. In seconds all her clothes are gone, and she's perched on top of me again, sinking down until I'm fully inside her.

"Fucking hell," she rasps, sinking her fingernails into my chest.

Mark me. Use me. Fuck me.

"That's right," I rasp, clutching her hips. "Ride me, River Blue."

River throws her head back with a groan, swiveling her hips several times. With each movement, my dick hits every inch of her pussy. My damn balls tighten embarrassingly early until I'm cumming deep inside her.

"Holy shit," I groan, emptying everything I have deep inside her pussy.

River slumps against my chest, brushing her lips along my flesh. "I think I'm addicted to you," she murmurs, working her way up my neck until her lips caress mine.

"You're not the only one," I whisper, weaving my fingers through her hair. "I'm hopelessly addicted to everything about you. And that'll never change. Ever again. Now, let's go enjoy a hot shower together and get cleaned up."

She grins, slowly rising off me, and stands by the bed. "You better wash me good, Knight."

And I fucking do. At least three more times against the shower wall. Once I had her in my clutches, there was no way I was letting her walk away without walking funny. By the time we're in bed, I hold her close to me, reveling in the feel of her flesh against mine.

"Do you care if I take Ly out for some ice cream tomorrow? Maybe some shopping... I..." My heart breaks when Lyric's questions from earlier ring in my mind. My poor baby has lived her life thinking we didn't want her when the opposite is true. If I had known about her, I would have been there from the second she started growing inside River's womb. Every day I'll live with this ache in my heart that Lyric's first years were taken from me. But I can't live in my past failures. I'll live in the now and make it up to her every second I get.

"Knight," she murmurs, running her fingers over my bare chest. "You don't have to ask. You can take her. She's yours, too."

"Thank you," I breathe, mentally planning out what we're going to do. "Night, River Blue. I fucking love you."

"Love you, too," she whispers before drifting off to sleep in my arms.

47

Kieran

"PICK WHATEVER FLAVOR YOU WANT."

Lyric's huge, mismatched eyes dart wildly around the tiny ice cream shop with wonder, latching on to the vast display of flavors under the glass container. Pinks. Blues. Hell, there are even sparkles in the damn ice cream. With every color she gazes at, the more excited she becomes, barely containing it as she bounces beside me.

Her tiny hand squeezes mine in excitement.

"Double scoop?" she whispers, staring at me with pleading eyes.

"Triple scoop, if you want."

The worker behind the counter flinches when Lyric's sweet squeal rings through the shop, catching the attention of several parents sitting with their families. Cue the curious whispers starting all around us, saying my name beneath their breaths to their friends, knowing exactly who I am.

"I wants a triple scoop of unicorn sparkle ice cream, pwease," Lyric says with confidence, standing on her tippy toes barely as tall as the counter. Her little eyes watch the redhead with the name tag—Penny—behind the counter, smiling at her.

"Of course. And for you, Sir?" A deep crimson tint takes over Penny's cheeks as she looks me up and down, biting her lip.

Shit. This is the downfall of being famous. I can't even have ice cream with my daughter without eyes watching our every move. The heated stare the worker gives me is nothing new. I'm used to women stopping me for autographs. Or soliciting me for a good time. It comes with the rock star territory. They don't see me as Kieran. They see me as the shirtless guy who walks around on stage doing what he loves. It's tiring.

My need to protect Lyric ramps up tenfold as I survey the room. It's nothing but families, friends, and their children, but you never know who is lurking in the background. Case in point, River, and her damn stalker. Nothing pleases me more than that asshole being off the streets and six feet deep. Now, I feel like I can protect both my girls better. A vow I will never break. They're my number one priority.

"I'll have the same." If my baby girl likes it, then I like it, too. Whatever she wants today is hers.

"Okay! Two triple scoops of sparkly unicorn ice cream coming right up. That'll be... $45.56." I blink several times, computing the amount she fucking said. Is this ice cream made with real gold flakes? What am I missing here? Fuck.

With a grimace, I dig in my pocket, pull out my card, and hand it to Penny as she swipes it. Even though I've got millions in the damn bank from working all these years, spending forty-five bucks on scoops of ice cream makes my stomach drop.

I think it's from all those years of scrounging for food after my dad left. My mother was never stable. Especially the following months after he was gone. We barely survived. Little to no food. Couldn't pay our damn heat bill. Luckily, power companies won't shut off the heat in the winter months due to not paying the bill. But when spring came? Yeah, we were out of luck for a few weeks until the church stepped in and helped us pay. Then came the eviction notice from our rental with thirty days to vacate.

"We'll be homeless," I mumble, staring down at the paper my mother threw at me with disgust.

A cigarette hangs from her mouth as she sits on the sofa, not doing a damn thing to fix it.

"Don't worry; I've got an idea." The smirk that lights up her face when she peels herself off the couch and heads upstairs without another word sends chills down my little body.

I'm way too fucking young to have to understand what's happening. But I know it all too well. Ever since Dennis—since I refuse to call him father—left us without a fucking goodbye, I've had to grow up. I've watched my mom continually dress herself up, bring men over, and then have a few bucks for McDonald's. Then, the process starts over again.

"Make yourself scarce, boy," Gloria says, fluffing up her brown locks. Makeup covers the tired lines and hides all the truths about our situation. "I've got company coming. Then, we'll go out and have some dinner. After that, we'll stop by and talk to the Aid Office. They'll have some sort of housing for us. Especially with this," she says, holding up the eviction notice. I blink several times when she lights up another cigarette and smirks like she's got it all figured out.

Somehow, my mother finagled her way into the government housing apartments after showing them her eviction notice and bank account. After that, we lived there for a few short years. But those short years were the most stable—and I use that loosely—we had ever been. With a roof over our heads and help with food and power, we never lived without the necessities again. Not to mention, moving into those apartments brought me to my best friend. The love of my damn life. Producing this cute little creature watching Penny behind the counter, furrowing her brows.

"I'm so sorry, Mr. Knight," she croaks, turning beet red again. "It says it's declined." Well. That's a first. My heart fucking stops. Declined? How the fuck does a bank account with that much money get rejected? Fuck. Just as it's declined, my phone pings in my pocket as I dig for my wallet again with a sense of dread pulling at my senses.

"Uh, sorry about that. Old card. Just use this one instead."

Thankfully, my financial advisor turned me on to having multiple bank accounts as a just in case, spreading my wealth among the five of them.

Penny loses the tint as my second card goes through, and she smiles, handing it back. "If you'd like to pick out a table, we can bring it right out to you," she says, gesturing to the sea of small red and white tables lining the shop.

I nod in thanks, taking Lyric's hand as she searches for the perfect spot to sit.

"Over here, Daddy," she says, yanking my arm toward the corner of the shop where a little red, sparkly tabletop with two matching chairs sitting across from each other rests.

"Perfect spot, Little Blue." I grin when she climbs into her seat, swinging her legs with a pleased grin.

"I love this place, Daddy. Can we come here again? They've gots my favorite ice cream. I love Unicorn Ice Cream." She grins bigger when Penny sets our bowls in front of us with a shy grin, turning her entire face red again.

"I...um... Could I get your autograph?" she asks with a nervous breath. Her eyes dart all around as she scratches the back of her neck. "Whispered Words is my favorite band of all time. And—"

"Sure," I say with a tight smile, trying to remain friendly.

Nothing grinds my gears more than fans interrupting personal time. I get it. They want to meet me. Get my signature. But it's irritating when Lyric sits across from me, watching our every move. I hate taking time away from my daughter. But I also appreciate my fans. I wouldn't be here if they didn't like our music so much. I wouldn't be able to afford the fifty-dollar ice cream my daughter loves so damn much.

"Kieran, thank you so much!" she squeals, pulling a notepad and a black marker out of her pocket. "This means so much to me. You guys are so friggin good!" She's breathless by the time all the words spew from her mouth.

"Thanks! Have you been coming to see us play at The KC

Club? We'll be there in two weeks." As she hovers above me, I quickly sign my name, trying to get a move on so others don't catch on that I'm handing out autographs.

River let us off the hook this weekend and next, letting us adjust from our trip back home. Next Saturday, we celebrate Lyric in the best way with tons of sparkly ice cream, her friends from school, and rollercoasters galore. Rad's really gone off the damn deep end with these crazy plans for her. Secretly, I love his enthusiasm. He's prepared to spend an arm and a leg just to get this crazy birthday party off the ground. He had a point, though. We've missed so much; it's time to make up for our absence.

"Yes-yes!" she stammers, taking the notebook back with trembling fingers. "We saw you guys a few weeks ago. You were amazing. Any plans to go back out on tour?"

I swear to fuck. My heart stops beating, ceasing to pump blood through my body. Tour. If we go on tour, we'll have to leave Lyric behind for months at a time. There's no fucking way we could take her and River with us. There wouldn't be time. It's nothing but eating, sleeping, and playing music twenty-four-seven.

Fuck.

"I, umm. We're on a break right now. We're taking some time off from touring. I'm not sure when we will again. But locally, we're playing."

My bright smile is an illusion of the turmoil spreading through me.

How could I have been so damn stupid to think this could all work out? There's no way in hell I can leave my daughter. Not even for music.

Music is the life force keeping me going. Or was it? Maybe Lyric is the only thing I need now to make life worthwhile. Since she entered my life like the little hurricane she is, the weight of everything has lifted off me. Internally, I'm so much happier than I was a year ago on the road in Europe, playing for sold-out shows.

"That's cool! I'm always watching on FlashGram to see your

pictures. You guys are so good. Gah! Thank you so much!" she squeals, running her words together as she backs away, grinning.

At least I could make her day with something so simple.

Lyric watches the exchange with inquisitive eyes, watching Penny's every move as she makes her way back behind the counter.

"One day I be famous," she says with a grin, digging into her first mouthful of ice cream.

Famous, my ass—is what I want to say. There's no way in hell my baby girl will live this lifestyle. It's rough being on the road for weeks at a time. It's more than that, though. Drugs run rampant. Fans are fucking crazy. And I don't want her exposed to the wildness of being famous. But I also want to give her a chance to spread her wings and make her dreams come true. I'll do anything for Lyric. Even if it means mentoring her through something as crazy as rock and roll. Or acting. Or modeling. Whatever she wants. She can have.

"What would you want to do?" I ask, tentatively tasting the crazy, sparkly concoction on my spoon. "Well, I'll be damned," I mumble, shoving the strawberry-tasting ice cream into my mouth. "I think you're onto something here, Little Blue. This ice cream is pretty good."

She grins at me, giggling when she shoves another bite into her mouth. "Told ya, Daddy."

While Lyric is distracted with her treat, I pull my phone out of my pocket. Immediately, my heart drops when a notification from my bank card displays on my screen. Fraudulent Charges Detected. Followed by an alert that my card was locked until I called in and spoke to my advisor. Fuck. What the hell? Has someone been using my account to buy things? Why haven't I been getting any sort of alerts on my phone?

Lyric and I fall into an easy conversation as I type out a message to my financial advisor asking about my accounts. Lyric talks on and on, telling me about her all-day preschool and how she's the youngest and smallest but claims to be the smartest. It makes me laugh when she grins, exposing her teeth full of sparkles.

"I'm the smartest in the class, Daddy. That's why I gots to start early this year."

"Oh, yeah?" I grin, setting my chin in my palm, watching with rapt attention as she hums into her ice cream and babbles more. I think I could listen to my baby girl talk all day long and never get bored.

ME

> Hey man, My card got declined. I got an alert, too, that there was fraud charges? Just looking in to see what's going on.

TEDDY

> Hey, Kieran. Let me take a look.

I tap my nail on the table, waiting patiently for a response from Teddy. It could be something as simple as fraudulent charges or something else.

I furrow my brow when my phone lights up with a call from Teddy. He never calls. It's usually just text messages or face-to-face meetings with this guy. It's fine by me, too. I loathe talking on the phone.

"Hey, Ly. Daddy needs to take this, okay? It's an important call." She nods, digging into more ice cream, and licks her lips.

"Hello?" I ask, leaning back in my chair, keeping a sharp eye on my daughter.

"Hey, Kieran. Sorry for the call. I was just checking over your accounts. And there's a problem."

"What is it?" My heart leaps into my throat at his hesitation. I know I'll still have money in other accounts, but years of living hand-to-mouth have me panicking. I know what it would feel like to wake up with nothing.

"It got declined because there's been a stop put on the card by the bank."

I blink several times, my head fucking spinning.

"I've been out of the city for a while. Why would the bank do that? And is that because of the fraudulent charges?" I try to get the world to stop spinning as his mouse clicks in the background.

"I'm looking at it right now. It looks like there were hundreds of charges at places around town within the last two weeks." With every word he says, the more strained he becomes.

"What places?" My jaw tics on instinct, no matter how hard I try to hide it. "And why wasn't I notified immediately?"

"Sorry, K. I'm not sure why you weren't notified. I'm looking into this immediately. There's been charges at Riggs. Jenni's Purple and Lace. Blooming Deals. There were more purchases at several clothing shops and even a purchase at the Coach and Prada stores..." he trails off, clicking more. "It looks like the last purchase was made about an hour ago at Florence's, a department store downtown. They tried to spend—" he chokes off, coughing into the phone. "Twenty grand there." Jesus. Fucking. Christ. Twenty grand? At a damn clothing shop? Who the hell has enough balls to not only spend my money but do it in the same town I reside in? Maybe that's why they didn't fucking call?

Either way, I'm fuming. That's my hard-earned money someone is blowing through. They have no right. I stood on stage for hours on end, singing my heart out. Sweating. Fucking losing my personal time. All for my career to pay for the things I need.

"It was just used?" My teeth clench together. "How is that fucking possible? I didn't give anyone access to it."

I had an extra card in my wallet for emergencies. A duplicate card to hand to my fucking mother so she could buy a few groceries. But I always made her give it back to me. Shit... Pulling my wallet out, I check through my cards, and my heart drops. It's gone. Someone used it in town. Someone took my card. Either Gloria stole it from right under my nose, or someone took off with it.

My stomach turns several times when my phone beeps, alerting me to a new call straight from Florence's Department Store.

"Hey, Teddy. I gotta go. Thanks for the information. The store is calling right now. I'm going to head there." We quickly say our goodbyes and hang up in time for me to answer the call from the store.

"Hello?" I ask, still watching Lyric happily eat the rest of her ice cream, oblivious to the murderous feeling churning inside me. She hasn't moved an inch since this whole shit show came to my attention.

"Hi, this is Angie, the store manager down here at Florence's. Am I speaking to a Mister Kieran Knight?"

"Yeah, that's me," I say, stiffening my spine as a wailing echoes through the damn phone.

"I'm calling to inform you that we've detained a Gloria Montgomery for theft of merchandise. She's asked us to call you before the police get here. We were also concerned after confiscating a credit card with your name on it after it came up as stolen. The police have been called."

I swallow hard. My rage swells like a violent storm pounding through me. I curl my fingers into a fist, ready to pummel my hanging bag to let out some of my aggression. But first, I'll have a few words with Gloria before I let them haul her conniving ass away.

Now, I need to focus on keeping this aggression locked inside so Lyric never sees this side of me.

Not only did Gloria steal merchandise from an upscale department store, but she also stole from me. Not only my money but she also robbed me of fatherhood. It's time to let her manipulative ass rot in jail. Because after today? She won't have anyone on her side to bail her out.

"Do you want to stop this? Or—" she trails off over the phone, knowing full well who I am.

Fuck that.

"Keep her there. Tell the cops I want to speak with her before I press charges against her."

"Okay, Sir."

And we hang up.

I heave a breath, running a hand down my face. My mother. Fucking Gloria. She must have done it at some point when she was desperate for my money. It's been like this since we moved her here with us. Constantly texting and calling us, begging for it. The only reason we've put up with her for this long is for our little sister, Cami. We've tried to protect her every step of the way. Including sending her to a private boarding school on the edge of town to get her away from Gloria's shitty parenting. After Asher's father went to prison, everything fell apart for them. We were the only people who picked Gloria up by her arms and coddled her ungrateful ass. It's not like she deserved a penthouse apartment or money from us. She's never been thankful. Always so damn greedy when it comes to what we earned.

She only saw us as dollar signs. Never humans. Never her fucking sons. So once and for all, the time has come to sever ties with the woman who gave me life.

"Lyric," I sigh, reaching across to clutch her little hand as she sets her spoon down. "I need to run an errand. It's right next door..." I hesitate a moment, not really wanting to take Lyric into this hostile situation. I want to protect her from Gloria's manipulating ways. But a part of me wants to show Gloria what she missed out on by sending River away. Not that she would have been a good grandma, anyway.

"Okay," Lyric says with a shrug. "But you didn't eat your ice cream, Daddy." She points to my melted ice cream glittering in the sun shining through the windows.

"We'll come back, and I'll try it again. I liked it, but Daddy has to take care of something important."

She nods, jumps down from the chair, and takes my hand as we walk to the last meeting I'll ever have with my piss-poor excuse for a mother. No... Gloria. She's no one's mother. She's a user. Manipulator. And her reign of terror ends now, including her hold over Camilla, our teenage sister who luckily lives in her own dorm at the local prep school. Our mother has never been there for her. Never protected her from Nigel's fists, like she should have. So, we did the only thing we could do on our end to keep her safe from Gloria's clutches. Since Asher's father went to prison and now, I'm sending my mother's ass there, Camilla will fall into our hands.

ME

> We're going to have to enact plan 'Save Camilla'.

AKA beg our lawyers to give us custody of Cami and prove our mother unfit. It shouldn't be too hard, but it'll be a huge leap for us. Another reason going on tour would prove harmful.

ASHER

What? What happened?

ME

> Get the lawyers on the phone...Gloria's been stealing money from me... And is getting arrested.

ASHER

Shit. I'll call the lawyer. The school. The landlord of Gloria's apartment...any other place?

ME

> Nah, man. Thanks, tho. I gotta take care of this. Can you meet me at Florence's? Apparently, she stole my card... And I've got Ly...

ASHER

Yes. On my way.

48

Kieran

NOTHING PREPARES you for facing down your own flesh and blood. Especially when that person is your mother. My life bringer. The one who carefully cooked me in her belly for nine months, shot me out, and then ruined my fucking life.

She's the one individual who is supposed to look after you. Not take advantage of you. Not steal from you—multiple times. Fuck. Her. The only person that matters now is Cami. I'll protect my sister from everything.

"Mr. Knight."

I stop dead in front of the manager's office with a grim expression, clutching tight to Lyric in my arms. Her eyes dart around, soaking in everything happening. Maybe it was a mistake bringing her with me. But I couldn't pass this up and let Gloria go straight to jail without knowing what I have to say.

Gloria and I are about to have a lot of words.

"Yes. I'm Kieran Knight," I say, holding out a hand to the police officer standing guard outside the door. "I was told my mother was here?"

His lips roll tight, and he nods. "Yes. We were told you wanted to speak to her before we took her in. And that you wanted to press charges?"

"I do. For using my credit card without permission. I have the records with my finance guy. He'll be able to prove without a doubt it was her who spent over fifty-K of my money." I seethe on the inside, thinking about all the cash her grubby hands got onto before I was alerted.

"Okay. We've got her for theft of merchandise with a value of over a thousand dollars," the officer says, looking down at his notepad.

"What exactly did Gloria try to steal?" I ask with a tic forming in my jaw again. Shit. Even saying her name now puts a bad taste in my mouth.

"Diamond earrings," he states flatly with thinned lips.

"I'm here," Asher says breathlessly, wiping his hand across his forehead as he jogs toward us.

"Daddy!" Lyric lights up at the sight of Asher, grinning at him over my shoulder where she's snuggly cuddled against my chest.

"Who is that?" the officer asks, eyeing Asher with concern.

"My brother."

At that, the officer drops his shoulders and nods.

Asher grins, stepping right into his element. Being a damn good father. Nothing lights up his face more than baking, cooking, and helping Lyric with whatever she wants.

It's like he's trying to prove the exact same thing I am. We are not our fathers. We take responsibility and love the little human we created. Or I created—but that's semantics. We're all fathers in Lyric's eyes.

"Did you have fun?" Asher asks, cocking his head to the side with a chuckle. "Looks like you ate some sparkly ice cream." Shit. I didn't even think to wipe her face off before we left.

She immediately nods. "Daddy and me had lots of unicorn ice cream. I ate all mines. Daddy only took a few bites." She side-eyes me with so much sass I choke on my spit.

How will I survive raising a tiny little River clone? At this rate, she's going to give me gray hair before I'm thirty. And so will

River. Lord. Thankfully, I have the other three guys to balance out the chaos.

"It was good, Little Blue. Daddy just had an important phone call." That's the understatement of the century. Vital. Life changing. All those words ring through my mind.

"Come here, Little One," Asher says, curling his fingers in her direction as she practically climbs over my shoulder and into his embrace.

"I'll—" I stare at the door holding Gloria, whose soft, pitiful voice wheedles through, infiltrating my damn ears and making them ring. She's crying inside, begging someone to believe her that she didn't do this.

"Take your time, man. Are you—" I know what he's asking without uttering a word.

"She stole from me." My lips roll together. "After everything we've done for her. She stole from me, and I can't..." I shake my head. "After what she did to River." My eyes cut to Ly, who listens to our conversation, tilting her head like she's soaking it in for later. "I'm done with her."

God. She's going to tell River everything that happened today. Not that I'd keep anything from her. But I know kids. They're little blabbermouths. So, it looks like I'll be having a good old-fashioned sit down with River about what's to come. Especially with us taking custody of Cami and having her stay with us through the summer and being financially responsible for her, too.

"Okay. We'll be here," he says, kissing Ly's cheek. "Why don't you show me your favorite YouTube videos? You can use my phone."

"Yay!" Ly claps her hands as they walk around the corner and away from me.

"Okay, I'd like to speak to her now." And with that, the officer opens the door to the makeshift hell housing my distraught mother.

"Mr. Knight?" a tall woman with the name tag Angie on it, indicating she's the store manager, asks as I approach.

"Yes, we spoke on the phone," I say, giving her a curt nod.

"Oh, Kieran! Thank God you're here! Tell them...tell them you let me use it! They don't believe me. They-they took your card, and then the police showed up. Tell them, Kieran, that I'd never take something that wasn't mine." Gloria heaves a breath, watching me with tear-filled eyes. Metal handcuffs clink against the table she's tied to every time she tries to reach for me.

"Sorry for the theatrics, Mr. Knight. We were alerted of fraudulent charges through our computer system. But we found this in her purse first." I scowl when Angie holds up a pair of diamond earrings glittering in the low, fluorescent lights of the room. "We watched your mother through the cameras walking around. It was brought to our attention by a few customers that they saw her tossing these into her purse after removing the packaging." She side-eyes Gloria, glaring at her with rage sparking.

Gloria thought she could pull one over on them. And if she couldn't have, she thought I'd talk them out of taking her to jail by paying for the earrings she stole.

No chance in hell.

My jaw tics. "Do you mind if I have a word with her before you take her?"

"Take me? No! Kieran, tell them, sweet boy. I didn't know those earrings were in there! I'm being framed!" she cries out, wrestling with her handcuffs again, trying to scurry away from the situation like the bug she is.

"Absolutely, Sir." Angie spins on her heel and closes the door, leaving Gloria and me alone.

The air shifts as my anger rises, snuffing out the warmth of the room. Cold shivers run down my spine as my fingers curl again at my sides.

"I swear," she breathes with big, pleading eyes filled with tears.

"You swear what? That you didn't take my credit card? That

you didn't spend thousands of dollars of my money? Or that you didn't steal those earrings. Tell me which one; I'm dying to find out." I raise a brow, pacing in front of her as she hunches her shoulders, looking as small as possible in my presence.

I'm not buying her sweet little mouse act. She's the fucking snake in the grass. And the orchestrator of my damn demise. Everything Gloria does is for herself. No one else matters in her eyes. We're all pawns in her little game of chess.

Well, not anymore.

Gloria sniffles, rubbing at her nose the best she can. "You gave it to me."

"Enlighten me, Gloria. When did I give you my card?" I cock my head when her bleary eyes meet mine, filling with more moisture.

She's not sad because she thinks she hurt me. There are only tears present because she is upset I found out.

Gloria scoffs, shaking her head in disbelief. "You gave it to me, don't you remember?" Fucking gaslighting bitch.

"Nope," I say with as much indifference as I can.

I learned a long time ago not to give into my emotions around her narcissistic ass.

She rolls her eyes. "Get them to drop the charges. You and I both know you can just pay for those earrings yourself. I didn't take that card. You gave it to me before you disappeared off the face of the earth. It hurt." More tears fall down her cheeks as she looks away, twisting her expression into anguish. "It hurt that you left and didn't even tell me about it. Did you go on another vacation? I could have come, too. You know?"

"Vacation?" I scoff, staring up at the ceiling. After a few big breaths, I look at her pathetic self again.

"Yeah. So, let's just go, Kieran. You know I don't belong in prison."

"See, that's where you're wrong," I say, placing my hands on the table she's attached to. "It is where you belong. I'm tired of bailing your grown ass out of situations you shouldn't have been in the first place."

She blinks several times, turning a beautiful shade of red. "Kieran Knight, you drop these charges against me and pay for those earrings, or I'll... I'll—"

"You'll what? Move away? With what money? And with what freedom? After this, Gloria, I'm going to walk out of this room and forget your existence."

"You'll never see Cami again," she hisses in a rage, pulling at her handcuffs again.

"I think you have that backward. As we speak, Asher and I are gaining custody of Cami. So, it's you who will never see your kids again."

"You can't fucking do this, Kieran!" she cries out, slamming her fists into the table. "I'm your mother!"

"My mother? Were you my mother when you brought strange men to our apartment and kicked me out without shoes on? Were you my mother when you got married and let some man put his hands on me? Leaving bruises and broken ribs? Were you my mother when you fucking offered Asher money to leave the love of my fucking life behind? Which instance were you my goddamn mother?" I heave every word, spitting my rage at the woman throwing a fucking temper tantrum in front of me. My lip curls back when she throws her head back, manically laughing in my face.

"Oh, please." She levels me with a thunderous look, losing all the theatrics from before. "If I hadn't done all those things, then you wouldn't be here. Life is fucking hard, Kieran, and it's even harder when someone leaves you with an ungrateful brat. I did you so many favors in life, including not informing you of River and the bastard child."

Don't hit your fucking mother. Don't fucking throw her into the river down the way and go to jail for murder.

"Bastard child?" I ask with a calm I don't feel. It's nothing but storms and fucking violence brewing inside me.

Gloria scoffs. "It wasn't yours anyway. She was fucking around with that damn Van Drake boy. Probably for the better. He seemed happy to help her raise the baby." My fucking blood boils to a dangerous rate at the sound of his name.

"So, that's why you did it then when you offered Ash the money? And forged restraining orders. So, River couldn't ruin the gravy train of money coming your way?"

"Those restraining orders were nothing. Judge Drake and I concocted that plan, and then he sent Van away so she couldn't poison anyone else with her lies. I also let Asher know about the videos Van had stashed on his phone," she says, rolling her eyes again. "It was easy to put the pieces together and rid you all of the vermin she was. Nothing but a slutty Central girl looking for an easy paycheck."

"That's rich coming from you," I say with a little chuckle. "Is that the whole reason behind it? Because you saw yourself in River and wanted to get her away from me?"

"She was only going to bring you down," she howls. "I knew girls like her."

"You mean girls like you? That's what you did. You sunk your claws into the first man who reeked of money so you could move us to a mansion on the greener side of town. But nothing was greener about that fucking house. You can't sit here and tell me that you enjoyed his fists?"

Her face hardens at the talk of the abuse she endured under Nigel's roof. "It doesn't matter anymore. He's in jail."

"Again, because of you. I'm curious. Did you think all his wealth was going to come to you once they slammed the prison door shut? I bet you never imagined they'd freeze every asset and sell it, did you?"

"It wasn't supposed to go like that," she says through clenched teeth. "All that was supposed to be mine. I..." She rolls her lips together.

"Do tell, Gloria," I say, spreading my arms wide. "There's no one here but me." And the cameras in the corner of the room. It seems my mother has a lot to confess to now that she's caught.

Her back stiffens, and her chest puffs out. "His partner and I had it all planned out. So, we called the feds and set it up so it looked like Nigel was the one skimming money. Once Nigel was out of the picture, we were going to take over and elope. It was all supposed to be mine, but he fucking...he fucking took off too, with the rest of the money. He left me." She sniffles again, heaving an angry breath.

"So, you both set Nigel up to go to prison and then, he fucking left you, too? That's hysterical." I can't help but fucking laugh at Gloria and the shitty life decisions she's made. Now, she'll go to prison for theft and more fraud.

"There's nothing funny about it! He took all the fucking money and left me homeless, hungry, and without a cent to my name! Kieran, he left me like everyone has always left me."

Ah, there it is. Gloria has always looked for love in all the wrong places. Manipulating herself into other people's pockets and circumstances. But the one thing she's always been afraid of is getting left behind.

Seems like her nightmare is about to come true.

"That's when I stepped in, huh? I offered you a cushy life here. All you had to do was sit back and let me take care of Cami. But you couldn't do that, could you? You had to go and fucking ruin it by spending money that wasn't yours. You stole my card. You stole my fucking money. And on top of all that, you stole my life with MY daughter."

Gloria's head snaps up, locking her gaze on me. "Your daughter?"

"If you had managed to do an ounce of research on the girl you were damning to a life without the boys and me, then you'd have found out that River West is Corbin West's daughter. You know, West Records' founder. Then, you'd have known that she received an inheritance. She's also our band manager now. And the baby she had? That was mine. She's four now. Well, five on Saturday."

"What?" she hiccups, staring at me like a deer caught in the headlights.

"So, thanks for all your meddling," I say sarcastically, tossing a hand in her direction. "But, I'm pressing charges now. You stole over fifty-K from my bank account, not to mention the additional twenty you tried to spend here. Don't expect any visits from us while you rot in prison." I stand straight up and waltz toward the door with a light feeling pulling my shoulders out of my ears. "Your lease is gone. Everything in your apartment is ours. You were afraid of people leaving you with nothing. Well, now you really have nothing. I won't bail you out. No one will. Your desperate acts won't work on anyone. Have a good life, Gloria. I hope you fucking rot."

Parting shots fired, I slam open the door with force, nearly knocking it off the hinges, and race out of the room. Once outside the door, I look over my shoulder at the devastation I left behind. There she sits, the woman who thought she had it all, but now, she has nothing. Her vacant eyes stare straight ahead, and she hasn't moved an inch since I walked away.

Good.

"I'm all done here, thanks," I say, giving the officer a tight smile. "Um. Did you happen to get that interview on camera?" I ask, shutting the door behind me. "Because it sounds like Gloria had a few sleazy things up her sleeve."

"Yes, Sir. We'll look into it with the feds and let them know what we caught." The officer extends his hand, and I grab onto it, shaking it with a breath of relief.

"Thanks, Officer. If you need anything else from me, here's my number." Quickly, I jot it down on his notepad and walk away.

I'm sure in the future there will be more I have to do. Maybe go on the stand and tell the court how awful she was. For now, I'm walking away with my head up and my anger gone.

Gloria is in the past.

"Hey, Man," Asher says, standing up from a bench outside. My eyes fall on Lyric as she smiles at his phone, swaying to an upbeat kids' song blasting from the speakers. "Everything good?"

"That was a shit show," I confess, rubbing at my forehead. "She stole earrings, but yet, stole my card, too. She..." Asher clasps my shoulder, gently squeezing in support. "She admitted to fucking everything. She set up your dad to go to prison."

"Good fucking riddance," he mumbles, shaking his head.

"She admitted to what she did to River and... Fuck... I don't know how to feel about this," I whisper, swallowing hard. "She was a horrible fucking mother..."

"But she was still your mother." Asher nods in understanding. "That's how I felt about my dad. I hated him with every fiber of my being. He was an abusive loser. But he was still my dad and... It's confusing."

"It is." I trail off, staring at Lyric, mentally making a vow to never be a bad fucking parent. I'll make mistakes, but I'll own up to them every time.

"We got this, man. Every step of the way. Okay? We'll make sure Cami is ours. We won't have to worry about her getting hurt by Gloria."

"You talked to the lawyer?" He gently squeezes my shoulder again, dropping his hands.

"Yeah. Talked to him earlier about applying for custody. He says we have a really good chance since we're the brothers, and no one else in the family would volunteer. So, we probably won't have a fight on our hands. It helps we're financially secure and can prove we've been taking care of her, anyway."

"Thanks, Asher. I don't think I could have gone through with this...with anyone else."

"What are brothers for?" he asks as a smile pulls at the edge of his lips.

"Brothers," I hum, clapping him on the shoulder. "How about we get this baby home? We've got lots to plan for."

"Plan for?" Lyric asks, staring between us.

"Yup!" I say, picking her up from the bench. "Let's go home."

Together. As a whole fucking family. No more Gloria. No more stalkers. It's just us rebuilding what we had before into something bigger and better.

This is our future.

49

THE SUN BEATS DOWN, warming us on one of the last September days. September 29th. The most special day in history. On this day, five years ago, I was blessed with the most beautiful surprise. My baby girl. The one being who majorly helped me through my depression and rage. It's because of her that I'm living.

Every morning, she brings a smile to my face. Every question she asks or piece of vital information she thinks I need brings joy to my life.

This is where I'm meant to be. Right here. Right now. At Lyric's ultimate unicorn dream.

The boys really came through when they promised they'd rent out the entire East Point Amusement Park. With little to no bribing, they were able to procure it for us at the last minute. Although the bastards refuse to tell me how much it cost them. Stating they were paying for the entire thing, and that I had better just smile and take it like a good girl.

Okay, that last part may have been during one of our few sessions in the bedroom. I may have thrown out the whole going slow thing, because it's not really working out for me. I've never been one to hold myself back from what I want. Or what my body craves.

My heart soars with what they've done for Ly already. And for me. They're proving themselves over and over again. Making me proud to have forgiven them completely and given them a much-needed second chance.

We've been happier than ever, figuring out our new life together. Slowly, of course. I'd never jump into this without caution. Only idiots repeat their mistakes.

Happy children's laughter echoes through the festive air only amping up at the promise of cake amusement park rides later. Family and friends gather around in large circles, catching up with soft drinks in their hands. As the kids play in a circle in front of us with glee.

Nothing beats today.

"You invited your mafia sister?" Rad hisses, not so discreetly staring at my sister, Journey, with wide eyes.

I snort, stepping into his side with a shake of my head. The four of us stand in a little circle on the blacktop, watching the chaos unfold.

The moment my brothers tracked each of us down and handed out our inheritances, we started a family group chat. Some participate fully and others don't bother at all. The ones who do respond to the texts have really become our family through blood and bond.

"She won't hurt you. She's harmless." I shrug, grinning when Rad shudders. From disgust or fear, I'm not sure.

My sister, Journey, may be a little out of her mind sometimes, but she wouldn't start anything here. Not at her niece's birthday party. Who she adores, by the way. Besides, I love Journey. Despite only knowing her for two years, she's become someone I can talk to and depend on.

A sister.

I have my brothers, but she gets me. Like really gets me. I would never tell my guys she threatened to come here and slice their toes off as a threat after she learned about what they did.

"You told me her and her boyfriends—"

"Husbands. They're her husbands." My eyes cut to her three husbands surrounding her like a protective wall, not permitting anyone from getting too close. Especially people they don't know. Liv casually hugs Journey in a tight embrace, rubbing a hand over Journey's engorged belly with a grin. I can't hear what they're saying, but they all seem to be smiling. You'd think three mafia kings wouldn't want a Veritas agent in their midst. And that'd be true if Liv wasn't their cousin.

What a weird West web we've created. It's gotten so big my damn head hurts just thinking about my siblings. All fourteen of them.

"That's Arrow, Jericho, and Shepp. And yeah, they're in some sort of mafia type thing." I shrug; I'm not sure what they actually do. I'd rather stay ignorant if they're committing crimes. Especially if they're sinking people in the river with concrete shoes.

They're family. That's it. They've never threatened us. Seger and Zepp seem to like them, too. So, that's a plus. Even Carter tolerates them to an extent. And he doesn't like anyone except his wife, Kaycee.

I point each of them out to Rad, adding in a little wave when Jericho narrows his eyes at me and then grins, waving back. See? For being the head of a gang, he sure is pleasant and polite. Maybe a little crazy, but that's a whole other book I can't dive into right now. Too much to tell and not enough time to explain the dynamic between my sister and those three. Let's just say they purposefully got her arrested, then bailed her out, and then... Handcuffed her to them so they could keep her forever.

Totally normal stuff. But she's happy. Even when she tells the story, she laughs her ass off.

"I've heard stories from that town..." Rad trails off when Callum snorts.

"Are you afraid of the Briar Cove Devils?" Callum asks in a soft voice, leaning in to kiss my cheek. "They're nice. You should talk to them."

"Yes. Yes, I am. I've heard what they do. They...they...pluck eyeballs, remove fingers, and—"

"Shut up," I mumble. "They're here to enjoy Ly's birthday party. They brought their kid."

I swear Journey hasn't been *not* pregnant since I met her two years ago. Including now. Her guys make a circle around her as she sucks on a large, chocolate ice cream bar like a protective entourage. They watch her every move with love in their eyes. Every once in a while, they gaze at their two-year-old toddling around, following his older cousins—Roman, Axel, and Dash— around with a grin. Ly giggles as the boys chase her, squealing when one of them taps her shoulder. Grabbing her cousin Maggie, she drags her away with a loud yelp as they all continue to run around.

"Miss West!" Kat, my assistant, calls out from behind me, hurrying along at a quick pace.

Turning, I raise my brows as she saunters forward with a grin on her face, holding tight to a large white box filled with Lyric's cake.

Perfect.

It's amazing to see how well she's come into her role as my PA. Not even a few months ago, I wasn't sure if she was going to make it. I'm not sure what happened in her life, but she was a trembling mess. Now, I'm more confident than ever that she's going to continue to help me in my department as the Fixer.

"Kat," I laugh, shaking my head. "Please, I've told you a thousand times to call me River."

She blushes when Rocco saunters up to her side and carefully helps her with the white box filled with Lyric's sparkly unicorn birthday cake.

"Hello, Doll," he says, kissing my cheek. "Mullet. Cal," he says, nodding a greeting.

"Rad. It's Rad. Hell, call me Ashton. But don't disrespect the mullet," Rad quips, fluffing his curly hair in his hands. "The mullet is sacred, dude."

"Sacred in the early 90s, maybe," Callum quips quietly under his breath.

"Heard that!" Rad hisses, lightly shoving Cal as he belts out a laugh while stumbling over his feet.

"I've got the cake," Kat beams, tapping the box. "It's perfect. Just like you ordered. Ly is going to love the unicorns!"

"Thanks so much for picking it up for me," I say with sincerity.

"It was no problem. Now, where do you want me to put it?" Her eyes dart around the enormous amusement park we've rented out. The only people admitted are the ones standing around this large, open courtyard.

The park graciously supplied a few security guards at the gates, turning around customers trying to enter. And keeping us all safe. Not to mention the plethora of Veritas agents wandering around and enjoying the party. They're no doubt packing heat under their shirts just in case anything happens.

Large roller coasters sit off in the distance, darting into the clouds and then plummeting to the earth. But those are off-limits with no attendants running them. The only rides we'll have access to are the small ones for the kids. Unicorn planes, the carousel, the fun house, and a mini-roller coaster make up our little Unicorn hell hole.

I'm not sure what it is about these magical horses with horns on their heads. She loves them, though. More than loves. She's mildly obsessed with them. Even that's putting it lightly. So much so we've had someone redecorate her room with the exact colors and unicorns she wanted as part of her birthday present. The moment she sees it tonight, she's going to flip her lid.

"We have a spot over there," I say, pointing toward a group of picnic tables nestled under a large pavilion.

"Thanks! I'll get it over there. Trevor is in the parking lot, grabbing the cooler of ice cream treats." She shyly grins, looking away at the mention of his name. Her boyfriend. The one we've only heard about and never seen.

My brows raise. They must have made up from the last time he went away without a word.

She's never brought him around. He's always working or busy when he's invited to places. Office Christmas party? He was out of town. New Year's party my brothers threw? Sick. The list goes on.

He's so damn elusive, and we've never even seen his picture. According to Kat, he hates having his photo taken. Seems odd to me in this day and age. Who hates their picture being taken? Or who doesn't have social media?

Joe from *You*, that's who.

"We finally get to meet the ever-elusive Trevor," Rocco quips, with interest flaring in his eyes as he walks in front of us.

"Yes," she blushes, ducking her head and taking off toward the pavilion without another word.

"I didn't think we'd ever get to meet him," I say, watching as she happily sits the cake down.

"Me either. Hopefully, he's a loser," Rocco quips.

"Pfft. With the way she's been getting happier, I think they're getting serious. Back off, Roc." I raise a brow when he pouts.

"Fine," he grumbles, pulling away. "Time to say hello to my Godchild. Oh, Lyric!" he shouts, jumping into the fray of kids and hoisting her into the air. She squeals at his antics, kicking her feet as they spin in a circle.

"I like him," Asher says, cocking his head and watching Rocco play with Lyric.

I snort. "You might be the only one." I point to Callum, Rad, and Kieran standing side by side with their arms crossed over their chests, watching Rocco's every move.

Fucking cavemen. They should know by now Rocco is nothing more than a very important friend. To me and Lyric. Besides, he's married to Christian and on the prowl for Kat's undying love.

"I need to make you another shirt," Rad grumbles, wrinkling his nose. "Property of Callum, Rad, Asher, and Kieran."

"Good idea," Kieran says with a smirk. "We'll force it over your head any time you leave the house."

"Everyone will always know who you belong to," Rad adds with a grin, high-fiving Kieran over their oh-so-brilliant idea.

I roll my eyes, raising my middle finger to them. "I'm not your damn property. I belong to no one. If anything, you're mine. Maybe I should make you a shirt that says... River's Boys. See how you'd like that."

"You're under the impression that we wouldn't wear a shirt with your face on it," Rad says, raising a brow. "I would, in fact, wear a shirt that says I am your property. In fact..."

Well then. That didn't hit like I thought it would. Who am I kidding? Of course, they'd want a shirt with my name on it. That wasn't a proper threat.

"We'll get them made," Callum snorts, covering his lips with his fist.

"Hell yeah! We'll wear it at our wedding. Speaking of... Will you marry us, Pretty Girl?" he asks, smirking at me.

I huff. It's been like that for the past week or so since we got home. Every morning, I have a text asking if I'll marry them.

"No."

"I'll ask every day until you say yes," he reminds me, kissing my cheek. "I'll wear you down, Pretty Girl. Then you'll be all ours. Forever and ever. I can't wait to stick a ring on that finger." His arm wraps around my shoulder, pulling me further into the side of his body. "Do you think anyone would be offended if I took my shirt off? It's fucking hot."

"Keep your clothes on, Cowboy. This is a children's party."

"Make me those fancy sleeves again, Pretty Girl. Or I'm going to drown in my sweat." Rad pulls his T-shirt away from his body, wafting air on his face. His tongue flops out of his mouth as he huffs. "I don't even care if you cut me with your knife. In fact... cut me a lit—"

"Kids party," I hiss, covering his loud mouth with my hand.

"He's going to start having to pay a fee every time he runs his mouth." Kieran side-eyes him with a smirk.

"Thirty thousand dollars!" Lyric says, passing by, doing a twirl in her pretty, multi-colored unicorn dress. Quickly, she darts off, laughing through a candy sugar high.

Lord help us when we have to tame this baby tonight.

My heart hurts as I watch her carefree smile light up the party. She's five now. Practically a teenager. Just yesterday, I gave birth with my brothers anxiously awaiting her arrival in another room and Kaycee generously holding my hand as I screamed. Even though it made her light-headed and awkward feeling. She stood by my side, knowing I didn't have anyone else to help ease the pain of having her and losing my boys.

My baby is growing too fast. And there's nothing I can do to stop it.

"Thirty thousand," Callum confirms, holding out his hand expectantly.

Rad licks my palm with a chuckle until I rip it away, wiping my hand down the front of his T-shirt.

"Fine. I'll keep my shirt intact," Rad harrumphs, pouting a little until his eyes fall on my face. "Pretty girl, what's wrong?" he asks, squeezing me tight.

"She's five," I groan, swallowing my emotions. "She's so big."

"She is," Kieran agrees, watching her with a big grin.

"That's a good thing, right? We want Little Pretty Girl to get bigger and grow older." Rad watches my glossy eyes, softening his confused expression. With ease, he pulls me into his side and kisses my temple. "She'll always be our baby."

Oh, swoon. Our baby. Fuck. Don't tear up. Don't show them how messed up your emotions are since having her. I swear I've turned into a pile of gooey feelings, crying at the drop of a hat. Damn hormones.

"I know. It just feels like yesterday that I went to the hospital and had her." I shake my head, reliving the memories again.

"Next time, we'll be there." Kieran's eyes fall to the ground. "I promise."

"Next time?" I ask, scrunching my nose.

"Oh yeah, Pretty Girl! You gave a baby to Kieran. Now the rest of us want a little one. Can you imagine my baby with a mullet? He's getting a mullet." He side-eyes the guys. "Don't laugh at me." I snort when they start to bicker amongst themselves.

"You really want more?" I ask with slight vulnerabilities.

"Thousands." Rad waggles his eyebrows.

"Or four." A slight red tint creeps up Callum's neck and onto his cheeks.

"We'll get to that bridge when it comes. In the meantime, we can practice as much as you want," Asher says with a cocky grin, winking at me.

"We'll enjoy the baby we have now," Kieran adds, grinning when Lyric spins in front of him with a giggle.

"Daddies, I wants to go to the fun house," she says, pointing toward the two-story unicorn house with funny mirrors and bright lights flashing.

"Whoop! Then let's go to the fun house!" Rad scoops Lyric into his arms, chuckling when she giggles more, and we all head off toward the fun house thirty feet away from the courtyard.

"After this, we'll do your cake and ice cream," I say, catching up to her and kissing her cheek.

"Hey, girl! Want me to get that set up?" Olivia asks, running up to my side. "Hey, cutie pie." She pinches Lyric's cheeks, much to her disapproval.

"Hey, Liv," I say, leaning in to hug her with a grin. "That'd be amazing. We're going there, and then we can do the cake."

She agrees, rushing off toward the cake as we leave the area, walking to the fun house.

"Wow, this is bitchin'," Lyric says with a grin, staring up at the house.

"I'm sorry. What did you say?" I huff, raising a brow at my baby girl, who has a knack for saying words she shouldn't.

"Bitchin'. Cousin Roman says it alllllllll the time." She raises her chin with confidence, huffing at my downturned face.

"Sorry, Little Blue. That's a bad word. You shouldn't say that ever again." Kieran shakes his head, using his best dad voice to get the desired effect. I can tell the moment sadness crosses his face. He regrets being so stern.

Lyric's lip pouts out, and she nods, sniffling. "Okay, Daddy. I'm sorry. But you says it all the time."

I put my hand up to my lips, holding back the laugh that begs to escape. She has them there. They curse all the time without consequence.

"Fuck she's right," Rad groans, quickly covering his lips. "I mean, she's right. No more cussing."

"I can't be mad at that," Kieran whispers in my ear frantically, watching her pouty lip.

"You have to be," I mumble, leaning into his side. "She won't learn unless you correct her bad behavior. You did good." He perks up, kissing me on the cheek when I applaud his effort.

"Let's go," Callum says with his eyes lighting up. "I'm going to take her through," he says excitedly, holding out his hand.

Lyric doesn't waste a moment, grabbing onto his hand and practically dragging him through the entrance of the fun house, which happens to be a rolling, dark tunnel.

I smile when she falls, giggling as the piece continues to slowly roll them. Thankfully, Callum grabs her and drags her through the curtain at the end, and they venture into the unknown.

"Shall we?" Kieran asks, sweeping a hand out with mischief behind his eyes.

"You want to go?"

"Why not, Pretty Girl? Let's go through the fun house and look at ourselves in those ridiculous mirrors. I haven't seen one of these in so damn long."

Without a second thought, Kieran grabs my hand, pulling me

forward. The three of us shake with laughter as we enter the turning tube, losing our balance halfway through.

I fall over my stupid feet, plummeting to the moving ground with a thump.

"Fuck," I grumble, trying to balance myself to stand, but it doesn't work.

And wouldn't you know it? Those assfaces didn't wait for me either. There they are, laughing their heads off at the end of the tunnel, watching as I continually fall.

"Crawl to me, Pretty Girl," Rad quips, wiggling his fingers in my direction as he stands under the black sheet hiding the rest of the attraction.

I grin, shakily moving forward on my hands and knees until Rad's hands grips under my armpits, and he pulls me into the darkened room, only lit by neon LEDs.

"Holy hell," I murmur, leaning my front against Rad's, heaving a breath. "This place is crazy."

Kieran chuckles, kissing my cheek from behind. "Let's keep going."

"Yeah. Let's... But you guys have to catch me," Rad shouts, taking off at warp speed out of the darkened room and through another set of curtains.

I blink through the darkness as Rad's body heat disappears, and he whoops in the distance.

Kieran chuckles, holding me close. "I think he's having more fun than Ly."

I grin. "It's nice to let loose some days and pretend we aren't adults." I lean my head against his shoulder, soaking in the warmth he's offering me in the midst of darkness.

"Should we keep going? You never know what he's going to do."

"Yeah."

Hand in hand, Kieran and I stumble through the dark room, listening to the echoes of giggles from somewhere above us.

Callum's deep chuckle, which I would recognize from anywhere, slips through as Lyric screeches with happiness.

"I'm beyond grateful we're a part of her life now," Kieran murmurs, pulling me through the next set of curtains and into a wacky mirrored room looking more like an unsolvable maze.

"Shit. Which way?" I groan, looking back and forth as nothing but mirrors filled with our bodies stare back at us. "And where the hell is Rad?" Who knows where that slippery fucker went off to. Knowing my luck, he's hiding in the shadows, ready to scare the shit out of me.

"I would have reached out," I whisper, twisting my face. "No matter how much I hated you guys, I wouldn't have kept her from you. But the restraining order...and that phone call...I'm sad you missed it all."

"Well, we won't anymore. Okay? We're here."

"Gotcha!" Rad screeches from somewhere, throwing his hands around me and pulling me back into his chest.

"Ashton!" I yell as the warmth of his body encases me, and the smell of his cologne pulls me in.

"God damnit, Rad!" Kieran hisses from somewhere in the distance.

The mirrored maze disappears completely as Rad drags me into a small room, closing the mysterious door behind us.

Stale air smothers me as I look around at the tiny room filled with excess parts and props. I blanch when a clown in the corner catches my attention, forcing my heart out of my damn ribs.

"Heya, Pretty Girl," he murmurs in my ear. "Fancy seeing you here..." he trails off with a menacing chuckle, promising me naughty things in the future. I swear my whole body relaxes the second he spins me around and places his hands on my hips.

His eyes darken further when he looks me up and down, staring at me like a delicious meal he's about to devour. Something I don't doubt. My body vibrates with anticipation. Not only with what we're about to do but with the wrongness of this, too. Here we are at a children's party and funhouse, about to fuck like bunnies.

"Where is here, exactly?"

"Storage closet," he says, grinning as he slowly backs me up against an oversized wooden box until my thighs slam into it. "I needed—" His brows furrow. "I needed some time with you," he whispers, kissing my cheek. "I'm desperate for you, Pretty Girl. So fucking needy."

"You just wanted to take your shirt off," I whisper, running my fingers through his silky mullet, pulling his curls between my fingers.

"Well, it is about to get even hotter," he murmurs, licking at my flesh with a satisfied groan.

"Rad!" Kieran shouts from outside the room, oblivious to where we are. "I swear to fuck, dude!" he grumbles, knocking so hard the walls of the storage closet bow with the force. "I'm going to kick your ass when you're done."

"Or you could join!" Rad shouts with a chuckle, darting his hand underneath my T-shirt.

"He's not invited to this party," I whisper, thrusting my tongue into his mouth.

Our breaths mingle in heavy pants as our tongues collide in a desperate dance of lust. I groan into his mouth, pulling my body even closer to his, feeling every inch of his want.

The warmth of his fingertips pinches my nipple through my bra, causing goosebumps to explode over my flesh. I buck my hips, chasing friction.

"Fuck me, Rad," I groan as his lips travel down my neck. "Make it fast. We gotta make this quick."

"Anything for you, Pretty Girl," he hums against my flesh, reaching down to undo my jeans.

His fingers dive into my denim, underneath my panties, and straight into my throbbing pussy, begging for him to fill it up.

"You're so goddamn wet already," he groans, hastily thrusting his fingers inside of me.

"Yes. Now, fuck me," I beg again, sinking my nails into his neck as I ride out his fingers thrusting roughly inside me.

"As you wish, my queen." Within seconds he removes both our jeans, tossing them to the dusty floor. Another problem for another time. All I care about right now is him taking care of this need brewing deep inside me.

My veins catch fire when he lines himself up with me. Toying with my entrance. The head of his pierced dick moves up and down my slit, teasing me until he's finally had enough.

Our moans fill the air when he enters me in one quick thrust, bouncing my body. My legs wrap around his hips as I lean back on my hands, letting him pound wildly into me.

My breath hitches when his lean fingers wrap around my throat, gently squeezing until my airflow is slightly constricted.

"I fucking love you, Pretty Girl," he moans, leaning in to take my lips hostage with his.

"I love you, too," I wheeze, squeezing my eyes shut.

"Look at me," he groans, forcing my gaze back to him. "That's it, Pretty Girl. I can tell how close you are. Your pussy is squeezing the hell out of me. So, cum with me," he begs, biting into my bottom lip, leaving behind the smallest hint of blood.

"I'm cumming," I cry out as my pussy contracts over his cock, ending his movements with a loud groan, filling the room.

Whoever else is making their way through the funhouse will know exactly what's going on inside this little closet. If they could find it, that is.

I shudder against Rad's hold, coming down from the aftereffects of my orgasm. The whole world tilts as I stare into the darkness of his eyes, reveling in the lust sparking there.

"I'm going to just live in your pussy. Little Rad likes his warm home," he rasps, brushing his lips lightly against mine.

"No," I laugh breathily, slightly shoving at his chest. "That's not going to happen." I groan, leaning into his kiss as he softens inside me.

"I love you, Pretty Girl."

I stare into his dark eyes, memorizing the moment. "I love you, too."

"Come on, asshole!" Kieran bangs against the outside again, still unable to find the door Rad snuck us through.

"Think we should head out?" Rad asks, reluctantly pulling out of me with a groan, pouting as he tucks himself back into his jeans.

"Probably. Ly was eager for her cake." Shit. We fucked inside a fun house while a whole ass party happened outside these walls. I guess that's the perk of having four guys in my life. They pick up the slack with the kiddo while I get boned within an inch of my life.

Well, when I put it that way...

I'm a terrible fucking mother. Guilt slams into me. This was supposed to be a quick, fun family adventure. And I let myself get caught up...

"You're doing something funny with your face, Pretty Girl. The one you do when you're feeling guilty about something," Rad says, bending down to grab my jeans from the floor. When he looks up, his entire face softens. "You're thinking something, aren't you?"

I wrinkle my nose, stepping into my jeans. "I...guess I feel guilty sometimes when I leave her to—" Do things like this. Drink wine with the girls. Go out with Rocco and leave her with Maggie. If it weren't for my brother's insistence I have a social life, I'd be a hermit.

"Pretty Girl," he murmurs, buttoning my jeans and straightening my bra and shirt. "You're an amazing mother. Even if you snuck off to have a one-on-one session with your boyfriend. She's probably having the time of her life. Cal has got her. We've got her. Ly will never wonder if she was loved and cared for. Sometimes moms have to take care of themselves. Or, let their boyfriend take care of them." He winks at me, kissing me one last time. "Now, let's put poor Kieran out of his misery."

I grin, grabbing his hand as he pulls open the door to the

mirrored room. Kieran stands beside it with a frown, shaking his head.

"Walls are thin," he grumbles, adjusting himself. "And Liv is looking for you."

"Okay. Let's go cut some cake," I say, leading them out of the fun house.

"Oh, thank fucking God!" Olivia shouts with tears in her eyes, throwing her arms in the air.

"What's wrong?" I ask, searching her concerned face.

She pales. "We can't find Lyric."

50

River

"WHAT?" I breathe, looking around the park, frantically trying to spot Lyric in the people milling around with their kids. "What the hell does that mean?"

Panic doesn't even begin to describe the feelings bubbling to the surface. My fingers tremble, unable to stay still. Possibility after possibility runs through my mind. All ending in the worst-case scenario.

"Deep breaths. We think Lyric just went to play some hide and seek," Olivia says, putting her hands up.

"Whoa. Wait. She was with Cal," Rad says, pulling me into his side and rubbing a hand up and down my upper arm in support. "Don't freak out yet, Pretty Girl. Kids do this all the time."

Freak out? I'm beyond freaking out. My breaths come in short pants. Adrenaline pours through my damn veins until I'm a trembling mess. My daughter is missing, and everyone thinks it's normal. It's not. This party is about her. Making her the center of attention. Something she can't pass up. If Olivia is frantic and pale-faced, then something is truly wrong. You can't convince me otherwise.

"Look at me, Riv. We're at a huge amusement park. She probably wandered off with one of the other kids, and they were playing. Cal turned his back for five seconds to grab a drink for them, and when he turned around, she had taken off. We'll find her." Olivia gives me that Veritas look she loves to give me when she knows she's right. Or wants to prove a damn point. She's awful fucking bossy sometimes.

"I'm so sorry, Little Star," Callum says with tears, looking on the verge of a freakout. "I didn't... I would never..." His gaze falls to the ground. Hiccups fall from his lips as he tries to take deep breaths.

"It's okay. She's probably trying to find her favorite ice cream," I say, squeezing his hand with reassurance. "You didn't do anything wrong. She could have done this with anyone. Even me. She's five. They're slippery at this age." I try to give him my best reassuring smile so he doesn't continue to beat himself up. But it doesn't work. His face falls, and tears slip down his cheeks.

Olivia claps a hand on his shoulder, taking control of the situation before we all start slipping into hysterics.

Ly is probably having fun somewhere with one of her cousins. That's it. She hasn't been kidnapped or abducted by aliens. There's a perfectly rational explanation for this.

"Believe me, that child wanders when she wants to. Something probably caught her eye. Maybe a balloon or a unicorn. We'll all split up and look for her," Olivia demands, looking each of us in the eye. "Calmly and collectively. The partygoers are helping, too. There's no need to freak out yet, okay? Last we saw her, she had come out of the fun house with Cal. They went to the hut, fifty feet away, to grab a drink. No one saw her slip away when Cal put in the order. Remember, she's wearing her unicorn dress. Riv, you've got a picture?" When I nod, she nods back. "Good, send it to all of us. We'll start canvassing the area and trying to find her. Since it's just us in the park, maybe call her name or call out her outfit."

My heart races in my chest when I bring the photo up on my phone and send it to everyone I can think of at the party.

Someone will see her. Or find her. They have to. She can't be too far away. It's her damn birthday party.

Right?

"You two, start over there," she says, pointing to me and Asher, who stands rigidly beside Callum with worry in his eyes. "And you two over there, you two over there. Okay? You all have your phones?" Everyone nods in silence as the situation sits heavy on our shoulders. "Good. Please message me. I put my number in each of your phones when I had them on your trip to Central City. And I'll meet you wherever. I will check over by the entrance and canvas, making sure she didn't make a break for it."

My eyes follow her finger, pointing to the right where the unicorn carousel stands still, and the tall roller coasters stand beyond that.

"Okay," I breathe, sucking in air, trying to clear my muddled brain.

"We'll find her, Little Brat. It'll be okay," Asher whispers in my ear, gently taking my hand in his.

Together we walk as a unit, splitting off from the rest of the group as Olivia directs them to different areas to search.

I swallow hard, remembering Lyric's words from this morning.

"Mommy, I can't wait to ride the unicorn ride. The one that spins in circles and has pretty music." I grin as she twirls in her dress, going round and round with a squeal of pure joy.

It was one of the first rides she begged to go on when we stepped foot in the park.

I heave a breath when we all separate. Echoes of Lyric's name being shouted through the park rattles my nerves. This isn't like her. She doesn't wander off. She...

"She's going to be okay," Asher says, clinging to my hand as we walk around the carousel, sitting hauntingly still in the middle of the day.

The sun blares down on us without a cloud in the sky. It's the perfect day to celebrate a birthday. If the birthday girl wasn't missing. How could this happen in such a short period of time? How could she just wander away without anyone noticing? Doesn't this place have cameras? My heart drops more. Desperation claws at me. I need her in my arms.

As we make our way around the ride, the operator casually lounging back in a chair catches my eye.

"Maybe," I mutter, pulling out my phone and bringing up the picture of Lyric from this morning. "Excuse me, Sir. Have you seen this little girl?" I ask the operator as he lounges back in his chair.

A toothpick hangs from his mouth, jolting around when his tongue rolls. He pushes his sunglasses down to the tip of his nose, staring at the picture of Ly in her pink, purple, and sparkly unicorn dress, smiling at the camera.

His brows raise as he checks it over and gives me a sharp nod. My heart leaps out of my chest with hope latching on.

"Yeah. I saw her about five minutes ago. She was walking with some guy in a red zip-up hoodie." He shrugs nonchalantly, pointing in the direction of the rollercoasters.

My heart drops. Red hoodie? Who the fuck was wearing a red hoodie? Everyone I saw was in T-shirts or dresses. It's seventy fucking degrees right now.

So, who the hell has my baby?

"What? What did he look like?" I stumble over my words, begging my heavy tongue to cooperate.

"About this tall," he says, holding his arm up. So not fucking helpful. "Brown hair. That's about it."

My eyes dart around when we take a few steps away from the operator. Someone has her. She could be anywhere. Fuck. With trembling hands, I let Olivia know what I just found out so she can keep an eye out in case anyone wants to leave.

Thoughts scramble in my head. Ly has never taken the hand of a stranger she...

"Up there," Asher rumbles, turning paler than a fucking ghost. His entire body vibrates, pointing toward a giant roller coaster in the distance as he squints against the sun. "She's up there with someone on the boarding platform."

With someone. It repeats in my fucking head. Someone. Not anyone we know. A stranger. I follow his line of sight, gazing at the tall roller coaster in the sky. My daughter sits at the entrance of the tallest ride in the park at the boarding platform. With a stranger holding her hand. High in the sky, barely visible from where we are. The only colors streaking in the wind are the multiple colors of Lyric's unicorn dress. And the dark red hoodie the person wears to conceal themselves from us.

It's her. But who the fuck is he? Who has Ly? It's not anyone in the family. They'd have sent a message.

"Who the fuck is it?" I growl, taking off in the direction of the rollercoaster. Fuck common sense. Fuck it all. My soul calls out to the little being I created, needing her to be with me.

Not him.

"I don't know!" Asher shouts frantically, chasing after me at a quick pace. "I just called Olivia about where we're headed and that we saw her."

"Good!" I shout, running toward the coaster and up the paved slopes carrying me up, up, and into the fucking clouds.

My heart pounds in my ears, drowning out everything as I run behind Asher at full speed. At some point, probably because he's athletic, he passed me, giving me his back and leaving me in the dust with my heaving lungs.

When we finally get to the top of the entrance, I stop dead, slamming into the back of Asher with a quiet umph.

"Shh," he murmurs, looking at me over his shoulder with furrowed brows. I nod shakily, swallowing hard when Lyric's little voice filters through. It takes everything inside me not to jump into action and scoop her up.

"I want my mommy," her little voice sniffles quietly.

"You'll see her again," the unfamiliar man's voice says, carrying through the rock-like surroundings encasing the entrance to the roller coaster currently not running.

It's deep. Gruff, even. No one I recognize from my life. Has some crazed person followed us here? The boy's fan? My brother's fan? Fuck! Another stalker? It can't be mine. He's fucking dead. All the possibilities run through my mind in overdrive.

"I want her," she cries again, yelping when he does something to her.

I tense. Every instinct inside my body screams for me to run in there and save her. I need my goddamn baby to be safe.

"She'll come!" he says in a sharp voice through heavy breaths, causing Lyric to sniffle hysterically again. "She'll come. Now, quiet."

"We need to do this slowly..." Asher's eyes fall on the man with his back to us. His red hoodie clings to his body, and the hood covers his hair.

Asher pulls out his phone and carefully checks his messages, updating Olivia on where we are and that we need help immediately. Also, snapping a picture of him and sending it on. With shaky fingers, Asher connects a call to Olivia and leaves it in his hand, letting Liv hear everything that happens. Hopefully, with her training, she'll record everything for later. In case this all goes sideways. But if the swooping in my stomach is any indication of how this will go, it won't end well.

"This room echoes. You know?" the man in the red hoodie calls out. "I can hear every word you say. It looks like your mommy finally made it," he sing-songs the last part mockingly. "Let's get this party started. I'm tired of waiting."

My heart falls into my ass when he spins around toward us with a black gun nestled in his hand, pointing it toward my baby clutched in his tight, unrelenting grip. Tears work down Lyric's face as she trembles, but she doesn't pull away. Whatever fear she has, she knows she needs to stay still.

The moment my eyes collide with his, I die a little on the inside—those eyes. I know them. I recognize that face. It's someone I saw a week ago at Dead End. Someone I just happened to run into. Maybe it wasn't such a fucking coincidence that he was there.

Donavon fucking Drake. That is the whole reason the boys left. The videos he kept. The way he stalked me back then. My nightmare has followed me here. But why? Why him? And why the fuck now? I already had one stalker. I don't need another psycho in my life. Besides, Olivia checked in on him multiple times, assuring me he was gone. He was in Europe. Away from here. But yet, here he stands with a weapon in his hand, smiling maniacally.

"Rivey, so good to see you again," he coos, tilting his head to the side with a sadistic grin.

My lips pop open, and I shake my head. "Van..." I trail off in horror, shaking my head. "I don't understand..." His grip tightens on Lyric's arm when my eyes dart to my baby in the clutches of madness.

"The one and only..." His eyes immediately dart to Asher, who stays in front of me, protectively covering my body with his. "What the fuck is he doing here?" His teeth grind together as his eyes narrow in on Asher frozen with his hands up. Van wildly waves the gun in his direction. "I told you! You are mine, River West! You both are!" Van shouts erratically, stomping his foot.

I stiffen at his words. "Y-yours?" I stammer.

My heart threatens to punch out of my chest when he throws his head back, laughing like a loon.

"Mine. All mine. You always have been. How do you feel knowing your guy here sold you out? He came to me. Begged ME for those videos..."

"Why did you take videos?" I breathe, stepping around Asher. "Why would you do that? That's gross." I shake my head, begging to keep his attention on me so Lyric and Asher can run away.

Now would be a good time for Olivia or Carter, or fuck, I'll take Jordy, to show their faces with guns blazing and take this asshole down for good.

"Stay back," Asher hisses through his teeth, trying to grab my elbow.

"No more," Van hisses. "You've touched what's mine for far too fucking long!" In the blink of an eye, he raises the gun in Asher's direction, waving it around.

"Whoa!" I shout, stupidly jumping in front of Asher. "Van. What the hell is going on? Explain it to me!" I scream, bringing his attention back to me. "Look at me, Van. Explain what's happening." I lower my voice, trying to sound as calm and collected as possible. Something I don't fucking feel right now. Panic takes me over when he doesn't lower the weapon, leaving it pointed in Asher's direction.

His face hardens—a twitch forms in his right eye, highlighting his loss of composure.

"Oh, right. I'll explain everything to you, Rivey. Just let me touch you. I need to fucking touch you," he pleads with desperation. "Let me feel you, baby."

Fat chance.

"Let Lyric go," I say, motioning toward my baby still in his clutches.

For as long as I live, the haunting expression holding her captive will keep me up at night. Somehow, Lyric has retreated inside herself, no longer blubbering, or trying to pull away. She's a shadow of nothingness. I need to take charge of this situation before she sinks too far into herself and I'm unable to pull her out. My baby doesn't deserve to live through the pain of Van's obsession. I've protected her from this for so long.

"No," Van snarls, baring his teeth. "I let our child go, and you'll take off again and let these assholes raise her. You are both fucking MINE!" His voice echoes off the walls, filling the room with his rage. It's so visceral, the tiny hairs on my arm stand on end.

My breath catches in my chest, refusing to refill my lungs. Our? He's delusional. Concocting this fantasy that Lyric and I are his. His? Really? My mind races out of control. What the fuck do

I do here? I'm so out of my goddamn depth. I need to get Lyric away from him. I have to think on my fucking feet to get his hands off of her and onto me.

It's time to save my baby and Asher. No matter the cost.

I inch forward, avoiding Asher's desperate glare to keep me within his reach. His head shakes with limited movements, like he's reading my mind.

"Okay," I say, holding my hands up, placating the asshole. "Let's just talk, Van. Okay? Let's work this out. You can touch me. Just let her go." I swallow razor blades when his eyes light up, traveling up and down my body with intense interest. Disgust fills every molecule of my body when he zones in on my breasts, licking his lips. I shiver, holding back the vomit threatening to spew from my throat.

I can do this. This is for Lyric and her safety. For Asher. For everyone else he wants to injure. I can only hope Olivia gets her ass up here before anything else can go wrong.

"River," Asher begs with choked emotions as I inch closer to Van. Every step I take is a nail in my coffin. "Don't," he pleads, reaching a hand out to pull me back.

But I'm too far gone now. Lyric is the most important thing in my life, and I can't lose her. She's my baby. I'll fight tooth and nail to keep her safe. Even if it means putting my own life on the line. Shoot me. Not them.

"Don't you fucking put your hands on her again! She is not yours! She has never been!" Van cries out, lifting the gun in Asher's direction.

I'd rather endanger my life than have any harm come to Lyric or Asher. It's my job to protect her. My fucking duty as a mother. And I obviously didn't do enough to keep her from his grasp. Somehow, he swooped in when no one was looking and stole her from us.

By why? How? How is he even here?

"What's going on, Van? Why are you doing this? Why are you

here?" I whisper, wincing when his angry gaze whips to me and he points the gun right at my heaving chest.

Sweat prickles along my neck the further I walk. With small, measured movements, I inch across the platform until I stand directly before him until the gun pushes into the middle of my chest.

A breath away—within reach.

I turn everything inside of me off, shutting down. If this is my end, then that's it. I've had a good life. Fought the good fight. If it helps Asher and Ly make a break for it, then it was all worth it. They're worth it.

"I had to get your attention somehow. You blocked my calls. I couldn't see you anymore! You wouldn't even talk to me without turning your nose up at me," he growls angrily in my face with a hint of betrayal sparking in his eyes. "So, here I am," he says, lifting his chin in victory.

Every ounce of emotion vanishes from his face when he looks into my eyes. Blank. Dark. Nothingness. Reminding me of his expression at Dead End when I watched him from afar. I try to hold back the flinch when his finger runs down my cheek, caressing me like he used to.

"I've been watching you, Rivey. Protecting you from the shadows. You should thank me for the pictures I took. I had to look at you through your cameras to make sure you didn't do anything stupid."

My lips flap open and closed at his words. My stomach drops at the realization. Sharp memories float through my mind of the stalking I endured at the hands of...

"It was you?"

"Finally, you get it. It was for your own good. I had to keep my girls safe, Rivey. I had to make sure you two were always protected..."

"But Adrian. That... that guy!" My stomach clenches, threatening to spill the treats I had earlier. "He-he..." I stammer, reaching for the words desperate to escape my lips. "No. No. Not you..."

"Killed himself? I know. It was so tragic. But someone had to take the fall. Your little agent friends were getting too close. I had to throw you off the trail. And my poor cousin needed to die." He scrunches his nose at the thought, turning my stomach more. "They took you away from me! You should have stayed in East Point. You should never have run from me! I can't believe you didn't like my gift."

Red blood flashes in my mind. My pictures splayed across my front porch. Dripping. Red. Lyric's screams. It all scrambles in my mind.

"It was always you?"

Hopefully, someone with a gun will get here soon before someone gets hurt. It's the only thing holding me together.

"When they left, he promised me I could have you! He said you'd run right into my arms like they never existed!" His shouts reverberate off the walls again when he yanks the gun from me and points it in Asher's direction with a snarl. "But you didn't. And I was sent the fuck away by my father. An internship. Like I fucking wanted anything to do with my father's career." He rolls his eyes, scoffing at the idea.

"I never promised you anything," Asher says with a fake calm, taking a step forward. His wide, hazel eyes dart to Ly, checking her over as she stands still in Van's grasp. "I never said she'd be yours. I said she might come running to you for support. But that's it." He swallows a lump in his throat, his eyes darting to me as if he's trying to convey a silent message meant for the two of us. "But I know now that I made a mistake that night. I should never have come to you for help." He shakes his head. "I never should have done what I did."

"Shut the fuck up!" Van howls, stiffening his arm. "You're a goddamn liar. You all used River."

"Like you did?" Asher retorts, cocking his head with confidence.

"I didn't use her!" Van shouts manically, waving the gun around. "I didn't do anything! She was mine!"

"Yours?" Asher scoffs, continuing to step even closer to us despite my silent protests.

No. No. Please. Step back. Don't come any closer. I've got this.

"Yes," Van growls, gritting his teeth. "I put my claim on her a long time ago. You had no fucking right to touch what was mine." He shakes his head back and forth, squeezing his eyes shut.

My heart drops into my ass when Asher lurches forward, grabbing Ly by her other arm and yanking her out of Van's death grip. She stumbles forward into Asher's arms with a frantic yelp, knocking her out of her stupor. It's a small reprieve from the craziness going on around us, like time stands still.

"Go," Asher yells. "Get help, baby!" He urges her, throwing her toward the door with tears in his eyes. "Please!" He begs, stepping toward her, frantically hurrying her along and herding her toward the opening.

Tears stream down Lyric's face when she stumbles away from us. Her eyes dart back and forth with uncertainty. Trembles roll through her tiny, frozen body, shaking every inch of her.

"Mommy," she sniffles, taking a step toward me with wide eyes, staring straight at the barrel of the gun, pointing at her tiny chest.

"No!" I shout, gluing my eyes to Van and his movements. Something depraved brews behind his dark eyes as he calculates his next moves. Lyric was his leverage. And now, she's out of his grasp. Will he harm her, too?

"If I can't have her, then no one will," he says, staring directly into my eyes. A void opens in his dark eyes. There are no emotions resting behind them. Just a black hole of nothingness. "No one touches what is mine, again," he says with a deadly calm—the calm before the shit storm about to rain on all of us.

An ache pangs across my chest when he cocks the gun and fucking fires it. No hesitation. No second thoughts. Like this was all a part of his plan. A small smirk pulls at his lips when my body flinches back and my gaze darts to my helpless child, standing stock still.

The bullet careens in Lyric's direction, like a fucking missile aiming straight at her little chest, which heaves out of control as sobs flow from her throat.

I can't fucking move to protect her from harm's way. I can't stop the bullet from speeding toward her little body. Everything is spiraling out of fucking control, and I can't stop any of it from happening.

"No!" I shout as the loud bang reverberates off the stone walls. My fucking ears ring as the noise from the blast blocks everything out. I cry out, covering my ears from the closeness of the sound, deafening everything.

My eyes dart to Lyric, checking her for injuries. I make a move to run to her, despite the gun still hanging in the air, but a strong grip grabs the back of my neck, halting my retreat. Helplessly, I watch from a distance, cataloging her body inch by inch. Her shrill, frantic screams fill the room, penetrating through the static in my ears.

"Go!" Asher shouts, jumping directly in front of her with a fierce expression, pushing her once again and knocking her back.

All the color drains from my face. With an umph, he gasps out, grabbing at his calf. Those wide, hazel eyes connect with mine, darkening as he shouts out in pain, and hops around.

"Again," Van chuckles, pulling the hammer back and firing directly into Asher's thigh.

The blast deafens me further, and I wince, trying to focus on Asher. I pull. I yank. I try to break free. I'm ten seconds away from kneeing Van in the nuts to flee, but he pulls me against him with a satisfied hum.

Asher's eyes widen, rolling into the back of his head when the pain takes him down to his knees.

"I'm sorry," he gasps out, barely audible for me to hear him.

"No!" I grasp Van's forearm, trying to force the gun from his hands. If I could make it fall to the ground then he'd stop shooting Asher, and I could break free.

"Oops," Van grins, firing one more shot into Asher's upper leg.

All the color drains from Asher's face when he falls over onto his back, staring up at the ceiling. He blinks several times, heaving desperate breaths, but the pain is too much. Every tight muscle uncoils in his body, falling limp until he's carried away into unconsciousness. Dark red blood pushes through the fabric of his jeans, staining the fabric at an alarming rate. I don't know much about anatomy, but getting shot isn't good. Even if it's just one leg.

"Asher!" I screech, trying to pull away from Van's embrace again. My foot stomps into his but does nothing to loosen his hold. If anything, he clings on tighter with his painful grip. Digging his fingertips into my neck and holding me hostage.

"Stop fighting me!" he grits out in my ear, pulling me further into him. "You'll never fucking fight me again after all these distractions are out of the way. You're mine. For fucking ever, Rivey."

Sobs wrack through my body as I helplessly watch my entire world fall apart. Tears roll down my cheeks. I can't get away. I can't save anyone in this room.

"Run," I croak out, trying to gain Lyric's attention.

Her saddened gaze locks on Asher lying lifeless on the cold ground with blood trickling out of his leg from the three wounds, no doubt ending his life. He doesn't twitch or fucking react. His chest barely moves with his labored breaths. If we're not careful and don't get the help we need, he'll be fucking dead.

Lyric is frozen, unable to move when she needs to run. Her soft whimpers spear through the room, infiltrating through the static clogging up my ears.

"Daddy!" she cries out, twisting her face in anguish at the sight of him. "Daddy," she whimpers again.

"NO!" Van shouts, huffing against the side of my neck when he raises the gun yet again. "He's not your daddy."

Lyric's eyes dart to mine, gliding over my tear-soaked face and onto Van. Her tiny head shakes at his statement, not understanding him.

"He is my daddy," she says through a quivering lip, standing tall. "And you hurt him." A fierce expression pulls at her face, narrowing her eyes at him. Her tiny fingers form fists at her sides, like she's about to pounce on the asshole behind me.

"Get help," I croak out again through my bubbling emotions. "Ly!" I shout, clinging to Van's forearm and digging my nails into his flesh. He doesn't budge, but the grunt in my ear lets me know I'm inflicting some sort of damage.

"Run!" I shout through my fear, waving a hand at her to get a move on. If Van has a chance, I'm sure he'll take her out, and I can't fucking witness that and do nothing.

"Mommy!" she quivers with uncertainty, wavering where she stands tall.

"Run, Lyric! Don't look back!" I grunt when Van grabs my hair in his tight grip and abandons my neck. His sickly long fingers weave through my locks, holding me firmly in place. I couldn't move even if I fought again. But it should be me. Not her. I can take this trauma—something she shouldn't have to endure. "Run and get help! Run, baby!" I shout when he lifts the gun again, pointing it right at her stomach.

My skin crawls—my heart races. Stars burst behind my eyes as I gasp for air. The walls close in on me rapidly when his hands land on me.

Lyric's eyes dart between us, frantically taking the picture in. She tries to step toward me. I'm her protector, the person in charge of keeping her safe. She wants to dive into my arms and never let go. But I can't right now. I shake my head as best I can, straining against Van's hold on me.

She needs to run before he does something stupid like hurt

her. He could fucking shoot her, and then my life would truly be over. She needs to get the fuck out of here.

"Run, baby! Don't look back at me. Please!"

Get Liv. Get the fuck out of this shit show—is what I want to shout. But I can't give Van any more ammunition. If he knows we have help just steps away, he might do something drastic.

With one last little whine of despair, Lyric runs out of the entrance. My ears ring again, overtaking everything when the gun explodes. My breath hitches when I try to pull away, desperate to chase after her. Or jump in front of the bullet myself. Relentless tears pour down my face when the dust finally settles, and Lyric is nowhere to be found.

A single hole rests in the stone wall with dust billowing from it. She's safe. Lyric is safe, running to get help for Asher. Van can take me. Do whatever he wants to me. As long as Lyric is safe. And Asher gets the ambulance he desperately needs.

My mind swirls as the room softens and all the noises come to a halt. The static in my ears eases away when Van lowers his gun, staring toward the entrance where the bright sun shines through.

Why is this happening?

Van was the one who broke up with me. He sent me away. All because his parents couldn't stand the thought of him being with some Central girl. So, why is he standing here, holding me against my will?

"You see him, Rivey? You see him now?" he asks with a false sense of calm taking over his tone. With the gun in his hand, he grips my chin, forcing my gaze to Asher, lying on the ground with blood dripping like a leaky faucet out of his leg. "He's bleeding and practically begging for his life. How about another shot to make sure he never fucking comes back?" he hisses in my ear, raising the gun again in Asher's direction.

How many more fucking bullets does he have?

His hot breath rolls over my neck as he holds me tight to the front of his body, letting me feel every disgusting inch of him.

Spiders crawl under my skin at the nearness to him. My mind begs me to run. Bile rises in my throat. Desperation claws at me.

"Please don't shoot him again, Van. I'll do whatever you want. Please don't hurt anyone else," I beg, with tears pooling in my eyes and rushing down my cheeks. "Van," I plead.

"I love it when you say my name," he whispers, pressing his lips on my hair. "Say you'll be mine forever."

"I'm yours."

For now. A gag sits at the back of my throat when I say those words.

Until I shoot you in the dick for ever laying a hand on Lyric, me, and for shooting Asher three fucking times. If only I had packed my knife. The same one Kieran gave me all those years ago so I could protect myself. But I left it at home, tucked in my dresser drawer with my other weapon. I was stupid to think I'd be safe at my own daughter's birthday party, surrounded by Veritas agents.

"Good. Rivey. This is going so well. It's funny... When you called Kat to let her know you would be in Central City, I was there. Right beside her, listening as you spilled where'd you'd be. I knew I needed to make my moves. And fucking fast. So, here we are, baby," he coos again, dropping his arm to his side, removing the danger to Asher's rapidly deteriorating state.

Everything seizes inside me, and I blanch. "Kat? My PA? Kat?"

"Yeah, baby. That's the girl. Your PA. I'm Trevor. Her boyfriend," he whispers in my ear, forcing me to step back with him into the darkness of the unknown.

I stumble over my feet, unable to fall forward when his grip gets tighter and tighter. My breaths barely have enough room to fill my lungs as the darkening room takes over my vision. How I long for the sunlight gleaming in. How I long to keep my eyes on Asher's unmoving body.

"I've been him for six months. Did you ever wonder why I never showed my face?"

Trevor, Kat's elusive boyfriend. The one she gushed about being in love with. She cried over him when he went away without a word. He never came to our company parties. Never took pictures. He was a fucking ghost in the waiting, preying on an innocent woman. No wonder we never met him and only heard about their time together.

"Why would you do that?" I croak, sucking in harsh breaths. "That doesn't make any sense."

"Kat likes you. She likes to talk about you and what's going on with you. She was my in. I knew where you'd be every fucking day of your life. I had to date her and be with her to get to see you. It was the only way. And God! Sleeping with her, well, it was a way to be closer to you, Rivey. I could close my eyes and imagine it was your face. Your moans. I still have our movies together. I watch them every night before I go to sleep, fucking her... Or fucking my hand to you. It's sad, but I had to get my info from her. After all, being close to her made me close to you. But don't worry, I don't love her like I love you. Poor pathetic bitch she is. I just had to show her a scrap of affection, and she was dripping wet." He tsks at his manipulation, solely putting the blame on poor Kat, who was head over heels in love with this asshole. "Especially today on our daughter's birthday. I wanted to be here to help you celebrate. You'll love the home I have for us. Well, me and you. That's okay, though. We'll have more children. Just you and me. Forever."

The impact of his words settles on my chest, caving it in. Oxygen refuses to enter my fucking lungs, seizing them every time I open my mouth.

"You dated her for the sole purpose of getting to me? You... You stalked me from the beginning?" I stammer, wrapping my brain around the idea that Van had been following me this entire time from afar, waiting in the shadows as he watched our every move. "Wait... Did you even go to Europe?"

Twisting me around, he forces my back into the roughly textured wall. I cry out when my head knocks into the stone, dazing me. Bright stars burst behind my eyelids. A sharp gasp rings out from between my parted lips.

Van cracks a smile, tsking at me in a cruel mockery. "Of course, I went to Europe, Rivey. Where do you think I picked up the cyber skills that allowed me to watch you from anywhere at any time? I was there for three years, eyeing your every move."

"Cyber skills?" I swallow hard at the information flowing from his mouth like a villain revealing all his moves before he executes them. If I'm not careful with this conversation, bad things could continue to happen. I need to keep him talking and make him reveal everything. "What cyber skills?" Please take the bait. Please spill everything.

It's a good thing this cavern echoes because Asher's phone should be picking all this up.

"My favorite was hacking into your camera system, which wasn't that hard, especially since it was my company that protected your precious home. A little slip of the business card to the perfect person had you right where I wanted you. But I couldn't stay away, Rivey. I was tired of watching you on a screen. So, I came back and created Trevor so I could keep a closer eye on you."

"But—I..." I swallow hard, willing my tears to go away. I have to keep him going and admit to everything he's done to orchestrate this entire thing. "I only got the cameras because of the pictures," I murmur with realization as vomit shoots up my throat.

He grins more. "I needed you scared and desperate for protection. Getting your picture wasn't hard, though. It was easy to follow you around and watch you shop or play with our baby girl. It made me want this more," he purrs with victory. "I'm so sorry I frightened you, Rivey. You were just so beautiful. I didn't mean to scare you; I just needed to keep my eyes on you at all times and keep you safe."

My body shudders at the thought of him watching my every

move through the cameras in my home. "Why... How?" Fuck, I can't get my damn brain to ask the right questions.

Van's teeth grit when his hand tightens on me. "But then they came back and fucked it all up! They were supposed to stay away. They were supposed to never touch you again. You are mine, River. All fucking mine. You'd never know that I've done so many things for you, Rivey," he whispers, putting his forehead against mine. "I saved you from Bradley's attack at that shitty bar you worked at."

"I saved myself," I say, curling my lip in disgust at the thought of my attack at Dead End, resulting in my hospitalization. "I stabbed that bastard. Not you..." I grunt when his hand slams over my mouth, blocking me from talking properly.

"I was supposed to save you!" he lashes out, spitting in my face with every word. "I was supposed to pull you out of that alleyway and be the fucking hero. Me! Not you," he growls again. "And definitely not fucking them!" The entire darkened chamber he's pulled me into lights up with his voice, echoing for what seems like miles. Only a sliver of light from buzzing bulbs above us illuminates his demented eyes. "I set it all up so I could win you back. But you see how fucking well that worked out?" He rolls his eyes, clenching his teeth so tight, I swear he'll snap them into pieces.

"You?" My muffled voice comes through his hand, widening his smile.

My stomach drops, thinking back to when I took out the trash at Dead End and was attacked from behind by Bradley. My former rapist. My abuser. The man who forced himself on me at the party where I drank too much, and Rad saved me.

"Me," he whispers. "You ever wonder why he was at Dead End that night? Why was I there to stop him? I was the fucking hero. And then that piece of shit Kieran beat my face in." He shakes his head erratically. "I hope he makes an appearance soon so I can give him the same treatment. One bullet for every asshole who has put their hands on you."

My breath hitches.

"You're fucking crazy," I murmur through his hand again. "You can't do this, Van. You can't shoot them. You can't take Lyric or me."

A frantic squeal falls from my lips when he presses the gun to my jaw.

"I don't think you're in any sort of position to make demands. This is how it's going to go. You're going to text your bestie that you're fine. Call off the dogs, Riv. Then, we'll go out of this emergency exit and start our lives together before anyone can come to save you." A sparkle lights up his eyes when his free hand digs into my pocket and pulls out my phone. "Unlock it," he grunts, gesturing to my thumbprint.

"Okay," I say, unlocking my phone with my thumb.

"Text her! They'll be here soon. I'm going to leave them with quite the distraction to stop them from making it here." He grins again when I grab my phone, bringing Olivia's name to the screen.

I stare at it for several long seconds, debating what to say. We don't have a code in place for situations like this. Now, I regret not having something. I can only hope Lyric gets to her quickly before Asher bleeds out.

ME
I'm fine. No rusH. Things are undEr controL... Please.

My heart stops when Van zeroes in on the phone, checking over my message before he allows me to hit send. I know the moment he sees my hidden message when he looks up at me and tightens his grip on his gun. He growls in my face—no doubt about to unleash a massive punishment for even trying to send that message.

"I'm not a fucking idiot, Rivey. I may be a little obsessive, especially when it comes to you. But any idiot would see the message hidden. Help? Is that really what you wanted to say? I have more than a gun in my artillery." My breaths quicken when he drops the gun on the ground with a grin and digs through his pocket—never letting me go. Confidence puffs out his chest like he has this entire thing under control.

My breath stalls when he holds up a small object, reflecting off the soft lights above us.

"Boom," he whispers manically, pressing down on a large red button. In the distance, a loud bang rattles against the walls. My spine stiffens as loud screams happen, and he beams more with pride at whatever the hell he just did. "You remember the night we met, Rivey?" he questions without giving me a chance to answer out loud.

It was a chance encounter at the record store. He came in, like he did often after, to purchase his favorite vinyl. Something he started collecting. One thing led to another, and I ended up ass over elbow in the backseat of his Mustang. The worst mistake of my life was ever entertaining this dickbag and letting him use my body for pleasure. The sex wasn't even that fucking great. But by the way he lights up; he thought I was the best damn thing he ever had. Maybe I was. I mean, he is standing before me with a possessed grin on his face, looking off to the side like the memory of our meeting snapped something inside him.

I stiffen when he drops his nose to the crook of my neck, forcing me still. His disgusting breath rolls over my skin, getting heavier by the second. I quickly ignore the hard piece poking into my abdomen when he inhales again and runs his tongue along my flesh. If I had my knife, I'd cut his boner in two and shove it up his ass where it belongs. But I'm a dumbass and left it.

Fucking bastard. Always taking what the fuck, he wants. If I could move a muscle, I'd knee him in the goddamn dick. Or stab him. I swear the next chance I get; I'm chopping that appendage off so he can never harm another person again.

"You don't have to say anything. I'll remind you of it all," he whispers, flicking his tongue over my ear lobe.

"The sun had just set, blanketing the party in thick darkness, which brought out all the freaks. Everyone was dancing and laughing and drinking their asses off. But they didn't notice the most beautiful piece walking through the party. You were by yourself. All doe-eyed and petrified looking. But goddamn, the way you looked so damn sexy. I knew you were a Central girl the moment you got closer. But you never fucking looked at me. You were watching him and his cronies' taking shots by the pool. I knew Knight from school. Hell, I had a fucking band, too! You never fucking noticed me..."

I soak in his confessions one word at a time, memorizing them for later. The truth is, I noticed him at one point in our lives. That we had fucked around so many times and had been in a relationship with each other. Until his parents intervened, we were a couple. Happy, too. But that's all semantics now. Because they did me a fucking favor by pulling him back.

"So I slipped something special into your drink when you got glass after glass. Nothing bad, just something that'd help you notice me."

The world stops at his confession. It was bad enough he was my stalker for the past three years. But this? He drugged me at a party. All these years I thought it was me who had drank too many glasses of alcohol.

I blanch, shivering at his words. "You did what?" My muffled reply comes out in a squeak.

He grins against my flesh. "Yeah, Rivey. It was me. You thought you drank too much, didn't you? Nah. It was the drugs. Me. All me. I knew how to make you fall to your knees and give me what I wanted. Funny, isn't it? You had no idea who took your V-card. Well, you're looking at him." He grins at that, cocking his head when tears flow freely from my eyes and down my cheeks.

I think I'm going to be fucking sick. Everything in my stomach sloshes, begging to cover his hand with my vomit.

"Why wouldn't you just talk to me?" I whisper, shaking my head as best I can. "I don't..."

"Then, I dragged you to a secluded spot... And well, you see where that goes. When I was finished, I tucked myself back in my pants with the intention of killing those mother fuckers who were waiting in the shadows to get a piece. Fucking Bradley. He had his eyes on you the moment he saw you stumbling around. You were mine to take over and over, and they were going to steal you from me. So, I decided to become the hero... I walked away for five goddamn seconds! They got you, and then Rad swooped in and put you in his car. But I never forgot about you, Sweetness. You were all I craved. So, we met again. This time, I made sure you loved me. And you did, didn't you?"

I swear his monologue goes on and on for five thousand hours. He could probably get off on his own damn voice. But the longer I keep him talking and in one place, the better chance I have at surviving this whole ordeal.

"Why the fuck would you rape me?" I hiss frantically, clawing at his forearm, begging him to release me.

The entire time he's been chatting away, he's held me down. Despite the hand still stalling in his pocket. I'm afraid to know what he has up his sleeve next. It can't be worse than the loaded gun by our side. Can it?

"And that's where my obsession blossomed. The feel of you around my cock. The blood you sacrificed for me, baby. It made me want you over and over again. No matter what."

Gag. Fucking hell.

"And my hatred for them was born. Fuck those assholes." He licks my face again, groaning at the taste of my tears. A deep, hollow chuckle vibrates against my body when he steps back, finally revealing the other part of his plan. In the dim light, he holds up a syringe filled to the brim with a clear liquid. "I had a feeling you wouldn't come willingly, so..." Using his teeth, he uncaps it and plunges it into my fucking neck. The second the liquid enters my bloodstream, my skin fucking boils. Heat spreads through my veins.

I cry out, scratching at him until he's finished. He chuckles, throwing it aside with pride puffing out at his chest. He's so fucking deranged; he thinks he did a good fucking thing.

"Have a good rest," he whispers, grinning as he removes his hand from my mouth, watching his masterpiece fall to pieces.

I suck in a few breaths, trying to stay conscious when he lets me go. He hums to himself, stepping back to observe his handy work with a sparkle in his eyes.

The moment he's off me, I slide down the rock wall with a groan. My head fucking pounds from the impact, and my face fucking burns from the barrel of the gun.

Whatever he gave me has my vision blurring, but not completely. No. I'm still in control of my limbs. For now, at least.

"What did you give me?" I slur, reaching around beside me as he hums again with happiness.

My tongue tingles as I try to lift it to ask the question again, but it doesn't work. My fucking time is running out. Along with the light blinking out around me.

"Just something to make you sleepy. Then I can get you to our home without fanfare. You'll love it!" he shouts, bouncing on his toes with excitement. I tune him out the moment he starts listing the things inside this magical house he built for the two of us.

I suck in oxygen as my vision blurs, producing two Vans prancing around in front of me. My ears start ringing, and numbness takes over my entire body.

I fight against the medicine, continuing to feel around me for the gun he dropped in haste to get the drug from his pocket. He threw it like he wouldn't need it anymore. But I do. I swallow hard, which becomes increasingly challenging as the effects wear on me. But determination spears through me as my numb fingers feel the gun thrown beside me.

With every ounce of energy, I have left, I bring it into my lap to hold it steady. All those times, Olivia took me to the range to perfect my skills in case something like this ever happened finally come to fruition.

My time has fucking come.

Just as the darkness takes over my vision and I'm clinging to consciousness, I use my remaining energy to point the gun in his direction. He doesn't seem to notice. Or maybe I'm too far gone. I grunt, squeezing the trigger, praying to the Gods above that this one shot buys me enough time. One shot fires off before the darkness completely takes over, pulling me under the spell of the drug.

I'm either a kidnapped girl walking, or I shot the man responsible for stalking me for three years.

I guess I'll find out which soon.

51

CONCRETE WEIGHS down every molecule inside me, refusing to let me move an inch. No matter how hard I try, nothing cooperates with me. I'm stuck.

A dense fog swirls deep in my mind, clouding my thoughts and erasing all rationale.

Every ache pulling at my nerves awakens, throbbing into existence the more my mind comes back to the land of the living.

What the fuck happened to me? And why do I feel like I got hit by a damn bus, backed over, and hit fucking again?

A softness encompasses my back like a mattress cocooning my body in a soft embrace.

I grunt, trying to move again. Nothing fucking works. My arms are useless. My legs fucking tingle. Fuck! Sludge moves through my veins toward my frantically beating heart, trying to break through my ribcage.

I have to move, or I'll die here. Wherever that is...

My breath hitches when I'm finally able to lift a finger. Fucking finally! That's one finger of many. Only nine to go. Tingling encompasses every digit, slowly waking up from the deep sleep I was in the more I move.

My breath hitches in my throat again as desperation claws at me to get moving. The faster I'm off this bed, the faster I can skedaddle out of this fucking nightmare I've been put in.

One by one, I'm able to shake off the heavy feeling weighing my limbs down and freely wiggle my fingers and toes. Thankfully, clothes rustle with every move. So, I'm not naked. That's a plus.

I blink several times through the grit crusting over my eyelashes, letting my sight adjust to the absolute darkness before me.

It's nothing but shadows. No lights. No sounds. Desolate. A fucking void of nothing.

Have I died and gone to Hell? God, I hope not.

A chill shudders my body as a cool sweat forms on my palms. Through heavy breaths, I manage to force my body into the seated position at the edge of the mattress I was left on. Or, I think it's a mattress. If I could fucking see to figure it out, I'd know more.

I groan as the darkness swirls, forcing my eyes to squeeze shut. What in the ever living fuck is happening right now?

My eyes dart around the fucking blackness, trying to latch onto anything I can. A shape. A light of any kind. But there's nothing. It's like I'm lost inside a damp basement that's a maze of corridors.

I inhale, trying to use my other senses to guide me in the right direction. Nothing but a sterile bleach scent filters through my nose. So, a clean basement? That doesn't make any damn sense. Basements are notorious for a mildewy stench. Has someone created this space just for me?

I shake my head, running my numb fingers over my tired face.

Goosebumps erupt over every inch of my body as I ground myself in the heavy darkness blanketing the entire room.

"Hello?" My brows furrow when my voice echoes through the room like a cavernous space lies before me.

Right. This is how every serial killer movie starts. Poor girl left in the basement. Next, a man with a chainsaw will pop out of the wall and grind my body to pieces as I scream. How fucking morbid... I shake those thoughts out of my fucking head. I don't have time to get all mopey about my newfound situation. I have to think and get the hell out of here.

Now, if I could only remember what the fuck happened to get me here, I'd be in a better place.

"Rivey, I knew you'd wake up soon."

My entire body freezes at the sound of his voice. I run a shaky hand over my forehead, wiping the cold sweat breaking out over every inch of my flesh.

"So glad to see you sitting up! We have so much planned today..." His voice echoes again with a manic laugh from somewhere in the distance. Yet, he sounds like he's all around me.

My fingernails dig into the edge of the mattress, grounding me to the spot. How the hell...

How did Van get to me? Where...

Like a whirlwind of memories, it all comes back to me at rapid speed. Nearly knocking me back from my seated position. My lips flop open, gasping for air.

The birthday party.

The needle at the rollercoaster.

The goddamn gunshot...

Asher!

"What did you do?" I shout through my sudden rage, shaking with every move I make.

I jump to my trembling feet, swaying like a tree in the wind. Fuck. Everything swirls again. I rub my temples, begging for relief from the constant wave of vertigo.

I grunt, stumbling through the darkness with my hand out in front of me. Come on, asshole. Show yourself so I can beat you to a bloody pulp.

My fingers prod my pockets, hoping without fail I brought my knife. Hope blossoms in my chest. Quickly popped by the reminder that I didn't have it with me. Why would I? It was my child's birthday party. I shouldn't have felt unsafe there. Liv was there. Jordy was there. A whole slew of Veritas agents attended as well. Somehow this psycho broke through all the safety precautions we had in place and smashed them to pieces by getting to me.

My brows furrow when his confession rings in my mind. He was Trevor. The elusive boyfriend of my PA. How could we have been so trusting and blind?

"I brought you home!" His voice rings out again from all around me, sounding like an ever-present entity haunting all sides of my life.

"No," I cry out in desperation. "This is not my home! Let me go, Van!" My fingers curl into fists.

Every ounce of fog dissipates into nothing, giving me back my sound mind. Replaced by massive amounts of rage boiling through my system.

I'll fuck him up before he touches me. There's no way I'll let him get his hands on me like he promised. Fuck that. Fuck this. I'm River goddamn West. No one is taking anything from me again. I'll claw his fucking eyes out until he's bleeding on the ground.

"Pretty Girl."

My chest heaves as my eyes dart around the darkened space. Where is he? God, where is he in this darkness? His voice caresses me through the shadows, knocking me back a step. Rad? Is he here to save me from Van's clutches? Or is he a prisoner, too?

Van shot Asher. Will Rad be next?

"Run," I rasp with tears streaming down my cheeks. "Don't come any closer. He's got a gun," I plead, nearly dropping to my knees as they knock together.

"Pretty Girl," he says with a sigh. I swear the faintest touch against my cheek has me jerking back.

My fingers graze against the phantom touch, instantly relaxing me.

"Mine!" Van's voice echoes through the space like a menacing ghost, growling the word. "You're mine! You'll always be mine!" My ears ring at the sound of his frantic shouts.

"No. No. No!" I hiss, covering my ears. "I'm not yours. Let me go!"

"Come on, Pretty Girl!" Rad's voice echoes through my skull with desperation. "You're having a nightmare. You need to wake up. Please wake up. It's been twelve hours already."

Twelve hours? Of what? My unconsciousness? My imprisonment?

I blink several times until a blinding light pierces through the veil of shadows. Squinting against the brightness, I gasp, jolting forward.

My eyes snap open, greeted by the bright lights and a loud beeping sound filling the room. Several articles of clothing rustle beside me, getting closer as I come back online.

"Little Star."

A yelp leaves my throat when I jerk back into a warm embrace. Heavy hands hold me steady, wrapping around my front side. A drum beats in my chest, moving toward my ears and taking over my hearing. My breaths shudder when the unknown hands travel up and down my arm in a soothing manner.

"We got you, Pretty Girl." His voice cracks with emotions, murmuring in my ear.

"Rad," I croak sharply, turning to look over my shoulder.

Warm brown eyes filled to the brim with concern and exhaustion greet my vision.

"Rad," I confirm with a sob, falling apart as he embraces me more. His fingers wipe the rogue tears escaping down my cheeks.

He's here. He's safe. Fuck. I'm safe. There's no longer a stark darkness holding me captive. Just this room. My boys.

"We're so glad you're finally awake, Little Star," Callum says with a quivering voice. His bottom lip trembles when he looks me over, checking for more injuries.

Callum rests in front of me with dark bags blooming under his eyes from lack of sleep. The faintest smile tugs at his lips when his fingertips brush the hair from my face.

"Thank fuck you're finally awake," he whispers with relief sagging his entire body on the bed.

"Awake?" My eyes dart around the room, taking in my surroundings.

"It's okay, Pretty girl. You're safe. You were having a gnarly nightmare," Rad whispers right into my ear. My body trembles from the rumble of his voice, vibrating through my back.

"Nightmare?" I croak, shaking my head.

The never-ending darkness crowds my mind, but I shake it away. I will not be a victim of my fucking memories.

"You were mumbling and twitching in your sleep. It was..." Callum trails off, putting his fist in front of his face.

"Fucking scary as hell. But you're here at the hospital with us. You're safe." Rad softly kisses my hair, squeezing his arms around me as we lie tangled in the hospital bed.

My body jerks when the door to my room swings wide, displaying a new face.

"Oh good! We were beginning to worry about you, Miss West. Your assailant really did a number on you." My muscles stiffen when a woman dressed in all-white scrubs saunters through my room like she owns it.

A mess of brown hair rests on top of her lifted head. A stethoscope rests around her neck, and glasses perch on the end of her nose. A warm smile crosses her lips when she takes the three of us in, easing my initial worry.

"A nightmare," I confirm again, remembering the thick darkness I was just in with Van's menacing voice and... "What about Van? Did they get him? Oh my god..." I trail off as the nurse resets my IV bag and turns off the beeping machine. "My daughter?" I rasp.

The need to see Lyric and make sure she's okay overrides everything. I'm ten seconds away from climbing out of this bed and hightailing it out of this stupid hospital. She's probably freaking out without me. I've been here for God knows how long, and she's been by herself. No. Not alone. She's had the four of them.

The nurse sends me a sympathetic smile, humming under her breath.

"I'll send in the agents stationed outside your door. You should be okay for a while. The doctor wanted to monitor your vitals and make sure you got fluids while the drug was in your system. I suspect he'll want you here for another day to make sure it didn't have any other lasting effects on you." She smiles one last time, squeezing my arm before she walks out the door.

As soon as she exits, Olivia bursts in with a frantic look. Normally, she hides her emotions behind a thick wall of professionalism. Not today. Her eyes glide all over my body, taking me in.

"Bestie," she murmurs, a hint of emotion filtering through her voice.

"Liv. What happened? Where's Ly? Asher? Where's Van? Did he..."

"Don't worry, Dollface. I shot him in the dick," Jordy quips, strolling in casually after Liv with a cocky grin plastered. "Don't give me that disapproving face," he says, pointing at Olivia, who huffs in response.

"He's on Devil Head Island with the rest of the Veritas prisoners. They mended his..." She pauses, twisting her face. "His uh...manhood." She grimaces, pointing between her legs.

"His dick. You can say it. D-I-C-K. Or what's left of it. He'll be permanently limp from now on." He beams with pride, setting his eyes on me. "You missed, by the way. But that's okay. Thankfully, Liv and I stormed the castle before he could drag you away to his lair." He shudders at the thought, looking away with a head shake. "You were a lucky girl, Riv."

"Super fucking lucky," Liv murmurs through a breath.

"What the hell is happening?" I mutter, rubbing my temple. "So, he's gone?"

"In prison for a very long time. The good thing about Veritas is he doesn't need a damn trial. Besides, thanks to Asher's quick thinking, we have his confession on tape. So, Van is there forever."

"With sickening pride, too. Where the fuck did you find this guy, Riv?" Jordy asks, shaking his head.

"He was my ex, but he dumped me," I groan, trying to process what they're saying about him. "So, what is he saying?" I question with curiosity.

Olivia sighs, having a silent conversation with Jordy. Eyebrows raise. Hands move. But their mouths never open.

"I'm assuming everything he told you. From the admittance to what he did to you at that party and to stalking you since that moment ..." Olivia trails off, pinching the bridge of his nose.

Rad stiffens behind me. His breath picks up and heaves at the mention of the party so long ago. Rad, my hero. The man who scooped me up and took me to the hospital after Van and his little friends had their fun.

I squeeze my eyes shut, vomit rushing up my esophagus. Van fucking raped me. He took advantage of me by dumping drugs into my drink and luring me away from the mass of people and witnesses. Then, as a love-sick teenager, I fell under his spell and into his bed. Again. He took advantage of me more than once.

"We went through his house, Riv. It's apparent he's had a thing for you for a long time. Probably has been following you for longer than the three years he let on. We found the pictures, the videos, and everything in between to help him get to you. We also found his security companies shit all over the place, too. The same company in charge of your safety. Overall, it's another dangerous criminal off the streets. He won't see the light of day for the rest of his life." As Jordy speaks, more anger seeps into his words. A red tint crosses his cheeks, and his muscles turn rigid.

"And Ly? Asher? Are they okay?" My heart pounds against my ribs at the last images I have of them running through a loop in my mind.

Her screams. His anguish. The gunshot. The threats. It's all right there at the forefront of my mind, reminding me I couldn't save anyone. Not even myself.

"Ly's fine. She's snuggled up with Asher right now, Pretty Girl," Rad says reassuringly, running his hands up and down my arms again.

"He got out of surgery hours ago. He's fine. She's fine. Although Ly might be a little shaken up. She hasn't really mentioned it. But Kieran took her to that therapist you have for an emergency appointment to make sure she's okay since you were out for twelve hours, and he said they had a good talk about everything. She wants to continue to see Lyric on a regular basis. Something you might want to keep in mind," Liv says with gentleness as she eases forward. "Shoo," she rasps, waving Rad and Callum off me.

"Only this one time," Rad grumbles, kissing my cheek. "We'll snuggle soon. I'll go check on the asshole next door. He's been worried sick about you but couldn't get out of bed."

"See ya soon, Little Star." Callum brushes his lips against mine, finally breaking away and removing himself from my hospital bed.

"I'll beat feet and check on our little captive. I wonder if he had anything else to say. My boys can be so creative with their torture," Jordy says, grinning as he manically rubs his hands together as he, too, exits the room. Leaving me alone with one of my best friends, fighting back tears.

"Oh, girl," Liv murmurs, wrapping her arms around me. "I'm so sorry I couldn't get to you sooner. That asshole blew up my damn car!"

"Fuck, Liv. Your car?" I wheeze, strangled by her tightening hold. I don't even remember hearing an explosion of any sort.

"We thought there was a security breach on the outside. Little did we know it was on the inside." Pulling back, water pools in her dark eyes, slowly falling down her cheeks. "I almost lost you," she hiccups.

"You didn't, though. You got there in time. Right? Everything is so damn hazy. All I remember is him cornering me, and then he injected me..."

"Yeah, just in the nick of time. We found Ash and called an ambulance and reinforcements as your gun went off. We... God, I was so goddamn scared he had shot you. I raced in there with my gun in the air with Jordy right behind me. He hadn't moved you yet. But he was getting ready to take you away. I shot a round in his back, but it didn't stop him. It only made him face us with a gun in his hand. So, Jordy shot him in the dick without hesitation..." She grimaces at the thought.

"He really shot him in the dick?" I ask, trying to hold back the laughter bubbling in my throat. It feels so damn inappropriate to want to laugh, but I can't help it. It bubbles out of both of us as we sit embraced on my bed.

"Yeah. Give Jordy any opportunity to shoot someone where the sun don't shine. He'll do it. We wanted some real answers. The ones we thought died with Adrian... Who happens to be his cousin, somehow." She shakes her head, disappointment pulling her expression down. "I'm so sorry, River. I don't know how he eluded us for so long. All records showed Van Drake was in Europe on business... I'm so fucking sorry we brought you home without further investigation and thinking it was only Adrian. I should have smelled a setup a mile away."

"Don't be sorry. You didn't know. But he was Trevor here, right? He said he was Kat's boyfriend. Jesus, how is Kat?" I swallow the razorblades in my throat, burning with every fucking swallow. This whole situation keeps getting worse and worse by the second.

"Well, she's staying with Rocco right now. Much to his delight. He and Christian are supporting her in any way they know how. She's shaken up. I'd be, too. The man she thought she loved was only using her for you."

I rub my hand along my chest when she pulls away, staring me up and down.

"Well, good. I'm glad she has them. I'll have to check in with her soon and make sure she's okay to come back to work or take some time away from me. God, I'll even give her a raise."

"Well, the good news is the doc should release you soon. You're awake and looking good."

"Is it possible to go see, Asher? Was there much damage to him? I just can't get the image of him lying on the ground with blood pouring out of him out of my fucking mind," I rasp as tears burn the back of my eyes.

"He's fine. They cleaned up the damage from the bullets to his calf and upper thigh and put him in a cast. Thankfully, it didn't do much damage, besides the blood loss, which he's being treated for right now. But other than that, Asher is fine. He's been so worried about you. So, I think a reunion would do him some good. You should see Ly. She hasn't left his side since. She really loves them... I'm so happy you gave them another chance."

"Me too," I murmur.

52

Asher

I sigh, sitting at the edge of my bed in the band house, running a hand through my unruly hair. I need a hot shower, food, and this stupid cast off my leg.

Two days. That's how long it's been since I left the hospital in a thick cast and instructions on how to care for my wounds.

For the same amount of time, River has been by my side with concern in her eyes, following me around. Every step of the way, she's helped me cope with this new reality I've found myself in. Sometimes, a little too much.

No one tells you how painful bullet wounds are when they pierce through your skin. They fail to mention the mental decline after someone points a gun in your face and pulls the trigger. Or how vivid the recurring nightmares become. Night after night his evil face flashes through my dreams, jolting me awake. Sweat cakes my skin every time I wake up with wide eyes, frantically searching the room for the cause of it all. It's only then do I have to remind myself that he's in prison and far away from us.

Through my newly found trauma, I've discovered the best coping mechanism for me. Something I never thought I'd enjoy. Or feel relief from. Our therapist.

I had doubts at the beginning when River gave us mandatory

sessions. How could I sit in a quiet room and tell a complete stranger about what my father put me through?

That first day, I think I sat in silence for ten minutes. Then, the floodgates opened, and I told her everything. The abuse. The betrayal. My mother's death. It was all out in the open and no longer hidden in the depths of my mind for only me to suffer through.

And wouldn't you know? The relief I felt when she validated everything and helped me learn how to cope with the past was a life changer. Even now, as something sits heavily on my mind, she was the first person I spoke to about it. The therapist smiled at me, letting me know that everything I'm contemplating is good. It's coming from a place of true concern. She told me she'd help me talk it over with the guys, but I opted to have the discussion myself, without her help.

It's a subject that's been on my mind for some time now and was only cemented further during my hospital stay. After surgery, I stayed for a few extra days, ensuring I was okay. The guys and River stayed by my side every step of the way, especially my Little Brat. She glued herself to me, even then. Refusing to leave when visiting hours were over.

One night, long after the others left, River climbed into my hospital bed where we talked for hours. The future. The past. Everything in between brought us closer together. But there was one sentence that struck me square in the chest.

"You and the guys are doing so well with our training. Before you know it, you'll be back out on tour. After this, of course." River *tentatively runs a finger over my cast, slowly working up my leg, and grabs my hand. "You'll be as good as new."*

Will I, though? Will I ever become as good as *new in her eyes?*

Fuck.

"What if they leave again? They'll go on tour. What if..."

Her words haunt me, chasing me everywhere I go. The amount of pain and uncertainty that rested in her tone reminds me every day that I gave her that insecurity. It will always be on her shoulder, reminding her of what we did. We left.

And we could do it again.

What if we go on another band tour? Far the fuck away from here. We'd probably go back to Europe or travel through the US for weeks at a time. But it wouldn't be here. Not with her or Ly, where we need to be.

An ache forms in my chest at the thought of leaving them. Years ago, I walked away with no problem. Now? I could never. Not again. They're too damn important to say goodbye to anymore.

Been there. Done that. And have the bruises to prove it.

How can we rebuild our life on the road, anyway?

Answer? We can't. It's impossible. We'll never connect with millions of fans screaming our names when our girls are here. Without us.

Since we left Central City, this exact argument has been in the back of my mind. Every time I think I'm going to bring it up to the guys, I chicken out. I'm afraid of what they'll say. Or how they'll react when I let them know—I'm done.

Anxiety swirls in my stomach. Images of their angry faces pop into my mind. They'll argue. Fight tooth and nail for what we've worked so hard for.

But I won't.

They can find a new guitarist to carry on our legacy. For once, I'll sacrifice my dream to be with River so she can pursue her dream as the Fixer. She's already done so much for herself. Now, it's time for us to step up and be her support system. We can still work as a band, playing local gigs. Hell, we can still have a small-scale contract with West Records. Something that doesn't take us away from this spot we've carved out as our home.

Music has been our life for years now. Even before we moved here. It runs through our veins, feeding us life. It's our escape from reality. A way to glide above our bodies and live in the moment.

Nothing exists when music is involved.

And I'm about to suggest something that throws us off the rails of our future and plummets us into the unknown. A life without music and freedom. A life here. With the girls we've fallen in love with.

If only they'll listen.

After getting dressed the best I can without asking anyone for help, I make my way out of my room and toward the top of the staircase.

I grunt, hobbling down the stairs, carefully maneuvering my crutches. One at a time. Every few steps, my damn leg throbs where the bullets pierced through, and they sewed me back up, fixing the ripped muscles, bones, and ligaments. They promised eight weeks of this cast and then physical therapy to regain my walking.

"You idiot," Rad grunts, coming up to meet me halfway up the stairs. "I told you to yell, and I'd help you." He shakes his head with disapproval, stealing a crutch from me and winding his arm around my shoulders. "Now, lean on me like a good boy."

I sigh, leaning into him for support. A pathetic feeling festers inside of me at the amount of help I need to get around. And shower. That's been the worst. Having to tie a damn black bag around my leg feels so weird and even weirder when River hangs out in the bathroom with me, making sure I don't fall over. I would have, too, the first night.

"Thanks, man," I say, taking my crutch from him as he tsks me like a child.

"Call for help, bro. You got shot. You're in a cast. I can carry you on my back everywhere I go. Don't make me do it," he quips, giving me his best dad look that might work on Lyric.

"I'm fine, seriously. I can do some stuff on my own. I'm a big boy." I roll my eyes when he points to the dining room table, demanding I sit across from Kieran and Cal.

"Bossy, asshole," I grumble, leaning on my crutches as I make my way to the long table.

"Morning, sunshine," Callum quips, leaning his elbow on the table.

I snort, situate myself in a chair, and lean my crutches behind me. "Morning."

Kieran nods in my direction, dropping his eyes to his steamy plate of food. He shifts uncomfortably, drawing my attention to his stiff posture. I've known the guy for a long time now. So, I can always tell when something is on his mind.

From the kitchen, Rad whistles a little tune, clinking plates and silverware together before emerging again with a plate full of every breakfast food imaginable. Eggs, bacon, hash browns, and even a massive side of biscuits and gravy.

My stomach rumbles when the smell hits my senses, and I swear, I drool a little.

"Breakfast is served," Rad singsongs, waltzing into the dining room with two plates and setting one in front of me. He hums more, wiggling his body as he finds his seat and grins. "God, I love cooking. There's even enough for my Little Pretty Girl before she has to go to school."

"Thanks," I say with appreciation, rubbing my hands together. I raise my brow when I look up from my plate, greeted by two concerned looks from Kieran and Cal.

"I'm fine," I reassure them again, shaking my head when they scoff in unison.

"You say that, but I don't fucking believe it," Kieran grumbles, digging into his food and shoving it into his mouth with a huff.

Rad snorts. "That's because this asshole is never okay. And now, he's been shot, by Donavan fucking Drake. That super bunghole," he grunts, roughly cutting into his biscuits.

"New rule. Never say his name again," Kieran says, shaking his head with disgust. "I'm just...I can't believe that happened," he whispers, keeping his voice low so we don't wake our two guests, still snuggled in bed upstairs.

That's another new development I need to discuss with our

girl. River hasn't left our house since this happened. Half of me thinks she's terrified to go home. Totally understandable, too. I wouldn't want to return to the place where my privacy was invaded.

The other half of me thinks she feels guilty for me getting shot. She shouldn't. It's not her fault. I did it to protect Lyric.

We were both at the same place. It could have been her or Ly. So, I'm glad it was me. I took it so they didn't have to.

So, the next time I see River, I'm suggesting the therapist and a good session with her and Lyric. It'll all help us fight through this in the end without losing our minds over it.

The four of us converse softly as we eat our breakfast, trying to stay as quiet as possible. Not only has River basically moved in here, but she hasn't been sleeping. More often than not, she plays bed roulette throughout the night. By morning, she's slept with all four of us and Ly, who also has her own bed here.

The conversation goes on around us as my thoughts bubble to the surface, nagging me to bring it up. Say it already. Tell them how you feel. Express yourself. They're your brothers, they'll understand.

Finally, I set my knife and fork down, staring between the other three stuffing their faces and blowing out a breath.

For the moment, they're happy, conversing about mundane things. The weather. The beach. Simple things. Until I complicate everything.

"I want to quit," I blurt, unable to hold it in any longer.

Shit. I curl my fingers into fists, silently wishing I could run away. But a soothing voice reminds me I'm expressing something important, and I'm allowed to say it.

My heart beats like a drum against my ribs when everything ceases around me. The noise halts. Their bodies stiffen when they exchange curious glances.

"Quit what exactly?" Kieran asks, furrowing his brows.

"Oh boy, I think I know where this is going," Rad murmurs, rubbing at his chin with worry.

"This," I say, gesturing to the house. "This entire thing... I... I want to quit the band. I want to stay here in East Point and be with River." I roll my lips together when Kieran sighs, digging his phone out of his pocket.

"Funny you should say that. I wasn't going to bring this up until later. But you know how Constance was looking into other deals for us when we first saw River? Something that might pay a little more. Well, EJ records sent her an offer this morning for a five-year contract with us. It's worth a hundred mil."

Rad whistles under his breath. "A hundred fucking million? That's like millions more than this contract." His eyes widen in disbelief.

I take his phone, reading the messages she sent him and the email displaying the offer. It's real. We could advance further with our career with another record company. We don't need this gig anymore.

All we have to do is walk away from River again.

I swallow hard, not wanting to hold them back from what they want again.

"What are your thoughts?" I ask, clearing my throat. My eyes fall to my empty plate in shame. I could be dragging them down again instead of lifting them.

"There's no fucking way," Kieran whispers, bringing my eyes back to him. He shakes his head, and his lips twist into agony. "Before all this," he says, waving a hand and gesturing toward the house. "I would have jumped at the opportunity. That's a lot of fuckin money, but..."

"Lyric and River," Callum murmurs. "If we go on tour... How much more are we going to miss? We'll be gone for months at a time, and there's no stopping. They'd have us on the road in a matter of months."

"And my Pretty Girl," Rad says with a sour expression. "I'm never leaving her again. I've been thinking about it for a while now. I love music. But I don't love it more than my girls," he says, swallowing a large lump in his throat. "They trump everything."

"She sacrificed a lot for us back in the day. She took time out to build us into what we are now. Even now... She's still working her ass off to get us back to our glory days..." I trail off with moisture pooling in my eyes. The fear from before evaporates into thin air.

Kieran's expression softens when he looks me over, giving me a sharp nod of approval.

"I get it," Callum breathes, setting his fork down. With a long look, he takes in all our faces and nods.

"I think it's time we sacrifice something for River," Callum murmurs with the smallest hint of a smile pulling at his lips.

Rad blows out a breath. "You mean, give it all up?" he whispers, blinking rapidly. "Everything?"

Kieran blows out a breath and nods. "Yeah. If we can't be here for them every day, then I don't want to continue on a big scale. We can still play around town and live through our music, but every night we'd get to come home to them. They're our life now."

"We should treat them like it," I say, finishing his sentence. "You guys are sure? We'd be..."

"Throwing it all down the drain. But they're worth it..."

"More than worth it," Rad says, slamming his fist onto the table. "I'm ready to give myself over to my girl!" He grins now, joy lighting up his face. "Maybe now she'll marry us." He waggles his brows playfully, looking around the room.

"Maybe," Callum chuckles with a glint in his eyes, letting me know he agrees with that sentiment.

"All right," I say, feeling the relief of our decision lifting all the weight off my chest.

"It'll be so weird," Kieran says, rubbing a spot on his chest. "Not having the tours or the recording time..."

"We still can. You know? We can rent out a studio and create albums. We just won't put on shows out of town. There are plenty of venues in town we could play at," Callum adds.

"We could have a big ass show every year at the stadium or

some shit. Like people will fly from everywhere just to come here and see us. River could be there, and Ly could get on stage with us," Rad says with renewed energy, practically vibrating in his seat.

"This isn't the end of anything. This is a whole new chapter in our band... Our fucking life," Kieran says, heaving a big breath. "Once we talk to her brothers and let them know, we can talk to her about it."

"If she finds out we're doing this now, she'll try to stop us," I say with a sharp nod.

"She wouldn't want us to give up our dreams." Cal says.

"But we've already lived that part of it. Now, it's time to live our River dream and help her raise Ly and be a fucking family," Kieran says.

"Shh," Rad hisses, putting a finger to his lips. "My Little Pretty Girl is stomping down the stairs," he chuckles when the sound of heavy little footsteps stomps our way. "We'll talk after River takes her to school. Maybe go talk to Seger and Zepp?"

We all nod in agreement.

"Slow down," River reprimands in her motherly voice, only earning a giggle in return.

Lyric bursts into the dining room with an enormous grin, running straight toward Kieran.

"Little Blue," he murmurs, pulling her into his lap. "Good morning."

"Morning, Daddies," she chirps, throwing her arms around Kieran's neck.

"Sleep well, Little One?" I ask, grinning when she spins around and nods with an eager smile.

"I love this house," she says, staring at Kieran's plate with big eyes.

"Don't worry, Little Pretty Girl. I got a plate for you," Rad says, jumping up and heading into the kitchen with a bounce in his step. "And you too!" he shouts, pointing at River, who winces from his loud voice.

"Coffee," River mumbles, stumbling into the dining room with a mug in her hand. She groans, taking the first drink with her eyes closed.

As she tilts her head back, I examine the remnants of Van's handy work. A small burn sits on her jaw from the barrel of the gun being pressed into her skin too soon after firing. Bruises sit around her lips from the force of his grip.

Everything in me wishes I could erase all the pain he inflicted on her. Hell, I'd settle for going back in time and taking him out before he got to her or Lyric.

But I can't.

So, I settle for taking her free hand and squeezing.

"Have a good sleep?"

River grins at my question, nodding. "Yes. I slept like a log." Liar. She was up more times than I can count checking on me. Or switching beds, trying to get comfy. The bags under her eyes don't lie. The dimmed light in her eyes doesn't lie.

"Breakfast, my ladies," Rad coos, setting a plate in front of River and a smaller one in front of Lyric.

"Pancakes!" Lyric celebrates with a tiny clap, digging into the food.

"She's going to become a pancake monster," River quips, grabbing a fork and cutting into her breakfast.

"I love pancakes, Mommy," Lyric says through a mouthful of food.

"You sure do," Kieran chuckles, moving her crazy hair out of the way as she eats some more pancakes and sticky syrup, getting it everywhere.

"We're going to have to hose you down before school," Callum chuckles, cutting a piece of pancake for her.

"No school," she pouts, opening her mouth when Cal holds his fork in front of her lips.

"Yes, school," I respond quickly, earning a frown.

I can tell there are more protests on the tip of her tongue, but

Cal doesn't give her a chance to speak as he feeds her with a wide smile.

This is how it should have been all along. Us. Our girl. Little Lyric. I like to imagine what it would have been like if we had stayed in Central City. If I had never betrayed River in such a big way.

Baby Lyric would have had four caring dads at her beck and call from the beginning. Night feedings. Diaper changes. Everything that comes with new babies. Kieran and I would have figured out how to handle Nigel and his demands.

It would have worked out. But I guess this is the ultimate journey we had to make. We're fundamentally changed. For better and worse.

"All right, Little Lady. Time to get dressed for school," River says, leaning her cheek on her palm.

"I'm sick," Lyric says with a fake cough, pouting even more.

"Heard that one before, Little Pretty Girl. You're going to have to come up with something better than that," Rad snorts, shaking his head. "There's five of us now."

"Let's not give your momma a hard time today, okay?" I ask, leaning forward and catching her eyes. "Go upstairs, get cleaned up, brush your teeth, and get dressed. I bet your friends have missed you."

She huffs when she jumps down from Kieran's lap and walks up the stairs, stomping the whole way.

"And you want more," River snorts, taking another sip of her coffee.

"It's five adults against babies. We got this, Pretty Girl. Now, go get dressed and take her to school." Rad gets up and kisses her cheek.

"Yes, Sir," she grumbles sarcastically, climbing to her feet and shuffling up the stairs.

"They've agreed to a meeting," Kieran whispers, holding up a text exchange between him, Seger, and Zeppelin West.

"When?"

Kieran licks his lips, looking around between us. "As soon as she leaves. We're going to tell them what we're doing."

Rad grins, rubbing his hands together. "I thought I'd be terrified of this... Losing our music." He shakes his head. "But I'm excited."

As soon as River walks out the door, we pile into my car and take off, about to decimate our careers.

But in the end...

It'll all pay off.

53

River.

BEING SCARED to enter my own house shouldn't be a thing. Right? Like I shouldn't feel my heart thumping wildly in my neck. Or the anxious swirl in my belly at the thought of walking through my front door.

But yet, here I am, standing in front of my house. By myself, wishing I had someone to hold my hand.

I peek at the quiet band house from over my shoulder. They're in band practice right now, working hard to get back into a routine. At least, that's what they told me they were doing before I left with Ly and dropped her off at school. I could march over there and demand someone help me walk into my house. They'd drop everything to help me. I'm sure of it.

But I won't.

Why? Because I'm a bad bitch who needs to get over the fear coursing through my veins. By myself. Van invaded my privacy here. Multiple times. But he's gone. Locked in prison until his very last breath. There's no way he's getting out now. Jordy made sure of it.

His security firm's equipment is gone from my home, too. Every camera. Every wire. Any trace of him has been erased like he never existed in the first place.

So, why am I so fucking terrified to go inside? He's not here anymore. I am. It's my home, goddamnit. The place I built so Lyric and I could have a paradise of our own on a beach to ourselves. We were safe here. Just us and my security guards. Useless bastards. They're gone, too, replaced by bigger and better people, guarding my driveway and walking the property. Carter gave me my own Veritas agents who will protect me no matter what. Or I'm sure Carter will murder them in their sleep.

So, I should feel safer than before. My stalker is gone. For real, this time. I have better guards. My guys are stuck to me like glue. So, why do I have this constant anxiety running through me, leaving me with sweaty palms and heart palpitations? God, my stomach churns, thinking about all the shit Van put me through, pulling the wool over everyone's eyes.

Van somehow snuck his way onto my property, putting his fingers in situations he shouldn't have. He tortured Ly for months with his constant tapping on the windows. Mine too. He watched us through the cameras. Probably every fucking day. I shiver, pushing the thoughts of what he did with those videos out of my mind. I have no doubt; he was a very sick man.

I don't know if I can ever live here again without feeling his eyes on me. Or his hand on my mouth. Or his body pressed against mine as he held me captive.

I take a deep breath, grounding myself. I'm free. I can do this. Totally can do this without any help. Fuck.

Looking over my shoulder again, I peek at the band house, which seems eerily quiet from here. Maybe Rad could come over and help? He'd hold my hand and—

No. I can't. I need to face this head-on so I can continue living my life. Van can't dictate my life anymore. I'm done letting him take up space in my brain. He can't scare me anymore.

With trembling hands, I unlock the door and step into the house. I nearly piss myself when the alarm begins to beep at a steady pace, echoing on the walls. Holy shit! My heart nearly leaps out of my damn chest and takes a walk.

Right. Carter added new security for me after dismantling

Van's.

After inputting the code and turning it off, I freeze in the living room. My eyes dart around, taking in my familiar surroundings. My home. The place I built as our paradise. I take a deep, calming breath and shake the eerie feeling pushing down on my shoulders.

The feeling of ants marching across my skin starting at my toes makes my skin crawl. It feels odd standing here by myself. My home closes in on me. The walls caving in. I squeeze my eyes shut.

Maybe I should have brought them over. Then I wouldn't feel so alone.

My guys appease me by letting me bed-hop in the middle of the night. Never protesting when I crawl in with one and then leave when I can't get comfortable. Or fall asleep. That's been the hardest part of coping. Every time I close my eyes, his voice rings in my head, and his face appears with that menacing grin.

They know something is wrong, but I just want to go back to normal.

Whatever that is.

I rub a hand up and down my arm, attempting to soothe the swirling nerves taking me over as I walk through the silent house. Nothing has changed. It's all the same as I left it the day we left for Lyric's birthday party.

A deep sigh rocks through me when I plop onto Ly's bed and grab the white bunny she's been asking for. I was too afraid to come here alone and grab it. Just that simple action threw me into a tailspin of panic. And I'm way too hardheaded to admit to the guys that I needed them to help me.

My fingers swipe over the beady little eyes of her white bunny as I contemplate our future. Ly's and mine. Plus, the guys. They're going to graduate from my program with flying colors in a few months. Meaning they're going to leave us again. For months on end. We may still be in a relationship, but they won't physically be here. I know we'll have video chats and text messages. But it won't be the same. I need to be in their arms.

And I guess that's what terrifies me. I've fallen down the same deep, dark hole of commitment with them. Last time, they left town without saying goodbye. This time... I don't know. I believe them when they say they're all in, but that nagging voice in the back of my head that's been burned before fucks with me.

I also won't be the person to rip their passion away from them with ultimatums. Rocking out on stage is their fucking dream, something they've wished for since they started in high school.

I also can't do that to myself. Sure, I could go on the road with them and bring Ly. But what kind of life would that be? Becoming a band manager has always been my dream. I shine here and finally feel like I'm doing some good. I thought I'd never achieve it. Not from Central City.

Here I am, doing what I wanted to do. Same goes for them. This has always been something they've wanted. They talked about it from the moment I met them.

We all got out of Central City. Now, I'm afraid of where it's going to lead.

Closing my eyes, I finally settle all the shit going haywire inside me. From the fear of the future to the fear of sitting in my house, I blow it all out. We'll deal with that when the time comes. Maybe we'll strengthen what we have further, and it won't be a problem.

Everything is okay. It will all be fine.

Except...

My head snaps up when what sounds like a dump truck makes its way up the driveway. Gears shift, brakes squeak, and its engine groans when it comes to a complete stop, idling loudly. Low murmurs sound outside as doors slam.

What the fuck? No one else should be here. Unless my new guard let them through.

Clutching Ly's bunny, I rush out of her room and into the kitchen. My heart sputters in my chest at the memories of watching Break leave the band house months ago, listening as their moving trucks pulled into the driveway.

And as I stand in my kitchen, the same spot I was in before, and peek out the window, it's happening all over again.

Moving trucks sit in front of the band house, with twenty or so movers walking straight into the house and grabbing items.

I scramble to grab my phone. There has to be an explanation for this. There's no way they...no. They're practicing. Right?

I bring the screen in front of my eyes, and a call with Seger's name on it is coming through.

"Seger," I say out a breath, unable to take my eyes off the shit happening across the street.

"River," he mocks back in a smooth voice.

"Why..."

"I need you to come to the office. We need to, uh, have a meeting," he says, clearing his throat like uncertainty is rocking through him.

"A meeting?" I ask, swallowing hard. "Wait. Where are Whispered Words, and why are there moving vans outside their house?" Emotions bubble to the surface as I bring a fist to my trembling lips.

Was this all too much? Have they decided that this can't happen anymore? Am I still too much baggage for them?

"Deep breaths," Zepp pipes up in a smooth voice. "Just come down here. Take your time."

"Don't fucking crash on their account," Seger quips playfully, not sounding the least bit worried about what is happening.

"Seriously? That's all you're going to give me? My band is moving out of the house... They...they..."

A sigh rocks through the phone. "I can tell you're overthinking whatever is happening, Riv. Just trust us, okay? And please get down here so they can explain what's happening. You might puncture my lung or something if I tell you. You need to hear everything from them."

"Are they quitting?" I ask, swallowing the thick lump forming in my throat. If they're quitting, then they probably got the offer they were looking for. We pay well, but they're probably due a raise.

"Jesus. Yes. Now, would you get down here so they can explain everything? It's not what it seems," Seger says in what he thinks is a soothing voice.

It's anything but.

Nerves take over when I hang up the phone and make my way to my car. It's not as bad as it seems?

Liar.

"Good, you're here. And shit, you're mad as fuck," Seger whistles, shaking his head.

Well, he's not fucking wrong.

My face tightens as I march through the halls of West Records with murder on my mind. The entire drive here consisted of anxiety and burial plans.

First, my brothers will go. Their wife may miss them, but she's got two more husbands to make up for their loss. RIP, West bros. It was nice knowing you.

Then, it's my turn to murder my baby daddies. All four of them. Whatever they've got up their sleeve is killable. I'll have their graves dug before they can say—River, please don't.

"Yeah! I'm fucking fuming," I grunt, moving past him as he catches my arm, stopping my movements in the middle of the hallway.

His green eyes dart around before he moves in, which is brave on his part. I narrow my eyes, ready to bite his nose off in retaliation.

"Riv," he says, forcing my gaze to his. "Listen to them. Don't just go off, okay?"

Don't go off? No, I'm going to decimate them for leaving my

program and walking away. For leaving me. They're supposed to graduate in a few months and live their dream. Now, they're giving it up or going somewhere else.

"In here. You're making a spectacle," Zepp grumbles, nodding us into the small room with the two-way mirror connected to the conference room.

The same damn room I saw them for the first time after five years of being apart. It's like we've jumped in a time machine and traveled back in time to the point at which this all started.

Seger grumbles and curses under his breath, dragging me like a rag doll into the closed-off room. The door softly shuts behind us, leaving us to view the guys sitting around the conference table through the two-way mirror. My heart speeds up. I can't fucking stand to look at them right now. I don't know what scares me more. That they didn't talk to me about this? Or that they're possibly leaving me?

I narrow my eyes. "Why are you so calm? If they quit, that means they're going somewhere else. Doesn't it?"

My eyes drift to them, finally taking in the four men who've come to take over my life. Again. A long time ago, I promised myself I'd never fall into their dirty trap. Or fall in love with them. It's so hard to resist their charms when all these old feelings have resurfaced with a vengeance, begging me to be in their orbit. I wonder if this is how fated mates feel when they finally find that perfect person their soul was made for.

Whispered Words may not be magically mine, but my entire being calls out to them and pulls me into them every time. No matter how angry I am at them, I still see myself with them.

As my eyes scan over the boys, my heart pumps faster, and sweat breaks out across my skin. The last time I viewed them from this angle, they were staring at their phones and barely talking. They fucking hated each other and loathed me even more.

And now?

Kieran smiles at Rad, who softly speaks in his direction, causing Asher to laugh and turn red. Callum leans his elbow on the table with a grin, shaking his head. Whatever they're discussing brings them so much joy.

"Go and talk to them. We'll be right here," Zepp murmurs, gripping my shoulder. "It's nothing bad. In fact, it's something we were expecting."

"Did you guys do this on purpose?" I whisper, looking between the two of them as they once again have a rude, silent conversation.

"No," Seger grumbles. "We'd never purposefully put you through that torture. Scouts honor," he says, holding up two fingers.

"You're not scouts." I roll my eyes, staring at the guys again with longing in my heart.

No wonder they didn't want to help take Ly to school. They were planning... Well, whatever this is.

"I could have been, but dear old dad shoved us into private schools, never giving us a chance to enjoy that kind of shit. Now, get in there before they combust."

"It'll be fine," Zepp says with reassurance, patting my shoulder.

"Fine. But if I have to kill them, you had better protect me with fancy lawyers and shit," I grumble, wrinkling my nose when Seger bursts out laughing.

"Always got your back," he chuckles, opening the door for me, and practically shoves me into the conference room.

I swallow hard when my guys freeze, watching me approach with caution.

"So, you called a meeting?" I ask, crossing my arms over my chest and walking further into the room. "When I left my house, there were moving vans sitting outside."

Rad slaps Kieran on the arm, gesturing for him to speak.

"We got another offer from EJ Records," he says in a deep voice, nearly knocking me off my feet.

An offer? From another company? What in the ever living fuck is happening right now?

"And you accepted?" Anger boils in my gut as his eyes widen, and he takes a step back. His eyes fly to my fingers, curling in my pocket where my knife rests. I'm never leaving without it again. No matter what. Thank God, too. I'm about to put this through each of their eyeballs.

"Fuck. River Blue..." he trails off, swiping a hand down his face. "We didn't accept the offer."

"He told them to shove it up their asses with a smile on his face," Rad snorts with glee, rising to his feet. "All one hundred million, too. That'd hurt." He cringes, shuttering at the thought.

"Is that what you really thought?" Callum asks, cocking his head to the side. I swallow hard when his gray eyes inspect every inch of my body, and he nods in confirmation. "Understandable, Little Star."

"Why else would you be vacating the band house without telling me? You..." I trail off, wondering what the fuck is going through their heads. If they aren't staying here, then where are they going? They don't have any prospects on the horizon. So, that means... "No," I choke out, shaking my head. "There's no way you're just..."

"We quit," Kieran says, coming to stand in front of me. His fingers brush against my cheeks, and he gives me a small smile. "We quit West Records. We didn't accept that offer. We're done, baby."

"What the hell?" I murmur with a trembling lip. "You can't just walk away from your dream. Guys, this is your fucking passion. You're living something everyone else wants. You're rock stars. You're—"

"Not anymore, Little Star," Callum says with a head shake.

Not an ounce of sadness rests on their faces as they look up at me with soft smiles.

"It was," Asher grunts, getting to his feet with the help of Callum as they situate his crutches.

"We have a lot more dreams, Pretty Girl," Rad says with a shrug.

"But music is your life."

"Was our life," Kieran adds, bringing my gaze to his. "River Blue. This band was our dream for years. Getting here to this place, it was fucking wild. We've soared on stage and sold-out shows. But nothing compares to the little girl that wraps her arms around me and calls me Daddy. That's the real dream with you and her."

"And you, Little Star," Callum murmurs, coming to my other side and moving a piece of hair from my shoulder. "You're the ultimate dream." His face softens when tears burn the back of my eyes.

"No. I can't let you quit because of me," I whisper, sucking in a breath. "You can't—"

"We can," Rad says with a shrug. "Plus, we kind of already did. We've signed the papers giving up our contract."

My eyes cut to the mirror, where I know my brothers are watching. Nosy bastards. They set it up so they could quit, and I'd have no say in the matter. Their death is still on the table. But my guys? Not so much.

"We knew you'd try to stop us if we talked to you about it. We were damn sure that this is what we wanted." Kieran swallows hard, continually tracing the freckles lining my cheeks.

"You'll regret it later," I whisper. "You'll..."

"Nope. No regrets, Pretty Girl. This," he murmurs, pointing between the five of us. "This is our new dream. We're going to build you a house on the beach with enough room for all of us."

"We're going to walk you down the aisle and say I do and make you ours forever," Asher says with glossy eyes.

"I'm going to put so many babies in you—" Rad grunts when Asher punches him in the gut. "Asshole! Why do you keep doing that." He sends Asher a scathing look.

"We're going to take you out to dinner. Make you breakfast in bed. Give you the best orgasms you've ever had," Rad says, wiggling his brows. "We have it all planned out, Pretty Girl. Every day. Just you, Lyric, and us."

"Those, River Blue. Are our dreams. Music will always be here," Kieran says, tapping his chest with his free hand.

"We don't have to go on tour or play for millions of people..." Rad wheezes, trailing off.

"We're right where we want to be. With you and Ly, building our future," Asher says with determination.

"Besides, your brothers offered us jobs," Rad beams, crossing his arms over his chest. "So, you can't say no."

"You're all serious?" I ask in disbelief as tears stream down my face. "You're seriously going to work here?"

"Yes," Kieran chuckles, brushing the tears from my cheeks. "We've lived our dream. You helped us with that, and we appreciate what you did for us. Back then, in Central City, helping us set up for Battle of the Bands. And now, helping us work through our shit. You've done so much for us, and it opened our eyes. We weren't happy because you weren't in our lives. We weren't happy because Whispered Words is nothing without River West."

"We'd give up the world for you, Little Brat," Asher whispers, licking his lips.

"But we're doing this for us, too. We want to be in your lives. We want to help take Ly to school every morning and pick her up in the afternoon. We want to wake up for the night feedings and let you sleep. We want the shitty diapers, long nights, and beautiful sunrises with you," Kieran adds again.

"We want all the things. Firsts, seconds, and lasts," Rad whispers, moving in on me. "We want it all with you at the center of it. You're our number one. You always should have been. Music can take a backseat. Everything else can get fucked. I mean, you can too; we'll help with that. But you're ours. Forever. Whether you like it or not."

I sniffle, leaning into Kieran's touch.

"I can't believe you're giving up everything for me."

"You did it for us," Asher says. "You gave up your whole life because we walked away. You raised our baby into an amazing child. You sacrificed your time and freedom to give yourself the life you deserved all along. Now, we're here to help you keep moving forward. We love you, Little Brat."

I close my eyes when their touches start softly stroking different parts of my body. Arms. Face. Back. Shoulders. They're everywhere, surrounding me, promising to never leave my side.

"I love you, too," I murmur through a ragged breath. "I can't believe it."

"Believe it, Pretty Girl. You'll be seeing our faces every day from now on." He wiggles his brows, forcing a laugh from my throat.

"So, what do you say?" Kieran asks, bringing my attention back to him. "Are you ready to start this new chapter in our lives?"

"Yes." A smile breaks free, stretching across my lips when he leans in and kisses my cheek.

"Good, because I think we would have just kidnapped you, anyway." Kieran shrugs, pulling back.

"I don't doubt it," I say with a laugh, shaking my head. "Well... Looks like I'm free for a day or two. What should we do?"

"Let's go get reacquainted properly," Rad quips, wiggling his brows. "My tongue wants to explore some new places."

I snort when something bangs against the mirror on the opposite side of the room. Serves them right for being nosy assholes.

"All right," I say, holding out my hand for him to take. "Let's go then."

The five of us slowly walk toward the door as a unit, with silence between us. Not the uncomfortable kind, either. It's the satisfied—we finally made it—kind of silence.

It's been five years of pure hell thinking they left without reason, leaving me with our baby and restraining orders. All we needed was time to patch ourselves back together and knit our relationship back to what it was. This time around, we're more cohesive and in better control of our emotions. From this moment on, we'll be a fucking family together. Forever in each other's arms.

"So, how about that wedding proposal?" I ask when we make it out the front door after saying our awkward goodbyes to my brothers.

"Wait, what?" Rad shouts, turning sharply on his heel to face me.

"You heard me," I say, waving a hand in his direction.

He swallows hard, eyeing the other guys, and pats his pockets. "I don't have a ring."

"That never stopped you before," I say, smiling when his face reddens.

"Marry us, Pretty Girl. Please be our wife. Our baby momma. The woman who lets me clean her up when the others are done with her," he asks in a low voice, taking my hand in his as the others gather around us with their hearts in their throats.

"Okay," I say with a grin, squeezing his hand. "I'll marry you all."

"YES!" Rad shouts, throwing his arms around me and lifting me in the air. After several spins, he sets me on my feet and captures my lips with his. "Time to celebrate," he chuckles, dragging me toward my car.

Whispered Words and River West. We started out as something impossible. Five broken people coming together and finding something other people long for. The love was there, but the timing was all wrong.

We spent five years apart from each other, growing into broken adults. We were people who depended on music, work, drugs, fighting, and fucking isolation to get us through the end of the day.

In the end, the five broken pieces patched themselves back together from the inside out and, in turn, connected again. The love is here. The timing is right.

And us?

Well, we're whole.

THE FUCKING END
SHUT THE CURTAIN.

Take a bow.
The boys and River are done for now.

Epilogue

River

SIX MONTHS LATER

"You're going to tell them tonight?" Olivia practically begs, bustling by with bright flowers in her hands. She grins when she sets them on the little table in my master bath.

"Yes. But they won't tell me what we have planned for the honeymoon," I say, wrinkling my nose when Ode brushes bright red blush on my cheek.

"Stop moving, bitch," Ode quips, flicking my nose. "Or I'll miss and poke you in the eye."

"She will, too," Rocco quips, leaning against the bathroom counter, watching intently.

"I will," Ode says, grinning, pointing a makeup brush in his direction.

I side-eye Ode, who grins wider, dipping the brush into the red blush again, preparing to paint my other cheek.

"But definitely tonight?" Kaycee asks, cocking her head to the side and letting her blonde curls fall down her back. "I don't know if I can hold my tongue anymore. This is the hardest secret I've had to keep in a long time." She makes a face, shaking her head. "And I don't keep secrets very well."

"Please tell them before we collectively die of secret-keeping," Rocco groans, shaking his head

I snort, ignoring his whines. "Well, the rest of them," I say with a shrug. "Kieran kinda walked in on me peeing on the stick."

Literally. The man knows no personal space when it comes to me sometimes. There I was, minding my own business and trying to be discreet. Then, walks in Kieran, tossing his shirt off and letting me know he's going to hop into the shower.

"And he's kept it a secret?" Ode snorts, brushing on the red to my cheeks.

I suck in a breath as another round of nausea rolls through my stomach. This has been happening more and more as the weeks have gone on. I mean, I'm only about seven weeks pregnant, but I found out two weeks ago. Just in time to get this wedding done and start our lives together.

"Like a good boy, yes," I quip, taking a sip of 7-Up. "He's been helping me ever since the morning sickness decided to come along."

He's been the sweetest man since he accidentally walked in on me in the bathroom. Right after I had set the test on the counter.

"Is that?" he whispers, plastering his front to my back. Those mismatched eyes peer down at the test, lighting up when the results finally appear. "You're pregnant," he whispers, wrapping his arms around me. "It finally happened."

I swallow hard, tracing the test with tears in my eyes. "You're only happy because you don't have to wear a condom anymore," I quip, sniffling.

"That too," he murmurs, kissing my cheek. "Oh, River Blue. I can't believe this is finally happening. We're going to be here every step of the way. I can't fucking wait." Emotions bubble in his throat, glazing over his eyes. Silent tears fall down his cheeks, expressing the joy he's feeling. "I'll always regret not being here the first time around," he confesses, rubbing a hand along my flat stomach. "Anything you need, My Blue. I'll be here."

"I want to wait to tell them," I say, catching his gaze in the mirror above the sink we're standing in front of. "Until after the

wedding." *A slight smirk pulls at the edge of his lip with satisfaction. "It'll be the ultimate surprise."*

"So I get to know before those other assholes?" His brows wiggle as his hand glides over my stomach. "I'll keep it a secret for now." He takes a deep breath, brushing his nose against the column of my neck. "They're going to be so fucking excited for this, especially Rad. That fucker's been throwing you in closets every chance he gets."

I snort, closing my eyes and leaning into his touch. "Ever since we decided to start trying, he's been fucking insatiable," I whisper as goosebumps spread across my flesh.

Since we decided three months ago to start trying to expand our family, Rad's been the clingiest. Deep down, I know it's his guilt tearing through him for not being here for Lyric. He's wanted more children since we went all in, and finally, we decided not to wait any longer. We started planning the wedding the moment they picked out a ring and slipped it on my finger.

This is our future, and we're finally settling into our new normal.

"That boy hasn't changed one bit, has he? Loyal as ever," Ode murmurs with sincerity, eyeing my makeup with a satisfied grin. "You're as beautiful as ever, bitch. I can't believe..." She turns away, putting a hand to her lips.

"Don't you start," Olivia sniffles, swiping a hand under her nose. "Every time you start the waterworks, mine starts."

"Nobody start!" Rocco sniffles, wiping under his eyes.

"Can't help it," Ode says through a quivering voice. "I never thought my girl would walk down the aisle after what they did. And now look at her, she's getting four dicks for the price of one," she wails, covering her face with her hands.

"Please don't cry. You'll make me cry, and then my makeup will be ruined for the wedding." Emotions sit in the back of my throat, burning my damn eyes.

"None of that," Ode says, shaking her head and wiping her eyes. "We've got to get you down that aisle and married before they fuck up again."

Olivia snorts. "Oh, they'll fuck up a lot, Riv. But that's the joy of marriage," she says wistfully, looking out the window of the bathroom. She swallows hard, watching the movements of the men outside, working together as they put my flower arch into the sand.

I couldn't have dreamed of a better place to get married than the sands behind my home, under the sparkling stars and moonlight. Even though I was once terrified after Van's invasion to resume living here, I'm not anymore. This is my home. Or will be for the next few months. Just a hundred feet away on two acres of my property, the boys and I are building our dream home. Fit with six bedrooms, four baths, a basement with a recording studio, and room to grow.

As the day progresses and the sun goes down, everyone clears out to get ready for the wedding. Olivia, Kaycee, and Ode get into their dresses for the ceremony. And Rocco leaves to put his suit on.

Our ceremony is simple. Just the five of us standing under the arch. No bridesmaids or groomsmen. We wanted something where people could just come and watch with their families and celebrate with us.

"Love you, Riv. I'm so happy they came around, and you guys were able to fix this," Olivia says, kissing my cheek. "I'm so happy for you." She grins, stepping out of my house, and takes a seat with the audience.

"Show 'em hell, bitch. Don't let those assholes get one over on you," Ode says with a wink, heading out to sit next to Olivia.

"If you ever need assistance. You know who to call," Kaycee says, cocking her head to the side. "But I have a feeling you're used to this."

"Just as used to it as you are, Angel," Seger says, sauntering into the bathroom with a cocky grin. He stops short, throwing his arm over Kaycee's shoulders and nods. "Wow. You clean up good, Sis. They're all ready for you. It's not too late to run, though," he quips, kissing Kaycee's head with affection.

"Like I wanted to run from you?" she asks, raising a brow when his face falls.

"You'd never, Angel..." he trails off, wrinkling his nose. "Would you?"

"She wouldn't," Zepp says, coming to stand beside me. "You look beautiful, Riv. Congrats on the big day."

I sniffle, leaning in to hug him. "Thanks, guys. For being here and for walking me down the aisle."

"What're big brothers for? Besides, Dad isn't here. We're the next best thing," Seger says.

"Well, shall we?" Zepp asks, gesturing toward the back sliding doors.

I nod.

"I'll be out there. You're gorgeous," Kaycee compliments before scurrying off out the door and taking a seat next to Chase and Carter, her other husbands. Leaving me alone with my two brothers, who are about to walk me down the aisle, giving me over to the four men I've loved, hated, and loved again.

"Seriously. It's not too late," Seger murmurs, offering me his elbow.

I snort. "What if I want to marry them? Hmm?" I hum, maneuvering my long, white dress as we take a few steps. It swishes with every movement I make, slightly sparkling under the living room lights.

"We're so happy for you," Zepp says with a grin, reaching for the back sliding glass door, but stops. "And proud, Riv. You've come a long way. You've worked hard. Been an amazing mother..."

"And sister," Seger interrupts. "You're fucking amazing, Riv. And I gotta say, they've really helped you shine these past six months since they quit. They've gone from cocky assholes to fucking amazing dudes."

I smile, peeking out the glass door at the four men who've stolen my heart standing under the flower arch. Tight suits fit against their bodies, showing off their toned muscles.

Since they quit their contract, they've really thrived within the music industry. Rad and Callum have turned into amazing West Records talent scouts, hitting all the small venues in a fifty-mile radius. Callum's eye for stardom and Rad's easy-going personality has drawn in some amazing talent.

Kieran has stepped up as my assistant, since Kat had to take some time off to regain herself emotionally and hasn't been back since. Rocco keeps me updated on her whereabouts and how she's holding up. Day by day, she's healing from the trauma Van put her through.

And Asher? Well, he's anointed himself as a stay-at-home father, soaking up all the love Lyric has to give him while we all work. He takes care of the laundry. Cooks us elaborate dinners, fit with appetizers and desserts. He makes sure all the housework is done and manages Lyric's school pick-up schedule. He's helped Camilla get used to her new life with us and not Gloria. Although, for the most part, she's opted to continue living at the prep school during the school year and will stay with us during the summer.

For the first time in a long time, Asher seems free of everything and is doing what he loves.

"Mommy! I look like a princess!" Lyric's small voice carries through the house as she clutches tight to Rocco's hand.

"You do," I rasp, leaning down to run my fingers through her curly, dark locks. "Are you ready to throw some flowers out?"

Lyric grins, nodding. "I am! Uncle Rocco gots me this basket with pretty red rose petals to throw everywhere!" She squeals, reaching into the basket with a grin. "I'm excited, Mommy. You're going to marry daddies."

"I am," I say with tears burning in my eyes. "Is that okay?"

"Of course," she says, nodding.

"All right, my little doll. How about we start walking down the aisle?" Rocco says, nodding toward the back door with a dopey expression.

"Okay," she says, looking me up and down. "You look like a queen, Mommy." Her grin lights up my fucking world, sending tears down my cheeks.

This is what we needed all fucking along. She needed them. I needed them. And now, we're all coming together as one unit. The guys, me, Lyric, and even their sister Camilla. The girl we adopted after Gloria's ass went straight to prison for her crimes. We're one happy family, just trying to make it day by day.

"Are you ready for this?" Zepp asks, opening the slider all the way.

The cool night air hits my face as we step out onto the back porch. Fairy lights wrap around the wooden structure, illuminating our way toward the small crowd gathered around the flowery archway. The small buzz of conversation halts when our feet hit the sand, and as one, all our friends and family stand from their chairs, watching with eager eyes as Zepp and Seger guide me down the make-shift aisle.

Lyric giggles every time she tosses her red rose petals onto the sand, finally making it up to the arch. Each of the guys kisses her cheek before Rocco guides her to the front row of chairs, sitting next to Christian and Kat. I smile, catching Kat's eyes and she grins, sending me a thumbs up. It's nice to see her out and about after everything that happened six months ago. She's slowly rebuilding herself with the two men surrounding her.

I heave a breath, break eye contact, and focus on my surroundings. Ocean waves act as our symphony in the background when the bride's music starts.

"What?" I murmur, startling when a soft guitar rhythm starts playing through the speaker at the front.

"You're not the only one keeping secrets," Zepp murmurs, raising a brow when I side-eye him.

Kieran's quiet, sultry voice echoes through the quiet crowd. Tears heat behind my eyes, catching on my lashes when his soft, loving words take root in my brain.

Loved you from day one
Time has been rough.
Broke up.
Repaired.
Now we're one.
The future holds bright
Like a candle steady in the wind
You're the one we want.
Forever.
Always.
Our wife.

"Fuck," I rasp, squeezing my eyes shut in hopes I don't ruin the mascara curling my eyelashes.

I will not fucking cry over a beautiful song they obviously wrote for our wedding day. I will not fucking cry in front of all these people! Fuck it. Who am I kidding? I'm borderline hormonal from the pregnancy, and they wrote me a fucking song. Who does that? The men of my dreams, that's who.

Slowly, we walk through the sand, making our way toward the four men who stare at me with tears in their eyes.

Asher glances away, rubbing away the moisture collecting on his lashes before looking back and smiling at me. He takes in my appearance. Inch by fucking inch, slowly making his way to my gaze. He nods in approval when we finally stop directly in front of them, under the flowery archway.

"I'm the luckiest guy in the world," he rasps, stepping forward with his hand held out.

"Jesus, Pretty Girl," Rad chokes out, covering his quivering lips with his hand. "You look so beautiful. I can't wait to rip that dress in half and then—"

"Don't fucking finish that sentence," Seger grunts, plowing his fist into Rad's stomach.

"Groom!" Rad wheezes, bending at the waist. "You can't punch a groom on his wedding day."

"When you make comments like that about my sister, I do, asshole," Seger grumbles, shaking his head.

I crack a smile when he slowly lifts my hand into Asher's, joining us together as one. Gently, Asher squeezes my fingers in his.

"You take care of my fucking sister, or you four won't have lives to live." He gives them a meaningful look when he steps back, running a finger across his throat for dramatic effect. "Grumpy knows how to dispose of bodies." He tilts his head in Carter's direction.

Carter grins from the audience, throwing an arm over the back of Kaycee's chair, nodding like he knows exactly what Seger is talking about. Casually, he lifts his fingers in a tiny wave, solidifying the threat further.

"Fuck," Callum murmurs, stiffening at the look of pure joy on Carter's face.

"He's going to kill us," Rad hisses, jerking his gaze to me. "Pretty Girl, tell your brothers we're good boys."

I shrug, biting the inside of my cheek to hold my smile. My stomach churns from either the nerves or my morning sickness, coming back with a vengeance. Up until now, Kieran's helped me hide the need to rush to the bathroom and puke my brains out. But nothing will hide it now if I spew all over the beach.

Please don't barf. I suck in a breath, breathing through the torment squeezing my stomach into knots.

"Stop it," I grunt at my brother, shoving him away.

"He will," Rad rasps, rubbing at his abdomen. "I have zero doubts he'll chop us into tiny pieces." He wrinkles his nose when Seger's grin grows, and he nods.

"Just be good," Zepp mutters, kissing my cheek.

Slowly, Asher pulls me forward, helping me maneuver my long dress through the sand.

"You really are gorgeous, Pretty Girl," Rad murmurs, leaning in to kiss my cheek. "This dress is...beautiful." Tears form in his eyes, and he sniffles. "I'm finally marrying my dream girl. My one true love." He cups my cheeks, swiping away the rogue tears dripping down my damn cheeks. Despite my efforts not to cry, it seems impossible at this point. "I knew from the moment I watched Kieran fuck you over that desk that you were the one for me."

"Dude," Kieran grumbles, shaking his head. "We have an audience."

"What?" Rad asks, wrinkling his nose. "It's true! You think we didn't stand there for the full thirty seconds..." Rad grins when Kieran rolls his eyes.

"Was longer than thirty seconds, asshole," Kieran huffs.

"Try three minutes," Callum says, side-eyeing Kieran as he turns beet red.

"I hate you all. I can't believe I'm strapped to you idiots for eternity. You know, River Blue. It's not too late. We can run away together," he says with a sly grin, falling over when Asher pushes him aside.

"I won't let you take my girl," Asher grumbles, straightening out his suit jacket.

"Psst. Get in your spots," Chase, Kaycee's other husband, whispers, pointing to a few spots in the sand. Without a second thought, the five of us take our spots.

Me in the middle with the four of them surrounding me, leaving me in the center of their circle. My stomach swirls again as hot acid leaks up my throat, begging to come out. I take a deep breath, working through the constant nausea. Nervous sweat leaks from every pore.

"Ready, Little West?" he asks with a megawatt grin.

I nod, not daring to speak when he begins the ceremony. The crowd settles into their seats, watching us with rapt attention as

Chase belts out the words animatedly.

Kieran squeezes my waist, staring down at me with furrowed brows. "River Blue, you're pale," he whispers right in my ear, not garnering the attention of the rest of the boys.

I shake my head. If I open my mouth, I'll...

"Fuck," I hiss, pushing through the boys, barely making it to a clear spot away from the prying eyes watching our every move.

"I got you," Kieran says, rushing to my side and holding back my hair.

"Well, I was going to say you may kiss the bride, but..." Chase's joking voice trails off as the murmurs start in the crowd.

"I'm okay," I whisper through a ragged breath, holding back the next wave of nausea threatening to pull me under.

"Maybe we should talk to the doctor about those pills?" Kieran says, helping me stand tall. I let out a sigh of relief when he rubs a tissue along my lips and cleans me up.

"Yeah. Might have to. Wait, how'd you know about those?" I whisper, wiping the moisture from my cheeks.

He smiles, fluffing my hair back out. "You mentioned you had to do that with Ly in the beginning. That it had gotten so bad you couldn't go to work or class."

"Pretty Girl, are you okay?" Rad asks with concern, finally making it to my side.

"Are you sick?" Callum asks, turning green when he blinks at the little pile on the sand.

Fuck. I press my lips into a tight line, breathing through the swooping feeling taking over my stomach.

Kieran hums, rubbing a hand over my stomach, which seems to soothe the waves of vomit attempting to come out again.

"Little Star," Callum says with wide eyes, watching Kieran's movements. "Are you..."

I smile, taking his hand in mine and gently placing it on my stomach over the dress. I do the same to Rad and Asher, bringing them in a circle around me again.

"Welcome to fatherhood, boys," I whisper with more damn tears falling down my cheeks.

Rad falls to his knees, pushing everyone away. Gently, he lays a kiss on my stomach, cradling it with his hands.

"I'm going to be the best father I can be, Little Peanut. Just ask your older sister Ly. I swear I owe her two-hundred thousand right now, but fuck, baby. I've longed for you." His dark eyes crawl up my body, meeting my gaze. "Thank you, Pretty Girl. For indulging me any chance you got. I loved helping to create this."

"It's not just possibly yours, dickface. It could be mine, too," Asher says with a grin, kissing my cheek. "Do you need anything, Little Brat?"

"Hmm. No," I murmur, leaning into his kiss.

"It-it could be mine," Callum stammers, staring at my stomach with big eyes. "Holy shit."

Kieran snorts, shoving his hands in his pockets. "Well, it can't be mine..."

"Back door or shut up," Rad quips, jumping to his feet.

"Yeah, that," Kieran cringes, gazing at the crowd watching.

"Do you guys want to continue getting married?" Chase asks, rubbing the back of his neck.

"Yeah," I say, taking their hands and leading them back to our altar. Turning to the crowd, I grin, soaking in their faces. "We're going to have a baby!" I shout, thrusting my fist into the air, laughing as they cheer us on.

"A baby," Rad says, clinging to my hand.

His eyes never leave my stomach, and that includes the entire nine months she cooks to the moment she comes out with rich, dark curly hair and dark eyes.

I guess all those extra moments he shoved me into closets, came to see me at work, and locked me in my bedroom really paid off.

The moment she cried her first breath, Rad scooped her into his arms and proclaimed her as his. And she was. Aria. Our little mischievous one, named for songs and melodies, living up to her father's legend.

Our family grew one by one over the next few years, happening almost right after another. Lyric. Aria. Alana. Maya.

Four girls for four men who helped make me whole.

Connect with Aly Beck